Praise for
POUL ANDERSON
and
THE STARS ARE ALSO FIRE

———

"One of hard science fiction's most consistently impressive writers . . . the bleak surfaces of distant asteroids and the nearer moon become beautiful and vibrant in Anderson's hands . . . Anderson's hard-science spirit imbues every page."
—*Omni*

———

It is the dawn of a new era of space exploration and colonization. Dagny Beynac, descendant of the legendary Anson Guthrie, becomes a heroine of a new Lunarian civilization that struggles to break free of the influence of Earth.

Centuries later, the entire solar system is dominated by a vast network of machine intelligences. On Earth and Luna, splintered fragments of humanity search for some way to survive in a system that no longer seems to hold a place for flesh and blood.

And the only solution lies in the distant past, in the life of Dagny Beynac.

TOR BOOKS BY POUL ANDERSON

Alight in the Void
The Armies of Elfland
The Boat of a Million Years
The Dancer from Atlantis
The Day of Their Return
Explorations
Harvest of Stars
Hoka! (*with Gordon R. Dickson*)
Kinship with the Stars
A Knight of Ghosts and Shadows
The Long Night
The Longest Voyage
Maurai and Kith
A Midsummer Tempest
No Truce with Kings
Past Times
The Saturn Game
The Shield of Time
The Stars Are Also Fire
Tales of the Flying Mountains
The Time Patrol
There Will Be Time

THE STARS
ARE ALSO FIRE

POUL ANDERSON

A TOM DOHERTY ASSOCIATES BOOK
NEW YORK

This is a work of fiction. All the characters and events portrayed in this book are fictitious or are used fictitiously

THE STARS ARE ALSO FIRE

A Tor Book
Published by Tom Doherty Associates, Inc.
175 Fifth Avenue
New York, N.Y. 10010

Tor® is a registered trademark of Tom Doherty Associates, Inc.

Cover art by Vincent DiFate

ISBN:0-812-53022-5
Library of Congress Catalog Card Number: 94-7020

First edition: August 1994
First mass market edition: October 1995

Printed in the United States of America

0 9 8 7 6 5 4 3 2

TO LARRY AND MARILYN NIVEN

ACKNOWLEDGMENTS

For advice, information, suggestions, encouragement, and much else I am indebted to Karen Anderson (first and foremost as always), Gregory Benford, C.J. Cherryh, Larry J. Friesen, Robert Gleason, Alan Jeffery, Mike Resnick, and S.M. Stirling. They are not responsible for any errors or other infelicities that remain in this book, but without them there would have been many more.

It is clear that I have also drawn on the thoughts of Freeman Dyson, Hans Moravec, Roger Penrose, Gunther S. Stent, and Frank J. Tipler. Again, nothing bad is their fault, the more so since I have often contradicted this or that in their writings. For that matter, some of their own ideas disagree with each other. All are immensely interesting and reach for the very heart of truth.

DRAMATIS PERSONAE

(Some minor figures are omitted)

Aiant: A husband of Lilisaire.

Annie: Former wife of Ian Kenmuir.

Anson Beynac: Oldest child of Dagny and Edmond Beynac.

Carla Beynac: Sixth child of Dagny and Edmond Beynac.

Dagny Beynac: An engineer, later an administrator, eventually a political leader on Luna in early days; her download.

Edmond Beynac: A geologist, husband of Dagny Beynac.

Francis Beynac: Fourth child of Dagny and Edmond Beynac.

Gabrielle Beynac: Second child of Dagny and Edmond Beynac.

Helen Beynac: Fifth child of Dagny and Edmond Beynac.

Sigurd Beynac: Third child of Dagny and Edmond Beynac.

Bolly: A henchman of Bruno.

Bornay: Son of Lilisaire and Caraine.

Brandir: Lunarian name of Anson Beynac.

Bruno: Mayor of Overburg in Bramland.

Caraine: A husband of Lilisaire.

Mary Carfax: Alias of a sophotect in Lilisaire's service.

Delgado: An officer of the Peace Authority.

Diddyboom: Pet name given Dagny by Guthrie.

Dagny Ebbesen: A granddaughter and protégée of Anson Guthrie; after her marriage, Dagny Beynac.

DRAMATIS PERSONAE

Erann: A grandson of Brandir.

Etana: A Lunarian space pilot.

Eyrnen: A Lunarian bioengineer, son of Jinann.

Eythil: A henchman of Lilisaire.

Fernando: A priest and leader among the Drylanders.

Fia: Lunarian name of Helen Beynac.

James Fong: An officer of the Peace Authority.

Miguel Fuentes: An engineer on Luna in early days.

Lucrezia Gambetta: Second governor general of Luna for the World Federation.

Petras Gedminas: An engineer on Luna in early days.

Anson Guthrie: Co-founder and chief of Fireball Enterprises; his download.

Juliana Guthrie: Wife of Anson Guthrie and co-founder of Fireball Enterprises.

Zaid Hakim: An agent of the Ministry of Environment of the World Federation.

Einar Haugen: Fourth governor general of Luna for the World Federation.

Stepan Huizinga: A leader among the Terran Moondwellers in early days.

Ilitu: A Lunarian geologist.

Inalante: Mayor of Tychopolis, a son of Kaino.

Iscah: A metamorph of Chemo type in Los Angeles.

Ivala: A wife of Brandir.

Eva Jannicki: A spacefarer for Fireball Enterprises.

Daniel Janvier: President of the World Federation at the time of the Lunar crisis.

Jinann: Lunarian name of Carla Beynac.

Charles Jomo: A mediator in East Africa.

Ka'eo: One of the Keiki Moana.

Kaino: Lunarian name of Sigurd Beynac.

Aleka Kame: A member of the Lahui Kuikawa, serving as liaison with the Keiki Moana and other metamorphs.

Ian Kenmuir: An Earth-born space pilot of the Venture.

Lilisaire: A Lunarian magnate of the Republic era.

Matthias: Lodgemaster (Rydberg) of the Fireball Trothdom.

DRAMATIS PERSONAE

Lucas Mthembu: Birth name of Venator.

Dolores Nightborn: An alias of Lilisaire.

Niolente: A Lunarian magnate of the Selenarchy era, leader of the movement against incorporation of Luna in the World Federation.

Manyane Nkuhlu: A spaceman for Fireball Enterprises.

Irene Norton: Alias used by Aleka Kame.

Antonio Oliveira: A spaceman for Fireball Enterprises.

Joe Packer: An engineer on Luna in early days.

Sam Packer: A consorte of the Fireball Trothdom.

Rinndalir: A Lunarian magnate of the Selenarchy era, co-leader of the exodus to Alpha Centauri.

Lars Rydberg: A spaceman for Fireball Enterprises, son of Dagny Ebbesen and William Thurshaw.

Ulla Rydberg: Wife of Lars Rydberg.

Sandhu: A guru at Prajnaloka.

Soraya: A metamorph of Titan type in Los Angeles.

Mohandas Sundaram: A colonel of the Peace Authority on Luna.

Alice Tam: Anglo version of "Aleka Kame."

Temerir: Lunarian name of Francis Beynac.

The Teramind: The apex of the cybercosm.

William Thurshaw: Youthful lover of Dagny Ebbesen.

Tuori: A wife of Brandir.

Uncans: Pet name given Guthrie by Dagny.

Valanndray: A Lunarian engineer of the Venture.

Venator: A synnoiont and officer of the intelligence corps of the Peace Authority.

Verdea: Lunarian name of Gabrielle Beynac.

Yuri Volkov: A former lover of Aleka Kame.

Jaime Wahl y Medina: Third governor general of Luna for the World Federation.

Leandro Wahl y Urribe: Son of Jaime Wahl.

Rita Urribe de Wahl: Wife of Jaime Wahl.

Pilar Wahl y Urribe: Daughter of Jaime Wahl.

Zhao Haifeng: First governor general of Luna for the World Federation.

What did you see, Proserpina,
When you were down in the dark?
Why speak you not of that hollow realm
Where the puzzled, quiet shades
Half-dreaming drift through starlessness
And you were their captive queen,
Now when we welcome you back to earth
For as long as you may abide?
The meadows blossom beneath your feet,
The world is awash with light,
But the springtime grass has roots that reach
To trouble the bones below.
Is this why you walk among us mute,
Is this the gift of your love,
To save us from knowing what you have known,
Until you descend again?

—Salerianus,
   Quaestiones, II, i, 1–16

Long afterward, there came to Alpha Centauri the news of what had happened on Earth and around Sol. How that news came, breaking the silence that had been laid upon it, is another story. At the time, few dwellers on Demeter gave it much heed, disturbing though it was. They were in the course of departure from the world their forebears had made home, for in less than a hundred years it must perish. However, one among them was a philosopher.

His young son found him deep in thought and asked why. Because he would not lie to a child, he explained that word lately received from the Mother Star troubled him. "But don't be afraid," he added. "This is nothing that will touch us for a very long while, if it ever does."

"What is it?" inquired the boy.

"I'm sorry, I can't quite tell you," said the philosopher. "Not because it's a secret any longer, but because it goes too far back," and because ultimately it was too subtle.

"Can't you tell me anyway?" urged his son.

With an effort, the father put disquiet aside. Truly, four and a third light-years distant, they need have no immediate fears about the matter; or so he supposed. He smiled. "First you must know some history, and you have barely begun to study that."

"It jumbles together in my head," the boy complained.

"Yes, a big load for a small head to take in," the philosopher agreed. He reached a decision. His child wanted to be with him. Furthermore, if he took this chance to describe certain key factors, a realization of their importance might dawn for the boy, and that might someday make a difference. "Well, sit down beside me and we'll talk," he invited. "We'll look at the beginnings of what you're wondering about. Would you like that?

"We could start anywhere and anywhen. Creatures not yet human, taming fire. The first machines, the first scientists, the early explorers—or spaceships, genetics, cybernetics, nanotechnology—But we'll start with Anson Guthrie."

The boy's eyes widened.

"Always remember, he was just another man," the philosopher said. "Never imagine him as anything else. He'd hate that. You see, he loves freedom, and freedom means having no masters except our own consciences and common sense.

"He did do more than most of us. You remember how it was his Fireball Enterprises that opened up space for everybody. Many governments didn't like having a private company that powerful, nearly a nation itself. But he didn't interfere much with them; he didn't want their sort of power. It was enough that his followers were loyal to him and he to them.

"This might have changed after he died. Luckily, before then he'd been downloaded. The pattern of his mind, memories, style of thinking, were mapped into a neural network. And so his personality went on, in machine bodies, as the chief of Fireball."

"Aw, it's not like that," the boy protested.

"I'm sorry," his father apologized. "Often I'm vague about how much of your education you've quite grasped, as young as you are. You're right, the truth is endlessly more complicated. I don't pretend to know everything about it. I don't believe anybody does.

"But let's go on. Of course you have learned how the Lunarians came to be. Human genes needed changing, if human beings were to live, really live and have children, on Earth's Moon. What you may not have heard much about is the other metamorphs, the other life forms that got changed too, many different new kinds of plants and animals and even people. You may not have heard anything about the Keiki Moana."

The boy frowned, searching memory. "They—they helped Anson Guthrie once—they swam?"

"Yes. Intelligent seals," his father said. The boy had encountered full-sensory recordings of the ordinary species. "They lived with a few humans like dear friends, or more than friends." The philosopher paused. "But I'm getting ahead of myself. That community wasn't founded until after the exodus."

"What's that?"

"Oh, you haven't met the word? Doubtless it is rather archaic. In this case, 'exodus' means when Guthrie led our ancestors to Demeter."

The boy nodded eagerly. "An' the an—ancestors of the Lunarians who live in our asteroids. They all had to go."

"Not strictly true. Probably they could have stayed. But they wouldn't have been happy, the way everything was changing and Fireball itself soon to be no more."

"Because of the machines?"

"No, that isn't right either. Don't forget, people have had machines of one kind or another for ages. They made the machines better and better, till at last they began to build robots, which can be programmed to do things without a person in control. And then finally they built sophotects, machines that can think and *know* that they think, like you and me."

Now the boy's voice took on the least tinge of fear.

"But the so-pho-tects, they made themselves better yet, didn't they?"

His father put an arm around his shoulders. "Don't be afraid. They have no wish to harm us. Besides, they're far away at Sol. Yes, Earth has come to depend on the cybercosm, all those wonderful machines working and . . . thinking . . . together. That's made Earth very different from what we have here—"

The philosopher stopped, knowing how readily dim fears arise in children and grow until they leap forth as nightmares. Already he had softened his utterances. He did not know what the cybercosm portended for humankind. Nobody did, maybe not even itself. Let him set the little heart beside him at rest, as well as he could.

"But it's still Earth, the Earth you've been told about," he said. "The countries are still all in the World Federation, and the Peace Authority keeps them peaceful, and no one has to be hungry or fall sick or go in fear." He wondered how much softening was in that sentence, for indeed he spoke of a world so distant that no ship had borne any of his kind across the space between since Guthrie spent the whole wealth of Fireball to bring a handful of colonists here. Communication with it had virtually ceased. "And we are just as different, in our own ways, from what Earth once was," he finished.

The boy's mother came into the room. "Bedtime," she told him. "Kiss Daddy goodnight."

The philosopher stayed behind, meditating. A violet dusk filled the old-style windows, for the companion sun was aloft, remote in its orbit. Presently he rose and went to his desk. He wished to record whatever ideas occurred to him while the news was fresh. As yet they were unclear, but he hoped that eventually he could write something useful, a letter to the man his son would be. Piece by slow piece, he entered:

"Few of us will ever fully understand what has come to pass—perhaps none, as strange as it was and is.

Surely we cannot foresee how far or how mightily the aftermath will reach, whether out among the comets or onward to trouble the stars. A man and a woman searched back through time, bewildered, hunted, alone. Two lives met across death and centuries. To ask what it meant is meaningless. There is no destiny. But sometimes there is bravery."

1

Lilisaire, Wardress of Mare Orientale and the Cordillera, at Zamok Vysoki, summons the captain Ian Kenmuir, wheresoever he be. Come, I have need of you.

From Luna her message rode carrier beams through relays circling millions of kilometers apart, until it reached the communications center on Ceres. Then the hunt began.

Out here in the deeps, vessels seldom kept unbroken contact with any traffic control station. The computer on the big asteroid knew only that Kenmuir's ship had been active among the moons of Jupiter these past seventeen months. It flashed a question to its twin on Himalia, tenth from the planet. Shunted through another relay, the answer spent almost an hour in passage. The ship had left the Jovian realm eleven daycycles earlier, inbound for a certain minor body.

Given the flight plan Kenmuir had registered, calculating the direction of a laser beam that would intercept him was the work of a microsecond or less. It required no awareness, merely power over numbers. Within that vast net which was the cybercosm, robotic functions like this were more automatic than were the human brainstem's regulation of breath and heartbeat. The minds of the machines were elsewhere.

Yet the cybercosm was always One.

The ship received. "A message for the captain," she said.

Kenmuir and Valanndray were playing double chaos. Fractals swirled through the viewtank before them, in every color and in shapes beyond counting. Guided more by intuition than reason, fingers stroked keyboards. Forms changed, flowed, swept toward a chosen attractor, tumbled away as the opponent threw in a new function. Caught in their game, the players breathed quickly and shallowly of air that they had ordered to be cool, with a tang of pine. They ignored the cabin-wide audiovisual recording at their backs, a view from the Andes, rock and sky and snowdrift on a shrill wind.

The ship spoke.

"Halt play!" snapped Kenmuir. The contest for a stable configuration froze in place.

He spent a moment beneath Valanndray's gaze before he decided, "I'll take it at the console. No offense meant. It may be a private matter." Belatedly he realized that the apology would have gone better had he expressed it in Lunarian.

He felt relieved when his passenger replied, in Anglo at that, "Understood. Secrecy is precious by scarcity, nay?" If the tone was a bit sardonic, no harm. The two men had been getting along reasonably well, but tension was bound to rise on a long mission, and more than once they had skirted a fight. After all, they were not of the same species.

Or maybe that saved them, Kenmuir thought flittingly, as he had often thought before. A pair of Terran males like him, weeks or months on end with no other company, would either have to become soul-brothers or else risk flying at one another's throats. A pair of Lunarians like Valanndray—well, alterations made in ancient genes had not brought forth any race of saints. But neither of this team found his companion growing maddeningly predictable.

Kenmuir doubted that their occasional encounters with sophotects had soothed them. An inorganic intelligence—a machine with consciousness, if you wanted to think of it in those terms—was too alien to them both.

He shrugged the reflection off and walked out into the passageway.

The ship murmured around him, sounds of ventilation, chemical recycling, self-maintenance of the whole structure. There went no sound or shiver of acceleration; the deck was as steady beneath his feet, at one-sixth of Earth weight, as if he were on the Moon. The corridor flickered with a chromatic abstraction, Valanndray's choice. When it was Kenmuir's turn to decorate, he usually picked a scene from his native world, contemporary, historical, or fantasy.

Where his path descended, he used the fixed ladder rather than the conveyor. Anything to help himself stay in trim. The command cabin lay near the center of the spheroidal hull. Its interior displayed ambient space, a representation better than reality. Solar radiance was muted lest it blind. Star images were brightened to overcome shipboard lighting. Unwinking, they beswarmed the dark, white, amber, coal-red, steel-blue, the galactic belt icy among them. Jupiter glowed like a lamp, the sun was a tiny disc rimmed with fire-tongues. Kenmuir settled at the main control board. "Screen the message," he ordered.

His voice sounded too loud in the encompassing silence. For an instant, bitterness woke anew. Command cabin! Control board! He told the ship where and how to go; she did the rest. And hers was a narrowly limited mind. A higher-order sophotect would not have needed anything from him. He knew of no emergency that even this craft couldn't handle by herself, unless it be something that destroyed her utterly.

His glance swung over the stars of the southern sky and came to a stop at Alpha Centauri. Longing shook him. Yonder they dwelt, the descendants of those who had followed Anson Guthrie to a new world, and so tremendous a voyage would scarcely be repeated ever again. From here, at least. Maybe their own descendants would find ways to farther suns. They must, if they were to outlive their doomed planet. But that wreck would not come for lifetimes yet, and meanwhile, meanwhile—

"Pull yourself together, old fool," Kenmuir muttered. Self-pity was contemptible. He did get to fare through space, and the worlds that swung around Sol should have grandeurs enough for any man. Let him thank Lilisaire for that.

Wryness bent his lips upward. Gratitude was irrelevant. The Lunarians had their reasons for keeping as much human staff of both races in their space operations as possible. He, Terran, served a genuine purpose, less as a transporteer who could tolerate higher accelerations than they could than as advisor, troubleshooter, partner of the engineers whom he brought to their work. A sophotect with similar capabilities wouldn't necessarily do better, he told himself fiercely; and if he depended on life-support systems, why, a machine had its requirements too.

The thoughts had flashed through him in a fraction of a second. The message grabbed his attention. Its few words rammed into him. He sat for a while dumbstruck.

Lilisaire wanted him back. At once.

He had expected some communication about the job ahead. To read it in isolation had been an impulse, irrational, a sudden desire to escape for five or ten minutes. Such feelings grew in you on a twenty-four-month tour of duty.

But Lilisaire wanted him straight back.

"Easy, lad, easy," he whispered. Put down love and lust and all other emotions entangled around her. Think. She was not calling him to her for his personal sweet sake. He could guess what the crisis might be, but not what help he might give. The matter must be grave, for her to interrupt this undertaking on which he was embarked. However mercurial some of the Lunarian magnates were, they all took their Venture most seriously. An alliance of entrepreneurs was their solitary last hope of maintaining an active presence in deep space.

Absently, as a nearly automatic accompaniment to thought, he evoked a scan of his destination. It was now about six million kilometers away. At her present rate of braking, the ship would get there in one more daycycle.

Magnified and enhanced, the image of the asteroid swam in the viewtank as a rough oblong lump, murky reddish, pocked with craters shadow-limned against harsh sunlight. Compared to the lesser Jovian moons where Valanndray, with Kenmuir's assistance, had led machines in the labor of development, this was a pygmy.

However, a robotic prospector had found resources worth extracting, not ices and organics but ferrous and actinide ores. A work gang was waiting for human direction—robots, of course, not sophotects: mindless, unaware, though versatile and adaptable. Skilled vision identified a landing field, a cluster of shelters, glints off polished metal skins.

Nearby loomed the skeletal form of a shield generator, big enough for its electrodynamic fields to fend particle radiation not merely off a spacecraft, but off an entire mining plant. Nevertheless it was small, when he compared those that had let him visit Ganymede and return alive.

A visit, and brief. The settlers there were sophotects, for only machines could function in such an environment and only machines that thought, that were aware, could cope with its often terrible surprises. In law the big inner satellites of Jupiter were territory of the World Federation Space Service. In practice they belonged to the cybercosm.

Kenmuir dismissed the recollection and stood up. His heart thudded. To be with Lilisaire again, soon,

soon! Well, if his feelings were like a boy's, he could keep his words a man's. He went back to the recreation room.

Valanndray was still there, toying with orbital mechanics variations. He turned to confront the pilot. His face, fine-boned, ivory-pale, lifted ten centimeters above Kenmuir's. On this crossing he had laid flamboyancy aside and clothed his litheness in a coverall; but it was of deep-blue perlux, and phosphorescent light-points blinked in the fabric. Recorded snow blew behind him, recorded wind beneath the musical voice: "So, Captain?"

Kenmuir halted. Tall for an Earthling, he had long ceased letting Lunarian height overawe him. "A surprise. You won't like it, I'm afraid." He recited the message. Within him, it sang.

Valanndray stood motionless. "In truth, a reversal," he said at length, tonelessly. "What propose you to do?"

"Set you off with the supplies and equipment, and make for Luna. What else?"

"Abandonment, then."

"No, wait. Naturally, we'll call in and explain the situation, if they don't already know at headquarters."

The big oblique eyes narrowed. "Nay. The Federals would retrieve it and learn."

Irritation stirred. Kenmuir had simply wanted to be tactful. Their months together had given him an impression that his associate was in some ways, down below the haughtiness, quite woundable. Valanndray might have felt hurt that the other man was so ready to leave him behind.

Just the same, Kenmuir had grown tired of hearing coldly hostile remarks about the World Federation, and this one was ridiculous. Granted, Lunarians had not rejoiced when their world came back under the general government of humankind. Resentment persisted in many, perhaps most, to this day. But—name of reason!—how long before they were born had the change taken place? And their wish for "independence" was flat-out wrong. What nation-states bred while they existed, as surely as contaminated water bred sickness, had been war.

"The message went in clear because it must, if we were to read it," Kenmuir said. "We don't have cryptographic equipment aboard, do we? Very well, it's in the databases now. Who cares? If somebody does notice it, will he send for the Peace Authority? I hardly think the lady Lilisaire is plotting rebellion."

Recognizing his sarcasm, he made haste to adopt mildness: "Yes, we'll notify the Venture, though I daresay she has already. It ought to dispatch another ship and teammate for you. Within a week or two, I should imagine."

He was relieved to see no anger. Instead, Valanndray regarded the spacefarer as if studying a stranger. He saw a man drably clad, lean to the point of gauntness, with big bony hands, narrow face and jutting nose, grizzled sandy hair cut short, lines around the mouth and crow's-feet at the gray eyes. The look made Kenmuir feel awkward. He was amply decisive when coping with nature, space, machines, but when it came to human affairs he could go abruptly shy.

"The lords of the Venture will be less than glad," Valanndray said.

Kenmuir shaped a smile. "That's obvious. Upset plans, extra cost." When everything was marginal to begin with, he thought. The associated companies and colonists didn't really compete with the Space Service and its sophotects. They couldn't. What kept them going was, basically, subsidy, from the former aristocratic families and from lesser Lunarians who traded with them out of Lunarian pride. And still their enterprises were dying away, dwindling like the numbers of the Lunarians themselves. . . .

He forced matter-of-factness: "But the lady Lilisaire, she's a power among them, maybe more than you or I know." His pulse hammered anew.

Valanndray spread his fingers. A Terran would have shrugged shoulders. "She can prevail over them, yes. Go you shall, Captain."

"I, I'm sorry," Kenmuir said.

"You are not," Valanndray retorted. "You could protest this order. But nay, go you will, and at higher thrust than a single Earth gravity."

Why that grim displeasure? He and Kenmuir had shaken down into an efficient partnership, which included getting along with one another's peculiarities. A newcomer would need time to adjust. But the Earthman felt something else was underlying.

Jealousy, that Lilisaire wanted Kenmuir and not him, though Kenmuir was an alien employee and Valanndray kin to her, a member of her phyle? How well the pilot knew that tomcat Lunarian vanity; how well he had learned to steer clear of it.

Or a different kind of jealousy? Kenmuir pushed the question away. Just once had Valanndray seemed to drop an erotic hint. Kenmuir promptly changed the subject, and it arose no more. Quite possibly he had misunderstood. Who of his species had ever seen the inmost heart of a Lunarian? In any case, they had a quivira to ease them. Kenmuir did not know what pseudo-experiences Valanndray induced for himself in the dream box, nor did the Earthman talk about his own.

"If you loathe the idea, you can come back with me," he said. "You're entitled." On the Moon, obligations between underlings and overlings had their strength, but it was the strength of a river, form and force incessantly changeable.

Valanndray shook his head. Long platinum locks fell aside from ears that were not convoluted like Kenmuir's. "Nay. I have sunken my mind in yonder asteroid for weeks, hypertext, simulations, the whole of available knowledge about it. None can readily replace me. Were I to forsake it, that would leave the Federation so much the richer, so much the more powerful, than my folk."

Kenmuir recalled conversations they had had, and dealings he had had with others, on Luna, Mars, the worldlets of the Belt, moons of Jupiter and Saturn. Few they were, those Lunarian spacefarers and colonists, reckoned against Terrankind. Meager their wealth was, reckoned against that which the machines held in the name of Terrankind. But if they leagued in anger and raised all the resources at their beck, it could bring a catastrophe like none that history knew.

No, hold on. He was being fantastical. Ignore Valanndray's last words. No revolt was brewing. War was a horror of the far past, like disease. "That's right loyal of you," Kenmuir replied.

"I hold my special vision of the future," Valanndray told him. "Come the time, I want potency in council. Here I gain a part of it." The admission was thoroughly Lunarian. "I regret losing your help, in this final phase of our tour; but go, Captain, go."

"Uh, whatever the reason the lady's recalling me, it must be good. For the good of—of Luna—"

Valanndray laughed. Kenmuir flushed. The good of Luna? Hardly a Lunarian concept. At most, the good of the phyle. Still, that could entail benefit for the entire race.

"As for me," Valanndray said, "I will think on this. We can finish our game later. Until evenwatch, Captain." He laid right palm on left breast, courtesy salute, and strolled out the door.

Kenmuir stood a while alone. Lilisaire, Lilisaire!

But why did she want unimportant him at her side?

Because of the Habitat? Remote and preoccupied as he had been, he had caught only fugitive mentions of that project. It seemed the Federation government was definitely going to go through with it. That would rouse fury on Luna—a feat of engineering that would make mass immigration from Earth possible—but what in the manifold cosmos could he do?

What *should* he do? He was no rebel, no ideologue, nothing but a plain and peaceful man who worked in the Venture of Luna because it had some berths for

Terrans who would rather be out among the stars than anywhere else.

Let him shoot a beam to Ceres and ask for an update on Solar System news, with special reference to the Habitat.

No. A chill traversed him. That call, hard upon what had just passed, might draw notice. Or it might not. But if the cybercosm, ceaselessly scanning its databases in search of significant correlations, turned this one up—

Then what? He did not, repeat not, intend anything illegal.

Still, best if he didn't get that update. Wait till he reached Luna, maybe till he and Lilisaire were secluded.

Kenmuir realized that he was bound for his stateroom.

To reach it felt almost like a homecoming. This space was his, was him. Most of his recreations he pursued elsewhere, handball in the gym, figurine sculpture in the workshop, whatever. Here he went to be himself. From the ship's database he retrieved any books and dramas, music and visual art, that he wished. He thought his thoughts and relived his memories, uninterrupted, unseen if maybe he breathed a name or beat a fist into an open hand. A few flat pictures clung to the bulkheads. They showed the Highland moor of his childhood; the Grand Canyon of the Colorado as photographed by him; his parents, years dead; Dagny Beynac, centuries dead. . . .

From a cabinet he took a bottle and poured a short brandy. He wasn't given to solitary drinking, or indulgence in glee or brainstir or other intoxicants. He severely rationed both his time in the quivira and the adventures he dreamed there. He had learned the hard way that he must. Now, though, he wanted to uncoil.

He took his chair, leaned back, put feet on desk. The position was more relaxing under full Earth weight. Yes, bound for Luna, he would most certainly go at that acceleration or better. Lilisaire's words implied he was free to squander the energy. So he wouldn't need the centrifuge to maintain muscle tone. Of course, he would keep up his martial arts and related exercises. As for the rest of his hours, he could read, play some favorite classic shows, and—and, right now, call up Bach's Second Brandenburg Concerto. His tastes ran to the antique.

As the notes marched forth, as the liquor smoldered across tongue and into bloodstream, his eyes sought the portrait of Dagny Beynac and lingered. Always her figure had stood heroic before him. He wasn't sure why. Oh, he knew what she did, he had read three biographies and found remembrances everywhere on Luna; but others had also been great. Was it her association with Anson Guthrie? Or was it, in part, that she resembled his mother a little?

For the thousandth time, he considered her. The picture had been taken when she was in early middle age. She stood tall for an Earthborn woman, 180 centimeters, against the background of a conservatory where flowers grew extravagant under Lunar gravity. A sari and shawl clothed a form robust, erect, deep-bosomed. He knew from recordings that her gait was free-striding. Her features were a bit too strong for conventional beauty, broad across the high cheekbones, with slightly curved nose, full mouth, and rounded chin. Eyes wide-set and sea-blue looked straight from beneath hair that was thick and red, with overtones of bronze and gold, in bangs across the forehead and waves down to the jawline. After half a lifespan of sun and weather and radiation, her skin remained fair. He had heard her voice. It was low, with a trace of burr—"whisky tenor," she called it.

If her spirit, like Guthrie's, had stayed in the world until this day, what might the two of them not have wrought? But no, she ordered oblivion for herself. And she knew best. Surely, in her wisdom, she did.

Hard to believe that once she too was young,

confused, helpless. Kenmuir found his imagination slipping pastward, as if he could see her then. It was a refuge from the present and the future. In the teeth of all fact and logic, he felt himself headed for worse trouble than anybody awaited.

2

The Mother of the Moon

It was always something of an event, reported in the local news media, when Anson and Juliana Guthrie visited Aberdeen, Washington. Self-made billionaires weren't an everyday sight, especially in a small seaport, twice especially after the lumbering that had been the mainstay of adjacent Hoquiam dwindled away. Not that this pair made a production of their status. On the contrary, they took ordinary accommodations and throughout a stay—usually brief, for their business would recall them—they avoided public appearances as much as possible. Dignitaries and celebrities who tried for their company got more or less politely brushed off. Instead, the Guthries were together with the Stambaughs and, later, the Ebbesens. This too caused wonderment. What could they have in common with people who worked hard to earn a humble living?

"We hit it off, we enjoy each other, that's all," Guthrie once told a reporter. "My wife and I aren't silver-spoon types either, you know. Our backgrounds aren't so different from these folks'. We've known 'em for years now, and old friends are best, like old shoes, eh?" Those friends said much the same to anyone who asked. The community learned to accept the situation. As the political climate changed, envy of them diminished.

The relationship came to seem truly remarkable when the Guthries bet all they had on the Bowen laser launcher and founded Fireball Enterprises. Their failure would have been almost as spectacular as their success was, if less meaningful. But after seven years their company dominated space activity near Earth and was readying ships to go harvest the wealth of the Solar System. Nevertheless they returned to Aberdeen every once in a while and were guests in the same small houses.

At last they even invited young Dagny Ebbesen to come along with them up the coast for a little vacation. Centuries later, Ian Kenmuir could conjecture more shrewdly than her neighbors ever did what the real reason was and what actually went on.

In the beginning the girl drew strength and comfort more from the woman. Toward the end, though, Juliana drew her husband aside and murmured, "She needs to talk privately with you. Take her for a walk. A long one."

"Huh?" Anson raised his shaggy brows. "What makes you think so?"

"I don't think it, I feel it," Juliana replied. "She's fond of me; she worships you."

He harked back to their own daughter—she was in Quito, happily married, but he remembered certain desperate confidences—and after a moment nodded. "Okay. I dunno as how I rate that, but okay."

When he rumbled to Dagny, "Hey, you're looking as peaked as Mount Rainier. Let's get some salt air in you and some klicks behind you," she came aglow.

The resort was antiquated, shingle-walled cottages among trees. Across the crumbling road that ran past it, evergreen forest gloomed beneath a silver-gray sky and soughed in the wind. A staircase led down a bluff to a beach that right and left outreached vision. Below the heights and above the clear sand, driftwood lay tumbled, huge bleached logs, lesser fragments of trees and flotsam. Surf brawled white. Beyond it the waves surged in hues of iron. Where they hit a reef, they fountained. A few gulls rode the wind, which skirled bleak, bearing odors of sea and bite of spindrift. At this fall of the year and in these hard times, Guthrie's party had the place to themselves.

He and the girl turned north. For a while they trudged in silence. They made an odd pair, not only because of age. He was big and burly, his blunt visage furrowed beneath thinning reddish hair. Her own hair, uncovered, tossed in elflocks as the single brightness to see. Thus far she still walked slim and light-foot, her condition betrayed by no more than a fullness gathering in the breasts. Whenever she crossed a sprawl of kelp she popped a bladder or two under her heel. When she spied an intact sand dollar, she picked it up with a coo of pleasure. She was, after all, just sixteen.

"Here." She thrust it into Guthrie's hand. "For you, Uncans."

He accepted while asking, "Don't you want it yourself, a souvenir?"

She flushed. Her glance dropped. He barely heard: "Please. You and . . . and Auntie—something to 'member me by."

"Well, thanks, Diddyboom." He gave her hand a quick squeeze, let go again, and dropped the disc into a jacket pocket. "Muchas gracias. Not that we're about to forget you anyhow."

The pet names blew away on the wind as though the wind were time, names from long ago when she toddled laughing to him and hadn't quite mastered "Uncle Anson." They walked for another span, upon the wet strip where the sea had packed and smoothed and darkened the sand. Water hissed from the breakers to lap near their feet.

"Please don't thank me!" she cried suddenly.

He threw her a pale-blue glance. "Why shouldn't I?"

Tears glimmered. "You've done so much for me, and I, I've never done anything for you. Can't I even give you a shell?"

"Of course you can, honey, and we'll give it a good home," he answered. "If you think you owe Juliana

and me something, pay the debt forward; give somebody else who needs it a leg up someday." He paused.
"But you don't owe, not really. We've gotten plenty
enjoyment out of our honorary status. In fact, to us,
for all practical purposes, you're family."

"Why?" she half challenged, half appealed. "What
reason for it, ever?"

"Well," he said carefully, "I'm auld acquaintance
with your parents, you know. Your mother since she
was a sprat, and when your dad-to-be married her, I
was delighted at what a catch she'd made. Juliana
agreed." He ventured a grin. "I expected she'd call
him a dinkum cobber, till she reminded me Aussies
these days don't talk like that unless they're conning a
tourist."

"But we, we're nobody."

"Nonsense. Your sort doesn't take handouts, nor
need them. If I gave a bit of help, it was a business
proposition."

Already in her life she knew otherwise. Helen
Stambaugh's father had been master of a fishing boat
till the fisheries failed. Guthrie put up the capital, as a
silent partner, for him to start over with a charter
cruiser that went up to the Strait of Juan de Fuca and
around among the islands. For a while he prospered
modestly. Sigurd Ebbesen, immigrant from Norway,
became his mate, then presently his son-in-law, and
then, with a further financial boost from Guthrie, a
second partner captaining a second boat. But the
venture collapsed when the North American economy
in general did. The old man was able to take an
austere retirement. Sigurd survived only because
Guthrie persuaded various of his associates and em-
ployees that this was a pleasant way to spend some
leisure time. However, Dagny, first child of two, must
act as bull cook when school was out. She graduated to
deckhand, then mate-*cum*-engineer, still unpaid, her
eyes turned starward each night that was unclouded.

"No," she protested. "Not business, not really. You,
you're just p-plain good—"

Her stammer ended. She swallowed a ragged breath, knuckled her eyes, and walked faster.

Guthrie matched the pace. He allowed her a hundred meters of quietness, except for the wind and surf and sea-mews, before he laid a hand on her shoulder and said, "Friends are friends. I don't gauge anybody's worth by their bank accounts. Been poor too damn often, myself, for that."

She jarred to a stop. "I'm sorry! I didn't mean—"

"Sure." A smile creased his face. "I know you that well, at least." He sighed. "Wish it was better. If I could've seen you folks more than in far-apart snatches—" It trailed away.

She mustered the calm, though fists clenched at her sides, to look straight at him and say almost levelly, "Then maybe you could've steered me off this mess I've gotten myself into? Is that what you're thinking, Uncans? Prob'ly you're right."

Again he smiled, one-sidedly. "You didn't get into it all by yourself, muchacha. You had enthusiastic help."

The color came and went in her cheeks. "Don't hate him. Please don't. He never would have if I—I hadn't—"

Guthrie nodded. "Yeah. I understand. Also, when the word got to me, I looked into the situation a bit. Love and lust and more than a little rebellion, right? By all accounts, Bill Thurshaw's a decent boy. Bright, too. I figure I'll hire an eye kept on him, and if he shows promise—But that's for later. Right now, you *are* too young, you two, to get married. It'd be flybait for a thousand assorted miseries, till you broke up; and your kid would suffer worst."

Steadier by the minute, she asked him: "Then what should I do?"

"That's what we brought you here to decide," he reminded her.

"Dad and Mother—"

"They're adrift with a broken rudder, poor souls. Yes, they'll stand by you whatever you choose, whatever the sniggering neighbors say and the dipnose government does, but what's the least bad course? They've also got your brother to think about. School alone could become an endurance contest, in the clammy piety that's settled on this country."

Momentarily, irrelevantly surprised, she wondered, "Piety? The Renewal doesn't care about God."

"I should've said pietism," he growled. "Puritanism. Masochists dictating that the rest of us be likewise. Oh, sure, nowadays the words are 'environment' and 'social justice,' but it's the same dreary dreck, what Churchill once called equality of misery. And Bismarck, earlier, said that God looks after fools, drunks, and the United States of America; but when the North American Union elected the Renewal ticket, I suspect God's patience came to an end."

Shared need brought unspoken agreement that they walk on. The sand squelped faintly beneath their shoes; incoming tide began to erase the tracks. "Never mind," Guthrie said. "My mouth's too apt to ramble. Let's stay somewhere in the vicinity of the point. You're pregnant. That's shocking enough, in the national climate today, but you're also reluctant to do the environmentally responsible thing and have it terminated."

"A life," she whispered. "It didn't ask for this. And it, it trusts me. Is that crazy?"

"No. 'Terminate' means they poison that life out of you. If you wait till later, it means they crush the skull and slice off any inconvenient limbs and haul it out of you. Yeah, there are times when that may seem necessary, and there are too many people. But when across half the planet they're dying by the millions of famine and sickness and government actions, I should think we can afford a few new little lives."

"But I—" She lifted her hands and gazed at the empty palms. "What can I do?" The fingers closed. "Whatever you say, Uncans."

"You're a proud one, you are," he observed. "I've a hunch this whole business, including your hope you can save the baby, is partly your claim to a fresh breath in all the stifling smarminess around you. Well, we've been over and over the ground, these past several days. Juliana and I, we never wanted to lay pressure on you, one way or another. We only want to help. But first we had to help you grope forward till you knew what your own mind was, didn't we?"

"I could always talk to you . . . better than to anybody else."

"M-m, maybe because we haven't been around so much."

"No, it was *you*, Uncans." With haste: "And Auntie. All right. What should I do?"

"Have the baby. That's pretty well decided. Juliana believes if you don't, you'll always be haunted. Not that your life would be ruined, but you'd never feel completely happy. Besides the killing itself, you'd know you'd crawfished, which plain isn't in your nature. Trust Juliana's insight. If I hadn't had it to guide me dealing with people, I'd be flat broke and beachcombing."

"You understand me too. You made me see."

"Naw. I simply remarked that considering how morons and collectivists breed, DNA like yours and Bill's oughtn't be flushed down the toilet." His tone, deliberately coarse, gentled. "That was no basis for decision. You were what counted, Dagny, and Juliana was who eased the confusion out of you. Okay, now it's my turn. We've settled the what and why, we need to settle the how."

Her stride faltered. She recovered, gulped, looked into the distances before her, and asked quietly, "You don't think I should keep the baby, do you?"

"No. You aren't ready to be tied down. My guess is you never will be, unless it's in the right place, a place where you can really use your gifts. It'll hurt, giving up the young'un as soon as you've borne it, but that will heal. You see, naturally we'll get the best foster parents we can; and I've got the money to mount a proper search for them. Not in this country, under this wretched regime, but abroad, Europe maybe. Don't worry, I'll find my way around any laws there are. You'll know you did the right thing, and can put the whole matter behind you."

Once more, briefly, she caught his hand. "I won't ever—not quite—but . . . thank you."

"Meanwhile and afterward, what about you?" he went on in methodical fashion. "Let's do what I should've seen to before and get you out of here, permanently."

She stiffened. Her voice came thin. "No. I told you when you first suggested it. Dad needs me."

"And is too proud to let me hire him the kind of labor you've provided for free. I know. That's how come I never pushed the idea of putting you in a school where they teach facts and how to think for yourself instead of the Renewal party line. But the chips are down, honey. If you stay home and have the child, I doubt the community will be habitable for your family. And the story will forever be in your file, available at a keystroke to any busybody. If you drop out of sight, though, more or less immediately, the petty scandal won't grow, it'll die out in people's minds. You'll just be a black sheep that left the flock, soon forgotten. As for your father's business, why, your brother's pushing fourteen. Quite able to take over from you, and eager, if I judge aright."

"I . . . I suppose so—"

They were mute for half a kilometer, alone between the sea and the driftwood.

Then she blurted, "Where? What?"

He chuckled. "Isn't it obvious?"

She turned her head to stare at him. Hope went in tides, to and fro with her blood.

Guthrie shrugged. "Well, I wouldn't come right out and say it till we had a notion of where you'd take your stand. But you know Fireball's more and more arranging for the education of its people's children, and we're starting up an academy for professional training. Me, I know you've always been space-struck. For openers, how'd you like to come to Quito with us, and we'll see what develops?"

She stopped. "Ecuador," she gasped—to her, Camelot, Cíbola, Xanadu, the fabled country that Fireball had made its seat because there the government was still friendly to enterprise, the gateway to the universe.

She cast herself into his arms and wept against his shoulder. He stroked the ruddy hair and shuddering back and made bearlike noises.

Finally they could sit down in the lee of a log, side by side. The wind whistled past, driving a wrack of clouds beneath the overcast, but the waters lulled, *hush-hush-hush*. The chill made them shiver a bit, now that they were at rest. She spoke in weary calm:

"Why are you so good to us, Uncans? Sure, you like Dad and Mother, same as you do Mother's parents, but you've told us about friends all over the world. What've we done to deserve this much kindness?"

"I expected I'd have to tell you," he said slowly. "It's got to stay a secret. Promise me you'll never tell anybody without my leave, not your folks, not Bill when you say goodbye to him—which ain't going to be easy, even if the affair is over—not anybody, ever."

"I promise, honest to Dr. Dolittle," she replied, as grave as the child who had learned it from him.

He nodded. "I trust you. The ones who make their own way through life, paying their freight as they go, they're who you can rely on.

"All right. I know your mother's mentioned to you that she wasn't born to the Stambaughs, she was adopted. What she's never known is that I am her father."

Dagny's eyes widened, her lips parted, she kept silence.

"So I can be simpático with you in your bind," Guthrie continued. "Of course, things were quite different for me. This was way back when Carla and I

were in high school in Port Angeles. Carla Rezek—
Never mind. It was wild and beautiful and hopeless."

"And it hurts yet, doesn't it?" Dagny murmured.

His grin flickered. "Mainly I cherish certain memories. Carla went on to marry and move elsewhere; I've
lost track and she hasn't tried to get back in touch,
being the good people she is. Her folks were less
tolerant than yours; they got her well and thoroughly
away from me, but on religious grounds they didn't
countenance abortion. When the baby was born, it
was adopted out. Neither Carla nor I were told where.
Back then, that sort of incident was no great rarity, no
enormous deal. Besides, I soon went off to college, and
on to foreign parts."

"Till at last—"

"Yeah. I came back, not to stay but to revisit the old
scenes, well-heeled and . . . wondering."

The girl flushed. "Auntie?"

"Oh, Juliana knew, and in fact urged me to try and
find out. I might have a responsibility, she said. A
detective followed up some easy clues and located the
Stambaughs in Aberdeen. It wasn't hard to scrape up
an acquaintance. I never meant to intrude, you realize, just be a friend, so I kept mum and swear you to
the same. Wouldn't have told you, either, if I could've
avoided it. Among other things, the secret will be a
burden on you, because I can't very well show you any
favoritism if you elect a Fireball career. Space is too
unforgiving. This day, however, well, you have a
pretty clear need to know. For your heart's sake,
anyhow."

Dagny blinked hard. "Uncans—"

Guthrie cut back to years agone. "Helen was growing up a charming little lady. Shortly after, she
married. We're a headlong breed in that regard, it
seems. You—Me, in my fifties, you're about to make a
great-grandfather of me!" Brief laughter boomed.

"And—and you'll make of me—"

"Nothing, sweetheart. All we offer is a chance for
you to make of yourself whatever you will and can."

They talked onward, until the cold drove them to
walk farther. The sun had gone low. It was still no
more than a brightening behind the cloud deck, but a
few rays struck through to kindle the waters.

3

He who sometimes called himself Venator was also
known, to those who had a need to know, as an officer
in the secret service of the World Federation Peace
Authority. In truth—for the ultimate truths about a
human are in the spirit—he was a huntsman.

In late mornwatch of a certain day on the Moon, he
finished his business with one Aiant and left the
Lunarian's dwelling. After the twilight, birdsong,
white blooms, and vaulted ceiling of the room where
they had spoken, the passage outside glared at him.
Yet it too was a place of subtle curves, along which
colors flowed and intertwined, ocher, mauve, rose,
amber, smoke. At intervals stood planters where al-
oes, under this gravity, lifted their stalks out of spiky
clusters as high as his head, to flower like fireworks six
meters aloft. The breeze had a smell as of fresh-cut
grass, with a tinge of something sharper, purely chemical. He could barely hear the music in it, fluting on a
scale unknown to Earth, but his blood responded to a
subsonic drumbeat.

Few others were afoot. This being a wealthy section,
some went sumptuous of tunic and hose or sweeping
gown, while the rest were retainers of this or that
household, in livery not much less fine. One led a
Siamese-marked cat on a leash—metamorphic, its
genes transformed through generations to make it of
tiger size. All moved with the same grace and aloofness as the animal. A pair who were talking in their
melodious language did so very softly.

They were doubtless a little surprised by the huntsman. Terrans seldom came here, and he was obviously not one who lived on their world but from Earth. Under the former Selenarchy his kind had been debarred from entering the neighborhood at all except by special permission. However, nobody said or did anything, though the big eyes might narrow a bit.

He could have given them back those looks, and not always upward. Many Lunarians were no taller than a tall Terran, which he was. He refrained. A huntsman on the hunt draws no needless attention to himself. Let them glance, inwardly shrug, and forget him.

What they saw was a man lithe and slender, in his mid-thirties, with light-brown skin, deep-brown eyes, and black hair a woolcap on a head long and high. The features were sharp, nose broad and arched, lips thinner than usual for his ethnotype. Clad in a plain gray coverall and soft boots, he carried at his hip a case that might have held a hand-size computer, a satellite-range phone, or even a medic, but which in fact bore something much more potent. His gait was unhurried, efficient, well practiced in low-weight.

It soon took him from the district of old and palatial apartments, through another and humbler inhabited mainly by his species, on into the commercial core of the city. Three-story arcades on plume-like pillars lined Tsiolkovsky Prospect, duramoss yielded underfoot, illusions drifted through the ceiling far overhead. Here there were more folk. Most of the Lunarians wore ordinary garments, although their styles of it—upward-flared collars, short cloaks, dagged skirts, pectoral sunbursts, insignia of phyle or family, colors, iridescences, inset glitterlights, details more fanciful still—would have been florid were it not as natural on them as brilliance on a coral snake. Three men came by together; their walk and posture, black kilts and silver-filigree breastplates, comparatively brusque manner and loud speech, said they were from Mars. Asterites were scarce and less readily identifiable.

Terrans numbered perhaps three out of ten. Some

declared themselves Lunar citizens by some version
of Lunarian garb, often the livery of a seigneurial
house. Others stayed with Earthside fashions, but one
could see by their carriage and by tokens more slight
that they were citizens too, or at least long-term
residents. Among themselves both kinds used ancestral tongues, unless Lunarian was all that they had in
common.

About a third of the Terrans were here from Earth
on assorted errands. Tourists were conspicuous by
their rarity as well as their awkwardness and stares.
Why trouble to come for pleasure when you could
have the experience more easily and cheaply in a
quivira? Your brain would register and remember the
same sensations.

These people were too sparse to be a crowd. Half
the shops, restaurants, bistros, bagnios, amusement
specialties, and cultural enterprises in the arcades
stood closed and vacant. Background noise was a
susurrus through which a gust of music would twang
startlingly strong or a drift of perfume entice the
nostrils. A conversation ahead of him resounded
clearly as the huntsman drew near.

"—sick of being second-class, all my life second-
class. So far can I go, so much can I achieve, then I
strike the invisible wall and everything begins to
happen in such ways that nothing further is possible
for me."

The language, Neudeutsch, was among those the net
had implanted in the huntsman. He slowed his pace.
Familiar though the complaint was, he might possibly
get a little useful input.

Two sat at a street-level table outside an otherwise
empty café tended by a robot. The speaker was plainly
a Terran Moondweller, though he wore a Han Revival
robe in a forlorn sort of defiance. He was as well-
muscled as if he lived on Earth; perhaps he worked off
rage with extra exercise. The skin stood taut on his
knuckles where he gripped a tumbler. His companion,
in a unisuit, was just as plainly a visiting European.

She sipped her own drink and murmured, "Not quite all your life."

"No, of course not. But we've lived here for two hundred years, my family." The man tossed off a gulp. His words tumbled forth. "My parents went back to Earth only to have us, my siblings and me." Evidently it had been a multiple conception, three or four zygotes induced, to spare having to repeat the whole expensive timespan. Probably, the huntsman thought, gestation had been uterine, to save the cost of exogenesis. "As soon as we were developed enough, they returned with us. Nine months plus three years they were gone. Should that have lost them what miserable employment they had? Should the need make us aliens, inferiors? The law says no. But what does the law count for? What is this damned Republic but the same old Selenarchy, in a disguise so thin it's an insult?"

"Calm, please be calm. Once the Habitat is ready, things will soon become very different."

"Will they? Can they? The Selenarchs—"

"The magnates will be overwhelmed, obsolete, irrelevant, within a decade, I promise you. Meanwhile, the opportunities—"

The huntsman went past. He had heard nothing new after all. The woman was involved in one or another of the consortiums already searching out potentials for the Moon of the future. Perhaps she had some use for the man, perhaps he was merely a chance-met talkmate. It didn't matter.

What did matter was that that future lay in danger of abortion.

Despite the service centers at Hydra Square, the fountain in the middle of the plaza splashed through its silvery twinings and fractals alone. The door of the constabulary retracted to let a uniformed officer in and a couple of civilians out, otherwise the fish below the clear paving swam about nobody's feet but the huntsman's. No paradox, though Tychopolis be the largest of the Lunar cities. Here, too, automatons,

robots, and sophotects increasingly took over such
tasks as medical care, maintenance, and rescue, while
the population requiring those attentions declined.
He expected the area would again be thronged once
the settlers from Earth had established themselves
(for however long that would last, a few centuries, a
few millennia, a blink in time for the Teramind but
long enough in human reckoning). Unless their hopes
died beneath the claws of the Selenarchs.

No, he thought, have done with those ideas. He had
found no evidence of any widespread conspiracy. It
seemed he had an adversary more capable than that,
brewing a menace less combatable.

He never knew fear. An organism born to be brave
had learned self-mastery on St. Helena and gone on
into the cybercosm. But when he considered what
might come of this, a thousand years hence or a
million, bleakness touched him.

Resolution resurged. He willed nonsanity away.
Rationally estimated, the odds were high in favor of
his cause. Let him proceed, and the future he had
imagined would be one that *he* aborted.

Besides—a smile played briefly—he expected to
enjoy his quest.

From the square he went on down Oberth Passage.
Industry, computation, biotech, molecular, and quantum operations proceeded in busy silence behind its
walls. Something was not perfectly shielded, and a
stray electromagnetic pulse happened to resonate with
the net inside his skull. Memories sprang up unbid-
den, dawn over a wind-rippled veldt, the face of a
preceptor in the Brain Garden, dream-distorted. He
leaped out of the influence and regained himself.

The disturbance had whetted his senses. He observed his surroundings with redoubled sharpness,
although there was little to see. Nobody else walked
this corridor. The only emblems of ownership were on
the doors of facilities now abandoned. An academic
part of him reflected how the seigneurs of the Moon
disdained the minor trades and businesses viable in a

post-capitalist economy and mostly lived off their inherited holdings. To be sure, some of those were far-flung in the Solar System and not insubstantial on Earth. Also, a few individuals continued active in enterprises they deemed worthy of themselves. The associated companies of their Venture were still breaking new ground on Mars, small moons of Jupiter and Saturn, the comets, the asteroids. . . .

The huntsman's mouth drew tight. He went onward in long low-gravity bounds.

Ellipse Lane curved off from Oberth. Fifty meters down it, he came to his lodgings. The front was as bare and undistinguished as the corridor. He put his right palm against the keyplate.

It looked like any other, but it did not merely scan lines in the skin. All standard security devices could be fooled in any of several different ways, if someone had the will and the means. Were such an attempt made here, the lock would alert headquarters. Meanwhile it removed three or four cells from him, which he did not feel, and shunted them to a DNA reader. This identified him, and the door retracted. The identification took a little more time than usual, but so little that a watcher who didn't know would not have noticed. A hundred milliseconds or five hundred, what difference? Speed like that demanded an enormous capability, but it was present, hidden. The huntsman entered his den.

After the door shut behind him, the place seemed barren. It wasn't really a home. Two inner cubicles held a bed, a sanitor, a nutrition unit, and whatever else was barebones necessary, but here were only screens, panels, receptors, and other unobtrusive outwardnesses of the great, thinking engine. The ceiling shone cold white, and air circulated odorless.

When the site was converted to an apartment—he had heard that it was formerly a tavern—the secret service of the Peace Authority acquired it under the name of a data-synthetic person and remodeled it, an unnoticeable piece at a time. That seemed a reasonable precaution, inasmuch as the Republic of Luna restricted the Authority to a single office and a platoon in Port Bowen. A listening post and center for safe communications was desirable elsewhere, in a nation this widespread and tricky. Later the huntsman's corps had installed their special gear, and at the moment he was using the fictitious name.

He went straight to work. More drove him than eagerness in the chase. For too many daycycles he had been just briefly and intermittently in synnoiosis. This episode of it would go longer and deeper, enough to sustain him until he returned to Earth and could again enter a full communion.

Or a Unity—no, he dared not yearn for that. Not now.

Opening the case at his flank, he took out the interlink, unfolded it, and adjusted it on his head. It fitted like a coif of closely woven black mesh with bright small nodules at a number of the intersections. Within was a complexity not much less than that in a living cell, and in certain respects more: crystals and giant molecules never found in nature, interactions down to the quantum level. It was best to be physically relaxed, however mild the demands of Lunar gravity. He reclined on a couch before a deceptively simple-looking control panel. "Is all clear?" he inquired.

"All clear," replied the sophotect that had kept watch on the room and the communication lines. "Carry on at will."

The huntsman plugged in his interlink. Wire and contact were structures comparably intricate. He willed. Synnoiosis began.

The net that nanomachines had woven inside his head, when he was a cadet in the Garden, came active. It traced out the ongoing, ever-shifting electrochemical activity of his brain, rendered the readings as a multiple-terabaud data stream, and passed them on to the interlink, which translated them into machine language and conveyed them farther. As the system

responded, the interlink became a generator of pulses
and dancing fields whereby the net directly stimulated
the brain.

The process appeared to be as uncomplicated as the
outward show of the things themselves. It was in fact
an achievement beyond the creation or the full understanding of any merely human intelligence. It joined
two orders of being that were utterly unlike—organic
and inorganic, chemical and electrophotonic, life and
post-life.

It was not telepathy, it was communication by
language through an interpreter. But to master that
language, the huntsman had paid with his childhood
and youth. And it was not a language that went
through the ears or the eyes, the sensor or the keyboard. It went directly between nervous system and
circuitry.

For him, its fullness was a transcendence higher
than ever he knew in sexual union, mortal danger, or
intellectual challenge. He had asked sophotects how it
was for them, but they had been unable to explain. If
nothing else, among them oneness was as normal an
occurrence as feeding was to him.

This was only a partial, almost superficial, interface. He dealt in straightforward information, material that could have been rendered in text, graphics, and
speech. The sophotects involved, the one here and the
one at headquarters in Port Bowen, were conscious.
They thought, but they were narrowly specialized and
focused, content to dwell immobile, essentially bodi-
less, with all input and output going along the data
lines. The system itself was limited in both databases
and capabilities. Even on the Moon, larger nets existed; but if he tapped into them, he might alert his
prey.

Nevertheless, this synnoiotic session was more than
a hurried report or query. Far faster and more com-
prehensively than could have been done in the flesh,
he gave out what he had learned and received what he
asked for. He need not trace a way through hypertext;

associated facts and ideas came to him as an integrated whole. Entire histories became his. A hundred variant plans of campaign developed, simulated their probable consequences, and left behind them what parts he deemed worth fitting into a new synthesis. Above and beyond loomed the sense of how it all reached through space-time, past and future and the ends of the universe, and how fateful it might yet prove.

The cool and luminous ecstasy had no counterpart among mortals, although religious enlightenment or a basic mathematical insight shared aspects of it. He was in a single mind that built its own memories and discoursed with itself by many thinkings on many levels conjoined. That polylogue was not for any human tongue to repeat. Even its material content grew cumbersome when set baldly and linearly down.

Aiant, husband of Lilisaire, resident here in Tychopolis, is seldom in contact with her and almost never meets her. They are second cousins. She succeeded her father in the ancestral estates by right of ontigeniture, but Aiant contested this and there is reason to suspect he had the father assassinated. Although she was only 23 at the time, Lilisaire undertook intrigue and occasional surreptitious violence on her own behalf. In the course of five years she outmaneuvered him, leaving him stripped of most of his conciliar powers and close to bankruptcy. Then she married him. The alliance works well. He is secondary but not subjugated, and profits by serving her interests, especially her share of the spacefaring Venture.

He and his city wife (probably chosen for him by Lilisaire because of her family connections, she being of the Mare Crisium phratry) received me courteously if not cordially and were as cooperative as could be expected. They were eager to convince me that there is no plot to sabotage the Habitat, as I had led them to believe we suspect. A full-scale investigation by the Peace Authority would inconvenience the Venture at best, and might turn up matters that really are being kept secret. They retrieved all the data I requested (not knowing me for a synnoiont, who could get more out of this information than an entire detective squad).

Conclusion: They are ignorant of any untoward activity, and their organization is not involved in any, although individuals and cabals within it may be.

It was already established that Caraine of Hertz-sprung, Lilisaire's younger husband, their adult son Bornay, and Caraine's other two wives are equally uninvolved. Although oftener together physically with Lilisaire than Aiant is, Caraine has little to do with her various undertakings. The alliance is useful to both, coupling Phyle Beynac and Phyle Nakamura in a genetically and strategically desirable bond between the Cordilleran and Korolevan phratries, and a personal affinity exists. However, besides his estate, Caraine is engaged in politics, being one of the few Lunarians, especially of Selenarchic descent, who has condescended to develop parliamentary skills.

As such, he is valuable to the aristocratic faction, machinating to keep them in effective power and the Terran minority effectively disfranchised. Lilisaire would likely regard it as wasteful to engage his energy and talents in anything else. Moreover, in recent months he has been fully and conspicuously occupied in the effort to mobilize opposition to the Habitat sufficient to force the cancellation of the project. Improbable though his success is, he would scarcely be wanted meanwhile in any clandestine endeavor. Nor have his wives and children left home or communicated with anyone off the Moon.

Thus Lilisaire may well be the only Lunarian magnate preparing trouble for us. This gives no grounds for complacency. She could prove as formidable, and is certainly as ruthless, as her famous ancestors Rinndalir and Niolente.

Evidence: Legal proof is lacking, and the case would in any event not be prosecuted by the present Lunar government; but the Peace Authority intelligence corps has ascertained that in younger days she killed at least two men in duels. One was fought topside in the wilderness with firearms, one in her castle with rapiers. She has traveled widely, even braving the gravity of Earth, where she has a large inherited property. She has gone out to Mars, the asteroids, Jupiter, and Saturn. She is enamored of deep space and of endeavor in it. (A more distant ancestor of hers was a grandson of both the explorer Kaino and the poet Verdea.) But she is coldly realistic about her part in the Venture operations.

She maintains connections throughout the Solar System. Some of these are with former lovers, especially influential Earthmen, who, if not actually her allies, are usually willing to oblige her with information and assistance. Her reckless, voluptuous youth is behind her, but her power to fascinate and mislead has, if anything, grown with the years. This is not a negligible factor. It is one which the cybercosm is ill suited to comprehend or control.

She is highly intelligent, possesses an extensive cybernet, and has at her call a variety of agents. About many of these we have only intimations, no knowledge of identity, location, or function.

Lately our watch program over her communications detected a message to a spacer in the asteroids, bidding him come to her immediately. (Not knowing precisely where he was, she could not beam it quantum encrypted. Nor would he likely have had equipment to decode it.) She may not be aware that we are monitoring. If she is, she doubtless means to pass this off as involving some service he can do her which is no affair of the government's.

But the matter is almost certainly not trivial. This Ian Kenmuir is an Earthman in the service of the Venture. His one distinction is that he has been her guest in Zamok Vysoki, and probably her lover. (That was not publicized in any way. Although Lunarians seldom like being in the public eye, they also seldom make any effort to conceal such doings, being indiffer-

*ent to gossip or contemptuous of it.) His very obscurity
may well recommend him to her for her purposes.*

*Or he may have knowledge, or access to knowledge,
that she wants. Those researches of hers are aimed at
deep space. Very deep space.*

I propose to visit her.

*I have a pretext prepared. The odds are that she does
not know that we know of her quiet inquiries. The order
to monitor her came from high in the cybercosm—
perhaps from the Teramind itself, when it observed
those questions being asked and foresaw where the
answers would lead.*

*She must know that agents of the Peace Authority
have called on associates of hers. It would appear
strange if none talked also with her. I do not expect to
discover much, if anything. Yet . . . I am a synnoiont.*

GO, THEN, the system of which he was a part told
him.

That oneness died away. The huntsman removed
himself from the net.

For a while he lay quiescent. Nothing felt real. The
facts and the decision were in him but he could not
remember them other than as fading wisps of a
dream. The physical world seemed flat and grotesque,
his body a foreigner.

The sense of loss passed, and he was human again.
Hunger and thirst nudged him to his feet. "Put me in
touch with the lady Lilisaire," he directed the
sophotect, and went to get his nutrition.

It was minimal. He could savor good food and
drink, if the amounts were moderate, but not when on
the trail.

Afterward he relaxed at the vivifer. The show he
summoned was a comedy set in the New Delhi of
Nehru. He did not set the speech converter; Indi was
among his languages. The story was shallow and not
especially believable—although he admitted to himself he had scant rapport with low-tech societies,

today or in the past—but sight, sound, scent, tactility were well done. To have a more lifelike experience, he would have had to get into a quivira.

A bell tone pulled him from it. So soon? He had been resigned to waiting hours before the system located Lilisaire and persuaded her to give audience to a constable.

He hastened to the eidophone. Her image met him, vivid as fire. He saw, above a long neck, a face nearly classic save for the high cheekbones, peculiar ears with blinking stardrops in the lobes, gold-flecked sea-green of the big oblique eyes, flared nostrils, wide mouth where smiles and snarls might follow each other like sun and hailwind. Startling against blue-veined white skin was the hair, auburn threaded with flame-red, swept up from her brow and falling halfway down her back. He knew from recordings that she was as tall as he, slender, long-legged, firm in the breasts and rounded in the hips. He saw a lustrous cheong-sam, a headband patterned on the DNA molecule, and hardly a trace of her fifty-odd years. Medical programs accounted for only a part of that, he knew. With Lunarian chromosomes, she might reach a fourth again of his projected 120.

If they both survived.

"Hail, my lady," he greeted in his fluent Lunarian. "You are gracious thus to respond."

For some reason, she chose to reply in Anglo. Her voice purred low. "Unwise would I be to linger when the Peace Authority calls."

He shifted to the same tongue. "You know full well, my lady, we have very little power within your country unless your government grants it. Wise you may be, but kind you certainly are."

She smiled. "A neat riposte. What would you of me, Officer?"

"An interview, if you please. I think you would prefer it be either over an encrypted line or in private person."

Arched fox-colored brows lifted higher. "What could be so critical?"

"I believe you have made a shrewd guess at it, my lady."

The mercurial visage refashioned cordiality. "Maychance I have. We shall see, Captain—Eyach, I have no name for you." The sophotect, pretending to be a robot, had declared that was his rank.

"My apologies, my lady. I forgot to instruct the communicator about that." It was true, and he felt annoyed at himself. His name had long ceased to have meaning for him and he used any that suited his purposes. His actual identity was a function within the cybercosm.

"Venator," he said, accenting the penult. Roving through the databases, his favorite recreation, he had acquired a jackdaw hoard of knowledge. It amused him to resurrect this word from a language dead and well-nigh forgotten.

Lilisaire inquired no further. Probably more Earthlings than not went without surnames these days, as Lunarians always had. He imagined her thinking in scorn: but the Earthlings have their registry numbers. Her courtesy remained smooth. "Then, Captain Venator, wish you to come directly to me at Zamok Vysoki? I will make you welcome."

Astonished, he said, "At once? I could take a suborbital and be there very shortly, but—"

"If you, of the Peace Authority, have a suborbital available at Tychopolis, your superiors look on this as important," she said, still at catlike ease. "Yes, do, and allow time for the taking of hospitality. I will await." The screen blanked.

He sat for a brief while recovering his equilibrium. How much did she know? What was her intent—to rush him along, to lead him astray, or merely to perplex him for sport's sake?

If she was on the attack, let him respond.

Quickly he stripped, stepped under needle spray

and dryer, and donned a close-fitting blue uniform with bronze insignia. Formality was his first line of defense. After hesitating, he decided to leave his interlink behind. He didn't anticipate urgent need of it, and he was unsure what detectors and probes Lilisaire kept in her stronghold. The less she discovered about him, the better.

The sophotect made arrangements while he was on his way to the flyport. A fahrweg took him below the ringwall, out to the drome. Antique installations like this remained in service in regions of lesser prosperity and population, also on Earth. His fellow riders were few. The vehicle waited in a launcher already set and programmed for its destination. A mobile gangtube admitted him to it. He secured himself in a seat. *Go,* he pressed.

Against this gravity, the electromagnetic acceleration was gentle. In moments he was falling free along an arc that would carry him high above the Moon and a quarter of the way around it.

Silence brimmed the cabin. Weightlessness recalled to him, a little, that ocean of thought in which he had lately floated. He looked out the viewscreens. Beneath him shadows edged a magnificent desolation of craters and worn-down highlands. Monorails, transmission towers, solar collectors, energy casters glittered steely, strewn across that wasteland. Few stars shone in the black overhead; light drowned them out. To north the sun stood at late Lunar morning. Earth was not far from it, the thinnest of blue crescents along a darkling disc. They sank as he flew.

Idly, he turned off the cabin lights and enhanced the stars. Their multitudes sprang forth before him, more each second while his eyes adapted. He traced constellations, Eridanus, Dorado—yonder the Magellanic galaxies—Crux, Centaurus . . . Alpha Centauri, where Anson Guthrie presided over his companion downloads and the descendants of those humans who had left the Solar System with him. . . . No, the

Lunarians among them didn't live on the doomed planet Demeter but on asteroids whirling between the two suns. . . .

Had that exodus been the last and in some ways the mightiest achievement of the Faustian spirit? A withdrawal after defeat was not a capitulation. Someday, against all believability, could it somehow carry its banners back home? What allies might it then raise? It was not yet dead here, either. He was on his way to meet with a living embodiment of it.

Revolt—No, nothing so simple. The Lyudov Rebellion had been, if anything, anti-Faustian. "Reclaim the world for humanity, before it is too late!" Keep machines mindless, create anew an organic order, restore God to his throne.

But Niolente of Zamok Vysoki had had much to do with stirring up that convulsion; and Lilisaire bore the same resentments, the same wild dreams.

A warning broke Venator from his reverie. Time had passed more quickly than he thought. Jets fired, decelerating.

The vehicle and the ground control system handled everything. He was free to observe. His glance ranged avidly ahead and downward. Images of this place were common enough, but few Terrans ever came to it. He never had, until now.

Eastward the mountains fell away toward a valley from which a road wound upward, with Earth and sun just above the horizon. Westward the castle rose sheer from its height, tiered walls darkly burnished, steep roofs, craggy towers, windows and cupolas flaring where they caught the light. It belonged to the landscape; the design fended off meteoroids and radiation, held onto air and warmth. Nevertheless, Venator thought, a Gothic soul had raised it. There should have been pennons flying, trumpets sounding, bowmen at the parapets, ghosts at night in the corridors.

Well, in one sense, ghosts did walk here.

The flyer set down on a tiny field at the rear of the

building. A gangtube extended itself from otherwise bare masonry and osculated the airlock. The huntsman went in.

Two guards waited. In form-fitting black chased with silver, shortswords and sonic stunners at hips, they overtopped him by a head. The handsome faces were identical and impassive. They gave salute, right palm on left breast, and said, "Welcome, lord Captain. We shall bring you to the Wardress," in unison and perfect Anglo.

"Thank you." Venator's own Anglo was of the eastern, not the western hemisphere. He fell in between them.

The way was long. An ascensor brought them to a hallway where the illusion of a vast metallic plain was being overwhelmed by blue mists in which flames flickered many-hued and half-glimpses of monsters flitted by, whistling or laughing. It gave on a conservatory riotous with huge low-gravity flowers, unearthly in shape and color. Their fragrances made the air almost too rich to breathe. Beyond was another corridor, which spiraled upward, twilit, full of funereal music. Ancestral portraits lined the walls; their eyes shifted, tracking the men. At the top, a vaulted room displayed relics that Venator would have liked to examine. What was the story behind that knife, that piece of meteoritic rock, that broken gyroscope, that human skull with a sapphire set in the forehead? The next chamber must have its everyday uses, for spidery Lunarian furniture stood on a white pelt of carpet; but the ceiling was a blackness containing an enormous representation of the galaxy, visibly rotating, millions of years within seconds, stars coming to birth, flaring, guttering out as he watched.

He came to Lilisaire.

The room she had chosen was of comparatively modest size and outfitting. One wall imaged a view of Lake Korolev, waves under a forced wind, dome simulating blue heaven, a pair of sport flyers aloft, wings outstretched from their arms. On a shelf, a nude girl twenty centimeters tall, exquisitely done in mercury-bright metal, danced to music recorded from Pan pipes. A table bore carafes, goblets, plates of delicacies. Lilisaire stood near it.

The guards saluted again, wheeled, and left. Venator advanced. "Hail anew," he said with a bow, in Lunarian, using the deferential form. "You are indeed gracious."

She smiled. "How so, Captain?" As before, her reply was in Anglo.

He went back to the Terrestrial language. Why make it clear how well he knew hers? But courtliness, yes. "The tension between—I won't say between our races or even our societies, my lady, but between your class and mine. And still you set privacy aside, though I understand full well how your people prize it, and you receive me in your home."

Her tone stayed amicable. "Also enemies negotiate."

"I'm not exactly an envoy, my lady. And to me you are no enemy. Nor are Earth or the World Federation enemies to you."

The voice stiffened. "Speak for yourself, not them."

"Who wishes you harm?"

"Wishing or nay, they make ready to wreak it."

"Do you refer to the Habitat, my lady?" he asked: a socially necessary redundancy.

She evaded directness. "Much else has Earth done to Luna."

"Why, it was Earth that brought Luna alive."

She laughed. The sound was brief and low, but in some sly fashion uttered with her whole body. "You have a quite charming way of affecting naïveté, Captain. Let me, then, denote us as dwellers on the Moon."

He followed her conversational lead, for his real purpose was to explore her attitudes. "May I speak freely?"

"Is that not the reason you came?" she murmured. Now she was playing at being an innocent, he thought. "When you say 'dwellers,' I suspect you mean Lunarians, not resident Terrans, not even those Terrans who are citizens. And . . . if you say 'Lunarians' to me, do you perhaps mean the Selenarchic families—or the Cordilleran phratry—or simply its overlings?" Try, cautiously, to provoke her.

The green gaze levelled upon him. The words were quiet but steady. "I mean the survival of the blood."

That should not have put him on the defensive, but he heard himself protest, "In what way are you threatened, your life or your property or anything that's yours?"

"My lineage is. You propose to make Lunarians extinct."

The shock was slight but real. "My lady!"

Lilisaire finger-shrugged. "Eyach, of course the fond, foolish politicians who imagine they govern humankind, they think no such thing, insofar as they can think at all. They see before them only the ego-bloated eminence that will be theirs, for that they opened the Moon to Terrans."

"The gain's much more than theirs," he must argue. "Those people who'll come are bold, enterprising sorts. What new work has been done here for the past century or longer? They'll build the way your ancestors did, cities, caverns, life—make the Moon over."

For they were the restless ones, the latent Faustians, he thought for the hundredth time. They found their lives on Earth empty, nothing meaningful left for them to do, and their energy and anger grew troublesome. He had wondered whether the Teramind itself had conceived this means, the Habitat, of drawing them together here where they could expend themselves in ways that were containable, controllable—in the course of lifetimes, tamable.

"They will swarm in," Lilisaire said, "they will soon outvote us, and all the while they will outbreed us."

"Nothing prevents you Lunarians from vying with them in that," Venator said dryly.

Except, he thought, their lack of the strong urge to reproduce that was in his race, that had brought Earth to the edge of catastrophe and was still barely curbed, still a wellspring of discontent and unrest. The Habitat would give its beneficiaries some outlet for this, for some generations. Lunarians were never so fecund. Why? Was it cultural or did it have a genetic basis? Who knew? To this day, who knew? You could map the genome, but the map is not the territory, nor does it reveal what goes on underground. He himself supposed that the effect was indirect. Arrogant, self-willed people did not want to be burdened with many children.

Again Lilisaire laughed. "At last a thousandfold worn-out dispute shows a fresh face!" Lightly: "Shall we leave it to twitch? Be welcome, Captain, as a new presence in an old house. Will you take refreshment?"

He had gotten used to Lunarian shifts of mood. "Thank you, my lady."

She poured, a clear sound against the Pan pipes, gave him his goblet of cut crystal, and raised hers. The wine glowed golden. *"Uwach yei,"* she toasted. It meant, more or less, "Aloft."

"Serefe," he responded. Rims chimed together.

"What tongue is that?" she asked.

"Turkish. 'To your honor.'" He sipped. It was glorious.

"You have ranged widely, then—and, I deem, as much in your person as in vivifer or quivira."

"It is my duty," he said dismissingly.

"What breed are you?"

Momentarily he was taken aback, then recognized the idiom she had in mind. "I was born in the southern end of Africa, my lady."

"A stark and beautiful land, from what I have seen."

"I was small when I left it." If you had the synnoiotic potential, you must develop it from early childhood, or it was gone. His mind flew back to the sacrifices his parents had made—his mother giving up

her career; his father, pastor in the Cosmological
Christian Church, seeing him bit by bit losing God—
to be with him in the Brain Garden on St. Helena, give
him some family life while he grew into strangeness.
But parents had always surrendered themselves and
their children to something larger. History knew of
apprentices to shamans, the prophet Samuel, Dalai
Lamas, lesser monks of many faiths, yes, boys made
eunuchs because only so could they advance in the
service of the Emperor. . . . "I do go back now and
then." It was indeed beautiful, that preserve where
lions walked and grass swayed golden beneath the
wind.

He must not let her pursue this subject. Lilisaire
stood pensive. How much did she know or guess at? It
was actually a relief when she said: "Maychance we
should consider your business, that later we can take
our ease. I think I would enjoy showing you about my
abode."

"I'd be fascinated," he replied, which was no lie,
although he realized he would see nothing she didn't
want him to see.

"You and your . . . lesser comrades?" (What intimation had she of his real status, not a simple captain
among detectives but a pragmatic of determinor
rank?) "have investigated Caraine and Aiant, as well
as others of the old blood." (How quickly she had
learned that!) "Now it is my turn, nay?" Her glance
might have seemed candid. "Well, short and plain, I
know naught of any plot to wreck the Habitat. True,
you would not await that I admit it. Thus let me lay
thereto that any such would be futile, stupid. Niolente
herself could not in the end stay the all-devouring
Federation."

Despite her resistances, intrigues, fomented rebellion, terminal armed defiance, no. Venator wanted to
say that the collapse of the sovereign Selenarchy, the
establishment of the Republic, its accession to the
World Federation and the rules of the Covenant were

not merely the result of political and economic pressures. Ultimately, it was moral force. When Rinndalir left with Guthrie and Fireball began disbanding, the heart went out of too many Lunarians. Niolente's had beaten rather lonely.

But: "We were not going to pick over dry bones, were we, my lady?" he advanced.

Lilisaire's smile could turn unfairly seductive. "You *are* an intelligent man, Captain. I could come to a liking for you."

"I certainly don't accuse or suspect you of wrongdoing," he said in haste. "I'm only, m-m, puzzled, and hope you can give me some illumination."

"Ask on." She gestured. "Shall we be seated?"

That meant more on low-*g* Luna than on Earth. He settled onto the divan before the table. She joined him. He was far too conscious of her nearness. A pheromonal perfume? No, surely nothing so crude, and so limited in its force.

"Taste," she urged. He nibbled a canapé of quail's egg and caviar. Her daintiness put him to shame.

He cleared his throat. "My service has found clues to some activity in deep space," he said. "Probably it's based in the asteroids, but we aren't certain."

He lied. He knew of no such thing, unless you counted that bitter resistance to Federation governance which died with Lilisaire's ancestress Niolente. The service had monitored this woman as closely as it was able because it knew she was equally opposed to most of what the Federation stood for, and she was dangerous. It learned that she had been ransacking every record and database available to her, and some of her queries had come near the matter of Proserpina. If she reached it, that could prove deadly. And now she had recalled Ian Kenmuir from yonder.

"It's not necessarily illicit," Venator continued, "but it is undeclared, apparently secret. If it's going to be consequential, the government naturally wants information about it."

"Yes," she said low, "to feed your computer models, to coordinate this also into your blandly running socioeconomic structure."

He heard but ignored the venom. "Since you have enterprises out there, my lady," and all the asteroid colonists were Lunarians, who could tolerate weak gravity, "I wonder if you might have some knowledge."

Her voice became teasing. "If the undertaking be secret, how should I?"

"I don't mean directly. Someone may have noticed something and mentioned it to you, incidentally."

"Nay. I am too distant from those realms. I have been too long away." Intensity: "Eyach, too long away."

Because she must stay here to wage her hidden war?

"A forlorn hope of mine, no doubt," he said. "And the whole thing may be a mistake, a wrong interpretation of ours." What it was was a farce. He had no expectation of really sounding her out. He was after intangibles, personality, traits, loves, hatreds, strengths, weaknesses, her as a living person. Given that, he might better cope with her. "I'll be very grateful if you'd look into your memory, put a search through your personal files, whatever may possibly call up something relevant."

"Indeed I have memories. Yet you must tell me more. Thus far this is vacuum-vague."

"I agree." He did have specifics to offer her, concocted details that might be convincing.

"Best we range it at leisure." Her fingers touched his wrist. She smiled afresh. "Come, you've barely tasted your wine, and it a pride of my house. Let us get acquainted. You spoke of your African childhood—"

He must be careful, careful. But with a mind like hers, it should not be too difficult to steer conversation away from the trivia that would betray him.

The daycycle passed. They drank, talked, wandered, dined, and went on from there.

To him, sexual activity had been an exercise desirable occasionally for health's sake. He discovered otherwise.

She bade him farewell next mornwatch, cool as a mountain spring. He was only dimly aware of his flight back to Tychopolis. Not until he had been in oneness and cleared his head did he see how she had told him nothing meaningful, and how he might well have let slip a few inklings to her.

For a while he had even thought there was some justice on her side. But no. In the long term, hers was the fire that must be quenched. In the near future—well, Terrans had brought the Moon to life, beginning before there were any Lunarians. They had their own claim, their own rights, on this world, won for them hundreds of years ago by the likes of Dagny Beynac.

4

The Mother of the Moon

The great meteorite that blasted out Tycho Crater had been richer in iron and nickel than most of its kind. Fragments lay far-scattered, shallowly buried under the regolith. The larger ones, chondrules fused together by the impact, thus became ore deposits such as are rare on weatherless basaltic Luna. When expanding operations demanded a Nearside base in the southern hemisphere, they were a major reason to site it in Tycho.

Dagny Ebbesen was helping build it when her boss sent her to the Rudolph lode. "We've promised the workers better quarters, you know," Petras Gedminas explained. "It will be a standard assembly, but you will get experience in directing a job." He paused. "No. We are far from the stage at which any task is standard. Expect the unexpected."

His warning was unnecessary. In the course of two

years, Dagny had learned it well. A habitations engineer, no matter how junior, must needs be quite a bit of everything.

Three daycycles after she reached the mine, about one-tenth of a Lunar day, the disaster happened.

A field van had newly rolled in. Calling ahead, the driver identified himself as Edmond Beynac, homebound from an expedition with his assistant. They would like a little rest and sociability before going on. Dagny was eager to meet the geologist. His reports had been important to construction, showing where the rock could be trusted, in what ways and how much. Moreover, his discoveries and analyses had changed several ideas about the entire globe. And then the adventure of it, roving and beholding where no human had ever trod!

The hour was 2130, mid-evenwatch. Her gang worked around the clock, sleeping in relays, to finish before the sun got so high that heat and radiation kept them inside full-time. Someday, she thought, technology would remove that handicap. (Yes, and it would do something about the damned, clinging, all-begriming dust.) Weariness nagged at her bones. However, at twenty-two years of age, under one-sixth Terrestrial gravity, she could ignore it. She could lose herself in what she did and what she sensed.

Her project was still a jumble of excavations, frameworks, life-support and power systems half installed, men and machines intricately busy. High-piled supplies dwarfed the shelters. Some distance off, the original camp clustered in domes and beehives, not much larger; most living space was underground. There the centrifuge stood idle. The miners were at rest, except for two or three who kept watch over the equipment that did the heavy labor, digging, breaking, and loading. That was two kilometers eastward, almost at the horizon. Sun, shadow, and upflung dust-haze obscured it; occasionally a piece of metal flashed.

The slim pylons of the funicular lifted clear to sight.

In double file, widely separated, they marched from the pit, passed within a hundred meters of her, and vanished beyond the southwestern rim of vision. Their cable strands made thin streaks across the sable overhead. A gondola had just been filled with ore and winched aloft to hang by its suspension. The cable was set in motion àgain. The gondola started its journey through heaven like a spider dangling from a strand. It was off to deliver its burden to the builders of Tychopolis, who would refine and use the metals. They in their turn sent back what the crews here needed. This was the most economical means of bulk transport, given the shortage of vehicles and ruggedness of the crater floor.

Rugged indeed: hillocks, shelves, boulders, pockmarks, cracks, clefts, a confused and darkling plain. Behind the mine, the uppermost ramparts of a ringwall segment hove into view. The sun having barely cleared them, they remained featurelessly black, their shadow a tar pool. Everywhere else, lesser shadows fingered stone. Stars were drowned in the glare. Soiled white spacesuits, bright-colored badges and tags, scuttled tiny amidst huelessness.

Earth, though, Earth ruled the northern sky. Waned slightly past half phase, the curves of it limned a blue and white marbling, an ocherous blur that was land, a luminance that lingered for a moment after you looked away from it as a dream may linger when first you awaken. Earth was glory enough.

Below it dwelt quietude. Without air, sound dies aborning. Sometimes Dagny's receiver conveyed a voice, but mainly work proceeded mute, skill set against time. Otherwise she heard air rustle in her recycler and nostrils, blood in her ears.

"Take over," she told Joe Packer, her second, and went toward the field van. Cabin and laboratory, equipped to travel hundreds of kilometers without recharge and sustain life for weeks, on its eight enormous tires it overtopped the main dome near which it had parked. As she approached, a ladder

swung down to the ground, an outer valve opened.
The new buildings would allow direct access, airlock
to airlock, but as yet visitors must walk across to the
entrance.

Dagny quickened her pace. Long since adapted, she
moved in her spacesuit almost as easily as in a
coverall, low-*g* lope, exultantly light. A similarly
garbed figure appeared above the ladder. "Hi, there!"
she called. "Welcome!"

The ground shook beneath her.

The violence went up through her boots and body
like a thundercrash.

Almost, she fell. The stumble threw her glance at
the sun. Her faceplate darkened to save her eyes and
she saw its disc pale in a sudden blindness. She
recovered her footing, sight flowed back, she stared
northward.

A cloud rose high above yonder horizon. It climbed
and climbed, roiled and sooty, thinning at the edges to
gray, a smear across Earth. Sparks tumbled from it in
long parabolas, as if stars fell.

Meteorite strike! Those were ejecta, flung rocks,
shrapnel. Soldiers under fire cast themselves prone—
No. When it came from the sky you were a smaller
target on your feet. And you must *not* run.

The rearview display strip seized her mind. She
spun on her heel for a direct look. Close to the pylon
nearest her, the loaded gondola was swinging in ever
wilder arcs. The column shuddered. Several meters
beyond, a stone hit, spurted its own little dust cloud
and gouged its own little crater. Another struck a
boulder, glanced off, and skittered murderously low
above the regolith.

The dust began to fall. Renewed blindness fell with
it. Dagny felt impact after impact somewhere hard by.
She stood fast and fumbled in a pouch after her scrub
cloth. Perhaps it was to stave off panic that there
passed through her: Power joints in spacesuits were
fine, took the curse off interior air pressure, but when

would the engineers develop tactile amplifiers for the gloves and let you properly feel what you were doing?

The Moon accelerates objects downward slowly, but has no atmosphere to hinder them. Within a minute, sixty mortal seconds, the local bombardment had ended and she could wipe her faceplate clean.

Relief flooded her in a wave, a sob, a looseness in the knees as if she would fall on them. Nothing worse than dust seemed to have reached the camp or the mine. Well, of course the odds had always favored that, else this operation would have been impossible, though nobody expected anything so big to strike in any given vicinity, not for hundreds or thousands of years—Her gaze traveled onward and stopped. She strangled a scream.

The pylon stood warped. The cable held but was drawn line-taut and immobile, the engine at this end surely badly damaged. The gondola lay on its side, three meters distant. Its mad gyrations had unhooked it and strewn its load afar. Metallic chunks were piled and tumbled throughout Dagny's worksite.

Somebody cried out, a hoarse and jagged noise of agony. It broke a hammerstruck silence; suddenly the radio band clamored. Dagny switched her transmitter to full power. "Hold on!" she made her voice go overriding. "Shut up! We've got rescue to do!"

Meanwhile she bounded back to the scene. A dim part of her wondered how she dared take charge, she who'd never met anything like this. Classes and simulations at the academy felt unreal. But the leadership, the duty was hers.

Then she was too busy for doubts or fears.

"Names, by the numbers." They snapped in her earphones, one after the next. Janice Bye sprawled dead, her helmet split open, her face ghastly under the long sunlight. Two people appeared to be in shock, slumped useless and shivering. And Joe, Joe Packer was on his back, right leg buried under a heap of heavy chunks.

Dagny knelt beside him. After the first animal shriek he had gone silent, apart from the gasping breath. His skin looked more gray than brown, studded with sweat that sparkled like dew. Against it his eyeballs stood appallingly white around dark irises and dilated pupils. Did Earth tinge them faintly blue? Dagny caught both his hands in hers. "How are you, Joe?" The question came forth steady.

He fought for the same control. "Like I'm choking," he mumbled. "Doesn't hurt . . . much . . . any more . . . but dizzy and—uh-h—"

The spacesuit leg must have been ruptured, she decided, probably at the knee joint. Air would have gushed out, more than the reserve tank could replenish, before enough gunk oozed free and hardened to plug a hole that size. Oxygen-starved on top of trauma, his heart might fail at any instant.

"Greenbaum, fetch an air bottle and coupling," Dagny snapped. You had to tell everybody exactly what to do, or they'd fall over each other's feet. "Royce, Olson, see to Etcheverry and Graf," the shock cases. "The rest of you, crowbars, spades, get this junk off of Joe. Carefully!"

"Bloody 'ell, 'ere, stand aside," she heard. It was a rumbling bass, startlingly like Anson Guthrie's but the English accented. In her rearview she saw the speaker loom above her. Behind him, another man carried something. They must be the geologists. Nobody from the main camp or the mine could have made it here this fast.

You couldn't let just anybody prong in. "What do you want?" Dagny demanded.

"*Sacre putain de l'archevêque anglais!* Sat man, 'e weell die wissout air. Get from se way." The newcomer stooped, grabbed her by the upper arms, lifted her and set her aside.

Dagny swallowed anger. Edmond Beynac, had to be him, should know better than she how to handle this kind of emergency. And, yes, his companion bore a tank with an attachment. From their elevation at the ladder head they'd probably seen what was happening, figured what was likely needed, and immediately gotten it. Christ, that was quick thinking.

The two men hunkered down on either side of Packer and went deftly to work. "Greenbaum, never mind, come on back and help," Dagny remembered to call.

Presently Beynac straightened. The crew were gathered with their tools. Two men started to shift rock. "Not like sat, imbeciles!" Beynac roared. "God damn! You could roll pieces down onto 'im. *Comme ci.*" He plucked a bar from the nearest hand and demonstrated.

Yes, Dagny thought, things did behave differently on Luna, lower gravity meant less frictional force and—She heard a mutter of resentment. "Obey him," she commanded. "He's straw boss now."

Evidently the men at the pit had received orders to stay and cope with the damage there, but the first ones from camp were arriving. Dagny went to get them organized. When she returned to Packer, he had been freed and lay in Beynac's arms.

"I take 'im to my van and geeve first aid," the geologist told her. "Per'aps sen se *médecins*—se physicians, sey can save 'is leg." Not waiting for an okay, he bounded off across the crater floor.

They were four who gathered in the main office. It belonged to Miguel Fuentes, chief of operations at Rudolph. Dagny Ebbesen was there as a co-ordinate supervisor and Edmond Beynac had been invited for his expertise. The fourth was Anson Guthrie. He spoke from Earth via his image in a teleset on the table.

Officially he had no business here. The mine, like Tychopolis and almost everything else on Luna, was the undertaking of an international consortium under UN supervision. But Fireball was the principal con-

tractor to all the consortiums, and not only for space
transport services. Besides, this was an informal preliminary assessment.

"The government inquiry will drone on for months
and set the taxpayers back more than the repairs will
cost," he predicted. "What we can hope for today is to
reach the same conclusions it will, and lay our plans
accordingly."

"What plans must we make?" Fuentes asked. "A
meteorite that large was a freak to start with, and then
it purely chanced to slam down close to where people
were. We can't let an accident like that stop us, can
we? Or are the politicians really so stupid?"

He made the three-finger *Wait* signal in the direction of the hologram, and all held their peace while
radio waves passed through space and back again.
Dagny grew aware of how small the room was, how
crowded with apparatus, relieved merely by a couple
of garish pictures stuck on the walls—Florida scenes,
she guessed, their lushness pathetic in this place. The
air recycler had developed a collywobble of some
kind, which gave the flow whirring from the ventilator
a faint metallic reek. She longed to be outside.

"Politicians aren't necessarily any stupider than the
rest of us, including corporate chairmen of the
board," Guthrie said. "I've studied the immediate
reports. That rock wasn't so big nor so near that it
should've done the harm it did. Obviously it found a
design flaw; but we thought we'd engineered for the
worst-case scenario, didn't we? What got overlooked?
If we can figure that out pronto, and how to correct it,
we'll know what to tell the commission. Then it can
fart around as much longer as it wants; we'll meanwhile be doing what's needed." He rubbed his chin.
"You're the folks on the spot. Got any ideas?"

Dagny looked across the table at Beynac. She noticed that she enjoyed doing so. He was about thirty,
she guessed, very little taller than her but powerfully
built, with long head, square face, straight nose,
prominent cheekbones, stiff brown hair, green eyes.

Not what you'd call handsome, no. But how he radiated masculinity.

With care, because their previous encounter suggested he might have a short fuse, she said, "You're the geologist, Dr. Beynac. Could the local rock have unusual properties?"

"It does not," he declared. "I investigated the area myself, two years ago. When the deposit was found, a student of mine, a good young man, he studied more precisely. If we had seen possible trouble, we would have warned." Free of extreme stress, he spoke English with an accent mostly in the vowels and the lilt.

"Of course," she said. "What I mean is seismic-type waves. How do they transmit hereabouts?"

"*Hein?* Moonquakes are negligible, of scientific interest only."

"I know. But I'm wondering how the shock wave from the impact might have arrived."

"Not enough to knock anything down," he snorted. "You saw."

Dagny bridled. "Yes. I also saw what did get wrecked. Forces had to cause that. Where'd they come from? The impact. How'd they get here? Through the ground." Impulsively: "That should be obvious enough for anyone."

He didn't explode. Instead, his gaze grew intent and he murmured, "You have a hypothesis?"

"Fancy word for a wild-ass guess," Dagny admitted. "Still, I have been thinking. How's this sound?" She addressed Fuentes as well, and especially Guthrie. "A resonant frequency set that particular pylon vibrating. This in turn sent a wave along the cable and made the gondola pendulum. If there was a rock layer down below that reflected the shock, the impulse would be repeated and the oscillations go crazy."

Beynac sat bolt upright. *"Pardieu!"* he exclaimed. "I sink per'aps—" He leaned back, eyes half closing. "Perhaps. Let me too now think if this is possible. A transverse component—" He withdrew into his brain.

"The probability is ridiculous," Fuentes objected. "The system would have to have had the exact suitable loading and configuration at that exact moment."

Dagny nodded. "Sure. What I'm proposing is a worse case than anybody imagined. It's just that I haven't got any better idea. Do you? They'll have to collect data, and run lab tests and computer models, to check it out. But maybe today Dr. Beynac can tell us whether it's worth checking."

Guthrie's words cut across her last few. "By damn, *my* guess is that you've got hold of its tail! Good for you, lass!" His grin and wink added: *How I wish I could brag you up, granddaughter mine.* "And if you're right, why, we needn't worry. I could draw a hundred royal flushes in a row before those conditions repeated."

Beynac stirred, reopened his eyes, and growled, "Not true, mister." Himself unwilling to wait out transmission lag, he went straight on: "This especial accident, yes, I must do an analysis, but I believe today that Miss Engineer Ebbesen is basically correct. However, I am interested in meteoritics. That object was a member of the Beta Taurid Swarm. Orbital precession is making it once more, after centuries, a menace. Other strikes may well kill people in other ways. Take this that has happened for a warning. In every month of June, close down topside operations from sunrise to sunset."

Fuentes stiffened. "Wait a minute! Do you realize what kind of burden that would be?"

Beynac shrugged. "Pft! I am a scientist. I shall make my honest recommendation. The costs, they are your department."

Deferential, not obsequious, Fuentes signalled a pause for Guthrie.

The lord of Fireball smiled his oddly charming smile. "Gracias," he said. "I'd been fretting about that on my own for a spell. Do me a favor and don't stampede into a press conference, okay? We'll assemble our facts and figures and calculations, and then go public. It's that important. Major strikes are a threat to Mama Earth herself. The dinosaurs learned that the hard way; and if the Tunguska object had hit a few hours later than it did, it would've taken out most of Belgium."

Beynac regarded the image with a freshened respect. Guthrie continued: "It could be that the human race makes a profit off the Rudolph smashup. We may get sentiment for a space patrol to track meteoroids, and deflect or destroy the dangerous ones." He laughed. "Fireball will bid on the contract."

Beynac surprised Dagny when he said, soft-voiced, "Another reason for humans on the Moon."

Reasons already aplenty, swirled through her.

Energy. Criswell solar collectors going up around the globe, to beam to Earth electric power clean and cheap and well-nigh limitless.

Science. Astronomy on Farside, a stable platform, a planet-sized shield against radio interference and light pollution. Chemistry, biology, physiology, agronomy under conditions unique and enlightening. Who could foretell how much more?

Industry. Today, small specialties. Ultimately, gigantic factories of every kind, with no surrounding vulnerable biosphere, their products easily launched for the mother world in aerodynamic containers that descended gently to destination. Or sent into deeper space—

Astronautics, building the fleet and homeporting the ships, at least until humankind had struck roots elsewhere. And so the future. Yes, Luna was poor in heavy elements, airless, waterless; but wealth of that kind waited unbounded in the asteroids and comets, along with the day when no more need be torn out of living Earth.

Adventure, discovery, deeds to do and songs to sing.

"We'll swing it!" she cried.

Heat rushed into her face. This was a business meeting. Why hadn't she felt such a childish outburst rising, and stopped it? Fuentes, that very proper man, looked the least bit embarrassed. Guthrie's image hadn't yet had time to show reaction. She foresaw him chuckling indulgently and moving the conversation onward. Beynac—Beynac's gaze had come to rest on her. And now he himself smiled. "Good for you, mademoiselle," he said.

5

Sunlight spilled from aloft and shattered into a million dancing brilliances. The sea ran sapphire-blue, turquoise-blue, cobalt-blue, amethyst, surges and swirls over long, gentle swells. It shushed and rumbled, noises as tender as the wind and as deep as itself. Westward a bank of cumulus towered white above a dim streak that was land. Elsewhere reached distances, moving hues, odors of salt and air.

Then the day went black. For a moment Aleka knew only the eidophone before her, the sights in its screen and the rage out of its speaker. Fuller awareness returned, but the warmth and breeze that washed her stopped at her skin.

Small loss, gibed a thought fleeting by. She had been in a mucho hard mood already, outbound to her rendezvous.

Now time was like a shark behind her. She sprang to her feet and leaned out above the port side. "Ka'eo!" she shouted. *"Hele mai! Aboard, āwīwī!"*

Her companion reared out of the water and thrust himself over the low gunwale. The boat canted. It rocked back as his bulk slithered across the deck to the middle, forward of the cockpit where she stood. *"Kāohi mai 'oe,"* she warned: Hold fast. The swimmer pushed his front flippers into a pair of cuffs secured to the framework. His dark sleekness dripped and shimmered.

They had been idling along at four or five knots, for Aleka was in no hurry to meet those people who awaited her. She made the boat leap. In a minute it was planing, up and down in eagle swoops, forward at a unicorn gallop. The engine purred quietly, being almost half as efficient as a spaceship's plasma thrust, but air brawled around the hyalon screen in front of her.

Through it, Ka'eo's liquid brown gaze met the woman's. He barked and grunted loudly enough for her to make out. The language was basically Anglo, with many Hawaiian and Japanese loan words and a number—larger year by year, it seemed—that were purely of the Keiki Moana. But no human mouth could have shaped just those sounds.

"[What hastens us, oath-sister?]"

Aleka touched a disc on the pilot panel and a supersonic carrier beam gave him her reply, clear through the racket, in her version of the same tongue. "A fight between the inspectors and some kauwa. At least two dead." She looked at the transmission in the flatscreen, tiny images, cries she barely heard amidst the booming of her speed.

To her eyes, the seal face did not change, save that whiskers stood straight out from the muzzle and fangs briefly gleamed. She had sometimes wondered what his kind read in the mobile features of hers. Maybe they were too alien for a play of expressions to convey much. She did sense horror in his tone. "[This is bad, orca-bad. Speak to them, sister mine! Make them stop!]"

Crazily into her mind lurched another question. Where did that phrase come from? Killer whales didn't haunt these seas. Keiki Moana had doubtless seen them on documentary programs and such, but why had their name entered the language, and as a word for evil? For centuries, her own race had pitied and protected what big cats remained.

Was the forebrain of the seal-folk so new and thin an overlay that an inborn dread of beasts which had preyed on their ancestors still dominated it? Then what other instincts also did?

"Metamorph" was an easy word to say. Was it that easy a thought to think? A strain of organisms in which the DNA had once been modified to bring forth something never seen in nature—Microbes that decomposed or sequestered toxic wastes. Trees with sap that was fuel. Exotic animals. Talking animals. Lunarians—But when you change the body like that, what changes do you make in the mind? The soul?

Maybe it was only that certain Keiki had wandered far north, unbeknownst to humans, and brought back tales of orcas. Or maybe not. How little she really knew of these people, her friends and fellows in the Lahui Kuikawa.

No matter yet, surely not if murder went on any longer. She forced steadiness upon herself, recited the Tulip Mantra seven times, felt the painful tension leave her back and the trembling leave her hands. "Major Delgado, por favor," she said at the phone, in mainland Anglo. A man's pale countenance entered the screen. "I'm coming, top speed. But can't you get this under control?"

The officer in charge of the Peace Authority's investigative team bit his lip. "We're trying," he grated. "They don't listen. Do they understand?"

"Maybe not. More and more of their younger ones have little or no direct contact with us. But what's *happening?*"

"At the moment, a standoff. See." Delgado swept a scanner around, and Aleka saw.

His party's craft, a small submersible with an observation turret, lay near the edge of a biorange. To starboard, the green, loosely woven mat of vegetation reached beyond sight, rippling to waves and currents, drinking light, weaving atoms together into material desired by its designers—in this case, Aleka knew, anticarcinoma virus base. In the offing an attendant glided about, agleam, oblivious of everything but its duties, a versatile machine with a program capable of some learning and much adaptation, nevertheless just a robot and unaware.

To port, blood streaks curled luridly bright. Repeated bursts of foam showed where a body plunged or broached or slapped the water as if it were the enemy. They circled the vessel, those shapes, around and around, more than Aleka had imagined, two or three score. The clamor out of their throats reached her faintly over the phone, hoarse and harsh. Delgado's team had spaced themselves along the rails, ten men and women in blue field uniforms. Each pair of hands gripped a firearm.

The view went back to the commander's face. "I've called on the amplisonor for peace, again and again," he said desperately. "They pay no attention. They're no real threat to us, of course, but—What should we do? Submerge? Leave the vicinity?" He tautened. "We can't let them suppose they've won, those lawbreakers."

"Hang on," Aleka said. She tapped for her location. It appeared on the pilot board. "I will be there in about ten minutes." She drew breath. "What exactly went wrong? Por favor, begin from the beginning, señor."

In the world beyond Hawaii she had learned the value of courtesy, even carefully measured deference. Besides, her brief meeting with him had given her the idea that this was a decent man. If his task put him at odds with her, that wasn't his fault; and today they could join to fend off more deaths. They must!

He nodded. "Ciertamente. On our cruise we've found considerable evidence of widespread violation, especially ecological; but you can hear the details later, when we enter our report. However, we saw nothing so blatant as here, where we've come on that band of seals—uh, metamorphs—openly plundering fish, kinds of fish necessary to the health of the range. You probably know which I mean."

Aleka did. They weren't the little darters developed to eat parasites, they were the grazers that kept the sea plants well pruned: fat, sluggish, temptation incarnate.

Delgado seemed to draw comfort from speaking methodically. "I called on them to cease and desist. They ignored me. I had us move closer, to no effect. Señorita, our duty is to the law and the general welfare. More and more seals were converging on us. It was clear a large gang had been poaching. I sent a man down onto a diving fin with a shock gun. The idea was to hit a few of them—only painfully, you understand, no serious injury—hoping they would disperse. Instead, two of them scrambled up onto the fin, before our man saw, and attacked him. Señorita, you know those are big animals, with sharp teeth. His squad mates on deck shot them dead. Quite rightly. He returned. Now the creatures act as if they think they're besieging us. Naturally, knowing you were on your way, I had you called."

He sighed. "I could wish, now, you had joined us earlier, yes, had accompanied us from the start. But that is hindsight, no?"

"Your plan was reasonable under the circumstances, Major," Aleka gave him.

Inwardly, to ready herself for the encounter ahead, she rehearsed those circumstances: complaints, suspicions, proven losses, violent incidents, not to mention the demographics. The Peace Authority was bound to look into them. If anything, the surprise lay in how long it waited. Delgado had dropped hints—about hopes that the Lahui could somehow resolve the problem among themselves—thereby helping people around the planet believe that the tribes and cantons and ethnoi of Earth worked, because that helped keep people happy and orderly—Yes, when at last there was no choice but to mount an official investigation, it made sense for the First inspectors to go forth on their own, as well prepared as databases and vivifers could make them. Consciously or unconsciously, a local guide might lead them astray.

Yet she was in fact a human liaison, within the

Lahui, between the Keiki Moana and the outer world. It also made sense for her and a metamorph to join the team after a while, discuss their experiences, conduct them to wherever else they two felt the inspectors should observe things. That they had been on their way when battle erupted was a coincidence.

Not a very unlikely coincidence, Aleka thought. Not when you recalled how conflict seethed in these waters.

Delgado scowled, as if deciding he had shown too much softness. "These are not the first killings," he stated. "Humans have died."

"Not just humans," Aleka countered.

She could well-nigh hear him thinking, choosing his words. After all, sentient metamorphs had full rights under the law, whether they descended from his species or another. Sophotects did, which could not really be said to have any ancestors—if "rights" in any traditional sense bore any meaning for inorganic intelligences, Aleka thought while she waited.

"The destructive activity has been . . . almost entirely . . . by the . . . seal beings," Delgado said. "Those humans who got killed were trying to stop it." They had come upon it mostly by chance, and reacted more strongly than was prudent. But who would have expected fury to respond?

"Seven altogether," Aleka answered. "And some nonfatal injuries. Keiki Moana lost many more." Humans generally had tools aboard their vessels, knives, tridents, boathooks, anchors, which could double as lethal weapons. The vessels themselves could, if driven hard against swimmers.

Delgado's visage congealed. "It is going to stop, señorita. And I did not say no humans are to blame."

She believed she knew what he meant. Something of the chill crept back into her. "Hang on," she repeated. "Don't provoke anything. My partner and I will be there pronto."

He nodded and went from the scanner field, though he left the phone transmitting. She peered ahead, past

Ka'eo's bulk. The submersible was now on the horizon, a fingerling to behold but rapidly growing in her sight. She switched to manual control and sent her hands in a dance across the board. The boat swung about to a precise aim and bounded onward.

"Did you follow that, Ka'eo?" she asked.

"[I think so, oath-sister,]" he replied.

"What do you make of it?" Since it was to a Keiki she spoke, that was literally: "How do your senses take this water?"

"[A riptide through reefs.]" He fell silent for a bit. Arrow-swift in the chase, his folk were oftenest slow and careful in their serious thinking, as though the skill was new enough to them that they still had great respect for it. Aleka had wondered if that might not be exactly true. A mere few centuries since the experimentation that brought this race into existence—Had the earliest humans likewise pondered their way forward?

"[Kauwa,]" he said, as nearly as he could pronounce the word. The judgment was self-evident, but what followed drew on his knowledge. "[They are not here at this same time by happenstance. No, they are a band, under leadership that planned the foray. Else they would by now have scattered. They must have nets or mesh bags down below, which they were filling with fish to take home. But home, to them, cannot be a fixed rookery, or I would have heard of it. They must shift about between islets, rocks, small uninhabited coves and beaches, according to some scheme. It is the germ of a . . . a nation, oath-sister.]"

Aleka grimaced. "Nomads. I was guessing as much." Hadn't it been inevitable, sooner or later? "Why did they attack when they were caught robbing, why didn't they flee?"

"[The attack must have been in rage, by those two of them. It is clear that the alpha bull commanded the others to hold back, yet also to stay. He must want to show strength, determination.]"

Her heart stumbled. It quickened again when the

croaking, ringing voice went on: "[But perhaps he hopes to bargain or, anyhow, talk. He knows he cannot prevail. If a little wisdom drifts within him, he knows as well that no kauwa nation can long survive, once the landfolk go on hunt. Nor can it be worth surviving, without anything more than what few poor things they can steal, without writing, pictures, robots, machines, tools.]"

Without hands, Aleka thought. Sadness closed teeth upon her. By what right had those scientists bulged out these brains, to make a creature that was neither a good human nor a good seal? Research into the nature of intelligence was no excuse. They should have been downloaded, those scientific minds, so that they could be burning in a virtual hell.

No. She overrode herself. Were it possible to go back in time, by what right could she annul the creation of beings she loved, oath-brethren of the Lahui and fountainhead of its identity? Ka'eo was what he was, a good Keiki Moana. Open a way for his race to find its own fulfillment.

Coolness took over. Her boat was approaching the Authority craft. She cut the drive. Noise died away, the hull came down, waves splashed alongside, casting brine on her lips, and she slid onward to the outlaws.

They had seen her coming and fallen quiet, darknesses awash in the swell. Sunlight gleamed off wet pelts and big eyes. Ka'eo freed his flippers, turned about, and barked at them.

Delgado's image entered the phone screen. Aleka saw him standing on deck near the turret, amidst his armed crew. "What are you doing?" he demanded.

"Trying to establish contact, Major," she answered. "With luck, we'll negotiate."

"What? No, you can't. These are criminals. We've been in touch with the station ashore. It's activated monitors in the range, and the damage that they report has been done—"

"Por favor. We two aren't about to make a treaty. We may find how to end this business without further bloodshed. Our chances are best if we aren't disturbed meanwhile. If *they* aren't."

Delgado flushed, then swallowed, nodded, and stepped aside. He was an able officer, Aleka realized. He'd simply been placed in a situation he didn't comprehend. How well did she?

Wake swirled behind a long form. It reached her boat. A scarred head lifted to look over the gunwale. After a moment, Ka'eo slipped overside to join the chieftain.

What happened in the next hour was not altogether clear to the woman, and sometimes unknown. The Keiki Moana communicated among each other by far more than speech. Often they dived below, remaining for minutes; or they swam off through the pack, touching noses here, stroking flipper across back there; or they floated mute and motionless. Two frigate birds cruised on high, wings and split tails like drawn swords. Clouds in the west loomed larger, glooms grew beneath them, a rainstorm fell blue-gray and she heard the whisper of it across the kilometers.

At the end, she too had her say. Thereafter, "[So shall flow this tide,]" the alpha bull grunted, and went back to his gathered followers. Brief raucousness resounded. As one, they plunged. Time passed before she saw them emerge, far off, bound north. Several of them towed pursed nets full of a harvest that glistened.

"What is this?" Delgado was crying. "What have you done?"

Aleka sighed. The hour had exhausted her, wrung her bloodless. "We agreed they could go—"

"Scot-free? Carrying off their booty? No!"

"Señor, they lost two camaradas, others of them are in pain, and their efforts have gone for very little. The fish they took are already dead. If you let them return home in peace, they'll leave the bioranges alone for three months as measured by the Moon, and won't raid fish herds either. They'll subsist as best they can on what they catch in the wild. Meanwhile their leaders will negotiate with . . . acceptable representatives of your side, trying for a permanent arrangement. You can pursue them and start real hostilities going, if you like, but *I* think you've come out of the affair mighty well."

Delgado gnawed his lip. Finally: "Would you come aboard and tell us more, señorita?"

"Oh, yes, yes."

As she slipped closer, Aleka's pulsebeat accelerated. She spoke the Thorn Mantra to herself and strength flowed back from some inner well. A single bound lifted her out of the cockpit; she caught a rail with one hand, pressed bare feet against the sun-warmed metal of the submersible, and swung herself onto its deck. Her boat drifted free, Ka'eo watchful beside it.

The constables stared at the visitor, the men with pleasure. They saw a young woman—twenty-eight—of medium height, clad in shorts and halter. Swimming, running, climbing, strenuous play had made her figure superb. Many breeds of human had come together in tawny skin, wavy blue-black hair bobbed just below the ears, round head, broad face, short nose, full mouth, big russet eyes. Disciplined, the squad members stayed at their posts while one man accompanied Delgado to greet her.

Stiffly, the commander shook hands. Her palm was hard to the touch. "Bienvenida," he said. "I don't believe you've met Dr. Zaid Hakim. He joined us to observe for the Ministry of Environment. Dr. Hakim, Señorita Aleka, uh-m, Kame?"

She smiled. "Alice Tam, if you'd rather speak straight Anglo," she said. "Buenas tardes, señor."

Hakim, in workaday civilian clothes, bowed. "How do you do," he replied. His usage was scholarly, his accent clipped. "My compliments on a remarkable performance. Do I understand correctly, you speak for your community, Mamselle Tam?"

"No," Aleka told him, surprised. "No one person can do that. I'm a, an interpreter, you might say." But why should he know much about her folk? How many different groupings were there in the world? Half a million? And a number of them changeable as foam, too. The Lahui Kuikawa amounted to about ten thousand humans on a small Hawaiian island and maybe fifty thousand Keiki Moana, maybe considerably more, prowling the greatest of the oceans.

Had their obscurity been what protected them, and was it now coming to an end?

"Let's go below and talk," Delgado proposed. To the crew: "At ease, but keep alert."

His cabin was cool and dim after the molten-bright water outside, cramped but adequately equipped. It extruded three chairs. "Do be seated," he urged. "Refreshment?" A servotube brought coffee for him and Hakim, beer for Aleka. She felt she'd earned it.

Was earning it. The catnip tingle vanished from her awareness as Hakim said, "Yes, you did amazingly, mamselle, but I fear it was basically futile." He raised a hand. "No, no, we shall not give chase. However, the Federation cannot strike deals with a bandit gang."

Aleka braced her spirit. "They aren't that, señor."

"What, then?"

"Nothing you—the Federation has a word or a law to fit, really. They are kauwa."

"Please explain."

"Where shall I begin? 'Kauwa' in modern Hawaiian usually means a servant, but it can also have its old meaning of an outcast, an exile, not necessarily a public enemy but someone who doesn't fit into society, maybe because his birth was irregular, or because he doesn't conform to the rules, or he's simply been too long away from his people."

"I must remember the word," Delgado said. "The world has quite a few like that." These men were not her enemies, Aleka thought. They did not want to oppress anybody. It made them the more dangerous.

"Bueno," she continued, "as the numbers of the Keiki Moana increased, they naturally had to range farther to support themselves. . . . Wait. Let me finish, por favor. They could not and should not have kept on being pensioners, fenced off and fed. They aren't pets or show animals, for Pele's sake, they're sentients! They had their, their own potentials to realize, their own culture to develop, and it couldn't be the same as ours. Do you expect sophotects to think or feel or act like you? Then why should metamorphs? And what might we learn, what might we get in the way of inspiration, from a nonhuman *organic* civilization?"

She had almost said "living," but checked it. Best not let out any antagonism toward artificial intelligence, no, call it electrophotonic intelligence. Otherwise her words were beginning to run smoothly. How often had she used them on outsiders, trying to explain?

"For that, they needed to be self-sufficient. You know about the fish ranches, dolphin domestication, aquaculture, recreational enterprises, salvage and repair and scientific survey work and all the rest, whatever they could do together with humans, at sea or on the reefs. It was labor-intensive, but viable because it spared the capital cost of robotization. The proceeds let us of the Lahui give a living to our poets, thinkers, singers, artists, dancers, inventors, dreamers. Our spirits.

"But robotization got to be cheap. And the Keiki population grew. Poverty did. More and more of them had to go hunting for food. Fewer and fewer were in regular, direct relationships with the Lahui, the core society. There's the origin of the kauwa, señores. The poor people, the fringe people. Yes, certain of them have gone back to a kind of savagery. But can you blame them?"

Aleka drew breath. "Pardon me if I've repeated common knowledge," she ended. "I know you've heard most of this before, Major Delgado. But sometimes it's hard to tell what is common knowledge, out in your Orthosphere."

Hakim raised his brows. "Then you consider your . . . Lahui to be of the Heterosphere?" he asked.

"Bueno, we don't have much to do with the cybercosm or the global economy. I suppose, yes, to you we may all look like kauwa." Defiantly, Aleka knocked back her beer.

Had the Lyudov Rebellion succeeded—or had it even won to a middle ground, where some bounds were put upon the machines—But that was a daydream. It had been a lost cause from the start; and maybe rightly. No sense romancing about a wildness that ceased long before she was born. Yuri Volkov had stopped doing so . . . and he and she drifted apart. . . .

"Your metamorphic friends could have ample food, and whatever else they require, for the asking," Hakim said. "They need only heed the law, quit damaging property and ecology."

"Give up their freedom?" she challenged. "Hunting is in their genes."

"Humans adapt."

"Humans have had far longer, and many more opportunities. Why, the world as it is *came* from them. And I'm not sure how well or happily adapted most of them are."

"Given proper population restriction, a limited amount of predation on wildlife would be allowable, integrated with the general ecosystem. But the seals' hunting is uncontrolled, and becoming serious."

"Birth control isn't in their genes either." Abruptly she felt how forlorn her arguments were in the face of this implacable reasonableness.

"Humans generally manage." Hakim paused. "There are exceptions. Your little society—your, ah, Lahui Kuikawa—has not reduced its birth rate much. I mean your part of it, the human members. Already you are crowded on your island, are you not? Soon you too will have to give up your freedom, as you put it."

"We need time," Aleka pleaded. "Of course we have to stabilize our numbers. The Keiki close to us know it too. We're working on it, both our species, and we'll bring the idea to the kauwa. They aren't stupid either. But—a life with so few children around us, so few pups—Give us time!"

She wanted to go on: It's not an either-or matter of personal choice and everybody making the correct renunciation. It's that we have always been a young folk. Merriment and recklessness, sudden moonlit lovemaking and houses full of growth, birthday festivals, carp flags flying in springtime, yes, and reverence for the aged, whose wisdom not many of us have reached to, all these things and more have always been our lives. We can't instantly become something else.

And then, the Keiki Moana are our spirit kin. Very likely we have learned more from them than ever they from us. Forebears of ours were caretakers of their colony, after it outgrew its Big Island refuge and was moved to Niihau. (Fireball, its original protector, had disbanded. Guthrie himself had gone to Alpha Centauri. Somebody must mediate between these beings and the human-machine world. Have you forgotten the history that made us, you men?) As they began to sustain themselves, other humans joined in, to help and to share. Selection: The new recruits were they whom sea and open sky, village and open boat, firelight and starlight, called away from the cybernetic world. They raised their children accordingly. Those of the next generation who did not like it moved elsewhere. Those who did like it stayed, and their children in turn became still more the Lahui Kuikawa, the Free People. And they were oath-siblings to the Keiki Moana, fared with them, foregathered with them, rejoiced with them, mourned with them, until those strong sea-born instincts roused human urges that they had believed were safely buried.

No, she wanted to say, we haven't gone into hiding. We haven't tried to bring back an ideal Stone Age that never was. I'm proof of that. But we have made a life that is our own, that is us, and we will not willingly let it die.

Useless, here. She had said quite enough.

Hakim smiled—a little regretfully, she thought. "I can sympathize," he told her. "I expect that after further study I will recommend that the government agree to your proposal and see if any arrangement can be made with the—the kauwa. At least, with this particular, perhaps unique band of them. We will rely heavily on you . . . civilized . . . Lahui, to help negotiate and afterward keep the arrangement in force."

His lips drooped. He shook his head. "But in honesty, mamselle, I do not expect anything important to result. At best, the robbers will agree to be fed and medicated and otherwise provided for. History suggests that this will demoralize them, encourage the criminal element, and do nothing to curb their breeding. There is also your culture to deal with. In many ways it seems admirable. But can it accommodate itself to—let me be frank—to the real world?"

Time, Aleka wanted to cry. Give us time, give us space, land, and waters where everything isn't owned or regulated; let us be alone a generation or two, till we have changed ourselves without destroying ourselves.

Useless, here.

Useless, likewise, to linger. After what had happened, the team wouldn't cruise farther. It would report and doubtless be ordered back to base, whence it would be dispersed on other duties. If the counsel of Delgado or Hakim was wanted, their telepresence would be immediately available, wherever they might be on Earth.

Aleka had a familiar sense of lying in a box while the lid closed.

Nevertheless she stayed for two or three hours. The men had questions for her, shrewd but courteous. They were more ready to listen than to talk. She found herself telling them unexpectedly much about her home.

—the island, a mountain looming above coral ground, orchards, meadows, parklands, once lovely in their sea-girt loneliness but now with little solitude anywhere, because the village had grown till it was—

—the town. Formerly a longhouse stood surrounded by the cottages of the dwellers, who had it in common for their ceremonies, celebrations, and mutual business. Today a dozen such clusters served as many 'ohana—

—extended families, whose members shared in caring for each other from birth to cremation. Yes, of course children knew who their parents were and took the most love and guidance from them; but uncles, aunts, cousins, grandparents, great-grandparents were nearly as close and you were always welcome in their homes. Yes, of course people quarreled, feuded, lied, swindled, stole, betrayed, perhaps more than among atomic individuals with easily made, easily dissolved relationships; but their 'ohana found its ways to compose matters. Besides friends, respected elders, and traditional mores, they had the influence of the luakini—

—the temple, where they attended the simple rites and heard anew the simple words of the Dao Kai that Kelekolio Pēla had uttered long ago, the Sea Way for a sea folk. They also held secular assemblies, where those adults who wished could debate and vote on public questions and where cases were tried. Criminals were handed over to the police on Oahu, but the worst punishment was exile, expulsion from the island, the 'ohana, the people—

—and their songs, stories, dances, games, festivals, solemnities, some of Keiki Moana origin, all special to the Lahui soul. The community did not try to wall itself off, but it did nothing to encourage casual visitation, and except for educational purposes children did not watch multiceiver programs before they had had their twelfth-year initiations. Afterward they might well go elsewhere for part of their schooling, as Aleka had done. Yet if their early lives had taken hold

in them, upon returning they would want their beloved ethos to abide. Whoever grew discontented was
free to move away. Increasingly many were doing so.
This was not always gladly—

—for indeed the Lahui, human as well as nonhuman, had grown beyond the numbers which their
permitted stretches of ocean and their industries
could support. Economic independence had been the
aim, the two races joining their different abilities to
win a living from the waters. Given robotics, biotics,
energetics, nanotechnology, trained minds, skilled
bodies, life went on with a beguiling appearance of
simplicity for generations. The products were traded
for manufactured goods from outside and a modest
amount of luxury. But as the island population waxed,
global demand waned; recycling and direct synthesis
accommodated ever more of it. When mining and
refining operations beyond Earth were dwindling,
how should a few minor enterprises on her sea much
longer endure?

"Oh, yes," Aleka said. "We can live on our Federation credit. We'll not starve or fall sick or go homeless.
Gracias for that."

Hakim overlooked the bitterness in her voice. His
stayed mild. "No, any thanks are due modern productivity. Credit merely shares out the goods. What have
your people been spending theirs on?"

Aleka shrugged. "Whatever a given person fancies.
Not uncommonly, something for their 'ohana. Keiki
usually order toys, unless they save to buy a piece of
capital equipment. I mean those who draw their
credit. They're the minority."

"Who is to blame if most are unregistered?"

"I'm not blaming," Aleka sighed. "I'm telling.
When none of us have anything but credit payments,
that will be the end of us. Lives will go on, no doubt,
but the meaning, the heart will be out of them, and
what we walking, swimming ghosts will do, I can't
foresee."

"You shall have to change," Delgado declared, his tone less brusque than the words. "It begins with your kauwa. We don't want to hunt them down—robots, guns—and imprison them. But they threaten the regional balance of nature and it must stop. So must their unrestrained breeding. By compulsory inoculation, if nothing else will do." He did not mention the historical precedents. He could rely on her to realize that the kind of popular opposition which several of those measures had had to overcome would not arise in this case.

"We will start by seeing what comes of the agreement you worked out today, Mamselle Tam," Hakim added. "It may lead to real progress, especially if your town cooperates. But the Lahui cannot continue as they are, either."

"You're asking us to transform ourselves faster than we can," Aleka remonstrated. "I tell you again, we are not tribeless neonomads of the Ortho. Our ways *are* us. Give us time to adapt them. Give us enough scope, enough access to resources, that meanwhile we can at least produce for ourselves what we want, instead of depending on you and, and paying your price for it!"

Hakim's look went stern. He too must be near the end of his patience. "I hear you again, Mamselle Tam, and I repeat that what you ask for is not possible. It would infringe on existing ranges, ranches, extractive industries, which are marginal already. It would disrupt ecology throughout this part of the Pacific. It would be incompatible with plans for adjustment and conversion as those industries are phased out. These are considerations of planetary significance, mamselle," beside which the death of one little culture was a quantum fluctuation.

"This argument is foolish, pointless," Delgado put in. "Dr. Hakim and I aren't going to decide anything. We'll report and recommend, along with hundreds of other investigators," including sophotects and surveillance robots, "but the decision will come from Hiroshima. Bring your case into the public communications if you wish. Get your representatives to try convincing their delegates in the Assembly. Appeal to the High Court and the President."

"Or to the Teramind?" Aleka jeered. The apex, the ultimate intelligence of the cybercosm—in an earlier era, she thought momentarily, she would have said "God."

She slumped. "No. I'm sorry, señores. You do mean well, by your lights, and you're quite right, I have no further business here. If you'll excuse me, I'll go home."

They made polite reply and escorted her back topside, these civilized men whose presence she could no longer stand. She used the informant on her wrist to call the boat to her. "Adiós," she said—not "aloha"—and sprang down into the cockpit. Ka'eo accompanied her as she drew away.

The rainstorm afar had passed with subtropical swiftness. Ahead of her the sun was descending. Gold shivered across waves that swung deep blue and violet. They lullabied, they rocked her. The air was cooling; green odors off the range fell aft and she breathed a subliminally fine salt mist. In limitless heights, sunset glowed off the wings of an albatross. For this while, she was free.

She did yearn homeward—her cottage, jasmine and hibiscus fragrant along the porch, palms murmurous overhead, gravel and bamboo and beautiful stones around the longhouse, the sweep of its roofbeams challenging Paniau's peak in heaven, lanes and gardens where folk strolled easily and talked softly and someone plucked strings or blew into a flute—shops and ships by the docks, worksteads closing at day's end and machines that never rested, the cenotaph to those lost at sea, for a measure of daring went with being of the Lahui—

—but first she wanted a time alone with her ocean and the silent nearness of her oath-brother.

There was no haste. She had instruments for night. Besides, a Moon not much past the full would presently rise. She stopped the motor and touched a command. Mast, boom, and centerboard extended, mainsail and jib deployed, rudder and helm came forth. The wind was fair for Niihau. She wasn't particularly hungry or thirsty; Delgado had been hospitable in his stiff fashion. However, she took a water bottle and a food bar from the cabin locker before she settled down to steer.

Bound on its own course, the submersible dropped below the eastern horizon. Ka'eo was hardly more than a roiling in the water, several meters to starboard. Often he went under for minutes at a time, while she refrained from wondering what he snatched for himself. Now and then an aircraft glimmered across the sky, no more than a spark afloat. She was free to seek peace.

It did not come easily. No loosening of muscles, no mantra was of great help. She set about understanding this past day as part of an entirety. Nothing really new had happened. It was only that things were coming to a head, which she had known they would. That knowledge grew in her throughout her life, with roots that went back in time to before she was born and in space to the ends of the Solar System. But she had seen, she had felt, for herself.

She searched out memories, less from here than from abroad, Russia, Yuri, the Lyudovite passion against the cyberneticized world that still smoldered deep down in her, missions to mainland America and the underground web of metamorphs that she touched upon, Luna and the cold Lunarian anger, the machines, everywhere the machines, and the sophotects in their multitudes and their oneness. . . .

History had become the next phase of evolution. No use railing against it, any more than protesting the doom of Alpha Centauri's Demeter. At least, on Earth, when the dinosaurs perished the mammals came into their glory; and a dinosaur lineage lived on in the birds. Might likewise a doomed people somehow find their way to some rescuing transfiguration?

She found no clear answer; but thought, perspective, together with wind and sea and the tiller athrill beneath her hand, granted a certain calm.

The sun sank, the quick night fell, stars glittered forth. Not everything was downfall. Had she lived in the early years of the Lahui, she would never have seen such a sky. Technology moved forward, global population diminished, global greenhouse came under control and there were fewer obscuring clouds, light pollution lessened. Of course, a haze of it remained. She did not behold the splendor her ancestors knew, those of them who took their canoes from end to end of this ocean or those whom Yankee ships brought afterward from across the same reaches, east and west. But then, she had stood on the Moon, on Farside where no Earth dazzled, and looked up into naked space.

She had stood within a single gigantic diamond, and through splintered radiance heard what might yet prove to be words of hope.

As if it followed her train of memories, Luna rose at her back. The mainsail filled with wan light, and glare cast a trembling road.

She put the helm over. Fabric crackled, water strewed brightness and gurgled, the boat came about.

"Aleka Kame," said the phone.

She started. Who might that be?

"Dolores Nightborn to Aleka Kame, to Alice Tam," ran the voice. Female, it spoke colorless Anglo, but instantly she knew where it came from. "Acknowledge."

The blood thundered in her ears. The finger shook that reached to touch the instrument. Its panel, going luminous, was like a tiny window. "I, I receive," she heard out of her throat.

While the stammer traveled, she had more than a second to imagine its paths. It responded to a message that must have been routed through Oahu, addressed to her personally. Since she had left the number of this phone in the local database, in case anyone wanted to make contact with her, the system did not need to instigate a search that might have gone around the planet. It passed the call directly out to sea. It likewise knew the central from which the call reached Earth. So her reply was riding a beam up to a relay satellite, was hurtling down to Luna, was surely passing through another station that encrypted it, was arriving at a place where waited the lady Lilisaire.

"Should we have occasion to communicate in confidence, I will be Dolores Nightborn. Should ever you be asked, that identity has been entered as a Terran resident of Tychopolis, and you may say you met her on your visit and share with her an interest in marine biology."

Photons crossed space. The flatscreen formed an image, the head and shoulders of a middle-aged woman, caucasoid, plump, totally undistinguished. And as synthetic as her voice, Aleka knew, an electronic phantom. "Hail," the face greeted. "Are you alone, and will you have time free in the near future?"

"Yes. Yes to both!" Aleka's heart slammed. She'd ripping well make free time, whatever demands anybody else tried to lay on her.

Transmission lag. She twisted about and stared at the Moon. Against its ashen-bright almost-disc, no points of light showed as they did on dark parts. If she took out her optic and magnified, she would see traces of human presence. No need. She knew what life laired yonder.

"It is well." The face smiled, the voice purred. "Aleka Kame, I want you to—" It broke off. Then, anxiously: "Dear, could I ask a favor of you? You remember me telling you about my kinswoman Mary Carfax in San Francisco Bay Integrate, don't you? Old and frail and living by herself. She insists she's all right, but when last we talked she looked terrible and I'm worried. Could you hop over, call on her personal-

ly, and let me know what you think? I'll be your
thank-slave, and next time you're on the Moon I may
have something rather wonderful to show you."

Lilisaire had remembered to switch on a program
that remade dialect as well as sound and sight. It was
oddly comforting, in this huge stillness, to discover
that she too could be momentarily forgetful.

Though what had shaken her self-command?

*"Should I have need to convey a message to you in
full secrecy, I will send you on a harmless pretext to
Mary Carfax, my Earthside agent nearest your dwelling place. She is another false identity, a sophotect.
From it you will receive instructions."*

Why this roundaboutness? Who might be listening
in?

Something rather wonderful. What Lilisaire had
spoken of, that day in the diamond pagoda at Zamok
Vysoki?

"Yes, I w-will be glad to," Aleka said. Her mouth
had gone dry. How to mislead the possible eavesdrop-
per? She seized an idea that winged past. "I've been
wanting a short vacation anyhow." Her taking it at
this crisis would earn her reproaches, but her kind of
service necessarily gave broad discretion, and she
could quite logically ask what difference her staying
on the scene would make. "Give me a few days to
disengage here."

Transmission lag.

"Good. You are . . . quick-witted," *as I judged you
to be.* "And as a matter of fact, it would be more
convenient if you paid your visit a week from now. I
am so grateful. How have you been?"

Because it would be a natural action, and because it
might be helpful there in the high castle, Aleka related
her day.

—"Yes, something ought certainly to be done
about this. Perhaps something can be done. We'll see.
Adiós for now, dear."

The screen darkened. Only wind and sea and the
hiss of the bow cleaving water spoke further. Aleka's

glance returned to the Lunar disc. Strange, if that was where her hope lay, hope for the ancient unreasonableness of life. Or maybe not so strange. Yonder, too, it had flourished from the earliest years, heedless of the machines that kept it in being.

6

The Mother of the Moon

Port Bowen had gained a few amenities, among them L'Étoile de Diane. The restaurant's menu was limited, but that was because all vegetables and fruit were fresh, raised in its own agro unit. Lately, as excavation and outfitting continued, it had become able to add fish and poultry. The proprietor spoke of wine which wasn't bruisingly shipped from Earth, beginning fairly soon. Dagny, who could ill afford the place, rejoiced when Edmond Beynac invited her. She recognized that that wasn't entirely on account of the dinner.

"Not bad," he said of his roast duck. "But if we chance to have Earthside leave at the same time, let me introduce you to a real *confit d'oie.* I know an inn at Les Eyzies where they make the best in the universe." He sipped from his glass and chuckled. "They should, by hell. They have been doing it for centuries."

Earthside together? Dagny told her pulse to behave itself. "Everything in those parts is old, isn't it?" she asked for lack of a brilliant response.

"No, no, we are living people, not museum exhibits or tourist shows." The broad shoulders shrugged. "But yes, that is an ancient land, and more survives than castles and archaeological sites. Most of my ancestors, they doubtless trace back to Crô-Magnon Man." He grinned. "Or further, if those geneticists are right who think Neandertal blood is in us too. I would not mind that, being descended from a little fellow who stayed alive in the face of the glacier and the cave bear."

She recalled a picture in a book, a hunter on those primeval barrens, and thought Edmond resembled him. Maybe the setting helped her impression along —not this small, warm, food-fragrant room where conversation buzzed low and music (Debussy?) breathed from the speaker—but the view in the ports and in the clear cupola. By day you dined underground; at night the topside section was opened for patrons who didn't worry about a bit of added radiation. Candles on the tables scarcely dimmed the splendor of Earth near the full; even some of the brighter stars gleamed through, unwinking and wintry. The ground was no longer bare and somber, it reached in a dream of luminance and shadows, as if every stone were alive and every craterlet a well where the spirits might give you your wish. Such works of humankind as stood in view became themselves magical, like shapes in a painting by a man who had slain mammoths. Edmond sat poised against a cold wilderness through which he pursued bigger game than ever walked the tundra.

"You're interested in prehistory?" Dagny ventured. "You sure keep a zoo of interests."

He had a smile that came and went quickly but brightly. "Well, my father is professor of the subject at the University of Bordeaux. Me, I thought I might go into the same science, but then I decided most of the great discoveries in it have been made, and—Fireball was giving us the space frontier."

She couldn't resist: "Not exactly giving, as Anson Guthrie would be the first to admit."

He grinned. "*Touché!* His prices, however, they are no more than the traffic will bear, and we do not have to deal with mole-eyed, lard-bottomed bureaucrats, we can simply pay and go. I envy you that you know him so well."

She had told him about her past, what parts seemed appropriate, in the course of their developing acquaintance. "I rarely see him any more. He and his wife put me in a good school, and they paid my expenses at the academy, but I had to qualify for it on my own and since I've graduated they've never shown me any partiality."

"I know."

She remembered she had already emphasized this to him, and flushed. A gulp of wine lent sufficient assurance for her to dangle bait. "Of course, we've stayed in touch, and I visited them on my last vacation and expect I will again occasionally." With a companion? Better swing the subject back. "We were talking about you, though, for a change. You mentioned something earlier about not having gone directly into your profession."

"I bounced about." His tone softened. "We had a summer cottage in the upper Dordogne. In my childhood I got so familiar with the local farmers they nicknamed me *Jacquou le croquant*, Jacques the peasant, from a famous novel. I believed I would become a farmer too, until I found out that technology long ago made the family farm extinct and my friends were just administrators. Besides, my father's work, it soon had more romance for me. But then my mother, she has an export-import business, textiles and artwork, through her I came at age sixteen to spend a year in Malaysia. That made me restless to see more of the world than tourists do, and at age eighteen I enlisted in the French section of United Nations forces." Could an unlucky love affair have given impulse? "We were sent to the chaos in the Middle East—you know, when Europe was establishing the *Befehl* there."

"You saw action?" Dagny dared ask, low.

"Oh, yes," he answered grimly. "Too much. Any amount of combat is too much. In between, I began really thinking. After two years I was wounded badly enough for discharge." So he'd stuck it out that long, having pledged his word, in spite of hating it, and must have been brave, because a man that smart could wangle a rear-echelon assignment if he tried. "The

physicians fixed me all right, I carry only some scraps
of metal in me and they do not bother. But I was quite
ready for civilian life, studies, field work on Earth, my
degree, and then, four years ago, a postdoctoral fellowship on Luna."

As he talked, he cheered up afresh. "Here I am
happy," he finished. "True, it is not perfect. Those
hours per daycycle in the bloody centrifuge, we could
very well do without them, *hein?* How do you spend
that time?"

"Going through the standard exercises," Dagny
said. "Doesn't everybody? Otherwise, read, write
letters, watch a show, whatever. In a big unit, I mean.
Not much choice on a field platform."

"On one of those, when I am alone except for a
counterweight, I turn off my transmitter and sing," he
confessed. "Then nobody else must suffer my voice."

She laughed. "You see, the necessity isn't a total
nuisance!"

"It is not too bad," he agreed, "not too high a price.
When they begin to study Mars and the asteroids in
earnest, I would like to go. But there is no limit yet on
what is to do here." He regarded her. "Nor, I find, is
there lack of good company."

Her heartbeat refused flat-out the order to quiet
down.

7

As the ship neared on her approach curve, Luna in
the viewscreens shifted from ahead to below, from
thickening crescent to dun stoneland scarred with
craters. Earth hung high and horned above the south.

Silence had grown heavy. Kenmuir cleared his
throat. "Well, Barbara," he said, hearing the awkwardness, "it's goodbye—for a while, at any rate."

"May your meantime be happy," replied the ship. He had ordered a female voice when she spoke with him alone. The Lunarian-accented Anglo sounded friendly, even warm. Valanndray had specified a whistling, birdlike, unhuman timbre for himself. He hadn't said why and Kenmuir had never asked. When all three talked together, the vessel used a neutral male tone.

"Thank you. And yours."

The absurdity of it struck at Kenmuir. His mouth twisted upward. What was he doing, swapping banalities with a sophotect? Yes, it was conscious, it thought, but in how constricted a range! By tapping the cultural database, it could give him an interesting conversation on any subject he chose, from the puns in Shakespeare to the causes of the Lyudov Rebellion, but he knew how purely algorithmic that was. Its creativity, its self lay in the manifold, ever-varying functions of a spacecraft.

And yes, he'd grown fond of this machine, in the way he'd formerly grown fond of his old laserblade or a particular plaid shirt or his and Annie's house on Earth, but that wasn't the same as affection for a human being or a live pet. Somehow he felt it would be wrong to leave without a farewell, but why?

Would the ship have been hurt? He couldn't believe that. Her words, comradely or concerned as the situation called for, gave simply the illusion of feelings like his. What were hers? Meaningless question. He imagined her taking pleasure in the challenge of a difficult maneuver, he imagined her longing to get back into full connection with others, with the cybercosm, and for that span share in a larger awareness than he would ever know; but this was anthropomorphism on his part. It was as inane as his naming her, privately, Barbara, after the first girl he had loved and never gotten.

Too long aspace, a man went a bit crazy. By Earth standards, anyhow.

"Commencing descent," she warned him. Also that was needless. Besides the instruments on the console, he sensed the swingaround. Had the algorithm computed that he would appreciate her gesture?

Signals flew back and forth. Electrophotonic intelligences meshed. Weight returned, settling Kenmuir in his chair, and the ship climbed down the sky to Port Bowen.

The thought of Annie lingered in him. His gaze sought Earth. Where was she yonder? Ten years, now, since last he'd heard anything; a dozen years since they parted. Mostly his fault, he supposed. Spacefarers were a poor risk for marriage. But theirs had begun so happily, nestled under Ben Dearg in a land whose heights and heather they had nearly to themselves. . . . He sighed. "It's space you love, Ian," she had said—oh, very quietly, with a bare glimmer of tears. "It doesn't leave enough of you for me to live on." Well, he hadn't quite given up hope of someday having a little touslehead or two of his own. But no woman whom a spacefarer would likely meet shared it as Annie once did, except dream-women in the quivira, and he dared not call those up very often.

Lilisaire waited! A surge passed through him, half lust, half fear, and left him trembling.

Touchdown into a cradle was feather-gentle. He saw just two other vessels on the field, a globular freighter and a small, slim suborbital that was probably his transport to Zamok Vysoki. In Fireball's day the number could well have been a score.

Seeking to master himself, and thinking of what Lilisaire might want him for, he looked westward, past the control tower. The spark that was L-5 stood above that horizon. But no, he hadn't set the screen to enhance the stars, and the sun-glare of early Lunar afternoon hid most of them, including the derelict worldlet. Symbolic, an omen?

Now there was an anachronism for you. Kenmuir's tautness eased with a grin at himself. Unharnessing, he went to get his luggage. After three daycycles of boost at a fourth again Earth's gravity, one-sixth was like blowing along on a breeze.

Stripped, his cabin had become a hollowness he gladly quitted. A single bag sufficed him. He had packed the rest of his effects; robots would fetch and stow them till he phoned instructions. He need not actually carry anything. His hostess could provide him clothes and such, lavishly. Too much. He preferred his plain personal style, as well as his independence.

As he was about to command an airlock to open, the ship surprised him. "Fare you well, Ian Kenmuir," she said. "May we travel together again."

"Why, why, I'd like that," he faltered.

Meaningless wish. If he was assigned a different craft, its intelligence would, routinely, get a download of everything Barbara knew about him. He would find the personalities indistinguishable—if personality, distinct individuality, could be said to exist in sophotects. What then led her to send him off this humanly?

He didn't really understand these minds. Did they? Beyond a certain degree of complexity, systems go chaotic, inherently unpredictable and unfathomable even to themselves. No doubt the Teramind saw more deeply, but was that insight absolute, and did it include all of the vast psyche?

He thrust the question from him. It always gave him an inward shudder. "Until then, Barbara," he mumbled, and signalled the inner valve. It contracted. He passed through the chamber. The outer valve had already withdrawn, when the portal sealed fast to an ascensor shaft in the cradle. Kenmuir stepped onto the platform. It bore him down to the terminal. He emerged.

The floor gleamed before him, wide and almost empty. The murals along it seemed to mock the triumphs they celebrated, Armstrong's landing, the

Great Return, Anson Guthrie founding the base that
would become this city, Dagny Beynac bossing construction of the hundredth Criswell energy collector. . . . None dated from the Selenarchy, although
that era had seen the Mars colony begun, interstellar
missions, Guthrie's and Rinndalir's exodus to Alpha
Centauri. Lunarians didn't flaunt public achievements; they were too catlike, individualistic, secretive. . . . The air felt cold.

A lone man waited, clad in form-fitting black and
silver. Kenmuir recognized him, Eythil, a trusted
attendant of Lilisaire's. Mars-bred, he stood less tall
and more broad than the average Moondweller of his
race, strong, dangerous when necessary. His complexion was dark, his hair black and curly, but that was not
unusual; many different stocks had gone into the
ancestry.

He saluted, hand to breast. "Greeting and welcome,
my captain." His use of his mother tongue, un-
prompted, was an honorific, implying worth—not
status, but inborn worth—equal or nearly equal to the
Lunarian. He also refrained from explaining that he
would bring the newcomer to his lady, and from
asking how the journey had been.

"To you I am indeed well come, Saljaine," Kenmuir
replied likewise. The title had no Earthside equivalent, for Selenarchs had never bestowed rigid ranks on
their followers. It might perhaps be rendered "officer," perhaps "faithful henchman."

They started across the floor. Being a Terran of the
Orthosphere, Kenmuir felt obliged to make some
conversation. "The port was not quite this deserted"
—eerily so—"when I left last year. Has traffic fallen
off more, or is it a statistical fluke?"

"Both are at work, I think," Eythil said. "I have
heard of three large ships retired from service in the
past thirteen-month, and might learn of more did I
consult the official database." The insinuation was
that he didn't believe every byte of information was

available to everybody, even in such apparently harmless areas as interplanetary commerce.

Kenmuir, who thought this was true, nodded. "Traffic must have grown sparse, or we'd not see random variations."

A part of his mind ran through the reasons—some of the reasons. Population decline wasn't one. The original steep drop (which had, for example, left spacious reaches of Scotland open to him in his boyhood and to him and Annie in their marriage) had long since flattened out and was approaching the asymptote of zero growth. Lowered demand for raw materials certainly was a reason: efficient recycling, goods made to last, few if any design changes. But what lay behind it? The old, driving dynamism had faded well-nigh out of people—How? Why?

Ferocity lashed in Eythil's voice: "Hargh, they will soon swarm again, the ships, when the Habitat comes with its Terrans breeding, breeding. Unless maychance you—" He broke off. Kenmuir couldn't tell whether that was due caution or because a robot was moving across the floor to intercept them.

Robot, or sophotect? The turret could hold a human-capability computer. If it didn't, the body could be remote-controlled by an intelligence. This was a standard multipurpose model, boxlike, with three different pairs of arms, the four legs lifting its principal sensors to a level with his eyes. Where organic components were not in supple motion, metal shone dull gold.

It drew close. Musical western Anglo floated out of the speaker: "Your pardon, Captain Kenmuir, Freeholder Eythil."

They stopped. "What would you?" the Lunarian rapped. It was obvious that Kenmuir, just in from space, would be known; but the system's identification of his companion must give, more than ever, a feeling of being caged.

"You are bound for your vehicle?" the machine

said. "Regrets and apologies. Clearance to lift will be delayed about an hour."

"What the Q?" Kenmuir exclaimed, amazed.

"An accidental explosion has occurred just a few minutes ago on Epsilon-93. Do you place the designation? An iceberg lately brought here."

Kenmuir and, stiffly, Eythil nodded. They hadn't heard of the object, but that was natural. Beneficiated pieces of comet stuff were, as a rule, set on trajectories that took them from the Kuiper Belt into Lunar orbit, there to be refined and sent down. Robotic, utterly routine, the operation hadn't been conducted much in recent decades, but no doubt the work was starting up on a larger scale. The influx of settlers after the Habitat was ready would want more water and air than the Moon currently recycled.

"Fragments are flying about," the machine continued. "None are expected to crash, but that is as yet not perfectly certain. Until every track is known, Traffic Control is interdicting civilian movement above ground, especially in this vicinity. For about an hour, is the estimate. You landed barely in time."

Eythil scowled. Kenmuir shrugged, although his impatience was probably sharper.

"Administration apologizes for any inconvenience," the machine said. "You are invited to spend the time in the executive lounge, with complimentary refreshments."

Eythil and Kenmuir exchanged a glance. Smiles quirked wry. "Never have I been there," the Lunarian admitted. "You, Captain?"

"No," Kenmuir replied. "Why not?" Satisfy a slight curiosity. Besides, the public bar and restaurant, big, well-nigh forsaken, would be spooky surroundings.

The room to which the machine led them was of a more intimate size. Its furniture, massive Earth-style, seemed somehow faded. Flat pictures of space pioneers hung on the walls. The air held a faint simulation of leather and woodsmoke odors. Kenmuir wondered why this retreat was maintained. How often had it seen use since the spaceport was completely cyberneticized? Well, it couldn't be much trouble to keep, and occasions like this doubtless arose once in a while. The system provided for improbabilities.

He and Eythil took chairs. The machine went to a dispenser. "What is your desire, señores?" it asked. Eythil wanted a Lunarian white wine—the vineyards under Copernicus still produced biologically—and Kenmuir chose ale. The machine touched the panel, the containers arrived, the machine poured into suitable goblets from off a shelf and brought them over. "If you wish anything more, call me, por favor," it said, indicating the nearest intercom input. "I trust you soon may be on your way."

"Thanks," Kenmuir answered. After all, either it or its controller was sentient. It departed. Kenmuir sipped. A goodly brew, yes. Never mind that molecular machineries had assembled it; the formula was tangy, the liquid cold. "Hadn't you better phone to say we'll be delayed?" he asked Eythil.

"Nay, not if the wait stretches no longer," the other man said. They both stayed with Anglo. Odd, Kenmuir reflected, what a relaxed attitude to schedules most Lunarians had, when survival might depend on precision. Well, with them timing was practically instinctive, as fast as recovery from a stumble was to an Earthman in his high-gravity home. You got to know your competences and their safe boundaries.

"I wonder what exactly went wrong," he remarked. "It sounded like the kind of accident that shouldn't ever happen these days."

"Thus the cybercosm tells us," Eythil growled.

"M-m, nothing is guaranteed, you know. The planning may be total, but—I simply wonder if this blowup was due to an oversight, or a runaway chaos, or a quantum fluctuation that got amplified. . . . I really don't know how these operations are conducted. In a few daycycles, if I have a free hour or two, I'd like to retrieve a full account."

"You will get one," Eythil said cynically. "Whether

or nay it relates what truly happened—if aught happened at all—will be for you to guess."

He was right, Kenmuir thought. The system could feed pretty much anything it chose into the database, complete with images, numbers, and mathematical analysis. It wouldn't be hard to bypass the human functionaries who were supposed to be in the loop. "Why should the mind lie," he protested, "especially when the story isn't to its credit?"

Eythil finger-shrugged. "Who knows? Incidentally to some broad design, maychance. Let us assume this happening will help make plausible the diversion of yet more resources to the Habitat project, and thereby hasten the destruction of Lunarian lifeways. Thus might the sociotechnic program esoterically calculate."

Kenmuir took a long, heartening draught. "Farfetched. You *are* bitter, aren't you?"

"Have I not cause?"

It surfaced in the minutes that followed, breaking through the normal reserve of Eythil's race toward Kenmuir's. The spaceman was familiar with most of it, but he listened throughout, because here was a need to speak. Moreover, he heard a few aspects that had not touched on him before.

—While the asteroids were invaluable sources of minerals, as the comets were of ices and both were of organics, by themselves they did not suffice. A large body is required for the chemical fractionation that creates usable concentrations of most industrial materials. Hence prospecting and mining on the moons of Jupiter and Saturn. On Mercury they were carried out entirely by machines—

—although even for them, Venus was too costly. In environments less horrific, humans were marginally employable: those humans whose desire for a frontier brought them there. Above all was Mars—

—to which Lunarians, especially, went in the high days of the Selenarchy. Terrans, too, could reproduce in that gravity field; but at first their numbers were less, because few were accustomed to land that could kill them. Mars remained a province of Luna until the Federation took them both over—

—"and we should yet be of Lunarian name," Eythil said. "Is not a member nation supposed to govern itself? But nay, afar on Mars we have less autonomy left us than here where we circle Earth."

"Well, you've gotten proportionally more Terrans," Kenmuir pointed out. "Whether or not they were born there, they'll think, act, vote according to their psychological bent and their culture."

"You speak like a sociotech." Contempt edged the word.

"I don't mean to," Kenmuir said mildly. "One is apt to read a lot on space hauls. It makes for a bookish vocabulary. Oh, I am not only a Terran by race, I'm an Earthling. But I do sympathize with you Lunarians. All the old, irreconcilable issues are rising again, aren't they?"

—which once made Luna declare itself a nation, independent and sovereign: birthright, property right, education, the survival of a civilization that openly rejected certain basic ideals. He had often wondered what would have developed if it had stayed clear of the Federation. Idle imagining, of course. When reaction to the War Strike doomed mighty Fireball, the end of separatist Luna was in sight, however long a delaying campaign Niolente and her cohorts might wage. Yet, in some hypothetical quantum-mechanical alternative reality—

"Under the Covenant, the Assembly and High Council should at least respect our constitution," Eythil maintained. "But nay, more and more they reshape the 'fundamental ethic' clause to bring down olden law and ways. Decision passes ever more from living beings to machines."

Intelligent machines, Kenmuir thought, not subject to human corruption and cruelty. Yet undeniably this

was governance by . . . aliens? The Teramind bore
something of the awesomeness of God, but it was not
God—too remote, not fallible enough. As for the
day-to-day details of life, maybe what gnawed some
people worst was just a sense of having become
irrelevant.

"It isn't due to any conspiracy," he argued. "It's
the, the logic of events. The former nations scarcely
exist any longer. They've broken up into thousands of
different societies, in fact and often in form. The
Federation has *had* to take over many of their duties.
Without an integrated world economy, everyone
would starve."

"Scant value has that economy had for us Martians
of late."

"Well, declining demand for minerals."

"We could adapt, in a self-chosen fashion. But nay,
it must be in Earth wise. You speak of the Federation
as the sole viable government that is left. But that
means that naught stands between the lone person
and it."

"I know. History shows your fear is reasonable.
Also, anomie is demoralizing. But you have to agree,
the Federation government doesn't try to run people's
lives for them. In fact, many of its interferences with
you Lunarians have been to curb arbitrary powers of
the Selenarchs that they aren't supposed to possess in
a republic—"

Perhaps fortunately, the wall speaker announced:
"Ambient space is now known to be safe. You may lift
when you please, señores."

Silence fell between them, and prevailed while they
went to the vehicle, launched, and flew. Eythil might
have been nursing his anger, or might have gone into
some unearthly mind-realm of his own. Kenmuir had
begun to feel a vague headache and feverishness. He
wondered whether it was nerves, dread that he might
somehow fail Lilisaire . . . whatever she wanted of
him.

The westering sun rose higher as the trajectory bore him in that direction. Earth, too, shifted across his sky, easterly and northerly. It shone at late first quarter, a blue crescent marbled with white clouds which, widespread over nightside, captured enough light from the stars and from below to make that part of it ghostly gray. So had it been when first she summoned him.

He did not yet know why she did—he, the most ordinary of men, an Earthman at that. "Ey, but you are far from ordinary," she had purred when he got up the courage to ask. "Your whole career, your doings in the yonder, your ties to the past. You live not in a void nor by illusions, like so many. You know what has gone before, the land and folk and deeds from which your being springs; for you, time has reality, even as space does." That had not seemed quite an answer to him.

True, in repeated talks she had drawn him out concerning the Fireball Trothdom. He wasn't sure why, and he knew nothing that a datasearch program couldn't have found for her. It wasn't much more than an association, after all, a lodge or fellowship rooted in wistfulness for a grandeur long vanished, not unlike the Ronin, the Swagmen, or the Believers. Like them, it had its rituals, social gatherings, mutual helpfulness, and little else. Whatever the secret lore was that was said to be passed down from Rydberg to Rydberg, it couldn't be of any importance, and it had certainly not been confided to Ian Kenmuir.

Maybe Lilisaire was trying to get an idea of what membership felt like. It was not a Lunarian sort of thing; it might provide a little insight into the other species. Or maybe she was interested because the Trothdom meant a great deal to Kenmuir, and in her fashion she liked him.

She had said he was a fine lover. (The memory flamed.) "No, except that you inspire me," he replied honestly. She laughed and rumpled his hair. He did

not delude himself that he was anything but an
agreeable diversion, at best.

And yet . . . she had called him back, urgently, at
no small cost to an undertaking from which she stood
to make a profit. In some way, however minor, she
needed him.

His heart thuttered. He didn't know if he was in
love—this was foreign to any such state anytime
earlier in his life—or in thralldom. At the moment, he
didn't care.

The flyer reached apoluna and descended. From
the Cordillera reared the witchy towers of Zamok
Vysoki.

Having landed, Kenmuir brushed past Eythil,
straight into the gangtube. The slight malaise had
faded out of him. If he was afire and ashiver, it was
wholly with Lilisaire. Not until later did he hope he
hadn't offended his proud escort, then wonder whether Eythil hadn't been amused.

No attendant waited in the room beyond. Clearly,
the flyer had sent word ahead, and a robot or a servant
would take his things wherever the Wardress desired.
A voice from the air said, "Hail, Ian Kenmuir. Betake
you to the Pagoda and be made welcome."

He knew that turret and the way there. How he
knew them! He bounded, he soared down the changeable corridors and through the multiform chambers.
Lunarians moved in them, male and female, on
various business of hers. Most were staff, whether or
not they wore the livery, but several came from
outside, and he recognized two magnates. No words
or gestures passed between them and him, save for the
swift and stylized eye contact that was courtesy. At the
end of his trek he did find a guardsman, standing at
panther ease, who saluted and let him through the
door.

Sunlight exploded from a blinding center into
sparks and flashes of every color his vision could
capture. They flowed and shifted all around him with
each least movement he made, across the glassy floor

and the few fragile furnishings, the walls and ceiling and his hands. He had come into the middle of a single million-faceted synthetic diamond. Odors drifted on the air, spice, honeysuckle. Barely audible wailed the minor-key melody of a canto of Verdea's.

By a table set with crystal, near a broad animate couch, poised Lilisaire. The auburn mane fell over bare shoulders and a full-length gown that sheathed her like a second skin. The wreckage of rainbows played on those whitenesses. Her only ornaments were stardrops hung from her ears and a finger ring whose jewel flickered with tiny flames. At her feet lay a pet he remembered, a black leopard with golden spots. It lifted its head and stared at him.

She smiled. "Yes, well are you come, my captain," she murmured in Anglo.

He stopped, suddenly helpless. She advanced. Her skirts whispered. He lifted a hand. She laid fingertips moth-lightly on the wrist. It signified that she was his superior, but he never thought to dispute that. The faintest of pressures urged him to the table. She lowered her arm and stood before him. "Pour for us," she bade.

He obeyed. The sound of it rang clear under the music. With a green glance she invited him to partake of the canapés—he knew they were superb—while she raised her goblet. *"Uwach yei,"* she said.

"Your service, m-my lady," he pledged. Rims belled together. They sipped. The wine sang.

Her gaze steadied on him. He forgot the diamond radiance. "Service," she said low. "Mean you this?"

He caught his breath before he answered: "I do. And not because I'm your employee."

"My captain." Her free hand reached to stroke his cheek. He would have felt a blow less keenly and shakingly.

He snatched after balance. "What is this about?" he asked in his driest voice. "What can I do?"

"You may well have guessed. It concerns the Habitat."

"Yes, I . . . surmised as much. You and your class have opposed it so hard."

The Selenarchic families must feel sore pressed, he thought, when they stooped to politics—what they called monkey dealings. Granted, it was for the most part indirectly. Those who, like Lilisaire, had substantial inherited property on Earth could raise up Terran advocates and get a few into the Federation Assembly —Useless. Public opinion (in such fraction of the public as paid any attention) excitedly favored what would be the first real pioneering their species had mounted in generations. Besides, the cybercosm had first proposed the scheme. Surely sophotectic intelligence superior to the human knew what was best for humanity.

Lilisaire's voice plucked him from his recollections. "Indeed. We waxed sufficiently troublesome that the government investigated us."

"Well, naturally, if you were making a fuss, a data scan—"

"Nay, more. Officers from Earth prowled about inquiring. One of them came hither soon after I had called to you. Nor was he an ordinary Peace Authority agent. He was of the best they have, a very synnoiont."

Startled, Kenmuir exclaimed, "That *was* serious!"

She finger-shrugged. "Ey, he said not his nature to me. But I scented he was no common man. Later I carried a hunt of my own through the databases and among folk. Have no fear. It is unlikely he knows I did. And he found naught of wrongdoing." Her laughter chimed. "For, I regret, there has been none. Whence might the opportunity for it have come?"

Abrupt, cold fury spat: "Nay, we lie bound, awaiting the knife. It will not even slit our throats cleanly. First the women shall be spayed and the men gelded."

The leopard snarled.

Kenmuir fumbled for words. "Matters can't be that bad, my lady."

She put on calm. "Think. What has preserved us

thus far, save that Terrans cannot breed on the Moon?"

His mind tried to resist her. What was preserved, it said, was the dominance of the Selenarchy, in fact if no longer in name. And that began to be eroded after biotech enabled his kind to live indefinitely under low gravity, healthy except for loss of muscle tissue if they didn't keep up their exercises. (For a second he imagined he could feel the engineered microbes implanted in him, their chemistry suffusing every cell.) More and more of the old species took up permanent residence. But, yes, their numbers remained limited by the inability of their women to carry a child to term, or raise one born on a larger world but less than about three years of age, nervous system still developing. However precariously, the Lunar aristocrats clung to dominion over the nominal republic.

"Now you expect a rush of settlers from Earth?" he asked stupidly.

"It will be unstoppable. The sociotechnic equations foretell it. Hundreds of thousands declare themselves ardent to go. Once the Habitat is ready—"

—abandoned L-5 refurbished, brought into low Lunar orbit, provided with lightsails to exert the forces that would keep it on that otherwise unstable path, set spinning again in order to give full Earth weight around its huge circumference. Lo, a place for Terrans to bear young and see them through those early years, while easily going to the Moon and back—

"—and that will be no long while hence. Time hounds us, Kenmuir." She never used his given name. He did not know whether it was due habit, hers being single, or a decision to avoid any true intimacy.

"But they'll be the flower of Earth," he argued. "The sort who want to do real work, live real lives, here, in space." Like himself, he acknowledged. He had been lucky, had gotten into the Academy, the Space Service, at last the Venture. How could be begrudge anyone else the stars?

Her lip lifted. "Yes, the lords of the world and their machine masters should well rejoice to see that restlessness bled away from the planet. On the Moon it will be more easily contained." Her tone went urgent. "But understand you not? They will make Luna over. Their vast new constructions will break its peace while they in their hordes impose the society they want."

"Uh, that can't happen overnight."

"Swifter than you believe, my innocent captain, and with entropic certainty. I say to you, it will destroy us."

"Mars—"

"Mars is already lost."

Recalling Eythil, Kenmuir didn't dispute that. "M-m, your colonists on the asteroids and the outer moons—no, those places could never hold more than remnants," powerless, impoverished, until ships from Earth came to remove them under the banner of charity and efficiency.

He glanced down at the leopard and pictured it confined for life in a cage full of apes.

"We, or our children, will cease wishing to live," Lilisaire went on, quietly. "Some will drag out their last years, some not," but go violently, in rebellion, crime, suicide. "None will bring young into that kennel of an existence. In two centuries, three, no matter, this mischief-making, unconforming breed will be extinct. How convenient for the cybercosm."

Kenmuir doubted her concern for her species. Yet how genuine was the despair he heard beneath the steel! If she was right, if the Lunarians perished, a certain magnificence would have gone out of the universe.

Shock: Could the cybercosm actually intend that?

The eyes regarding him were tearless, the slim body unbowed. "You must have some recourse in mind," he said slowly.

She nodded. The ruddy hair rippled. "A forlorn

venture," she replied in the same level voice, "belike in quest of a treasure that shall prove to be a myth."

Leaning slightly forward, suddenly tense: "Will you dare it?"

Almost, he gasped at the impact. "T-tell me," he stammered.

She straightened, relaxing her flesh. "It need be naught unlawful . . . on your part," he heard. "Nevertheless there is a thing you can seek to learn for me, which has lain hidden away for lifetimes."

"What?"

"In this house abides a fugitive tradition. Yet I have also fact to relate. Come, drink, calm yourself, hear me out."

He was amazed at the deftness with which she reviewed history. It was familiar to him, but she brought it into perspective—her perspective—and touched on matters about which he had known little.

She recalled to him the long, Machiavellian struggle to keep Luna sovereign, out of the Federation, waged by Niolente and her cohorts after Guthrie and Rinndalir left for Alpha Centauri and Fireball began disbanding. He had not known of several missions into deep space, whose purpose was never divulged, nor that those were what seemed to have given Niolente the confidence to keep striving.

Of course, in the end it had not helped her. Events torrented, the proclamation of the republic by one faction, its instant recognition by the governments of Earth, the dispatch of Peace Authority troops to its aid. No doubt the old woman had then resolved to die fighting, for the armed force she whistled up had no hope whatsoever. It was inevitable that the Authority would afterward ransack every site she had ever occupied, including any databases kept in them.

Kenmuir had not been aware that all the material was confiscated, that what was later released was incomplete, or that the official story about the accidental wiping of some files was inconsistent with the methodical procedures of the man in charge. Nobody had taken any special notice. The whole business was soon forgotten, except among certain of her direct descendants.

"She was working on something in far space?" he breathed.

"It must have been," Lilisaire said. "A weapon or—I know not what."

"Then how should I?"

She drained her glass and beckoned him to pour another. First he finished his own. The leopard got up and padded about the room, black and gold among the light-shards.

"Hear me," Lilisaire said. "The tradition I spoke of goes further back still, to the time of Dagny Beynac. A son of hers made an expedition into the deeps from which he did not return. Naught of real explanation was ever given. The family held to itself whatever knowledge had been gained."

In hopes of eventual profit? That would have been quite Lunarian. But so, too, would have been keeping the secret for a memorial, an enduring sacrifice to sorrow.

"Searching what records remain, for the conquerors did not find everything, I have come to feel sure that this discovery was what Niolente had intent to make use of," Lilisaire continued. "Could we acquire it, we might achieve a part of her hope. But time is short, and even before the Habitat makes everything too late for us, the enemy's suspicions may lead him to take forestalling action. Thus, as soon as I had this clue, I sent for you, who will be able to look further."

"I, uh, I've no idea where to begin," he demurred.

Again her look pierced him. "On Earth."

"What?" He realized he was gaping, and snapped his jaw shut. "How?"

"Well do you know that the first Rydberg was the first child of Dagny Beynac, and came to be in her close confidence. And . . . to this day, the Fireball lodgemaster guards some arcanum, which appears to go back to that time of upheaval."

"You mean—"

She sighed. "A thin possibility, yes; but I see scant others."

"A weapon—" Chill tingled through Kenmuir. It was bad enough when Fireball turned spacecraft against the Avantists. Justified though the action might have been, the outrage it globally provoked brought on the end of Fireball and of sovereign Luna. A teratonne nuclear warhead, an asteroid made dirigible—"No!"

"It may not be that," she said quickly. "Or if it is, the menace alone should win us our freedom. In any case, why, since the powers on Earth are so anxious to keep it secret, the simple threat of disclosure would be a weapon for us, nay?"

He tossed off a long drink. The wine deserved closer attention, but he had to brace himself. As the glow spread through his blood, he became able to say, almost thoughtfully, "Y-yes, if the information's been buried that deep, there must be a strong reason. . . . It could be a good reason, though."

"I ask no betrayal of you," she said with a flick of scorn. "Find what you can and choose what you can."

It hurt worse than he would have expected. "I scarcely believe the Rydberg will confide in me just for the asking," he said.

Warmth returned, and with it a smile. "If you explain, maychance he will. If not, or if what he tells is of no avail, then—" She let the sentence trail off like music.

"Yes?" he prompted out of his pulsebeat.

"I have other agents on Earth. Would you be willing to join forces with one of them? Your ken of space may greatly help."

This was demented, he thought. He was no spy, no rebel, nothing but a middle-aged, law-abiding technician whose audacity was all in the head, interplay with

impersonal forces, out among stars which the conten-
tions and griefs of humankind would never touch. Yet
she flung him a challenge, and—she wanted it, she
needed it, this might be her life that he could save.

"I will try," he heard himself mumble.

She shouted, cast her goblet shattering against the
diamond, and was in his arms.

The living couch received them and responded to
them.

In his heart he could only praise the terrible necessity that had brought her race into being.

8

The Mother of the Moon

Night on Lunar Farside is a glory of stars. With
neither sun nor Earth to override them, you need only
walk away from human lights and your sky will brim
with brilliance, six thousand or more stars revealed to
an eye that has nothing between it and them but a
clear plate and a few centimeters of breath. They
gleam unblinking where they crowd the crystal dark,
and the brightest are not all white; many burn steel-
blue, gold, amber, bronze-red. The constellations are
no longer geometrical diagrams so much as they are
prodigally marshalling hosts, planets ablaze among
them. Nebulae rear thunderhead-black or float softly
aglow. From horizon to horizon arches the galactic
belt, not milky to sight but icy, a winter river banked
and islanded with night. Beyond it you may spy its
nearer sisters, the clotted Magellanics, Andromeda
vague and huge, perhaps one or two more glimpsed
across yet greater deeps. Turn off your receiver and
you are wholly of this vision, in a silence as vast as its
reaches; far, far beneath it, the murmurs of your body
declare that you are alive, you are what is beholding.

Sometimes a spark hastens aloft, a satellite. It is
quickly lost in the Moon's shadow.

Dagny Beynac sighed and turned back toward camp. She couldn't stand long agaze, she had work to do.

First, scheduled whirly time. The boss ought not to keep anybody waiting. She swung into kangaroo pace, eight or ten kilometers per hour across the murky lava, an easy and exhilarating rhythm. The lamps ahead glared the stars away from her.

The other three were already at the centrifuge. In undiffusing vacuum, not entirely helped by reflection off surroundings, light and shadow, whiteness and dust made their spacesuits a goblin chiaroscuro. Like every newcomer, Dagny when she arrived on the Moon had had to learn how to *see,* especially after sunset on Farside. Today she effortlessly identified yonder shapes, the supply depot and shelters in their background, the crews and machines, the widespread complexities they were creating. A multi-facility astronomical observatory was under construction in Mare Moscoviense, and she in charge of housing for its personnel. Advancement was fast if you were able, if you survived.

She turned her radio back on. Switching it off in the field had been dead against regulations, but now and then she needed to be alone for a short while with heaven and the life inside her. "Hi," she greeted. "Prepared and eager?"

Wim den Boer mistook the cheerful sarcasm. "No," he grumbled. "Damnation, a full three hours? I'm busy! You know how that hitch in delivering the pumps has thrown my section behind schedule."

Dagny came to the group and stopped. "Friend," she replied, "when this job is done and we're back in Bowen, stand me a beer in the Fuel Tank and I'll tell you tales of woe that'll freeze yours in your stein. Meanwhile, don't fret your pretty little head, or I'll decide it is pretty little. The zeroth law of thermodynamics says that everything takes longer and costs more."

"We are rather badly delayed, though, aren't we?"

Jane Ireland argued. She was a good electrical engineer—had helped troubleshoot the grid that carried power from sunlit Criswells to the transmitters on Nearside—but overanxious about political questions. "Do you appreciate how hard Eurospace and Eco-Astro lobby against awarding contracts like this to any private company, ours above all? If we fail here—"

"We won't," Dagny vowed. "Let the chief fight his particular battles. If Guthrie can't outwangle, outconnive, and outroar the combined governments of Earth, we may as well go back there and the North Americans among us embrace the Renewal. Our way of helping him is to meet the contract in spite of whatever Murphy slings at us."

She had learned early on that her position required even more human skills than technical ones, and set herself to master them. Edmond had been a wonderful counselor at first, but soon she must necessarily grope her own way forward, trial and error, by feel rather than rules, because each individual is unique in the universe.

Pedro Noguchi came to her assistance: "Listen, Wim, Jane, you cannot serve if you fall sick. We have been skimping these sessions as it is. Instead of wasting time complaining, shall we get it done with?"

That quieted them. Strange, Dagny often thought, the loyalty so many of its people bore for Fireball, maybe more than for their countries. She had her personal reasons, but what about the rest? The wellspring couldn't merely be exciting work, high pay, simpático management, no limit on a career except your ability and luck. In Fireball, somehow, you belonged, you shared a spirit, as few did anywhere on Earth.

She sought her place and got busy.

The field centrifuge sheered its column above her, 250 centimeters from the broad, gripfooted base to the four rotor arms. Portable, it didn't have much in common with the giant stationary machines in the settlements. The arms were hollow, flaring trumpet-like from the pillar. Out of each dangled a cable, at the end of which hung a cage, its floor a 150-centimeter disc knee-high above the ground. Within this were simple items of exercise equipment, secured by brackets. Beneath the disc was welded a box for the makeweight.

Nobody present, complete with suit and gear, massed the 125 kilos—21 kilos Lunar weight—that made a standard load. Dagny stepped onto a scale built into the base. Disdaining to punch the calculator on her left sleeve, she figured her deficit mentally, and selected the bricks needed to equal it from a stack nearby. Having slid the right amount into the box, she dogged it shut and mounted to the cage. There she closed the door, made herself fast just in case, and commanded, "Report."

"Ready. . . . Ready. . . . Ready," she heard.

"Centrifuge to Overview, commencing three-hour operation," she called. The man in the skeletal tower a kilometer distant acknowledged. He'd keep an eye on them as he did on the worksites, also just in case. "We're off," Dagny said. Each cage had a start and stop button, but she, being senior, pressed hers.

The motor in the column base awoke. The rotor began to turn. The gripfeet flexed their metal toes and extended their claws over ground that was neither smooth nor level and that might have been rubble rather than hard stone. Sensors monitored shifting forces and gave orders to effectors; the machine held itself in dynamic balance. As the rotor increased speed and the cages lifted, their cables unreeled to full length and flew well-nigh horizontal. When the system had reached steady state, each occupant stood under an Earth gravity of acceleration.

Dagny unbuckled. For a minute or two she looked between the bars, upward from Luna. Some persons faced the ground, some sideways, some kept their eyes mostly closed, whatever gave them the least vertigo; she chose the heavens. Stars went in a wild wheel whose hub was above her head. Her breathing and that of her companions had loudened. Vibration was a faint thrum in her bloodstream. Heaviness laid a hand on her suit, flesh, bones, every last cell of her.

It felt pleasant, actually. She reveled in low-weight, but nature had not meant her for that freedom.

Standing there, she wondered how long ago her fate was set. A third of a billion years, when her ancestors crawled from the sea and must uphold themselves? 'Mond could tell her exactly. She knew the end result all too well, the multitudinous, marvelous, imprisoning adaptations that evolution forged on its single world. Lunar gravity simply was not enough for the creature from Earth.

Oh, nowhere near as bad as micro. You didn't get nauseated, your countenance didn't puff, muscles and skeleton dwindled rather slowly, you could go years before the harm was irreversible and then have a few years more until you died—or so the extrapolation from lab animals and computer models forecast. But the decay was pervasive, a matter of fluid balance and cell chemistry, cardiovascular degeneration, blood-brain barrier malfunction, tumorous growth of various tissues, sclerosis or necrosis of others, the earliest effects clinically detectable after a twelvemonth or less.

If you wanted to keep your health, you'd better subject yourself often to the heft for which you were born.

Born. Dagny's hand stole to her belly. Memories tumbled through her like the stars overhead.

They hadn't intended this, she and 'Mond, not till they were sure it was safe. Her booster shot wasn't due for half a year. Could that failure be another consequence of low-g? (Perhaps idiosyncratic, because Lord knew plenty of love got made on Luna, frequently in delightful ways impractical elsewhere.) The doctor suggested abortion. Dagny demanded violently to know what the alternative was. The doctor called a conference across orbital distance. The specialists opined that the pregnancy would probably be normal.

After all, embryo and fetus would be afloat in the amniotic fluid, the little primordial ocean. Mammals, including a monkey, had borne young on the Moon, and the young lived, once experiment had established what the proper centrifuging regime was for a given species.

The specialists guaranteed nothing, of course. Knowledge was too scant. Science would be glad of the opportunity to observe and learn, but Mrs. Beynac must understand that this eventuality was quite unanticipated. The regimes and treatments collectively dubbed biomedicine could extend life expectancy to well over a century, but biomedicine could not alter the basic human organism. That required modification of the DNA. A scheme was under development, offering the sole realistic hope for a genuine Lunar colony—highly controversial, not relevant to Mrs. Beynac, who might find her infant's welfare requiring she move back to Earth. . . .

Okay, if absolutely necessary. Only if. Anyhow, she could get one more field job under her belt before the belt stretched too wide to fit in a spacesuit. Morning sickness—racking, an order of magnitude beyond that now half-unreal first time—had been outlived. The signs and tests reassured. Fireball would never dismiss or demote or reprimand her if she transferred Earthside, but Fireball had urgent need of her on Farside. So here she stood, at her second trimester, alert, able-bodied, carrying Edmond's child.

Juliana, she said within herself. It was going to be a girl. Juliana, Moon baby, welcome to the future.

Enough remembrance, enough sentiment. If you wanted to maximize the benefits of high-g and minimize the time you must spend under it, you didn't only stand or sit, you exercised.

Hunkering down, Dagny unfastened the bar bells and rose holding them. She moved with care, to avoid dizziness. The Terrestrial pseudo-weight was a waistline average, the differential between head and feet nearly ten percent. Coriolis force posed less of a nuisance; still, you had to allow for it too. The big centrifuges were far more comfortable in both respects. Downright luxurious, the largest at Port Bowen—private compartments, couches—Dagny grinned. She strongly suspected Juliana was begotten there.

Raise the bells, lower them, raise, lower, swing them crossways, commence the stationary jogging. Flex, tense, flex, let your body enjoy while your mind rides the carousel of stars. Breathe deep, flush out the lungs, smell the sweet sweat, savor the growing warmth. The heart beats high, the blood quickens, and is that another quickening below, does Juliana also dance?

No, Dagny remembered, way too early, not yet, not yet.

The pain went through her like a harrow through a field.

The hospital in Port Bowen was small, austere, and superbly equipped. By the time Edmond Beynac got there from his current expedition, his wife was almost ready for discharge.

"You needn't come," she had said to him over the phone when first he called. "I'm okay. I'll be out of here fast."

"Bloody 'ell!" he had replied, his accent thickened. "You 'ave—*un avortement*—se meescarriage, een a, a God damn *spacesuit*—and I should stay from you?" While the radio link carried an image, it was poor and the screen tiny. She couldn't be certain, but thought she saw tears on his cheeks. She never had before.

Aborting as convulsively as she did, incompletely till her team got her inside and the armor off, had in fact torn her up considerably. She was young and vigorous, though, and the hospital staff had more than surgery at their command, they had the latest molecular biotech.

She was sitting up in bed after a walk along the corridors when he arrived. The reader in her hands displayed *The Sea-Wolf;* she liked adventure stories, and hardly any were being written these days. The room was private, but on that account a cubicle. Edmond's bulk crowded her. Not that she minded. His arms went strong around her, trembling a bit, and his kiss gave her a dear scratch of stubble, and when she laid her head against his breast she felt the slugging behind the ribs.

After a while he sat on the edge of the bed and simply held her hand. "Honest, 'Mond, you poor worrymaker, I'm fine," she insisted. "They tell me I can be back on the job in two weeks, this time with no personal deadline on me." That last was a mistake. Her voice cracked. Immediately, she lowered her lashes and made a purr. "Before then, I'll be fit to screw. I *have* missed you, darling."

Starkness remained in him. "We will be careful, always."

"Oh, yes, oh, yes."

His look dwelt on her. Silence lengthened.

"But you wish for children," he said at last.

"Well—Not unless you do, really, truly."

"Two have you lost." He had not hitherto spoken of the one adopted away since she told him, that evenwatch when he asked her to marry him. Then he had likewise been still for a while, until he said that it didn't matter, that it was long past, and changed the subject.

"Do not lie to me," he ordered rather than begged; but how compassionate was his tone. "I know very well you have wept, alone in this bed."

"That's done with" was all she could find to say.

"There shall not be a third loss."

"No." Resolution held firm. She had done much thinking. "We want the Moon more than anything else."

"Including children?"

"Yes, if it comes to that."

"You understand the trouble, no?"

She nodded and spoke quickly. "Dr. Nguyen drew me the picture. Computer models flipflop when you input changed data. They took those data off me. Examinations, tests, specimens, electrochemical monitoring, my God, I'll be in the scientific journals for the next five years. Sure, I'm the single case, but I seem to have supplied critical information that was missing. The revised opinion is that what happened was inevitable. Contraceps wear off before they would on Earth, with a random time distribution, and no pregnancy will go to term. The lab animals fooled us. For one thing, humans are a lot bigger, which makes fluid management an entirely different engineering problem, at least in a weak grav field. For another thing, the human brain, as complicated as it is, gets tricked into sending the wrong signals to the whole muscular-glandular-nervous female reproductive system. The placenta's chemical defenses break down, allergic reactions build up, the fetus gets expelled but it's dead or dying anyway. Our kind will never breed naturally on Luna."

There, she'd said it, in a rush but without a quaver. She leaned back on the pillows, abruptly exhausted. "You've heard this?" she whispered.

"Yes, I was in communication the whole while I drove here." Edmond paused. "They think medications can be developed to compensate and make birth possible."

"I know," she sighed. "I also know it'd be unpleasant and expensive and condemn the next generation to the same. No."

She saw and felt how he tautened. "Dagny," he said, word by word, "we can move to Earth . . . before we are too old."

"You were prepared to do that for Juliana right away, if need be," she answered low.

"I was. For children born—I do want children for us."

She shook her head. Calm welled up in her, and

with it a new, quiet strength. "Juliana *was*. She had happened, and we would not kill her nor forsake her. But I saw—You were so kind, so gentle in your gruff way. You never hinted what it would mean to you, tossing out this top-level scientific career of yours and returning to where everything's cut and dried, where you could hope for no more than to drone through a professorship in a mediocre academic department. But I knew, 'Mond. I knew how you'd be taking long walks by yourself so you could shout your blasphemies, and you'd drink hard and your wholesome cynicism would sour into alienation—and you'd stand by me, because you said you would, and you'd never blame the child. 'Mond, I wished I could believe in God, so I could pray we wouldn't have to return. Well, we don't."

"Bienaimée," he said shakenly.

The strength rose higher. She sat straight. "It does not follow that we have to be sterile." No, "barren" was the word she wanted, dead end, double death, and to hell with the population-reduction fanatics.

His bowed head lifted. *"Qu'est-ce*—what do you mean?"

"Obvious," she said. "Genetics. A race for which the Moon is the normal environment. I began investigating this damn near as soon as I knew I was pregnant, because—It can be done, 'Mond. The knowledge is there, in genome maps, molecular biology, histology, plain old-fashioned anatomy and physiology. The computers have shown what changes in the DNA are necessary, practically atom by atom. How to do it, that's no different in principle from what's standard in biotech when they want any special kind of new organism. The whole thing's been roughed out, as a scientific exercise and a contingency measure. The details can be refined in a year or two, once the project is go."

"And you, you would—"

"Why not? Why the hell not? Take a fertilized

ovum, treat it, implant it." Impulse swept her along.
"Why, I'll bet we can do the fertilizing in the usual
way."

"No! The risk to you. And . . . the cost, we could
not afford this."

"Nonsense. No more risky than an outing topside.
I've studied the matter, I tell you. A, a Lunarian fetus
would interact differently. I'd need chemical support,
true, but far less than for our kind of child, nothing
that'd handicap me in any way. As for cost, why, as
long as the Guthries are in charge, Fireball will look
beyond the annual profit sheet. In fact, it underwrote
the research to date. It'll cheerfully pungle up to
produce a next generation that *won't* need help."

"You are too crazy sure," he growled.

"Oh, maybe it won't work out every time. That'll
hurt, but I'm willing to take the chance if you are,
because we'll be on the way to our kids, our Lunarian
children, 'Mond. Our blood living here forever."

Hers drummed in her veins. She gripped both his
hands. For a moment more he hung back. "Dagny, it
has powerful opposition, experimenting with humans.
Me, I feel trouble in my conscience. What of the
people and politicians on Earth?"

"If anybody can get approval pushed through, the
Guthries can. Darling, say yes, do say yes, and I'll send
them a private-coded message tomorrow."

Anson Guthrie's blood alive on the Moon.

That he was her grandfather was the last real secret
she kept from Edmond. She hoped that now he would
let her share it.

9

Guthrie House seemed older than its centuries, the
stone of it almost as if shaped by wind and rain and
frost rather than human hands. That mass belonged

here, among the firs to right and left and behind, the sweep of lawn and flowerbeds down to the water. Dock, boat, outbuildings fitted as well into the island. Even the spaceship and its shelter were right for this ground.

But that was all within him, Kenmuir thought. It was because of tradition, sanctity, about which nature knew nothing. And nature itself, the sense of coming home to a living ancientness, was an illusion. Clouds lifted like snowbanks into radiant blue; a breeze blew cool, with savors of woods and salt, above summer-warm soil; waves gleamed and murmured, forest soughed; a few gulls went soaring aloft—in a carefully tended and restricted enclave. It was happenstance that he saw no aircraft pass overhead. When the declining sun had gone behind the ocean, he would spy satellites on their ways across what stars the sky-glow let him see.

Maybe that was why the spaceship stood not as an intruder. Instead, a guardian of this peace? A totem, a rallying point, at least. She wasn't obtrusive to sight anyway. Occupying a clearing several hundred meters inland, she and her transparent cover would not have shown if the terrain had not risen. As it was, only her bow appeared, a spearhead above treetops and roof.

Leaving his hired volant on the airstrip and walking toward the house—gravel scrunched beneath his feet—Kenmuir found his gaze and mind dwelling on her. *Kestrel*, the little Falcon-class that Kyra Davis piloted, she who long and long ago rescued Guthrie from the Avantists and did battle with his doubleganger. Kenmuir himself had once partaken in the annual rite of inspection, cleaning, recharging accumulators, the benediction that ended, "Be always ready to fly." Beneath the solemnity, a chill had coursed through him and the hair stood up over his whole body. He was very young then. . . . But something of the same stirred anew today. His race did live and die by symbols. And the Lunarians by theirs—But what of the sophotects?

It occurred to him that he had never looked up the history of this relic. What struggles and chicanery had it taken, not to obtain her, but to win leave to keep her in alert condition? Oh, she was totally obsolete now, but she had not been then; and to this day, license for storing any amount of antimatter on Earth was not otherwise given unless the machines were fully in charge of it and its containment.

Well, Fireball Enterprises, which had dominated the Solar System, did not dissolve quickly or without many concessions granted its folk. Let them have their memorial. Already in their lifetimes, they were becoming no more than a harmless sodality. After a generation or two, hardly anyone else remembered that *Kestrel* existed. To the cybercosm, she was an entry in the database.

Nevertheless, she was. And—Fireball, harmless? That remained to be seen. Kenmuir's pulse and footsteps speeded up.

A guard waited on the verandah. She was unarmed, ceremonial, a girl serving her apprenticeship before initiation into full consorte status. Matthias liked to have visitors greeted in style. She saw the Fireball uniform he had donned, the same gray as hers, and snapped him a salute, which he returned. (Meanwhile he reflected that in the days of the company there had been no formalities. Such things accreted, like coral growing on a sunken hull.) "Captain Ian Kenmuir," he identified himself unnecessarily, except for her sake, "with an appointment to meet the Rydberg in private."

"Aye, señor," she responded. "Por favor, follow me."

He had not been here in years, but as he entered the vestibule, memory billowed over him. The oak panels, the glass window where Daedalus and Icarus spread their wings—and down a hall, the great dark room with its antique furniture, carpeting and hangings, candelabra and crystal, pictures, books, traditions. In an armchair at the stone fireplace sat Matthias.

Kenmuir drew to attention before him. "Hola, señor," he greeted as was customary here.

The old man nodded. "Bienvenido," he said. His voice was a bass rumble. Nor had much else changed since Kenmuir last encountered him. The frame was still massive, paunchy but not withered in the limbs or in the heavy, hook-nosed features; hair was a white cockatoo crest, eyes deep-set and unwavering. A Fireball emblem on the left breast made his plain blue robe uniform enough for him.

Fleetingly, Kenmuir wondered if Matthias had ever borne more than the single name. Many Earthlings didn't. He knew little about this master of the lodge. Given longevity, a person could serve for such decades that his or her past receded into obscurity.

"At ease," the Rydberg said. "Be seated if you wish."

"Thank you—gracias." Kenmuir took a chair facing him.

A chuckle grated. "Have we had our fill of Americanisms and anachronisms? What would you like for refreshment, Captain?"

"Uh, well—"

"As far as I'm concerned, it's not too early for a Scotch and water."

"Beer, please," Kenmuir made bold to reply.

Matthias gestured at the guard, who went out. The house had a small human staff as well as its machines, but for her this service was an honor. "You're seldom hereabouts," he remarked.

"No, sir. I've not been much on Earth, and when I am—" He simply was not a very sociable animal. He'd call on a few friends here and there around the globe, seek out historic sites and daydream, go on days-long tramps through the preserves, that sort of thing. Sometimes he patronized a joyeuse, but not often. It always struck him as rather sad, even when she found pleasure in the specialty by which she prospered. "I ought to participate more in the Trothdom, yes."

"It's voluntary." Matthias leaned back, bridged his fingers, drooped his lids, and went on ponderously, "Let me see. When you called to ask for an interview, I retrieved what data the outfit has on you, but they're meager and parts may be incorrect. Check me out. Your ancestors include consortes of Fireball since it was a business, but your parents were Earthsiders and not deeply involved in our affairs either."

Pain twinged in Kenmuir. They should still have been alive. He, their single child, was just fifty-five years of age. But accidents happen also in cybernetic societies. Two volants under manual control, being above an Arctic sports ground where traffic was light, collided—and he out beyond the orbit of Pluto, helping to herd a comet.

"If I haven't been so active, sir, that's not because I don't value my membership." He was quite sincere.

"Agreed," Matthias said. "To continue, you won admission to the Academy. Starstruck from birth, eh? And, what's more, gifted for it. You began your career in the Federal Space Service, then shifted to the Venture."

Since Kenmuir knew that Matthias' own employment had been entirely in the Service, he said half defensively, "Well, sir, everything Earth-based has grown so—uh—"

"So efficient." Matthias nodded. "Hardly a place left for humans, except on the ground and that mostly makework. No place at all left for initiative. The Service wasn't that far gone in my time. But as I approached retirement, I stopped envying the young."

Kenmuir's pulse jumped. "The Lunarians, they keep space human."

"Their kind of human."

Not to truckle. The Rydberg would despise that. "They do it for our kind too. They need us."

"Because their style of operations goes against all practicality."

"Not when it's their nature, sir. And Terran nature, too, for many of us, even these days."

"Yes, a flicker of the old spirit survives. For a while yet, a while." Matthias brightened a trifle. "The Habitat should revive it. I may live to watch in the flesh a bit of what I've only seen in vivifers and quiviras."

Kenmuir tensed. "That's what I've come here about."

Eyes probed him. "I suspected as much."

What did he actually know?

The girl returned with a tray, set the drinks on end tables, saluted, and left. "Good liftoff," Matthias toasted. The men brought vessels to lips. The tingle in his mouth gave Kenmuir impetus.

"You know what the Habitat will do to the Lunarians," he said.

"Civilize them, gradually," Matthias snorted.

"Not into a civilization they'll find endurable."

"So they claim." The tone was rough. "Have they really so little adaptability, or is this a handful of Selenarchs yelling and clawing because they'll lose their privileges?"

Kenmuir mustered his words.

"Sir, with respect, I know the Lunarians, every class of Lunarians, about as well as any Earthdweller—any Terran can. When you've been to the ends of the Solar System with somebody, over and over, it gives you an understanding of them." And he had met them at home and in Mars and in their tiny colonies clinging to asteroids that whirled among wintry stars, or dug into ice and rock beneath the majesty of Jupiter or the jewelwork of Saturn.

"You've come to love them, then?" Matthias asked softly.

Taken aback, Kenmuir could merely say, "Well, I, I feel for them."

Matthias lifted a finger. "Mind you, I don't hate them. I agree they're admirable, the way a tiger is.

And, yes, they are a leaven in this thickening world of ours." He paused. "But we have our own race to think about." With a shrug: "As if what you or I think, what we do, will make the slightest difference."

Kenmuir knotted a fist. "The Habitat is *wrong.*"

Matthias raised his brows. "Wrong, to give thousands of humans, and whole generations after them, once again a frontier?"

Yes, Kenmuir thought, he'd heard it before, the renewed dynamic, humankind looking outward from its games and shadow shows, to the endlessness of the universe. He was pleading the case of native Americans as the whites rolled across them on the way to the Pacific. But what was it Lilisaire had said, about a wave of Lunar colonists being directed into a holding tank? He had spent many a watch in space exploring the past of Earth. After the white Americans filled their new land, vested interests and demagogues did not take long to make citizens into subjects.

"Sir," he persisted, "I'm an example of what Lunarian freedom can mean to Terrans. If we're ever to go to the stars—" where download Guthrie was, but how barely! "—it will have to be together with them."

"Maybe. Speak your piece."

"They deserve a chance, the same as we do."

"I'd not deny that, if it be a fair chance. Though, to repeat myself, what choice in the matter do you or I have? Say on."

Kenmuir drew breath and plunged ahead. In the course of three daycycles, Lilisaire had filled out details of what she first told him, but mostly she had kindled him for her cause. He said nothing about what happened when they were not talking. Did Matthias, impassive in his chair, guess?

The Rydberg made a single comment: "Remarkable, that those activities Niolente got carried out in space could stay a secret."

"Well, sir, you know how basic the etaine is there." Kenmuir chose the Lunarian word because its usual translation as "family" or "clan" was not really right.

Nothing that quite corresponded occurred in any Terran culture. Sometimes he had speculated that "pride" might serve—but no, Lunarians weren't lions either. "Apparently the expeditions were highly cyberneticized, the few organic personnel chosen for ties of blood as well as their skills. They'd keep silent. Niolente presumably meant to reveal her design at the right moment, under the right circumstances, which would give Luna the advantage she was working for, with her and her phyle in firm control of it.

"At the final catastrophe, it seems everyone who knew perished with her. They were holed up together under Delandres Crater, and you surely recall how the missiles collapsed their shell around them even though the Peace Authority was only trying to force them to surrender. I think she kept them in a group like that precisely to retain the secret, and threatened to catapult warheads only as a bargaining counter that might win favorable terms—amnesty, at least. Instead, it got her bombarded.

"Apparently, also, she'd wiped what files on the project she could. The record that the Peace Authority laid hands on was fragmentary. All that her adult children knew was that something major had been under way. You'd expect them to be close-mouthed about it, wouldn't you? They passed it down through the generations, under pledge of secrecy, very much like . . . the Rydbergs in the Trothdom."

Hoarsened, Kenmuir drained his beer. A stillness followed, wherein his blood beat loudly through his veins.

"And now this female wants me to give you the Founder's Word, for her benefit and in hopes she can use it to thwart the Habitat," Matthias said at last.

"If, if possible, and if—"

"Exactly what does she fantasize it is?"

"Information. Long before Niolente's time, Dagny Beynac's son Kaino led a mysterious mission into deep space. The family never let out what it had been. Most likely it became the basis of what Niolente undertook. Meanwhile, Lars Rydberg had learned something, probably from Beynac herself, which he considered to be of the first importance."

"Concerning a giant weapon in remote Solar orbit?" Matthias scoffed. "To revive an impolite word, lunacy."

"I didn't—Lilisaire didn't necessarily mean that—"

"She'd like it. For her personal gain. Judging from your account, she's let slip no hint to many of her fellow magnates, if any."

"Sir, I'm not asking for—I wouldn't condone—"

"But you are hoping for a way to keep the Terrans on Earth."

"Not even that, sir, not in itself. Is it right to suppress information relevant to a matter as important as this? A decision made in ignorance could cost lives later on. I'm sorry if—if I—"

Matthias gusted a sigh. "Don't apologize. No reason to. No such knowledge exists."

"None?" Kenmuir protested.

"Lars Rydberg brought a secret home to Earth, yes," Matthias said heavily. "He charged his eldest son with preserving it against a possible hour of great need. It has gone down the succession ever since." That was not by descent, although every lodgemaster had some Rydberg blood. "This is as much as the world has been told. I will not be the one who betrays it."

Kenmuir saw adamantness. "Can you give me any hint?" he pleaded. "If nothing else, can you tell me Lilisaire was mistaken and it could not help her?"

The old man nodded. "Yes, I believe I can truly say that." Again he sighed. "By now, after all the time that has passed, I wonder if it means anything whatsoever. We keep the faith, we Rydbergs, simply because this is one more tradition, rite, bond holding the Trothdom together, so a ghost of Fireball Enterprises can haunt living memories. . . . I'm the one who's sorry, son."

Abruptly Kenmuir felt wrung dry. "I see. Thank you, sir."

"It was never a real hope for you, was it?"

"I suppose not."

"What will you do?"

"Report back."

"You're welcome to call from here."

"Thank you, but—"

"Ah. You want encryption?"

"Well, actually, I was to call a number on Earth, but—a secure line—"

"Tell me no more. For groundside communications, we have good security. Now and then, you know, the outfit gives aid to a consorte whose trouble is best kept confidential."

Overwhelmed, Kenmuir mumbled, "Sir, when you're opposed to my whole purpose—"

"Not entirely. I don't approve of the government concealing possibly critical information either. But mainly, you're a consorte yourself. I owe you troth." The gaze was keenly gauging. "I trust you not to break yours."

After a moment: "If you're not in too big a hurry, let's have another drink. And dinner. Spend the night. I'd like to hear you yarn about where you've been."

No, Kenmuir thought, assuredly he would not violate his oath. He would follow Lilisaire's next instructions as best he was able, to the point where he saw them leading toward a public menace. He did not expect they would. She ought to know him better than that. But he must stay wary. Events might flare out of control. And always—he harked back to his classical reading—the Lunarian spirit was Lucifer's.

10

The Mother of the Moon

Seen from the Taurus Mountains, Earth hung low in the southwestern sky. Its crescent was thinning with the sun's slow climb over eastern ridges. Shadows had shrunken across the bench where the Beynacs were encamped, but still picked out uncountable pockmarks in the level grayish rock. Above and below, the slope was likewise scarred, as were the heights around. Not yet lighted, the valley beneath lay as a lake of blackness. All contours were gentle, worn down by the meteoritic rains of gigayears, nothing here of Terrestrial crags or Martian steeps, an aged land withdrawn into itself and its secrets.

For Dagny the view, like everything on Luna, had splendor. Maybe the very bareness uplifted her heart, a challenge. At the moment she was giving it no thought. Her attention was for Tychopolis, some 2700 kilometers hence.

Joe Packer's face confronted her, clear to see through the new-model fishbowl helmet that topped his spacesuit. Its hyalon had self-darkened at the back against sunlight which would have blasted his eyes had he glanced straight and unprotected in its direction. The big holoscreen showed an excavator at work behind him, hazed in the dust it continuously stirred up. The images weren't perfect. No fiber-optic cable ran to these man-empty parts; a satellite relayed. The pictures were adequate for practical purposes.

"—satisfactory progress in general," Packer was saying. "However, we've got a decision to make. This past nightwatch, over at the northwest corner of the Complex Three site, they hit a pretty huge boulder. It's evidently got more or less the same composition as the surrounding rock, so it didn't register on the ground-wave probe, but Pedro Noguchi says we'll have to get it out, and that'll leave a hole in the side, plus a lot of cracks that must be due to it. I told him to hold off there till you called in." His smile flashed, vivid white against the chocolate skin. "Don't worry, I found plenty other things to keep him and his gang out of mischief."

"You would," Dagny agreed. Packer was every bit as competent as she was, slated to succeed her when she moved into general administration. For that reason, as well as to give him added experience, she felt free occasionally to accompany Edmond on his field trips—adventure, family life, helping out in his research. Still badly undermanned, the work was as basic to engineering and future habitation as it was to pure science. Building the structures for the University of Luna ought not to pose any extraordinary problems anyway.

But of course no project on the Moon failed to spring its surprises, and the ultimate responsibility was hers. Even ten years ago, she'd have been tied to the spot. Telepresence capability was like having another avatar.

Yes, flitted through her, history in space moved headlong, ever faster, like a comet plunging sunward. Not only here. An L-5 under construction, spaceport, industrial center, home for Terrans where they could bear children wholly Terran. The wealth of the asteroids ingathered. Ice from the deeps of space, soon water in abundance wherever humans wanted it. Not too many years later, antimatter produced so copiously that ships could burn it to accelerate through an entire voyage, bisecting Pluto's orbit in a trio of weeks. But when that liberation was won, Guthrie said, Fireball would first launch probes to the nearer stars. . . .

Her mind sprang back to business. "Muy bien, let's have a look."

Packer spoke a command. The computer shifted the viewpoint. Dagny beheld rubble, the rough-hewn angle of a pit, a mass suggestive of a clenched fist partly protruding, broken-off pieces of it scattered below. Packer turned the scanning over to her. She made the camera move in and out and around, illuminate murky recesses, magnify, induce fluorescence.

"M-hm," she murmured at length. "It's what I thought, and I imagine you guessed." She, though, had learned from Edmond Beynac. "A meteorite, ancient, buried in later lava flow. The plutonic character—unusual, to say the least. My husband will be *most* interested."

"Beg pardon?"

"Didn't you know? He studies meteoritics, besides what's under his feet. Believes we won't understand the basics of how the planets formed till we understand the asteroids better." Dagny clicked her tongue. "Swears that one of these years he'll get out into the Belt and fossick around personally." Her heart stumbled. Too many had already perished in yonder distances. "This rock will be evidence for his idea, his minority opinion, that there was once a body in that region big enough to get really hot before it cooled off again. He thinks the nickel-iron object that gave us the Tycho mines was a piece of its core." Dagny shook herself. "But I'm wandering. Pedro's right, we'll have to remove this thing. The hole, and the fissures where the lava congealed around it, will be a potential weakness in the foundation. We can't simply fill in and feel safe." Not after the Rudolph strike, or the more recent, similar but worse disaster at the Struve Criswell.

"What, then?" Packer asked.

"Got any idea? A couple occur to me, but you've had longer to think. Between us, we ought to come up with something worth pursuing." A cry interrupted. "Oh, damn. The joys of motherhood. 'Scuse a mo'. I'll be right back, I hope."

Rising, Dagny slipped from the office compartment and aft through the outsize, purely household van she had dubbed her kidmobile. The family often traveling in it—recreation, mainly, with friends along, though this was not their first serious expedition together—it was well furnished, from the pilot house in front to her and Edmond's bed cubicle at the rear. Beyond the pantry, kitchenette, and dinette, she found the main room and her children.

It offered a space ten meters long by six wide. Foldout tables, collapsible chairs as thin as Lunar gravity permitted, chests that doubled as seats allowed passage, occasionally zigzaggy, no matter what was going on in the way of games, partying, entertainment, education, or simple ease. Duramoss made a living green carpet. Reserve tanks of water and air on the roof forbade any view straight up, but the windows on either side gave ample outlook. She saw the regular field van parked nearby, the whirly, strewn geological specimens and other clutter, the mountainscape, Earth big and lovely, the sun opposite stopped down to a wan disc. Music twanged from the speakers, for Dagny mercifully low—the newest fenghuang, she assumed. Her youngsters' tastes were not hers. She sometimes wondered what their generation would compose when they were grown.

Anson was outside with his father and the two grad students. Gabrielle, at seven the next oldest, sat before one of the computer terminals. That was in order, her regular schooling session. But why did five-year-old Sigurd hunker beside her? He should be at his own lesson. Francis, three, was curled up with a reader. That was nothing strange; all of them had acquired literacy by his age, except for Helen in her cradle, who doubtless would too, and Francy seemed a natural-born bookworm. What had he chosen today? He never cared for the ordinary stuff. . . .

Her eyes took aim on Gaby and Sigurd. Intent, they had not noticed her arrival. She recalled past incidents, a quick switcharound when she appeared, an air of surreptitiousness, baffled half-suspicions. In two kangaroo bounds, she was there. The baby's noises weren't of the sort that meant emergency.

The girl registered dismay, immediately masked.

The boy's mutinous expression stayed on him. He was the hell-raiser among them. Dagny peered at the screen. No, it did not carry an interactive math program. ARVEN ARDEA NIO LULLUI PEYAR— "What the devil is going on here?"

Her daughter blanked the display. "Nothin'," she muttered. Color came and went in her face. She was outwardly the most Earthlike, chubby, topped with light-brown curls. Quiet, studious, was she inwardly the most paradoxical? "Just a game."

Easy, Dagny thought, take it slow, don't drive them into hostility. They bore alien genes, but that DNA had come from two mighty self-determined parents. She caught Sigurd's glance and held it. "Doesn't seem like your kind of game," she said mildly to this large, strongly built, redhaired muchacho.

He flushed in his turn. "Aw, we wan'ed a break."

"If I were playing hooky, I'd do something more interesting. Unless this is. May I ask what it's about?"

Gaby was getting back some composure. "Per—per-mu-ta-tions," she said. Triumphantly: "See? I did study."

Having the machine produce random combinations of, no, not words, syllables? Dagny shook her head. That couldn't be right. Her glimpse had suggested a pattern, as if those were words in an unknown language. Could the pair be creating a fantasy world? Gaby showed gifts of that kind, insofar as she revealed any of herself. Sigurd, restless, resentful at being cooped up when his older brother had gone forth, might be finding an outlet in a shared dream.

If so, it was nice that these utterly unlike two had set their fights aside and made something in common, for however brief a spell. Childhood secrets that had lain three decades forgotten stirred within Dagny. She'd better not push her invasion further.

"Good for you, as far as it goes," she said. "However, you are not supposed to study sets today, you're to practice the mechanics of arithmetic. And you, Sigurd, are to improve your deplorable spelling."

"Bo-oring," he whined. Gaby nodded, again and again.

"I know," their mother replied. "And you wonder why you have to, when a computer can do such jobs for you. Bueno, listen. You may not always have a computer handy, when you badly need to figure out something or write something that comes across unmistakable. More important, learning the systems is the single way you'll get to understand them. If you're ignorant of how the machines work and why, they won't serve you, they'll boss you. And you'll be shut away from all kinds of wonderful things. Mainly, remember: Independent people have got to *be* independent.

"Play games on your own time. You're on Fireball time now. Prove that we can trust you."

Thus she led them back to their tasks. Francis, slight and blond, had barely glanced up from his reading. Past experience made Dagny believe he'd observed much more than he let on.

Helen wailed. Dagny ascertained she didn't need changing but was hungry, undid her tunic, and laid the infant to her right breast. (An excellent feature of life on the Moon—except when centrifuging, you could leave off the bra and yet never begin to sag.) "I'm busy too, dear," she said, and returned forward.

The dark little head pumped milk from her. Warmth and love flowed back. Yes, never mind all the extra trouble during pregnancy, she wanted anyway one more, another life to brighten hers and 'Mond's before it flew out into the unbounded future.

Unbounded in space. What was there for Earth? It shone so blue-and-white resplendent above the mountains. How much misery, how much terror and despair did the clouds veil? Poor North America, impoverished and stultified, the Renewal clinging like pitch to a semblance of power while the reality crumbled away in lawlessness. Poor Middle East, *Befehl* withdrawn, chaos loose, fanaticism a tide rising higher for every day that passed. . . . But in lands more fortunate civilization flourished, prosperity, liberty, and the true renewal, the healing of the planet, paid for by the riches that Fireball brought home. . . . The woman held her baby close.

When she seated herself again at the office com, fears slipped away and Helen became simply a sweet presence on the fringe of awareness. Packer's eyes widened appreciatively, then he too got straight back to work. They were occupied for the next couple of hours, save when Dagny took her offspring back to the crib. She found Gaby and Sigurd at their education. They did not act especially chastened.

"Um, yes, this sounds reasonable," Packer said at last. Don't just cut out the unreliable rock and replace with concrete. The metal frame of the building would carry downward the blaze at midday, the space-coldness at midnight; in the course of years, differing coefficients of thermal expansion could have fatigue effects. Therefore, seal a heat exchanger grid into the plug, such as automatically equalized temperatures. It would take some designing, but probably no more than an off-the-shelf program could handle, and the concept might well prove useful at other sites.

"Oh, sure, first we run a simple model through the computer to see whether the notion's loco," Packer went on. "No, first we hear what Dr. Beynac thinks." He was forever deferential to the man who saved his life and limb, not in any servile way but in an abiding gratitude that Edmond and Dagny respected.

"He's due back soon," she said. "Overdue, in fact. I'll talk with him and call you this time tomorrow, okay?" Earth's tomorrow; the sun over Lunar Taurus would stand a dozen degrees higher. "Happy landings."

She switched off, rose, stretched cramped muscles, and wished for an extra go in the whirly. No, too much trouble, and dinner to fix. Later, this evening, early bedtime—She grinned. Horizontal exercise didn't count, officially, but damn if she didn't wake at dawnwatch perkier than after anything else.

She went aft. Study time was past. Gaby and Sigurd had not resumed their curious game. Dagny wondered if they would before they were home in Tychopolis and the privacy of their rooms. The girl slouched on a seat, staring beyond the windows, an electronic pad on her knees. Her lips moved, she scribbled something with the stylus, then again she was in reverie. Dagny decided not to pry. Francy had put a show of fractals on one terminal, or gotten a sibling to do it for him, and watched fascinated. Hunched over a table, Sigurd moved his toy soldiers and their machines through a battle. "Ee-ee-*pow*," he breathed. "S-s-s-s. Crack." They represented UN peacekeepers and imaginary villains, but Dagny doubted that was what he had in mind. She hardly dared ask.

Not that she and 'Mond let their youngsters terrorize them. Not that affection and cheer were missing. But these, and their kind being born to other couples, would inherit the Moon, which was not Earth.

Helen slept peacefully. Yet already you could see, in the big oblique eyes, the odd convolutions of the ears, the bones underneath the baby fat, that this too would become a face such as none of her forebears had worn.

Sigurd turned his head. His countenance was going to be rugged, bearing at least a memory of his father's. "Hiu-yo!" he piped, as if the small clash earlier had never happened. "Madre, you promised you'd tell 'bout Jefe Guthrie at Mars. Now?"

He could reach out and take hold of her heart any time he wanted. All of them could. Though he didn't know about his kinship, and maybe never would, Fireball's lord was as much a legend to him as to everyone else. Dagny, who had stories directly from her grandfather, couldn't stop mention of them from slipping free once in a while.

"This instant?" she demurred. "I've soon got to rustle the rations."

"*De*-tails later."

"Tell, tell!" Francy cried.

Dagny yielded. It *was* a funny story, how Anson

Guthrie shot himself into orbit around Deimos and thereby confounded his opponents. What the incident had meant to politics and policy did not matter to this audience.

"—and that's why spacefolk call the crater Whisky's Grief." What was keeping the geologists?

"Why didn't the gov'ment want Fireball there?" Gaby had joined the group. Her mother couldn't well fob the girl's question off, could she?

"That's complicated to explain, darling. It wasn't one government, it was three of them at loggerheads. Space is supposed to belong to the whole human race, but everybody is a citizen of some or other country— you and I count as Ecuadorans, your father's French, the Guptas are Indian—and our governments make demands on us that often aren't the same. Then, if we're with Fireball—Hoy! There come our wanderers."

Through a window Dagny saw the camión trundle around the eastern flank of this mountain. Absurd, the relief that washed through her. If 'Mond's party had met trouble, they'd have called to let her know. Nevertheless, they were notably later than usual, and Anson had been with them. . . . "Another time," she pledged. "Right now I'd better hustle."

She had no real need for haste, but making ready worked the tension off. Start dinner. When she had leisure for it, she cooked according to standards she had learned from Edmond, unless he wanted to himself. In the field, and she riding herd on the gangs at Tychopolis, they settled for prepackaged stuff. But bring forth apéritifs and glasses. Change her coverall for a dress. 'Mond would do the corresponding thing, after a shower, and the kids would be quiet, though welcome to join in the talk. Happy hour, Guthrie called it. Oh, but nearly all her hours were happy.

At odd moments she watched the vehicle arrive, the riders unload what they had collected, the graduate assistants carry those boxes into the field van. Ross and Marietta slept there, and generally had their meals there. It wasn't exclusion on the Beynacs' part. The young people rated some privacy; eating, sleeping, and laboratory studies weren't everything they did in those quarters. Father and son approached their roving house. Against dun rock and long shadows, their spacesuits dazzled with whiteness. What a liberation dust-repellent impregnants were! "Don't snub technofixes," Guthrie used to say. "Progress consists of 'em. Has, ever since Ung Uggson chipped his first flint."

Dagny lost sight of them as they stepped onto the gangramp. Noise followed, outer airlock valve opened and shut, gas pumped back into the reserve tank while boots banged down the companionway to the lockers. A bass grumble drifted up, "God damn, I smell like a dead goat," and Dagny smiled.

Skinsuits went into the washer, which began to purr. Edmond and Anson returned to deck level. Dagny met them at the hatch. Both wore bathrobes. No puritan, the man remained uncomfortable with the casual nudity common among Moonfolk. At least, he felt adults should avoid it before children of the opposite sex.

Dagny sprang to him. "*I* think you smell exciting," she laughed. "C'mere, you." She cast her arms around his neck and her mouth against his.

After a second or two she let go and stepped back. "Hey," she said, "that was like kissing a robot. A sweaty robot, but otherwise not programmed for it. What's the matter?"

He scowled. Anson stood sullen. "Clean yourself," Edmond ordered him. "Then go to your bunk."

"Hold on," Dagny exclaimed. "What's this about?"

"No supper for him," Edmond snapped. "He was insubordinate and reckless." To the boy: "Go."

"Wait just a minute," Dagny countermanded. "What did he do?"

"He left us," Edmond said. "We were sorting our specimens into the boxes and did not notice before he was gone. We called and got no answer. His tracks went upslope to bare rock where we could not trail him. For more than an hour we searched, until we found him in a cleft. He had not answered us, that whole while."

"I couldn't receive you." Anson spoke with a clipped precision which in him registered fury. "The ridges screened it. That overhang below your site must have blocked the satellite relay."

"You told me already. And I told you—bloody hell, how many times?—you do not leave your party without permission."

"When I started off, you didn't call me to stop."

"You knew we were not watching. *Hein?* I told you, if you want to walk around, you must stay in line of sight. If you get into a no-reception zone, you retrace your steps. Immediately! *Mon Dieu,* you could 'ave been lost, somesing could 'ave 'appened—" The father's voice wavered. "After daycycles, we might 'ave found your mummy."

Dagny wondered whether this was their first real exchange or they were going over the ground again for her. Undoubtedly Anson had received an awesome tongue-lashing, but it had only stiffened his spine. "That's far too true," she said to him, keeping her tone low. "Why did you do it?"

The boy met her gaze. He was the beautiful one of her brood, slim, straight, cat-graceful, bird-soaring in this gravity for which he was made. Already the great height that would be typically Lunarian had brought his head even with his father's. Ash-blond hair fell in bangs over milk-white temples wherein a vein stood as blue as the big, slanty Lunarian eyes. The cheekbones were Asian, the nose and mouth and chin Hellenic, though neither blood was in him; it went with the altered genotype and had surprised the geneticists themselves. They talked of chaos inherent in biological systems, but she gathered this meant "We don't know."

At her he smiled, to her he spoke gently. "It was all right, Madre. I wasn't in danger. The sun gave me a direction, and the high, jagged peak south of us, that'd be a landmark any time I climbed to where I could see it."

"Merde!" Edmond roared.

Dagny shushed him with a gesture. "But why did you go, dear?"

"Bueno, I got out of sight before I noticed, and then I thought how I wanted a better look at those formations we found in the cleft, that Padre doesn't think are interesting." Anson shrugged. "Honest, I'd have come back before they were ready to leave."

"If you did not bloody lose your way in that—that jumble, that labyrinth." Edmond's hands trembled a bit. He'd want comforting tonight, Dagny knew.

"I wouldn't have," Anson argued. "I never do."

It could well be the truth, she thought. Not that he'd been anywhere alone before now, but on guided excursions he acted as though he'd drawn maps in his head. Virtually no visitors, and few long-time residents, could do that, on this world that was not Earth.

This world that was to be his.

She mustn't undercut 'Mond. "You could have discovered the hard way that it's possible," she said. "In any case, you were selfish and inconsiderate, you made a whopping lot of trouble, and most especially, you breached discipline. If you don't learn better, someday you may cause somebody's death. Go wash and lie down."

Mute, haughtily erect, the boy departed. When he was out of sight, the man embraced the woman. She laid her head against the hard solidity of him, inhaled his warmth and male smell, clutched him tightly. "I 'ate sis," he whispered in her ear. "But we are obliged."

"Oh, yes, oh, yes," she breathed. "For their sakes."

If he and she knew what was right. How many of the old rules held? These were not children like any that had ever been before. In a sense, they were not human. They'd never be able to breed with her kind, nor even abide for very long on Earth. Not for them were wind and wave, blue heaven, thunderheads, rainbows, the great wheel of the seasons; theirs were the naked stone and the scornful stars and a life to make from a new beginning. She had not believed the otherness of their flesh would matter too much. Else she would not have borne them. But how foreign were their souls?

11

As soon as she left the tubeway that had taken her from the airport, Aleka Kame realized she needed a warmer garment than she had brought along. The sky hung low and leaden. A raw wind harried tatters of fog borne in off the sea. Earth's atmosphere didn't always respond as it should to the nudges it got from Weather Control, and sometimes even short-range local prediction failed. Ultimately, the planet was chaotic.

Having noticed a dispenser in the station, she went back. The booth was basic, but she didn't want anything fancy. In fact, she did not need to strip for the scan, as lightly clad as she was. When she had specified a brown calidex coverall and debited herself, the system took three minutes to prepare it and drop it out the chute. She put it on over her blouse and shorts, picked up her bag, and went forth again.

The carrier had let her off within a few blocks of her first destination. Walking up Fell Street, she saw that more of the houses that lined it had gone empty since her last visit. They stood shingled, turreted, painted, sealed and silent in their eld, museum pieces. What tenants remained were generally old, caretaking to earn a bit of extra credit. However, a number of small businesses were interspersed: personal services, entertainment, curio shops, hand-prepared food and drink, a place to linger and chat over coffee. Traffic went sparse, pedestrians, motorskaters, minicars, the occasional machine on duty at which she could only guess.

Passing Steiner, she saw what was new, a quivira opposite Alamo Square. It was designed to blend in with its archaic surroundings; she would not have known its nature except for the schematic cosmos discreetly flashing above the entrance.

So people were now coming here to lie in the tanks and enjoy the dream-lives they could not find in reality? Then the neighborhood wasn't actually dying . . . unless a sociotechnic computation had shown that this might restore a little vitality to it, and that that was desirable for some larger end. . . .

The Albergo Vecchio filled a building which the occupants had gotten permission to remodel. A sign-board creaked in the wind, with a garish amateur painting of peasants in a harvest field passing a leather bottle around. The walls behind the door, similarly decorated, enclosed a tiny bar and several tables with red-checked cloths. Cooking odors drifted from a reconstructed primitive kitchen. Mama Lucia bustled out to cry, *"Benvenuta, carissima!"* and hug Aleka to her vast bosom. Nothing would do but that the guest immediately have a tumbler of wine and a slab of bread and cheese.

Upstairs in her room, which was also small and meticulously antiquated, Aleka sighed, shook her head, and smiled a bit sadly. She always stayed here when she came to San Francisco Bay Integrate. It wasn't fake, not really; it was a family's gallant effort to keep themselves independent, doing work they could care about. And, yes, it offered a haven from the machines. Her window overlooked a vegetable garden. As far as she knew, the plants were all traditional.

If you wanted this kind of respite, a quivira could give it in totality; but the real thing, though limited, cost rather less.

Of course, you didn't get away from a multiceiver and an eidophone. Aleka called the Mary Carfax number. An aged female face appeared on the screen. "Buenos tardes?" it quavered.

Aleka named herself. "I'm a friend of your grandniece Dolores Nightborn," she said. "She suggested I come by, since I'm in town, give you some news you may not have heard—nothing major, but nice—and see if you need anything. I'll be glad to help wherever I can."

"Oh, yes, yes. Dear Dolores. Gracias, mil gracias, señorita. Can you come over pronto, for tea?"

Hard to believe that this was an electrophotonic intelligence speaking while a program modulated the transmission. Aleka held her own features stiff, her voice calm. The effort made her forget and say, *"Mahalo"* by way of thanks, but no matter; she herself wasn't playing identity games, not yet. "Sure, I'll be happy to. In about half an hour, bien?"

Quickly she changed to a decorous unisuit, flipped the coverall together around it, and went back downstairs. "I've a lot of errands," she told Mama. "Don't know when I'll be in." Beneath the easy words, she shivered.

The display at the station directed her to a stop on Columbus Avenue. She had never seen that district before. It busied itself, but not directly with human concerns. On her right a wall rose a sheer hundred meters and ran for a kilometer or more, like a palisade, windowless, seemingly doorless. Recesses and flutings made a subtle pattern over which smoked the hues of a thousand different sunsets. Light also played, in coruscant sparkles, across a building on the other side, whose soaring intricacy suggested a fountain. Complementing it with height and grace, a metal framework reared beyond, where cables made a moving network around silvery control nodes. Aleka sometimes wished she had the brains to understand sophotectic esthetics, not simply admire it or stand bewildered.

A sense of enormous energies filled her, though the wind whistled through silence and traffic was still thinner than along Fell. The cybercosm sent communications to work scenes far oftener than it dispatched material bodies. Perhaps a score of machines were in her visual field. A huge, torpedo-shaped transport murmured by, self-steered. Two little flyers buzzed overhead, optics bulging out of bluish metal, arms trailing aft below the wings. A fractally dendritic manipulator glided past, three meters tall; its finest extremities quivered and shimmered in the gusts. A wheeled, multiply tentacular globe was a sight new to her. And on and on. . . . Which were robots, which were intelligent and aware, which were puppets of a thing that might reside halfway around the planet? How much did the question mean? Electrophotonic minds could mesh at will in every possible configuration, achieving every potential—

She was not quite the sole human. A man strode by, so purposefully that he must have some occupation here. A consultant, a technician? A woman stood at a distance, apparently discoursing with an anthropomorph that could almost have been taken for a spacesuit. Could she be a synnoiont? Two other men, grizzled and vaguely shabby, walked in surly conversation. Local residents? Probably. Those would be few, because flesh and blood tended to feel uncomfortable in environs like this, but on that account lodgings in side streets would be cheap.

"Mary Carfax" had one. The seething data traffic everywhere around must help screen hers. She'd be free of people living close by, who might wonder why she never left home. All that had been necessary was to smuggle the apparatus in and install it. The precaution of slipping a false registry into the database would have been more difficult to take, but, given Lilisaire's connections, not impossible. Aleka knew something about that kind of trick.

She turned on Greenwich and, a few blocks down, found the place. It was a leftover house in the sleek pastel-plastic style of eighty or ninety years ago. Those flanking and facing it looked deserted. Evidently city robots kept them in good repair, but Aleka wondered fleetingly how long it would be before other machines obliterated them to make room for more machines.

Or would they? Why? Sophotects didn't proliferate for the sake of proliferation, as humans used to. The growth they strove for was ethereal, capabilities of the intellect, up toward the Teramind and beyond. Aleka shivered in the bleak wind.

She confronted the door and spoke her name. Carfax had obviously entered instructions, with a recorded image, for it retracted at once. She ran tongue across lips, clamped teeth together, and went inside.

A cramped room held obsolete furniture and banal pictures. Surprised, Aleka then decided this was for the benefit of any unwanted person, a constable or whoever, who could not be refused admission. She passed on into a space big and still. Walls had withdrawn to make a single chamber. Windows had blanked. The ceiling imitated sunlight and the air lay warm, but she guessed that was on her account, likewise a lounger in the middle of the otherwise empty floor. At the far end she saw a large gray panel, blank except for sensors, a screen, a speaker, and sliders that doubtless covered specialized outlets. A general-purpose robot stood in a corner adjoining. She assumed the sophotect took direct control of it. The mind itself, the physical system, was—elsewhere in the house.

"Salud," she greeted out of a tight throat.

The voice that replied had become a resonant baritone. "Bienvenida, Señorita Kame. Por favor, remove your outer garment, be seated, make yourself comfortable. What can I offer you? Food, beverage, narcotic, stimulant? I regret the choice is limited, because visitors like you are rare, but the usual things are on hand."

"N-no, gracias." Aleka feared that if she tried to deal with a cup or plate, it would tremble. She felt grateful for Mama's wine.

Reaction flared. Why the Q should she be nervous? Here was no god, but a machine—a single machine, sealed off from the rest of the cybercosm. Yes, it had awareness, it had gifts that in certain respects must be greater than hers, but in other ways it was surely circumscribed, naïve, dedicated to this one service. When that ended and a new program was entered, it would not be the same mind, the same being, at all.

True, she was on the verge of what might be a dangerous enterprise. But she'd taken risks before. Generally she'd enjoyed them. And the possible stakes—

She grinned, for the sake of bravado. Peeling off her coverall and dropping it on the floor, she sat down. She would rather have kept her feet, but figured obscurely that this showed her more at ease, more in command. She did set the lounger straight upright and ignored its sensuous self-adjustments to contours and skin temperature.

"Are you ready?" asked the machine. She nodded. Her heart thumped. "I speak for the Wardress Lilisaire. She has provided me·a file of her information about you."

Aleka frowned. "Was that safe? I mean, if she's being watched—"

"How do you know she is?"

"She has a reason for these precautions, doesn't she?"

The voice made a chuckle. "Excellent. You confirm her impression of sharp wits. The file was not transmitted from Luna, it was carried as a recording to Earth by a messenger. He privately gave it to another person, who brought it here."

Then presumably Lilisaire had no cause to suspect Aleka was under surveillance. That came as a pulse-lowering relief. "Are you, uh, empowered to make decisions?"

"As far as feasible, yes. Why do you think you were called?"

"It has to do with the Habitat, right?"

Lilisaire had talked enough about that, with enough venom, when they met, although mainly she had set herself to charm and, under cover of it, inquire. Besides, everybody knew how opposed to the project the large majority of Lunarians were.

"Yes," the machine said. "What is your opinion of it?"

"I, I hadn't given it much thought," Aleka confessed. "The idea seemed—exciting—till I heard her. Since then . . . I sympathize. If Earthlings want to colonize, let them go to Mars."

"A long, expensive haul."

"What does expense mean, when you can pretty nearly grow your ships in the nanotanks, and they don't need human crews? Nor would you need a Habitat at Mars."

"Shrewdly put. I was quoting the argument advanced by proponents. They are humans too, you know, in the government and out of it."

Bitterness lifted. "What has the cybercosm bribed them with?"

The tone was matter-of-fact. "Essentially nothing. Most of them are sincere. They accept the cost-benefit analysis produced for them because they trust the cybercosm. You know why. This *is* a more stable world, with more social and economic justice, than ever was before sophotectic intelligence developed. Do not be so hostile to it."

Aleka's emotion subsided a little. "Oh, I'm not, not really. I'm . . . skeptical. At least, I often wonder where we humans are bound, and how much control over the course we have left to us."

"Your Lyudovite background?"

"I never was a Lyudovite!" she exclaimed. "How could I be? The Rebellion happened lifetimes ago."

"But when you were studying at the Irkutsk Institute, you encountered persons whose ancestors fought in it, and who still hold it was a rightful cause wrongly crushed."

Memory rushed back, campus, the Russian plain, glorious Lake Baikal, Yuri, Yuri, and the village to which he took her, more than once. "I had a, a close friend, a fellow student. He came from that kind of family, yes. They tried to keep the old ways alive, handicraft, agriculture, it was pitiful to see. He introduced me to them. We were very young." Aleka sighed. "Later he . . . changed his mind." And they drifted apart, and finally she went home to Hawaii. By now he seldom troubled her dreams.

"And you?"

She shrugged. "I've got my work to do."

"I am only familiarizing myself with you," the machine said mildly. "I know what Lilisaire has informed me of, but it is incomplete and abstract."

However, Aleka reflected, it probably went beyond what she had revealed. Agents on Earth must have looked into her life before the Wardress decided she could trust her. Or earlier, yes. Lilisaire would have had more than a casual reason, a couple of mutual acquaintances, for inviting her to Zamok Vysoki that time she vacationed on the Moon, and bedazzling her.

Aleka felt she ought to resent such snooping, but couldn't. She didn't even resent it that the ancestress Niolente had taken a part in fomenting and prolonging the Rebellion. A cold-blooded move, granted, in hopes of weakening the Federation until it gave up on incorporating Luna. But Lyudovites and Lunarians had a great deal in common.

Aleka stiffened her will. "All right," she said, "I admit I've kept the sympathies I acquired then. To a degree, anyhow. I don't personally believe we can turn history backward. Nor that we should." It had indeed been a desperate cause: Keep humanity in charge. Do not permit the making of fully conscious artificial intelligence. Stop before it is too late, and then consider how much mechanization and automation is really desirable. "Too late," she repeated her thought.

"But I live with what the system is doing to my people."

"So you told the lady Lilisaire."

She bewitched it out of me, Aleka almost replied. She had never confided like that in anyone else, feelings too deep to have clear form until she uttered them. Not Father nor Mother nor sisters nor Yuri had worked thus upon her. She did not yet know just how the Selenarch had.

She curbed her words. A silent half minute went by.

"Shall we proceed to the matter?" asked the machine.

"*'Olu'olu!*" burst forth. Aleka caught her breath. "Por favor."

The calm tone helped steady her: "You have an uncommon knowledge of peculiar byways in these parts, as well as of the global datanet."

"I, I'm no . . . spy, or any such thing."

"Would you care to describe your experiences? Again, I know of them from the Wardress, but hearing you in person gives depth to the information," the machine said.

And it had to judge whether or not she actually was what Lilisaire required. Responding in a half-organized fashion stabilized Aleka further. "Details, anecdotes, they'd take the rest of this week. But—oh, in my student days I was exposed to a wide variety of places and folk around Earth, besides getting a technical education. You see, the Lahui need people like that, and the elders thought I had the talent, so they encouraged and supported me to knock around. Since then I've served as a liaison, with the Keiki Moana on the one hand and the outside world on the other hand. I've come to the mainland quite a lot on that account, because—bueno, metamorphs don't like to use telepresence, especially for important business. Among other things, they're afraid of eavesdroppers."

Not without grounds, she thought. The authorities would want to keep an eye on them. They were a chaotic element, which might by sheer chance disrupt carefully laid social plans.

"Your Keiki Moana seek cooperation with other Terrestrial metamorphs?" It was more a statement than a question.

"The core, the—I hate to say 'civilized' Keiki, yes, they do." And therefore Aleka did, on their beloved behalf. "Nothing criminal, nothing revolutionary. But . . . we'd like to quietly establish communication, find our common interests, work toward an organization that can promote and defend them."

Lunarians were metamorphs too.

"Nothing criminal, nothing revolutionary," the machine echoed. "Yet to Lilisaire you hinted at underground activity."

"Self-protective secrecy." Not absolutely true. "I've been let into a little of it—" partly because that was expedient, partly because she had pressed herself on the leaders, being interested and eager. Adventures into strangeness.

"Those connections could prove valuable. As for your access to databases and communication lines—"

"That's straightforward," she interrupted, for impatience was rising in her. "I *am* an officer of a recognized community, who has to deal with government officials. Sometimes that's best done under administrative confidentiality. You know, so the discussion can be frank and undistracted. Accordingly, I've learned my way around in the datanet. But I don't have unlimited access."

Supposing she theoretically did, how could she tell what was being kept hidden from her, or what was engineered to delude her?

"Muy bien," said the machine. "Let us get to the point." At last, at last! "The lady Lilisaire has found clues indicating there is a secret. . . ." It went on.

Aleka sat mute for a while before she whispered, out of her amazement, "I'd no idea. I don't know what to say. Or what to do."

"The hope is that you can discover the truth, and that it will give back to Luna some power over its future."

She shook her head. "Impossible, if they—" *they* "—want to keep it from us."

"Necessarily? You will have what help we can provide, beginning with a confederate highly knowledgeable about space."

Lilisaire and this thinking engine would not throw her away on a totally absurd endeavor. Arousal thrilled. She leaned forward, hands gripping knees. "Tell me about her."

"Him." With her senses whetted, she took in every word of the succinct account that followed, every lineament of Ian Kenmuir's displayed image.

But. "I'm afraid—" she began uneasily.

"That doesn't sound like you."

"I'm afraid he may be, uh, compromised. If he's been to see Lilisaire recently, and she's under suspicion—"

"We are aware. Could you not make him disappear with you?"

"Um-m." She considered. "Yes, maybe. Whether anything will come of it, I can't say, except that the odds look poor."

"Will you make the attempt?"

Go slow, she warned herself. Hang onto independence and common sense. "Why should I?"

That was curt, but the machine didn't seem to take offense. Could it, ever? "Granted, the risk will be significant. You shall not assume it without compensation."

"What am I offered?" A Lunarian attitude, she thought.

"If you make an honest effort and fail, a substantial sum. Before you refuse, think what it might buy for your people."

"Depends on the sum." They could wrangle about that later. She thrust onward. "What if somehow I succeed?"

"How would you like a country of your own?"

"What?"

The machine explained. At the end, she was on her feet, sobbing, "Yes, yes, oh, Pele, yes."

The machine started to discuss details.

When she left, emotionally exhausted, dusk was creeping out of the east. By the time she got back to Fell Street, night had fallen. The clouds made darkness heavy; the glow from the pavement could not entirely raise it. Fog streamed thicker on a wind grown colder.

She felt unable to cope with Mama's good cheer. In an autocafé she got a hasty supper, paying no attention to the taste. At the inn she went straight to her room.

Try to relax, try to get sleepy. A pill could knock her out, but she'd wake in the same turmoil as now. She had already decided against patronizing the quivira. Matters were amply complicated without adding memories of things that never physically happened. A vivifer would have been ideal, but this place didn't have any. Bueno, the multiceiver could engage her eyes and ears, while imagination supplied additional inputs.

But what to watch? She retrieved a list of major broadcasts. None appealed, and she didn't care to check out hundreds of lesser channels. The informant on her wrist, then. Thousands of entries in it, both text and audiovisual, both facts and entertainments. Many of them she hadn't yet seen, only put in because she thought she might like to someday.

She keyed for the sort of thing she wanted and pushed the bezel against the scanner. Titles and brief descriptions marched across the screen. Having chosen *Sunrise Over Tycho,* she directed the multi to get that from the public database, and settled back. This was a comedy she remembered favorably, set in the early days of Lunar colonization, when life was simpler, entirely human.

12

The Mother of the Moon

Spacious and gracious, the Beynaçs' living room gave a near-perfect illusion of being above ground and on an Earth long lost. Flowers on shelves splashed red, yellow, violet, green against ivory walls, above deep-blue carpet. Their perfume tinged air that went like a summer breeze. Furniture was redundantly massive. A giant viewscreen could have presented the outside scene or someplace within the Moon, but instead held an image from the Dordogne; trees stirred in a wind that blew up a hillside to a medieval castle, their soughing an undertone to peacefulness. Opposite it hung family pictures, not activated at the moment, and a scan-reproduction of a Winslow Homer seascape. A cat lay asleep on one chair.

But you moved with unearthly ease, and if you dropped something, it fell dreamlike slowly.

Three people entered. "Welcome," Dagny said. "We'll give you the grand tour later. Right now it's time for a drink before dinner."

"I see already, this is quite a place you've got," Anson Guthrie replied. "Bueno, you've earned it."

"We have built much of it ourselves," Edmond told him. A little bragging was allowable. The job had never been easy, often damned tough, what with shortages of materials, equipment, and, above all, leisure. It had taken years.

Again Dagny felt glad of how lightly those years seemed to have touched her grandfather. She had not encountered him in person for five of them, and pictorial messages or the occasional phone conversation didn't convey enough reality. Besides, his recent loss was of the kind that can break a spirit. But when she met him at the spaceport, his bass still boomed and he hugged her as bear-vigorously as ever. Though the hair was white and thin, the craggy face deeply furrowed, he bade fair to keep the helm of Fireball for decades more.

Which was well for her and hers, and for everybody everywhere who loved liberty. Why care about skintraces? Lines now radiated from the corners of her mouth and eyes when she laughed, 'Mond had gone frosty at the temples, yet neither of them had noticeably slowed down.

"Yes, Dagny's supplied me gossip along with business talk," Guthrie said. "Good workmanship here. It's got a solid feel to it, the sort you seldom find any more. Meant to last beyond your own lives, eh?"

The woman nodded. "So we hope. Of course, it's nothing like your home on Earth."

"Which one?"

"Hm, well, I happened to recall the Vancouver Island estate. The sea, the woods—" Her stay there had probably been the happiest of her infrequent visits to the planet, apart from times when she and 'Mond were together in his France. She gestured at the screen. "We have to pretend." Quickly, lest he get a false idea that she felt the slightest bit sorry for herself: "But we've got plenty you don't," more and more as Tychopolis grew. Bird-flight in Avis Park. Beautiful Hydra Square. Wonders, bred for Luna, in the zoo and botanical gardens. Outside, stern grandeur, sports—dashball, rock skiing, mountain climbing, suborbital flits, exploration—and the excitement, bewilderment, and occasional heartbreak of a civilization coming to birth.

"Right," Guthrie agreed. "Wish I could've called on you before. Too busy. Always too backscuttling busy." He took a turn around the room, glancing at things. "I do miss books," he remarked. "Antique bound volumes. When I was young, dropping in on somebody, if they were readers, what you saw on their bookshelves would tell you more about them than a month's palaver."

"I remember from your houses," Dagny said. "No

need to remind you about the transport problems we had till lately."

"Nevertheless we can oblige you," Edmond said. He took a hand-held cyberlit off a table, where it rested beside a small meteorite full of metallic glints, and started it. Titles and authors' names appeared on the screen. "Here, play with this." He gave it to Guthrie.

The jefe unscrolled part of the catalogue, darting to and fro among its items. Most were in the central library database, listed here because they interested the Beynacs. Some were personal property. He evoked a few pages, including representations of texts and pictures centuries old. "Fine collection," he said meanwhile. "This gadget's not the same as holding a real book, but then I daresay the Egyptian priest told Solon, at boring length, how much more character hieroglyphs had than any spindly alphabet."

He was no clotbrain, Dagny reflected, in spite of his sneers at self-styled intellectuals.

A door opened. The housekeeper robot scanned in, sensed people, and, in the absence of orders, withdrew, closing the door again.

"Ah, your professional publications, 'Mond," Guthrie observed. "Impressive clutch. M-m, I see you're stiff-necked as ever pushing your theory about a big ancient asteroid."

"The evidence accumulates," the geologist answered. He sought the miniature bar. "But we are being inhospitable. What will you have to drink?"

"I'm told they've begun brewing decent beer since I was last on the Moon. That, por favor, to go in hot pursuit of a cold akvavit, if you've got some."

"Dagny would disown me if we did not, especially when you were coming." Edmond prepared the same for her, a dry sherry for himself.

"But where's your real writing?" Guthrie asked him.

"Hein?"

"Those novels Dagny's mentioned, under the name —uh, blast, I'm getting senile—"

"You are not, Uncans," she declared. "You've simply got so much else in your head. Jacques Croquant, that's his pen name."

"My secret is out!" Edmond groaned. "I did not know you had told him."

"I'd like to read 'em," Guthrie said. "'Fraid my French has gone down a black hole, what little there ever was of it, but if a translator program won't mangle the style too badly, I gather they're fun."

Edmond shrugged. "Style, what is that? They are deep-space adventure stories I write in spare time for amusement. The pseudonym is because academics are snobs. They respect my Lunar work, yes." As well they might, Dagny thought fiercely. It had revolutionized selenology. "But I want also my ideas about the early Solar System taken seriously, investigated."

"That might well be arranged, now we're setting up a meteoroid patrol." Guthrie continued his random retrievals. "What, three biographies of Charles de Gaulle? And his collected works. Hero of yours?"

"In the twentieth century, exactly two leaders of major nations deserved the name of statesman, he and Konrad Adenauer. The rest—" Edmond shrugged again. *"Eh, bien,* I can imagine several of them meant well."

"'Mond's got more regard for authority than I do," Dagny put in.

Guthrie smiled. "Yeah, you're a natural-born, two-dominants rebel, Diddyboom. So how does it feel to be turning into a power yourself, here on Luna?"

"I'm not," she denied. "Not really. It's just that, you know how the governments load us with politicians and bureaucrats who can't tell a crap from a crater. Being in administration forces me to deal directly with them, and if my friends and I can get the residents to support Fireball's positions, and the right candidates into what few elective offices we're allowed

—ah, you know. The drinks are ready. Sit down, please do."

All three took chairs, though on Luna it was as easy to stand and gatherings often did throughout a social evening. The Beynacs preferred to maintain a few gestures, customs, symbols. Dagny wondered whether they would be able to through the rest of their lives.

When Edmond cared about something, he cared passionately. "We must accept legitimate authority," he argued. "Else society ablates itself until people welcome the warlord who will enforce a brutal kind of order that at least gives them security. The problem is not what makes a government legitimate. There have been many ways in history, royal or noble birth, priestliness, popular vote, a sociological theory, et cetera, et cetera. The problem is, how does a government keep legitimacy? How does it lose it? I say the breakdown comes when it begins doing more *to* people than *for* them. This has happened, it is happening, in more and more countries on Earth. In space, the disorder that soon or late follows breakdown, it would mean extinction. Fireball has more right to power than most of the governments that today claim power, because Fireball's masters honor their obligations to Fireball's people."

He wasn't what you'd call handsome, Dagny thought, but when he kindled, a nova lit in her too. She sent a chill caraway nip over her tongue, followed it with the tingle of beer, and was not much calmed.

"Gracias," Guthrie said. "We try. Don't thank me, however. Thank the folks who're actually doing it, like this wife of yours. Or you personally, 'Mond, even if you avoid politicking. I've kept track, sort of. You two don't scamp your responsibilities, you go out and look for more."

"If we do well, it is because of you, sir. You make us want to. You make it possible."

Guthrie shook his head. "Not me. Never think that. Those who believe in an indispensable man don't survive long, nor ought to." He grinned, tossed off a considerable draught, and added, "Mind you, I'm not modest. I do a braw job where I am. But that's in an outfit which is sound because its members are."

"And they are because it is."

Dagny nodded to herself. She had watched mutuality grow and strengthen, year by year. This new, fast-spreading, altogether spontaneous practice of swearing troth to the company, which in the person of an officer pledged faith of its own—

"You started Fireball, Uncans," she said softly. "You kept it going through every terrible trouble."

"Juliana more than me," Guthrie answered, low in his throat.

Her eyes stung. "We all miss her. You—" She leaned over to lay her hand briefly upon his.

"Don't worry about me," he growled. "I soldier on."

"She would have wanted you to," Edmond said.

"It's your nature," Dagny murmured.

Guthrie shook his heavy shoulders. "Hey, this is in danger of turning serious," he protested.

Dagny saw how he wanted to veer from the intimate. But when would another chance come to talk quietly? "Please bear with us a little while longer," she appealed. "We've so been wanting to hear your thoughts, your knowledge. Earth is in such a bad way, and Fireball seems to be almost the only strong force for good that's left."

"Hoo-ha, lass!" he exclaimed. "Jesus Christ couldn't live up to that kind of billing. You know better. You could name as well as me plenty who haven't let power short circuit their wits."

"Yes, they keep progress alive, at least in science and technology," Edmond said. "Foremost, those of the super-rich who are enlightened, like you. The 'Savant Barons.'"

"And a few in government, much though I hate to admit it."

"But what of the populace? What of the vast majority, in every land, who can find no real place in this high-technology universe you have created?"

"Yeah. The High World versus the Low World. It's more than a journalistic duck-billed platitude. Count yourselves lucky. Everybody in space is High World. Not as a pun. Necessarily."

Dagny felt her brows draw together. "That may be why we have trouble making sense of what's going on on Earth," she ventured.

"Sense there is mighty thin on the ground, honey. Day by day, scarcer and scarcer, in spite of the best efforts of us whom you want to canonize."

"Newscasts, analyses, books, personal communications—here on the Moon, it all seems . . . abstract? Surreal?" Dagny forced herself: "Is there really going to be a war?"

"Wars are popping already, around the planet," Guthrie replied somberly. "We call 'em disorders or revolutions or whatever, but wars is what they amount to. And, yes, I'm afraid the big one is on the way."

"The Jihad?" Edmond's tone went hoarse. "Those preachers—But it is not Islam against the infidels, not truly, is it? Nothing so simple."

"No, sure not. I'd call it the last full-scale revolt of the Low World against an order of things it doesn't understand and feels forever left out of. The High World will have its share of Muslim allies, and the Mahdis will have theirs of every creed and none."

"What will come of it?" Dagny whispered.

"Not a general blowup," Guthrie assured her. "I expect nukes will get fired in anger, but not many nor high-yield. The whole hooraw is too complicated, changeable, scrambled geographically and ethnically and economically and you-name-it—too much for any clear-cut showdown. My guess is we'll see years of fighting, minor in some areas, a blood tsunami in others. The High World countries will end on top, but they'll be so shaken that things can't go back to the same for them either."

He paused, then finished: "I doubt there ever was or ever will be a war that was worth what it cost, when you figure in the costs to everybody concerned, including generations unborn. But what comes out of this might be better in a few respects than what we've got now. For instance, I don't see how that rattlebone, patchgut Renewal can survive the strain.

"On the whole, though, be glad you're on the Moon, you and yours, with nothing worse to worry about than vacuum, radiation, meteoroids, life-support failure, and bureaucrats."

"Most glad for our children," Dagny said.

"Of course."

Now they all wanted to change the subject. "Where are the youngsters, anyway?" Guthrie inquired.

Dagny seized on the relief, the lightness. "That question has more answers than kids."

Edmond nodded. "They scamper about, when they do not—*vont à la derobée*—go very quietly, like the cat. And they have their private things we know little about." He sighed. "Less and less, the more they grow."

"Yes, I've gotten that from Dagny," Guthrie said. Once, after she thus confided in him, his return message spoke of a mother hen he'd seen when he was a boy, given duck eggs to brood and the hatchlings to raise, helplessly watching them swim off across a pond. "But where are they at the moment?"

"Well, Brandir's in Port Bowen," she told him. "He aims to be a structural engineer, you may remember, and I arranged for him to work a few weeks on a new cargo launch catapult they're building, hands-on experience. He's eager to meet you, but unless you can stay longer than you said, or seek him out, it'll have to be by phone. Verdea's at a friend's, probably trying out a composition on her. Kaino's wingflight stunt team—"

"Hold on, por favor. Brandir, Verdea, Kaino? You've described this fad among the Lunarian youngsters for taking invented names and insisting on them—so have the journalists—but I can't recall which of yours is which."

"It is more than a fad," Edmond said. "They are totally serious about it. In fact, they are developing a whole new language for themselves. Not slang, not an argot, a language."

"They don't reject us," Dagny said. "Not really." She had to believe that. And they did remain amicable toward their parents, in their individual ways, and if an aloofness dwelt beneath it, was the pain this gave her more than she had given to hers? "It's just that they are—different, more different than anybody foresaw. They're trying to learn what their natures are, and, and we can't help them much."

Guthrie rubbed his chin. "Not simply adolescent rebellion, then, eh? Though Lord knows, looking at Earth and Earth's officials on Luna, they have a fair amount of justification." He knocked back his beer. Edmond took the mug and the shot glass for refills. "Gracias, amigo. Can you sort of fill me in on them?"

Dagny put recent sequences onto the screen, in succession, and found a few words about each.

Brandir. Anson. Sixteen. Two meters tall, wide-shouldered, supple; ash-blond hair, silver-blue eyes, marmoreal skin on which no beard would ever grow. His face was not purely Lunarian, it bore traces of his mother's. He often clashed with his father, but not too seriously, and she thought he stayed emotionally closer to her than his siblings did or could. It didn't stop him from cutting a swath among Earth-gene girls. As for females of his kind, what happened was their choice as much as his. They appeared to have parallel interests of their own, an independence taken so for granted that they didn't bother to assert it. Whatever had become of school-age sweethearts?

Verdea. Gabrielle. Fourteen. Almost Earthlike in looks, of medium height, buxom, round snub-nosed countenance, brown eyes, brown curls bobbed short. Quiet, studious, and, when she wanted something, steely determined about it. A literary gift, expressed in poems and prose sketches that baffled Dagny. (*Starstone freedom: Achilles/Odysseus*—) While a couple of other young geniuses had written the program that constructed the basic Lunarian language, she seemed to be among the leading contributors to its expanding and ever more subtle vocabulary. Dagny had cause to wonder whether she was sexually active, but what did a mother know? Lunarian children kept their doings to themselves, and Verdea scorned Earthgene boys.

Kaino. Sigurd. Twelve. Big for his years, strong, redhaired, blue-eyed, features sharing much of his father's ruggedness. The athlete of the bunch, the loudest, impulsive, sometimes wildly reckless. In sibling rivalry with Brandir, but it seldom manifested itself in quarrels. They would stalk by one another for daycycles on end, unspeaking, and then abruptly, for a while, be the closest of comrades. Kaino's all-dream was to pilot spacecraft. He would not, could not accept that the heredity which made Lunar weight normal for him likewise made high accelerations a death barrier.

Temerir. Francis. Going on ten. Slight, platinum-blond, gray eyes oblique and enormous in a visage ascetic save for the full red lips. Even more than Verdea was he a reader, a student, soft-spoken, asocial. He showed great scientific talent.

Fia. Helen. Seven and a half. Still entirely a child, though you saw that she would be beautiful, black hair, umber eyes, face a feminine version of Brandir's. Already almost as reserved as Temerir. She might be highly musical, but it was hard to tell, and she disliked most of what she heard. Maybe she'd create the first truly Lunarian music.

Jinann. Carla. Four. A little redhead, as her mother had been, vivacious and affectionate. Her Lunarian name she had from her siblings, and often forgot to use it. But who could say what she would become?

"Are the youngest at home?" Guthrie asked.

"In the playroom, I suppose," Edmond answered.

"You will meet them soon, when Clementine has made them presentable."

"They demand that," Dagny explained. "They're excited about your visit, but none of them likes . . . outsiders . . . to see them at a disadvantage."

Guthrie raised his brows. "You've found an actual nurse for them? My impression was the servant problem on Luna is so intractable nobody remembers what the word means. An *au pair,* maybe?"

"No, no. Clementine's what we call their robot."

"A robot nurse? Housekeepers are tough enough to program."

"This is a new model, lately developed by a small company in the city," Edmond said. "We consented to test it. To date it goes fairly well."

"Huh! I hadn't heard a thing. Ah, hell, who can keep up?"—when computer models and nanolevel experiments compress former years' worth of R & D into hours. The obstacle that progress must overcome wasn't innovation, Dagny understood; it was capital investment and market acceptance. "Isn't this a tad dicey?"

"We've got plenty of fail-safes, never fear," she said. "Besides, it's just a guardian, a doer of simple chores, and an entertainer. That is, it has a repertory of song and story elements to combine. We aren't making it a substitute for us, only a helper. We wouldn't want more."

"You'd scarcely get more anyway. This much surprises me."

"Is advancement in artificial intelligence slowing to a halt?" wondered Edmond. "I have seen it claimed, but the man who had Clementine built, he does not agree."

"Oh, we're getting remarkable machines, amazing programs. You know from your field trips what the top-chop robots are capable of these days, and better are in the works. Yeah. Including a kind of—what you might call thought, creativity. But that's still basically stochastic, no different in principle from your nanny's kaleidoscope method of plotting new stories. Real thought, consciousness, mind, whatever you dub it—the way I read the accounts and reports that've come to me, we're as far from that as ever."

"Strange," Dagny mused.

"Could it be the fundamental approach is mistaken?" Edmond speculated.

"I suspect those thinkers are right who say it is," Guthrie replied. "You may remember, according to their school of thought, the mind is not completely algorithmic. If that's true, then the ultimate Omega that fellow Xuan has been touting, it'll never come to be. Not by that route, anyhow."

"Are you sure?" Dagny asked. "You don't believe in a disembodied soul or anything like that."

Guthrie laughed. "To be exact, I have a bare smidgen more faith in the supernatural than I do in the wisdom and beneficence of governments."

Dagny frowned, intent. She had long puzzled over this. "Then the mind does have a material basis. In which case, we should be able to produce it artificially."

"I s'pose. However, the job may be trickier than the algorithm school imagines. For openers, 'material' is a concept full of weirdities. Read your quantum mechanics."

"What about downloading?"

"You mean scanning a brain and mapping its contents into a neural network designed for the purpose? Well, again judging by what reports I've seen, that does look promising. Though I'm not sure it's a promise I'll like to see kept."

"Then we *would* have a machine with consciousness."

"Sort of, I reckon." Guthrie drank beer while he assembled words. "But you see, if my guess is right, we wouldn't have created that mind ourselves. It'd be something that came from, that was a functioning of, a live body and everything that body ever experienced. The whole critter, not an isolated brain. If we

can someday impose its . . . molecular encoding . . .
on an electronic or photonic matrix, maybe that'll
help us figure out what a mind really is, and maybe
then we can generate one from scratch. I dunno." He
grimaced. "Me, I'd mainly feel sorry for the downloaded personality, what shadow of it there was in the
machine. No belly, no balls, no nothing."

"It would have sensors and effectors," Edmond
pointed out. "And it need never grow old."

"I'll settle for what nature gave me, thank you."

"Plus antisenescents, ongoing cellular repairs, and
the rest of the medical program," Dagny gibed gently.

"Okay, I admit I'd rather not spend my last ten or
twenty years doddering," Guthrie conceded. "And a
download of me might find existence interesting after
all. But I think I'd be glad it wasn't *me.*"

Dagny glanced at her watch. "Not to interrupt—"
she began.

"Do," Guthrie urged. "As Antony said to Cleopat-
ra, I am not prone to argue. I came here to relax for a
bit in good company."

"An intelligent argument, that is among the high
pleasures in life," Edmond reminded him.

"So is a proper meal," Dagny said, "and this will be
on the table very shortly."

"It is her cooking," Edmond told Guthrie. "Let us
finish our apéritifs. I state as a Frenchman, you have a
treat in store."

13

Seen from the air, Los Angeles was a monstrous
wasteland, kilometer after kilometer of ruins sprawl-
ing eastward until it scattered itself against summer-
brown mountains and dull-hued desert. Things leaped
out of the jumble into Kenmuir's notice: hummocks
that had been houses, bits of glass agleam, timbers

thrusting up parched and warped; snags of larger buildings; others almost whole, but raddled and empty; a freeway interchange, partly collapsed in some past earthquake; a water conduit, choked with rubble, dry as the sources on which the city once battened; overhead, a cloudless sky softening with evening, crossed by the meteor trail of a transoceanic.

Hitherto he had just glimpsed this on documentary shows, and seldom. The reality shocked him more than he would have expected. He twisted the scan control of his viewscreen, searching for life. It was there, he knew. The slow abandonment had never been total, and eventually, bit by bit, people crept back in, squatters, entrepreneurs, outlandish little groups of the special. Yes, a cleared space, palm trees, grass, ringed by homes mostly built from salvage, not unattractive. And another settlement, in a very different style, its center a pyramid—a religious community? And a third, a single big edifice suggestive of a fortress. And in the offing, fanciful shapes that marked Xibalba. . . . Probably the colonies were as many as the desalinization plant at Santa Monica could supply. Few; but then, the olden population pressure was gone.

Nevertheless he wondered why no reclamation was under way. Flying down from the north, he had seen a flourishing biome in the Central Valley, suited to its aridity, although habitation was almost as sparse as here. Did nature in these parts not deserve restoration too?

A matter of cost-benefit and priorities, he supposed. No doubt the regional parliament had once discussed it, in cursory fashion, and accepted the recommendations of the appropriate commissioners. The commissioners in their turn would have relied on the findings of a cyberstudy, conducted by everything from nanorobots permeating the soil to climatological monitors in orbit, and on an analysis of the data conducted by a mind superior to theirs.

If that mind saw things in a larger context, and

found reasons beyond ecology for leaving this area forsaken, would it have explained? Quite possibly no human being could have understood.

Kenmuir shoved the question aside. His flyer was slanting downward.

Santa Monica perched neat above the ocean, several hundred three- or four-story viviendas ringing their cloister parks, intermingled with bubblehouses, red-tiled Spanish Revival casas, and occasional eccentrics. He had heard of it as mildly prosperous, a place of small-time entertainers and other professionals, retirees who had accumulated funds to supplement basic credit, and the people who provided them their live services. Now he spied boats at a marina, the sands of Malibu Beach across the Bay and the gardens behind them, a bioinspector's snaky form broaching in a welter of foam. Westward the sea rippled silver and turquoise. Light blazed along it, out of a sun that smoldered as it sank.

Public transport to these parts had been discontinued since Kenmuir was last on Earth, ground as well as air. One by one, faster and faster, it was happening to minor communities, and some that maybe were not so minor. Insufficient demand, he was told. It was more efficient to use one's own vehicle or engage one or, oftenest, simply communicate. He had wondered whether this would make for community spirit and whether that might be the underlying purpose. On the field below, three volants were parked. They must belong to transients like him, or be hired by them. Those of residents would be in the big garage.

His set down. He unsnapped, rose, stretched. After the faint noise of the flight, silence rang in his ears.

Better get going. He'd overlingered a bit on Vancouver Island today, enjoying Guthrie House and its memories, water and woods and *Kestrel* forever ready to leap back at the stars. Rendezvous at 2100 hours, was the word from Lilisaire's agent in San Francisco Bay Integrate. (The number she had given him revealed that that was the location, but nothing more specific, and the reply from there was pictureless.) He didn't know exactly how long it would take him to get from here to Xibalba.

Nor did he know the person he would meet there. Or what they would speak of. Or where he would spend the night. He'd better leave his luggage behind.

Although he was properly clad, in an inconspicuous gray unisuit and soft boots, he felt naked as he stepped forth.

Nonsense. The air lay soft, barely stirring. He thought he sensed fragrance in it. Jasmine, growing somewhere nearby? His hearing captured a murmur. Gentle waves, gentle traffic, or maintenance machinery at work throughout the town? Sunset gilded field and walls.

But what was he bound for?

Why was he?

He squared his shoulders and marched.

Had the terminal been of any size, its stillness and emptiness would have ratcheted the tension in him. A single woman was leaving. She cast him a half-curious glance. Unthinkingly, he gave it back. Brown-complexioned caucasoid, middle-aged, well-dressed, doubtless a local person who'd landed a few minutes before he did. To what contentments was she returning? A door made way and she disappeared from Kenmuir's sight forever.

He went to the service panel. "A cab, please, uh, por favor," he said, automatically courteous, as if he were addressing an awareness.

"Where to?" asked the operations robot.

"Xibalba."

"Post number five, señor."

He went out. The designated spot was about four meters to the right. Very soon, a car slid up to the curb. He'd had lengthier waits. Maybe population here was declining rather fast, or maybe the residence had the political energy to get a large fleet assigned them.

The car was intended for this region, chassis

mounted on tracks rather than wheels and with a ground-effect motor in case of major obstacles. It opened itself and extruded a gangway. He got in, sat down, set the informant on his wrist to give an account number and touched it to the debit scan. "Xibalba district," he said. "Uh, the Asilo."

The car purred into motion. A screen displayed a map, on which a red dot crawled to show his position. "Advisory," said a voice. "The Asilo is a gathering house frequented by metamorphs, numbers of whom live in the vicinity. Unpleasant incidents involving outsiders have occurred. On 3 August last year, a patron of standard genome was badly beaten in a fight before police could arrive. Por favor, think about this."

Evidently the robot was programmed to refer questionable destinations and the like to a central intelligence. Kenmuir's pulse quickened. Nevertheless, "Thank you, but I should be all right," he said. He wasn't the sort to go looking for trouble—on the contrary—and if it sought him out, well, at worst he had his martial arts to fall back on. In friendly contests he didn't do badly.

"As you wish, señor."

Dusk thickened into night. The ride became slow and lumpy, on lightless pavement cracked, potholed, littered with debris. Twice the car lifted above a heap of wreckage. The glow from riding lamps glanced off remnant walls, then dropped them back into shadow. When he passed through a village, shining windows made the dark beyond seem deeper yet.

It seeped into Kenmuir. What business did he really have here? He had been Lilisaire's emissary to the Rydberg, and gained nothing. What more did he owe her? What had she given him, what would she in future? His career among the planets, yes; but always the stars taunted him, always Alpha Centauri gleamed out of reach. Her presence, yes, embraces like no other woman's whom he had known or imagined or even met in quivira dreams; but he did not delude himself that she loved him, and never could he have a child by her. The salvation of her race? So she said; but did she say rightly, did she say truthfully? And was it a claim on him? If somehow he gave her the means of forbidding the Habitat, might that deny *his* kind its last chance to get back and abide in the outer universe?

Guthrie's colony didn't count, he thought. In a few more centuries, Demeter would be shattered. Although transmissions across the light-years swore that folk yonder had not given up hope, neither did they know any means of saving their descendants. Would they ever?

Lights glared ahead. Buildings clustered together, a longhouse on four arches, an octagon white below an iridescent cupola, a corkscrew spire. A measure of heart came back. He straightened in his seat. Let him at least hear out this Irene Norton who was to meet him.

The cab stopped. "The Asilo, señor," it said. "Will you want further service at a particular time?"

"N-no." He got out. The cab departed.

The street, narrow but clear and clean, had scant traffic, pedestrian or vehicular. The bistro occupied part of the ground floor of a square masonry structure; the rest might be apartments, or might have uses more peculiar. A lightsign danced surrealistically above the door. He went in.

The chamber beyond was broad and long. Tables and chairs filled a splintery wooden floor. At the rear were a bar and cuisinier. The air lay blue-hazed. Among the reeks Kenmuir recognized tobacco and marijuana, guessed at opium and sniph. Customers sat at about half the tables, by themselves or in small groups. Synthesized music, at the moment tinkling not unlike a pi pa, wove beneath a buzz of talk. A live waiter bore a tray of drinks. Kenmuir hadn't seen a dive like this in years. Downright medieval.

He tapped his informant for the time. 2032. Half an hour to go, if Norton was punctual. He took a place off to one side but not so obscure that she'd have to search for him. The agent in San Francisco would have recorded his eidophone image and played it for her.

The waiter delivered his order and came over. He was a metamorph himself, a Titan, his shaggy head 250 centimeters up into the smoke, the body and limbs bole-thick to support his weight. Upon such a mass, shabby tunic and trousers were somehow pathetic. One had better not pity him, though, Kenmuir thought; he could pluck an ordinary man apart. Had the management lately engaged him to stop violence, or had he stood by while that fellow was beaten last year? "What's for you?" he rumbled.

"Uh, beer," Kenmuir said. "Sun Brew, if you have it." Most establishments did, and it was drinkable.

"Cash."

"What? Oh, uh, yes." Kenmuir fumbled in his pouch and brought out a ten-ucu note. It had lain there for quite a while, but the fabric still showed startlingly clean against this tabletop. The waiter nodded and went off. The floor creaked to his tread.

Kenmuir looked around. Although he wasn't the sole standard human here, this certainly was a hangout for metamorphs. Several Tinies chattered shrilly. A party of Drylanders held likewise to themselves. A Chemo talked with two Aquatics, who huddled unhappily in garments that the water tanks on their backs kept moist. Why had they come so far from the sea? Was the Chemo, easily breathing this tainted atmosphere, taking advantage of their discomfort to work some swindle? ... The impression of poverty was not universal. It was surprising how sumptuously dressed four Chimpos were, and what a meal they were tucking into. Yet they didn't seem joyous either. ... The saddest sight was perhaps a bulge-headed Intellect, playing a game of heisenberg against a computer. He'd have had to make it employ a low enough level of competence that he stood a chance.

"Hola, amigo."

The throaty trill brought Kenmuir's attention around. Another metamorph had come to his table, a female Exotic. Otter-slim save for hips and breasts, attired in a string of beads and her sleek brown fur, she smiled at him with great yellow eyes and sharp teeth. Her plumy tail arched up above the delicate features and tumbling black mane, seductively sinuous. "Are you lonesome?" she murmured. "I am Rrienna."

"No, thank you," he said clumsily.

"No-o-o? A handsome man like you shouldn't sit all alone. You must have come here for something."

"Well, I—"

"I don't think you'd care to meet a Priapic. It could be arranged if you want, but—" She leaned close. Through the smoke he scented her musk.

"No! I'm, I'm waiting for somebody."

She straightened. "Muy bien, I only thought I'd ask."

"I'm sorry." How lame that sounded. "Good luck."

She undulated off. He caught a snatch of what she sang under her breath,

> *"Gin a body meet a body*
> *Coming through the rye—"*

and then she was out of earshot, half lost again in the haze.

Ruination, he *was* sorry. These poor creatures, living fossils, victims of regimes long since down in the dust with Caligula, Tamerlane, Tchaka, Stalin, Zeyd—genomes modified for purposes of science, industry, war, pleasure—why did they go on, begetting generation after hopeless generation?

Lunarians were metamorphs too.

Why did Terrans go on, when sophotects did everything better?

Except being human.

He had wondered if those opposing presences and examples might be the underlying reason why few of his species had ever made radical changes in themselves. Technologically it was quite possible. A person might almost casually shift body form, sex, temperament, anything. But no real demand existed, and therefore the means did not, and whoever did wish for transformation must do without. Could the sheer blind instinct for survival make people, metamorphs included, hold fast to the identities they had? Societies had likewise never become as different from what the past had known as he could imagine them having done. Were they also both driven and bound by a biological heritage that went back to the prehuman?

The waiter interrupted his reverie by bringing his beer. He paid and gulped it.

"Buenas tardes, Captain Kenmuir."

He looked up. The heart thuttered between his ribs.

"I am Irene Norton," the woman said in a musical, young-sounding contralto. Otherwise she was undistinguished, pale face, shoulder-length brown hair. Of average height, she muffled her shape in a slit poncho and wide-bottomed slacks. That wasn't uncommon, but he didn't suppose she intended stylishness.

He half rose. She waved him back. "May I join you?" she asked. When she took a chair, the motion was lithe.

"D-do you care for a drink?" he stammered.

She gave a steady look out of a visage held expressionless. "No, gracias. This is simply a, a convenient place to meet."

"No eavesdroppers?" What an idiotic question.

She shook her head. "And I know the neighborhood and those who live in it, a little. Let's not waste time. We'll have to go somewhere else for serious talking, but first—" She leaned forward. Her arms came out of the poncho to rest on the table. "Has anything unusual, anything at all, happened to you on this expedition?"

"Why, uh, well—" He barked a laugh. "The whole business is unusual, isn't it?"

"I mean, have you noticed something that could suggest, oh, you're being watched?"

It came to him with a start. He should have seen earlier, when she first gestured. The hands and wrists before him were well-formed, strong, and . . . golden-brown. That was a life mask on her head.

She should have been more thorough about her disguise, or more careful in her movements. And she spoke almost as hesitantly as he. No professional, then. Another amateur, maybe just as bewildered and anxious? What was driving her?

The sense of equal responsibility braced him. He saw what a funk he had been in, and how much it was due to feeling like a pawn—he who had taken a boat down through a gravel storm, on his own decision, to rescue five men stranded on a cometary nucleus.

"I don't know," he said slowly. "Let me think." He did, aloud, while he stared into his beer mug or sipped from it. "If Lilisaire is under suspicion and monitored, they could know she called me back from space. Have you been told about that? And of course they'd know I visited her at the castle. I took the regular shuttle from Port Bowen to Kenyatta. Somebody could have ridden with me or called ahead and had somebody else waiting to trail me. But—I'm no expert at this, you understand. However, she and I had discussed my procedure at length. When I rented a volant at Kenyatta, I debited the account of an Earthside agent of hers. I left it in a part of Scotland I know, with instructions to return home next day, and went on foot about thirty kilometers across uninhabited Highland preserve to where another volant was waiting for me. That had been arranged by messenger or quantum-coded transmission, I'm not sure which, but in either case it ought to have been secure. I saw no sign of anyone else, and cloud cover—which had been forecast—hampered satellite surveillance, if they were zealous enough to order that. In Lake Superior Hub I changed vehicles again, and proceeded to a resort community on Vancouver Island, where I made a local call to Guthrie House and arranged an appointment with the Rydberg. I phoned San Francisco from there. The Rydberg told me it was safe, and I do believe it would take a special operation to tap that line. Today, according to the orders I got, I flew here without incident."

He raised his glance. His grin was wry. "I should think," he said, "if they considered making the kind of effort needed to track me through all that, they'd have done better to arrest me on suspicion and interrogate. Simpler and cheaper."

The life mask barely frowned. She wasn't practiced in using one. *"I* think," she said, "that they may be more clever. Lilisaire's agent warned me a very high-powered agent had come to see her, Lilisaire, in person."

"Yes, she told—"

Urgency cut across his words: "Search your memory. Has anything happened, no matter how trivial it seems, anything you can't quite explain?"

A slight shudder passed through him. He pushed his mind back into time. Nothing, nothing. . . . Wait.

"Not really, but—Well, when I first landed on the Moon and her man met me, our flight was delayed about an hour because of an accident in orbit."

"What happened?" Beneath the poncho, she crouched.

"Nothing. We were taken to the executive lounge and given a drink while we waited. Then we were let go."

"A drink. And you never mentioned this to Lilisaire?"

"I don't remember. Maybe, maybe not. With everything else to talk about—"

"Pele!" She sprang to her feet. "Come on!"

"What?"

"Āwīwī!" She grabbed his hand and tugged. "I could be wrong, b-but I'm afraid I'm not. Come *on!"*

Numbly, he obeyed. They threaded among the tables, rearward. The waiter loomed in front of them. Norton gave him a few rapid words in a language Kenmuir didn't recognize. His massive countenance turning grim, he stepped aside and waved them to go ahead.

"I picked this place to meet because I know it," Norton said in a voice slurred by haste. "I picked a time after dark because we might need darkness. Now, if we hurry, if we're lucky, we may—Here."

They had passed through a hinged door to a storeroom. She swung another such door aside. A stairway descended into murk. She touched a switchplate, feeble fluorescence glimmered forth, she drew Kenmuir along and shut the door behind them. They started downward.

But he was no criminal, he protested silently, wildly. He had done nothing unlawful, nothing to make him a fugitive. Why was he in flight? Only this morning he'd been conversing with Matthias over breakfast. The lodgemaster had admitted, grudgingly, that Lunarians might after all be the best hope of humans for getting to the stars, or even of humans becoming less than totally dependent on sophotectic intelligences—if that was desirable. . . . It seemed impossibly long ago, another age, well-nigh as lost to him as the lifetime of the first Rydberg.

14

The Mother of the Moon

Homebound from Jupiter, the *Caroline Herschel* passed within naked-eye range of L-5. Nevertheless the gigantic cylinder gleamed tiny athwart space, half in light, half in darkness, its tapered ends pointed at the stars, jewel-exquisite. Firefly sparks flitted about it, spacecraft, machines. Earth and Luna were crescents to sunward, large and small, opalescent and ashen.

"We should have arrived a few months later," Eva Jannicki said. "We might have inaugurated the dock and drunk liters of free champagne." Though the orbital colony was an East Asian, mainly Japanese project, Fireball was inevitably a full partner and would dominate its commerce.

"I think our people will always gather mostly on Luna, when they do not on Earth," Lars Rydberg replied. "That is where our traditions have struck root."

"Oh, you!" The little full-figured woman gave the tall rawboned man a look of comic despair. Blue eyes returned her glance, from beneath cropped yellow hair and above jutting nose and lantern jaw. "That was a joke. I hoped you might know. Three times in these past four months I saw you smile. Once I distinctly heard you laugh. I thought my efforts were finally bearing fruit."

"You exaggerate, my dear, as usual." Rydberg's lips turned upward, ruefully. "But maybe not much. I fear we Swedes are like the English of legend. If you want to make us happy in our old age, tell us a funny story when we are young."

"There, you see, you can, if you try. Besides, you told me you aren't Swedish by ancestry."

He looked from her, out the port to the sky. His tone harshened. "That was a mistake. I should not have. Could you please forget it?"

Silence fell, making the ventilators sound loud. The two who manned *Herschel* floated adrift in it, weightless, while the ship moved on trajectory toward the point where final maneuvers were to commence. At this point in its cycle, air renewal had increased the ozone; there was a slight odor as of thunderstorm.

Jannicki reached to touch Rydberg's sleeve. "I'm sorry," she said low. "I didn't mean to offend you. Especially now, of all times."

He faced her anew. "You did not," he replied with some difficulty. "I should apologize for snapping at you. You touched a nerve, but you could not know, it was not your fault."

"Well, you've never talked much about yourself," she agreed. "And nerves do wear thin," during fifteen weeks with hardly anything to do but maintain health in the centrifuge, read, watch recorded shows, listen to recorded music, and pursue what other recreations are possible in free fall. "Our sheer uselessness—"

"No. We could have had an emergency, something the ship could not cope with alone. And before then—" Outbound eagerness, study, preparation. Supplies and support borne to Himalia Base. Participation, helping explore and prospect the outer moons, sharing in the telepresence when humans directed robots through the radiation rain upon the Galileans and into the king planet itself. The knowledge that this remoteness and unknownness required humans, were they to find and understand and someday make use of the stark wonders around them. Rydberg pondered. "Again I apologize. Memories ran away with me. It's another bad habit of mine, repeating the obvious."

She smiled. "I forgive you."

"Really?"

"That has perforce become one of my habits."

"Amazing, that you have not cut my throat."

"Oh, I probably lack a perfection or two myself. Were you never tempted to cut mine?"

"Of course not. Quite apart from the mess and the legal consequences, what a terrible waste."

"My feeling exactly." She paused. The lightened mood left her. "When the new ships replace these, when it's a few daycycles at one g to most destinations—"

"And the automation is so advanced that a single person is enough—Yes," he sighed. "I too will often miss the long voyages. But maybe before this comes to pass, we will be retired to planetside duty and living off our memories."

"Memories indeed."

"Indeed."

She fluttered her eyelashes. Her voice went husky. "We can still add to them, you know. Hours yet before we'll be wanted at the controls."

He smiled. "Now it is you speaking the obvious."

Together they kicked the bulkhead and soared aft.

When presently they rested at ease, harnessed against drift, otherwise in one another's arms and warmth and breath, she said, "Yes, the psych staff took a correct compatibility profile of us."

"I trust we will be teamed again, more than once," he replied in his solemn wise.

"I too. And as for our leave—You haven't told me, not really, how you plan to spend yours, aside from visiting your . . . parents . . . on Earth."

He stared before him at blank metal. "I am not sure. It depends."

"Nor am I sure. My ties are all Fireball, you know. I'll meet friends, doubtless make new ones, variety—" Her tone grew wistful. "But afterward, we two, a rendezvous?"

"I don't know," he repeated.

Being of a size for Luna if not Earth, *Herschel* was just a short while in parking orbit, then descended to Port Bowen. Since discussions had gone on beforehand by radio and a quick inspection showed everything apparently in order, her crew were soon finished at the office. As customary, they took separate quarters in the Hotel Aldrin—privacy, total privacy, any time they wanted!—but she was hurt when he declined to make straight for the Fuel Tank with her. He didn't notice. "I may join you later," he muttered, and hurried off to his room.

Alone, he put through a call to Geneva. Business hours obtained in Europe, and he got the live contact he wished. "Hold a moment," he said, and debited for quantum coding. "Now, please, what have you learned?"

When the detective told him, he whistled long and low and sat for a span mute, until he commanded, "This is to stay strictly confidential."

The reply after transmission lag came stiff. "Sir, you knew the reputation of our agency when you engaged us."

"Yes, of course." Fireball's were not the only people touchy about the outfits to which they belonged. Because that *was* where they belonged, far more than in their countries or any other part of an impersonal civilization? "No offense. You did an excellent job. Keep the file encrypted, please, till I can get to Earth and study it in detail." Not that that would likely make any difference. "After which, I suppose, I'll want it wiped and forgotten."

Having switched off, Rydberg jumped to his feet and paced, not Lunar-style paces but short, jerky steps as if to make the room feel larger than it was. Finally he observed the time and swore. Late duskwatch. Aside from police and the like, nobody administrative was at work. He couldn't very well call the Beynac home, could he?

No, wait, this might be for the best. The phone found the office number he wanted and made contact for him. An assistor responded. That wasn't necessarily fortunate. The machine might not be programmed with the flexibility to consider his request and decide. However, this one was. It said the mayor could receive him at 1530 tomorrow. It even scanned the transport database and advised him about schedules.

Well, he'd heard that the incumbent ran things in free and easy fashion. From what he'd also heard, if his business wasn't worth her attention, he wouldn't last but a few minutes.

And if it was—considering what it was—he'd meet that when the hour came, and endure whatever he must.

Meanwhile he had an obligation. Honoring it would

be a distraction for his mind, a balm for his heart. The call to Stockholm found both Sten and Linnea Rydberg. The old couple had inquired when he was due and stayed in their place waiting. Their joy made his eyes sting. It was hard to tell them, *"Nej, ack, jag vet ej*—No, I'm sorry, I don't know when I can come. I must see to something here first. I will come as soon as possible. I promise."* He meant it, though he did not know what "possible" was going to mean.

His room had become a cage. He considered the pub. Eva Jannicki was getting an uproarious welcome there. Why not he? No. Ordinarily he was happy among comrades, but tonight he'd have to force it, boosted by alcohol or cannabis or levitane. Experiments in youth had left him with a dislike of intoxication.

He went instead to the public gymnasium. Nobody else was using the springball court. That suited him well. Its robot gave him a game that left him pleasantly tired. After a shower and a light supper in a cafeteria, he slept better than he had expected.

In dawnwatch he boarded the monorail to Tychopolis. The system was newly completed, and in spite of regathering tension he enjoyed this, his first ride. Not simply faster than the semitrain, it was spacious and comfortable, its ports affording a sublime view. By day, when Earth was narrowed to a sickle and stars flooded out of vision, the heavens were not a sight to hold you unmoving for hours, certainly nothing comparable to what he had beheld near Mars, Jupiter, Saturn; yet his glance kept returning. The satellites he had lately betrodden had no real landscapes. They were too small; their stoniness toppled away. Here he looked across plains and up heights, here he spied energy dishes like triumphal monuments.

A fellow passenger struck up a conversation which Rydberg found himself likewise enjoying. The man was a tourist, but intelligent, an ecological engineer fresh from an aquacultural project south of Greenland. Though he worried about the troubles in the Near East and Africa and hoped they wouldn't erupt into full war, mainly he was indignant. Damned fanatics, delaying the reclamation of a continent and a half!

"Did you follow the news, out Jupiter way?" he asked.

"When we could," Rydberg said. "We would cluster around the screen—they still do, I am sure—each time the beam brought a 'cast, if we were on hand. We do have kinfolk and friends on Earth. But mostly we were elsewhere, or too busy. It came to seem distant, half unreal. We felt ashamed of that."

"You needn't have. I'd be a spacer myself if I'd had a chance when I was young. The future is here."

Rydberg wondered. How much of humankind would ever live off Earth? Aside from science and industry, how much would it ever mean?

He reached Tychopolis in ample time to get lodging and lunch. Appetite was lacking, though. He prowled the city. Everywhere he found activity, growth, ongoing improvement. It wasn't all government's or Fireball's. Three arcaded levels of businesses lined Tsiolkovsky Prospect. A doorscreen advertised that *King Lear* would be performed within, live. The ballet had acquired a theater of its own. Apartments in residential sections were being remodeled to suit their tenants, who often held title. Other units had evidently become places of worship, Christian, Jewish, Muslim, Buddhist, Hindu, Shinto, Gaian. A Cinco de Mayo picnic filled the bamboo grove of Kaifungfu Park with music and merriment.

Among the crowds passed the Lunarians, the new generation, in their late teens or younger, comely, graceful, and apart.

Rydberg's hour drew nigh. He entered city hall.

Those three or four rented rooms in the Fireball Complex hardly rated the name. Municipal government had no more authority than the nations had jointly chosen to allow it, essentially the overseeing of

services. That thought raised a brief smile on his lips.
What had been delegated was most of what touched
the lives of the Moon's inhabitants.

Human workers were few. They went about their
duties informally. The assistor in the mayor's office
scanned Rydberg, heard his name, and opened the
inner door for him. He passed through. The chamber
beyond was uncluttered. A large desk held a phone, a
computer terminal, and some personal items—a picture, a chunk of deep-blue mineral, a notepad
bescribbled and bedoodled. Background music lilted
soft from a speaker; Rydberg recognized "Appalachi-
an Spring."

The woman behind the desk met his gaze steadily.
He had seen her before on newscasts, her image in
articles and books. The person had the force that he
had awaited, but also a balance, a quiet alertness that
somehow slowed his heartbeat for him.

Dagny Beynac in her forties had put a little more
flesh on the big bones, but only a little. The face,
broad, curve-nosed, high in the cheeks, remained
fair-skinned, slightly creased at the blue eyes and full
mouth. White threads were like highlights in the
red-bronze hair that fell to her shoulders. She wore a
plain gray tunic and slacks, a silver-and-opal pin at
her throat.

"Pilot Rydberg?" Her voice was more low than
when she spoke in public, the burr more evident.
"Salud. What can I do for you?"

Unconsciously, he came to attention. "I don't
know," he said.

The ruddy brows lifted. "What do you mean by
that?"

He was faintly astonished at how levelly he too
spoke. "I am your son, madame."

The elevator to the centrifuge was for the disabled or
lazy. He and she used the staircase that wound around
its shaft. Most of the numerous people they encountered knew and greeted her. She gave back a smile, a

wave, perhaps a word, while moving onward. Rydberg didn't see how she managed it. He'd have used up his stock of affability in the first hundred meters.

In form as well as in size, this machine was as unlike the devices in a spacecraft or on the surface of a low-*g* body as those two kinds were unlike one another. At the bottom of the shaft, you stepped onto a narrow band, then more in series, each rotating more rapidly than the last. Cuddlers were available to cushion acceleration shock, but an accustomed person of normal agility didn't need them. However, when you reached the primary disc, you must get onto a pathway as it went by, and then you did well to lay hold of its right or left rail.

Silent on maglev, the great wheel endlessly turned, burnished, majestic, beneath a ceiling that was a single screen and simulated an Earth sky, clouds blowing white across blue, birds on the wing. Given such a mass, precise balancing was unnecessary. As you walked outward, centrifugal weight changed in force and direction. Spiraling, the path canted to stay under your feet, until at last you got to the flange and Earth weight. Almost perpendicular to the Lunar horizontal, it bore a wide circular roadway, paved with yielding duramoss. Folk crowded the walking lane, spaced themselves more carefully in the running lane, did stationary aerobics or weight lifting in the frequent bays. On the opposite side of the path, compartments ringed the disc. From the center you saw their continuous roof, here you saw their doors. Anybody could use the open circle at any time, but one of these you must reserve and pay for.

"I often bring somebody to a whirly booth for a private conference," Beynac had said. "Might as well get in some *g*-time while making sure of no interruptions." She laughed. "If today they notice me sequester myself with a good-looking young man, why, *envieuse soit qui mal y pense.*"

Yet earlier, briefly, she had been more shaken than he was. He didn't think he could have mastered his emotions so fast, nor donned such a cheerful manner. Impassivity was his defense.

The crowd moved spinwise, to gain a little extra drag. He and she wove their way along until they came to the Number Nineteen bespoken. They went in and shut the door behind them. The interior, ventilated, lighted, held a couch, a screened-off toilet and washbasin, and a scrap of carpeted floor space.

Beynac cast herself against Rydberg and clung. He felt how she shuddered. "Oh, God, God," she stammered at his breast. "You. I never dared dream—" He embraced her. The realization came that this was why she had hurried him off, minutes after he arrived. It had bewildered him. Did she mean to question him, flay him open, learn whether he was an impostor and what he wanted from her? Instead, through his blouse he felt tears.

"Mother," he said in awe.

After a while: "Have I done wrong? Maybe this hurts you, a ghost that should stay in its grave. Then I beg you forgive me. I will leave here and never speak a word to anyone, ever."

"No. Don't. Please. Lars—" She let go, stepped back a little, smiled up at him, still within his arms. The smile trembled, tears glimmered in lashes and on skin, but she cried no more and began to breathe evenly. "Lars," she whispered. "What a pretty name. Pretty, but masculine. I'm glad they gave you it."

"My foster parents were always good to me," he said.

"I knew they'd be. Anson Guthrie picked them. He never told me more, though, and I f-figured he knew best, he and his wife."

"They did. You had your life to make. I asked myself over and over if it was right I track you down. I still know not."

"It was. I am so happy. I thought, yes, over and over about trying to find you, but was afraid it might do harm somehow. You've settled it for me. Thank you, dearest."

She disengaged, ran a hand across her face, and gusted a sigh. "Smash! What a mess I must be. 'Scuse a mo'." She disappeared into the wash section. He stood in his own enchantment.

She emerged neatened, self-possessed, radiant. "Hoy, don't look that earnest," she chided with a grin. "Sit down and let's talk. We've got, what is it, twenty-six years' worth of talking to catch up on."

"We can hardly do that today."

She cocked her red head at him. "Okay, I'll consider you as having finished your 'Goo-goo' and 'Wa-a-ah!' and we'll get straight to business. *Mon Dieu,* you are a sobersides, aren't you?"

She settled at the right end of the couch. He thought she must understand how shy he felt, and took the left side, leaving a meter or more between them. She twisted about, shin under opposite knee, arm along the back, to face him. He kept both feet on the floor and leaned on his palm to regard her.

"You have the advantage of me," she said. "I know your name and that you're a space pilot for Fireball. And my first-born. Period."

"You do not know that, except for my word," he answered. "I had better prove it. I have not the evidence with me, but you can easily trace my path from what I tell."

"Easier than that. I'll ask Uncle Anson." She gave Rydberg a close look. "M-m, but I see you're anxious to establish your bona fides. Methodical type. Okay, let's get it out of the way. How did you find me?"

To relate it brought further calm. "My foster parents are Swedish. Far—Father—he was an engineer, his wife taught school, before they retired. They were childless and middle-aged when they adopted me. They made no secret of that, but said they had me from an agency that did not tell them anything about my, my biological parents, because this is wisest. They told the truth there, I have learned, except for not mentioning that Anson Guthrie was involved. Perhaps he bribed someone in the agency."

Beynac chuckled. "Very likely. In the government too, I wouldn't be surprised. Go on."

"I think, now, Far and Mor suspected this but were never sure and decided they had better not inquire. He was in a firm that had several times done Earthside work for Fireball, such as enlarging the Australian spaceport, and he had met Guthrie in the course of it. A few times afterward, over the years, Guthrie paid us short visits. That was when he simply happened to be in Sweden. Or so he said. At last I began to wonder. Why should he, a mighty man in the world, countless claims on his attention, why should he remember us? He was no snob, I knew; he had friends in every walk of life; but these far-apart social calls were not such a relationship. And . . . when I applied to Fireball, I was admitted for training, although hundreds of those who were turned away must have been at least as qualified.

"Therefore, when I decided to try learning who my real parents were—I have not told Far and Mor, they would be hurt—*jo*, it was natural to seek a clue in Guthrie. I gave the job to a detective agency, but it was not very difficult. Most of what trouble they had was due to the chaotic conditions in North America, which was where the trail led. A public figure like Guthrie, his whereabouts are always a news item, at least potentially. Afterward the information will lie forgotten in a journalistic database for decades, no reason to wipe it. I knew my year of birth, since I was adopted out immediately, and the birthday we celebrated for me must be approximately correct. Since I was almost certainly illegitimate—Forgive me, M-mother—"

Beynac reached to pat Rydberg's hand. "Quite all right, you wonderful bastard."

"Uh-hm! Where was Guthrie and what did he do in the nine months previous? It turned out that six months earlier than that, the local news in a small Pacific Northwest town called Aberdeen reported that once again the community was honored by the distinguished presence of Mr. and Mrs. Anson Guthrie, who were visiting their friends Mr. and Mrs. Sigurd Ebbesen. A detective on site jogged various people's memories, consulted the database further, and learned that Miss Dagny Ebbesen moved at that time to Quito, Ecuador, under the tutelage of the Guthries, where she was to receive a first-class education in the Fireball school before being offered employment in the company. There was no record in Ecuador of her giving birth, but it would have been easy for them to conceal, and investigation showed she did not enroll in the school until months after she left Aberdeen. The probability seemed high, and your career was a matter of public record. In fact, you are rather famous; I have long heard of you."

The dry, rapid recital jerked to a halt. Rydberg's glance had turned from Beynac while he spoke. He sat staring at the wall.

"Were you surprised?" she asked mildly.

"Well," he said, "I thought . . . if my mother was a protégée of the Guthries . . . she would not live in poverty. Otherwise I had no idea about her."

"Many children fantasize about real parents who are far more glamorous and important than those they know. I'm afraid I can't live up to that."

His head swung back toward her. His right hand clenched on his thigh, the left grabbed at the edge of the couch. "I don't want anything from you!" he cried. "I don't need anything! I'm well off!"

She lifted a palm. "Easy, dear," she said low. "I didn't mean what you suppose. If you're a space pilot, sure, you're highly paid, and your share in the company is appreciating like an avalanche. Nor did I imagine for one second you've come sucking after preferment or special privilege. Credit me with that much insight."

"I am sorry," he said, contrite. "I am clumsy with words. Will you forgive me?"

"Nothing to forgive, darling. You're pretty well ashiver. Think I'm not? What I meant was just that I'm nothing extraordinary. A wife and mother. Former engineer. They asked me to take over some administrative chores. That was *faute de mieux,* but gradually the administrating crowded out the engineering. It involved me in politics, because somebody had to speak up for the ordinary resident, buck the assorted governments, try to get taxes and regulations held in some relationship to reality. So now, for my sins, I'm serving a term as mayor here, and I'm afraid there'll be another term or two before I can locate a suitable successor who can't run fast enough. That's all."

"That . . . is plenty, . . . I would say."

"Your life is bound to have been much more interesting."

"I doubt that."

"Tell me about it."

"And I am not a very interesting person," he said doggedly.

"I'll be the judge of that, if you please." Beynac shifted position, leaned back, crossed her legs, an attitude that invited easiness.

He found his tongue moving more readily as he talked. "Well, you have heard the basic facts. I was raised as a Swede. We traveled, I saw a good deal of Earth, but I was always . . . starstruck. I wanted out, as the North Americans say, and at age eighteen I was admitted to Fireball's academy. My talent and wish were for piloting, and it has become my work. I have flown both regular and exploratory missions, and am newly back from Jupiter."

"And you call yourself dull. Huh! How about your Earthside life? Married? I lust to start having grandkids."

"No," he replied harshly. "I was, for three years. It ended."

Her tone went like a hand that stroked his hair.

"Didn't intend to pry. I won't discuss anything you'd rather not, nor investigate it. A promise." After a moment: "Pilots are dreadful marriage risks. Everybody knows it. She must have been a brave and loving girl."

"She deserved better. I hope she will find it."

"Drop that remorsefulness, will you? Switching back—again, not to pry, but—you said you were starstruck, but you must have been too smart not to know the hazards and sacrifices and miseries of space, as well as the glamour; and you've described a pleasant life on Earth, by no means boring. You could have gone into a career that would soon provide you the money to taste space as a tourist. I mean the kind of tourist who trains for it till he can have real experiences. Nevertheless, you say you wanted out. Why? What was wrong?"

"I—I felt, well, cramped, restricted."

"Really? I remember Anson Guthrie remarking once that when he was young, Sweden was what he called a nanny state, but it got rid of that and nowadays people there are more free than in most countries, including North America. Which is obviously one reason why he placed you where he did."

"True. Still, everywhere on Earth—everywhere fit to live in—you have a feeling that everything is settled, everything important has been done, anything truly new can only make us uncomfortable. And that, what is the word, that smarmy Neoromantic movement, claiming to bring back traditions that for hundreds of years have existed only in books, if they ever existed at all—it made me gag. In space they are not afraid of newness and greatness. They have their customs, their genuine traditions, and those are growing, they serve a purpose, they *live*."

Beynac nodded. "I realize it wasn't anywhere near as simple as that, and probably your motives never were clear to you and never will be, but I see your drift." With a smile: "I also see you are not a bore. I'll bet in your teens your age mates found you an intolerable, stiff-necked nonconformist."

After a silence she went on, carefully, "I do need to ask what made you search me out. It was not idle curiosity."

"No," he said. "It was that same feeling of rootlessness, of belonging to nothing and nobody. Yes, I am fond of my foster parents, but in every other way I have grown apart from them."

"I know how they feel," she said half under her breath.

He decided not to pursue that. "Fireball is my real family now, as for so many of us. And yet, maybe it is that I have not quite matured out of a lonely adolescence, yet there was this emptiness in me. It made no sense, but I could not fill it. At last I thought that if I could learn who my true parents were, where and what I came from, it might make healing. But I did not want to disturb them. Simply knowing who you are, meeting you this once, that is a miracle."

"You don't have to go away, Lars," Beynac told him. "You won't, if I can help it."

After another moment she went on: "You don't seem to have identified your biological father. His name was William Thurshaw. It was a summer's love affair, wild and beautiful and of course impossible. I resisted having an abortion, and the Guthries saved me and you as you know. That was because—no. Maybe someday I can tell you.

"Bill was a gifted boy. That was maybe the main thing that drew me to him. He was also gallant and caring, and he went on to become the same sort of man. We never heard from each other again, but Guthrie told me this much. Now that I can tell what to look for, yes, I see a lot of Bill in you. And I think in your spirit, too."

Her tone hardened. "He could have gotten into Fireball like me and later you, no doubt, but chose differently. Two years ago, Guthrie told me he was dead. You must know how the Renewal is getting more frantic, more ruthless, as the country goes to pieces beneath it. Bill spoke too freely in defense of freedom. He was killed 'resisting arrest,' the police reported."

"I am sorry," was all Rydberg could find to say.

Beynac's voice gentled. "For me, he wasn't much more than a dream I'd had. I cried a little. My husband held me close and made the world good again. I am very happily married, Lars. But you can be proud of your father."

She took Rydberg's hand. They sat thus for a space.

"I am glad you are happy," he said at last. "I must not threaten it. I will go. Today has been more than enough."

"No!" she exclaimed. "Bloody hell, no! You stay!"

"But your husband, your children—"

She regained control. "Please. I can't just let you orbit back into the swarm and think no more about it. Not that I'll lay any claims on you, either. Can't we get to know each other, though?"

"At your home? I would feel like an invader."

"Don't." Her laugh wavered a bit. "Oh, Edmond will be taken aback at first, but not badly, and he'll recover fast. He's so absolutely a man, you see. The children will just be interested, not deeply nor for long, I'm sure; about like a cat when a visitor arrives. That's all.

"Lars, I love those children with my whole heart, but you are the only one of mine who's completely human."

15

Westward the lake sheened blue, reaching like a sea
off beyond the horizon. A few last shreds of dawn-mist
smoked across its quietness. A waning Moon floated
pale above several islands. Eastward the shore stood
boldly and the sun filled intensely green highlands
with shadows. Musoma town lifted white at the
mouth of its bay. Three pelicans and a heron passed
overhead. The air lay cool and hushed, with an odor of
fish that would become strong later in the day.

A boat drifted some distance out. Two men sat at
ease in it, facing one another. Lines trailed from the
rods in their hands.

"A lovely morning," Charles Jomo said conversa-
tionally.

"Yes," Venator agreed. His body could savor it as
well as any other human's could. Nevertheless the
hunter stirred within him. "But will we ever get a
bite?"

They were speaking Anglo. Jomo wanted to practice
his. Venator had not admitted to his knowledge of any
languages current hereabouts. Capabilities were best
kept in reserve till needed, and surprise was a potent
weapon.

"Oh, yes," Jomo said. "The fish here behave differently from the fish in the shallows. Designed for sport.
You shall have your excitement, I promise you. Meanwhile, patience. We have the whole day." He was a
gray-haired, deep-brown man with a comfortable
paunch. Like his companion, he wore only a tunic.
Sunburn was no hazard to either of them.

Venator repeated earlier politeness: "It's very kind
of you to take this much for an outsider." If the fellow
knew what kind of outsider! he thought sardonically.

Jomo chuckled. "The professional guide you would

otherwise have engaged may have a different opinion."

Venator reckoned he should pretend a bit of concern. "I'm sorry. That didn't occur to me."

"Not to worry. He's not desperate for ucus. Who is?"

"I have known some."

"Ambitious types." Jomo's tone grew interested. "And wouldn't you say—isn't it the same in your home territory?—the hard workers are not after extra purchasing power so much as fame or personal satisfaction or something else emotional? How important are material goods and services when everyone receives basic credit?"

Good, Venator thought. He had hoped to draw his acquaintance out. Educated, philosophically inclined persons, who were active in the affairs of their societies, were apt to reveal the most. Occasional perceptions they gave him had been startling.

Not to them. Nor did he show his reaction. That would have defeated his purpose. It wasn't just that a synnoiont was too awesome a figure for casual talk to be possible, it was that a synnoiont grew too remote from common humanity. A police officer needed to understand people, in their endless variousness as individuals and as cultures. Whenever he could escape the demands upon him and the desires within him, Venator forced himself to return incognito to his species.

Jomo hadn't said anything extraordinary thus far. However, if nothing else, he probably typified the attitude of local residents toward many aspects of their existence. It wasn't likely to be identical with the attitudes of Australians or Brazilians or even southern Africans.

Keep this going. "Some work hard because the kind of thing they do requires it," Venator pointed out. "Professional athletes. Certain artists. Spacefarers," such few as were left, mostly in Lunarian employ. "Et cetera."

Jomo nodded. "That's what they choose to do. What I said. Personal satisfaction, prestige, the approval of one's peers."

"M-m, you don't impress me as either a lazy man or one greatly concerned with status."

"Few of us hereabouts are lazy. It's frowned on. But neither are we fanatic strivers. We take our leisure. For example, my mediation practice. The cases aren't many or deadly serious. I can generally set them aside when I've a better way to spend a day, like this expedition."

"Do you mean most of you have jobs? Are there enough to go around?"

"Many occupations are unpaid, private pursuits or public service."

"Yours, if I may ask?"

"I'm on the municipal recreation committee, with emphasis on children's activities." Of course, Venator thought. Children were always special, as few as they were, here too, here too. "I garden. I'm studying Kikuyu, to experience the ancient compositions in the original."

Archaism seemed popular throughout Africa, Venator reflected. Was that precisely because most of the continent was so well adjusted to the modern world? Or did it go deeper, was it a quest for something lost, forgotten, yet inwardly felt? When tribalism, the whole primitive heritage, perished in the Dieback, it had enabled the old Protectorate to lay a firm foundation for a new and rational life—but did a rootlessness linger and hurt after all these centuries, like ghost-pain from an amputated limb in eras before medical regeneration?

No, that was absurd, totally unscientific.

But the human mind had its own dark mathematics, which was not that of logic or causality. It was chaotic.

His task was to hold chaos at bay.

Jomo's voice drew him from his momentary reverie. "What about you, Mr. Mthembu?"

The name with which Venator was born frequently served him as an alias. He made a smile. "Currently I am on holiday, you know," he replied. But forever observing. "And I've told you I do liaison work with the cybercosm."

"That covers an extremely wide field. Your position—"

Venator sensed the buzz in his breast pocket more through his skin than his ears. Emergency? Alertness went electric along his nerves. He raised a hand. "Excuse me. I seem to have a call."

Jomo looked with curiosity at the little disc he took out. It wasn't the usual miniphone. Nor was it limited to the usual functions. Venator laid it against his head behind the right ear.

"Report on subject Kenmuir," he heard by bone conduction.

Outwardly he sat relaxed, flicking his fishing rod. The float danced; quicksilver droplets arced off the water. Inside, he had become entirely hunter. Beneath the machine lucidity of consciousness, blood throbbed.

"Proceed," he subvocalized. For added caution, he used the generated language that was a high secret of his corps.

"We have lost contact with the subject. Apparently he has been taken into a well-screened section by an opposition agent, who doubtless plans to remove him from the vicinity."

We was a misrendition, but so would *I* have been. The pronoun referred to those aspects of an awareness that, mutably as occasion required, devoted themselves to this business; and the awareness itself was a changeable part of a vastly larger whole. Ripples upon waves upon an ocean.

"H'ng!" escaped Venator. Jomo gave him a quizzical glance. "Summarize for me." He had last been in touch three days ago. It was pointless—counterproductive, in fact—to monitor an operation hour by hour when nothing untoward was happening. That

was what high-level robots were for. He had plenty
else to engage him. This stop at Victoria Nyanza
was only half a respite. Word still came in, sporadi-
cally, from half a dozen different, ongoing investi-
gations.

"Kenmuir left Guthrie House today, American
Pacific time, and flew to Los Angeles. It seems clear,
now, that while in the house he made a call on a secure
line and got further instructions."

"Yes, yes. I rather expected that." It was unnecessary to say, the sophotect knew it quite well, but
Venator didn't waste energy suppressing every ape
impulse in himself.

There hadn't been time to penetrate that line. The
Fireball Trothdom had had centuries in which to
develop its private channels and vaults. A wariness of
government that went back to Fireball Enterprises
had led it to keep those defenses up to date. Venator
hadn't worried. The odds were enormous that Matthias would give Kenmuir nothing. What most plausibly
mattered was what Kenmuir did next. Still, it could be
worthwhile to study the Rydberg. . . .

Kenmuir had disappeared. *That* mattered. "Go
on," Venator directed.

"In Los Angeles he went to an obscure cantina. A
woman using the name Irene Norton met him. Their
conversation was brief before she hastily conducted
him off."

"Replay it."

When he had heard: "Tell me about this meeting
place."

And afterward: "Obviously she suspects he's been
implanted—anticipated the possibility, and chose
that rendezvous because she knew of just such a
bolthole as she's taken him into. That may give clues
to her identity. She's quick-witted and has had some
experience, but didn't sound to me like a professional
at this."

"A datascan shows that she cannot be any of the

persons registered under the name Irene Norton. It is an alias. Orders?"

"Sweep-surveillance of the area. It may find them fairly soon. Kenmuir has to surface sometime. He may even turn himself in. He's dubious about the whole affair. Meanwhile start inquiries at that Asilo den. Discreet, tactful. It doesn't impress me as having a staff or a clientele overly friendly to us. Still, detectives may learn who this woman really is."

"Yes, pragmatic. Further orders?"

"Inform me immediately of any new developments. I will be on my way to Central to take full charge."

Venator pocketed the disc. Sky, water, sunlight, breeze crowded in on him.

"I hope that wasn't bad news," Jomo said slowly.

"Emergency," Venator answered. "Work-related. I'm not free to say more, and I'm afraid I must leave at once."

"Pity." Jomo reeled in his line while his visitor did the same. "Come back again."

"I hope to." It was peace and sanity like this that Venator fought to preserve.

Incidentally to the main purpose, to the cosmic meaning of his life.

Jomo started the motor. The boat skimmed shoreward.

This wasn't really a dire situation, Venator deemed. Not yet. Probably not ever. What could two fugitives do?

It was plain that Fireball knew nothing about Proserpina. Otherwise the truth would have come out long ago—irresistible, to spirits that still yearned after the stars. The arcanum on which the Rydbergs brooded so dragonlike must be some trivial piece of long-irrelevant history, if it was that much: on a par with the unpublished diary of an ancestor.

Lilisaire, intensely researching, had found indications of a mystery in deep space. She thought the object of it might, barely possibly, give her power to block the Habitat, or actually break Luna free of the Federation.

It could do nothing of the kind, of course. It threatened far worse.

But those data that survived were well safeguarded. Venator himself had not been granted an access code—and it biological—until the cybercosm had concluded that Lilisaire's activities were disturbing enough that he had a need to know. How could two amateurs tell where to begin looking, let alone how to break in?

No, they were not important in themselves. They were leads to Lilisaire and her underground—clever, dangerous Lilisaire.

(Assassination? Difficult, maybe infeasible, disastrous if an attempt failed. Besides, she might well leave word behind her, and others carry on. Arrest? On what charges, with what repercussions? Wait a while. Play the game. It was good to have a really challenging opponent.)

Nonetheless, because they were walking clues, Kenmuir and Norton must be captured. And there were loose ends elsewhere, securities to make secure. For that, communication facilities here were ridiculously inadequate. He would return to Central.

To oneness. The knowledge pierced him like love.

The reasoning brain went on in its work. It was vital to take back control over events, now, before they got out of hand, before crisis led to crisis as in the distant past.

16

The Mother of the Moon

The room in Port Bowen was overlarge for two persons, but Dagny Beynac appreciated the courtesy of a meeting there rather than in an office. It softened a little the fact that she had been summoned. Likewise did spaciousness, the sheer expanse of carpet. A conference table stood offside, with a console for data and communications in the adjacent wall. Of the several free armchairs, at each of the two that were in use an end table bore a cup and teapot.

The governor general for the Lunar Authority had given the chamber a personal touch as well. A big viewscreen played a recorded scene, houses on precipitous green mountainsides, the Chiangjing flowing majestic between. Opposite hung a scroll. Its black-and-white picture was of an old man in a robe, seated, probably a sage. Did its calligraphy embalm a poem?

The attendant who brought the tea bowed and left. He was young, in hard condition, his civilian clothing suggestive of a uniform. Dagny suspected he was secret service. The door slid shut behind him. For a moment she heard silence.

"Please be seated," Zhao Haifeng said. His English came fluent, in a choppy accent and high voice. He was tall, gaunt, white-haired, austerely clad. "Does tobacco annoy you?"

"No, go ahead," Dagny replied. She refrained from expressing a hope that his cancer shots were current. If Luna must have a proconsul, he could be worse than this former professor of sociodynamics. Or so she supposed. Today might change her opinion.

They took their seats. Zhao brought forth a cigarette, touched his lighter ring to it, inhaled, streamed smoke from his nostrils. Dagny wondered if he was as tense as she was. A hint of acridity reached her.

Ventilation sensors took note and it blew away on a piny breeze.

"You were most kind to come in person," Zhao said. "I know how busy you are."

"Your Excellency's . . . request . . . was somewhat pressing," Dagny answered.

"Quite apart from the security of communication lines," the governor explained, "I am archaic enough to find a holographic image an inadequate substitute for flesh-and-blood presence, when matters of grave import are to be discussed."

Also, Dagny thought, her coming to him was a symbol, an act of submission. Did he expect it to quell her, however subtly? When she called Anson Guthrie about the demand, the jefe had grinned and said, "The lamb requires the she-wolf to visit him." But that was a jape. Behind the Confucian façade, this was no sheep whom she faced.

"Can we do that?" she asked. "You realize I no longer have any official standing of any kind."

Zhao lifted a palm. "Please, Madame Beynac. We are in privacy. You know full well that in some respects you have more power on Luna than I do."

Draw him out. "How? I was the Tycho Region delegate to the Coordinating Committee. That's all."

"You were elected its chairman—" Zhao inclined his head "—by which it did itself honor." He pulled hard on his cigarette. "Let us not continue the public charade. Time is as valuable to you as to me. The Committee lives on in the hearts of the colonists. It is what saw them through the anarchic years. Most of its former members have close ties to Fireball Enterprises, which has become unhealthily dominant in space." Dagny bridled inwardly but let that pass. "The Lunar Authority is new, unwelcomed by many, often perceived as irrelevant to their real concerns, or as a burden. My duty is to improve this situation."

Surprised despite herself, Dagny murmured, "Your Excellency is very frank."

Zhao smiled. *Entre nous, madame.*

Since hearing from him, she had prepared her thoughts and words as best she was able. "But may I then say you exaggerate? The Committee was never more than *ad hoc,* formed because we were getting one emergency after another and somebody had to take charge." Her mind completed the sentence: Take charge, when the Grand Jihad erupted across Earth, an interwoven economy collapsed in country after country, revolutions and lawlessness ripped whole societies asunder, the brittle old United Nations broke into shards, nobody on the planet had serious attention to spare for a few tens of thousands on the Moon. "Fireball helped, yes. You might even say it saved us. But it didn't take over government. It couldn't have."

"At any rate," said Zhao dryly, "it chose not to. Perhaps that was because M. Guthrie foresaw that you Selenites would perforce set aside the conflicting fragments of national authority and establish your own."

"Señor, you know we never meant the Committee to be permanent. Didn't we cooperate in full with you and your people after you arrived?"

"You did not resist."

"We're as glad to have a single law here as we are to have a World Federation and a Peace Authority on Earth." In principle, Dagny thought. In practice, it depended on how that law read. "Anyway, to get back to the subject, you've dissolved the Committee."

"I am not certain it was wise to do that so soon." Zhao lifted his teacup. "However, such was the decision in Hiroshima."

Dagny sipped likewise. The fluid went hot and flowery over her tongue. "I can understand their reasons. It's hard enough settling what national autonomy is going to amount to, without adding the germ of a whole new nation."

"And thus we come to the present exigency," Zhao said. "You Selenites are scarcely in a position to threaten anyone else—not that I accuse you of wishing to. But if you set an example of defiance, a successful example, which virulent nationalists on Earth can make into a precedent, that could open the gates to new horror. Consider, for example, how many people will perish miserably if the African Protectorate is overthrown." He sighed. "The Federation needs time to gain strength, to take firm root, before it is severely tested."

Temptation beckoned. "Meanwhile," Dagny snapped, "Luna's a nice, small, comfortably distant laboratory for trying out this or that theory of international governance."

At once she regretted her outburst. Relief brought warmth when he said merely, mildly, "Pray do not be bitter."

"Oh, I'm not," she made haste to answer. "Some among us are, true, but I do believe—yes, I am glad you wanted a meeting in person—I believe you mean well, señor." She spoke sincerely, within limits. His good intentions were not necessarily identical with hers.

"Thank you. Gracias." Zhao dropped his cigarette down the disposer in his table and reached for a replacement. "Then please help me." ·

"How? I'm nothing but a private citizen, these daycycles."

He measured out his sentences. "Your influence is global. The colonists respect you, they listen to you, as they do not my officials or me. Furthermore, you know what they want and, more important, what they need. After three years, I continue to be an outsider. Advise me. Support me—" he inhaled twice "—to the maximum extent your conscience permits. For my part, I promise that when you disagree with me, I will listen."

"Advise?" Dagny asked in astonishment. "Señor, anything I can tell you, you've heard a thousand times before."

Her mind leaped. She was here on account of her sons. If he offered her an opening, jump through it! "What do we on Luna want and need?" she said.

"Why, it's simple, obvious. For openers, removal of a lot of rules and restrictions left over from the former regimes. We thought we'd gotten rid of them, but then your Lunar Authority came in and declared nearly all were back in force."

"Those that have justification."

Boldness, short of insolence, might well be the safest course. "Such as?"

"Taxes paid to the respective governments on Earth. Yes, you Selenites complain that you do not receive commensurate services. Perhaps adjustments should be made. Nevertheless, the fact abides that without viable nations on Earth you would have no markets and indeed would not long survive. Consider that a service."

"We're self-sufficient by now in air, water, food, energy. We managed during the Jihad. We're looking spaceward."

Zhao stayed by his argument. "Furthermore, you have an obligation to humankind at large, the civilization from which you sprang and that is still your spiritual home."

"I don't dispute that myself," Dagny said with care.

"Certain people do. Above all—pardon me, I intend no offense—above all, in the younger generation, the metamorphs."

Dagny nodded. "They'd feel less alien if—less alienated if the educational requirements laid on them were better fitted to . . . their natures."

"Again, adjustments are possible," Zhao said. Sharply: "In fact, they are made. My office is not ignorant of what goes on in colonial households. More and more, that is where children learn their major lessons, from programs written at home and from their elders and their peers. True?"

"Yes. It's only right and natural."

Zhao frowned, drew on his cigarette, made a stabbing gesture with it. "Up to a point, madame. That alienation to which you admit must not evolve much further. It is taking an ugly, yes, dangerous turn."

Dagny had known the talk would come to this. Let her play for time, though, keep him among generalities a few minutes more while she marshalled her wits and will. "Not just the young are protesting," she said. "Many of us were doing it for years before the Jihad. The grievances are genuine, your Excellency."

He went along with her tactics. She wondered whether that was because it suited his. "I take it you refer principally to the regulation of Lunar industry?"

"Well, that's one thing. Enterprise feels stifled."

He raised his brows. "You colonists do not unanimously claim that this unique, scientifically and culturally priceless environment deserves no protection."

"Of course not." She thought of Edmond's rage at what might happen to various geological sites. She thought of what their son Temerir had to say about the astronomy he was newly entering; those few glacial words struck deeper than all his father's pyrotechnic profanity. "Just the same, it's time for some trade-offs," she said.

"We are not discussing a slight pollution of pristine near-vacuum, nor the damage mining can do to areas of interest, nor any other inevitabilities. What we touch on is whether they shall be kept within bounds." Zhao's gaze drilled at her. She forced herself to meet it. "Beyond this, we have the fundamental principle that the Solar System is the common heritage of humankind."

It was a shopworn retort, but she could find no better: "And therefore nobody outside of Earth may own any part of space."

"On the contrary, the concessions are generous. Perhaps too generous. Fireball has grown monstrously off much more than space transport. Many other companies and individuals have too."

"Yes." In her reluctant political career, Dagny had often needed to speak with more sonorousness than directness. The skill came back. "But no one among us may stand on a piece of land, even a piece of orbiting rock, and say, 'This is mine. I made it what it is. I bequeath it to my children and to their children.'"

"Strange," he murmured, "that so primitive a wish has been reborn in space."

"Primitive, or human? We're still the old Crô-Magnon." Edmond stood suddenly forth in her, waiting at home for her, hunter of the unknown, he whose folk had left their bones in the caves and valleys and up the steeps of his Dordogne since ice cliffs barred the North and mammoths walked the tundra. It was as if he spoke from her throat. "We still bear an instinct to possess our territories."

Quietly seated, soft in his voice, Zhao lashed out: *"We*, madame? Is the desire of the new generation, the generation created for Luna, that simple and straightforward? Can you tell me what they in their inmost beings want? Can you themselves?"

For a hundred heartbeats there was again silence in the room. Dagny's look strayed to the viewscreen. In the image a bird sailed past, a wisp of cloud blew across a rounded peak. It was beautiful. She wished it were of surf and sand and driftwood.

Returning her heed to Zhao, she said: "Muy bien. Let's get serious. You did not call me in because I'm a fairly big frog in this little dry puddle the Moon. No, I'm the mother of Brandir and Kaino."

"Of Anson and Sigurd Beynac, technically," he answered with the same restraint. "And of Gabrielle Beynac, who is perhaps more to be feared. I have studied Verdea's writings." Yes, Dagny thought, he did his homework. "They are not overtly subversive, no. Nothing so resistible. What they nourish is a new and foreign spirit."

"Is that bad?"

Was it? Did not every small and dear person grow at last into a stranger? And yet it was Lars Rydberg, when he visited, who set aside the bleak face he turned

on the world, to give her and, yes, 'Mond something of
himself, the warmth that came from feeling you were
wanted. Not her Lunarian children.

"Well, but this is not time for philosophical mus-
ings," Zhao said. "The fact on hand is that your two
older sons and their associates are in grave violation
of the law. My hope is that you can bring them to their
senses before something irrevocable happens. You
and your husband, of course. I did not invite him here
today because he has avoided politics, and because,
hm, a man of his temperament might have been
uncomfortable."

Might well have exploded, Dagny understood.

"Invite" was another cute word. "What exactly
have they done?" she demanded.

"Madame, you know. Everyone does."

"We've been in touch with them, their father and I,
briefly. We did not argue rights or wrongs." They
never did any longer. "And we've followed the newscasts." She must not go passive, she must keep the
initiative, make Zhao respond to her. "Por favor,
though, brief me on what you see the issues to be. We
can't talk sense before we've straightened out what
each of us is talking about."

He nodded. "As you wish. I am anxious to make
peace."

"Peace hasn't been breached, has it?"

"Not yet—openly—not quite. I cannot help speculating whether their aim is to force the Authority to
take the first unretraceable step." Zhao made an
understated production of drinking more tea. "Let me
show you a recorded presentation. I have not permitted its release thus far, because it could prove inflam-
matory."

"Good of you, your Excellency. Look, I don't want
trouble either. Nobody in their right mind does."

His glance hinted that that might not include the
young, the true Lunarians. What he said was, "Stipulated. This sequence was meant for transmission to
Peace Authority headquarters on Earth, as a three-

dimensional account of what happened. It was prepared by order of Chief of Constabulary Levine, under the direction of the officer who had been in command of the mission. Anticipating difficulties, he had had a continuous record kept. For purposes of clarity this has been edited and commentary added, but it remains objective and unbiased."

"Does any such thing exist where people are concerned?"

His smile flickered wry. "True, they would not interpret it in Hiroshima as your Selenites would. Therefore I have sequestered it. I have not decided whether to release it. Please try to see my dilemma."

He rose and went to the console. Dagny got up too and took a bounding low-*g* turn around the room. It darkened. The scene from China went out of the viewscreen. They moved their chairs to face that way and sat down again. She breathed deep and made her muscles ease, like undoing a row of knots.

A man's image appeared, uniformed, standing in a Spartanly functional studio. Lip movements showed he was not speaking the English that a translator program furnished: "Mohandas V. Sundaram, colonel, Peace Authority of the World Federation, reporting on an incident—" He went on to give date, hour, precise location, and then, in the same clipped voice, background.

"During the Grand Jihad and the chaotic period afterward, the effective government on Luna was a self-created Coordinating Committee." Unfair, Dagny thought. Colonial officers had agreed on the necessity, but the delegates were elected. Admittedly, several Earthside governments denounced the action, though they'd been in no position to do anything about it. "This confined itself to matters of public safety and essential services." What else could or should it have done? "Numerous colonists and associations of colonists took advantage of the situation to commence operations hitherto illegal, notably in extractive and manufacturing industries. Indeed, the

Committee turned a number of facilities over to them." Somebody had to operate the plants. "They used these not only to produce needed goods, but to make new capabilities for themselves." The multiplier effect, thrice powerful when you started with robotic and molecular technology.

The reflection flashed through Dagny: The Renewal had simply been an extremist faction on an Earth gone generally ideological. People everywhere had been apt to regard productivity the way the medieval Church regarded sex, as inherently sinful, destructive, to be engaged in no more than was required for the survival of the race. Anyway, such was the ideal, and ideals could also constrain the thinking of the majority who didn't really live by them. Wherefore people on the Moon must conform. And Fireball folk, who did not accept this, grew closer, more loyal, to each other than to an unfriendly society around them . . . like medieval Jews?

Her attention had wandered. She snatched it back: "—claims to 'administration' of large tracts were routinely franchised by the Committee. These franchises gave exclusive rights to exploitation, forbade trespass, and could be bought and sold. To all intents and purposes, they were the property rights in extra-terrestrial real estate that the United Nations had enjoined. The World Federation has affirmed the prohibition. The Lunar Authority must enforce it."

Again Dagny's focus drifted. Her Lunarian children were not altogether sundered from her. Anson/Brandir told of mighty works to be wrought, and for Sigurd/Kaino shipyards were among them, spaceships for him and his kind. . . .

"—most notorious case, in the Cordillera range. Pursuant to the governor general's declared policy, every effort was made to reach agreement." At least Sundaram did not cite those back-and-forth, multiply connecting calls and faxes, the pussyfooting, the bluster, the queries, the evasions, the temporizing, the thunderheads piling high with lightning in their caverns—but no, that was a wrong figure for these lands which had never known a wind. . . . "—at last ordered a mission to the area in dispute."

Abruptly the scene was there, pockmarked bare hills rising toward mountains dappled and gashed by shadows. The camera, inside one of two large vans, swung about until it looked back east. Earth stood at the waning quarter just above yonder horizon. The sun blazed at mid-morning. A road, little more than regolith smoothed and roughly graded, wound up over the kilometers toward this halting place. The camera swept through a half circle and came to rest, scanning out the front of its vehicle. The road went on until lost to sight amidst ruggedness. Here, though, an arch made of native rock bestrode it, filled by a gate of steel bars, shut. Dagny well remembered that portal. Brandir had taken her and Edmond through it when he showed them his realm and what he was building there.

That was four years ago. Since then the newscasts had now and then replayed satellite pictures. Like others on Luna, the complex grew swiftly and greatly. Its inhabitants and workers said very little about their doings within. Brandir's parents had learned not to ask him.

Four spacesuited forms stood before the gate. Slung at their shoulders, jutting above the lifepacks, were things with tubes. Behind the bars waited the car that had brought them, a moondodger, fast and agile.

The camera zoomed in on their helmeted heads. Three were unknown to Dagny. One was a man of her kind, bald, stocky, tough. Two were young, male and female, unmistakable metamorphs—Lunarians. The fourth, the leader, was her Kaino. His unruly red hair shouted against the dun rockscape.

"Greeting," came Sundaram's voice, machine-rendered into English. He identified himself. "I am in command of the inspection team you have been notified to expect."

"You were detected afar." Kaino's own English did

not ordinarily bear this strong an intonation of the language his breed used among themselves. "Greeting, and may your homefaring go well."

Another camera had been aimed at Sundaram in the control cabin of his vehicle. The presentation split in two, he on the left side of the screen, the Selenites on the right. Mostly the center of the latter was on Kaino, but sometimes it moved across his companions, as if to catch them in any sinful action. The two Lunarians poised panther-quiet, the terrestroid human shifted from foot to foot and scowled. Kaino himself gestured while he talked, as was his wont.

"Thank you," the colonel said stiffly. "I take it you will conduct us to the settlement. Shall we proceed?"

"Nay, we have but come to warn you against continuing."

"What?" Dagny suspected Sundaram registered more surprise than he felt.

"As you must know from highview, presently this road tunnels, dividing into several before any of them emerge. Belike you would lose the proper route."

"Not if we follow you."

Kaino grinned. "Ah, but you shall not. I said we came to give you a cautioning. Now we will turn about." He shrugged in the Earth manner. "You can drive around this gate, yes. It is a mere boundary marker. But you cannot match our speed."

"So you refuse to guide us?"

"We do, either to Zamok Vysoki or through it." The castle that was arising yonder was already spectacular, but Dagny knew that it must be the iceberg-tip of underground hugenesses, and they shielded against instruments.

"This is the constabulary of the Lunar Authority."

"And this is the domain of the lord Brandir and the lady Ivala, and I am his brother who speaks for them."

"'Domain,'" Sundaram said low. "That word tells a great deal about your attitude."

"We are not hostile, Colonel. Nay, let me urge that

you never thrust onward unguided. You know not the safe ways to fare. Satellite maps and inertial navigation reveal naught of the treacheries—rubble pits, crevasse skins, infall-broken screes that any disturbance may bring down in a landslide. For your sake, I pray that you turn about."

"Such hazards are exaggerated in . . . folklore."

"You seem more knowledgeable about this ancient world than us its dwellers."

"If we should come to grief, would you assist us?"

"We respect the law that makes abandonment a felony first class, but we cannot promise to be aware of your trouble or able to rescue you if we learn."

Sundaram paused before he rapped, "You break the law as you stand there. Those are weapons you carry, are they not?"

Kaino waved a hand. "Sporting devices," he replied airily.

"They look like none I have ever seen."

"Nay." Kaino donned seriousness. "Weapons are not supposed to be in space, true, save small arms for police purposes. During the troublous years, we thought it advisable to develop better models. We do not yet feel assured that those years are quite behind us. It seems well to stay practiced in arms. But never gladly will we fire upon living targets."

"So you say." The officer sat silent for a time. The broad forward port framed his head in blackness.

"Let me talk to your brother," he then said. "The . . . lord Brandir may be . . . realistic."

Kaino smiled. "You may call, certainly. If none respond, I will give you a code for his private quarters. I know not whether he is at the fasthold and willing to converse."

"He knows full well we are here," Sundaram said roughly. "How many hidden monitors do you have spotted around these parts?"

The presentation skimmed over the next few minutes. The connection had been made through a buried relay cable. A face appeared in the phone screen before Sundaram. In the screen that Dagny watched, it replaced the view of her son.

Ivala, who had been christened Stephana Tarnowski, was Lunarian-beautiful, as white of hue as Brandir but with amber hair that fell to her shoulders, the big oblique eyes hazel, the countenance narrow and thinly chiseled. Iridescence played over the garment that sheathed her slenderness. Behind her a giant orchid bloomed against a crimson drape. Dagny caught her breath. This was the mother of her and Edmond's grandson.

"Greeting," she almost sang. "The lord Brandir is absent—" was he? "—but he and I are as one."

Dagny admired Sundaram's quickly regained equilibrium. "You are the lady Ivala? My pleasure, madame, I trust." He named himself. "I am sure you realize what our mission is."

The woman nodded. "You would inspect throughout all installations and operations at Zamok Vysoki."

"Yes, exactly. Persons here at the gate are obstructing our passage. Please direct them to assist us."

Ivala's lips curved upward. "In our earlier conversations, we explicitly did not pledge collaboration."

Sundaram stiffened. "You are now required to, by warrant of the Lunar Authority."

"You bear a search warrant?" Laughter trilled. "Has the Authority recognized these lands as our freehold? I am delighted."

"Kindly do not play games, madame."

The timbre grew cold. "Then shall I, rather than use the word 'inspect,' say, 'Invade, interfere, imperil?' We assert our right to refrain from partaking."

"That is not a claim the courts will grant."

"Are you a judge advocate?" she gibed.

"I am an officer of the law, given a duty which I intend to carry out." Sundaram paused again. When he spoke once more, it was evenly. "If you have nothing illegal to hide, why do you put yourselves in violation like this? Let my group conduct its survey, and we may well recommend that you receive a concession to regularize your status."

The fluid features congealed. "Rape of privacy is a violation."

Sundaram frowned. "I do not understand."

"Nay, you would not, would you?"

"Do you—you people—do you positively refuse to cooperate? Would you actually resist?"

"Some questions are best left unanswered, Colonel," Ivala said.

Kaino's voice broke in: "Before we go further, I pray your heed. You inquired about our equipment. Wish you to see a demonstration?"

Sundaram started where he sat. "What's this?"

"A demonstration. Maychance it will interest you, a military man."

Sundaram made his visage a mask. "Yes," he said without tone. "It will, very much."

The view shifted outside. In kangaroo bounds, Kaino and his followers deployed. They unslung the things they carried and opened fire on the hillside. Silently, silently, an automatic rifle stitched pox across a bluff. Another blew chips off a boulder, set it rolling, whipped it on with slug after slug. A miniature rocket streaked forth, a flash erupted, dust fountained aloft from a new-made crater a meter wide. The fourth instrument woke and the scene dissolved in flashes and buzzes, scrambled electronics.

When it cleared and steadied, Kaino stood limned athwart the sky, gun in hand, flame-head thrown back, joyously laughing.

The view regained Sundaram and Ivala. The officer held himself expressionless. "Thank you," he said. "That was most interesting."

"I do not believe your service possesses anything similar," she purred.

"No. We did not foresee a need to develop infantry weapons for space. Until now."

"Now? Why, what you saw was naught save sport."

Sundaram gazed straight at the lovely image. "You do not threaten us?"

"Positively not." Her amicability went grave. "We do caution you."

"Against what?"

"Against the unforeseeable. Too easily can events break free of all bounds. Not so? Let me suggest, Colonel, that you consult with your superiors. Thereafter, fare you well." The face disappeared.

Zhao rose and went over to blank the screen. He did not bring back the scene from home. "The rest we need not play," he told Dagny. "You know what passed. After some debate, the team received orders to turn back."

She nodded.

He stood tall above her. "That was by my direct command," he said. "I do not wish to provoke hotheads."

She looked up at him. "I wonder if those aren't inhumanly cool heads," she replied. "But thank you, your Excellency. You are a wise man."

His smile flickered. "Thank you for that. In fact, I fumble my way ahead, like everyone else." Somberness: "You must agree I cannot let this defiance go ignored."

"What can you do about it?"

"I begin by appealing to you, madame. Those are your sons. You are highly regarded everywhere on the Moon. If you make them see reason, I will see to it that no charges are brought."

Dagny weighed out her words. "I asked, what *can* you do?"

"I beg pardon?"

"They'd no more hear me or my husband than grown, headstrong men ever heard their parents. Probably less."

Zhao sat down again opposite her. "I am not convinced of that. You are you."

"Gracias. But don't you be convinced, either, of what I might say to them. This does involve a basic principle." Dagny sighed. "Yes, I could wish they'd been more . . . tactful, politic. But they are what they are. Don't you see, that's the heart of the conflict. You're trying to make them into what they are not, what they cannot be."

"'One Law for the Lion and Ox is Oppression,'" Zhao recited.

Dagny gave him a questioning glance.

"Thus wrote the poet William Blake some centuries ago," he explained. Her respect for him waxed further. "But I am lawman for the oxen," he went on. "For poor, wounded Earth. Have you no compassion for us?"

Dagny shook herself. "You're not that dependent— Well, never mind. No, I don't want a showdown, let alone an armed clash. It'd be lunacy." She intended no humor. "I'm just telling you that to avoid it, you'll have to give more than you get. Not more than you can afford, though."

"I fear that to yield would provoke further encroachments. What then of the future?"

"We can't control it. The grand illusion, that human beings ever could."

He smiled anew, a bit. "Now it is you who quote. Anson Guthrie."

"Why not? Fireball's a vital factor too." She leaned forward. "Listen, please. You want me to use my good offices to make Brandir give in. Well, they aren't worth much for that end, and if they were, I might not employ them. However, I can and will use whatever influence I have with Guthrie. You've doubtless heard we're close friends. He in his turn will . . . think of something. A stable Luna is in Fireball's interest also. Besides, he wouldn't let a fire burn people up when he could put it out."

Zhao sat bolt upright. "Can he persuade them to obey the law?"

"I think maybe he and I between us can get them to compromise, if you can get the Federation policy makers to," Dagny replied. "I have in mind something like the Lunarians admitting Sundaram's team. Afterward, maybe they'll agree to stop two or three disapproved projects." She didn't mention that the inspectors might not find everything there was to find and that an undertaking halted could always be started afresh. "You, the Federation, would have to make a credible promise beforehand, of a concession giving them and others like them control of their territory."

Zhao bit his lip. "'Their' territory. Private property, *de facto* if not *de jure*. No, worse than that. A feudal domain. Those four at the gate were a detachment of what amounts to a private army. And what of those other Lunarians? Once the precedent is set, what will they seek?"

Dagny resisted a temptation to reach over and pat his hand. "Don't worry so. You'll never get uniformed Lunarian thugs parading around intimidating voters. They're no more interested in politics as we understand it than my cats are. That is, it affects them, they react to it, but it's not a game they really care to play."

"Cats." This time Zhao's smile came easier. "I keep parakeets myself."

Dagny smiled back. "I'd enjoy meeting them."

"You shall be welcome." His mouth lowered. "You, though, have cats."

She decided to push her luck. "Bueno, what about my proposal?"

"That you consult Guthrie? Yes, do. I could not prevent you in any case. Beyond that, we must see. At best, the details to hammer out will be stubborn and countless."

"Uh-huh. And surprises jumping up at us all along the way. Still, we can hope to build a launch pad for a peace effort, can't we?"

"I must think."

He was a sensible, kindly man, she thought. He would almost certainly come to admit the need for yielding ground while preserving forms. Probably he could persuade them on Earth. Of course, he'd retain his deep doubts. She did. What about those long-range consequences?

Unforeseeable. You could only deal with the future as it came at you.

17

In a storeroom underground, Kenmuir saw another door and started for it. "No, not there," Norton said. "That'll take you back to the street. Here." She pushed at a shelf loaded with containers. It must double as a switch, for a section of wall slid aside. A passage reached beyond, bare, bleakly lit, surfaced with dull-green spray plastic. He followed her in. She touched a second switch and the entrance closed behind them. Air hung chill and stagnant. It smelled dusty.

"Come on," she urged.

Doubt flared into rebellion. He stopped. "What is all this, anyhow?" he demanded.

"It's our way out. If my guess is right, we have to hope they'll assume you went the other way, screened somehow. But if we stay this close, detectors could spot us—motion, infrared, transmitted through the wall—and that'd be that. Let's go."

He shook his head. "I mean, what's this all about?"

She tugged at his arm. The grip was strong. *"Kahuhū,* move, you tonto! We may have only minutes."

He resisted. "Not so fast, I say. Who are we running from? What am I being hustled into, and why?"

She released him, clenched her fists at her sides, and drew a shaky breath. The expressionless pale face turned up toward his contrasted uncannily with the intensity of her voice. "Are you afraid this is some-

thing criminal? Listen. We're in the service of the lady
Lilisaire, aren't we? Has anyone accused her of any
wrongdoing?"

"Well, I—she—"

"You're thinking the Peace Authority wouldn't be
investigating her without a reason, aren't you? Bueno,
of course there's a reason. She's told you, hasn't she?
She wants to get the Habitat project stopped. Since
when has the Covenant of the Federation denied any
citizen of any member republic the right to have a
political opinion and work for it? Since when was it a
crime to search for information? So far, at least,
anything unlawful has been on the other side. Most
especially if I'm right about what they've done to you,
Kenmuir. Find out and then decide!"

"Do you mean—" He fumbled for words. This was
like a nightmare from which he could not rouse
himself. "A cabal inside the government—"

"I don't know," she said starkly. "If we hang
around here till they come after us, we never will
know. Now, I'm on my way. Come along or stay,
whichever, but don't anchor me."

Lilisaire. And action, almost any action was better
than standing in helpless bewilderment. It might even
be a civic duty to learn more and then, as opportunity
offered, report to the proper people . . . whoever
those might be. The woman was bounding off at a
vigorous jog trot. He overtook and accompanied her.

"Good," she said. "I figured you must be the right
sort, or you wouldn't have been picked for this."

Right sort for what?

The passage branched in a T. She took them to the
left. A short distance onward, it terminated. They
halted. The air went harsh through his nostrils. He felt
sweat trickle rank down his ribs, more than the run
warranted. "Wait here," she ordered.

Stubbornness returned. "Why?"

She sighed. "The tunnel is screened. I asked Juan,
the waiter, to call and have a screened car sent to this
end. I'll go upstairs and meet it. When it arrives, I'll

come back for you. If you make a dash, maybe you won't be detected. Regardless, with luck we should be gone before they can get here." She opened the exit, slipped through, and closed it on him.

He stood his ground, shivering. Questions whirled. Screens? Against what? "They?" And why chase him and not her?

She'd asked about anything unusual that happened on his journey. When he told her—Hold! He lifted his hands, as if to fend horror off. No, that couldn't be, mustn't be. The woman was delusionary. What nest of dements had he stumbled into, and why hadn't they gotten themselves cured long ago? But, but Lilisaire had engaged Norton. Hadn't she? Then Norton— Was Lilisaire above using dements for purposes no sane person would touch? No, he'd not think that, not of her. And Norton seemed competent, maybe terrifyingly so. . . .

She returned. A metallic fabric lay across one arm. Did he hear laughter seethe below the urgency of her tone? "It's here already. And it brought this for you. Good old Iscah. Sharp as a shark's tooth. Put it on."

He took the object from her and shook it out. A kind of gown with a coif unfolded, made of fine mesh in which nodules glittered against the dark shimmer. "Portable screening," Norton explained. "Nothing ought to pick you up now. And we'll go in an ordinary car, which won't register suspicious on any monitor. Iscah's got to have called somebody nearby who could dispatch it here pronto. He knows folks everywhere around town." The laughter rattled out, shrill for the contralto voice. He realized what stress she too was under.

He slipped the garment over his head. It hung loose and light, halfway down his shins. Chain mail, he thought: an anachronism no more weird than the rest of this night. Norton led him into an empty basement, up a stair to an empty room lighted only by what trickled through grimy windows. Vacant house, he guessed, reserved for an occasional hideaway or

bolthole—by whom? They went on into the street.
The vehicle parked there resembled the cab he had
taken, except for being nicked and battered in the
body, dingy inside. Opposite gloomed a tenement.
Two of its own windows shone, with a cold bluish
brightness. Kenmuir wondered who lived there.

Three firefly glints darted to and fro above the
roofs. Norton glanced at them. "The pursuit, maybe,
scouting for us," she said. "We're none too soon."

Would they scan Kenmuir's outfit and drop down to
check? He made haste to enter. Norton was right
behind. "Ready," she told the car, and it started off.
He twisted his neck to look backward. The fireflies
stayed aloft. At short notice, over unfamiliar territory,
no matter how well equipped, a squad couldn't instantly identify everything. It wasn't as if the
resources of the whole cybercosm were marshalled.
Relief billowed through him.

Should it? he wondered. Were he seen and seized,
would it actually be a rescue?

He slumped back, willing his pulse to slow down,
counting again his reasons for doing what he did.
Norton sat equally still beside him. Lights that they
passed flickered across her pseudo-face, then left it
once more in an uneasy dusk.

With an effort, he asked at last, "Where are we
bound?"

"To Iscah's laboratory, I suppose," she answered in
the same monotone. She addressed the car: "Is that
right?"

"I do not have that information, nor may I speak
the address," it responded.

She shrugged, turned toward Kenmuir, and said,
"All I could tell Juan was to call Iscah and tell him this
felt like an emergency, that I had a party with me who
might be radiating, and that we'd go to the place on
Pico in hopes he could send a screened carrier." Her
head drooped. "If we'd waited there till morning and
nothing came, I don't know what I'd have done." The

head lifted, the words regained a little color. "I'd have thought of something."

"Concealed doorways, screened tunnel, screened transport," he said slowly. "You're quite familiar with this, this underground, aren't you?"

"Not really." She regarded him a while before continuing. "I'm not in any illicit operation. Nor am I involved in a revolutionary movement or any such *pupule*—such nonsense. Nobody I know is. It's just that I work with metamorphs. Not here, mostly, but the work brings me here from time to time, and it's caused me to meet some of these people."

She paused. When she went on, her voice had more emotion in it. "The metamorphs of Earth . . . they've got a hard fate, you know. Prejudice, discrimination, and there's very little the state can do to help them because in fact they *don't* fit in. They can't. Think how the Lunarians, the lucky ones, don't."

Again she fell silent. He waited. A spacefarer grew good at waiting.

"They form their organizations, their societies— cultures, even, or the germs of cultures," she resumed presently. "Yes, part of what goes on is illegal, but any victims are usually other metamorphs, and often there are no victims, it's a matter of helping each other toward a life that suits the species better. Most of the different leaders are trying to work out a . . . commonalty, a way for all metamorphs to cooperate, openly and lawfully. It isn't easy, it's not progressed far, in the long run it may be impossible, but we have to try, don't we? That's what I've been involved in, on behalf of my people." He wondered if she was a changeling herself, beneath the mask. What breed? If not, how closely did she identify with one of those races, and which? "It's led me into odd byways, yes, I've been initiated into certain secrets, because I needed the information so I could go home and suggest to my people the best courses for them to steer. Don't ask me too much."

"I have to ask a few things," he rasped. "You, they, were very quick, very well prepared to react against . . . official actions. That doesn't sound like legality to me."

"I admitted some activities are covert," she replied. "We, the leaders I've dealt with, we hope to phase those out, but meanwhile we've got to collaborate with the—you can call them gang lords if you insist, but the fact is that their ordinary, decent followers trust them." After another stillness: "The gang wars have practically ended. And the outright persecutions and the mob attacks by straight-gene humans. But metamorph history remembers, and tells metamorphs to stay prepared."

Also, he thought, the maintenance of protections and of a communal structure was a strong moral factor by itself, giving cohesion, hope, meaning to life. Fireball—

Norton sank back. "Por favor, I'm wrung dry," she whispered. "Can we just rest a while?"

Compassion touched him. "Surely." His own bones seemed to go liquid.

The car drove on, kilometer after kilometer, mostly through darkness and ruin. After a while Kenmuir made himself stop looking at the time.

Norton sat leaned into her corner, eyes closed, maybe asleep. She had drawn the poncho close about her, revealing a shapely frame. Remarkable person, formidable, but he had an illogical sense of an inward vulnerability. Why was she engaged in this unhopeful cause? For the sake of her creatures, whichever they were? Hardly that alone. What had Lilisaire promised her?

What had Lilisaire really promised him?

—The stop jolted him from his inner darkness, back to the outer. Norton sat up. "I guess we've arrived," she said. Eagerness throbbed in the words. As the vehicle opened, she scrambled lithely out, all her energy regained. Young, Kenmuir decided. He himself felt stiff and chilled. Fifty-five wasn't old, not nowadays, but probably the years wore away the spirit as much as ever in the past. He followed her.

Sky-glow above walls told of a settlement not far off. No doubt the building before him tapped its utilities. Windows steel-shuttered, the brick façade appeared in good condition, as nearly as he could tell through the gloom, but its neighbors crumbled empty and one was a rubble heap. Iscah wanted isolation, did he?

Norton moved toward the door with a sudden hesitancy not due to the poor seeing. "I've never been here," she admitted. "I just met him once, at a . . . an organizational conference, and heard a little about what he does. Assorted technical jobs." For people who perhaps couldn't afford a regular service, or perhaps did not wish the work known, Kenmuir thought. "Carfax—Lilisaire's agent who briefed me mentioned him too, among possible contacts."

Yes, Kenmuir thought, the Wardress had more operatives on Earth than Norton, some of them likely more active than she. He had a strong impression that she was carrying out her first mission for the Lunarian, because she happened to be the best qualified for these special circumstances. Or because she was the most powerfully motivated? . . . The others, though, at least gathered what information they could, information of every sort that might conceivably someday prove useful. Much of it would concern the Heterosphere, where unregistered facilities and unconforming lives were many. . . .

The door swung back on hinges. Light spilled around the hulk of a female Titan. She gestured them to come inside, and closed the door behind them.

The entryroom seemed too small for her. But if you allowed for the stockiness demanded by the mass, she was a handsome woman, evidently of Near Eastern descent, neatly clad in blouse and trews. A knife at her hip, with knuckleduster haft, was the single disagreeable feature. When she spoke, the bass sounded educated and quite feminine: "Bienvenida, Señorita Tam and señor. I hope everything went well?"

Tam? Kenmuir shot a glance at Norton. Yes, she'd have given her right name to the waiter, else he'd never have cooperated. "As far as I can tell, we got clean away," she answered.

"Muy bien. Would you like to shed that coat, señor? The house is thoroughly screened and shielded." The Titan helped Kenmuir take the garment off while she added: "I am Soraya. Por favor, follow me." She laid the mesh across a chair and started down the hall, so soft-footed that the dry old floorboards made hardly a sound. He did feel them tremble.

At the end of the house, a modern door contracted. The chamber beyond also belonged to the present era, cluttered though it was. Several rooms must have been demolished to make this large a space. The ceiling shone white on shelves, cabinets, benches, consoles, apparatus of physics, chemistry, biology, medicine, computation, and things Kenmuir did not recognize. Despite ventilator grilles, the air kept a faint acridity, smells of what happened here. Something in the background ticked.

A man got up from a computer terminal. He was a Chemo, totally hairless, skin obsidian-black. The lean body, long skull and visage, pale eyes were nordic. He wore little more than a gray smock over a shirt and hose, but somehow he made it imperial. Yet he spoke quietly, in a rather high-pitched voice: "Buenas tardes, señorita and señor. Will you be seated?" He waved at tall stools. Clearly he did not mean to shake hands, bow, or otherwise salute. "Would you care for coffee?"

"Gracias, no," Norton said. "I'm too charged." She turned to Kenmuir. "You?"

"Nor I," he replied, truthfully enough. Something wet would have been rather welcome, as dry as his mouth had gone, but he didn't want to delay matters and wondered, besides, whether he could get anything past his gullet. The weariness in him had become a pulsing tension. Like Norton, he perched himself. Soraya loomed at their backs.

"I am Iscah." Facing them, the man folded his arms, leaned against a lab bench, and talked methodically. "I take it that you, señorita, are Alice Tam, known too as Aleka Kame. It is prudent to make sure. Would you remove your mask? Soraya will assist you."

Norton—no, Tam?—hesitated for an instant, then jerked a nod. "Might as well, I suppose." She accompanied the Titan on a labyrinthine course to a medical couch and counter.

"It is equally wise from your standpoint," Iscah remarked as she passed by. "If the pursuit inquires among patrons at the Asilo, it will obtain a description of you in your disguise. I assume it will find no reason to associate that with your real persona—" he grinned "—insofar as 'real' has meaning in this context."

"Oh, I'm Aleka, all right," she flung back over her shoulder. "Anyhow, I was the last time I looked." The forlorn attempt at a jest appealed to Kenmuir.

Iscah focused on him. "How shall I address you, señor?" he asked.

The spaceman considered. What the Q, he wasn't a character in a historical thriller on the multi, required to act mysterious. He snapped forth his name and profession. "And I'd like to know what this rigmarole is about," he added. The roughness surprised him. Not his normal style.

Iscah stayed cool. "We share that desire. Let us try to learn. What can you tell me of the situation, Captain?"

Kenmuir swallowed. What should he tell, in this den of grotesquerie?

"Go ahead," called the woman who tagged herself Aleka. "It's nothing to be ashamed of." After a moment: "And you won't proceed blindfold, will you, Iscah? Besides, I suspect having the facts spread around will upset those bastards."

In for a penny, in for a pound, thought Kenmuir, harking back to centuried texts that had beguiled daycycles in space. But—He smiled ruefully. "I'm afraid I have very little in that line," he said. Indeed, a few sentences delivered his tale. "In spite of Lilisaire's animus against the Federation, I had no idea its police were aware of me till Mamselle Nor—Tam hauled me off."

"'Animus,'" Iscah murmured. "I can like a man who uses words of that kind."

"I've no wish to become an outlaw, either," Kenmuir stated. "If the government is trying to stop this business, it must have a reason."

"Necessarily a good reason?" rumbled Soraya. She took instruments from a case.

"Let us first collect what further data we may," Iscah said. He walked off. "Over here, por favor."

Electronic equipment was ranked along one wall. Kenmuir knew the object Iscah first picked up, a magnetic field mapper. He couldn't see what it read as it was moved across his torso, and Iscah's midnight countenance had turned expressionless. Across the room, Soraya worked with a delicacy incredible for those gigantic hands, teasing the life mask skin free of Aleka's. You could do the job alone, and no doubt Aleka had donned it thus, but removal without help took a long time if you weren't to hurt the delicate organism.

Peculiar partnership, Kenmuir thought. Titan, gene-bred for strength and endurance, infantry to go where war machines could not; Chemo, hardy against radiation and pollution that would sicken or kill ordinary humans; both stemming from a few ancestors engineered to deal with things as long vanished as the governments and the fanaticisms that had ordered it. Beings obsolete, purposeless, except for what they could make of their lives by themselves. He could only guess at that. Plainly, Soraya was more than a bodyguard. Was Iscah more than a technician? Might they even be lovers? The idea seemed freakish at first, then touching, then tragic.

Various instruments had been busy about his person. Iscah laid the last of them down, stepped back, and nodded. "You were right, Señorita Tam," he said, still imperturbable. "He carries a spy."

The notion had barely skimmed over Kenmuir's mind. The utterance hit him like a fist. He snatched after breath. "No, impossible!" he cried. "How could anybody—no way—"

The ice-colored glance laid hold of his. "Let me explain," Iscah said. "The technique is not publicized, but a part of my business is to know such things. A conjoined set of molecular assemblers was slipped into you. You may think of it as a pseudo-virus. Obviously, the servitor in the lounge put it in the drink it gave you. A single drop of liquid would be ample to hold the nanomass involved. I would guess that the dropper was in a substituted finger. Did you later feel a trifle ill and fevered for a short while? . . . I thought so. The pseudo-virus was taking material from your bloodstream to multiply itself. When there were sufficient assemblers, they set to work, again using elements in your body, carbon, iron, calcium— I won't bore you with the list. The process was harmless *per se,* because the device they built masses less than a gram, neatly woven into your peritoneum near the diaphragm, and taps less than a microwatt from the metabolism of surrounding cells. Essentially, it is a circuit controlled by a simple computer with a hardwired program, although it does include a transponder for sonic-range vibrations."

"I didn't have those details," Aleka said. Her voice came muffled through the skin being pulled over her head. "I'd just seen reports of tracers planted in people or animals for study purposes, and Lilisaire's agent warned me it can be done clandestinely."

Yes, passed through Kenmuir. Lilisaire would think of that possibility. It was a trick she'd gladly play herself. "The, the thing can't radiate . . . enough for pickup at a distance . . . across background noise," he protested.

"No, no," Iscah replied. "What it does is to detect

an ordinary transmission line nearby—which means almost anywhere on Earth, you know—and tap in with a microsignal, an imposed modulation. Special equipment is necessary to recover, amplify, and interpret that weak an effect; but the cybercosm does not lack for special equipment. Hence it tracks your movements—through the air, too, since every vehicle must always be in contact with Traffic Control. And it conveys your speech. To listen in on what you hear, it has run a line up to the auditory canal—a submicroscopic thread, I assure you. Interruptions of the surveillance will be accidental and transitory, unless deliberately arranged as we have done for you."

Rage exploded in Kenmuir. Suddenly he believed he understood what it meant to be raped. Not that he'd said or done anything intimate these past days. Nevertheless!

Vaguely, he heard Iscah muse aloud: "I wonder whether the spy was able to eavesdrop on you inside Guthrie House. I have heard that that place is well screened, and you mentioned being lent a secure line when you called for further instructions. Presumably the number you called activated a shuntaround program as well. Still, I suggest you bear in mind the possibility that that agent of Lilisaire's is now compromised."

"It's a, a violation of my Covenant rights," Kenmuir choked. "I never consented. I'm going straight to the nearest ombud and—" He strangled on his words.

"And what?" asked Iscah sardonically. "Do you expect the miscreants will be found and punished? They are agents of the government, remember."

"Why? Why?"

"The secret's got to be that important," Aleka said. "Which means Lilisaire is right about the size of it."

Unmasked, she came over to the men. Kenmuir stared. She had doffed her poncho too, revealing a body hard-muscled beneath spectacular curves, clad in plain tunic and slacks. The features were nearly as arresting. It was as if every bloodline on Earth had flowed together, harmoniously and vibrantly. Anyone who paid for biosculp could have any face desired, of course, but he felt sure hers was natural. Only nature had the originality to create all the little irregularities and uniquenesses that brought it so alive.

"What are you going to do to get justice?" she challenged him.

Energy drained away. His shoulders stooped. "What can I do?" he mumbled. "I'm marked. A medic will have to dissect this thing out of me."

"That would take at least a day, probably more, in a clinic where they have healing enhancements," Iscah said. "I don't, and to go there would defeat the purpose. Fortunately, I can set up a resonator that will burn out the circuit by overloading it. No significant damage to you, as low as the power levels are. Any discomfort will be slight and brief. Later, when it is convenient, you can have your surgery. I do not think I would take the trouble. The remnants will be inert and unnoticeable."

Heartened, Kenmuir drew himself erect. "What then?"

"We'll talk about that," Aleka said. "You two will help us, won't you?"

Soraya rejoined them. "We certainly will," sounded above their heads like summer thunder.

"Why?" Kenmuir floundered.

Iscah gave a parched chuckle. "In due course I shall present the lady Lilisaire with a substantial bill."

"No, I mean—the risk—"

"We live with risk all our lives, here," Soraya said quietly. "I have a feeling this is a gamble more worth taking than most."

"Is it?" Kenmuir wondered. "What can you, your people, gain?"

"Maybe nothing. Maybe much. We'll see."

He looked from eyes to eyes. The fury had left him, unless as a coldness deep inside. He was confused, and a peaceable man, and the doubts were swarming afresh. "You can't have any notion of . . . over-throwing the Federation. You aren't dement. And I, I wouldn't go along. There may after all be a, an excellent reason to keep the secret."

"In that case," Aleka said, "they could have told you so like honest *po'e*. Plenty of information's not allowed loose, but everybody knows why. How to scramble a driver robot to make the vehicle crash onto a target, for instance. But no, they broke in on you, your perfectly legitimate inquiries, before you'd even begun them." She was still for a moment. The hidden ticking seemed louder than before. "I don't want anarchy either," she finished low. "But I believe we've run afoul of a criminal conspiracy."

"And we alone will oppose it?" he jeered.

She stepped close and caught both his hands. Hers were warm and firm; he felt small calluses. "Listen, I beg you. Maybe, somewhere along the line, we should go to the proper authorities. But who are they? What can we prove? That you were bugged . . . by someone who can't be traced. Someone well positioned to strike at us, though, and afterward bury the story in a subduction zone. We need more information before we surface. I think I know where and how to search for it. Come along with me that far, Kenmuir. You're a man, a free man. Come!"

Freedom, Lilisaire, and a regathering sense of outrage to avenge. If they had done this to him, what might they do to others? He cast his mind back across history, terror that could have been crushed when it was newly hatched but instead was let grow and grow. What had Burke said? "The only thing necessary for the triumph of evil is that good men do nothing." Something like that.

Was this actually evil that he had met? How could he tell, save by hunting the truth down? If he could. Aleka believed it was possible, and she was better informed than he was, and—

"Very well," he heard himself say, and saw joy blaze

up before him. "For a while, reserving my right to opt out when I choose."

—and, laughed a devil in his head, he was most infernally curious about this secret that went back to the dawn of Lilisaire's world.

18

The Mother of the Moon

Lars Rydberg had soon come to feel that when he visited his mother and stepfather he was at home, more than ever elsewhere, even with the old couple who gave him his upbringing and all their love. The Beynacs were spacefolk, Fireball folk. His missions that sundered him from them, so that they rarely and briefly met in the flesh, also bound him to them.

On this occasion the big viewscreen in their living room played a record from the Stockholm Archipelago. Sailing was his great pleasure on Earth. Waves danced and glittered among the islets; wind tossed the crowns of trees, sent clouds scudding across blue and boats heeling and dancing before it. Sound went soft, rush and whistle. The air cycle had been set for a tang of salt and sunlight to join the perfumes of Dagny's flowers. She wanted to gladden him. Today everybody needed that.

It had gone much as she hoped, from the moment she bade him welcome. True, his smiles came seldom, but he always was a solemn, undemonstrative sort. Now they sat with drinks, hearing him tell of his latest faring. Altogether the company numbered four. Jinann, her youngest, still lived here.

"—nothing special on the way out," he said. "The common long, lazy haul."

"But it was urgent, you told us," Jinann interrupted. "Why ran you not at one *g* the whole way?"

She was less educated about such matters than most

Moondwellers. Her interests were art, notably the jewelry work from which she was beginning to earn pretty well; and men, a series of stormy affairs; and, paradoxically, a search for truth and meaning. Withal, she was closest to her parents of that whole brood and most nearly Terrestrial in appearance—at twenty-four, not unlike the young Dagny Ebbesen.

Rydberg's look at her was discreet but unmistakably enjoyable. "With such a mass, the fuel cost would have been ridiculous for the time saved," he explained.

Dagny reminded herself that usage had changed of late. "Fuel" didn't mean simply antimatter, but also the reaction material it torched forth. Although superb capabilities were coming on line, she must remember, too, that it was taking a while, that the capital investment in older vessels couldn't just be spouted away—She was thinking in Guthrie's words. Pain stabbed.

She pulled her attention back to Rydberg: "—and we had constant full weight once we'd spun up the hull."

Jinann's eyes widened. As she sat straighter, her hair passed like a flame over the sight of clouds and water. "Eyach, a spider ship? Sheer beauty, they. I've sought to make a brooch in the form of one, a minimotor to turn it, but there lacked a universe around."

"Would you like to see ours?" Rydberg asked. Beneath his reserve, Dagny thought, he had more feel for people than he let on, or maybe than he knew. "If I'm going to show you my pictures, we can start there. It's a standard scan, you've seen the same kind a hundred times. But it is . . . cheerful."

"We could use some cheer, by damn," Edmond Beynac growled. He reached to close his hand around Dagny's.

"Hush," she murmured aside. Not to break the fragile mood in the room. Nonetheless his concern

lifted her heart. He felt the loss himself—who didn't?
—but he knew how deep it went in her.

Rydberg kept his tone dry: "A large spacecraft
routinely sends a bug to observe from outside,
supplementing her instruments and sensors, making
sure everything is in order."

Space did not forgive, Dagny thought. Memories
trooped down the years, her dead and they who had
come near dying.

Rydberg took a pocket databanker from his tunic
and activated the multiceiver screen. Before them
appeared what a tiny robot had recorded as it jetted
about. Distance-dwindled, the hull was a teardrop
amidst blackness and frost-cold stars; the four
fullerene cables, each extending a kilometer from its
waist, were gossamer, the pods at their ends were
glints. They turned like second hands on an antique
clock, measuring off time while they fell between the
planets.

"Wondrous," Jinann breathed.

Rydberg grinned a bit. "Less wondrous to live in."
He played a close view, synchronously rotating. A
man climbed downward, radially outward, by rungs
in the flexible airtube that lay alongside the cable. The
camera followed him to its pod, which he entered.
Another scene succeeded this, taken within the
cramped and crowded quarters. "Here I am." Limited
facilities for hobbies existed. Rydberg in image sat at
a workbench, using a variety of tools to hand-carve a
length of wood. The shot focused on his design,
intricately intertwining vines and leaves. "This will be
a frieze for an armoire I will make on Earth."

"Ah, for your home there?" Beynac asked.

"For the home I hope to have there." Rydberg
sighed. "I'm tired of apartments."

Yes, Dagny thought, he hadn't many years to go in
space. If you started young in that game, you ended it
half young. Never mind longevity meds, nor even the
robotics that made human slowness and frailty almost

irrelevant. Beyond a certain point, no biotechnology would compensate for cumulative radiation damage. Someday an electromagnetic screen would be perfected, to fend off cosmic rays and solar wind, but meanwhile they set their limits on careers. Fifty was the usual cutoff age, to assure a normal, healthy span afterward. Already, his silvering hair—

It meant less that 'Mond's was wholly grizzled, while hers stayed red because she made it, not so much in vanity as in defiance. They had spent most of their lives inside the Moon, far better protected.

Her heed went back to the scene. Whoever had been shooting it, doubtless by request, drew back for a longer view. An attractive woman came up behind Rydberg, leaned over to watch what he did, laid a hand on his shoulder. "Um, that is Leota Mannion from North America, one of the engineers we were conveying," he said a little quickly.

Dagny brightened. "Friendly sort," she observed.

Rydberg shifted his glance. "Well, on a lengthy mission—"

A prospective wife for him? He really should start having children soon. Especially being a spaceman. Dagny wasn't convinced that nanorepair could entirely fix mutated DNA. Not that she and 'Mond hadn't been getting grandchildren and didn't expect more— from Brandir and his two wives, Verdea and the Zarenn (once Jiang Xi) she'd wedded in an eerie ceremony, Kaino in his communal arrangement (though there you needed genetic analysis to be certain who'd fathered whom, and the members didn't seem to care), Temerir and his colleague Hylia (once Olga Vuolainen), maybe Fia and Jinann in future. . . . But Lars was the Earth human.

It'd be nice if he took a North American wife. Of course, more and more people in that country felt the constitutional republic wasn't coping with its problems. But you could move abroad if you had to. While Lars wasn't exactly young any more, neither was he too old to start afresh. Plenty of life ahead of him yet, an estimated seventy-five years if he followed his med program and didn't come to grief. . . .

Oh, if only Uncans had been born enough later for the treatments to take full hold and give him that much!

But then everything would have been different, Dagny would never have known him, in fact never have existed—

She blinked away tears and heard Jinann: "Do you truly thus and altogether shut yourselves away as you fare? Gives a journey no scope for samadhi?"

Youthful earnestness, Dagny thought. A slight, comforting smile touched her lips. Jinann had been a Buddhist, afterward a Cosmicist; now she wandered and mused on her own beneath the stars of Luna. Would she someday become a prophetess to her kind?

"We get a sufficiency of the universe on the job," Rydberg said. "Here is the far terminus of our voyage, out beyond the orbit of Saturn."

The camera had scanned a small comet. At first it was unimpressive, well-nigh ugly, a dark, rough lump against the galaxy's glory. When the edited sequence swept close, you realized with your senses as well as your mind that "small" meant something else in these depths, multiple billions of tonnes of rocks, frozen gases, and ice, ice. The view passed breathtakingly over a pitted surface to the clustered human works. What the robots had built for the engineers was not dwarfish either. Those buildings, machines, and tall frames would have stood out in any landscape.

The view steadied. Rydberg activated a pointer image to show where girders were buckled or skewed. "You see how the foundation gave way below the mass driver," he said: damage exceeding the repair capacity of the system or its machine attendants. "Probably you remember from newscasts that it was caused by a major quake, which the continued stress of reaction triggered."

Beynac snorted. "I told those bloody fools at the start, they should study the interior of the comet more thoroughly before they began. *Têtes de merde!*"

"Well, it was a judgment call, as Leota Mannion would say," Rydberg replied, mainly for Jinnan's benefit. "At its original distance, with few torchcraft then available, more investigation would have taken years of expensive time. Meanwhile its position would be getting less and less favorable, until the window of opportunity closed. The decision was to proceed on the basis of what appeared to be reasonably good knowledge, and get started nudging it sunward."

"I know, I know," Beynac grumbled. "If they had sent me and a few of my students out, we could have warned them."

How he would have reveled in that, Dagny thought. He'd solved too many of the Moon's riddles. He had scant taste for filling in details; more and more his field trips reminded her of a wildcat pacing its cage.

"Actually, as you also know, fail-safes were built in, and this mishap was not catastrophic," Rydberg said needlessly. "We got it fixed in time." *We.* Dagny was impatient to see the record of her son and his crew aiding the team. "It's bound back again for its new orbit," he finished.

"For its transfiguration," Jinann murmured.

Rydberg raised his brows. "Do you disapprove? Some people do," holding that comets should be left inviolate, to salute the sun with a flare of beauty. But this one would never have done that, Dagny thought. Never in eon after eon while it swung through the Kuiper Belt, out beyond Neptune and Pluto where Sol was merely the brightest among the stars.

Jinann shook her head. "Eyach, nay. I said 'transfiguration.'"

Into life. The thrill went through Dagny anew. Ice mined and brought to Luna, water, a harvest more abundant than any from the asteroids, the beginning of a lavishness that would at last bestow rivers, lakes, maybe an interior sea, upon habitation; and living things are mostly water.

She bore no pride more high than knowing she had been in the forefront of the battle for this, the call, the politics, the bargains and connivances, setbacks and despair and toilsome return, until the World Federation agreed that a wholly alive new world was worth paying for.

Not that she claimed too much honor. Without Fireball at their side, the Moondwellers would have been a handful of flies, to be brushed aside when they buzzed.

Her man spoke it for her, quietly: "We have Anson Guthrie to thank."

"Yes," she whispered.

Jinann's regard of the older three grew troubled. "What think you will happen now he is gone?" she asked. Lunarian soul or no, to her it must feel as if a great tree had fallen, leaving an emptiness in the sky.

It did not quite to Dagny. Maybe it would later. First she had her Uncans to mourn.

"Fireball will go on, have no fears," Rydberg assured. "We are lucky he didn't die before he agreed to be downloaded, but even without that, Fireball would keep his strength, his dream."

"Dreams can die," Jinann said, "and then the strength dies."

What was Guthrie's download, his ghost, like? Dagny dreaded the hour when she must meet it.

"We will see that they don't," Rydberg vowed. He turned toward Beynac and spoke with a briskness that Dagny knew guarded him against unleashing whatever grief was in him. "'Mond, earlier I promised you some interesting news."

The geologist was likewise glad to change the subject. "Yes?"

"While the repair work went on, naturally we mounted an intensive sky survey. The comet's new path would be different enough from what was origi-

nally planned that we must make sure there would be
no serious meteoroid impact. When the computer
analyzed the observations, it reported no such danger.
However, I had idle time, and I remembered your
ideas about asteroidal debris in far space. I programmed a search for indications that would otherwise have been ignored."

Beynac leaned forward. "Yes? What did you find?"

"Nothing picturesque. The reflection spectrum,
barely readable, as faint as it was, of an object that
standard theory does not believe ought to have the
orbit this one does. Excuse me, please, while I interrupt the show," said Rydberg to the others. He keyed
his databanker. The image from the comet gave way to
a band of dim lines, numbers below them indicating
wavelengths, and more numbers in columns. At the
bottom stood a listing of that which calculation had
distilled from the raw data.

Beynac peered, started half out of his chair, sank
back, and mumbled, *"Mon Dieu. Enfin, enfin."* After a
moment, into the air: "But it had to be. If I was right,
this must be. It was only that no one looked as hard as
they should. Too much else to search after."

A song for him erupted in Dagny. She seized his
hand.

"What means this?" Jinann inquired.

"It is a nickel-iron asteroid, at present about thirty
astronomical units from the sun," Rydberg told her.
"We don't yet have the figures to compute a very
accurate orbit, although I ran a probecraft to high
velocity and got a parallax. Roughly, perihelion is at
about five a.u., aphelion forty or fifty thousand—
ultra-cometary. The inclination to the ecliptic is forty-
three degrees."

The young woman was not ignorant of basic astronomy, no Moondweller was, and she had sometimes
heard her father talk about his heresy. "There should
be no such thing, should there?" she said.

"No, no, *rien là-bas*—nothing yonder but ice
dwarfs," Beynac answered, almost automatically, as if

he spoke in sleep or a daze. "According to the standard picture. I agree they are nonsense, notions of colonizing the comets. Too far apart, too little mineral buried too deep in ices. But this—" His voice trailed away. He stared before him and breathed heavily.

"It could not have originated that far out, especially in an orbit so skewed," Rydberg said to Jinann. He spoke awkwardly, unsure what she might already know, wishing neither to insult her nor exclude her. She gave him an amiable attention. Peripherally, Dagny admired how she could put on Earth-human femininity whenever she wanted to. "Your father's idea, I suppose you are aware, his idea from studying the distribution of asteroid types in the inner System —he thinks there was at least one more than the accepted ten original bodies between Mars and Jupiter, which collisions reduced to those we know." He gulped. "I thought the object we found might provide evidence."

Beynac's head swung toward them. How well Dagny knew him in that mood, his intellect aprowl after quarry to pounce upon. "I suspect those *eleven* began as three," he boomed. "From this body perhaps we may find out. But it is not the major one that was lost. It is too small. And such an orbit is unstable. In a few million years, the planets will change it radically. My large, dense asteroid, it was exiled much longer ago, early in the life of the Solar System. Else we would have more pieces like what you have found, Lars. No, yours was perturbed back inward, probably by a close encounter with a big comet. That suggests the large one is still out there somewhere, not lost to interstellar space after all but in a wide and canted orbit. Perhaps someday we can find it. First we go to this little fellow."

Rydberg shrugged. "I don't know when we can do that, if ever."

Beynac bristled. *"Hein?"* he barked.

Rydberg picked up his neglected beer, took a draught, collected his words. "The existing situation," he then said. "Guthrie would have underwritten an immediate expedition, but he was a dying man, and now he is dead. Everything is confusion while his download takes over, if his download can. Factions in Fireball maneuver for advantage. Politicians fish in our troubled waters. Oh, even in far space we got plenty of news on the beams, and on my way home I was thinking what it meant. Besides, the Alpha Centauri project engages most of Fireball's discretionary resources, and will until it is well under way."

As was right, Dagny thought. Was not a launch to Sol's neighbor star Uncans's memorial to Juliana, whose vision it had been? A flyby miniprobe, followed by a versatile little craft packed with molecular-level instructions for building the robots that would do the science on those planets—

"Meanwhile your asteroid recedes, each daycycle harder and more expensive to reach, until it may well be lost forever." Beynac's rumble ascended to a roar. He sprang to his feet. "No! Bloody hell, no!" He shook a fist aloft, bounded to the wall and back, stood glaring around.

"You can apply for a research grant," Rydberg began.

"We can agitate for it," Dagny said.

She was surprised when Jinann spoke. She had known the girl shared the bitterness of her brothers. "If we but had a ship of our own to go! Yet nay, never have they licensed us more than a few orbiters. Fear they we might smash down on Hiroshima?"

Well, how much did their parents know of anything in the breasts of Lunarian children?

"Getting approval would very likely take too long," Rydberg went on. "If nothing else, suitable robots are booked far in advance. That includes those not yet made and programmed. A human or two would have to go along in any event, to make the quick decisions when transmission lag is so great. I think you should first try if you can charter a vessel for a manned expedition. Fireball has three or four to spare, if you can pay."

A tingle went along Dagny's nerves. "Brandir has plenty of money these daycycles. We could ask him." For the honor, or the aggrandizement, of his house and of Luna, he might be willing to lay some out. And maybe for love of his father?

Rydberg, her Lars, said soberly, because he disliked dramatics, "Besides the scientists, a qualified crew would be necessary. I could arrange it, and be the captain myself. That is if this is possible at all, which I do not promise."

"And I will be the chief geologist," Beynac said.

They stared at him. "What?" Rydberg exclaimed and, "You have won enough, Dada," Jinann protested in a voice she had not used for well-nigh two decades.

Dagny sat mute, remembering certain verses.

> *What is a woman that you forsake her,*
> *And the hearth-fire and the home-acre,*
> *To go with the old grey Widow-maker?*

Standing above them, her 'Mond looked into her eyes and said, "Yes, I."

19

Wake up, man. Up! Time's a-wasting."

Dreams clung. Kenmuir struggled with them. They broke apart as he felt another quake. He opened his eyes. Aleka hunkered by the pallet, shaking his shoulder.

"C'mon, sleepyhead," she urged. "You've had a few hours. We've got heavy seas to weather."

He blinked. The shelter arched faintly mother-of-pearl, enclosing him in its small dome. The ground beneath was hard and cracked, the air hot and mummy-dry. Seas?

Memory returned. It felt almost like another dream, the long drive from Iscah's place through night, he and she silent, fitfully dozing, till they reached—here—and after a few mumbled words with somebody he stumbled into this refuge. She'd joined him, nearby lay her own mattress and bedding, but now she was on her feet and outrageously refreshed.

He peered at his informant. The hour was 1310. He tried to whistle, but was too thirsty. Bit by bit, he climbed erect. He barely managed to fold a blanket around his waist. Aleka laughed. "Good boy," she said. "You knew you could do it if you tried."

"What's the program?" he croaked.

"Lunch with the padre. Be intelligent, or at least polite. I've fairly well got him talked over, but he wants to meet you before he agrees to anything. Understandable." Aleka cocked her head and smiled. "All right, I'll have mercy and let you clean up." She turned, parted the doorflap, and disappeared from him.

Padre? he thought vaguely. Oh, yes. Between them, Aleka and the two metamorphs had decided to send him and her to a Drylander camp—communications available—and, yes, this particular tribe, or whatever the word was, were Biocatholics. He'd once seen a documentary on that sect. Its members were few, sparsely scattered, intensely religious—what other force could drive their way of life?—but by no means retrograde. He'd better make a good impression.

A curtain hung in front of a portable washstand and sanitor. He noted the outlets by which they could be attached to a water reclamation unit. Losses to anything but evaporation and accidental spills must be rare. No, perspiration surely dissipated a lot. As quickly as possible, he availed himself, ending with a washcloth over his face and body. A comb hung on a chain. His last dose of beard inhibitor wouldn't wear off for a while yet. The clothes into which he scrambled had gotten a little grubby, but there was no help for that.

Feeling more alive, he trod forth. The sun stood furious in a sky like blue metal. He could barely make out the waning, westering Moon. No wonder Aleka was in a hurry. They needed to make contact while it was still above this horizon. Relaying through stations on the ground could alert the system to them.

She took his arm. The touch was more cheering than it ought to be. "This way," she said. He accompanied her through the camp.

Hemispheres of varying size, according to how many occupied each, had been raised in an orderly array around a space left clear. Behind them, a transportable desalinator worked in a muddy remnant of the Salton Sea. Gray-white desolation stretched onward in that direction. Elsewhere, though, the land bore life, shrubs, cactus, gaunt trees, all growing widely apart in alkaline dust. Some, he knew, was native, but most was metamorphic, designed to thrive under these conditions and produce food, fiber, fuel, pharmaceuticals. He spied individuals out there, afoot or on minicycles, inspecting, tending, applying the equipment that harvested the products. Vehicles not in use stood parked offside, half a dozen trucks, two volants, four rugged cars besides the one that had brought him and Aleka.

Heat-shimmer blurred the distances. The air lay full of harsh aromas.

"Hola," greeted a passerby courteously.

"Uh, buenos días," Kenmuir responded. Or was that correct? He wasn't a North American.

The man was a typical Drylander, thin, black-haired, yellowish-brown complexion, broad face, slit eyes, aquiline nose. A hooded white robe draped proudly over the huge buttocks. Such women as Kenmuir saw were similarly clad and even more steatopygous. In children the water-hoarding cells were less developed. People moved quietly, with an innate dignity, saying little. Not many were around.

The temperature didn't bother them, but those that weren't out in the field were generally busy in the shelters. A group recital in sweet treble voices, from a large dome, told that a part of the activity was schooling.

The open space, common ground for meetings and for sociability after sunset, had four lamps on its perimeter. At the center, a crucifix lifted three meters tall. The cross was carved to represent a leafing tree, and the Christ was—not exactly metamorphic, but he had a suggestion of the alien about him—Startled, Kenmuir realized that he looked almost Lunarian.

That might not have been intended, the spaceman thought, but the underlying idea certainly was. A faith that sought to expiate man's sins against Mother Earth. . . . Inevitable, he supposed. When the first Drylanders were engineered to tolerate conditions like these, the deserts were still on the march. The rollback that later began deprived their race of any ultimate purpose in existence. So some among them created it for themselves. He wondered if any appreciated the irony that their credit was what enabled them to buy those necessities they couldn't produce or trade their meager output for.

Or was it irony? After all, they pooled their individual payments; material possessions were of small concern; distinction came from personal accomplishments, strength, skill, holiness. Maybe the difference between these neonomads—Legionarios was what the members of this tribe dubbed themselves, he recollected—and his Fireball Trothdom was they lived their ideals, while his kind played at their dreams. Who was happier? Who had better adapted to the cybercosm?

"We're here," Aleka said.

A shelter facing the square bore a fish symbol painted above the entrance. She went to stand before it and call softly, "Hola. Visitantes, por favor."

"Entrad en el nombre de Dios," replied a man's voice.

They obeyed. The inside was nearly as plain as where they had slept, two pallets, a stump-legged table, a portable cuisinier and utensil rack, the curtained wash space. At the back was a primitive desk with shelves holding various items, including a reader and a miniature crucifix. A boy stood watching coffee brew; the fragrance reminded Kenmuir of how long ago it was he last ate. Near the middle a man sat cross-legged on his great fundament. Though the hair was white and countenance deeply lined, he kept his back straight. From a chain around his neck hung an ankh carved out of coral.

"Padre Fernando, el capitán Ian Kenmuir," Aleka said.

The priest raised his hand. "Bendecidos, hijos míos," he greeted.

"I, uh, pardon me—no hablo," Kenmuir faltered. Not for present purposes.

Fernando smiled. "We do deal with the outside world, Captain." His Anglo was only slightly accented. He gestured. "Pray be seated."

They lowered themselves to a pad, across the table from him. Kenmuir wondered if Aleka's garb counted as immodest here. But these folk didn't live in isolation, they watched their public multi and received occasional outsiders. "I hope you are well rested," Fernando said to him.

He shrugged. "Enough, *I* hope." That drew a chuckle. "Thank you."

A carafe and tumblers stood on the table. "We have a custom of welcome," Fernando said. He poured water and offered it. Remembering the documentary, Kenmuir sipped in respectful silence with the others.

"And now," Fernando laughed when they were done, "I imagine what you truly want is coffee." He beckoned. The boy carried over a tray with pot and cups, knelt to put them down, and retired.

Kenmuir barely restrained his eagerness.

"Padre," Aleka began after a minute, "I explained—"

Fernando nodded. "Your time is short, if you are to call the Moon directly this day."

"You have the equipment."

Kenmuir's heart knocked.

"We do," Fernando said. "Not that transmission takes much wattage. It is our quantum-coding capability that you ask for."

What did these simple wanderers want with eavesdropper-proof communications? wondered Kenmuir. He thought back to Iscah and Soraya. Evidently the Legionarios weren't that simple either. Intertribal messages—maybe ritual and knowledge reserved for church initiates, maybe coordination of plans to cope with the commerce and politics of a globe largely indifferent to a few eccentrics, or maybe just precaution left over from the times of active hostility— and the high-bandwidth channels available for this sort of thing were limited, so their license must go far back. . . .

Fernando continued, gravely: "The question is whether we should grant it. Forgive me. I neither accuse nor insinuate. But poor ones like us dare not get embroiled in quarrels."

"Nobody has to know," said Aleka brashly.

Fernando frowned. "They could learn." Indeed they could, Kenmuir reflected, if he or she was captured. Or would the hunters actually resort to brainphasing? He didn't want to believe that.

Nor did he want to sit passive. "Aleka," he inquired, "what have you told our . . . our host?"

"Not everything by a long haul," she admitted. "Nor should you. As you say, Padre, your people ought not to be put at risk. All we want is to make a confidential call in a, uh, a cause worthy of your help." Mostly to Kenmuir: "I've explained that we're working on behalf of a certain Lunarian association." Well, Lilisaire had her henchmen. She might also have a coequal ally or two on the Moon. "We're trying to find out about a matter involving the Habitat project, which everybody knows they oppose. The information appears to have been concealed without any justification being publicly given, as the Covenant requires. We need to call for further instructions, while not being noticed by whoever is responsible."

"If anyone is," Kenmuir said. "It could be a misunderstanding."

"Or it could be too bloody right," Aleka snarled. "Maybe the sophotects are all morally perfect, but humans average as corrupt and greedy and power-hungry as always."

Fernando stroked his chin. "There is considerably more than that to your story," he said shrewdly. "Don't fear, I will not interrogate you. Let us relax and talk of pleasant things."

The boy served a vegetarian meal. After a brief blessing, Kenmuir discovered most of the food was new to him, and exotically seasoned. A decent white wine accompanied it.

Meanwhile, with intelligent questions and remarks, Fernando encouraged him to tell about his life. He in his turn learned more about the Drylanders than he had known there was. No doubt Aleka had, earlier, similarly described her own background. Kenmuir much wanted to hear that himself.

At the end, Fernando said quite matter-of-factly, "Yes, you may make your call. Let me conduct you." Kenmuir realized with a slight shock that in this past hour the priest had been sizing his visitors up till he decided they were genuine.

They walked together through the camp. People crossed arms on breasts at sight of Fernando, and he signed benediction. Otherwise he commented along the way. "—desert rats are becoming an ecological problem, but a new disease of the protein tubers poses the immediate threat. Life simply will not stop mutating and evolving for our convenience, will it? Bioservice has developed a counteragent but naturally wants to study possible side effects before releasing it to us. . . . Our solstice festival. . . . Younger people moving out, more and more. I wonder how many we would keep in this hard life if everybody had an alternative—"

The laser was in a truck, which Fernando unlocked. "Do you need help?" he asked. "I can send for our communications officer."

Kenmuir looked inside. "No, thanks. I'm familiar with this model." It was rather an antique, but so was most of the remaining Lunarian space fleet. To modernize would have meant going entirely cybernetic, no more humans crossing space except as infrequent passengers. He could understand why the Legionarios held by their Legion, those who still did.

"And I know the encryption," Aleka added. One key, out of however many were in Lilisaire's possession.

"Muy bien, I will leave you," Fernando said. "Por favor, lock again when you are done and come back to me." He went from them, lonely under the huge sky.

Kenmuir and Aleka climbed into the body of the truck and shut the door. A breathless furnace twilight dropped over them. They went to the set and stood for a moment unspeaking.

He cleared his throat. "Well!" he said against the hammering in his chest. "Let's get this done before we stifle."

"The beam can't go straight to her castle," Aleka told him. "It might be traced back, if they're watching as closely as she thinks, and suddenly a squad would pounce on us. It'll skip randomly among several—"

"Yes, I know, and in any event I'm not a defective." Kenmuir stopped. "I'm sorry. That was uncalled for. I'm drawn too tight."

She smiled through the dimness. He grew aware of sweat beading her upper lip, the swell and cleavage at her partly open tunic, an odor of healthy flesh. "You're a *kanaka 'oi*, Kenmuir," she murmured. Running a hand through her damp dark hair, she sighed. "As you say, we should get on with it."

Their fingers had little to do on the keyboard. The

computer behind was only robotic, but it comprehended the task and went directly to work. The signal sought its first address, a relay satellite in Lunar orbit. This was not an official station, but Selenarchic, a tiny solar-powered automaton. It passed the coded message on according to instructions received, and so forth shiftingly, until the last transmitter took aim at Zamok Vysoki. To trace that changeable zigzagging back to Earth was quite impractical, and interception would be not just difficult but pointless. The laws of quantum mechanics protected the secrecy from anyone who did not know the key.

"I daresay somebody's wishing hard that the Covenant didn't guarantee privacy rights," Aleka remarked.

"It was drawn up in another era," Kenmuir replied absently. His attention was welded to the screen. "I've seen arguments for amending it to fit new conditions."

"To control us closer?"

"M-m, they talk about conflicts between societies getting out of hand, sometimes murderously, and plots by one to harm another—" Human disorder, human unreason, dangerous anachronisms.

The screen brightened. A Lunarian face appeared. Kenmuir recognized Eythil of Mars.

"Captain," he acknowledged in Anglo. "How fare you?"

"Not well, as should be obvious," the Earthman retorted. "My associate and I must consult with the lady Lilisaire."

The image had gone impassive, as was Lunarian wont while waiting for photons to fly across space. After about three seconds it frowned and said, "I think she is at rest."

Nightwatch; Luna didn't have time zones. Kenmuir wondered if Lilisaire was not in fact at carousal, or some subtler pleasure. "I assure you, this is urgent, and for her alone," he declared. "If she can't come to a pickup, tell me when I can try again. But I don't promise I'll be able to."

Lag.

"I will seek," Eythil said. "Hold." The screen blanked.

"I guess we could stay here till tomorrow." Aleka's voice was subdued in the silence. "We've probably broken our trail. But if they decide to bring in the entire system—"

Survey satellites, which could identify a man on the ground and see whether he laughed or wept. Data searches, which could list virtually everybody on Earth who had ever had to do with Lilisaire, directly or indirectly. Inquiries called in to their unsuspecting communities. More data searches: Traffic Control's recent entries of whose vehicles had gone where. "Let's hope we're not that important," Kenmuir said.

Yet.

Time crawled. They found themselves standing hand in sweaty hand.

A head and shoulders in the screen, beautiful as a snowpeak, vivid as a flame. The auburn tresses were tousled but the green eyes altogether wakeful. "Hail," purred the Wardress. "What will you two of me?"

Kenmuir's clasp dropped free of Aleka's. His tongue locked. It was she who stood erect and gave a succinct account.

Lag. Lilisaire was smiling the least bit. Kenmuir stared and stared. Through the back of his head swirled bits of news he had gathered—Aleka was from Hawaii, she'd met an agent in San Francisco and that agent was a sophotect—what kept it from abandoning the Lunarian cause and merging with the cybercosm, if it had full intelligence?—but before him was the sight of Lilisaire.

She stirred. Her smile gave way to bleakness. "I belabored my wits most mightily about Pragmatic Venator," she said, half to herself. Who? For an instant, a grin flashed. "I did somewhat about him, too. A minor wile, but maychance we shall find a use for the outcome." She went serious again. "You deem truly, swift action is vital, else are you lost. Aleka, the Carfax machine laid out for you my skeleton of a plan. Do you still think it bears any possibility?"

"Yes, if, if we can get access to the file," the Earthwoman answered. "I wonder now if that isn't double-guarded."

Lag. Lilisaire looked thoughtfully before her. Kenmuir lost himself in her eyes.

"I believe I have a means to that end," the Lunarian told Aleka. "Hear me. Captain Kenmuir shall go to a place where the pursuit will not likely seek him soon. Pick one that is not far from your ultimate destination, which you and Carfax have discussed. Let him abide there while you double back to—Kamehameha is the spaceport nearest you. I have prepared a thing which an agent of mine shall bring on the mornwatch shuttle. He will be a Terran, I do not at this instant know precisely who but he will carry the name Friedrich and take a room at the Hotel Clarke. Meet him there, receive what he gives you, and rendezvous with Captain Kenmuir. Thence proceed according to plan and your own cunning. May fortune fare with you." Her tone glowed. "If you win to the truth, you shall have what was pledged you, in full and overflowing measure."

She settled back to wait, like a lynx for its prey.

Aleka swallowed. "I, yes, I'll try," she got out. "They don't suspect I'm involved, oh, surely not. Nobody will take any notice of me. Yes, I'll try, my lady."

The fear that she was mastering reached out into Kenmuir. *He* was being hunted. "What of me?" he cried. "What's my reward?"

Lag. Heat, thirst, longing, Aleka breathing at his side.

Lilisaire smiled anew. "I have told you, my captain," she answered like a song. "The cause of liberty and of humankind going to the stars. But you have right, that is abstract, and this is no longer a simple canvass you make but a fight that you wage. Eyach, then, would you be the chieftain over my emprises in space, and dwell with me as a seigneur among the Selenarchs? That will I gladly give you, my captain, if you come to me victorious."

Seconds drained away while he stood stunned.

Aleka nudged him.

Decision could not wait. He could say, "No," make his way to the authorities, and damn himself till he died. Or he could take the crazy hazard, jump into the unknown, very likely gain ignominy or death, at best go into a future of endless grief, jealousy, intrigue, homesickness—but he had no real home any more, did he?

"Yes," he called.

Through the time lag he looked at her face and understood, piece by hurtful piece, that whether or not he actually loved her, he desired her as a man lost in wilderness desires water and fire.

"Again will I kiss you," she said. Never in his knowledge had a Lunarian spoken thus to a Terran.

The screen blanked.

After a long while: "Bueno," blew from Aleka, "we're committed for sure, aren't we?"

"Why are you?" he asked dully.

"That's a long story, and we have to move. First, to get out of this oven." She plucked his sleeve. "Listen. It shouldn't take me more'n a couple of days to run her errand. What I'll do is take the car we came in to Santa Monica. At the airport I'll direct my volant to fly here and put itself at your service. That'll be tomorrow earlyish. Oh, yes, first I'll've bought a change of clothes and suchlike for you and left them in the volant. And I'll send the groundcar back to Iscah, and catch a flight to Hawaii. Meanwhile you should be safe here, if you stay mostly under cover and put one of those cowls on you whenever you go out. The Drylanders have a code of hospitality, and their padre favors us. But once you've got transport, you'd better scramble."

"Where to?" he asked, powerless in his ignorance.

"Um, let me think. I oughtn't tell now where we'll be going when we've gotten back together, just in case. But Lilisaire's right, we should start from within an hour or two's hop of it. I'm not acquainted with the region either, but—C'mon, let's go conduct a data sweep."

Fernando directed them to the dome that held computer terminals. They were for general use, but nobody else was there at the moment. Aleka set up a search for communities in midcontinent that were relatively isolated and self-contained. Predictions of cloud cover for the next few days were another factor. Before long she had made her choice.

"Bramland. Not too nice a place, according to this, but by that token, not apt to be friendly to the police. We'll flange up a plausible reason for you to give the locals, why you've flitted there to spend a while and why I'll be joining you. I'll put a chunk of cash in with those spare clothes and things I've promised you. Mainly, from now on keep your head down and your mouth shut. I know you can." She caught his hand. "I know *we* can."

Uncover what had been centuries hidden? Not for the first time—not for the first time—Kenmuir's mind withdrew pastward, blindly casting about for whatever clues might lie buried in history.

20

The Mother of the Moon

The view from the café terrace was glorious. High on its hillside, Domme—stones brooding over narrow streets through which once rang the hoofbeats of knightly horses—looked down at the valley, across woods and fields and homes, to crests afar and the lordly summer sky of Earth. From the western horizon the sun wrought shadows and luminances; the river flowed molten gold among trees whose crowns were green-gold. A breeze awoke in what warmth yet lingered. Traffic sounds rolled muted beneath quietness.

Dagny sipped of her wine, a fragrant Bordeaux, set the glass down, leaned back, let her eyes savor. She and Edmond had the place nearly to themselves, which deepened her content. "Beautiful," she sighed. "How glad I am you chose this."

Across the little table he drank likewise. When he lowered his own glass, she heard how it clicked against the tiles. "You would rather have gone somewhere else?" She heard, too, the trouble in his voice. "You did not say."

She met his gaze and smiled. "I wanted the choice to be yours," she answered, "and knew you'd most want to see your Dordogne again."

"But it is your holiday also."

"Well, you knew I've liked the area whenever we've visited." A misleading way to speak, she thought. Their times on the planet had been so few, so brief, and he always ready to go along with her wishes. How often to southern France? Thrice, counting now. She wanted to say something about that, but something else was more important. "This trip I've come to love it." She was being honest, though she understood how much of the reason lay in him, his joy that made her joyful. "Thank you."

He smiled back, just a bit. They were silent a while. The sun went down. A flight of rooks crossed a heaven still blue.

Edmond stirred. "Dagny—"

She waited, expectant without urgency, in the manner she had learned was best. Quick with assertion, rage, laughter, he could have difficulty uttering what lay him closest.

"I have meant to say this," he went on after a few

seconds, "but I was not sure how. I am not. But I should try."

"Your tries generally work out fine, *mon vieux,*" she told him.

He struggled. "I am going soon to space because of you." Hastily: "I mean, thanks to you."

A disclaimer might ease things for him. "Really, you owe a lot more to Lars and Brandir."

"They did well, and I appreciate it," he said, "but you made their efforts possible. You—pulled the wires, cleared the path." He forced a chuckle. "Can you today help me with my metaphors?"

She wondered what he was leading up to. He'd acknowledged her role often before. Memory flitted back across those past months. Governor Zhao, yes, he'd been the main opponent, issuing his decree that forbade the expedition, insisting that this was the law and exemption must be gotten from the High Council of the World Federation, knowing full well how easily that could be choked in committee. A problem of hers was that she continued to like the old bastard and believe he meant well. She thought he was more than half sincere about the hazards that might arise if Lunarians took to space in any numbers. As for the rest of his motivation, he'd told her that there was enough nationalism, dangerous enough, on Earth, without allowing anything that might encourage the tumor to grow on the Moon. Maybe he had a point. Besides, he and she usually ended their private talks with his playing some music for the sake of their spirits, and it was through him that she had come to Beethoven's last quartets. . . . Occasionally she must needs fight him.

She recalled her mind to the present. Edmond had made a joke. Let her too try lightening things. She grinned. "I know where various bodies were shoveled under." She had, in fact, enjoyed putting the screws on Commissioner Zacharias till he leaned on the governor.

Seeing Edmond serious again, she released what rose within her: "And eventually, you know, eventually I got through to . . . the download. In spite of the woes he's having with Fireball, he found time for whatever he did behind the scenes to get the ban lifted." Guthrie's analog, the ghost of Uncans, had remembered—She swallowed. "I think mainly you've got him to thank."

"Speaking with him that first time, it was not easy for you," Edmond said. "None of this was. I could feel. Sometimes at night, beside me, you caught your breath."

He had been aware, then. He had been so fully aware that he kept still. Her eyes stung. "Oh, darling, you, you've thanked me aplenty already for my part."

"Yes," he replied slowly, "but never before have I thanked you for why you did it."

"For excellent reasons," she said in her briskest tone. "Science. Adventure. Kaino's wish as well as yours. A liberating precedent. A healthy kick to the fat gut of the Lunar Authority. All in all, a very worthy cause."

"*My* cause. *I* am going. I will be gone for months, perhaps in danger. You do not want this."

She looked straight at the Crô-Magnon face. "However, you do," she said.

He nodded. "Exactly. I am not glad to leave you, but I am glad to go. Does that make sense to you? You hate it, but for my sake you worked for it. You—you love me that much."

The blood beat in her temples. "I don't hold with caging eagles," was the best response she could find. "No, bears, in this case." She leaned across the table and rumpled the iron-gray hair. "Good ol' bear!"

"I . . . only want to stay . . . I understand," he mumbled.

"And I understand that you understand, and that makes me happy," she said, blinking the tears away from the sight of him. "Okay, 'Mond, let's enjoy. Drink up and we'll go in search of dinner."

Day was becoming dusk. When they rose, Dagny felt the weight on her bones. In none of her earlier returns had Earth been this heavy. Well, time in the centrifuge and time in the medical program did not stop time. Maybe she'd never again come back here from the Moon. But not to worry about that, she told herself. Not now, this now that she had with her man.

Sacajawea was the best that Fireball could provide, a Venus-class transport, well-designed, soundly built, but not one of the fantastic new torchcraft that would have made the crossing in a pair of weeks. Those were still few and committed for long periods ahead. *Sacajawea*'s main service had been in the Asteroid Belt. For the journey to Rydberg's rock she accelerated at less than one-fifth *g*, to spare the Lunarians aboard, until she attained trajectory speed; thereafter she fell free for more than a hundred daycycles before the hour came to brake for rendezvous.

Weightless that long, no matter how diligently he exercised, a Terrestrial would have taken six or seven rehabilitative weeks back on Earth to regain his full strength, skeletal and muscle mass, coordination, reflexes, body chemistry. At that, he would risk some of the changes being irreversible; resilience varies among individuals. A Lunarian, returned to his own home, would have done better, but not recovered overnight. To meet whatever they were going to meet, Beynac and his men should arrive in good condition. Besides, gravity would be feeble at their goal. Thus everyone was much in the whirly.

That machine had barely room in its compartment for a three-meter swing radius. Wire strands held a narrow platform, opposite which a one-tonne lead sphere counterrotated at the end of an adjustable arm. You did most of your drill parallel to the board, pushups, bicycles, mass-lifting with arms and legs. For the standing motions you rose very carefully; if the brain goes fast through a sudden drop in weight of some sixty percent, vertigo and nausea are the least of the possible consequences, and you must likewise be wary of Coriolis force. Although your belt and its leash, attached to the center post, kept you from being slung off, a bone-breaking accident could easily happen. It was well to hold onto that post during your knee bends and jogs. You certainly required it when you stood on your head and your heart pushed blood upward more or less as nature intended.

Beynac was among those who could keep their eyes open meanwhile without getting sick. Being alone, he could sing songs when he had breath to spare, the bawdier the better. Nevertheless he disliked such sessions; and here, in microgravity, they demanded more time per daycycle than on the Moon. Eventually he wearied of his repertory, fell silent, and combatted monotony with memories and thoughts.

They went back to Kaino. "Had we Lunarians our ships, this were no necessity," the young man had said, a few watches ago at mess. "For us, at any rate; and for Earthling passengers, no worse than on our world. We would accelerate throughout the voyage."

"If you could afford a fleet of torchcraft, you would have no need to trade across space," Beynac bantered him. "You could just wallow in your money."

Kaino scowled. "Does Fireball sit back idle?" His words shook with longing. "To go—And we'd not buy the ships, we'd build them."

"Even then, my son, it's not economic to boost the whole way, except for special purposes."

"We'd make it be! But who dares set us free? Often did Guthrie sneer at government, but never did he move to push it off us. He too feared us."

Beynac was about to reply that that was nonsense. A spacefaring enterprise ought rationally to welcome able newcomers. Competition would be no problem; the existing lines had more calls on them than they could meet. However, powerful though Fireball was, there were limits to its influence.

Rydberg forestalled him. "I have looked at the parameters of Lunarian astronautics," the captain said in his methodical fashion. "Given access to antimatter at a reasonable price, torching may well become profitable for many kinds of haul, if not every kind. Accelerating at a constant one-sixth *g*, a Lunarian crew would not need centrifuge time. Therefore they could be fewer, perhaps solo. Speed at turnover would be proportionately lower than for a full *g*, therefore less fuel-costly. Of course, transit time would be greater, by a factor of approximately the square root of six, but that would make no large difference in the inner System. Even this crossing of ours would have taken only about a month."

He had been right to steer the conversation away from politics, Beynac thought. When six men, two of them Lunarian, were cramped together for week after week after week, nerves wore thin.

Would it have helped if two or three were female? That was common practice on missions for Fireball, if not every spaceline. But no, Dagny had doubtless been right when she argued against it (and, her husband suspected, was the one who got the company to make all-male a condition of the charter). Given the Lunarian temperament, whether you believed it was genetic or cultural, the potentialities might be explosive.

Beynac laughed a little. She needn't have worried about him on that account, if she did. From the first, she had been woman enough for him, "and then some," as her North Americans would put it.

His duty to his body was done for the nonce. He could go toss this drenched, smelly sweatsuit in the cleaner, sponge-bathe, don his coverall, and, oh, seek his cubicle, he supposed, play a show before next mess. He hadn't watched *The Marriage of Figaro* for years. Earphones. He was the single man aboard who cared for opera. Terrestroid Moondwellers, isolated both from Earth and from their children, were apt to keep archaic tastes.

He touched the off switch. His weight dropped as the centrifuge whirred to a halt, until he hung in midair between the slack cables. Reaching out for a handhold, he pulled himself and the platform to a stanchion, used his safety belt to secure the gymnastic equipment, and started for the door.

It opened. Ilitu looked in. "Ah, sir, I awaited your loosing," he said.

"Is anything wrong?" Beynac asked. He became conscious of how lonely the ship was, a metal bubble adrift through the thin seething of the cosmos.

"Nay. It is but that they have acquired a good optical of the asteroid. I thought you would like to see it at once."

"Yes, indeed. Thank you." Beynac followed his graduate student forward through the axial passage. The consideration touched him. This wasn't the first friendly gesture Ilitu had made. He was more—all right, more human, more open than most Lunarians. Sometimes Beynac felt closer to him than to any of his sons and daughters.

Lars Rydberg, Antonio Oliveira, and Manyane Nkuhlu had evidently watched their fill. Kaino floated alone in the control cabin. He was always eager to stand pilot watch, including somebody else's, when he wasn't increasing his skills in a simulator he had insisted be taken along. His red head nodded curtly, eyes held hard on the viewscreen. Beynac came to it, checked his flight, stared, and softly whistled.

Radar had already established the dimensions of the asteroid. Rugged, lumpy, broader at one end than the opposite, it would have fitted inside a cylinder about 300 kilometers long and a hundred wide. At maximum useful magnification, as yet it seemed tiny in the night everywhere around. The hue was slaty, spotted with blacknesses that must be the deepest irregularities, save for a broad flat grayness near the middle. At the edge of this jutted something like a needle: a crag or peak, sharp against the dark. Rotation was just perceptible. Falling outward from the sun, the body wobbled around a skewed axis once in about five hours, as if tossed by a careless giant.

Seen in the Belt, it would have been fairly interesting. *Sacajawea,* though, had come four billion kilometers farther, out near the marches of the comets.

"Oui, tu voilà," Beynac whispered; and louder, for the rest to hear: "We tracked you down, by bloody damn."

When her chime sounded, Dagny went in Lunar leaps down the hall to the vestibule. At the door she hesitated. Her heart thuttered. Nobody in Tychopolis felt they needed a peephole or exterior scanner. This might be a casual, unannounced visitor—She didn't want it to be. Not really. She set her jaw and retracted the door. Beyond ran Hudson Way, a corridor lined with planters where roses grew against trellises, a neighbor's entrance catercorner across it. Every sense heightened, she caught the odor of the flowers as acutely as a swordthrust.

The robot that loomed there, two meters tall, was startlingly humanlike, suggestive of a medieval suit of plate armor. (No, not when you paid heed to the joints, the powerpack, the turret with its speaker and sonic sensors and ring of optics.) She had seen it on a newscast, because it was unique, an impractical shape for a machine unless the machine had some such purpose as this today.

For a moment she and it stood motionless. The city hummed low in their hearing.

"Hello," the robot said.

Dagny had heard that voice before, on a broadcast, on her phone, in her memory. It was Anson Guthrie's, not hoarsened as in his last years but strong and resonant. Defying every resolution, a wave of weakness passed through her.

She fought it down. "W-welcome," she said.

"May I come in?"

The robot spoke shyly, half unsurely. It must have been forceful enough, making whatever arrangements it did to keep a gaggle of curiosity seekers from tailing it here, but she realized that now it didn't know quite what to say either, and drew strength from the knowledge. That's what you came for, isn't it? she was tempted to reply. She curbed the impulse, mumbled, "Of course," and stepped aside.

Ought she to shake hands?

The robot passed by, a graceful movement, marvelous design behind the bluish-white metal. Dagny shut the door. "Gracias," the robot said, and stopped. She imagined it scanning this entry, oak-paneled walls, antique mirror, picture of the Washington coast, a tiny monument to an Earth that scarcely existed any longer. The turret didn't move. The computer within transferred its regard from the input of one pair of lenses to the next, around a full circle.

By itself out in the open, Dagny recalled, the computer had just two optic balls, protruding on stalks from the case that housed it. The robot was not its body, was not *it,* was merely a vehicle in temporary use.

Suddenly she could not, would not, think of "it." Something, at least, of Guthrie was here, and he had been totally male. By right of inheritance, the download bore the name. Let him also bear the gender.

"Same layout as before," he said, a little easier in his tone. The experts claimed he had moods, feelings, maybe different now but nonetheless real. "I wondered whether you'd changed things. Been a long time, hasn't it?"

"Yes," she answered. "Six years, seven?"—since last he, the original he, guested her and 'Mond. Afterward they had met once on Earth (how aged he had gotten, though salty as ever) and had talked occasionally by phone almost until the end . . . "This way, please." She led him through the hall to the living room.

He halted near the center. She had set the viewscreen for a direct presentation, an outlook from the top of the ringwall. A wilderness of shadows and softly lighted upthrusts fell away to the near horizon. A Criswell collector shouldered above yonder worldrim, the single brightness in all that land. Overhead arched night, Earth waxing through the second quarter, blue-and-white majesty. She wasn't sure why she had chosen this, rather than one of her usual scenes recorded on the mother planet. Maybe, down underneath, she hadn't wanted to raise any pretense, or hadn't dared.

"Nothing much changed here, either," Guthrie observed.

She found that she too could make conversation. "Well, you know how old married couples get set in their ways."

"I'd hardly say that of you and 'Mond. Not yet. Probably never. Him off to hell-and-hooraw in space. You directing the construction at Astrebourg and, I gather, making the governor's life miserable whenever he deserves it."

No pretense! But what instead? Dagny bit her lip. "I don't know what to—to offer you—"

A short laugh boomed. "Not a cup of tea." A hand gestured, that looked as if it were forged in a furnace but had been grown in a nanovat. "Sit down if you like." The voice dropped. "I can. I won't crumple your chair, here on the Moon."

"No need for me, really—here on the Moon," she said.

They fell mute.

Guthrie broke through: "Is Carla—is Jinann still living with you?"

"Yes," Dagny said, "but she's tending her jewelry shop. I told her to phone before coming, and that I might want her to sleep elsewhere."

"Why, for Pete's sake?" he exclaimed, precisely the way the man would have done. Her heart cracked. "I'd like to see her again, and your whole family."

"Again?" broke from her. She gasped, appalled. "Oh! Oh, God, I'm sorry."

"Don't be," he said gently.

"I didn't mean—"

"I know you didn't."

"Excuse me." She sought the table on which she had set out a decanter and several glasses. They were several because either a single glass or a pair would have uttered what had escaped her lips. Shakily, she poured a stiff slug and tossed off a fourth of it. The whisky smoked over tongue and gullet, bound for the bloodstream. She'd guessed the need might arise.

"No offense taken," he was saying. "I make no bones about my condition." A chuckle. "Nope, no bones at all."

This had been his favorite Scotch. He had introduced her to it—how long ago? And now he would never taste it, never, unless maybe in an electronic virtuality-dream. Dagny turned about to confront him. "I shouldn't be like this," she protested bitterly. "Stupid old bat."

He stroked hand across lower turret, as Guthrie had stroked his chin, and drawled, "I wouldn't apply any of those words. You're not just smart, you remain a damn sexy wench, Diddyboom."

She blinked and blinked. She would *not* cry.

Doubtless he noticed, for he added in haste: "I speak abstractly about such things, these days. But I've got my memories."

"Y-yes."

"His memories," Guthrie said, once more serious. "Should I have put it that way?"

"I don't know." She took another swallow.

"It's true. Sure. They pumped his nervous system full of nanoscanners, encoded what came out, used that to program a neural network custom-built to be an exact analog of his particular brain . . . Bueno, no point in rehashing it for you. I'm his aftermath."

How much could a download hurt? Dagny drew breath. "Nevertheless, you soldier on." His words, after Juliana died. What comfort might there be for a download? "Because they made you to be him."

"To be like him, in certain ways," Guthrie corrected. "No more than that." He was quiet for a space.

"When I called on him at his deathbed, I learned, or I was reminded of, several things about being a man."

Against her will, Dagny shivered. "The world's gone eerie, hasn't it?"

"I figure it always was," came the familiar tone. "How'd one of 'Mond's cavemen have reacted, seeing you in your simple small-town girlhood? What changes is just the kind of eeriness."

The whisky began to warm her. "You are—quite a bit like . . . Uncans," she ventured.

She believed that he thought a smile. "Gracias. I try."

"Because Fireball needs you. We all need you."

"That was the general idea. Personally, I take no stock in Santa Claus, the tooth fairy, or the indispensable man. But, yeah, there are loose ends to tie up before I can quit in reasonably good conscience."

The chill struck back. "Quit."

"Stop," he said almost lightly. "Turn off. Wipe out. Whatever you call it."

Cease to be. She drank afresh and gained courage to ask: "Do you want to?" When he could abide for thousands of years, maybe forever.

Mostly the robot stood moveless. Sometimes he appeared to remember body language. He shrugged. "Oh, I'm not sorry for myself. Por favor, credit me with analog guts. This is a hell of an interesting universe yet. But between us, and swear by Dr. Dolittle you won't quote me, being alive was better."

She shuddered. Never for her!

Yes, he was powerful, he had wonders open to him that mortals could barely imagine. Poor, brave wraith. "You always did your duty as you saw it, didn't you?" Dagny said. "Coming to me, in person, when you're so busy and harassed, that's Christly kind of you. That's my Uncans."

Again he spoke awkwardly, while he shuffled a foot. "Um, well, my image when I make a public speech— it was a mistake using it when I phoned you, Dagny. I saw right away what a mistake it was, and I'm no end sorry."

She recalled the pain, but dimly, as if across more than the few real-time daycycles. A synthesized audio-visual of Anson Guthrie in his vigorous middle age, controlled by the download as the living brain controls the living face, could inspire thousands or millions of watchers, or knife a solitary granddaughter. "That's okay," she mumbled.

"No, it isn't, and I aim to try and set it right," he insisted. "You're not one for smarmy fakes." He lifted his hands toward her. "Let's get straight with each other, you and me." The timbre levelled. "Because I hope we'll be working together pretty often in the future, same as you did with him."

Him? she thought. A separate and lost being? What was a mind, a self, a soul, anyway?

"Thank you," Dagny breathed. "Thank you more than I can ever say."

He had laid the ghost in her to rest.

With a long low-weight step, she went over to him and took the outreaching hands in her own. They felt a little cold, but their massiveness reminded her of Uncans's hands.

"Oh, Dagny," he said. When she let go, he hugged her, very quickly and gently.

That was the real reason he came, she thought. He had loved her. He still did.

It was a senseless accident that killed Edmond Beynac. But then, every accident is senseless, as is most of history.

"No, this is not the ancient lost body of my hypothesis," he had explained to Manyane Nkuhlu after his first quick survey upon it. The spaceman knew little geology but was interested in learning. "Bloody hell, I made that clear even before we left. No? *Eh, bien,* you were busy at the start, and later did not chance to listen.

"What we have here, it is principally metals, iron,

nickel, et cetera, which were once fused. That means it is a piece from the core of a body large enough to have melted and formed a core—which it is not itself, do you understand? The flat section, that is the fracture where it was broken loose in a great collision. But I do not think that collision shattered the big planetoid entirely into minor objects like this. Such an impact would leave different traces. Quite possibly the force did push the major part and the fragments knocked off it into a more eccentric path, and this was when Jupiter seized them and flung them outward. If they did not escape the Solar System, the new orbit was enormous, and during billions of years, passing stars would raise its perihelion farther yet."

"The new orbit?" asked Nkuhlu. "You can't mean that the pieces stayed in a group, on an identical course."

Beynac's hand chopped air. "No, no, of course not. However, the tracks must have been closely similar. And off in the Oort Cloud—yes, the comets there are many, but how far apart, in that huge volume! The pieces would seldom be much perturbed, the massive one least. Gradually, true, their cluster would disintegrate. Doubtless a comet changed the orbit of this piece drastically. Now its perihelion is scarcely more than it was in the beginning.

"That cannot have happened very long ago, a few millions of years perhaps, because the present orbit is unstable. The encounter was most likely near the former perihelion. Closest to the sun, the density of comets is a bit higher. This suggests the major body is not at its most distant from us. We may be able to compute backward through time and get an idea of where to search for it—"

Beynac lifted his palms and threw back his head. "But plenty of lecture!" he laughed. "My academic habits took me over. I will find you educational practical experience, my friend."

That may have been among the factors which, weeks later, joined to destroy him. Unlike most of the others, it was not random. Shorthanded, under-equipped, his research needed whatever help he could marshal. He and Ilitu were not able to handle the drilling, digging, and collecting that it demanded. Their time in the field went mainly to general exploration, search for promising sites. In their laboratory aboard *Sacajawea*, they prepared samples for examination, studied them, built piecemeal a knowledge of the asteroid and its story. Once in a while they exercised in the centrifuge, washed, ate, or slept.

Doctrine required that a man who could singly bring the vessel home be always shipside. This meant either Rydberg or Kaino. Actually, it oftenest meant both, the former working to heighten the skill of the latter. Nkuhlu and Oliveira were free.

The arrangement had been planned at the outset. Beynac welcomed such an opportunity for his son, now when Fireball's leaders were beginning to see what advantages might lie in having a few Lunarian pilots. Nkuhlu and Oliveira were experienced rock-jacks. They had acquitted themselves well in operations on stony bodies and treacherous comet ice.

They were technicians, not scientists or engineers. But probably no one could have foreseen the danger. Our sole sureness is that every fresh venture into the universe will meet with surprises.

Never before had humans walked on anything quite like the fracture plane across this cosmic shard. About ten kilometers long and twenty wide, it gashed transversely near the middle of the rough cylindroid. Around it was rock, lighter material that had overlain the primordial core and stuck to it through the sundering crash or, immediately afterward, fell back in a half-molten hail. Dark and rough reached that surface. Meteoritic strikes to wear it down and crater it had been rare in those realms where the fragment wandered. The plain of the plane stood forth stark amidst this stonescape, its sheen faintly grayed by dust, its pockmarks few and wide-scattered.

On the Orionward edge of that scar reared the peak

Beynac had seen from space. The collision must also have formed it, a freakishness of forces at this special point. Maybe a shock wave focused by a density interface had hurled liquefied metal upward in a fountain that congealed as it climbed. The height was not a mountain but a spire, swart, outlandishly twisted and gnarled, a sheer 1500 meters from the rubble at its base to the top, which hooked forth like an eagle's beak over the flat ground of the fracture.

At its back, rock wasteland lay in tiers and jumbles. When you fared yonder afoot, you saw a strip that was barely thirty meters wide between the jagged horizons to left and right but that lost itself in murkiness for more than a hundred kilometers ahead. Standing beneath the spire and gazing in the other direction, you saw the plain, well-nigh featureless, bordered by stars on either side and by a riven escarpment opposite you, twenty kilometers away. Above loomed a dark that at night was crowded with constellations, glowingly cloven by the Milky Way, haunted by nebulae and sister galaxies. Then the sun tumbled aloft, shrunken to a point but still intolerably fierce, radiant more than five hundred times full Moonlight on Earth. The visible stars became few, but the spindle of *Sacajawea*, in her companion orbit, might gleam among them. Weight likewise gave a faint sense of not being altogether lost from manhome. It was ghostly at the ends of the asteroid, but here, close to the centroid of a ferrous mass, it exceeded a tenth of a *g*.

Thus the scene where Edmond Beynac died.

"Go up onto the peak," he ordered Nkuhlu and Oliveira. "Along the way, take pictures and gamma readings as usual. What I want you to bring down in your packs is some pieces of the top—exact locations laser-gridded, do not forget this time, by damn! Yes, and a core, a meter or two deep. Plus a seismic sounding. I need to know the inside of this thing. Just how in bloody hell did it *happen?*"

He respected the men, therefore he did not add

what was obvious, that he had given them a difficult, perhaps dangerous assignment. Himself, he went with Ilitu into the badlands on the farther side of the scar. There he had found another enigma to investigate, strata where theory said no strata should be.

The ascent by Nkuhlu and Oliveira turned into a small epic of the kind that goes as undertones through every heroic age. Gravity was low but gear was massive and the faces to climb precipitous. An hour might be spent in peering at the next stage before attempting it. At that, thrice one man or the other would have fallen to his death, had he not slammed short on a line attached to his well-anchored partner. Life support labored, spacesuits grew hot, breath harsh, mouths dry; rest was measured in minutes on a ledge, doles of water sucked from a tube, rations and stimulants pushed through a chowlock—until at last, shaky-kneed on the summit, the pair looked down at desolation and out into immensity.

Thereupon the real work began. Never before had they wrestled with such stuff as this. It was not rock, it was metal; it was not uniform but multiply and intricately alloyed, a tangle of layers, encysted lumps, and vacuoles. When an ion torch cut free a sample, white-hot gobbets might spit back. When a sonic pulse went downward, the whole footing might tremble.

What caused the disaster was a shaped minicharge. It should simply have split an anomalous plumbic vein, to produce recoverable specimens. Instead, the explosion found a resonance. Weaknesses unstressed for billions of years gave way. The eagle's beak broke apart. A dozen huge, a hundred lesser chunks fell.

Beynac and Ilitu had emerged back on the plain, out of a crevice where their headlamp lights touched on mysteries. They were bound diagonally across, toward the dome shelter at the far corner and the gig that should bear them again to their ship. The walls around them had screened out radio. Else Beynac would have heard his helpers, vocally recording each thing they did. He might have warned them. Or he too might not have guessed.

He and his companion were well into the open when the overhang sundered. Tiny at their distance, the rocks went slowly at first. They accelerated, though, worse than a meter per second for every second that passed. They hit bottom at over two hundred kilometers per hour. In most places they would have bounced to a quick stop. Here the ground was smooth and hard. Friction, never much in low gravity, was almost nil. Moreover, the plain was not truly level. The increase of weight toward the asteroidal center of mass gave it a slight but real downslope.

Oliveira and Nkuhlu went on their bellies and gripped anything they could while the peak shook beneath them. Dust, cast high when the stones landed, briefly obscured heaven. It arced down. Rising to their feet, they saw boulders and gravel fan outward across the iron of the plain, a sleetstorm aimed for the two figures at its middle.

Now they heard a radio cry. *"Nom de Dieu! À bas, Ilitu!* Drop you, drop, God damn!" No man could dash clear of what was coming. The geologists flung themselves prone. Still they saw the rocks leap, bound, roll toward them. They felt those soundless impacts as drumbeats up through suits, flesh, bones. Sparks flew, momentary stars below the stars. There was time to think, remember, even speak.

Ilitu, Lunarian, hissed defiance. Beynac called, steady-toned, "If I do not survive, tell my Dagny I loved her." Otherwise he ignored the frantic voices from spire and ship. But when the storm reached him, he transmitted, surely unawares, *"O Maman, Maman—"*

Ilitu was lucky. A pebble pierced his garb, drew blood from a shoulder, and exited. The holes promptly self-sealed. As for Edmond Beynac, a lump the size of his fist smashed open his helmet. Air puffed away into emptiness.

That is a kindly death. You are unconscious within seconds, gone very soon thereafter.

His sons met with their mother in her home on the Moon.

"Later, yes, we shall bring more folk into the circle," Brandir said. "This evenwatch must be ours alone."

Like her and his brothers, he was standing. Behind him stretched the big viewscreen. Its mobile view of the River Dordogne, green valley and a castle on the heights beyond, seemed doubly remote from his tall, black-and-silver-clad form, the long pale hair and the features that were not wholly Asian nor of any other race upon Earth. And yet, Dagny thought, he too dwelt like a baron of old in his towered mountain fastness.

"Why?" she asked. Why not, at least, his sisters?

Because, she realized, these men had not come to mourn with her. For she heard: "We have our father to avenge."

"What?" she exclaimed. Punish a barren bit of wreckage?

No. This new generation was strange but sane. If anything, below the cavalier style lay an inborn realism colder than she liked to think about. Language mutates. "What exactly do you mean?" she demanded.

Kaino was the most outspoken among them. Through his lifespan she had heard him enraged, rancorous, sarcastic, hostile, but never so bleak: "We've a reckoning to make with them who wrought his bane."

Chill touched her. "Wait!" she cried. "Those two poor guys who touched off the rockfall? No!" She filled her lungs, captured his eyes, and declared to them all, "I forbid you."

When the ship returned, she had taken the pair aside to give what consolation she was able. "I don't pardon you," she said, "because I have nothing to pardon. Nobody could have known." Oliveira wept and kissed her hands. Nkuhlu saluted as he would have saluted Anson Guthrie.

Brandir swept an impatient gesture. "Needless," he replied. "Innocence is theirs. I grant them my peace." His arrogance bore for Dagny a curious innocence of its own, akin to a cat's. "It is the Earth lords to whom we owe ill."

"Had we had a vessel that was ours," Kaino said between his teeth, "and a Lunarian crew—"

"I would have sent him afare well-manned, and geared with the best that technics offers," Brandir stated.

By now he could probably afford the cost, Dagny thought. His enterprises—the undertakings of those mostly young persons who had pledged fealty to him—were enwebbing the globe. Barred, though, among many things, were the building of spacecraft and any Moondweller enterprise more distant than to Earth.

"Lunarians would have had a sense for whatever traps lay in wait," Kaino said.

"Belike not fully they, either," Temerir answered.

Dagny's glance went to him. Her third son generally kept silent until he saw reason to make some pointed remark. Slight, gray-eyed, pallid, he stood in his plain blue coverall as a contrast to Brandir's elegance and Kaino's flamboyancy. But his was the most purely Lunarian face of the three.

"Nay," Brandir agreed. "Yet would the odds have been better."

"And the venture *ours,*" Kaino added.

Brandir turned to Dagny. "This be the vengeance we take and the memorial we raise," he said, "that we break the ban of the overlords and set Luna free in space. Mother, we ask your aid."

Dagny's pulse wavered, recovered, and beat high. They could not bring about a change in the law without her, she knew. They might amass the wealth of dragons, but politically they were dwarfs, in large part because they lacked the gifts of born politicians.

Not that oratory, truth-shading, backroom bargains, wheedling, compromise, blackmail, bullying, bribery, promise-breaking, lip service, and self-puffery were very natural to her. "I, I don't know," she stammered.

Her look went past Brandir to the Dordogne view. It had moved to a mossy spot along the shore, oh, could this be the same spot where she and 'Mond came walking hand in hand, stopped, skimmed stones across the water, sat down on damp softness and let sun pour through them while he laid his arm about her waist and kissed her? His chin was a little scratchy . . .

It was as if ice abruptly thawed. She had wolf-howled that first nightwatch alone after the news came, but things beyond counting were necessary to do and say, smiles beyond counting were necessary to manufacture, therefore let the automaton run through its program and at bedtime switch off. The emptiness could await her leisure, it would never go away.

At this instant—

Abide a little longer, only a short while more. Then she could loose the tears. Then she could go through his desk, his clothes, his books, the database of his calls and messages to her when he was in the field, all of their years, daycycle by daycycle. Then she could know with her whole being that he was gone into forever, and come to terms with the fact, and warm her hands at his memory.

Not yet, not quite yet. At this instant, the eyes of his children toward her like guns, she had work to do. The triune god of Edmond Beynac had been kinship, truth, and freedom.

She straightened. Her muscles pleasured in the movement. "Okay," she said. "I'll try. I'll do my bloody damnedest."

Politics was more than fraud and brutality, she

thought. In fact, most of it was honest, was simply the means by which people ordered the affairs they had in common. Suppose she started by approaching Technocommissioner Lefevre. He and 'Mond had been pretty close . . .

Kaino embraced her. He hadn't done that since he was ten.

She would *not* cry.

He drew back. She said quickly, "Don't expect miracles. I may or may not get something going. At best, it'll take a long time, and we'll have to scrabble for allies."

Brandir nodded. "Aught you may need that we three can provide, you shall have," he said, "including our patience."

"Well, to begin with, your sisters—Verdea, anyway. She might stir up the kind of general sentiment we'll want," as Shelley and Byron did for the liberation of Greece, Solzhenitsyn for Russia, Jaynes for North America.

"And Fia, yes, I think Fia," Brandir murmured.

Helen, black-tressed, russet-eyed, reserved, formal, secretive, save where it came to music . . . Carla-Jinann, no, until matters got to the stage of emotional pressure, speeches, parades, demonstrations, appeals, at which point she could be a valuable link between Moondwellers, demonstrative Terrestroid and aloof Lunarian. . . .

"How long estimate you?" Kaino blurted at Dagny.

His yearning cut at her. "I don't know, I told you," she sighed.

"I also must drink of time," Temerir said.

Surprised, she regarded him where he stood limned against her flowers and asked, "What? Why?"

"I mean to search after the great planetoid that Father dreamed of," the astronomer answered. Brandir was having his personal observatory built for him on Farside. "The hunt will likely consume years. That is the more so because it shall be our secret."

"Huh? A scientific project secret? You'll sneak time for it when nobody's looking? How come, for Christ's sake?"

He spread his fingers. His parents would have shrugged. "Father's emprise won clues for me to follow. But few ever paid much heed to his notions about the early Solar System. Those were taken for the idiosyncracy of an elsewise mighty mind. It should be easy to let the matter slide back into obscurity—with your help, Mother. Who foreknows what a Lunarian may someday discover?" The wintry gaze sharpened upon her. "Unless all here tonight pledge muteness, I will not make the seeking I wish to make in honor of Edmond Beynac."

A shiver passed through Dagny. Was this, in his way, the most formidable of her sons?

21

Seen from above, the plains reached endless, a thousand mingling hues of green below a summer sky of the same vastness. Often a wind sent waves through the grasses, swift and shadow-delicate; Kenmuir could well-nigh hear them rustle, smell the odors of growth and of sun-warmed soil. Where terrain sank to make a wetland, trees walled the water-gleam and more wings than he could count wheeled above. A few roads ran spearshaft-straight, with hardly any movement upon them. Transmission towers stood as lonely. They seemed no violation of the landscape. Rather, those soaring, gracefully crowned slendernesses brought to the fore the life around them.

Which, in a fashion, they also guarded, Kenmuir thought. They were integral to the technology and, yes, the social system that kept all this in being. It hadn't been enough that population decline, plantations genetically engineered for efficiency, and direct synthesis had, between them, emptied many old agricultural regions. To restore a sound ecology—oftener, to create a new one—and then maintain it, that took more than a wish and an economic surplus. It demanded an analysis, a comprehension of the totality, beyond the scope of unaided human brains.

Yes, he thought, the cybercosm was doing a better job of ruling the biosphere than man had. As long as governments heeded its counsel, Earth would stay green.

Counsel? Or command? Was there a difference? You accepted a policy recommendation because it made sense, and presently you found there was no going back, because it had become a basis of too much on which people depended; and so you accepted the next recommendation. But hadn't that always been the case? And purely human politics, short-sighted, ignorant, superstitious, animally impassioned, forever repeated the same ghastly mistakes. Kenmuir had once read a remark of Anson Guthrie's: "Is it freedom when you're in a cage bigger than you want to fly across?"

He shook off his reverie and glanced about him. Three volants were visible afar, and a suborbital went as a rapid spark through heaven. Below him he spied other gleams, machines on their business of ground transport, inspection, tending the country. Trees shaded a small town. How white and peaceful it looked. He supposed the dwellers were all folk who enjoyed surroundings like these. Those who didn't simply live on their credit probably worked through telepresence, except for local service enterprises. And they had their hobbies, sports, tours, civic affairs, maybe some special ceremonies and observances; and surely, beneath the placid surface, private lives now and then got as tangled and stormy as ever. So, in its own manner, was the community where he grew up.

But on clear nights he would walk out of it and from

a hilltop yearn toward the stars. How many were they who still did? By what right would Lilisaire deny them a meaning to their lives?

"Damn!" Kenmuir muttered. "You've a real gift for fribbling away time, haven't you, lad?" He'd brooded enough in the Drylander camp after Aleka left and before her flyer arrived for him. If he meant to honor his commitment, and he did, then indecisiveness amounted to betrayal.

After all, the purpose was only to recover information that might well be illegally secreted. If it was important, and if the Federation Council and Assembly possessed it, then everybody who cared to inquire would soon have known too. But nobody did. And democracy, rationality itself weren't possible without adequate data.

He could complain to his legislators or ombud; or he could issue a public statement calling for disclosure, and be shrugged off as a crank.

If the matter came out into the open—As vague as Lilisaire's hopes were, she must be desperate. Certainly she didn't expect it would by itself cause the Habitat project to be cancelled, did she? No, she dreamed of somehow gaining the power to force a termination. But how? An old weapon she could commandeer? Monstrous absurdity.

True, the Lunarians in space, few and scattered though they were, had a rather terrifying military potential. Anybody with ships did. But to rouse them, rally them, get them together in resolution and discipline, before the Peace Authority could stop it—what imaginable revelation might do that? They were never crusaders. To see Luna overrun by Terrans would sharpen the embitterment of Lunarian spacers, asterites, Martians, satellite colonists, but it wouldn't provoke them to a war they'd almost surely lose. Not even the Lunarians in the Moon would rebel.

Kenmuir had already decided that Lilisaire's quest for the truth had brought her to hints of it that she wasn't sharing.

Alone in the desert, he had cursed his bond with her. He had sworn to himself that it would not lead him to do anything really harmful. He'd rather live without her than that. By now he might well have resigned, were it not for Aleka. While he scarcely knew the girl, she didn't strike him as a criminal, a fanatic, or a dupe. She had her own cause, whatever it was, but he couldn't believe she'd link it to one she saw as bad. Therefore let him go along at least a little further, through this haze of unknowns.

Briefly, he considered running a data search on her. He had clues to begin on, Hawaiian background, involvement with metamorphs—yes, he recalled something about a unique society in those parts . . . But no. Going through regular channels, that could conceivably alert the opposition. Besides, he needed to know more about his destination. Such an information retrieval would be expected of a visitor, and draw no attention; Bramland was another peculiar place.

Clouds rose over the horizon ahead as he flew. At first they shone like snow, then he was beneath them and the greens had dulled, the sky gone featureless gray. The overcast was predicted to last some days. It wouldn't block everything from monitor satellites, but it would fairly well blind their optics. If the system was scanning the whole planet for him.

Though in that case, he was defying someone or something that could order it to do so—the Federation? He suppressed a shiver. His jaw clamped. If they wanted him to stop, let them enjoin him officially, honestly, by a public announcement over the global net if need be. And let them jolly well explain the reason to him.

Meanwhile, he could do with an explanation from Aleka . . . But start at Bramland.

The volant's terminal screened a short history. Most of it was familiar, sociotechnic cliché. Various groups, ethnic, cultural, religious, or merely eccentric, strove to keep their identities alive. They seldom refused the basic advantages and services of the modern world, and in fact its productivity and peace were generally what enabled them to exist; but they turned their backs on its impersonal rationality. Humankind evolved as a tribal creature, and the need to belong to a tribe is almost as strong as sexuality. What price the Fireball Trothdom—? The very Lunarians had their feudalistic allegiances.

The movement toward such partial secession had been particularly marked in North America in the period of upheaval that followed the fall of the Avantists. Among those who found themselves involved were ex-guerrillas of the resistance, assorted nonconformists, and certain outlaws who hoped to gain legitimacy under the new conditions. They pooled their resources and acquired a large tract of land.

The Third Republic did not hinder them. As fragmented as the nation was by that time, it couldn't, aside from requiring observance of environmental regulations. The Bramlanders didn't mind that. They were seeking a life they could feel was natural. They founded villages, wide-spread over the territory, few of them with a population above 500 adults, a size at which all could participate in public business. In the course of generations, like-minded outsiders joined them while the dissatisfied departed; and thus the culture evolved. There was no dearth of parallel developments.

Evolution, though, takes its own blind courses, and selection working on random mutations and genetic drift can go in curious directions. Today, what vestiges of democracy survived in Bramland were purely ceremonial. It was rituals, taboos, and rankings that satisfied the ordinary member's desire for a well-defined station and purpose in life, a sense of community and of worth. Some men practiced crafts and trades, but incidentally to their real callings—as warriors, sacerdotes, occasional hunters. Women found fulfillment in their mystical sororities and as housewives, sexual artists, occasional mothers. The mayor of a town might or might not listen to its elders, but he was its absolute ruler. He had won to that status by challenging and defeating the former incumbent in a set of athletic contests that frequently ended in death. Quarrels with his counterparts led to equally violent "games" between villages.

Any complaints never got past their authority in any form that would force the North American government to intervene. After all, few of those deaths in duel or war were permanent. Chillcoffins were kept handy, and the fallen were rushed to the nearest medical station for revival and repair. Maybe sometimes, Kenmuir thought, it was lesser injuries that took more time and effort—surgery, regeneration, physical therapy.

Besides, whoever didn't like what went on was free to leave. When a society posed no threat to outsiders, meddling in one would set a precedent dangerous to the rest. They shared an interest, and their political influence, in deterring it. The cybercosm never advised otherwise. The bad old days were long past when law restricted voluntary association. The Bramlanders were content, weren't they?

Yes, Kenmuir thought, obviously most of the Bramlanders were. They were not very intelligent. Self-selection had seen to that.

So much for background. He summoned recent news of the different settlements. It rarely got on the regular broadcasts—who cared?—but of course the sophotects that served there passed their observations to the general database.

They reported nothing of special concern. Well, Joetown and Three Corners were at game. A pitched battle had not ended it, and now bands of men hunted each other across the fields and along the riverbanks. No weapons, oh, no, nothing but sport . . . with well-shaped clubs and staffs, karate chops, winked-at stones . . . Casualties were mounting. Avoid.

He decided on Overburg. Its mayor was at odds with Elville's, but as yet no fights had occurred and an agreement might possibly be reached. Besides, Overburg, larger than average, boasted an inn. Travel and trade did occur between villages, as well as visits from outside. Kenmuir instructed the volant and felt it change course.

Cultivation appeared. Inhabitants raised, processed, made various things for themselves and to sell. They called it "independence," and perhaps it was—spiritual, another set of rituals. The actual necessities were ferried in, paid for by credit.

"Message," announced the volant. Kenmuir tautened. Into the screen before him sprang a man's face. He was thin, pale, and stiff-lipped. A headband curled upward in a silvery filigree, a necklace with a pendant hung over his blouse. Badges of office, Kenmuir supposed. "Po't Commissioner f' his Pot'ncy Mayor Bruno o' Great Overburg," he identified himself in Anglo of sorts. "Y'r ve'icle signals intent to land. You got clearance?"

"I beg your pardon?" Kenmuir said.

"Clearance. Pe'mission. You don't? Who you, señor? What you' business?"

"Since when has a public field demanded a permit? Are you having a problem?"

"You will, if you try. Name y'self an' state y'r business."

Kenmuir checked his temper. Bureaucracy, too, was a way to make people feel important. "No offense, sir. My name is Hannibal, I'm on my way from the west coast, and I'd like to stop here for a day or two. I can't be the first person to come without asking leave beforehand."

"You don't soun' No'merican."

"I'm, uh, European, and—What the Q? May I land or may I not?"

"Awright. You'll have to go befo' the Mayor. Temporary pe'mission granted."

The town was in view. The houses along shaded streets didn't look very different from those Kenmuir had spied earlier, archaic design in modern materials, steep-roofed and slab-sided. At the center was a paved square, surrounded by larger buildings. Kenmuir assumed those were for markets, assemblies, storage, and the like. The biggest, ornately pillared, must be city hall or the mayoral palace or something of that kind. A small airfield, with garages and terminal, lay just beyond the habitations. He set down, took in hand the suitcase Aleka had bought him, and debarked into humid warmth.

The port commissioner awaited him, with four burly men in attendance. In this weather, their garments were loose and gaudy. Long, braided hair trailed below fillets beaded in patterns that presumably signified rank or descent. Each bore a sheath knife and a staff topped with a bronze ball that could fracture a skull. "This way fo' customs 'spection," said the commissioner, and strutted off to the terminal.

It was a standard automated structure, deserted save for his party. He made Kenmuir open his bag and pawed through the contents. They were what Aleka had supplied, a toilet kit and some changes of clothing. Almost reluctantly, he returned it and said, "I phoned. His Pot'ncy's gracious pleased t' receive you right away. Esco't him, Jeb." A slim, graying man, alone and unarmed, didn't need much guarding.

It was a ten or fifteen minute walk to the centrum. Kenmuir's attempt at conversation fell flat. Jeb was too full of the dignity of his assignment. A few cars passed by, but traffic was mainly pedestrian. Women wore flowing gowns and often carried baskets. Groups of them went chattering together, sometimes with one or two of the few, cherished children. Men likewise stayed with their own sex, or sat on porches drinking and playing games. A number of them were elaborately tattooed, and none seemed to have had scars eliminated. Emblems of pride, then.

Here and there Kenmuir passed a workshop and glimpsed a man making something—an implement, a piece of furniture, a decoration—with no tool more complex than a power drill. The style and execution struck him as crude. Yet on the whole, folk appeared happy enough; he saw smiles, heard laughter and animated talk. What words reached him concerned gossip, weather, crops, fishing, the iniquity of Elville, "yump . . . sho' right . . . haw . . ." He thought that if he had to stay here any length of time, he'd hope for a miniwar to enlist in before he went berserk from boredom.

The palace columns represented ferocious monsters. Two sentries flanked the entrance. "Now you be real respec'ful," Jeb warned. "Bend yo' knee."

A chamber stretched broad and long. Kenmuir made out painted shields on the walls and banners hung from the crossbeams. A strip of crimson carpet led to a dais at the far end. There, on a canopied throne, sat Bruno, mayor of Overburg. Four young women, thinly and luxuriously clad, displayed themselves on cushions at either side. Six warriors stood guard. Pages waited for orders. Half a dozen older men were also present; Kenmuir wasn't sure whether they were councillors, courtiers, petitioners, or social callers. He advanced with his escort through silence and stares.

Jeb halted a meter from the dais. Kenmuir did too. Jeb snapped a salute, palm to brow, and announced, "The stranger, señorissimo." Kenmuir remembered to genuflect, awkwardly.

"Ah, yuh," rumbled the mayor. "Yo' name an' pu'pose."

He was a huge man, massively muscular. A blond mane dropped past prognathous features, where a beard bristled, apparently unique in this place. A sign of office, like the horned headband and gold chain? A greasy shirt gaped open around the shaggy breast. The knife sheathed against his trews was outsize. His feet were bare and unwashed. In his right hand he clutched a wooden goblet.

"Hannibal, sir," Kenmuir replied. He and Aleka had agreed on the alias. It gave no clue to his identity, while being distinctive enough for her to be certain of the message he would put in the public bulletin base, informing her of his whereabouts, as soon as he could after learning what they would be.

"Hannibal, huh? Not Cannibal?" Bruno guffawed. Men and boys dutifully laughed. The women giggled. Kenmuir thought that two of them forced it, and that the looks they gave the mayor were frightened. The others were perhaps content with their status.

Bruno hunched forward. "Why you here? Spy? Gummint agent? Hah?" He sat back again, expectant, and glugged from his goblet.

He couldn't do worse than expel the newcomer. Could he? Maybe. Anyhow, that would be an infernal nuisance. "I assure you, sir," Kenmuir sighed, "I'm a harmless private person. A friend and I are going to spend a while in Lake Superior Preserve. At the last minute, she was delayed. I've heard interesting things about your community, and would like to take a day or two here till she can meet me." Curious outsiders must come occasionally, if not often. "You see, I deal in uniques, handmade work, and I gather you have skilled craftsmen." When was flattery ever unwelcome, or money?

Bruno raised his brows. " 'She,' d'you say?"

"Well, yes, a young lady," Kenmuir replied, hanging onto his patience. Somebody sniggered. "Could I arrange permission for her to land and look around too?" Somewhere along the orbit, he and Aleka must have a serious talk. This might be their last chance before jumping off into the irrevocable.

"Young. Hum. Yuh." Bruno pondered. Kenmuir thought of slow wheels turning. "Yuh. Awright. You see the health off'cer, it clears you, awright, you can stay. At the inn." Spend money.

The interview hadn't been too bad. No big surprise. Kenmuir was clearly not from hated Elville.

Bruno leered. "Landing tax. Near forgot. Landing tax. Ten, uh, fifteen ucus. Apiece. You can pay it f'r you both. To me."

Extortion, but Kenmuir decided not to invoke the law. "Do you object to cash, sir?" If he debited his account, that was a giveaway to any search program.

"Cash? Huh? Naw, naw, cash's fine." Bruno's manner suggested it was better than fine. Perhaps he had transactions of his own that he didn't want traced. He accepted the bills and counted them twice, moving his lips. "Awright, guardsman, take'm to the health off'cer, and when he's cleared, show'm to the inn." Half cordially: "Maybe we'll talk later, Hannibal. Maybe I'll 'vite you f'r a drink. Yuh, maybe even—" He nodded and winked, right and left, at his women. Two of them smiled.

Jeb saluted and led Kenmuir back out. "This way," he directed. "'Cross the square. The clinic there, see?"

Understanding smote. "The health officer" hadn't registered a meaning, unless as a vague idea of still another tribal functionary. But Bruno had said "it." Yonder waited a sophotect.

Kenmuir stumbled. He had almost dug in his heels. Jeb gave him a questioning glance. No. He must go through with this. Suddenly to return to his volant and take off, that would cause wondering. "Excuse me," he muttered and strode on.

Why did Bruno want the machine to approve him? Officiousness? The mayor, like the port commissioner, didn't get many chances to throw his weight around in the presence of strangers. Or was Bruno anxious to stay on the good side of the government, leaning backward to look cooperative? He might fear that sometime, policy or no, there would be a crackdown on local practices.

No matter now. What Kenmuir must do was pass himself off as what he claimed to be. He swallowed, cleared his throat, and told the muscles in his back to slack off.

Outwardly the clinic resembled its neighbors. The reception room was reassuringly if rather hideously decorated with Bramlander art. Behind it, Kenmuir knew, was up-to-date equipment for treating most hurts and ills. Likewise was what the sophotect used to monitor sanitation, automated services such as energy, and the biological well-being of the land around. The town of his childhood, also isolated, had had just such an attendant. People there had called it the caretaker, when they didn't say "Auld Angus."

The form here was hauntingly similar, boxy, four-legged, six-armed, with turret for sensors and electrophotonic brain, housing for powerpack, and retractable communications dish. The voice was male, deep and resonant: "Hi, how c'n I help you?"

"Got this guzzah wants 'a stay a couple days," Jeb explained. "Mayor wants you awright him."

"Ah." The accent became educated. "Bienvenido, señor. Por favor, be seated. A formality, I'm sure. Everybody's tense, what with this unfortunate friction with Elville. My opposite number there and I are trying to get it composed, but—" The flexible pair of arms rippled through a shrug. "Jeb, you can go."

"Not need me?"

"Certainly not. You may go, I said." The tone had sharpened the least bit. Jeb bent his head, perhaps unconsciously, and left.

"Do take a seat," the sophotect urged. "I suspect you've had a slightly unpleasant time. Would you care for coffee, tea, or a short whisky?"

Kenmuir took a chair. His body resisted its form-fitting embrace, but he kept his face steady. "No, thank you. I'm on trajectory, really I am."

The machine seized on the expression. "Ah, are you concerned with space? How interesting. You'd be our first visitor who wasn't of this Earth earthy." A chuckle ran forth.

Kenmuir swore at himself. "No, I, I have a friend in the Service, and I've gone once to the Moon. That's all." He retailed his story and waited belly-painful. That he chose to go by a name like Hannibal was nothing unusual, it could be whim, but what if the officer asked him for his registry number?

That still might not be fatal, he thought beneath the

thunders. For the time being, this was a distinct, separated personality that stood before him. It could not have received any reason to be suspicious. (Unless the cybercosm had contacted every last unit on the planet . . . but that kind of effort, at the present stage of things, was unlikely. The channels and the data-processing capabilities that would be tied up—) It might not call in to query whether the man thus identified was wanted for anything. After all, if it did, that would entail a global data search to determine whether the number he gave was false.

"I see," the sophotect said quietly. "Bueno, let me repeat, bienvenido. Or, in your idiom, welcome. I hope you and your friend to come will enjoy your stay."

The voice was warm. Could the wish be sincere? Why not? Kenmuir harked back. Auld Angus, comforting him when he was small and had broken a rib, telling him a fable and singing him a song . . . Auld Angus, counselor, arbiter of quarrels, patiently listening to a boy who was one-sidedly in love . . . Auld Angus, courteous as he told the town council that it must enforce limits on mussel gathering if it didn't want the government to station a patrol at the bay . . . Auld Angus, advising a youth that he indeed seemed to have the potential of becoming a space pilot, and he should go for it. . . .

Did they give their sophotect in Overburg a name and their affection?

Kenmuir stirred. "I'll be on my way, then," he said.

The officer raised a humanlike hand. "A moment, por favor. I would like to caution you. This is a difficult society. The conflict between chiefs has not improved matters. Have a care, always. Especially after your friend arrives. You've indicated she's female. I get the impression she's attractive. Best she stay inconspicuous, and no longer than she must. Do you follow me?"

"I . . . think so," Kenmuir answered.

Mostly he was thinking how well the machine had

read him. But why shouldn't it? If the glands weren't there, an equivalent was, conation, intuition, together with an intellect probably superior to his.

Certainly superior, if you understood that this was an avatar of the cybercosm, merging itself again and again with the whole, sometimes reshaped thereby, always bearing back memories of that gigantic oneness, even an intimation of the Teramind. Of course it interpreted his overtones, body language, things left unsaid: and not without what you might as well call empathy, or actual sympathy. It, Auld Angus, every electrophotonic intelligence—and, yes, the humble unconscious robots—were all waves on the same ocean.

The optics gleamed. How much did they note of his face and body? How much about him would the mind enter in the database, when next it reported what it observed?

For him to wear a life mask would have been an exercise in futility, as untrained as he was in it. Worse, it would have singled him out. After that, a quick check of somatic data that were surely on file would give cause to arrest him.

His hope lay in remaining utterly undistinguished. In the sheer immensity of the databases was refuge—for a while. No matter how carefully designed a search tree was, scanning, retrieval, and evaluation took finite time. Until the hunters got a clear idea of what to seek for, their machines could spend days, weeks, among the permutations of two billion humans. Not that that would happen. Too much of the system was needed to keep civilization running.

Give this kindly being no reason to want more information about him.

"Yes. Thank you. But, uh, you mean—"

"A mayor in Bramland may command any woman to join him for as long as he chooses. It's the custom; they seldom object. In fact, it's considered an honor." Those who did object could, theoretically, catch the next airbus out of town. Theoretically. Therefore the authorities ignored the whole business. "Ordinarily, a visitor would not be bothered. Our current mayor, though—Perhaps you'd like to meet your friend somewhere else."

Kenmuir considered. Another move could by itself draw attention, the more so if Bruno took offense and started phoning around about it. "No, thank you again, but I expect we'll be all right. He won't want charges filed against him, will he? Chances are, anyway, he'll never see her." He rose. "Good day, Officer."

"A good day to you," said the sophotect.

Jeb waited outside. Doggedly, he guided Kenmuir to the inn. Regardless, the heart rose within the spaceman. He'd made it this far. Weren't he and Aleka exaggerating their danger? What lay ahead could prove fairly straightforward, until—excitement thrummed—it brought them to whatever had been discovered and done, long ago on Luna.

22

The Mother of the Moon

From its height Temerir's observatory looked widely over the crater wilderness that is most of Farside. A low sun filled the land with intricate shadows and dun highlights. He had set the viewscreen in his living room to show that scene, not as the eye would have beheld it but with glare stopped down and lesser radiances enhanced. There the solar disc glowed soft between zodiacal wings and stars were like fire-drops flung off the tumbling Milky Way. Otherwise the room was sparsely furnished, as austere as its owner. An abstract lava sculpture on a table resembled a thick twist of smoke. The air, a little chilly, bore a tinge of ozone and subdued music on no scale ever heard on Earth. When Dagny noticed it, she thought of ghosts in flight before the wind.

Temerir had not said where his one wife and their

children were. He alone received his guests, Brandir, Kaino, Fia, and his mother. Crystal glasses and a decanter of wine were his scanty concession to custom. Nobody cared or poured. They entered and stood unspeaking for perhaps a minute. Nor had any among them talked much on their way here in Brandir's yacht; but then crew had been present.

Dagny broke the crust. "Now can we get to business?" she asked as gently as might be. She knew full well what the business was. Sadness edged her pleasure. 'Mond should have been at her side to hear.

She put the wish from her. In six years she hadn't stopped missing him, but it was no longer so that every small thing that had been his, every place she had ever seen him, cried aloud to her. She had dear friends, captivating work, lively recreations, a grandstand seat at humankind's ventures into the universe. From Anson Guthrie she had learned early on that self-pity is the most despicable emotion of any.

Nevertheless wistfulness touched her. "Maybe afterward we can be sociable a while?" she added. "I don't see you a lot." Nor the rest of her offspring, or their mates and children, now that Jinann was with that Voris who had been Reynaldo Fuentes. It wasn't that they were estranged or even indifferent, it was that their lives were no longer close to hers and, she believed, it seldom or never occurred to them that she might wish it were otherwise. Lars, her darling bastard, understood; but he wasn't on Luna very often.

Brandir's voice rippled at Temerir. Dagny caught that he put a question.

The astronomer cast her a pale glance and replied in English, "Yes, of course we are safe from listeners. I assured that before I called you."

Brandir's short golden-hued cloak swirled from his shoulders as he bowed. "Your pardon, lady Mother," he said. "I forgot me."

The inconsequential gesture made Dagny's eyes sting. "Oh, that, that's okay," she faltered. "I can follow Lunarian pretty well, you know, when I set my mind to the job."

"Yet not readily, nay?" blurted Kaino.

No, she thought. It was a mercury language, swift-flowing, shimmery, fluid also in its meanings, impossible for her to quite close hands on. She had borne these brains within her, but little of what was in them had passed through hers or Edmond's. "Admitted," she said. "Gracias."

From between her dark tresses, Fia frowned a bit at her brother's impetuosity. To Temerir she said, "The matter is simple for either tongue. You have found the planetoid our father foretold."

Yes, Dagny thought, at last, after these years. How long they seemed, looking back. But, true, he'd had to search on what amounted to stolen time, inventing pretexts and manufacturing their justifications. Though he ruled this place entirely, his fief from Brandir, those who worked with him and for him were not readily fooled.

She hadn't kept track of how it stretched on. Her existence had been too crowded. Personal matters, everyday jobs and joys, the occasional sorrow, a friend in need or a youthful confidence. The growth of Lunar population, industry, undertakings, the rewards they brought and the demands they made. Her engineering administrative work for Fireball becoming entangled with the whole society around her, resources to find and allocate, conflicting plans and ambitions. Friction worsening among Moondwellers, be they Lunarians, Terrans born on Earth or in L-5, avowed Earthlings. . . .

"I have," she heard, "if 'planetoid' be the rightful word for a thing such as yonder."

"What know you for certain?" Brandir snapped.

Temerir met the gaze of the taller, more powerful man as does an equal. "That which instruments and computations can tell," he replied. "Telescopic quest brought a huge harvest for winnowing." Yes, Dagny recalled, he could publicly mount a program to investigate the remote reaches of the Solar System, sketch-map and estimate-count the comets of the Kuiper Belt beyond Neptune and the Oort Cloud beyond it. What he held to himself were certain of the results he got. "Some few appear to be asteroids, but small and rocky, not what Father meant. When a candidate was promising, I must take what faint spectrum I could. Then, be the promise not immediately shown false, I must find occasion to send robotic probes far enough, fast enough to get a parallax. But you know of these procedures, you who are here this daycycle. In the end, one and only one body manifested the possibility."

"What is it *like?*" Kaino nearly shouted.

Temerir stayed ice-calm. "Seemingly akin to Father's bane, far larger. The form is spheric, diameter approximately 2000 kilometers. Much surface is overlaid with dull material, but sufficient reflects in ferrous wise to suggest that thus is the most, giving a high mean density. The orbital inclination is a few minutes less than forty-four degrees, about the same as for the lesser object that we came to know too well. This too implies a similar composition. Perihelion is 107 astronomical units and a fraction, eccentricity is above 99 one-hundredths." Judas priest, Dagny thought, that made the aphelion point something like thirty or forty thousand a.u. out. This fitted also with 'Mond's asteroid. Oh, 'Mond, 'Mond! "At present the body is 302 astronomical units hence, spaceward bound."

She could not hold back: "What do you propose to do about it?"

"What would you, Mother?" Brandir asked. It was not a retort, she felt, it was a response. All four were looking at her with a strange—eagerness?

"It was, was kind of you to invite me," she stammered, overwhelmed. "You didn't have to."

"You knew of the search from the outset," Fia said, she maybe the most coldly practical of the brood. "You would in any case have guessed what is now afare."

"Above that consideration," Brandir said, "we honor you."

Dagny wondered how sincere that was. How candid were they ever, even among each other?

Unworthy thought. She thrust it from her and spoke slowly. "Well, this is . . . scientifically fascinating, isn't it? Gives a whole new insight into the early history of the Solar System. What a memorial to your father."

"It is raised in our hearts, which are ours only," Brandir replied.

"What do you mean?" Already she knew.

Temerir confirmed it for her: "I foreglimpsed that the thing might have immense potentialities, and hence required secrecy. Should we give it away to Earth? Nay."

"But what could you *do* with it?"

"We'll find out!" Kaino cried.

Temerir nodded. "If naught seems valuable, then may we set the knowledge free."

And he was the scientist of this bunch, Dagny thought. Was his generation really that alien to hers? Or that alienated?

"We shall need a shipful of robots strong and subtle," Fia said.

Brandir drew a hand slantwise through the air, a negation. An Earthling would have shaken his head. "Nay. We could not assemble and prepare that much, that costly, unbeknownst," he said. Clear before Dagny stood the fact that he had been thinking about this for a long while.

"So, a manned expedition?" flared from Kaino. "Eyach!" He threw back his head and laughed against the stars.

It happened he stood nearest to Dagny. The vision flitted through her, the contrast, those red elflocks beside the hair that hung to her shoulders. Since Edmond's death she had let it go white. The future beside the past—

No, by damn. She wasn't yet ready for—what was

the phrase people used in her childhood? Senior citizen. She bloody well refused to be any sniveling senior citizen. She was an old woman, and she'd soldier on as one till the Old Man came for her.

These folks had not asked her here out of pure goodness. There was something she could do for them.

"To go on trajectory would need too much time and too much supply, as noticeable as robots," Brandir was saying. "We shall abide until we possess a torchcraft."

That wouldn't be soon. Only lately had Dagny and her allies gotten pushed through the Federation a grudging permission for Moondwellers to buy, build, and operate spaceships with the thrust and delta v for full interplanetary service. They must do it in stages, slowly raising capital, training crew, acquiring fleet; and the earlier vessels would be relatively short-range, used for easy missions. To be sure, Brandir would hold a large share in most of the enterprises.

Kaino sprang about the room. "Come the hour, I'll recruit me a trusty gang," he jubilated.

"How will you cover the departure?" asked Fia.

They spoke as if it could be tomorrow, rather than years hence, in ardor joined with frosty calculation.

"We will give out that Temerir has identified several possible lode comets in the near Kuiper, and I am bound forth to examine them more closely," Brandir said.

A reasonable story in itself, Dagny considered. The Moon could use a bunch more water and raw organics than had yet been brought to it. Comets of suitable composition and orbit weren't plentiful. Indeed, the Federation had decided that it had done enough of that and if the Selenites wanted more they'd have to help themselves, unsubsidized. That might put their uppity noses out of joint. . . .

The surprise struck through. Fia spoke before Dagny could, brows lifted over russet eyes: "Your very self, Brandir?"

"Yes," he said. "Since the emprise will be chiefly mine, I want a full input before I choose what we shall do afterward." His laugh purred. "Furthermore, I fear life on Luna will be flattening," as he achieved other goals, wealth, power, and desires more inward. "My mood will be no secret, and will help explain why men go, rather than robots. By then, sister mine, you ought to be able to manage the cityside affairs of Zamok Vysoki in my absence, under the direction of Ivala and Tuori," his wives. Evidently Fia had proven her worth in the subordinate executive position she currently occupied. It involved some tough, risky work.

And she just twenty-three, Dagny thought. But Brandir, the oldest, was just forty-one. And she, his mother, took her first job on the moon at age nineteen. (Forty-eight years ago, was that it? Time went, time went.) Well, pioneering eras stand open to youth.

"None of this can we swiftly or easily achieve, nor by ourselves." Brandir addressed Dagny: "Again we must draw on your wisdom and your aid."

"Me?" she countered.

"None other could do so well," Kaino avowed.

"You know your way about among both Selenites and Earthlings," Fia said. "You have the linkages to high persons and the skill to use them. Through you, we can win a cooperation from Fireball that it would not elsewise see for profitable."

"You can make sure our course toward the planetoid remains veiled," Temerir added.

"Yours is our blood," Brandir finished.

He smiled. He was beautiful.

Dared they take for granted she would turn on Earth?

No, wrong thinking. Helping Luna would be no treason to her kind. Would it? What harm to anyone —except self-infatuated politicians, busybody bureaucrats, and magnates enriched by their franchises and monopolies—if more freedom came to these children of hers and 'Mond's?

That wasn't fair, she reminded herself. Once you

started taking your own propaganda seriously, you were headed for fanaticism. Earth had made an enormous investment in Luna. All history shrieked how right the Federation was to dread a resurgent nationalism. The Lunarians chafed at laws written with good intent, when they did not violate them, covertly or more and more openly. Common heritage was only the most obvious sore point. Environmental concerns, weapons control, educational requirements, taxes, licenses, regulations, most of them reasonable —from the viewpoint of a civilized Earthling—but the civilization aborning here was none of Earth's, was maybe not quite human—

Wasn't it wise at least to make the cage larger, before the beast tried breaking altogether loose?

She couldn't tell. She wished she could seek counsel of Guthrie. But she was sworn to silence, and these were her children.

"Well," she sighed, "we'll talk about it."

23

Drums boomed and thuttered. A chant pulsed among them, now organ deep, now shrill as the whistles that interwove, *hai-ah-ho-hee*. At the landing field the noise went low, like a distant thunderstorm, but its darkness thickened the twilight closing in.

Thunderstorm, yes, Aleka thought. Air pressed downward from the cloud deck, hot, heavy with unshed rain; her skin gleamed wet under blouse and shorts, and prickled as if from gathering electricity.

For a moment she stood beside the hired volant, unsure. Likeliest she'd leave with Kenmuir in hers, which had brought him here. But that wasn't certain. The news had been a shock when she retrieved it while approaching Overburg—negotiations suddenly broken off, Mayor Bruno calling a game against Elville, a government advisory not to visit the area. She might need to flit in a hurry.

"Wait here," she directed the cab. "If I haven't told you otherwise, return to your station at, oh, hour seven tomorrow."

"In view of the hazard the charge for that will be double the standard rate," the robot warned.

The debit would put quite a nick in her modest personal account. However, Lilisaire ought to reimburse eventually. Besides—her head lifted—she was playing for almighty high stakes. "Authorized." Her voice pattern was sufficient signature. She gripped her two suitcases hard and set forth across the field.

It reached empty. When she got in among the houses, at first the sole light came from equally deserted pavement. Was everybody downtown, working up enthusiasm? Best would be to skirt that section. But she didn't know how. She had simply projected a street map from the database and memorized the most direct route to the inn. It lay beyond the square.

If only she could have talked with Kenmuir beforehand. They'd have arranged a safer meeting place, maybe an arbitrary spot in the countryside. Bueno, he had had no way of telling where she was en route. To set the communications net searching would have been to provide any hunters with a major clue. After she got the bad word, she tried to call him from the flyer. The innkeeper told her that Sr. Hannibal was out. Not knowing when to expect her, he must have gone to eat or something. She saw no point in leaving a message. On her second attempt, nobody replied. By then she was so close that she decided to go ahead with the original plan.

Rightly or wrongly. Probably there was no real danger. She stepped onward. Gloom canopied the buildings and crouched between them. Ahead, though, light strengthened wavery over the rooftops. Drums, whistles, song, stamping feet grew louder, till the racket beat in her marrow.

The street ended at a large edifice, a pile of night. She turned left, then right at its edge, hoping to stay clear of the crowd without getting lost. Unfamiliarity tricked her. All at once she came forth into the next street and found she was at a corner of the square diagonally across it. The spectacle jarred her to a halt.

At the center flared a bonfire, flames roaring three meters aloft, smoke washed red with their glare. Around it danced the young men, stripped to the waist, shining with sweat. They waved knives and staves, they ululated, their faces were stretched out of shape with passion. At the corners squatted the drummers and whistlers. Along the right side clustered the women, children, and elderly, a shadowy jumble wherein firelight glistened off eyeballs. Their keening wove like needles through the male chant. *"Ee-ya, ho-ah, hai-ah, ho!"*

Through Aleka whirled recollections of ceremonies at home, solemn or merry, cheering at sports events, and a police parade. This too was human.

Better get away. Fast.

A hand clamped on her shoulder. In her amazement she had not noticed anyone behind her. "Who you? What you doin' here?"

The man was gray and portly, unfit for campaign, but his muscles were still big and he carried a knobbed staff as well as a dagger. Yes, she realized, a few guards would be posted, even in this dement hour. "P-por favor," she choked, "I'm a, a visitor. Bound for your inn."

"Ungn? Spy, mebbe. We see. Come." He took hold of her arm and wrenched. Biting back fear and anger, she obeyed. They skirted the left side of the square.

A man came dancing solitary down that street. He was swathed in a knee-length hooded coat. As he passed, Aleka saw by the veined hands and withered face that he was aged beyond any further help from biotech. Then she saw that his coat was identical front and rear, and that on the back of his head he wore a mask of himself as a young man. That face bore the same blind ecstasy. He jerked his way on out of her sight. She wondered what magic he was working.

The guard took her up the stairs of a big, grotesquely colonnaded building. On the porch stood several men, also old but as richly attired as the four young women with them. At the middle hulked another man, in the prime of life, huge and shaggy-blond, a horned fillet and a gold chain declaring his rank. Beside him, a table held a jug and goblet. He was taking a long draught.

Gazes went from the warriors to the newcomers. The guard bent a knee and dipped his staff. "'Scuse, señorissimo," he said through the noise. "I caught this here moo over yonder. Dunno who she is or wha' she wants."

"Yah?" growled the giant.

Aleka mustered resolve. "Are you the mayor, señor?" she asked as calmly as she was able. "My respects. I didn't mean any harm or, or offense or anything. I just came to meet another visitor here. Nobody was at the airfield, so all I could do was make for the inn where he is."

"Ah-h. Yah. That there Hannibal, huh?"

"Yes. He messaged that he'd gotten permission for me."

"I know. Yuh." The mayor's glance slithered up and down and across her. He grinned. "Yuh, sure. You goin' to the inn, um? Awright. Stay there. I can't leave yet, but I'll see y' later. Stay, y' hear?" To the guard: "Follow 'long, Bolly, an' watch t' make sure they stay inside."

Unease quickened. "Why, señor?" Aleka protested. "I assure you, we're only transients, we have nothing to do with—"

A slab of a hand chopped air. "I know. I wanna talk wi' you, tha's all. Move on. Don't hurt her none, Bolly, long's she behaves. You got me? Awright, move on."

Evidently the mayor's part in the celebration must

not be interrupted any more than necessary. The guardsman led Aleka back down the stairs. He had released his grip, but sullen silence told how he resented being posted away from the fun. She suspected he would have found ways to take it out on her except for his orders. The database had said the chief enforced an absolute governance, personally and brutally.

But it was limited to his subjects, who could always leave, she told herself. It existed on sufferance. Unless he was a total fool, he wouldn't provoke national intervention.

Still, relief streamed through her when the escort stopped and mumbled, "Here y' are. Go on, get inside." He hunkered down on the grass by the steps and brooded on his wrongs.

The hostel was an ordinary-looking house, not much more sizable than average. A single window showed light from the second floor. An entryroom was illuminated but empty. When the hinged door had shut, quietness drew in on Aleka. Dust, a few pieces of weary furniture, a musty smell—no robots, then; two or three humans in charge. A role for them to play. Tonight they were playing another and frenzied one. However, that shining window—Her blood thrilled. Baggage or no, she ran upstairs.

Doors lined a corridor. They lacked any kind of scanners or annunciators. Mentally orienting herself and recalling historical shows, she chose which to knock on. It opened, and the sight of Kenmuir's simpático face set her spirit free. *"Aloha, aloha,"* she gasped.

"You!" he exclaimed. "Cosmos, but you're welcome. Come in, do." He took her suitcases and secured the door behind her.

The room was about four meters square, with an attached bath cubicle and a woven carpet underfoot. It possessed neither phone nor multi. A bed, a dresser, and two chairs were as primitive in workmanship as in design. The sash window was another anachronism, full of the night that had fallen. Kenmuir shut it against the sounds, to which he must have been listening, and turned on the air cycle. Coolness blew sweet into an atmosphere that had begun to stifle her.

He took both her hands. "How are you?" he asked anxiously. "I've been so worried since this trouble broke. I was hoping you'd sheer off and post a new message for me."

"I thought of it, but that would've cost more time and I don't know how much we can afford," she explained. "Maybe I should've. Too late now."

He sensed the grimness. "What do you mean?"

She told him about her arrival. He scowled, paced to and fro, shook his lean head. "Let's hope Bruno has nothing more in mind than a bit of farewell sociability, to show off his importance."

"What else might it be?" she asked with a flutter in her throat.

"I . . . can't say. Of course, he can't detain us, or anything like that. We can point out the legal consequences of trying. I'm afraid that ruffian outside is too stupid to understand, and we could end with a broken bone or two. But Bruno—I've come to know him a little, this past couple of days. He's been . . . cordial, in his clumsy way. Eager to impress me, the man from the wide world. Cultural inferiority complex, I think, fuelling a lot of the bluster and violence." Kenmuir's tone had gone scholarly. He curbed it and his unrest. A laugh rattled out. "But I say, what kind of host am I? Do sit down, or lie down if you'd rather. Would you care for a drink? I acquired a bottle of whisky."

Aleka took a chair and smiled up at him. "Gracias. Plenty of water in it, por favor. Don't worry about me. I've been through far worse. This was unpleasant but short, and I've already bounced back."

Charging the tumblers, he regarded her and said slowly, "Yes, you are an adventurous lass, aren't you? A great deal to tell me, I'll wager. Well, we've hours to wait, and we can talk freely. This room is one place—

one of the very few places on Earth—we can feel sure there's no surveillance."

"We do need to talk," she agreed.

He gave her her drink, pulled the other chair close, and folded himself onto it. Tenser than she, he took a stiff swallow before he began: "Who are you, Aleka? What are you doing in this affair, and why?"

"I'd like to know you better, too, Kenmuir."

"But you've been briefed about me. Haven't you? While to me you're a complete mystery."

She couldn't help grinning. "Woman of mystery? That'll be news to all my folk. How do I go about it? Should I put on a foreign accent, or find me a low-cut gown, or what? No, that's Lilisaire's department."

His lips tightened for a moment. Did she see him wince? She remembered what had been in his eyes when they spoke with the Selenarch from that furnace enclosure in the desert. Sympathy welled forth. By every evidence, he was a decent man, a quiet man, pitched into a situation for which he was no more fitted than a Keiki was to climb a mountain, yet going bravely ahead, without even the hope that drove her.

She gentled her voice. "I'm sorry. Don't want to play games with you. Go on, ask what you want. I'll answer anything that's not too personal."

He flushed. "I . . . wouldn't dream of intruding on your privacy." So he valued his own. "But as for your background and, and your motivation—"

Time lost itself in memories. He had a gift of evoking them from her, she couldn't quite tell how, the shy smile or the questions that could be awkwardly phrased but were always intelligent or the bits of his years and dreams that he offered in return. She believed that little by little he came to some knowledge of her Lahui Kuikawa, the two races of it that she both loved, small dear homes enfolded by immensities of sea and weather, ancient usages and youthful joys, a life with a meaning and purpose that went beyond itself, which no machine could share but which the world of the machines and their followers was going to confine and make over. . . . "Oh, I can admit the necessity, even the justice of it," she said, and blinked furiously at her tears, "but give us a while yet, give us a chance to find a new way for ourselves!" . . . She wasn't sure whether she would ever fully imagine his feelings. Though he had gone in pride among splendors, the faring seemed harsh and lonely. But he held her to him, briefly and tenderly, when grief was about to overwhelm her, and it receded.

He deserved better than Lilisaire.

The time came when they sat quiet, until he asked, "And what did she promise you, if somehow this crazy venture succeeds?" His tone was calm, with a hint of the academic style that he often fell into. His mouth creased slightly upward.

Doubts shivered away to naught. She straightened in her chair and cried, "A home!"

"Where? How?"

"Nauru." His glance inquired. Words spilled from her. "No, I don't expect you've heard of it. An island in mid-Pacific, barely south of the equator, northeast of the Solomons. It was a nation once, tiny but rich, because it had plenty of phosphate to export. But that got used up," before molecular technology had bridled the voracity of global industry. "The population, ten thousand or so, tried to build a new economic foundation, but didn't really succeed and became poorer and poorer. When Fireball offered to buy them out at a good price, they were happy to accept and move away. Guthrie had an idea of building another spaceport there. But things went to wrack and ruin on Earth, what with the Renewal and the Grand Jihad and all; and when they were starting to make sense again, Guthrie died, and it was a while before his download had full control over the company; and by then, so much space activity was based in space itself that a new Earthside port wouldn't pay. Eventually Fireball sold Nauru to Brandir of Zamok Vysoki. That was in the early days of Lunar independence.

Several Selenarchs had gotten superwealthy and were looking for investments. They picked up a fair amount of property on Earth, including real estate. Some of it is still in their families."

"This island being Lilisaire's, eh?" Kenmuir murmured. "What has she done with it?"

"Nothing much. Fishery and aquaculture, maintained by robots and a few resident Terrans. Not especially profitable. But you see, it was always important to have people there, if only a handful. Because technically, Nauru is still a distinct country."

Kenmuir's eyes widened. "I think I do see." He chuckled. "I'd love to know what maneuvers Guthrie went through to arrange it. Wily old devil."

Aleka nodded vigorously. "That was the idea. The Ecuadoran and Australian governments were cooperative with Fireball, but if he could have his very own—Bueno, as I said, it didn't work out. The Selenarch owners used it as a way of getting a kept politician into the Federation Assembly, but it never did them any noticeable good. And now—" She caught her breath.

"A-a-ah. You shall have it for your people."

"Yes. An atoll, with a couple of big float platforms to add some area. But more than a quarter million square kilometers of territorial waters. And the neighbor states, they long since granted rights in theirs to Nauru, on a basis of mutuality that they don't take advantage of any more.

"Oh, yes, we'll have to abide by environmental rules under the Covenant. But they're flexible enough when . . . we are the local supervisors . . . and we do want to bring our Keiki into balance with nature, it's just that we can't do it without destroying what we are unless we have time and elbow room and . . . freedom—" She couldn't go on.

She had not yet been there in person, but before her rose the vision she conjured out of the database. Nauru was not Niihau. It lay solitary, 200 square kilometers, a plateau scarred by the former mining, walled by coral cliffs, ringed by sandy beaches and the outlying reef, a wilderness where remnants of dwellings stood desolate under the sea wind and the screaming sea birds, the only habitation a few cabins. But trees swayed in that wind, flowers glowed, in the southwest was a freshwater lagoon, everywhere around reached the living sea. The English had named it Pleasant Island.

"What we can make of it," she whispered after a minute.

"I daresay the deal will raise an uproar in Hiroshima." Kenmuir stroked his chin. "But, hm, I'd guess you can plead your case on more than legalistic grounds. Popular sentiment will favor a cause that romantic. Also, not least, because you'll be taking the country out of Lunarian hands, back into Earthlings'. Yes, the prospects look good to me."

His dryness was just what she needed. Had he known? Aleka settled into reality. "First," she said, "we've got to carry out our mission, and hope the result will seem worth it to Lilisaire."

His countenance drew into furrows. "Right. *We* do." Then: "What exactly is your plan?"

"The plan I was given, actually," she replied, "and there's nothing exact about it, only a briefing on what to expect and a suggestion or two about how to proceed. We can try something different if we choose. But this does strike me as our best bet. Does the name Prajnaloka mean anything to you?"

"No-o. . . . Wait. Some kind of cult or fellowship?"

"Stranger than that. I hardly knew of the movement myself till the agent in San Francisco told me. Later, before going to meet you, I retrieved more details. It's worldwide, though it hasn't many members, and its name depends on the language—in Anglo, it's Soulquest. Prajnaloka is the center for North America, a settlement in the Ozark Mountains, not far east of here. For our purposes, it's got superb data facilities, and they often get used in such peculiar ways that we can hope the system won't look closely if we—"

A knock crashed on the door, again and again. Aleka and Kenmuir jumped to their feet. For a terrible half second, she felt this must be their enemy, who had no face. Then she thought to see what the time was. She hadn't noticed how the hours slipped away, noise and flicker from the square died out, the night grew old.

"Bruno," Kenmuir said. He walked stiffly over to unbolt the door and open it.

The mayor's bulk filled the frame. Aleka glimpsed the guardsman Bolly behind him. "Good evening," Kenmuir greeted. "Or I could better say, 'Good morning.'"

"Good, yah, good," Bruno replied slurrily. His face was flushed, he breathed hoarsely, but he advanced with iron steadiness. Kenmuir must step aside. Bruno's gaze sought Aleka and clung. "Ho, th' li'l lady," he boomed. "B'env'ida." He approached, stopped, laid hands on her shoulders. "Happy here?"

She slipped from her chair and his touch. He came after her and loomed. Sweat and drink swamped her nostrils.

"Not happy, huh? Yah, stuck in this room. No fun. Sorry. For y' own safety. Things got kin' o' wild. Quiet now. Come on out 'n' I'll show you our fair city. You'll like it."

She would *not* let her voice tremble. "Gracias, but I'm afraid we must go. Urgent business."

"Naw. Not that urgent. Later t'day. When I start off for th' game. First, fun." Again his hands were upon her, enclosing her hips, sliding up to her breasts. "Come on wi' me. You'll like it."

She writhed free. He grabbed her wrist, bruisingly hard. Through nausea she heard Kenmuir: "I say, this won't do. Let her go."

Bruno glared at him. "Huh? You gimme orders? You?" Bolly growled in the doorway and hefted his weapon.

"Please let us go," Kenmuir clipped.

"Why?"

"You have no right to keep us. You're being abusive. Have a care, sir, or you'll be under criminal charges."

Bruno tugged Aleka against his belly. She submitted. At least in this position he couldn't fondle her. "I'm not hurtin' nobody," he said, and farted. "Jus' gonna pleasure the li'l lady. Like she never been pleasured before."

"You're drunk."

Monumentally drunk, Aleka thought. Unless it was mostly the hysteria of the war dance still upon him. She could not stop a shudder.

"Shaddup!" he bawled. "Shaddup 'fore I shut you up wi' y'r teeth!" Aleka felt him slacken a bit. The hair around the lips scratched her cheek. He laughed. "You were ready enough t' enjoy a woman o' mine yestiddy. My turn."

"I warn you," Kenmuir stated, "if you don't release her this minute, you'll soon be under arrest. What then is your glory worth?"

Was that the wrong thing to say? Did it egg the creature past every border of reason? Bruno spat on the floor. *"That* f'r you!" he roared. Chortling: "Naw, no force. She'll like it, I tell you. You'll beg me for more, li'l girl. You'll wanna stay here. C'mon." He forced her around, her arm still in his grasp and twisted behind her back. "Bolly," he commanded, "make sure this yort don't give no trouble. Got me?"

"Yah, señorissimo," replied the guard happily.

Kenmuir ignored him, strode to stand in the doorway, and said to Bruno, "Very well, sir, you leave me no choice. I challenge you."

"What?" The mayor jarred to a halt.

"We'll settle between us who has the authority," Kenmuir told him.

Bolly raised his staff. "Hey, you can't talk t' him like that," he rasped.

"Is the mayor afraid to fight me?" Kenmuir retorted.

"No!" Aleka screamed out of nightmare. "Don't!

You can't—" The giant would pluck the slender middle-aged man apart. And then what recourse would be left? Both she and Kenmuir could disappear, permanently, and nobody else ever know what had become of them. "I'll go along. I will." And maybe later she could call on the law. Or maybe Bruno would wake up dead.

"You're loco," he was coughing.

"No," Kenmuir answered. "I simply challenge you to meet me, bare-handed. If you aren't man enough, let your follower here so inform the people."

Bruno bellowed.

And somehow, in a rush and clatter, they all got downstairs, out into the street. Bruno sprang backward and took stance, a monster blot on the pavement luminance. A breeze had arisen, sighing between darkened walls. Lightning had begun to flicker above roofs to the west. Bolly stood aside. He held Aleka by the wrist, not too tightly, and she saw a dull bemusement on him. Kenmuir patted her hand, a moth-wing touch, before he chose a position for himself. O Pele, how slight were his bones!

Maybe Bruno would be content to disable him, rape her, and release them. Not likely. Sober, he'd think of the aftermath. Aleka glanced skyward. Maybe Lilisaire would track down what had happened and avenge them.

Bruno charged. Kenmuir waited. Bruno reached him, twirled, launched a karate kick.

Kenmuir's forearm slashed. The leg went aside. Bruno tottered, off balance. Kenmuir's foot took him behind the knee. He howled and crashed.

Kenmuir sprang after him and gave him a heel in the torso. He gasped, but rolled clear and bounded up again. Incredible strength, Aleka realized. Let him close in, and he would smash his opponent as a maul breaks a cup.

He must have been a little dazed, though. Fists doubled, he struck for the stomach. Instantly Aleka saw the mistake. Kenmuir's hand darted like a knife to block the arm, which punched air. His shin made a sweep, and the mayor went back down.

Or so it seemed. Aleka had never studied combat. Her sports were gentle. She saw mostly a savage confusion.

Bruno tried once more, failed once more, groaned and shook. Blood smeared his face, matted his beard, dripped onto the street to shine luridly red. With an animal noise, he drew his knife. "No, can't!" wailed Bolly. Bruno lurched to attack. Kenmuir captured the wrist with his right hand, stepped in sideways, and as he moved smashed an elbow to the neck. The knife clattered free. Bruno became a bag of flesh that lay on the pavement and fought for air.

Kenmuir walked over to Bolly. Sweat sheened on his visage. He breathed deeply and his smell was—powerful, male, Aleka thought as dizziness rushed through her head. Yet his movements were easy and his words calm. "I believe that takes care of the matter. Release the woman."

Bolly did. He stared and stared.

"I'll take that stick of yours, if you please," Kenmuir said. He plucked it from unresisting fingers. "I'm not interested in anything else hereabouts, of course. Why don't you help your master?" To Aleka: "Can you fetch our luggage?"

She could. She did. Not until she returned did she understand, clear-minded once more, that they were free.

Kenmuir had been talking further to the guard, who crouched over the fallen and pawed unskillfully. Aleka arrived in time to see the staff twirl. Kenmuir must have demonstrated he could use it, too, if need be. He nodded at her and took his suitcase. "Let's be on our way," he said.

His pace was brisk but not hasty. Not to show fear, Aleka realized. Their escape depended on an emotional equilibrium that could break at any instant.

The walk to the airfield went on and on. Wind moaned, lightning blinked, thunder muttered.

—They were in her volant and airborne.

Uncontrollable shivering seized her. He held her close, stroked her hair, murmured. At last she could sit beside him and whisper, "I'm sorry. That was ch-childish."

"Not at all," he replied. "A very natural reaction. You were in trouble more foul than I was, and stayed in charge of yourself. That always carries a price."

She glanced at him. By now they were above the clouds. His profile was etched against a sky going pale and the last few stars. "You don't seem shook up," she said low.

He turned to smile at her. "Oh, I am. Exhausted. Let's stop over somewhere and sleep the sun down."

Her body ached, but the clarity within had come back, sharper still. "No, better not. Every place we could be noticed is an extra danger. Have the flyer cruise around a few hours while we rest, then make straight for Prajnaloka."

He slapped his forehead. "Q! You're right. The Overburg service sophotect will hear of the set-to, investigate, report; and it's met me, we talked." That brain could project the moving, speaking image of him into the database.

At least it had not seen her. By lucky chance—some luck was about due, Aleka thought—she had given her name to nobody in the town. True, it would come to light that a second outsider had been there. After that, a check with Traffic Control could reveal that the vehicle had been hers, and its present whereabouts.

But why should the authorities take that kind of trouble over an incident with no particular consequences, in a society that as a matter of policy was pretty much left to itself? They didn't know that a few among them were covertly hunting Kenmuir. They'd have no reason of their own to track him down. If he wanted to file charges, he'd call them; otherwise, it was logical just to leave what the sophotect related in the file. Maybe in due course that file would hold enough entries of this kind to make them take a closer look at Bramland. Aleka hoped so. But it wouldn't likely happen soon.

Her companion was smiling again, with what she guessed was an effort, and adding, "You see, you are in full command of your wits."

"You—" she marveled, "when you challenged him, I thought you were—*pupule*—crazy, suicidal."

He shrugged. "Spacers have to spend a great deal of time exercising, if they're to stay fit. Martial arts are a favorite program of mine. When I'm alone, I work against a generated image, which does wonders for developing the reflexes. Not that I ever expected to use them violently, but I've done fairly well in competitions. Bruno's knowledge is rudimentary. I'd ascertained that in conversation." Just in case he might find need for the knowledge, Aleka decided. A forethoughtful man. "Besides, he was drunk. I had no serious worry.

"He was stupid from the beginning, when he tried to kick. That's powerful but slow, and by itself it leaves you open to several different counterattacks. My problem was simply to keep him at a distance, unable to grapple or land a real blow, while I demolished him. And, yes, I had to try not to kill him, especially when under the circumstances that could well have been irreversible."

Kenmuir grimaced. "Hateful. The arts had never been anything to me but exercise and recreation. I never wanted them to be anything else." He sighed. "Well, I don't imagine Bruno has suffered permanent damage, other than to his ego and perhaps his social position."

She laid her hand over his. "Just the same, you were wonderful," she said.

"I couldn't have stood by. Could I? The more so when I was—not responsible for the mess, but a, a factor in it."

"You did accept his hospitality pretty, uh, thoroughly, didn't you?"

At once she knew the remark was illogical, unfair, something that slipped free before she in her exhaustion saw it coming. He looked away. "I didn't know how I could well refuse," he mumbled.

"I'm sorry!" she blurted. "None of my damn business."

Although . . . had he enjoyed it?

"Shall we try to sleep?" he proposed.

Still calm, still judicious, still the captain. Why should she vaguely resent that? Better be glad she had such a man at her side. Were there many spacers like him? (No, spacers were few, few, and most of them Lunarians.) How much of him was not inborn but was Fireball, ideals, rites, trothdom, a tradition as old as its Guthrie House?

24

The Mother of the Moon

In summer the little Rydberg fleet lay at its dock when not in use, a ketch, a ten-seater hydrofoil, a dinghy for knocking about in the sheltering cove. Winter's boathouse stood to one side. Behind it were an airstrip and a hangar that could accommodate three flitters. Lawn and flowerbeds led up to the dwelling. Stone-built, slate-roofed, it did not dominate the grounds with its size: for at its back the land rose beneath old fir forest, while westward the ocean swept across a fifth of the planet.

On this day a north wind blew strong. The treetops tossed and rustled with it, waves ran upward and inland through their murkiness, a hawk rode above the high horizon they made. Clouds flew in tatters, brilliant against the sun, gray when they passed over it and their shadows scythed below them. The sea ran steely in the distance, white and green where it roared

into surf. Chop on the cove threw sunlight back and
forth, blink-blink-blink, while boats rocked and their
mooring lines creaked. Warmth still lay in the earth,
but a chill went through the air, harbinger of autumn.

The flitter landed neatly. Lars and Ulla Rydberg
waited nearby. They were clad much alike, in tunic
and trousers over which they hugged cloaks. The wind
fluttered stray locks of hair, his whitening blond, hers
wheat-gold. The flitter door opened. A robot climbed
out. It was a small multipurpose model, four legs
under a cylinder which supported a control turret; two
arms ended in hands, two in attachments for various
tools. The optics in the turret gleamed about 130
centimeters above the ground. Ordinarily the computer inside would have been a neural net adequate for
manual tasks that were not too demanding. This unit
had been modified to hold a download.

The voice that rolled from it was Anson Guthrie's:
"Hola! Good seeing you again."

"Welcome—" Ulla hesitated for an instant "—
jefe." The honorific did not yet come quite naturally
to her. She had only been Fireball for seven years,
mainly by virtue of her marriage, and resident in
North America for three; the English she learned in
Europe was not Hispanicized; her direct contacts with
him had thus far been comparatively few and brief.
"You honor us." That was meant for courtesy. She
was a big, bluff, handsome woman, no sycophant.

"Gracias." Guthrie must have been scanning the
scene. "Uh, aren't your kids here? I'd've thought
they'd come on the gallop, except the baby, and she'd
crank up her buggy to full speed."

"We sent them off on an outing, together with
Señora Turner," Rydberg explained. He referred to
the single assistant he and his wife needed, aside from
machines, to run house and household comfortably.
"When you called, you gave me to understand you
wanted a confidential meeting."

"Oh, not that hush-hush," Guthrie said, shaking
hands. "We could go for a sail or a walk in the

woods—I'd enjoy that—or just close the door to a room for a couple of hours. The reason I came in person, instead of squirting my image through the usual code, was that I'd like to be with you for a short spell."

His tone was matter-of-fact. It generally had been too when Ulla saw the simulation of living Guthrie in her phone screen. Sometimes, though, it had gone soft, and the face had crinkled into a big grin, as when she showed him her children. "Stay as long as you want," she told him. "Oh, please!"

"'Fraid that can only be overnight, querida. Too flinkin' much to do. Also, if I was absent any length of time without carefully arranging it beforehand, the news pests would go into a feeding frenzy. I'm in this dinky body just so's I could sneak off without them noticing. Give me a rain check for a proper visit sometime, okay?"

Lars smiled, a little stiffly. "Do you need one, for your own house?" he said. "We can take that walk now if you wish."

"Aw, we might as well go inside. I've looked forward to poking around the old place on my personal feet."

The house where mortal Guthrie spent his last years, and where he died.

Until then he had kept in touch with his great-grandson, especially after Lars was told of the kinship. It was never made public, and Guthrie never showed favoritism to him. In fact, they spoke less often than either did with Dagny Beynac. Yet theirs was a genuine bond.

The download continued it, and it strengthened after Lars perforce retired from piloting. Groundside, his experience soon joined with administrative talents he had not known he possessed, to make him more important—above all, to Fireball's exploratory ventures—than ever when he ranged the Solar System.

Their images, the real and the synthetic, had chatted one evening in Stockholm, afternoon in Quito. "I gather you and your wife want to move," Guthrie said. "May I ask how come?"

"We grow restless," Lars answered. "I have found Europe is as I remembered. Too . . . too tame, everything too controlled. And if space, for me, will be no more than visits to Luna or L-5, well, then I would rather have the true Earth around me, Old Earth, as nearly as possible. Ulla agrees. She grew up in Lapland, a forest girl." He paused. "Besides, we want a big family. That is frowned on here, you know, and heavily taxed. Already we have social problems. We think of North America."

"Um-m, it's a fairly free country these days, yeah. Dunno how long it'll stay that way."

"Oh? Why?"

"The Renewal pretty well destroyed its middle class. The Second Republic is tinkering too much, trying too hard to restore a productive society and bring the underclass into it, by actions from above, instead of letting people alone to heal things for themselves." Guthrie projected a shrug. "But liberty ought to last a while yet. And whether it does or no, our company communities should stay autonomous, in fact if not in name."

"Jefe, I said we would like nature around us, Northern nature, not an enclave. Most of the time, anyhow."

"Hm-m . . . Hey, an idea! Listen, I once bought myself a beautiful preserve on Vancouver Island, Pacific Northwest, built a big house, spent as much time there as I could wangle. The poor thing's stood empty ever since, aside from a caretaker. I bet it'd love some clatter and chaos."

Lars stared. "What? But this is—is—"

"If you find you like it, I'll make it over to Fireball and you the trustee, with the right to bequeath your position. It's isolated, but a short hop by air to Victoria or Vancouver, not a lot longer by fast boat. The kids can go to school, call on their friends or invite 'em over, as often as you can stand. The winters are no worse than Sweden; or you can spend them in a southerly clime. Think about it, talk with your wife, make an inspection trip, let me know at your convenience. I hope you'll give it a try."

"This is, is very sudden."

"When factors click together for me, I don't stall around." Guthrie's created gaze gentled. "Keep things in the family, as near as may be, hm?"

Going up the path to the verandah, he remarked, "I'm glad to see how well you maintain things. You still like the place?"

"Oh, yes," Ulla said passionately.

"So do quite a few of our consortes, I hear. Don't you ever get tired of all those house guests?"

"No, no, they are friends. And it is good for the children to meet such different kinds of people, not in a screen but here, alive."

"And they bring space home to us in a way that recordings, writings, nothing else can do." Wistfulness tinged Lars's voice.

"I understand," said Guthrie quietly.

"Business as well as pleasure," Ulla continued. "It is necessary to know everything one can, when so much is always unknown. The house is becoming a center for informal, rank-free conferences—But why am I telling *you?*"

"Because you're feeling a tad nervous, ma'am. Don't. This is not the boss coming to dinner." Guthrie laughed. "Absolutely not." In seriousness: "Lars and I are closer than you realize. I think the time's ripe, you've proved you are reliable, for you to learn how close that is. But first, what I've mainly come about, I ask for your help."

"Whatever we can do!"

They mounted the steps, crossed to the door, opened it, and passed through into the vestibule. A cloud left the sun. The colors in a window blazed, Daedalus and Icarus aflight.

Cloaks removed, Lars led the way to a room whose ceiling was the roof itself, beams two stories above a parquet floor, oak wainscots, stone fireplace where logs were burning. Light fell soft upon furniture ancient and massive, thick carpet and drapes, paintings from centuries ago, wrought brass and silver. Smetana's "Moldau" flowed out of speakers. The robot entered like a spider into a sanctuary.

"Shall we talk here?" Lars proposed.

"Okay," Guthrie said. "I see you haven't changed anything to speak of. Do by all means, if you want. Isn't the décor kind of heavy for you?"

"No, no," Lars replied. "We have felt free to adapt the rest of the house, but this—it feels right as it is."

"Not a shrine," Ulla added. "We use it, it is the center of our home. But it is also like a heart or a root, not only for us but for Fireball."

Neither of them mentioned the other unaltered chamber, the one where Guthrie died.

"Can we . . . offer you anything, sir?" she went on, suddenly awkward.

"Just your company," Guthrie answered. "Wit and wisdom, or whatever else you've got in stock. Look, por favor, relax. Pour a Scotch or coffee or something, put your feet up, let's be our plain selves."

He guided them for a while through gossip and minor affairs: what had lately happened in the Hawaiian compound where the Rydbergs spent some of their winters; their recent vacation in L-5, the burgeoning arts and amusements of variable weight; a carefully unpublicized comic incident at Weinbaum Station on Mars; mining operations on Elara, Jupiter XI; the new Lake Aldrin park in Luna—

"It is about Luna, is it not?" Lars asked. "Why you have come."

By then he sat beside Ulla, a glass in his hand, a cup in hers. Guthrie faced them, standing before the hearth. Firelight shimmered on the metal of him. Words moved readily.

"Yeah," he said. "I daresay you guessed right away

when I called about getting together." Lars nodded. "After all, Dagny Beynac is your mother."

"And virtually coequal with the governor general," Ulla observed.

"Not legally," Lars reminded her. "She has no official position these days, aside from her berth in Fireball."

"The much greater her power."

"You're a wise lady," Guthrie said. "She's only half concerned about Fireball these days."

Shocked by the outspokenness, Lars exclaimed, "She would never break troth!"

"I didn't say that. Of course not. On the contrary, you know how since her supposed retirement she's stayed on tap as a consultant for us, but maybe you don't know just how badly the outfit would hate to lose her advice."

Guthrie fell silent for a span before he resumed, "However, like everything else human, 'troth' can be taken in a number of different ways."

Lars went defensive. "Please, what do you mean by that?"

"Nothing bad. She doesn't figure Fireball can be hurt by her Lunarians getting more of what they want, mainly home rule and scope for action. She claims we'd benefit. But she is more and more involved with the effort to get it for them." Guthrie made a sigh. "As a result, we're no longer as close as we used to be, we two."

"Since—" Ulla broke off.

"Since my original cashed in his chips and I took over?" Guthrie replied. "Don't be afraid to say it. Sure, that was bound to change the relationship, but it did less'n you might have expected. In the last several years, though, she's—well, she's gotten out of the way of sharing with me everything that's big on her mind."

"She grows old," Ulla said low. "People change with age."

"Hard to imagine her old. I remember her like yesterday, a little curlytop—" Guthrie stopped. That was not quite *his* yesterday. "But no. Time has only honed Dagny Beynac sharper."

"Then what is worrying you, jefe?" Lars inquired.

"That calls for a review of the background." Again Guthrie paused. "Look, you're both well aware of how, ever since they got leave to, Lunarians have been making a strong push to get into deep space on their own hook. Her sons are at the forefront. Purchase, manufacture, training—small-scale stuff to date, but energetic and ambitious."

"Yes," Lars mused. "Ambitious. An ambition that puzzles me, I confess. It isn't really economic. We have never—Fireball doesn't want to suppress them, for God's sake. But when I try to persuade them that at this stage, chartering vessels and hiring out jobs is better—they are polite, but it is as if they do not hear."

"Your experience isn't unique," Guthrie said dryly.

"I have told you, dear," Ulla recalled to her husband. "This is a matter of pride, self-assertion. When will you learn that not everybody is as rational as you are?"

Guthrie laughed once more. "The besetting irrationality of rationalists. You're right, my lady. I'm doubtful what is and is not rational to a Lunarian, that wild-ass breed, but basically you're right.

"Okay, let 'em go ahead. There's sure no dearth of things to do in space, even if the rich Lunarians have to subsidize their part of it. But—you wouldn't know, you two, because it was between Dagny Beynac and me—you wouldn't know how she's leaned on me about it, throughout this long while, on behalf of those folks."

Lars rubbed his chin and took a smoky sip of whisky. "M-m, I have wondered at some of the assistance Fireball has given, loans of money and facilities and so forth. How could it pay? But I am no economist."

"You aren't alone in wondering, either," Guthrie

said. "Others have been more vocal about it, or downright obstreperous. Not being the absolute dictator of the company that the news media make me out as, I had several knock-down-and-drag-out fights behind the scenes, getting this or that operation okayed and holding it on track."

"Why?" inquired Ulla.

"Trust a woman to ask an embarrassingly straight question. Why'd I go along with Dagny's requests? Well, as you might guess, partly I looked beyond the money side of it. The nations of Earth, the whole fat Federation, they need somebody in a position to cock a snook at them. At least, we the people do, if we aren't to see government growing all over us again like jungle rot." Guthrie's phrase went past his listeners. He hesitated. "But, well, also . . . it was Dagny who asked."

"And now she has asked for too much?" Firecrackle mingled with Lars's muted words.

"N-no. But it is pretty radical this time, enough to make me wonder real hard. So I thought I'd check with you."

"I am not—an intimate of hers. Not truly. Has she had any since Edmond died?"

"You know her better than most. And you, Señora Rydberg, seem to have a better than average feel for people. Let's try."

Lars leaned forward. "What does she want?"

"A torchcraft, designed and built to order, suitable for a Lunarian crew. That's nothing off the shelf, you realize. Financing it, complete with R and D, would be a tad burdensome for us, and repayment slow, if ever."

"Can't they wait until they are able to produce it themselves?"

"Evidently not. That could be a decade or more. They're too antsy. Anyhow, that's what Dagny claims. They want to get out and explore on their own. *Really* explore."

"That is . . . not unreasonable, is it?" Lars said. Ulla heard the longing and took his hand.

"I s'pose not. Still, to go this blue-sky at this earlyish stage of their space program—It looks like betting the store. For what?"

"She gave you no hint?"

"None, except that because her children bodaciously want this, she does. Oh, there was talk of it as a symbol that'll help quiet down the rebellious mood in the younger Moon generation. A sop, I'd call it. And there was talk of it as an investment, training, experience, et cetera. But mainly, she admits, they're impatient."

"They grow no younger," Lars muttered. Ulla tightened her grip on his hand.

"I thought you might have the information or ideas to help me decide."

"I am sorry, no. That Lunarian generation is as foreign to me as to you."

Ulla raised her head. "I suspect this is no simple impulse," she offered. "They have something specific in mind."

"My selfsame hunch," Guthrie agreed.

Lars repeated himself: "I cannot believe my mother would endorse it, so wholeheartedly, if it were any threat to us."

"No, no, certainly not," Guthrie said. "But a substantial expense, recoverable maybe, and for me a royal ruckus with my directors."

"A treasure trove? Perhaps they have learned of an extraordinary lode on some distant body?"

"That's the obvious guess. I asked Dagny forthright. She said no, and asked me in return how the hell they could get wind of any such thing if they didn't have a ship to prospect in or even robot probes with the needful capabilities."

"A spacecraft in orbit is potentially a terrible weapon. One like that—"

"No!" Ulla cried.

"No is right," Guthrie said. "The Lunarians may in

assorted ways be crazy, but they aren't insane. Nor stupid."

Lars nodded. "I didn't mean that seriously," he explained. "I simply wanted to dismiss it. Also because of what my mother is. They could not hoodwink her, and she would never allow——" He drew breath. "Aside from the economics, what harm, jefe? Knowledge or wealth or whatever they hope to gain, does it not in the end come to all humankind?"

"That's a natural-born explorer talking, and, I'm afraid, an idealist. I'm less naive. Nor is Fireball in the business of do-gooding."

"It does do good," Ulla insisted.

"Sort of, in the course of doing well," Guthrie said. "Though Lord knows we've got our share of short-sighted greed, hog-wild foolishness, and the rest of the human condition. They weren't left out of my program, either. . . . But this wanders. Should we or should we not underwrite the venture?"

"I am inclined to think we should——" Lars began.

"In hopes of satisfying our curiosity about it, hey?" And again Guthrie laughed.

"That may never happen. I am thinking of discovery, and diversity, and—But we must talk together more. Can you really only stay until tomorrow?"

"Unfortunately, yes. Well, in what hours we've got, we'll puzzle along as best we can. I'm inclined to think we'll end up with 'Damn the torpedoes! Full speed ahead!'"

Ulla looked a while at the robot and then said to the mind within it: "Because you too are what you are."

25

Venator had returned to Central after his interview with Matthias, less than satisfied. He had no simple need to do so. He could be as closely in touch with

developments, including any thoughts from the cybercosm, anyplace on Earth where there was an
interlink terminal. But he felt that here he would find
the calm and sureness from which his mind could win
total clarity.

He well understood the reason for that feeling. This
was holy ground.

He was among the few humans who knew of it,
other than vaguely. He was among the very few who
had ever walked it.

The morning after his arrival, he set forth on an
hours-long hike. Though athletic, he was not accli-
mated to the altitude. However, the evening before he
had gotten an infusion of hemoglobin surrogate and
now breathed easily. The air entered him cold, quiet,
utterly pure.

Domes, masts, parabolic dishes soon dropped from
view behind him. They were no more than a cluster, a
meteorological station. Nothing showed of what the
machines had wrought underground. Instruments
aboard a monitor satellite could detect radiations
from below, but those were subtle, electromagnetic,
infrared, neutrino; and the cybercosm edited all such
data before entering them in the public base.

Seldom visiting, Venator was not intimate with the
territory. From time to time he took out a hand-held
reader to screen a map and a text listing landmarks; he
used his informant to check his exact position and
bearing. That was his entire contact with the outer
world. He wandered untroubled, drawing serenity
from magnificence.

His course was northward. Around him as he
climbed, scattered dwarf juniper, birch, rhododen-
dron gave way to silvery tussocks between which
wildflowers bloomed tiny and rivulets trilled glistening. Sunlight spilled out of blue unboundedness;
shadows reached sharp from lichenous boulders.
Sometimes for a while he spied an eagle-vulture on
high, sometimes a marmot whistled, once a cock

pheasant took off like an exploding jewel. Ahead of him rose the Great Himalaya, from left horizon to right horizon, glaciers agleam over distance-dusky rock, the heights radiant white. A wind sent snow astream off one of those tremendous peaks, as if whetting it.

Venator's muscles strained and rejoiced. His breath went deep, his sight afar. From the might of the mountains he drew strength; trouble burned out of him; he was alone with infinity and eternity.

But those were within him. The highland had only evoked them. Among the stars, it was a ripple in the skin of a single small planet lost in the marches of a single galaxy. Life was already old on Earth when India rammed into Asia and thrust the wreckage heavenward. Life would abide after wind and water had brought the last range low—would embrace the universe, and abide after the last stars guttered out—would in the end *be* the universe, the whole of reality.

For intelligence was the ultimate evolution of life.

He knew it, had known it from before the day he was enrolled in the Brain Garden, not merely as words but as a part of himself like heart or nerves and as the meaning of his existence. Yet often the hours and the cares of service, the countless pettinesses of being human, blurred it in him, and he went about his tasks for their own sakes, in a cosmos gone narrow. Then he must seek renewal. Even so—he thought with a trace of sardonicism—does the believer in God make retreat for meditation and prayer.

Now he could again reason integrally and objectively. When he stopped for a meager lunch, on the rim of a gorge that plunged down to a sword-blade glacial river, he called up for fresh consideration the memories he had brought with him from Vancouver Island, halfway around the globe.

Rain blew off the sea, dashed against the house, blinded the antique windowpanes. A wood fire crack-

led on the hearth. Its flames were the sole brightness in
the high, crepuscular room. Their light ghosted over
the man in the carven armchair.

"Yes," Matthias rumbled, "Ian Kenmuir was here
last week. And spent the night. Why do you ask, when
obviously you know?"

Seated opposite him, Venator gave a shrug and a
smile. "Rhetorical question," he admitted. "A courtesy, if you will."

Eyes peered steadily from the craggy visage.
"What's your interest in the matter, Pragmatic?"

Equally obviously, it was considerable. Venator was
present in person and had declared his rank in order
to impress that on the Rydberg. Nevertheless he kept
his tone soft. "My service would like to find out what
his errand was."

"Nothing criminal."

"I didn't say it was."

"Ask him."

"I wish I could. He's disappeared."

Brows lifted. The big body stirred. "Do you suspect
foul play?"

This might be a chance to make use of the loyalties
that bound the Fireball Trothdom together. "It's
possible," Venator said. "Any clue that you can give
us will be much appreciated."

Matthias brooded for a minute, while the rain
whispered, before he snapped, "A man can drop out
of sight for many different reasons. We're not required
by law to report our whereabouts every hour. Not
yet."

Did he dread a stifling future? "Not ever, sir,"
Venator replied. He was sincere. Why should the
cybercosm give itself the trouble? "Police protection is
a service, not an obligation. It does, though, need the
cooperation of the people."

"Police. Hm." Matthias rubbed his chin. He
scorned cosmetic tech, Venator saw; the veins stood
out upon his hand, under the brown spots. "If one
individual may have come to grief, it concerns the

civil police, not the Peace Authority." Had he been fully informed, he would doubtless have added: *Most especially not a synnoiont agent of it.* "You're being less than candid, señor."

Venator's preliminary data retrievals had led him to anticipate stubbornness. "Very well, I'll try to explain. To begin indirectly: Do you support the Habitat project?"

"You mean putting L-5 in Lunar orbit?" The voice quickened. "Of course!"

"I should think your members all ought to," Venator pursued.

Matthias scowled. "Some among us have Lunarian sympathies. That's their right."

"Do they include Kenmuir?" Venator intensified his timbre. "Doesn't he care about other Terrans who hope to go where he's gone, make their lives where he's made his?"

"Spare the oratory, por favor," Matthias said.

Venator assembled words. "It's no secret how hostile most Lunarians are to the Habitat. Nor is it a secret that Kenmuir not only pilots for the Venture, he has . . . close personal ties to his employer." Venture, Venator, passed through him. What an ironic similarity. "We have reason to believe he came to Earth on her account."

"To sabotage the project?" scoffed Matthias. "Pragmatic, I'm an old man. Not much time's left me to spend on stupid games."

Venator suppressed irritation. "My apologies, sir. I'd no such intention. Nor do I accuse Kenmuir of anything unlawful. It's only—the potentialities, for good or ill—" He let the sentence trail off, as if he forbore to speak of spacecraft and meteoroids crashed with nuclear-bomb force on Earth, malignant biotech and nanotech, every nightmare that laired at the back of many a human skull.

"What ill?" the Rydberg snorted. "At worst, the Habitat gets cancelled. I agree that for a small minority of us, that would be a disaster, or at least a heartbreaking setback. But let's have no apocalyptic fantasies, eh? Kindly be specific."

That was no easy task when Venator could not hint at the truth. "We're trying to understand the situation," he said carefully. "It appears the Lunarian faction has something in train. But what? Why don't they proceed openly, through normal politics or persuasion? Call this a bugaboo if you wish, but the Peace Authority dares not stand idly by. Events could conceivably get out of hand, with disastrous consequences." So had they done throughout history, over and over, always; for human affairs are a chaotic system. Not until sophotectic intelligence transcended the human had there been any hope of peace that was not stagnation, progress that was not destruction; and how precarious was still the hold of the steersman's hand! It was encouraging to see the white head nod. "At the same time, we have no legal grounds for direct action. We cannot prove and in fact we do not claim that Captain Kenmuir, or any particular person, has evil intentions. They may be . . . misguided. Inadequately informed. As we ourselves are at present."

"You may be on a false trail altogether."

"Yes, we may. Without more information, we cannot just assume that. You know what duty is."

"What would you have me do?"

"Tell me what Kenmuir wanted of you."

The face congealed. "It's normal for consortes to pay respects at Guthrie House when they get the chance."

"I doubt that Kenmuir was making a pilgrimage or seeking help in a private difficulty. Else why has he disappeared?"

Matthias sat unyielding. "The Trothdom honors the confidences of its consortes."

Venator eased his manner a little. "May I guess? You keep a secret here. You have for centuries, the same as you've kept that historic spacecraft."

"We're far from being the only association that has

its mysteries, sanctuaries, and relics," Matthias said low.

"I'm aware of that. But did Kenmuir perhaps ask you what the secret is?"

Silence responded.

Venator sighed. "I don't suppose I may ask the same thing?"

Matthias grinned. "Oh, you may. You won't get an answer."

"If I came back with an official order and asked?" Venator challenged.

Implacability: "Still less would you get an answer. If necessary, I'd blow out my brains."

Venator shaped a soundless whistle. The fire spat sparks. "Is it that large a thing?"

"It is. To us." Matthias paused. "But not to you. Nothing important to you. So much I will say."

"If you did tell me, and if you're right about that, which you probably are, I'd take the secret with me to my cremation," Venator promised.

"Would you? *Could* you?"

Venator thought of screened rooms and sealed, encrypted communication lines. "Why do you mistrust us like this?" he asked softly.

"Because of what you are," Matthias told him. "Not you as an individual, or even as an officer. The whole way things are going, everywhere in the Solar System. It makes small difference to me. I'm old. But for my grandchildren and their children, I want out."

"How is the Federation government oppressing you? It means to give you the Habitat."

"The purpose of government is government," Matthias said. Venator recognized a quotation from Anson Guthrie. "Muy bien, this one meddles and extorts less than any other ever did, I suppose. But that's because it isn't the real power, any more than the national and regional governments below it are. The cybercosm is."

"We rely on the cybercosm, true—"

"Exactly."

"But that it plans to enslave us—there's an apocalyptic fantasy for you!" Venator exclaimed. "How could it? In the name of sanity, why should it?"

"I didn't say that. Nothing that simple." The heavy voice was silent for a moment. Outside, wind gusted and the rain against the house seethed. "Nor do I pretend to understand what's happening. I'm afraid it's gone beyond all human understanding, though hardly anyone has noticed as yet. For my race, before it's too late, I want out. The Habitat may or may not be a first step, but it's a very long way to the stars."

Alpha Centauri, Venator thought, a sign in heaven. Without Guthrie and his colonists yonder, the dream —the chimera—would long since have died its natural death.

"Meanwhile," Matthias finished, "I'll keep hold as best I can of what's humanly ours. That includes the Founder's Word. Do you follow me?" His bulk rose from the chair. "Enough. Adiós, Pragmatic."

The odds were that it didn't matter, that the lodgemaster had spoken truthfully and his defiance was symbolic. Indeed, what real threat did Kenmuir and his presumptive companion pose? Venator had guessed she possessed an expertise to which the spaceman would add his special knowledge; between them they might be able to devise a strategy that would find the Proserpina file and break into it.

Unlikely to the point of preposterousness, at least now, after it had been double-guarded by DNA access codes. More and more, Venator wondered if the whole business was not a feint, intended to draw attention from whatever scheme Lilisaire was actually engineering.

Other operatives were at work on the case, both sophotectic and human. He was their chief, but he knew better than to interfere. If and when they wanted his guidance, they'd call. Until then he'd assimilate their reports and get on with what he could do best himself.

Kenmuir and his partner were worth tracking down for the clues they could maybe provide to Lilisaire's intent. Besides—Venator smiled—it was an interesting problem.

Striding along, he reconsidered it. They could not forever move around hidden from the system. Already spoor of them must be there, in Traffic Control databases, in casual encounters, perhaps even in an unusual occurrence or two. People observed blurrily, remembered poorly, forgot altogether, or lied. The cybercosm did not. For instance, any service sophotect that had chanced to meet Kenmuir would recognize his image when it came over the net and supply every detail of his actions.

But machines of that kind were numbered in the millions, not to speak of more specialized ones, both sentient and robotic. The system was worldwide, hopelessly huge. A search through its entirety would take days or worse, tying up capabilities needed elsewhere. And during those days, what might Lilisaire make happen?

Well, you could focus your efforts. Delineate local units of manageable size. Inquire of each if anything had taken place fitting such-and-such parameters, within its area. That should yield a number of responses not too large, which could then be winnowed further. It would still devour time, but—

Whatever he did, he must act. However slight the chance of revelation was, he could not passively hazard it.

Venator shook his head. Sometimes he still found it hard to see how Proserpina could possibly mean that much.

The short-range politics was clear enough. Let the fact out, and the Terrans who wanted the Habitat would suddenly find themselves in alliance with the Lunarians who abhorred it, or at any rate not irresolvably opposed to them; and how could the Teramind itself make the mass of humankind realize that this threatened catastrophe?

Because *why* did it? Revival of the Faustian soul, how vague that sounded. How many dwellers in this mostly quiet, happy world knew what it meant, let alone what it portended?

And did it really spell evil? Reaching for the stars, Faustian man had well-nigh ruined his planet and obliterated his species. Yet the knowledge he wrested from an uncaring cosmos, the instrumentalities he forged, were they not that from which the age of sanity had flowered?

Venator shivered in an evening going bleak. Westward the thinnest sickle of a new Moon sank below the mountains. Eastward, night was on the way.

He had lived the horrors of the past, wars, tyrannies, fanaticisms, rampant crime, millstone poverty, wasted land, poisoned waters, deadly air, the breaking of the human spirit, alienation, throngs of the desperately lonely, the triumph first of the mediocre and then of the idiotic, in civilization after suicidal civilization. He had lived them though books, multiceivers, quiviras, imagination, guided by the great sophotectic minds. Not that they had told him what to think. They had led him to the facts and told him he must think. Against the past, he had seen the gentle present and the infinitely unfolding future. Therefore—yes, he was a hunter born, but nevertheless—therefore he became an officer of the Peace Authority.

But did an arrogant and unbounded ambition necessarily bring damnation? Fireball Enterprises had created a fellowship of shared loyalty and achievement whose remnant endured on Earth to this day.

At Alpha Centauri too, a remembrance and a lure.

Venator hastened his footsteps. Another beacon shone before him, the lighted station.

As if inspired by the sight, an idea came. He snapped his fingers, annoyed at himself. Why hadn't he thought of it earlier? Probably because the contingency against which it would guard was so remote. Still, it was an easy precaution to take, and if somehow it justified itself, why, the reward would be past all measure.

Evidently it hadn't occurred to the cybercosm either. The higher machine intelligences could well have come up with it, if only by running through permutations of concepts at the near-light speed of their data processing. But they had loftier occupations than this. The lower-level sophotects were as capable as he was, but in different ways. The electrophotonic brain did not work like the chemical neuroglandular system. That was the reason there were synnoionts.

Venator entered the main building and descended. Underneath it he went along a corridor where strange abstract shapes glimmered in the walls and strange abstract notes sounded out of them. Linked into the net, he could grasp and savor a little of what such art evoked. Isolated in his flesh, he could not. He was the sole human here, monastically lodged and nourished. That was by his choice. Mortal indulgences belonged among mortals.

A detached sophotect passed by. The body it was wearing rolled on wheels and sprouted implements. "Greeting, Pragmatic," it called courteously. He answered and they parted.

Elsewhere he had worked side by side with beings like this, and afterward sat in actual conversation. Not often, though. It had been agreeable and fascinating to him, but both knew how superficial it was. Direct data exchange was the natural way of the machines. Venator longed to begin upon it.

When he reached his communion room, he was trembling with eagerness. But that was the animal, which knew that soon the brain would be in rapture. Endorphins. . . . Somatically trained, he willed calm, donned the interlink, lay down on the couch, and requested clearance.

Although his purpose was simple and straightforward, he sensed the cybercosm as a single vast organism with a hundred billion avatars. The point-nexus that was his awareness could flash through strand after strand of the web, the ever-changing connectivity, to join any existence within it.

A bank of instruments at the bottom of the sea tasted the chemistries of a black smoker and the life it fed. A robot repaired the drainage line of a village in Yunnan. A monitor kept watch over the growth, atom by atom, of fullerene cables in a nanotank. A service sophotect chose the proper pseudo-virus to destroy precancerous cells in an aging human. Traffic Control kept aircraft in their millions safely flying, as intricately as a body circulates blood. An intelligence developed the logical structure needed for the proof or disproof of a theorem—but from that work the flitting point must retreat, half dazzled, half bewildered.

It was in wholeness with the world.

After a split second more full than a mortal lifetime, it moved to its purpose. From the net it raised the attention of a specific program, and they communicated.

In words, which the communication was not:

SHOULD THERE BE ANY ENTRY WHATSOEVER OF THE PROSERPINA FILE, AUTHORIZED OR NOT, TRACE THE LOCATION OF THE SOURCE AND INFORM AGENT VENATOR. ALERT THE NEAREST PEACE AUTHORITY BASE FOR IMMEDIATE ACTION.

DO NOT SPECIFY THE REASON FOR THIS.

APPROVED, responded the system. ENTERED AS AN INSTRUCTION.

And then, like a mother's anxious voice:

You are troubled. You are in doubt.

—I do not doubt, Venator saw. I do not quite comprehend, but I will believe.

(How can the system, even the Teramind, *know* what the outcome would be? Humankind is mathematically chaotic. We can learn no more than that history has certain attractors. Attempts at control may send it from one to another, unpredictably. A new element, introduced, may change the entirety in radical fashion, from the configuration to the very dimensionality. Is it possible to write the equations? If they be written, is it possible to solve them? A danger is foreseeable, but a disaster either happens or it does not. We exist as we are because those who existed before us ran fearsome risks. How can we be sure of what we are denying those who exist after us, if we dare not set ourselves at hazard?)

We cannot be sure.

—But in that case—

You shall know.

And the cybercosm took Venator into Unity.

Twice before had it done so, for his enlightenment and supreme rewarding. Anew it opened itself entirely for him. He went beyond the world.

He could not actually share. The thoughts, the creations that thundered and sang were not such as his poor brain might really be conscious of, let alone enfold. The intellects, star-brilliant, sea-fluid, rose over his like mountains, up and up to the unimaginable peak that was the Teramind. Yet somehow he was in and of them, the least quivering in the tremendous wave function; somehow the wholeness reached to him.

Reality is a manifold.

He became as it were a photon, an atom of light, arrowing through a space-time curved and warped by matter that itself was mutable. He flew not along a single path but an infinity of them, every possibility that the Law encompassed. They interfered with each other, annulling until almost a single one remained, the geodesic—almost, almost. Past and future alike flickered with shadows of uncertainty. He came to a thing that diffracted light, and the way by which he passed was knowable only afterward. He met his end in a particle of which he, transfigured, was the energy to bring it anywhere. The course that it took was not destined, but was irrevocable and therefore a destiny.

You have learned the theory of quantum mechanics as well as you were able. Now behold the quantum universe—as well as you are able.

The identity that guided him was a facet of the Unity; but it communed with him as no sophotectic mind ever might. For this was the download of a synnoiont who died before he was born, which the Unity had taken unto itself.

Yang: The continuum is changeless, determined at the beginning, onward through eternity. For the observations of two observers are equally valid, equally real, but their light cones are not the same. The future of either lies in the past of the other. Thus tomorrow must be as fixed as yesterday.

Yin: The paths are ultimately unknowable. The diversities are unboundedly many. To observe is to determine, as truly for past as for future. Mind gives meaning to the blind evolutions that brought it into being. Existence is meaning. Within the Law, the configurations of the continuum are infinite. All histories can happen.

Yang and Yin: Reality does not branch. It is One.

He could no more look into the universe of the Teramind than he could have looked into the heart of the sun. He could know that it was there, in glory, forever.

Afterward he lay a long while returning to himself. Once he wept for loss, once he shouted for joy.

At last he rose and went about his merely human business.

He had the promise. This body, this brain must someday perish. The self, the spirit that they generated would not. It too would go into that which was to find and be the Ultimate.

But omnipotence and omniscience were not yet, nor could they be for untold billions of years. He knew now why their reality required that Proserpina be forgotten.

26

The Mother of the Moon

Here the sun was only first among the stars, a hundred-thousandth as bright as over Luna, less than a tenth of full Earth. Still, when lights had been turned off in the observation cabin, eyes adapting to dusk saw shadows cast, faint and shifty. On the little world that crowded the primary viewscreen, peaks and crags reared gauntly forth, while glints and shimmers showed where metal lay naked. Dark vision was needful to make the rock surfaces something other than a mottled murkiness. It found a scene like a delirium, mountains, plains, valleys, cliffs, rilles, pits, crevices, flows frozen in their final convulsions, things less identifiable, wildly scrambled together.

After months under thrust, acceleration and deceleration at a steady Lunar gravity, weightlessness came strange even to this crew. Brandir and Kaino floated, gazing, in silence. Air currents seemed to rustle no louder than their blood. Low and slow, torchcraft *Beynac* orbited her goal. It turned faster than she revolved, a rotation each nine and a half hours. Feature after feature crept over the leading horizon.

"Behold!" cried Kaino.

He pointed to a sootiness not far below the north pole, as it hove in sight. From a distance they had seen that it spread halfway around the globe. This close, they picked out the foothills and steeps of it. Where the range was tumbled or riven, they saw depths that gleamed bluish white. "What *is* that?"

"A comet smote," Brandir judged. "This is the debris. Radiation caused exposed organic material from the comet to form larger molecules." He was quiet a few seconds, as if quelling a shiver. How long had that taken, in these outskirts of the Solar System?

The lines in his countenance deepened. He forced matter-of-factness into the melodious Lunarian language: "Belike most is water ice."

Kaino nodded eagerly. His question had been unthinking; he knew as well as his brother what the sight probably meant. "A hoard of it! And if that prove not enough, why, I've observed another comet within a few hundred astronomical units." He gestured at auxiliary screens full of stars, Milky Way, nebulae, night. "A fortunate happenstance, amidst all this hollowness."

"Should we want it. We have tracked down our father's dream; we know not what new dreams may spring forth." Brandir spoke curtly. His mood was harsher than fitted this terminus of their expedition. He returned his attention to what he had been studying before Kaino exclaimed.

He forsook it again, and glared, when Ilitu entered. The geologist's brown hair was rumpled, his clothes carelessly thrown on. He checked his flight at the main screen and the contentment on his thin face flared into joy.

"So your heed is back upon science," Kaino greeted. Ilitu and Etana had gone off together, exultant, while *Beynac* was completing the approach.

The younger man ignored the jape, or pretended to. "Have you obtained a good value for the mass?" he asked breathlessly.

Kaino nodded. "Twenty-nine and three-fifths percent of Luna's."

"A-ahh. Then indeed the body is chiefly iron. The core of a larger one, shattered in some gigantic collision, just as my mentor believed." Ilitu stared and stared. "But he could not foresee everything," he went on, almost as if to himself. "It is a chaos, like Miranda. It must itself have been broken in pieces, many of them melted, by that fury . . . and then shards of both rained down upon each other, fusing— Yes." A fingertip trembled across the images of a scarp two hundred kilometers long, a gash that gaped for three hundred, a highland that was a jumble of diverse huge blocks, chunks, and rubble. "The welding could not be total. The interior is surely veined with caverns and tunnels between ill-fitting segments. Sustained heavy bombardment would have collapsed them, making the spheroid still rougher than we see. Hence we know that Jupiter cast it afar soon after it formed. We have found a remnant of the primordial."

"There have been strikes since then," Brandir snapped. "Any witling could tell." He chopped a hand at the sight that had particularly interested him. Though craters were few, a big one with a central peak loomed in the southern hemisphere, receding from view as ship and planetoid wheeled.

"True," Ilitu agreed, conciliatory. "No matter how sparse, bodies must meet on occasion, in the course of four billion years or more. Yon great meteoroid, and the comet, and others; but seldom, and of scant geological consequence."

"Not to a man who can think. Piss about as you wish, groundside. I know what I will seek."

Ilitu's slender frame tensed. "Best we plan our field work before we start it," he said.

"When I desire your opinion, I will inform you," Brandir retorted.

Kaino plucked his sleeve. "Come," the pilot murmured. "I've need of you aft."

Brandir bridled. "I'm scanning the terrain."

"The cameras will do that better. Likewise Ilitu. Come." Kaino put a slight metallic ring into his voice. Sullenly, Brandir accompanied him from the cabin. In space, the pilot was master.

They did not push off and fly, but used handholds to pull themselves along the passage beyond, side by side. "What do you intend?" Brandir demanded.

"To calm you, brother mine. I smelled a fight brewing, and we cannot afford it. Relations have grown too strained already."

Brandir cast a sharp glance at the redhead. "*You* speak thus?"

Kaino finger-shrugged and grinned lopsidedly. "After a person has crossed the half-century mark, the fires damp down a little. I should have thought yours were cooler from the outset—and you my senior, and Etana companionate with me, not you."

Brandir flushed below his thinning ashen hair. "Do you suppose me jealous? Nay, it's his insolence."

"It's that, sitting in your castle, you've become too wont to have what you want when you want it. Yes, my own self-importance was stung. But we've both had plenty of women, inside our group or outside it. If Etana's come to favor a new man above me—I suspect his mildness appeals to her—why, there will be no lack of others to welcome me home. Meanwhile, Etana does not disdain either of us two, does she? Ease off, you. We should both carry too much pride to leave room for vanity."

Brandir parted his lips, clamped them shut again, and shook his head angrily.

The copilot emerged from a companionway, spied them, and drew near. She was in her thirties, dark, fuller-bodied than usual among Lunarians. Like Ilitu, she had dressed hastily, and the black locks floated unkempt about a face that remembered Oceanian ancestors. A faint muskiness clung to her skin.

The three poised in confrontation. She recognized the ill humor in Brandir and offered him a smile. "I was bound forward to see what we've found," she said.

"You felt no urgency earlier," he answered.

Resentment kindled. "Off duty, I choose my trajectory for myself."

Kaino meowed. They gave him a surprised look.

"R-r-rowr," he voiced. "S-s-s-s. Pity that you've neither of you the fur to bristle or the tails to bottle."

After a moment, Etana laughed. Brandir's mouth twitched upward. *"Touché,"* he muttered.

"I meant no offense, my lord," the woman told him softly. Never hitherto had she used that honorific. Her only allegiances were to the companionate she shared with Kaino and to this ship; she could and would leave either when she saw fit. "I did not suppose you especially cared."

"I ought not," Brandir replied with some difficulty. "You are a free agent."

Comprehension flickered into Kaino's eyes, and perhaps as much compassion as he was capable of. He drifted aside and kept quiet.

Etana touched Brandir's hand. "We shall be here for a span, and then it's a long voyage home," she said. "There will be time for talk and for other things."

"You are . . . kinder than I knew." He put on the reserve of the aristocrat. "I'll seek to arrange matters as may best please you, my lady."

Groundside, he, the major partner in Selene Space Enterprises and the most experienced leader aboard, would be in command.

He stood on that height he called Meteor Mountain and rejoiced.

As small as this world was, from here he could barely see parts of the crater ringwall, thrusting above the horizon. Under his feet the dark, lumpy mass went down to a plain of almost glassy smoothness, its gray-brown webbed with cracks and strewn with boulders. Over his head and around him gleamed the crowded constellations. Though night had fallen, they gave sufficient light for a person accustomed to Lunar Farside after sunset. *Beynac* was in the sky, free of the shadow cone, a spark gliding through Auriga toward the galactic belt.

Below him on the slope, he spied one of his robots at work, cutting loose a sample for analysis. The task was essentially finished, however. Soon he could seek his van and take the crew back to camp. He transmitted, for the ship to receive and relay:

"It's established now beyond doubt. The impactor was ferrous, probably itself a remnant of the original body, which went out on an orbit close to this and eventually collided. Between its composition and the material forced up from the interior, the central peak is a lode of industrial metals, both light and heavy, even more easily recoverable than they are at other locations."

"That makes two treasures, then!" rang Kaino's response. He meant the cometary glacier which he and Ilitu had been exploring. Not only had they found immense quantities of water ice and organic compounds, they had identified ample cyanide and ammonia intermingled, frozen or chemically bound. Hydrogen, oxygen, carbon, nitrogen: the fundamentals of life. "Never before, anything like! I could well-nigh believe in a god who meant it for us."

"That is not a necessary hypothesis," Ilitu said in his gentle, precise fashion. "Nor has coincidence been involved. Given Edmond Beynac's idea—a planetoid massive enough to form a core, smashed, then most of the pieces perturbed into Kuiper-Belt paths—the rest seems probable, perhaps inevitable. There were bound to be further encounters during gigayears, with rich fragments and with comets. This, the largest body, would attract more than its share. Weak irradiation and ultra-low ambient temperatures preserve volatiles as they cannot be preserved in the inner System."

"Thus speaks the savant," chuckled Etana affectionately from the ship.

"When will you be done where you are?" Brandir asked the men. Discoveries and what they would require were wholly unpredictable; and he had been too engaged with his to follow theirs in any detail.

"We prepare to depart," Kaino answered. "Let our successors trace out everything that's here. After a short rest and resupplying, Ilitu wants to investigate the Great Scarp and the Olla Podrida. That's good in my mind, if we can go by way of Iron Heath." Those were features noted before anyone had landed, but not yet betrodden.

"Well, we'll talk of it in camp," Brandir said. "We

near our limits of accomplishment in the while that we have left to us."

"I'll trust Ilitu to persuade you," Kaino laughed. Brandir heard the *click* of signoff.

Etana's voice stormed at him: "How's this? They wander straightway to a new land, and I remain caged?"

Doctrine. A qualified pilot must always be on standby. Tiny though the chance was of a meteoroid strike in these parts, and the solar flare hazard nonexistent, Brandir chose to abide by the rule. "It would be a long walk home," he had said. Besides, when they were just three persons and a few robots on the ground, it was well to have a watcher aloft, ready to mount a rescue.

"Let Kaino take his turn here," she said. "He promised me. You all did."

"Khr-r, he has done rockjack work in the asteroids, you know," Brandir pointed out.

"And I have not? Admitted. But this is no asteroid. Not in truth. It's more akin to Luna. And I have ranged the outback at home as much as ever he or you."

"Y-yes—"

She laid rage aside. "It's merely fair," she argued. "You have spirit, Brandir. Would you care to sit idled week upon week, in the ghost-companionship of recorded screenings, while your mates roved free?"

"Later, yes, certainly you shall."

"Now! The hour is ripe, two surveys completed, the next to be readied for." Etana's tone sweetened. "It could be you I fare with, could it not? Ilitu has scant need of more than the robots to help him do his science. You and I are aimed toward whatever may prove useful to the future."

"I must think on that."

"Must you? Is it not star-clear? And . . . Brandir, I've grievously misliked our being at odds. You kept yourself so masked. We should find our way to something better."

In the end he yielded. Knowing this, he spoke more stiffly than might have been necessary when he called the other pair.

The sun burst into sight. Farther stars vanished around it. Westward they still gemmed a majestic darkness, for the solar radiance was wan where no heights reflected it. This country was not altogether a plain of dull-colored rock, though. In places it sheened amidst the shadows that puddled in its roughness. Here and there the shadows reached long from formations whose laciness came aglitter and aglisten.

The anomalous region bordered rather sharply on the sort of terrain common on the lowlands of this world—coarse regolith, like shingle, virtually dust-free. A field van rolled to the marge and stopped. Two spacesuited forms climbed out. A robot followed, four-legged, four-armed, thickly instrumented, burdened with gear. For a minute they stood looking across the strangeness ahead of them.

Then: "Come!" rapped Kaino, and started forth afoot.

"Is this wise?" wondered Ilitu. "Send the robot first."

"We've no hours to squander on probing and sounding. Would you see what we're here to see? Get aflight!"

After an instant's hesitation, the geologist obeyed. The machine lumbered behind. While Kaino was furious at Brandir's decision, his haste also had an element of reason. He had insisted on detouring, and Ilitu backed him, in order that he might be sure of visiting Iron Heath before he arrived at camp and took a flitsled up to *Beynac*. Otherwise he, at least, probably never would, given everything else there was to do in the limited time remaining for it and the unlikeliness of another expedition here soon. The roundabout route overland stretched both food and fuel cells thin; the men were on half rations, which doubled his impatience. They could not dawdle.

After they had long been cramped in their vehicle, freedom to move brought exuberance as abrupt as the sunrise. "Hai-ah!" Kaino shouted. Forward he went in panther leaps. His spacesuit, state of the art, flexed around him, almost a second skin. Powerpack and life support scarcely weighted him. The dense globe pulled with a force 86 percent that of home, ample for Lunarian health and childbirth, liberating in its lightness. Landscape rivered from the near horizon to flow away beneath his feet. Breath sang in his nostrils, alive with a pungency of sweat.

He halted at the nearest formation. Ilitu joined him. They gazed. The robot trailed forlornly in their direction. It was built and programmed for a certain class of scientific tasks; at everything else, if it was capable at all, it was weak, slow, and stupid.

"What *is* this?" Kaino whispered.

From space, the travelers had simply become aware of curious protrusions on an unfamilar sort of territory. They could not untangle the shapes. Seen close up, the thing was sheerly weird.

An Earthdweller would have thought of coral. Lunarians knew that marvel only in books and screens. An intricate filigree rose from the ground, thin, its topmost spires some 150 centimeters high, its width variable with a maximum of about 100. Variable too was the brightness of strands, nodules, and rosettes; but many gleamed in the hard eastern light.

Ilitu walked around it, leaned close, touched, peered, hunkered, rose, took a magnifying glass from his tool pouch and went over the irregularities bit by bit. When the robot reached him, he ignored it. The sun climbed higher, breakneck fast to a Lunarian. More stars disappeared.

Kaino began to shift about and hum a tune to himself.

"A ferrous alloy, I think," Ilitu said at length. "You observe whole metallic sheets strewn across the regolith. I deem they're overlays, not the inner iron bared, although we must verify that. I would guess that this and its fellows are spatter formations. An upheaval flung molten drops and gobbets about. When they came down in a group, they welded together as they solidified, which they would have done very quickly."

Kaino went alert. "A meteoroid strike? We've no sign of a crater."

"It may have happened when the planetoid was forming out of fragments, itself hot and plastic. . . . Hai, that suggests the original, catastrophic collision occurred near Jupiter, because I should think a strong magnetic field was present to urge so many gouts along converging arcs. And *that* suggests enormously about the origin of this body and its orbit . . . about the early history of the asteroid belt, the entire Solar System—" Ilitu beat fist in palm, over and over. He stared outward at the fading stars.

"If Father could have known!" broke from Kaino.

"Yes. I remember. He would have jubilated." Ilitu's softness went thoughtful again. "This is but a preliminary, crude hypothesis of mine. It could be wrong. Already I wonder if this unique planetoid may not have had, in the past, a kind of vulcanism special to itself. It does possess a significant magnetic field of its own, you recall, and the formation here has several resemblances to the Pele's Hair phenomenon on Earth."

"Eyach, we can take a few hours," Kaino said. "Gather more data."

Ilitu raised his upper lip off the front teeth. His parents would have grinned differently. "I will."

He took out a reader, keyed a map onto the screen, and studied it. His eyes darted about, correlating what he saw with the cartography done in orbit. Iron growths were scattered across the plain. About two kilometers hence, close to the southern horizon, a metallic band glistered from edge to edge of vision, some three meters wide. On the far side of it reared a whole row of coraloids, up to five meters tall.

"We'll go yonder," he said, pointing.

Kaino laughed. "I awaited no less. Ho-hah!"

They set forth, as swiftly as before. In a few minutes Kaino veered. "Where go you?" asked Ilitu without changing course.

"That bush there." It was small but full of sparkles.

"I'll study the major objects first. If time remains and you've found this one interesting, I'll come back to it." Ilitu continued.

Kaino squatted down by the pseudo-shrub. Particles embedded in the darker iron caught sunlight and shone like glass. Maybe that was what they were, he decided after examination: fused silica entrained in the drops that had made the thing. Or they could be another mineral, such as a pyrite. He was no expert. Clearly, though, the geologist's intuition had been right. Here was nothing notable, merely beautiful. Kaino straightened and started off to rejoin his comrade.

Ilitu had just reached the metallic strip in front of his destination. A leap brought him onto it.

It split asunder. He fell from sight.

"Yaaaa!" screamed Kaino. He went into full low-gravity speed. Barely did he check himself at the border of the ribbon.

Ribbon indeed, he saw. This part of it, if not all, was no deposit sprayed across the rocks. It was, or had been, a cover for a pit—a cavern, a crevasse, or whatever—one of the emptinesses that seismic sounding had shown riddled the planetoid, as Ilitu predicted.

It must have been a freak, a sheet of moltenness thrown sidewise rather than downward in those moments of rage when Iron Heath took form. Low weight let it solidify before it dropped into the hole—unless the hole had appeared simultaneously, the ground rent by forces running wild—The layer was thin, and the cosmic rays of four billion years, spalling, transmuting, must have weakened it further—

Kaino went on his belly, crept forward, stuck his helmet over the gap. He failed to notice how the shingle slithered underneath him. Blackness welled below. "Ilitu," he called. "Ilitu, do you receive me? Can you hear me?"

Silence hummed in his earplugs.

He got a flashlight from his kit and shone it downward. Light returned dim, diffused off a huddled whiteness. Kaino played the beam to and fro. Yes, a spacesuit. Still no response. It was hard to gauge the distance when murk swallowed visual cues. He passed his ray slowly upward. The little pool of undiffused illumination wavered among shadows. An inexperienced man would have been nightmarishly bewildered.

Kaino, intimate with the Moon and certain asteroids, interpreted what he saw. He couldn't tell how long the fissure was, nor did he care, but it was about 175 centimeters broad here at the top and narrowed bottomwards. Ilitu lay forty or fifty meters below him. A nasty fall, possibly lethal, even in this gravity; but friction with the rough walls might have slowed it. There seemed to be depths beyond the motionless form. Ilitu might be caught on a ledge.

So.

Kaino got his feet and aimed his transmission aloft. The ship was not there at the moment, but her crew had distributed relays in the same orbit. "Code Zero," he intoned. Absolute emergency. "Kaino on Code Zero."

Etana's voice darted at him: "What's awry?"

Tersely, he explained. "Raise Brandir," he finished. "We'll want equipment for snatching him out—a cable and motor to lower a pallet, I'd guess—as well as the full medical panoply."

"Can't your Number One robot rescue him?"

Kaino glanced at the machine, which had arrived and stood awaiting his orders. "Nay," he said, "it's useless." That body could not clamber down, and the program could not cope with the unknowns hiding in the dark.

"You may need to haul me up too," he said. "I'm going after him."

"No!" she yelled, "Kaino, you—" He heard the gulp. "At least fetch a line for yourself and have the robot hold it."

"That may well take too long. Ilitu may be dying."

"He may be dead. Belike he is. You don't hear him, do you? Kaino, stay!"

"He is my follower. I am a Beynac. Raise Brandir, I told you." The pilot switched off his widecaster.

He did take a minute to instruct the robot: Go back to the van, bring that wire rope, lower it to him if he was still down in the hole. Meanwhile he removed the bulky pack that held food, reserve water, and field equipment. Having activated his head and breast lamps, he went on all fours to the edge of the gap and set about entering it.

Stones kept skidding around. Twice he nearly lost his hold and tumbled. That made him laugh, low, to himself. On the third try he succeeded, bootsoles braced against one wall, life support unit against the opposite side. He began to work his way downward.

It was wicked going. He could not properly feel the surfaces through his outfit. The lights were a poor help, sliding off lumps, diving into cracks, mingling with shadows that dashed about like cat's paws of the gloom. Often he started to slip. Only low gravity and quick reflexes let him recover. As he descended and the crevice contracted, his posture made him ever more awkward. Stressed muscles hurt. Sweat soaked his undergarb and stung his eyes. Breath rasped a throat gone dry. He toiled onward.

Wait. Had it grown a touch easier? More flex in the legs—He realized what he had been unable to see from above, that on the side where his feet were, the rift was widening again. If it broadened too much, he could fare no deeper. Unless—

Somehow he maneuvered about until by twisting his neck he could look the way he was bound. Light picked out the sprawled form there and sheened off jagged pieces of the broken roof. Ilitu had indeed fallen onto a narrow shelf projecting from the wall at

Kaino's back. Its ends vanished in the same darkness that gaped beside it. Pure luck. . . . No, not quite. That being the wall which slanted inward the whole way, and nearer to where the geologist fell through, it must have acted as a chute, its ruggedness catching at spacesuit and pack, slowing and guiding him.

Now that Kaino saw his objective half clearly, he could estimate dimensions and distances. The ledge was about ten meters below him, an easy drop in this weight, but it was less than a meter wide, and next to it yawned a vacantness a full two meters across. Low acceleration would give him a chance to push or kick at the iron, correct his course, but he'd have just three or four seconds, and if he missed his landing, that would doubtless be that.

"Convenient, being 98 percent chimpanzee," he muttered. After a moment's study he thrust and let go.

His drop was timeless, utter action. But when impact jarred through his bones and he knew himself safe, he glanced upward, saw the opening high above him full of stars, and laughed till his helmet echoed.

To work. Carefully, lest he go over the rim, he knelt. Ilitu lay on his back. A sheetlike piece of metal slanted across the upper body. It had screened off transmission. Kaino plucked it away, tossed it aside, and heard wheezing breath. He leaned forward. Because he had come down at Ilitu's head, he saw the face inverted, a chiaroscuro behind the hyalon, lights and shadows aflicker as his lamps moved. The lids were slit-open, the eyeballs ghastly slivers of white. Saliva bubbled pink on the parted lips. "Are you awake?" he asked. The breathing replied.

His search found the telltales on the wrists. "Eyach," he whispered. Temperature inside the suit was acceptable, but oxygen was at 15 percent and dropping, carbon dioxide and water vapor much too thick. That meant the powerpack was operative but the air recycler knocked out and the reserve bottle emptied. "Hu," Kaino said, "I came in time by a frog's whisker, nay?"

He couldn't make repairs. However, accidents to recyclers were known and feared. There was provision. He reached around his shoulder and released the bypass tube coiled and bracketed on his life support module.

More cautiously, hoping he inflicted no new injury, he eased Ilitu's torso up. His knee supported it while he deployed the corresponding tube, screwed the two free ends together, and opened the valves. Again he lowered his companion. They were joined by a meter of umbilicus, and his unit did duty for both.

He wrinkled his nose as foul air mingled with fresh. That took a while to clear. Thereafter, as long as neither exerted himself—and neither was about to!—the system was adequate.

He could do nothing more but wait. Curiosity overwhelmed him. Although the surface was metal-slippery and sloped down, he put his head over its verge and shot his light that way. A whistle escaped him. Somewhat under the ledge, the opposite wall bulged back inward and the two sides converged. He could not see the bottom where they met, because fifty or sixty meters below him, where the gap was about one meter wide, it was choked with shards from above. Most, bouncing off the walls and this shelf, had gotten jammed there. Some were pointed, some were thin and surely sharp along their broken edges. Even here, to fall on them would be like falling into an array of knives. Space armor could fend them off. His flexible suit could not. Kaino withdrew to a sitting position.

Ilitu's breath rattled. The minutes grew very long.

A motion caught Kaino's eye. He flashed his beams at it and saw a line descending. The robot had been obedient to his orders. The line slithered across the ledge and onward before it stopped. With limited judgment, the robot had paid out all.

Kaino saw no stars occluded. Nevertheless the machine must be at the rim of the chasm and thrusting an antenna over, for he received: "Your command executed. Pray, what is next?" On a whim, he had had the synthetic voice made throaty female. He wished now he hadn't.

"Drag the cable, m-ng, north," he directed. Inclined though its orbit was, the planetoid had a pole in the same celestial hemisphere as Ursa Minor. "I can't reach it. . . . Ah. I did. Stop." He secured bights around his waist and, with an effort, Ilitu's, precaution against contingency.

The program had a degree of initiative. "Shall I raise you?"

"No. Stand by." No telling what the damage to Ilitu was. A major concussion at least, a broken back or rib-ends into the lungs entirely possible. Rough handling might well kill him. That would be the end. The expedition had no facilities for cellular preservation, let alone revival. Better wait for a proper rig, trusting that meanwhile he wouldn't die or that cerebral hemorrhage wouldn't harm his brain beyond clone regeneration.

Again Kaino composed his mind. Time trudged. He remembered and looked forward, smiled and regretted, sang a song, said a poem, considered the wording of a message to somebody he cared about. Lunarians are not that different from Earth humans. Often he looked at the stars where they streamed above him.

And ultimately he heard: "Kaino!"

"I am here," he answered. "Ilitu lives yet."

"Etana loaded a flitsled with medical supplies, took it down to camp, and returned to the ship," Brandir said. "I've brought it here. She thinks she can land nearby if need be."

"Best get Ilitu to our van, give him first aid, and then decide what to do." Kaino explained the situation. "Can you lower a pallet?"

"Yes, of course."

"I'll secure him well, then you winch him aloft, *gently*. Lest we bump together, I'll abide until you have him safe."

"Once you were less patient, little brother," Brandir laughed.

"I will not be if you keep maundering, dotard," Kaino retorted. A wild merriment frothed in him too.

The pallet bumped its way down the slanting wall, out of blackness and onto the ledge. Kaino took advantage of weak gravity to hold Ilitu's back fairly straight as he moved him. He undid the bight, closed and disconnected the air tubes, fastened the straps. "Haul away," he called. The hurt man rose from his sight.

"I have him," Brandir transmitted after a few minutes.

"Then let the robot reel me in," Kaino whooped, "and we'll go—go—go!"

The cable tautened, drawing him toward the stars.

Afterward Brandir determined what happened. He had rejoined his machinery, which rested well back from the crevasse rim. The robot was very close to it. At the moment of catastrophe, four billion-odd years ago, rocks as well as metal were thrown on high. The horizontal gush of molten iron that made the deck over the crack had a mistlike fringe that promptly congealed into globules along the verge. The stones dropped back on these and hid them. The planetoid swung out into realms where meteoroids are fugitively few. None ever struck nearby to shake this precarious configuration.

Low gravity means low friction with the ground, and here the shingle rested virtually on bearings. The weight at the end of the line tugged at the robot. The regolith underfoot glided. The robot lurched forward. It toppled over the edge and fell in a rain of stones.

Below it, Kaino tumbled back to the shelf, skidded off, and plunged into the lower depth. The knives received him.

In the big viewscreen, surf crashed on a winter shore. The waves ran gray as the sky, burst into white, sent water hissing up the sand almost to the driftwood that lay bleached and skeletal under the cliffs. Wrack flew like smoke low above; spindrift mingled with rain-spatters; the skirl and rumble shook air which bore a tang of salt and a breath of chill. It was as if Dagny Beynac's living room stood alone within that weather.

She thought that maybe she shouldn't have played this scene. It fitted her mood, she'd had it going since dawnwatch, but it was altogether alien to the young woman before her. Might Etana read it as a sign of hostility, of blame?

"Won't you be seated?" she asked. Unusual on the Moon so early in a visit, that was an amicable gesture. Besides, her old bones wouldn't mind. She'd been pacing overmuch lately, when she wasn't off on a long walk, through the passageways and around the lake or topside across the crater floor. High time she started returning to everyday.

The guest inclined her head, more or less an equivalent of "Thanks," and flowed into a chair. Dagny sat down facing her and continued, "Do you care for tea or coffee, or something stronger?"

"Grace, nay." Etana looked at the hands tightly folded in her lap. "I came because—I would be sure you understand—" Lunarians were seldom this hesitant.

"Go ahead, dear," Dagny invited softly.

The dark eyes lifted to meet her faded blue. "We thought of how we could leave him . . . in his honor . . . beneath a cairn on Iron Heath. Or else we could bring him home, that his kinfolk cremate him and strew his ashes over his mountains. But—"

Dagny waited, hoping her expression spoke gentleness.

"But a freeze-dried mummy!" Etana cried. "What use?" More evenly: "And although we must perforce lie about where and how he ended, to do it at his services were unworthy of him, nay?"

"You'd have attended?" wondered Dagny, taken unawares. Lunarians didn't bother to scoff at Earth ceremonies, they simply avoided them. Christmas without grandchildren got pretty lonesome.

"Ey, your friends would have come and misliked it did his siblings and companionates hold away." Etana paused. "But without a body to commit to its rest, our absence is of indifference, true?"

"Actually, I wouldn't have staged a funeral," Dagny said. "My man didn't want any. I don't for myself. It's enough if you remember."

"Nothing else? His companionates will—No matter."

Dagny didn't inquire about those rites, or whatever they were. The younger generations weren't exactly secretive; they just didn't share their customs with outsiders, in word or deed. Recalling the frustration of several anthropologists, she felt a smile skim her lips, the first since she got the news.

Etana went on: "In the end, Brandir and I did what we judged was due his honor and ours."

Dagny nodded. "I know." The brother had told her. When the velocity of the homebound ship was optimal for it, Kaino departed, lashed to a courier rocket, on a trajectory that would end in the sun.

Etana struggled further before she could get out: "I feared Brandir might not have made clear how—*I* felt—and therefore I have come to you."

"Thank you," Dagny said, genuinely moved. They weren't heartless, the Lunarians, her children, their children. They weren't, not really. But wisest to steer clear of anything this personal. "How is Ilitu?"

She had been too busy to inquire, after learning that he returned alive but in need of spinal cord regrowth and lesser biorepair. Too busy with grief, and handling condolences, and blessed, blessed work.

Etana brightened. "He fares well, should soon be hale. Thus he becomes a memorial unto Kaino."

That sounded rehearsed. However, the girl's happiness about the fact appeared sincere, so probably her gratitude was also. "You care for him, then?"

Etana went masklike.

Dagny made haste to change the subject. "That world my son helped explore, I'd like to think he'll be remembered there as well. If only—" No, better not pursue this either.

Etana did, turning sympathetic while remaining firm. "Nay, you realize it must wait in the knowledge of a chosen small few. Else would Earth close it to us."

Paranoia? Maybe, maybe not. Temerir's discovery did have the potential of a colony—for Lunarians. The gravity was right; the minerals were abundant and easily available, not buried under many kilometers of ice as in comets; water, ammonia, and organics were present, with more to be had in the same general region of space.

Who, though, would want to dwell that far from the sun, in a cold close to absolute zero?

Dagny supposed Brandir and his confederates were being cagey. After all, today Lunarians weren't forbidden, but neither were they encouraged to prospect and develop the asteroids of the Belt and the lesser moons of the outer planets. And that was in spite of their being far better suited for the conditions than Earth-type humans, in some respects possibly superior to robots.

She couldn't resist probing a bit: "When will you open it to yourselves?"

"When the time is befitting. That may well be long after we today are dead."

It was inhuman to think so far ahead, and to feel assured the secret would stay inviolate. Dagny sighed. "Yes, Brandir, Temerir, Fia, they've discussed it with me. Never fear, I'll keep my promise, I won't betray you."

"Honor shall be yours," said Etana with rare warmth.

She clearly didn't want to talk about Kaino, she who had shared him. What now was in the breasts of his other mates? It had been good of this one to come speak, however briefly, with his mother. Dagny wouldn't risk pushing her any further. Just the same, here was a chance to set forth something that could be . . . his invisible cenotaph.

"I do have a suggestion," Dagny began. "Have you decided on a name for your little planet?"

Etana showed surprise, which was gratifying. "Nay. Brandir and I touched on it once during the voyage, but reached no idea. Nor have others considered it since, to my knowledge." And that wasn't quite human either. The young woman sat still for a bit. "A name will be useful, yes."

"Proserpina," Dagny said.

"Hai?"

"As distant and lonely as it is, out beyond Pluto, who was the god of the underworld and the dead—his queen sounds right to me."

"Have we not already a Proserpina?"

Dagny shrugged. "Probably. An asteroid? I haven't checked. Never mind. Duplications exist, you know."

"What suppose your children of this?"

"I haven't asked them yet. It only occurred to me yesterday. What do you think?"

Etana cradled her chin and gazed into air. "A musical name. The goddess of the dead—because you lost a son to her?"

The sea noises roared and wailed.

Dagny sat straight as she said, "And because every springtime Proserpina comes back to the living world."

27

Prajnaloka was as lovely as its setting. From that mountaintop you looked far across the Ozark range, forest-green below the sun, down into a valley where a river ran quicksilver and up to cumulus argosies scudding before a wind freighted with earthy scents. A mockingbird trilled through quietness, a cardinal flitted like flame. These were old mountains, worn down to gentleness, their limestone white or pale gold wherever it stood bared. The life upon them was ageless.

A small community clustered around the ashram, service establishments and homes. Those buildings were of natural wood, low and rambling under high-pitched roofs, most of them fronted by porches where folk could sit together as twilight deepened. Flower-beds bordered them with color. They seemed a part of the landscape. The ashram itself rose at the center, its massive edifices surrounding quads where beech or magnolia gave shade; but the material was native stone and the architecture recalled Oxford. A trans-ceiver-winged communications mast soared in harmony with them, the highest of their spires.

Kenmuir and Aleka were still too exhausted to appreciate the scene. Tomorrow, he thought. At the moment he had all he could do, accompanying the mentor who guided them over campus and following what the dark, white-bearded, white-robed little man said.

"No, por favor, don't apologize. We were informed in advance that you didn't know exactly when you would arrive—"

—by Mary Carfax, which had made the reservation for Aleka Kame and Johan. Kenmuir reminded himself once more that that was his name while he stayed here.

"—and in any event, we have a relaxed attitude toward schedules. There are usually accommodations to spare. Most participation in our programs is remote."

Most participation in most things was, Kenmuir thought dully. Eidophone, telepresence, multiceiver, vivifer, quivira, how much occasion did they leave anybody to go any real distance from home?

"I am not quite sure just what you are seeking," Sandhu continued.

"Enlightenment," Aleka answered.

"That word has many meanings, and the ways toward any of them are countless."

"Of course. We are hoping to get a glimmering of it from the cybercosm. For that, we need the kind of equipment you have." Kenmuir wished he could talk as brightly and readily as she did. Well, she was young, she could bounce back fast from tension and terror.

The mentor came close to frowning. "None but synnoionts can achieve direct communion with the cybercosm."

"Certainly, señor. Doesn't everyone know that? But the kind of insight, guidance, the understanding of space-time unity and mind that come from the database and sophotectic teachers—" Aleka smiled. "Am I sounding awfully pretentious?"

Sandhu smiled back. "Not really. Earnest, naïve, perhaps. The explorations and meditations you speak of, they are what most of us here undertake. But they are the work of a lifetime, which is never long enough to complete them. And you say you have but a short while to spend."

"We hope to try it, señor, and find out whether we're . . . worthy. Then maybe later—"

Sandhu nodded. "Your hope is not uncommon. Bueno, I can see you are both weary. Let us get you settled in. Tomorrow we shall give you preliminary instruction and test your skills. This evening, rest." He gestured about him. "Drink beauty. Drink deep."

He showed them to dormitory-style quarters. The men's section was sufficiently full that Kenmuir would share a room—two cots, two desks, two chairs, a cabinet—with a novice from the Brazilian region. At a simple meal in the refectory, Aleka whispered to him that she was alone. This was a piece of luck although, had it not happened, she could have made her arrangements anyway, less conveniently.

Talk at table was amicable, not very consequential, in several languages. Afterward a number of the fifty or sixty visitors and some of the permanent Soulquesters mingled socially or relaxed with sedate

games. Kenmuir, who didn't feel up to it, went
outside. Nobody took that amiss; these people were as
diverse as their Daos. He stood on a terrace, breathing
summer odors. Below him the lights of the village fell
away toward darkened woods, above him shone stars
and the thin young Moon, around him danced fireflies. At last he sought his bed.

His roommate had already arrived and sat studying
a text in a reader. He was an intense youth who
introduced himself as Cavalheiro. Kenmuir saw no
way out of a conversation. It proved interesting.

"I search for God in the quivira," Cavalheiro tried
to explain. The surprise on his listener's face was
unmistakable. "Ah, yes. You wonder, am I dement? A
quivira gives nothing but the full-sensory illusion, the
dream, of an experience. True. However, one does not
passively let the program run. One interacts with it,
not so? The result is that the episode affects the brain
and goes into the memory just as if it were real."

"Not quite," Kenmuir demurred. "That is, whenever I've been there, well, afterward I knew I was
actually lying in the tank."

"All you want is entertainment, or sometimes
knowledge," Cavalheiro said. Not always, Kenmuir
thought. On long space missions, sessions in the
quivira were a medicine for sensory impoverishment.
Their input helped keep a man sane.

"I seek the meaning of things," Cavalheiro went on.
"The programs I use were written by persons who
spent their lives pursuing the divine. They had the
help of sophotects long intimate with humans, that
draw on the whole of every religious culture in history
and think orders of magnitude more powerfully than
us. The conceptions in the programs go beyond words,
images, consciousness. They go to the depths of the
spirit and the bounds of the cosmos. I think the
Teramind is in them."

"Um, may I ask what it . . . feels like?"

"It is no single thing. I have cried to Indra and he

has answered me out of the thunders. I have questioned Jesus Christ. I have felt the compassion of Kwan-Yin. I have—no, it is not possible to speak of nearing samadhi. But do you not see, it is interaction. In a little, little way, I give form to the divine, while it fills me and shapes me."

"You are both finding and making your God, then?" Kenmuir ventured.

"I am trying to understand and enter into God," Cavalheiro replied. "I am not unique in taking this path. None of us has lived to walk it to the end, and I do not imagine any human ever will. But it is what our lives are about."

Aleka having demonstrated high competence and sketchily described what she and Kenmuir claimed were their intentions, they received permission to proceed. By then the sun stood at mid-afternoon. They said they would like to relax with a walk now and begin next morning. "An excellent idea," Sandhu approved. "What you desire lies as much in the living world as in any abstractions." He signed the air. "Blessings."

Trails wound down the mountain through its woodland. They chose theirs because it looked unfrequented. Their goal was solitude in which to plan their strategy. Time passed, though, while they fared in silence.

High above them, the greenwood rustled to a breeze. That and their footfalls on soil were the only sounds at first, except when a squirrel chittered and sped aloft or a bird-call came liquid from shadowy depths. Light-flecks danced. Air beneath the leaves lay rich and warm. They passed some crumbling, moss-grown blocks that Kenmuir guessed were remnants of a highway; but if a town had once been hereabouts, it was long abandoned, demolished to make room for the return of nature. Presently he began to hear a trill of running water. The path reached a brook that swirled and splashed in a small cascade, down to a hollow where blackberries beckoned robins.

He and Aleka stopped for a drink. The water was cool. It tasted wild. Straightening, he wiped his mouth and sighed, "Bonny country. And so peaceful. Like a whole different planet."

Aleka gave him a quizzical glance. Here, where the canopy overhead was thinner, her skin glowed amber below a faint sheen of sweat. "Different from what?" she inquired.

He grimaced. "Those places we've lately been."

"You've got it wrong, I think. They are the alien planets. This is the normal one, ours."

"How?" he asked, puzzled.

"Why, what you said. Here things are beautiful and peaceful. Bueno, isn't most of Earth?"

"Why, uh—"

He harked back. The heights and heather and bluebells, glens and lochs, old hamlets and friendly taverns of his earlier life. Immensities of forest, prairie, savannah, splendor of horned beasts and lethally graceful predators, birds in their tens of thousands aflight across the sky. An antique walled city, lovingly preserved. A city that was a single kilometer of upwardness triumphant amidst its parkland. A city that floated on the sea. A village where each home was a dirigible endlessly cruising. A guitar plangent through tropical dusk or in an Arctic hut. And nobody crowded, nobody afraid . . . unless they wanted to be?

"Y-yes," he admitted. "Most of it. And where it isn't, by our standards, maybe that's what the people choose." He thought of the Drylanders. "I'm not sure how much choice they have, given what they are. But they're not forced."

Aleka cocked her head—the obsidian-black hair rippled—and considered him. "You're a thoughtful *kanaka*," she murmured.

Unreasonably, he flushed. "You make me think."

"Naw, with you it's a habit."

"Well, you open my eyes to what's around me on Earth."

Suddenly in the sunshine, he felt cold. What did he know of Earth, really? Of common humanity? His universe had become rock and ice, the far-strewn outposts of beings whose blood was not his, and one among them whom he utterly desired but who he knew very clearly did not love him. How glad he was when Aleka pulled him back from the stars: "I don't claim this world is perfect. Parts of it are still pretty bad. But by and large, we're closing in on the Golden Age."

In argument was refuge. "How can you say that, when you yourself—"

Aleka stamped her foot. "I said it isn't perfect. A lot needs fixing. Sometimes the fixing makes matters worse. Then we have to fight. Like now."

Kenmuir recalled the bitterness of Lilisaire and other Lunarians against the whole smooth-wheeling system. He recalled how the machines of that system were competing them out of space. Asperity touched him. "I take it you don't share the standard belief in the absolute wisdom and beneficence of the cybercosm?"

She shrugged. "Never mind the cybercosm. We deal with people, after all. And they're as shortsighted and crooked as ever."

"But the system—the advice, that governments never fail to take—the services, everywhere around us like the atmosphere, and we as dependent—" Services that had lately included doping a drink, it seemed; and what else?

"You mean, do I imagine the machines are pure, and humans alone corrupt the works? No." Aleka's laugh sounded forlorn. "Maybe I'm eccentric in not thinking the Teramind has anything particular to do with God."

"Then I'm eccentric too," Kenmuir agreed.

Through him went: What was the Teramind? The

culmination, the supreme expression of the cyber-cosm? No. The lesser sophotectic intellects, some of them outranging anything the human brain could conceive, took part in it, but they were not it, any more than cliffs and crags are the peak of a mountain. A single planetwide organism would be too slow, too loose; light-speed crawls where thought would leap. The machines, ever improving themselves, had created a supreme engine of awareness, somewhere on Earth—

White on a throne or guarded in a cave
There lives a prophet who can understand
Why men were born—

and it engaged in its mysteries while, surely, heightening its own mightiness; but it was not omniscient or omnipotent, it was not everywhere.

Its underlings, though, might be anywhere.

He must assume that none were here. Else his battle was already lost.

"I do admit, basically this is a good world," Aleka said. Her gaze sought peace in the boisterous water. "I don't want to overthrow it. I feel guilty, lying to our decent, kind hosts. All I want is freedom for *my* folk to be what they are."

For which end she did indeed lie, Kenmuir thought, and she would defy the whole civilization of which she spoke so well, until she had won or it had convinced her that her cause was wrong.

Why had it not? Why this secrecy, these . . . machinations?

"I'm no revolutionary either," he said, while rebellion stirred within him. "I'd just like to see things, well, shaken up a bit."

Her look returned to him. During their hours in Overburg they had barely begun to know one another. He became acutely aware of her fullness, lips and breasts and hips and round strong limbs. "Why would you?" she asked.

"Oh," he floundered, "too complacent—When was the last scientific discovery that amounted to more than the next decimal place or the newest archeological dig? Who's pioneering in music, graphics, poetry, any art? Where's the frontier?"

"Regardless," she gainsaid him—how spirited she was—"you're trying to stop the Habitat."

Lilisaire's mission, he thought. His selfishness. But he couldn't confess that. Most especially not to himself. "Lunarian society deserves to survive," he replied lamely. "It's different from anything on Earth, a, a leaven." He stared about him, randomly into the forest. "It's created its own beautiful places, you know."

28

The Mother of the Moon

They were a trio that drew glances as they passed through Tychopolis—the big, white-maned woman, her broad countenance lined across the brow and at the mouth and eyes but her back straight and her stride limber; the tall man, also Earth-born, his locks equally white and the gaunt face weathered, likewise still in full health; and the Lunarian, coppery-dark of skin below the midnight hair, making the slanty sleet-gray eyes seem doubly large. In flare-collared scarlet cloak, gold-and-bronze tunic with a sunburst at the belt, blue hose, he might have been setting youthful flamboyance against the plain unisuits of the elders; but his expression was too bleak.

At the lifelock he identified himself to the portal. It opened on an elevator terminus. "This is a service entrance," he explained. "The public access is closed for reconstruction." His English was less idiomatic and lilting than that of most among his generation, perhaps because in his work he necessarily called on many Terrestrial databases and consulted with many Terrestrial experts.

"I know that, of course," Lars Rydberg answered. "I am not sure just what sort of reconstruction it is."

Eyrnen led the way into the elevator. "We can ill allow animals, seeds, or spores from low-level to get into the city. Think of bees nesting in ventilators, squirrels gnawing on electrical cables, or disease germs which the high mutation rate here may have turned into a medical surprise for us."

Dagny Beynac sensed the implied insult. "My son is quite well acquainted with the obvious," she said tartly.

"I pray pardon, sir," Eyrnen said to Rydberg. He did not sound as if he meant it. "I did but wish to ensure that the problem stood clear before you. Some folk confuse our situation with that of the L-5 colony. Yonder they have no more than large, closely managed parks. We are fashioning a wilderness."

Rydberg went along with the half-conciliation. "No offense," he answered. "I do know this, but wondered about the technical details. It's very good of you to show us around."

It was, even if the bioengineer's grandmother had specifically requested it for herself as well as her visitor, and a request from Dagny Beynac had on the Moon somewhat the force of a royal command. Quite a few Lunarians would have refused anyway, or at least taken the opportunity to display icy, impeccably formal insolence.

Odd that this son of Jinann should show what hostility he did. She was always the most Earthling-like of the Beynac children, the most amicable toward the mother world. Well, Eyrnen belonged to the next generation.

And was he actually hostile? Rydberg thought of a cat asserting itself before a dog, warning the alien lest a fight erupt. Could that be Eyrnen's intent? Rydberg smothered a sigh. He didn't understand Lunarians. He wondered how well his mother did.

"A pleasure," the engineer was saying. "My lady

grandmother has not guested these parts in some time. We have much new to reveal." He did not add outright that he'd rather she'd come unaccompanied. Instead: "She has been overly occupied on behalf of her people." Against the encroachments of Earth, he left unspoken.

Rydberg's ears popped. They were going deep indeed.

He admired the deftness with which Beynac intervened: "About those technicalities, I'd be interested to hear, too. Okay, you've got a long tunnel, for trucking bulky loads and numbers of passengers to and fro. Valves at either end keep the noticeable animals on the reservation. As you said, it's the bugs and seeds and microbes and such that could sneak by. But I thought your sensors and minirobots were keeping them well zapped. I haven't heard of anything escaping that couldn't easily be taken care of."

Maybe she was giving Eyrnen a taste of his own medicine, no matter how innocent her smile. He accepted it, replying, "The improvements in the lifelock are partwise qualitative, better technology, but mainwise quantitative, more of everything. As the ecology below strengthens and increases its fertility, and as the region grows, invasive pressures will heighten. We must anticipate them."

The elevator hissed to a stop, the door slid open, and the three emerged onto a balcony from which a ramp spiraled on downward. Rydberg caught his breath.

He stood near the ceiling of a cavern whose floor was almost two kilometers beneath him. The inset sunlike lamps that lighted it shone, as yet, gently, for this was "morning" in their cycle. They made warm a breeze that wandered past, bearing odors of forest which must be thick and sweet on the ground. Distance hazed and blued the air; seen across tens of kilometers, the other walls were dim, half unreal. Cloudlets drifted about. Birds flew by. So did a human a ways off, wings spread iridescent from the arms, banking and soaring not in sport—that was for such places as Avis Park—but watchful over the domain. It stretched in a thousand-hued greenness of crowns, and meadows starred with wildflowers, and a waterfall that stabbed out of sheer rock to form a lake from which a stream wound aglitter. . . .

Eyrnen let the others stand mute a while before he said, "Let us go and walk the trails. Shall I summon a car for the ramp?"

"Not for me!" Beynac exclaimed. She took the lead, in Lunar bounds, as a girl might have.

"It's a wonderful creation," she had said the duskwatch before. "I look forward on my own account, but still more to seeing you see it for the first time."

Having finished supper, they lingered over coffee and liqueurs. Drinks had preceded the food and a bottle of wine complemented it, for this celebrated the beginning of several daycycles she had arranged free of duties. Her son had completed his business for Fireball and meant to spend that period with her before going home. They were all too seldom together. A glow was in their veins, an easiness in their hearts.

She had cooked the meal herself, to a high standard, but served it in the kitchen. Now that she lived alone, except for visits like his, she saved her baronial dining room for parties. The kitchen was amply spacious, an abode of burnished copper, Mexican tile, and fragrances. A picture of Edmond Beynac in his later years, at his desk, looked across it to a Constable landscape reproduced by molecular scan. A Vivaldi concerto danced in the background.

"I'm eager," Lars said. "From everything I have screened about it—" He hesitated. "That's not much."

If only the Lunarians would cooperate with the news media, at least about matters as harmless and to their credit as this, he thought. If it weren't for the Earth-gene Moondwellers, what would Earth ever learn?

Dagny let his remark pass. "I've been far too long away from it," she mused. "I do miss natural nature."

"Most of your communities have lovely parks."

"Oh, yes." Her glance went to the painting. "But no living hinterlands."

He smiled. "If that's what you wish for, come see us again on Vancouver Island."

She smiled back, shaking her head a bit. "I've probably grown too creaky for the weight."

"You, at a mere ninety? Nonsense." Not just because of faithfulness about her biomed program and regular vigorous exercise in the centrifuge, he thought. She'd had luck in the heredity sweepstakes, and shared the prize with him. He did not feel greatly diminished in his own mid-seventies. "Do come."

"Well, maybe." She sighed. "There's always so bloody much to do, and the months go by so fast."

"Come for Christmas," he urged.

Her face kindled. "With your grandchildren!"

She had great-grandchildren here, but they were Lunarian.

She loved them, he felt sure, and no doubt they liked well enough the old lady who brought them presents and had the grace not to hug them or gush over them; but did they listen to her stories and songs with any deep feeling, did they ever care to romp with her?

"I'll bring along a great-grandchild of mine to help you celebrate your hundredth birthday," he said impulsively.

She laughed low. The light caught a glistening in her eyes. "You're a darling, once you've had a smidgen of alcohol to dissolve that Swedish starch." Her look sought her husband's image. "Oh, 'Mond," she whispered, "I do wish you could've known him better."

The picture was an animation. Because of the

comfort between them, Lars asked what would otherwise never have escaped him: "Do you activate that very often?"

"Not often any more," she answered. "I know it so well, you see."

"All these years," he blurted. "Nobody else. You must have had offers."

Sudden merriment rang forth. "Lots, though the last one was a fairish time ago. I was tempted occasionally, but never enough. 'Mond kept right on being too much competition for 'em."

The smile waned. She looked elsewhere. "Although," she said, "he's become like a dream I had once long ago."

"We live by our dreams, do we not?" he replied as softly.

It was a temperate-zone forest. Near Port Bowen, a tropical environment was under development, less far along because excavators did not have the fortune of starting out with hollows as big as were here. Talk went of making a prairie, or else a small sea, below Korolev Crater, but probably population and industry on Farside would remain too sparse for decades to support such an effort.

Eyrnen guided his kinfolk down a path along which elm and ash and the occasional oak arched leaves above underbrush where wild currants had begun to ripen. Deeper in the wood, birch gleamed white and light-spatters speckled shade. Butterflies fluttered brilliant in the air; the call of a cuckoo rippled its moist stillness. Where leaves from former years had blown onto the trail, they rustled underfoot. Smells were of summer. Yet this was no Terrestrial wild. Biotechnology had forced the growth; low gravity would let it go dizzyingly high.

A winged creature swept past and vanished again into the depths. It had been small, brightly furred, with a ruddering tail. A shrill cry died away in its wake. "What was that?" Rydberg asked.

"A daybat," Eyrnen told him. "One of our genetic experiments. Besides being ornamental, we hope it will help keep the population of necessary insects stable."

"It'll be quite a spell, with quite a few mistakes along the way, before you have a real, self-maintaining ecology," Beynac predicted.

"It is evolving more quickly than was forecast," Eyrnen replied. "I will live to walk through a true wilderness."

"Oh, scarcely that," Rydberg demurred. At once he regretted it. Bad habit, correcting other people's impressions.

Eyrnen glared at him and snapped, "How genuine is any of your so-called nature on Earth?"

"Down, boys," Beynac said. She could bring it off. To Rydberg: "Don't be persnickety, dear. What *is* nature, anyway? There'll be life that can do without human or robot attention, as long as the energy comes in; and don't forget, that's solar energy, good for several billion years."

Rydberg nodded. "True." The optical conduits that led it from the surface wouldn't likely give out. The molecular resonances that imposed a twenty-four-hour night-and-day cycle and the changing of the seasons might get deranged, but while some species would die off, others would adapt.

And, eventually, new breeds appear? As the sun grew hotter until runaway greenhouse effect seared and boiled Earth barren, could this forest endure, gone strange, in the deeps of the Moon?

He made his remark prosaic: "From what I have heard, a solidly viable ecology requires more space than this."

"So the scientists declare," Eyrnen conceded. "I think forms can be bred that would not need it. However, the point is moot, because the realms will in fact be vastly increased. At last, perhaps a century hence, all will be linked together."

"Hm, what a monstrous job."

"In future we will not depend on machinery to carve out volumes where geology has not provided them. Bacteria already in the laboratories can break down rock, multiplying as they do. It will take more energy than is available today, and of course they must be modified to fit into the ecology, but these are matters readily dealt with when the time comes."

Although Rydberg had encountered such ideas before, it had been as speculations. To hear them calmly set forth as certainties was exciting. "How much expansion do you suppose will happen in your lifetime?" he asked.

A supple shrug raised and lowered Eyrnen's shoulders as his hands flickered. "Less than might be. We have too many various demands on our resources, and Earth is a sink for them."

Beynac lifted a fist. "I told you, God damn it, no politics today!" she cried.

Eyrnen cast Rydberg a rueful, almost friendly grin and relaxed. The Earthling returned it.

Inwardly, though, he knew a cold moment. He wanted, he truly wanted kindliness between himself and the other children of his mother, and their children. Never had he won to more than a polite tolerance. It wasn't simply that they were different. He had gotten along well with metamorphs more radical than these. She knew what the overt problem was, and had just given it a name—politics, the wretched politics. But it was itself merely a symptom, a working, of the real trouble, like fever and buboes in medieval plague.

Property; the common heritage issue. Taxation. Education. Census. Home rule: legislation, legislature, the very concept of democracy and its desirability. Exclusivism. Legitimacy of power: negotiation, criminal law, sanctuary. And more disputes and more, some trivial in themselves but salt rubbed into the wound. . . .

What brought conflict on, Rydberg thought, was a heightening strife between an old civilization and one that was nascent; no, between an old biological species and one that was new, perhaps unstable.

While Dagny, his mother, stood torn between them.

Why had she hushed and shunted aside his questions about the death of Sigurd-Kaino, his half-brother? Somehow, on some remote asteroid—He had asked no further, because that was clearly what she wanted. But why?

Her Lunarian children claimed silence of her.

His mind went to his half-sister Gabrielle-Verdea, still in her sixties as fierce, as insurgent a speaker as her gene-kindred possessed. Through him keened a song of hers. Lunarian, it could not well be rendered in Terrestrial words, and his knowledge of its native tongue was limited to the practicalities in which all languages are about equal; but—

> With your Pacific eye, observe my scars
> Of ancient wars.
> Your bones remember dinosaurs.

29

Morning light brought alive the mandala of many colors in an arched window. White walls shone, relieved by pilasters that rose to join with the vaulted ceiling. Duramoss carpeted the floor, green and springy. Chairs, couches, table, desk were of wood and natural fiber, graceful as willows. Nothing in the chamber defied the complex of consoles, keyboards, screens, and other equipment that ruled over it. All was like a declaration that life, humanness, and the cybercosm belonged together.

A declaration much needed, Kenmuir thought. This multiple engine of communication and computation, advanced beyond anything he had ever encountered before, was a daunting sight at best.

The wordless reassurance did not speak to him. He was come as an enemy.

Aleka at his side, he entered into cool quietness. The doorway contracted behind them. They were shut away, sealed off, private, until they opened the gates to the cybercosm.

She swallowed, squared her shoulders, and walked forward. He went more slowly. His heart thudded, his tongue lay dry. This bade fair to be the day of victory, failure, or ruin. Again he knew himself for a fool, who ought to flee and confess it. But no, then he would be less than a man.

Aleka settled at the primary console and gestured him to take the seat beside hers. When he did, she caught his hand and squeezed it. He felt her warmth, as if blood flowed between them. She smiled. "Bueno," she said, "let's go for broke." He had turned his face toward her. She leaned over and kissed him.

Before he could really respond, she had drawn back, laughing a little, and her fingers were on the keys. Knowing it wasn't quite logical, he had disdained to take a tranquilizer. Now all at once the fears and doubts were burned out of him. That wasn't logical either, but what the Q. When committed to a course of action, he had always gone calm. Never, though, had he felt more clear and quick in the head than now.

"Direct me," she said.

Yesterday they had drafted a general plan. Afterward he had spent much time alone, pondering when his mind did not drift freely in hopes of inspiration. Nonetheless, they must grope their way forward, improvising, his knowledge of space and astronautics guiding her skill with the system.

"The history of interplanetary exploration," he told her unnecessarily. "For openers, a summary." That should make their undertaking seem an innocuous bit of research, perhaps by someone with nothing better to do.

Hypertext appeared in three-dimensional configuration. Aleka entered the commands that led topic by topic outward from the asteroid belt to the Kuiper and beyond. Casualties. . . . Sigurd Kaino Beynac did not come home. The purpose and destination of his voyage were never put in any public database. Whatever tale was kept sequestered was probably lost in the disastrous ending of Niolente's rebellion. So the computer said.

"We knew this stuff," Aleka complained.

"Yes, but I want it in an entire context, or as nearly entire as exists," Kenmuir replied. "Next we'll focus on scientific missions to asteroids."

The established associations quickly brought up Edmond Beynac and his death. Kenmuir nodded. He had expected that. "Beynac was after confirmation of his ideas about the early Solar System. Let's check on exactly what they were. It's vague in my memory. I'm beginning to realize that that's largely because I've scarcely ever seen it mentioned. Because he was in fact mistaken, or because there was something there that somebody would like to suppress? He was too important in his science for all record of this to be erasable."

When he had studied the précis, which took time, Kenmuir whistled low. "M-m-*hm*. I get a suspicion of what kind of body Kaino went out to. But that was years after his father died, and he wouldn't have taken off blind. First, an astronomical search. But nobody's ever heard—" He sketched instructions for Aleka to track down the account.

And: "Ah, yes, I'd forgotten, or maybe never knew, a brother of Kaino's directed the major Lunar observatory of that period. We'll run through a list of what reports and papers came out of it between those two deaths."

And: "Some curious gaps, wouldn't you say? Distant comets discovered and catalogued, nothing anomalous, but . . . I should think the surveys would have found more of them. We know they're out there. Were certain findings left unreported?"

And: "If I were seriously interested in spotting,

m-m, Edmond Beynac's hypothetical mother asteroid, I'd get better parallaxes than you can from the Moon. Robotic probes—those launches will be recorded, even if the results are not."

Aleka giggled. It sounded like a guitar string breaking. "How lucky for us the cybercosm is a data packrat. It hoards everything."

"Aye, but a part of the hoard stays permanently underground." Kenmuir was silent a while. "Duck back to Kaino. The departure date of his last voyage, exact type and capabilities of his ship, initial boost parameters as far as they were routinely tracked, date of the return without him. That will all have been public."

And: "Yes, it's consistent with an expedition to the Kuiper Belt, though that still leaves an unco huge region." Kenmuir frowned. "The last decade or two of the Selenarchy. Missions dispatched by the aristocrats of Zamok Vysoki: Rinndalir till he left for Alpha Centauri, Niolente afterward. Very little information would ever have been released about them, but we'll see what's available, including whatever the Peace Authority found in her files."

"You've told me they claimed a lot of that was accidentally destroyed," Aleka said.

"They claimed. Let's look. Again, ship types and launch parameters. Those could not have been hidden, at least not if they left from the Moon. And maybe you can locate a few cargo manifests or the like, scraps of fact, pointing to what they may have carried. . . . Uh, I'd better explain how such matters work."

Having assembled the figures, Kenmuir turned to an auxiliary board and calculated trajectories, fuel consumption, the range of what could have happened. When he was through, he sat back and said in his driest voice, "Plain to see now, Lilisaire's suspicions and mine are right. Some sort of project in deep space, involving construction. Clandestine, which means trips to the site had to be few and far between and minimally manned. But even in those days, you could do quite a lot with well-chosen, well-programmed robots, if the raw materials were handy."

He rose and paced. His hands wrestled one another. "Yes," he said in a monotone. "Do you see, Aleka? It's almost got to be Edmond Beynac's giant iron asteroid, orbiting out where only dust and gravel and cometary iceballs large and small are supposed to be. His children kept the discovery to themselves, thinking it might prove valuable. The secret was passed down the generations, doubtless to just one or two each time, else it couldn't have been kept so long. Finally Rinndalir and Niolente decided to try making use of it."

"A long shot, a what's-to-lose move," the woman breathed. "Otherwise somebody would have tried earlier. After Fireball made war on the Avantists, it was doomed, however slowly its dying went. The Selenarchs were threatened too. Without Fireball, they had no realistic hope of maintaining their independence against a determined Federation. Unless—Beynac's world—but how? What help was there?"

"Something the government doesn't want known."

"Not the whole government. How could it, century after century, and nobody blab?"

"The cybercosm. The—" Kenmuir decided not to say, "Teramind." Instead: "It could rather easily keep the knowledge to itself, except for a few totally trustworthy human agents. When Lilisaire grew curious, that synnoiont Venator took charge of investigating how much she might have learned and what her Lunarians might be thinking of."

She nodded. His last sentence had been automatic, unnecessary.

He halted. "Well, I believe we've gotten everything we can out of the open files," he said. "In remarkably short time, thanks to these facilities." Indeed, so thorough a probe into a quasi-infinity of bytes would hardly have been possible to a less-equipped station. "Still, several hours. Do you want to take a break, or shall we plunge ahead?"

"I couldn't relax, waiting. Could you?"

"Frankly, no." He rejoined her. They exchanged a cold grin.

Hers faded. As if reaching out for comfort, she murmured, "I wonder if Dagny Beynac knew."

"You've heard of her?"

"She was quite a power on the Moon, wasn't she?"

"Yes, I rather imagine she did know. The siblings would have needed her help in covering the trail. But she took the secret with her to the tomb."

Aleka shook herself. "C'mon. Anchors aweigh."

They spent minutes formulating their question. It was simple enough, but it must look like one onto which she had stumbled, a bit of aroused curiosity. Kenmuir put in what specifics he had been able to guess at, such as the broad arc of heaven in which the object most likely was wandering, but in its final form the query amounted to: *Does a very large ferrous asteroid, perturbed out of the inner Solar System, orbit through the Kuiper Belt?*

Aleka straightened, moistened her lips, and entered it.

A sharp note sounded. A red point of light blinked in the screen. Below it, words leaped out:

FILE 737. ACCESS IS RESTRICTED TO AUTHORIZED PERSONS. DNA IDENTIFICATION IS REQUIRED.

The Anglo changed to a series of other languages. Aleka shut the display off.

She and Kenmuir sat for a span in silence. Again he felt a steely steadiness. "Hardly a surprise, eh?" he said at length. "Shows we're on the scent." He gestured at the little bag Aleka had carried along. "Shall we?"

"One minute," she answered. Her voice was as level as his, but he saw sweat on her forehead. He thought it would smell sweet, of woman, were the reek of his not smothering that. "An ordinary scholar would wonder why."

"Good girl!" His laugh rattled. "You've a gift for intrigue, evidently."

Her mouth quirked. *May I ask for the reason the file is classified?* she tapped. Throughout, they had left vocal connections dead, so they could talk freely, and likewise the visual pickup. Besides, a real researcher would avoid distractions like that.

CONSIDERATIONS OF GENERAL SAFETY NECESSITATE THAT CERTAIN ACTIVITIES AND CERTAIN REGIONS OF DISTANT SPACE BE INTERDICTED TO ALL BUT PROPER CYBERNETIC ASSEMBLIES. OTHERWISE THE DANGER WOULD EXIST OF STARTING SOME OBJECTS, WHICH HAVE UNSTABLE ORBITS, INWARD. THAT COULD EVENTUALLY HAVE SERIOUS CONSEQUENCES. IT IS A CYBERNETIC RESPONSIBILITY TO PROVIDE AGAINST FORESEEABLE MISFORTUNES, NO MATTER HOW FAR AHEAD IN TIME. DETAILS ARE WITHHELD TO AVOID TEMPTATION.

HOWEVER, IT IS PERMISSIBLE TO STATE THAT NO BODY RESEMBLING YOUR DESCRIPTION IS KNOWN, AND ON COSMOLOGICAL GROUNDS IS IMPLAUSIBLE. SEE—The screen proffered a list of references. Kenmuir knew by the titles and dates that they were papers published in Edmond Beynac's lifetime, arguing against his theory.

"You lie," he muttered at the machine. "You lie in the teeth you haven't got."

"That takes sentience," Aleka whispered. "We've contacted a sophotect."

"Highly specialized, a node in the network," Kenmuir deemed. "It's best to have some flexibility, not a simple, blank refusal." He sighed. "We could continue the pretense, I suppose, and call up those ancient disputes, but I'm for going straight on ahead."

Aleka raised a hand. "Wait a minute. Let me think."

Quietude lasted. The faint colors thrown by the mandala window onto the wall opposite had noticeably shifted downward since she and Kenmuir arrived.

He glimpsed that she had turned her regard upon him, and looked back. Her eyes were gold-flecked russet. "This is mucho important business," she said very softly.

"Yes," he answered for lack of a better word.

"Somebody high, high up wants it kept *kapu*. The *haku*, the *kahuna*—I don't know who or what, but I think that in the past it got the Teramind's attention, and can get it again."

Chill touched him. "Could well be."

"Is the purpose bad?"

"Perhaps not. Why mayn't we decide for ourselves?"

"Do you still want to go through with this?"

He considered for an instant. "If you do."

She nodded. "Yes. But listen. You remarked that keeping information squirreled away—for a long, long time, as this has been—that needs more than a lock. It needs flexible response. Bueno, will the guardian really be satisfied with a DNA scan?"

"That was all it demanded."

"Anything more might be too clumsy." And anything less, Kenmuir reflected, such as a facial or fingerprint identification, was too easily counterfeited. "Still, if I were in charge, knowing that Lilisaire is on the prowl, I'd take an extra precaution or two. Like instructing the guardian to notify me if anybody does make entry, legitimately or not."

Kenmuir started where he sat. "Huh! That didn't occur to me."

"Nor to me till just now. I may be wrong, of course."

"But if you're right—" Thought searched wildly. "Venator wouldn't sit and wait. He'll be busy, quite likely far from here."

"So he'd want the guardian to contact not only him, but agents closer, who can pounce fast."

"The police?"

"Not local police. They'd wonder why they were ordered to arrest a couple of persons harmlessly using the public database. Those persons might tell them why, and they'd tell others, and folks would wonder. Me, I'd have the crack emergency squads of the Peace Authority alerted, around the planet, to be prepared for a quick raid, reasons not given but the thing top secret."

"As a recourse—" Protest rose in Kenmuir's throat like vomit. "Are we going to let this possibility paralyze us?"

"No," Aleka said. "But we'd better scout around first."

She gave herself anew to the equipment. It told her the nearest Authority base was in Chicago Integrate. "Allowing time to scramble, an arrowjet could bring a squad here inside half an hour," she reckoned. Kenmuir, who knew virtually nothing about constabulary, mustered courage. Maybe he could at least flash a message to Zamok Vysoki. It must go in clear. However, since the Moon was in the sky, it could beam directly to a central receiver there, and—and be intercepted by a surveillance program, and provoke immediate counteraction—"What we'll need to know is whether they do scramble," Aleka was saying. "Hang on."

Her fingers danced. The patience schooled into a spacer had strength to hold Kenmuir motionlessly waiting.

After a time he chose not to number, Aleka leaned back, wiped a hand across her face, and mumbled, "Good. We will know."

"How's that?" he croaked.

"I've set it up. Traffic Control will inform us if and when any high-speed unscheduled flyer leaves CI in this general direction." She shook her head. "No, no, nothing special, no break-in. The sort of information a civilian might have reason to want. For instance, we could be studying atmospheric turbulence effects, or some such academic makework. I just had to figure out how to request it."

His belly muscles slackened a trifle. "Then . . . if it happens . . . we'll have twenty or thirty minutes to get to your volant and away?"

"Not that simple. TrafCon will oblige a *maka'i* every bit as readily as us, if not more so. Easy enough to get the registry of a vehicle that left here a short while back, and know exactly where it is while it's moving. We'll've got to land somewhere close by and be off like bunnies." Aleka sighed. "I trust Lilisaire will ransom my poor flyer, or buy me a new one. Unless you and I end up where we won't have any need of personal transport."

Kenmuir refused to think about the ugliest possibilities. This was the modern world, for God's sake. Thus far he and she had done nothing illegal. If they were about to, well, it was not technically a serious offense, not in a society that recognized every citizen's right to information. They'd be entitled to a public hearing, to counsel, to procedures that might well be too awkward for the secretkeepers. It wasn't as though they were dealing with an instrument of an almighty state, KGB or IRS or whatever the name had been—

He wished he could believe that.

"What we must do is escape, and then take stock," he said. A detached part of him jeered that he could also tell her the value of pi to four decimal places. "How?"

"That's what I mean to check out." Once more she got busy. Schedules paraded over the screen.

After a while: "All right. There's no public transport out of Prajnaloka, and it's sparse everywhere close around, as thinly populated as the area is. Mostly it's local, which does us no good. Figure ten minutes to run to my volant. Ten or twelve minutes airborne before anybody can intercept us, no more.

"The single place in range is Springfield. It has a

twice-daily airbus to St. Louis Hub. There we could vanish into the crowd and quickly get seats to somewhere else big and anonymous. Trouble is, the opposition will know this too, or find out in a hurry. We'll have to time our arrival at Springfield and departure from it ve-ery closely. The next bus is in about half an hour. Otherwise we'll have to wait till evening."

"That gives us time to prepare," he said reluctantly.

"And it gives time for things to go wrong," she retorted. "Obviously, the fact that we bounced off the edge of the no-no hasn't raised an alert. Else we'd be under arrest this minute. But is a query going along the lines? Or—we *are* being chased. The data could be starting to point this way." Her voice rang. "I say keep moving!"

He weighed it. If they must immediately cut and run, it meant abandoning their spare clothes and things in the dormitory. But those were easily replaced, all their cash being on their persons, and stuff left behind might even divert suspicion for a critical short span. Impulsively, he thrust out his hand. "Go."

She returned the clasp, hers hard and warm. "Okay, *aikāne.*" Then he understood why humans throughout history had time and again staked their lives on ventures that later generations saw as fantastical. It was the nature of the beast.

Aleka took up her bag, set it on her lap, and plucked forth a thing that appeared to be a brown cloth. Unfolded, it revealed itself as a gauntlet of thin material—material that was alive, like the mask she had earlier worn. She slipped it over her right hand.

"Lilisaire's agent gave it to me in Hawaii," she had told Kenmuir that night in Overburg while the fire died away. "Prepared special. She thinks we may find use for it."

"What is it?" he asked.

"An organism with tissue reserves to last a couple of weeks. Made from a biospecimen of that synnoiont who visited her—Venator, she said is his name. It

carries his DNA. If we should need to get past a
biolock, won't its keys be likely to include that high-
powered a fellow, who's working on the case?"

"But, but how'd she get a useable sample?" The
scraps of skin and other tissue that everybody shed in
the course of a day wouldn't do. They were tiny, dead
and degraded, mingled with dust and other debris. It
took delicate equipment, most of which was only in
the possession of police forces, to find such stuff; and
once you had mapped the genome, you would have to
have independent means of ascertaining whose it was.
"If she drew blood somehow, maybe faking an
accident—but wouldn't he surmise her intentions?"

Aleka grinned. "I didn't ask. I did guess."

He felt his cheeks go hot, and was angry that they
did. "No, wait," he snapped, "that's ridiculous. A
gamete has just half the chromosomes."

He saw his error even as she responded: "Ah, but
we're talking about lots and lots of gametes. Between
them, a lab can quickly enough work out the complete
original genome. Then it synthesizes one, and—
You're not trying to clone the human, you know, just
some skin for a simple substrate. Not much of a trick.
Slip your sample to a technie in your pay, who goes
and does the job in any of a lot of genetech labs. I
daresay this wasn't the first occasion of that general
sort for Lilisaire. When the thing was ready, he'd
bring it to her under his shirt or whatever. We'd better
not underestimate friend Venator, but in this particular business with her—" Aleka laughed. "Poor, unsuspecting superman!"

Soon afterward, events exploded and Kenmuir forgot the pain.

Of course this station had biolock capability. That
belonged with its inclusiveness. Not all sealed files
were official. You might well want to enter highly
personal information in the public database or a
private one, for use in conjunction with other facts

already there. The cybercosm would know, in the sense that it scanned everything, but it would not betray your confidence.

Aleka keyed in and presented her life glove. After a moment the screen displayed PROCEED TO FILE 737.

To avoid the appearance of being the same person who inquired before, she tapped out *Give me full information on the giant ferrous asteroid in the Kuiper Belt.*

PROSERPINA. THIS IS THE NAME BESTOWED BY THE LUNARIANS WHO DISCOVERED AND FIRST EXPLORED IT. SUCCESSORS OF THEIRS PARTLY DEVELOPED IT FOR SETTLEMENT. ITS MASS IS—

Kenmuir hunched forward, as if he could haul the words out of the terminal. His pulse racketed. Yes, yes, Edmond Beynac's—

—REMNANT OF A PROTOPLANET, PER-TURBED INTO AN ECCENTRIC ORBIT WITH HIGH APHELION. BY COLLISIONS DURING GIGAYEARS IT HAS ACQUIRED SUBSTANTIAL DEPOSITS OF WATER ICE, ORGANICS, AND—

Generalities. When would the bloody program get down to the numbers?

—POTENTIAL OF COLONIZATION BY LU-NARIANS—

On Kenmuir's right, a second screen flashed. Aleka leaned past him to read. The breath hissed between her jaws. She shook him out of raptness. "That's it," she said. "A speedster just took off from Chicago base. *Hele aku.*"

"A minute, a minute," he gasped. "The orbital elements—"

"You want to mull them over in a nice quiet cell? Move, boy!" She was on her feet. She slapped his shoulder, hard.

He clambered erect and stumbled after her, out the door, across the quad, toward the communal garage.

Sunlight dashed over him, overweeningly bright, but eastward above a roof he spied the wan Lunar crescent.

Do strifes ever end? he wondered in the turmoil. Was he waging a war that began in the days of Dagny Beynac?

30

The Mother of the Moon

The swimming pool filled most of its chamber. Mist lay over it like a blanket, white in the bleak light that shone from fluoropanels and reflected off tile, for the water was very cold. The vapors scarcely stirred, as still as the air rested. So had Jaime Wahl y Medina ordered this place be kept for him. It was his refreshment, his twice-daily renewal, exercise to rouse the blood and shorten the times he must spend in the damned centrifuge. God knew the governor general of Luna needed whatever gladness he could find. Peace and quiet, too. Nobody else came here; family and friends used the older, larger, warmer pool at the opposite end of the mansion.

He entered as he was wont, late in dawnwatch, kicked off his sandals, hung his robe from a hook, and slipped his goggles on. For some minutes he went through his warmup routine, a powerfully built man of middle height and mid-forties age, big nose and heavy chin underscored by the blackness of hair, brows, mustache, brown eyes crinkled at the corners by years of squinting into the winds and tropical brightnesses of Earth. Chill raised gooseflesh on shaggy arms and legs. Having finished, he climbed the ladder to the diving board at the deep end of the basin, bounced—less vigorously than he would have liked, lest his head strike the ceiling—and plunged.

He also fell more slowly than he would have preferred. But the water received him with a liquid crash that echoed from the walls. It surrounded him, embraced him, slid sensuously around every movement, and now gravity made no difference, he was free, more free than in space itself.

Down he went to the bottom and streaked along just above. His flesh responded to the flowing cold, lashed into utter aliveness. The tile pattern, his hands where they came forward to thrust him on, passed stark in their clarity, transfigured by refraction. His eyes needed the goggles, they could not well open straight onto the purity, it would have washed the salt out of them. Like all Lunar water, this came totally clean from each recycling. Not in its comet had it been so unsullied, not since its ice-dust glittered in the nebula that would become the Solar System, and something of that ancient keenness had returned to it as well. He drove himself through a reborn virginity.

When his lungs could strain no more, he broke surface, breathed hard, went around and around the rim until he felt ready to go under again. And thus he reveled until his body warned him he would soon begin losing too much heat.

He swung out, leaped to the bath alcove, and let a nearly scalding shower gush over him. A vigorous toweling followed, and he was ravenously ready for breakfast.

He did stop a minute before he went off to get dressed, and looked at the instrument panel. There had been some trouble lately with temperature control. The thermometer was holding steady. Probably Maintenance had fixed the system so it would stay fixed. Well, it was simple enough. Coils under the pool tapped whatever cooling the thermostat called for from the municipal reservoir of it, a liquid-air tank which itself drew on space during the long Lunar night. Still, Wahl habitually kept track of everything he could for which he felt in any way responsible.

Too little of the first, too much of the second! He grimaced and went headlong down the hallway.

In his bedroom he donned not civilian garb but the

blue uniform of the Peace Authority. He was entitled, being a major in its reserve, and today such a reminder of what he represented, what power ultimately stood behind him, could be helpful.

The legislature was convening next week. Deputy Rabkin had announced that he would introduce a bill to give the tax agency warrant-free access to business databanks, making it harder to cook up falsifications. Most delegates with Terrestrial genes favored the measure; evasion was getting out of hand. Speaking for what she called the free folk, Deputy Fia threatened that if this proposed rape of privacy came to the floor, she would lead the Lunarians out, form a rump parliament, and nullify any act that passed.

It could happen. She was the sister of the Selenarch Brandir and his chief agent within the cities. (Jesus and Mary, if the arrogance of the feudal lords wasn't checked soon, they'd make that honorific into a title!) Maybe nothing too serious would come of this, but maybe it could be the neutron shot into the fissionables.

It must be headed off. The parties concerned must be argued, cajoled, browbeaten, bribed, blackmailed —whatever it took—into some kind of mutually face-saving compromise. Wahl would be meeting with them, by ones and twos, personally. No telephone image could stand in for the living presence, the life laid on the line. If necessary, he would go to that citadel in the Cordillera, yes, alone, to stare the great troublemaker down.

Chances were, matters wouldn't come to that. However, Wahl had a busy stretch ahead of him. As always, the prospect of action heartened. Maddeningly much of his two years' tenure had gone in frustration, defiances to which he could not even put a proper name. It was like trying to grip and hold a stream as it rushed on toward its cataract. He entered the breakfast room in a fairly good mood.

His wife and son were already there, she transferring the meal from autococinero to table, the boy slumped sullen in his chair. Aromas rolled around Wahl, omelette, toast, juice, coffee, coffee. His taste buds stood up and cheered.

The viewscreen was also bracing. The vista was from above the city, mountainside rolling down to Sinus Iridum, monorail a bright thread across its darkness to the spaceport, elsewhere a cluster of industrial domes and, on the near horizon, a power transmitter aimed at Earth. The mother world hung in the southern sky, a blue-and-white arc not far from the stopped-down sun disc, incredibly beautiful. It was scenery better than the crowded constructions around Port Bowen.

Of course, that wasn't the reason he had lately moved his residence and the seat of government to Tsukimachi in the Jura. Port Bowen was a company town, in Anson Guthrie's ghostly pocket, and half the time Fireball was at loggerheads with governments, the national, the Federation, the Lunar Authority. Not that that had ever led to disorder, but the lesser companies centered here were more cooperative. If the percentage of resident Lunarians was higher, that had its advantages as well as it drawbacks.

"Buenos días," Wahl greeted his son. Rita he had kissed when they woke.

Leandro mumbled an answer. He kept his face turned downward. His gaudy outfit was at odds with his behavior.

"Where is Pilar?" Wahl continued in Spanish.

"She said she wasn't hungry," Rita replied.

Wahl frowned. A wound reopened and a part of his pleasure drained out. Again the girl was moping in her room. It had been happening too often to be mere sulk. What was the matter, then? Depression brought on by loneliness? Fourteen was so vulnerable an age. How could he tell, what could he say? Pilar was a good child, she deserved to be happy. If, just once, she brought herself to confide in him, or at least in her mother—When did children ever give parents that overwhelming gift?

He sat down. Rita poured coffee before joining him. He crossed himself and sipped. The flavor went robust and friendly through his mouth.

"What are your plans for today?" he asked Leandro. Saturday, no school. Homework? If there was any, it would be scamped, or neglected altogether. The boy's scores were terrible. It wasn't due to lack of intelligence; he'd been bright and eager on Earth.

Leandro didn't look at him. "Nothing special."

The father forced a smile. "I have trouble believing that." In fact, Leandro was more sociable than his sister. But Wahl didn't like the lot he went about with—louts, loudmouths, no credit to the Earth genes they bragged of. More than once, quarrels with their Lunarian classmates had exploded into fights. Not that the Lunarians never provoked it.

"When I was sixteen," Wahl said, "I'd have been outdoors by now." Horse at a gallop, hoofs drumming, surge of muscles between his thighs, grass in billows beneath the wind, a hawk overhead—if only such spaciousness existed anywhere in space!

Leandro tossed his head. "That was then."

"Hold on," Wahl rapped. "We will have courtesy here."

The boy started to rise. "I'm not hungry either."

"Sit down. You will finish what's on your plate and you will answer my question."

Leandro yielded, knowing he'd spend the daycycle confined to quarters if he didn't. Tone and expression conveyed his resentment. "Pardon me . . . sir. I am meeting some fellows in about an hour. We are going to Hoshi Park."

Not likely, Wahl thought. Not those decorous amusements. The Ginza? Or worse? Unwise to insist on knowing. "Be home for dinner."

"I am not sure I—"

"You heard me. Hour 1900, in time to dress properly. No later."

Leandro flushed fiery. He wolfed his food, mouthed a formal request for leave to go, and stalked out.

A meal in silence had little savor. "You were too hard on him, dear," Rita ventured sadly.

"I didn't enjoy it," Wahl reminded her. "Without discipline, he could get into serious trouble."

"I understand. This horrible atmosphere, conflict, racial tension, and too few safe, healthy outlets—" She touched his hand. "But perhaps we should be gentler. It's not easy being young. Here, it's very hard, for both of them."

He regarded her. She was short, well-formed, round-faced, always an excellent helpmate and hostess, but her bubbliness had dwindled on the Moon. More than the social and political situation oppressed her. She was among those who could never quite be physically comfortable in low gravity. "Harder on you," he said, "and you don't complain."

She smiled a little. "Nor you, old duty lugger."

"I've enjoyed past duty more," he admitted. Even police actions and relief efforts in stricken corners of Earth. Even the niggling negotiations and boring parties that a Federation delegate must endure. He hadn't wanted to enter politics, but they persuaded him that Argentina needed someone of his caliber in Hiroshima, and, yes, he had gotten several worthwhile things accomplished. For those, his reward was first to be talked into administration of the African Protectorate and now into this cauldron called Luna.

He took several mouthfuls, consciously tasted them, and vowed, "I'll have things under control within five years. God willing, no longer. And then we'll go home and never leave again." To the lively life in Buenos Aires, the serenity of the house in San Isidro, the freedom of the ranch in La Pampa.

She smiled once more. "Oh, surely now and then to Guangzhou. Where else shall I buy my frivolous clothes?" He chuckled back at her and they finished their breakfast in mildness.

But then it was time to start the daycycle's work. See the news; play whatever communications had arrived; answer those that required it; at the appointed hour, call Sato Fujiwara. The shipping-line executive was a friend of Philip Rabkin and willing to brief the governor about the deputy. By all accounts, Rabkin was a reasonable man, but best to come well prepared to the lunch with him later today. Groundwork, and also a practice run for meeting the really difficult cases like Fia.

Wahl's private office comforted him with its mementos, pictures from home, a Noh mask, a Moshi-Dagomban figurine in wood, his archery trophies (it had been a minor triumph, adapting his skills that well to Lunar conditions), an eighteenth-century crucifix on the wall. He settled down before his terminal and keyed for tidings.

URGENT, CONFIDENTIAL flashed at him. What the devil? His nightcycle staff had entered an override. He keyed afresh. The report smashed forth.

"¡Madre de Dios!"

It was as if he had dived into his pool and it had turned to ice around him. He caught his breath, exhaled most carefully, willed muscles to slack off, felt his pulse drop to a hard slugging. The forebrain took over.

Constabulary headquarters had sent notification: About 0130, as per his orders, a vehicle was bound across Mare Imbrium for Archimedes Station. Aboard it was the accused murderer Darenn. (No proper name. He was among the many Lunarians whose parents, scofflaw, had not registered the birth. Nor had he made good their omission. His ident as George Hanover was false, although some of his race did still use Terrestrial names as alternatives. A fake registry was easy to arrange. The datalines were infested with subversive operators and the computer worms they planted.) The transfer was being made in secret because, detained in Port Bowen pending trial, he had become too flammable a symbol. Earth-gene Selenites in a mutinous humor might riot, or Lunarians might organize an attempt to free him, or—Violence, breakdown of law, while outside waited the vacuum and the radiation. Archimedes was a strongpoint; one could control who went in and out. At the same time, telecom of every sort guaranteed the killer his rights. He should have been sent to Archimedes in the first place. But who could think of everything?

The screen showed a recording made on the spot. A jetflyer came down. Half a dozen spacesuited men sprang from it and by nearbeam demanded admission to the police van. They bore weapons that could blow it open. Surrender was the only option. The men entered, helped Darenn into a rescue capsule, and carried him off to their flyer. It rocketed away before any constabulary vessel could reach the scene.

Wahl struck fist against knee. This meant that the corps, Earth's guardians of order, had been infiltrated.

He refocused on the report.

Monitor satellites had likewise recorded the incident, from above, but they weren't equipped to interpret what they saw. Data retrieval showed that the flyer had launched from Tychopolis spaceport. (No use inquiring further. Given today's volume of traffic, Control was satisfied with preventing collisions and had stopped asking for surface-to-surface flight plans.) After taking Darenn and his liberators aboard, the flyer hopped over to Farside, Gagarin Base. From there, ground transport could carry the gang anywhere, anonymously. They left their craft behind. Therefore somebody had been willing to write it off, not a negligible cost, for the sake of this operation.

Detectives found that the registration was false and the inboard database had been wiped. They would try for fingerprints, stray hairs and skin cells, any possible clue, but were not optimistic. By now, Darenn must be in concealment, perhaps getting a new face, new loops and whorls and every other mark short of his DNA—or perhaps only lying low until the next time Brandir wanted a killer.

Brandir? That might be unfair. Another of the magnates could be behind this. Or it could be quite a different sort of conspiracy. But Wahl doubted that. It had the earmarks: a Selenarch ordering justice executed, then standing loyal to the executioner as a Selenarch stood loyal to all his vassals.

Earth people commonly likened the Lunarians to cats. Wahl thought about wolves.

Before he went any further, he had better review the entire case. It had not seemed major. Tangled, nasty, potentially dangerous after emotions began seething up around it, but not worth his close attention. That had changed. He keyed for background.

Constabulary headquarters had organized the file well. He got a swift and incisive narrative.

Rafael Adair was Earthborn, but a twenty-year resident. He went into partnership with the Lunarian female Yrazul. Probably they were lovers, a situation unusual but not unknown though seldom stable. They meant to prospect along the fringes of Mare Australe, broken country where they had found reason to think valuable concentrations of minerals might be; and that *was* rare on Luna. According to acquaintances who were afterward willing to talk, the relationship was going from tempestuous to embittered. Perhaps the couple hoped this joint venture would help them reconcile, perhaps they simply hoped to get rich.

Adair chanced to be in camp, seeing specimens through analysis, while Yrazul was in the field. Her vehicle was a moondodger, fast, nimble, but unshielded. A solar flare was predicted. She planned to get back under shelter before the proton storm hit. Lunarians delighted in skimming the edge of danger.

A meteoroid struck her car, smashed through, disabled engine and communications. Self-seal must have acted fast enough, closing off the drive section where she was, to preserve breathable air long enough for her to don her spacesuit. After that, she was stranded. Her contact with the robots she had been directing was gone, not that they could have done much to help. A satellite recorded the accident and transmitted to Monitor Central; but the transmission was continuous, the program was not set to flag an event so unlikely, and besides, the flare soon had Emergency Services fully occupied.

When she failed to return or to contact him, Adair should have taken their well-shielded van and gone in search. Instead, he waited hours. (Rage, cowardice, greed?) Finally he went. Later he claimed that he assumed she had driven into a cave or beneath an overhang. Else why had he not received a call for help? Storm or no, a satellite would have relayed it.

A reasonable, if rather discreditable story. The trouble with it arose from the traces. Inspector Hopkins studied them too closely.

As he reconstructed the story, Adair came within sight of her vehicle. She left it and ran to meet him and go aboard his. He turned about and drove off.

Then Yrazul knew she would die. Already she had taken a radiation dosage that would keep her hospitalized for months while the nanos rebuilt her cells. Soon she would be over the threshold that cannot be recrossed. In the Moon dust she scrawled with a finger what had happened. Thereafter she forced her helmet up and drank vacuum. It was a death more merciful.

Adair came back after the flare was gone and wiped out the message. Presently he called in to say that, grown worried, he had finally followed her tracks and discovered her, too late. He assumed she had chosen to perish in the open under the stars.

Wahl came doubly erect. It was the astronomer Temerir, that cold brother of Brandir, Fia, and Verdea, who pried the case open. Yrazul had been a granddaughter of their sister Jinann. They hung together, those Beynacs. . . . Temerir went over the ground and thereupon summoned Stanley Hopkins.

Would Yrazul really have left her moondodger, where she had some slight protection, unless she saw rescue coming? Why was the dust scuffled around her? Why did Adair's van approach, retreat, and return? Its tracks showed its course. Left undisturbed, they might endure for a million years.

Hopkins ordered the shell of the van checked for residual radioactivity. He learned that it could not have been out under the flare nearly as long as Adair related.

Confronted with the evidence, the man broke. He pleaded fear. Well, nobody went willingly out into such a gale, armor or no. Inquiries in depth suggested he had other motivations. He was definitely guilty of abandonment, which on the Moon was a first-class felony. The law demanded he be imprisoned and rehabilitated.

The old Lunar law, in force during the years of the Jihad, the chaos, and the Coordinating Committee, demanded death.

Once established, the Lunar Authority had abrogated that, together with certain other practices. It seemed a largely *pro forma* betterment. How often did abandonment occur? Scarcely ever.

Yrazul was of Selenarchic family.

Maybe she could have been any Lunarian, or anybody at all. Wahl didn't know.

What he knew was that Adair, free on bail, had been knifed dead. (You didn't trigger firearms inside a settlement. The old law made that too a capital offense.) It was a murder quick and clean; Darenn should have been able to leave his note explaining the reason for it and escape. Unfortunately, a burly Dutch spaceman happened to witness the job and in a flying tackle captured the Lunarian.

Unfortunately indeed. What was becoming a *cause célèbre* had threatened to touch off a political crisis. Now it positively would.

Wahl switched off the playback, rose, went around and around the room. You couldn't really pace here, you bounded, airily, a wisp of dandelion fluff—you and your concerns mattering no more than that? But he must prowl his cage, and he would not whine.

What to do?

God be thanked, the hijacking was not yet in the news. He could keep it out for hours more; they were good people on his staff. Meanwhile he must prepare for the public reaction.

A hunt for the gang and its master(s?) would be hopeless, merely infuriating the seditiously minded. Yet the government could not dismiss the outrage as a bagatelle. Such a sign of weakness would dismay the law-abiding, on whose support the Authority depended as every government does. It would incite new violations, more blatant than ever. The extremists would take fire; they might well rupture the legislature, give the entire system a possibly fatal wound, in spite of anything the governor and the moderates could offer them.

Surely no sensible member of any faction wanted that, or an uproar, or a crime wave. They must make common cause, issue a joint call for order and reason, hold their followers steady.

Who were the sensible ones? He needed an individual who could tell him and could bring them together, fast, before things disintegrated.

Dagny Beynac.

Had she the forcefulness, the sheer physical strength for these hours ahead? How old was she, anyway? A hundred and five, a hundred and ten? Something like that.

Still, the last time he saw her, she had seemed hale enough. And she headed the Council for Lunar Commonalty, which she had taken a lead in forming. (*Lunar,* Wahl reassured himself, not Lunarian.) Unrecognized by the Authority, the Federation, any single nation, or the Selenarchs, it had become in several ways the most influential organization on the Moon; and that was largely due to her.

Quick! Call Beynac.

Easy, though. Take a minute and think. Was this really his best approach to controlling the damage? He should reconsider his relationship with her, and everything he knew about her. Begin with that talk they had had, the two of them alone, shortly after he assumed office here. He had asked if she objected to its being recorded, and she had grinned as she answered, "No, provided you keep it clean."

Having canceled his appointments, he played that part of it which to him epitomized the whole.

Her posture remained erect, but the big bones stood forth in her spareness—not ugly, he thought; no, beautiful, like a strong abstract sculpture. Against the pale skin, her eyes seemed large and bluely luminous, as if from a star behind them. Rather than unisuit or tunic and slacks, she wore a caftan of gray iridon. Her only jewelry was a Saturn brooch at her throat and a worn golden ring.

"Understand, por favor," she said, and her voice still resonated, "I claim no legal status. The Council is a forum. When its members reach basic agreement on an issue, it advises and urges, *pro bono publico.*" She laughed. "That doesn't happen too often."

"Hm, I shouldn't think so," Wahl agreed. For courtesy's sake, although he had heard that she knew Spanish well, he used English too, despite the fact that his was colorless. "Two genetic types, more unlike than any races on Earth."

"We all live on the Moon," Beynac replied sharply. "It is our country."

She sat in this conference chamber as the spokeswoman of her fellowship, its representative to him. To what degree did she speak for her world? He had better explore carefully. But not timidly. Absolutely not.

"A Lunar nation? I am afraid, madame, that is impossible. At least within . . . my lifetime. May I speak frankly?"

"I've been hoping you will," she said.

"From my studies and briefings, and from what I have observed at close range for myself, I suspect Lunarians and Terricolas will never be able to form a durable society."

"I've seen unlikelier metals alloy." Beynac shrugged. "And if in the end it's the Lunarians alone who inherit Luna, what's bad about that? They're our blood."

Daycycle by daycycle as he dealt with them, Wahl had begun to question it. In lineage, yes; but how much did that mean? How akin are mastiff and dachshund? Wrong comparison, he thought. Terricola and Lunarian were not the same species, perhaps not the same genus. They could never breed, not even a mule-child.

"Well," he temporized, "conceivably someday in the far future—"

"The future has a way of arriving sooner than we expect," said Beynac. "But let's get to business and save the philosophy for dessert. Of course we aren't talking revolution or any such foolishness today, neither you and I nor they and I. What I'm here about, Governor, is how to keep from encouraging foolishness."

Wahl inclined his head. "I appreciate your guidance, madame," he told her, quite sincerely. "You have had a long experience."

Beynac smiled. "I collect governors."

"I the third, ay?" Japing faded. "You said you wish to talk honestly with me."

"And you with me, right? We size each other up."

"I see." Wahl tugged his chin, looked beyond the human before him at an image of his garden at home where roses nodded to a breeze, and marshalled words. "Tell me, if you will, how do you—how did you—judge my predecessors?"

The reply came prompt and blunt. "Zhao had a fair amount of wisdom. I always respected him. *We* always did, whether or not we liked some particular action of his. Gambetta was a politician. Well-meaning, but to her this was one more step toward the presidency of the World Federation."

"Would you like to see her win it?"

"We wouldn't mind, on Luna," said Beynac dryly.

"I should think not. She gave you everything you wanted."

"Correction, por favor. Half of what the assorted groups among us wanted."

Piecemeal, reluctantly. Forced by connivance, tricked by semantics, and maybe to a degree psychologically intimidated—anything to avoid trouble. Not that Wahl believed Beynac had engineered that pressure. It came from the barons, the businessfolk, the multitudinous malcontents, unorganized but vocal, who were the atmosphere that rebellion breathed.

The intelligence Wahl had received declared that this woman sought ever to mediate, to work out compromises. After all, while most of her descendants were Lunarian, it had long ceased to be a secret that she had an Earthside son from whom stemmed also a family.

The trouble was, not every one of those compromises had proven viable, nor had every one of them been lawful.

Wahl chose his words. "Notwithstanding, madame, my impression is that for Gambetta you have little respect."

"That's as may be, and it doesn't matter any more," Beynac said. "You're in charge now."

"Exactly." Appeal to her. "And, madame, I too mean well. With my entire heart, I do not want conflict. As for my wisdom, I hope you will lend me yours."

The blue eyes looked straight into his. "But."

He nodded. "But the situation is growing impossible. My duty is to get it corrected."

"I have a notion," she said quietly, "that what's growing is that new society you don't suppose can be."

"Perhaps. In which case—I speak plainly, madame, because I respect *you* too much to, m-m, pussyfoot—"

She smiled at him. Suddenly he understood a part of why so many men heeded her. "Gracias," she murmured. "I think I'm going to like you."

He cleared his throat and hurried on. "If it is a

society, it is a society in flagrant violation of the law, hostile, unruly—"

She stopped him by raising a hand. "If you please, señor, let's just go over this point by point. What are the Lunarians and quite a few Terran Moondwellers hostile and unruly for? Mind you, I don't claim they are always in the right. For openers, I admit what's obvious, that they are not a solid bloc, most especially not the Lunarians. But their grudge curve is Gaussian, so to speak. It does have a maximum.

"Officially, or what passes for officially in the Council, I'm here to discuss with you, in a preliminary and informal way, a petition we're drawing up to present to the World Federation and world opinion. You see, we don't want to spring it on you as a surprise, as if we had no use for you and everything you stand for." Surely she had taken the lead in evoking that attitude, Wahl thought. "Maybe you can convince us that such-and-such a demand is out of line. Well, no, you won't, you can't, on certain of them, any more than you can yield on others. But maybe between us we can work out a document that explains the Moondwellers' position in a sensible way. Then maybe real, honest dickering can begin."

Wahl doubted it. The important differences were irreconcilable. The larger good required that some practices, some beliefs, be suppressed, as the Conquistadores had suppressed the human sacrifices of the Aztecs.

Too strong a metaphor. By all means, give the Selenites—not the Selenarchs, the Selenites— whatever legitimate rights they were being denied. The problem was to find precisely what those were, and how to make the populace accept that the rest were illegitimate.

"Pray proceed, madame."

Beynac sighed. "You've heard it before, over and over. Bear with me. I promised them I'd spell it out for you." The tone of apology gave place to confidence. "Besides, it can't hurt for you to hear it from across the fence. That might make it more real, bring it closer to home."

He felt himself stiffen at the underlying condescension.

No. That was wrong. She was simply aware of her capabilities. "I listen," he said.

"Do interrupt," she urged. "I've doubtless heard every argument you can raise, but I'll be interested to know how you, Jaime Wahl y Medina, go about the job.

"I won't say much about the biggest issue of the lot, because it's been talked over aplenty. I'll just warn you that we've decided it is the biggest. The right to own real property. 'Common heritage' is an anachronism. It has to go, on the Moon and throughout the Solar System."

"You will not find substantial agreement to this on Earth," Wahl said. "There most people don't look on it as an anachronism, but as a foundation stone of a more hopeful future."

"I know. If individuals can own pieces of celestial bodies, that means jurisdiction gets carved up among the countries they're citizens of, and nationalism gains a new lease on life. Look, the details can be adjusted. Federation law could be the sole law off Earth, provided it recognizes and guarantees private property rights. Besides, we're not convinced the average Earthdweller cares about common heritage any longer. We know for a fact that a lot of them would like it abolished; and they don't all work for Fireball, either. When will your politicians have the guts to admit it's become a shibboleth?"

Wahl arranged his expression as well as his words with care. "Frankly, Mrs. Beynac, the conduct of many Selenites is not helping toward that end. You speak of Federation law for the planets, satellites, asteroids. It already applies, and is being systematically flouted. That is done by everyone from the great baron or mine operator who occupies his leasehold as though it were his freehold, to the ordinary person not only evading his taxes but cooperating in a network of organized, data-falsifying evaders. How much confidence does this give those politicians you seem to consider so venal?"

She nodded. "Well put, sir. But the taxes are another of our main grievances. They're excessive."

"They are commensurate with the increasing prosperity of Luna, which is linked to the well-being of Earth."

"Yes, yes. Listen, por favor, I'm not personally unsympathetic to the poor, nor unwilling to help relieve them and cope with the rest of Earth's problems. After all, I'm North American by birth and Ecuadoran by citizenship. But the Terran Moondweller who seldom sets foot there, the Lunarian who never does, they don't feel that way and it's not reasonable to expect they should. Where's the *quid pro quo* for them?

"Furthermore, they hate income tax, and would hate it no matter how modest it was, because it's an invasion of privacy. We value personal privacy very highly here, Governor. It was scarce and precious in the early days. We still often have to forgo it, sometimes for long stretches like on a field trip or a space voyage. The desire for it is downright fierce in the Lunarians, I suppose because our Moon culture reinforces a predisposition that got built into their genes. What people here do about the income tax, they don't think of as cheating, but resistance."

Wahl frowned. "It will be difficult to pass legislation exempting them from it. Even if the Federation waived it, the countries of their citizenship scarcely would. Income tax is essential to the modern state."

Beynac smiled crookedly. "Some would say that's the best reason of all for abolishing it."

"Please, let us be realistic." Wahl paused. "I daresay that privacy fetish is also the cause of widespread obstructionism toward the census and other governmental information-gathering activities?" She nodded. "And yet I hear that the Lunar magnates have quite efficient methods of their own."

"In Lunar eyes, that's different. Don't blame me, I'm only telling you. But think. You're a Catholic, right? Well, then you tell your priest things you'd bloody anybody else's nose for asking about."

He contemplated her for a while before he said low, "What you mean is that the conflict is, at bottom, not economic or political but cultural. We do not have brewing anything like the First North American Revolution. No, it is to be a rising against occupation and exploitation by foreigners, aliens."

"You are an intelligent man," she replied gravely.

His tone went grim. "The analogy I see is the First North American Civil War. My duty is to do everything I can to prevent it. If this requires aborting a distinct Lunar civilization, then that is what must be. Now do you see why I have ordered full enforcement of the Educational Standards Act?"

"I knew that was your motive." She sounded half regretful. "Requiring private schools, as well as public, to teach—to try and instill—ideals like democracy and the equal worth of all human beings, what decent person could object to that? Not I. But it doesn't go down well with Lunarian children. They hear different at home. Furthermore, it's like telling cats they ought to behave like dogs. The whole thing was quietly phased out because it was causing too many problems. Not much violence, truancy, or even insolence. Subtler. A, a contempt. I myself could feel it in the kids. And now you're demanding the mistake be revived."

Wahl sighed. "You Selenites agitated year after year for home rule. You, madame, took a forefront role in that. And now you have it. How shall you maintain it, if your younger generations don't learn the principles and procedures of civilized self-government?"

"Pretty limited home rule, given that the governors general are charged with keeping it inside Federation and assorted national law, and that appeals from their rulings are regularly denied in court." Beynac gazed past him—into the past? He heard a measure of sorrow in her voice. "I confess this has been the greatest disappointment in my life." Even greater than when her children developed into . . . Lunarians? "Federation law *is* for the most part humane and rational. What parts of it are not, as far as the Moon is concerned, I thought we could get gradually changed by democratic means. On the whole, our Terran legislators are still hoping, still trying. But the Lunarians—they don't seem to have the right stuff for politics. Those who do go in for it are apt to be their worst, corrupt, quarrelsome, egotistic, short-sighted. Our legislature is working very poorly, and I've come to doubt it can improve."

"That may not be a completely bad thing," he risked saying, "in view of what measures it has attempted to pass."

"Like restoring the death penalty for criminal abandonment? Even Gambetta had to veto that one. There I agreed with her. The rest of my family did not. They aren't monsters, Governor. They have a high standard of—honor, I suppose is the nearest English word. But they are children of a world that is not Earth."

"A curious kind of honor," he rejoined. "It causes men to order the flogging or murder of offenders, without trial, and then shield the agents. Madame, that cannot be permitted to continue."

"Right of justice and right of granting sanctuary. That's how they regard it. I think it goes too far, which hurts me. But unless you want to keep it underground, growing worse and worse, some compromise with it will have to be negotiated."

"Why? You ask me to concede to the Selenarchs powers they have taken illicitly for themselves. That can only encourage them to claim more. Already some among them deal directly, not just with companies, but with governments, those governments that are—I say between us two—less than ideal members of the

World Federation. Shall they at last declare full sovereignty? Build their own nuclear weapons? Fight their own wars? No, madame, no."

"I can't conceive of them wanting to. They are not insane. What they want—what ordinary, peaceful Moondwellers want—is freedom to be what they are and become what they choose to be. I'm sure that's possible within the framework of the civilization you and I share, and in fact will enrich it in ways we can't imagine. But that's only if they are not compelled, confined, twisted about to the point where they see no other way than violence."

"They will be well advised to avoid driving the Authority and Federation to that point."

"Yes. You have your legitimate rights and claims. I understand them as clearly as I do theirs, I who belong to both worlds. We're here today to search for roads to reconciliation."

"We will not accomplish that in a few hours."

"Nor in years, if ever. But if you're willing to keep on talking a spell, I am."

"I've set this daycycle aside, madame. Er, can I offer you any refreshment?"

She laughed aloud. "Can you! A cold beer would put me in Heaven, and a shot of akvavit to go with it would admit you to join me there."

The conversation did indeed become long. It didn't stay entirely serious, nor had she intended that it do so. She asked him out about himself and his life, reminisced about hers, quipped, told jokes, introduced him to a bawdy ballad concerning a spaceman named MacCannon, and left him, at the end, thoroughly charmed.

Since then they had come together a number of times, alone or in the presence of others, in business or sociability. He felt that the sociability was at least as important. It let him meet eminent Selenites personally, informally. It gave him her sanction—well-nigh her protection, he often thought—and thus his initiatives and efforts did not encounter automatic resistance. For Rita, above all, it lessened the loneliness a bit.

Maybe, too, it slowed the upward ratcheting of tension and increase of ugly incidents. It did not halt them. Supposedly the Lunar Petition was under consideration in Hiroshima. It had gone to several committees. None had yet reported. Wahl gathered that they had deadlocked on various points and tabled it pending further studies. They felt no need of haste. The Moon was distant, its population was small, there were huge and urgent problems everywhere around the home globe. Meanwhile Wahl's own deadlock seemed to him in danger of breaking apart.

Today, when he called Dagny Beynac, her phone informed him that she was unavailable until hour noon. He guessed she was resting, old and frail as she was. He didn't like wondering what would happen after she died.

While he waited—hm—should he try for Anson Guthrie? Fireball had an enormous stake in keeping the peace. Besides, apparently the download had not lost normal human sympathies. But Wahl might well be unable to raise him on short notice. He might be unable or unwilling to intervene. What could he do, actually? If he took a direct part, perhaps that would worsen things. Better get Beynac's opinion first. If she approved the idea, she could certainly put him in touch with Guthrie and probably persuade the revenant; they were close.

Restless, Wahl left his office and stalked down the corridor. Never mind the countless other demands on him. It was too soon for a second icy swim, but he'd take a long walk through the city, maybe even fetch his spacesuit and go topside for a hike. That ought to clear his buzzing head.

He came by Pilar's room. The door was open. She sat at her telephone. Her slight frame shivered. Blood came and went in her cheeks. "Oh, Erann," she breathed.

The face in the screen was youthful, with the exotic Lunarian handsomeness. Wahl recognized it. He had met the boy once or twice when the youngsters had a party in this mansion. It had seemed good to promote friendship between the races.

Erann. A grandson of Brandir.

He smiled, seductive as Lucifer, and murmured something. Pilar strained forward, hands outheld, as if she could seize the image to her.

Her father stood where he was for a thunderful minute. She didn't notice. Almost, he broke in on her. But what to do then, what to cry out? He continued down the hall. His fists swung at his sides. Breath struggled in his throat.

He must speak with Rita. Today. Get this thing stopped before the damage was irretrievable. Tactfully if possible. Otherwise by whatever means proved necessary. Maybe create a reason to send the girl, the innocent child, to school on Earth, where she would be entirely among humans.

31

The cybercosm woke Venator about midnight. "Attention," called a speaker. "The Proserpina file is opened."

Instantly alert, he sprang from his cot and ordered light. Bare and narrow, the room seemed to radiate chill. "Who has done it?" he snapped. Hope flickered. He was not the sole human who knew. Another might have found cause to review those data.

The voice stayed flat. Thus far, the mentality engaged was little more than a high-capacity automation. "The DNA pattern belongs to—" Venator's identification followed.

No!

With an almost physical thrust, he denied the denial. "Location," he demanded.

"Prajnaloka, a community in south central North America." A screen lit, displaying a regional map. An arrow pointed. It was redundant. He knew that place, although he had never visited in person.

The intruder or intruders could not belong there, he thought. Soulquesters were the last people in the universe who'd challenge the system in any way. Besides, how would one of them have gotten the genetic key?

Lilisaire's agents, then. Fiendishly clever. Skilled, at least. They would never have come near the file unless their search strategy was so well-designed, with questions so natural and cogent, that it took them past every point at which the program might have detected a possible spy and blocked the line of investigation. Yes, this matched the picture he'd formed. Kenmuir, for spatial background; someone else, for a wide and deep knowledge of the information net, together with much past experience.

They felt their way to the portals of the secret, and—

"Has the nearest Peace Authority station been contacted?" Venator asked. He stepped to a peg and took a robe off it. The floor was cold and hard beneath his feet.

"Yes." He shouldn't have wasted time inquiring, he should have taken it for granted.

"Get me the captain of the emergency division. Crash priority." Venator slipped the robe over his nakedness. He needed to impress the man. Inwardly, he needed to cover himself, hiding from rage and shame. It was clear to him, now, where that DNA had come from.

A face appeared in the screen. "James Fong, captain of emergency services, Peace Authority, Chicago Integrate," the voice said in Anglo. Two names; old-fashioned; it suggested solid reliability.

"Pragmatic Venator, intelligence corps." Aside: "Verify." The system signalled that this was true. "We have a crisis. I am a synnoiont. Verify. It's that serious, Captain."

Fong sucked breath in between his teeth. "Yes, señor."

"Two persons—I believe they are two—are making an illicit break into a top secret, from Prajnaloka. The consequences could be disastrous. Fly a squad to capture them before they finish the job and escape. Take them back and hold them in solitary, pending further orders. Do not question them or permit them to talk with anyone, including you and your officers. With the personnel of the ashram, be courteous but discreet. Tell them they have been deceived by enemies of sanity, get them to describe those persons' actions, and ask them to keep quiet about the whole affair."

"Yes, señor. We can't suppress everything. People will see us. Rumors will fly."

"That ought not to matter if the operation is quick and thorough. Report directly to me by name." The cybercosm would route the call. "Begin."

"At once, señor. I'll lead the raid myself. Service!" The screen blanked.

Good. Fong was trustworthy. That was reassuring. It was even promising. A tingle went through Venator. Within this hour, the quarry should be his. Thereafter—

He put his feet into sandals and went out, down the corridors of shifting light-shapes and silent machines. His task required much better equipment than a phone and a terminal. He might well have to consult with the whole cybercosm.

Certainly he must soon do so. The issues were of the gravest. Fong and his followers would realize that. Arrest and temporary isolation were permissible under the Covenant, barely, by invoking the Emergency Provisions Clause. But they'd wonder why Venator wanted the prisoners straightaway whisked off. Why no news, later, about the charges against them? Were their rights being violated? Answers must be devised, more or less satisfactory.

His heart demanded it too, Venator thought. He'd try persuasion first, of course, but if Lilisaire's agents were stubborn and insisted on public proceedings, what then?

He didn't know. Whatever was necessary, he supposed. It would depend on their behavior, and how much they had learned, and on Lilisaire's next move, if any, and—more unknowns than he could list, no doubt. Chaos.

At worst, he guessed, the cybercosm would tell him to have their recent memories wiped. He bit his lip. That would be nearly as gross a violation as killing them, and it risked terrible side effects. And after they were released, how was their amnesia going to be explained?

Might the cybercosm order actual killing?

Maybe. If necessary.

Necessary to preserve sanity in the near future, and preserve the far future itself.

He reached the main communication chamber and settled down before the console. It curved around the swivel seat, a flatscreen on his left, a holoscreen on his right, and a viewtank in front. When Fong called back, the eidophone would relay to that. Venator dismissed the urge to talk with him as he flew. Pointless. Distracting. Hunters should wait before they spring.

However—With voice and fingers, he made connection to the Proserpina file. The program was still unrolling. Well, if it held the pair in place, that should suffice. It would have to. And why not? The spies would go over it more than once, excitedly discuss it, take notes. For Lilisaire.

A machine entered, carrying a tray. It was humanoform, suggestive of a man wrapped in foil, except for the turret, the two extra arms, and the inhumanly graceful movements. "Would you care for refreshment?" it asked musically.

A teapot steamed on the tray beside a plate of protein cakes. "Thank you very much," Venator said, for this was no robot, it was a sophotect using the body. "A long night ahead of me. Of us."

"Yes. What else can assist you?"

"Nothing at the moment. I'll let you know." Venator glanced up at the shining facelessness. "How fully are you involved?" It was the cybercosm to which he spoke, through this avatar.

"A minor part, but a standby signal has gone out to the whole system."

Venator nodded. He had instructed the half-mind guarding the file to notify him and alert the constabulary if it was activated. That went automatically; but it was extraordinary enough that a higher-level intelligence in the net was bound to have noticed and sent appropriate messages of its own.

The machine departed. Venator sipped the tea and munched a cake. Coarse, homely fare. A symbol. That which controlled the world and comprehended the universe had also thought of this ordinariness.

Universe—On a sudden impulse, he retrieved the Alpha Centauri file. In a blind way, he felt it could strengthen his resolve.

It was prodigious. He could only skip about, semi-randomly asking for this scene and that, while he waited to hear from Fong.

Far and far. The newest sight transmitted from Sol's closest neighbor was more than four years old. Guthrie's handful of colonists spent half a century making the passage, and readying for that one voyage had consumed every resource at his command. What was left, the World Federation took over, and Fireball Enterprises became a memory. There would be no more such argosies.

Venator chose a view from an earlier time, when the first unmanned probe arrived. That in itself had been no mean achievement. The double sun blazed brilliant against blackness. Fast-forwarded, the scan swept inward until Alpha A was a disc of light and the probe orbited the single life-bearing planet in the system.

Demeter was no Earth. Or else it was a primordial Earth, or an Earth that might have come to be had not population control, molecular technology, and clean energy saved it. The seas of Demeter swarmed with organisms, true, enough to create and sustain air that humans could breathe; but just a few primitive plants and creatures clung precariously to existence along the shores. Inland were rock, sand, dust blown on scouring winds, as stark as Mars. Why? Many factors, strong among them the absence of a huge moon to stabilize the rotation axis; and Luna was the child of a cosmic accident, a monster collision, back near the beginning.

No wonder that search had never found spoor of other thinking races. Life was a rarity. Sentience must be infrequent to almost the vanishing point. Maybe, in the whole of the universe, it had evolved on Earth alone.

It would make itself be the meaning and destiny of that universe.

Venator advanced the scene through time until he found an image of Demeter as it was now—four and a third years ago. Cloud-swirls marbled sapphire and turquoise ocean. Snows whitened a wintering north country and the crowns of mountains. Southward and lower, continents and islands lay soft green and brown, hues of forest, meadow, marsh, pastureland for mighty herds and breeding grounds for mighty flocks.

The scan magnified, focused, sped close above the world. He glimpsed a stand of birch, their leaves snaring sunlight; wild horses in gallop; a hillside blue with cornflowers; a village of small homes; a town lifting spires above a harbor where pleasure boats rocked at their moorings and a freighter unloaded its cargo; traffic on roads and aloft; a contrail like a road to heaven, slowly breaking up, where a spacecraft had ascended.

All this had Terrans, with their proliferating robots and molecular machinery, wrought in less than three hundred Earth years, while in space their Lunarian allies made the asteroids blossom. All this, despite the fact that on a day not very much further ahead, another senseless cataclysm was to destroy the planet, and nobody knew how or if any creature upon it could survive.

Deep within himself, Venator felt a shudder. Here, if ever, the Faustian spirit had made its absolute manifestation and seized its ultimate home.

No, he thought, the thing went beyond even that. It was not simply sheer, unbounded will, demonic energy and brazen laughter. ("We've decided the motto and guiding principle of our government shall be *'Absit prudentia nil rei publicae profitur,'*" Guthrie had communicated once. "Gracias to the database for fancying it up into Latin. What it means is 'Without common sense you ain't gonna have nothing.'" The insult to every concept of a guided society stood brutally plain.) It was that the necessities of the adventure had brought forth something altogether new and strange.

The scan winged onward. Cultivated fields passed beneath, goldening toward harvest. They were few and mainly for chemical production. Basic food and fiber were manufactured, as on Earth or Luna. Those who wished—on Demeter, most people—supplemented with kitchen gardens, orchards, the bounty of wild nature. The scan showed another woodland. It was that nature, the global web of life, which had made this world fit for humans.

But technology could not in a few centuries do the work of evolution through gigayears. The ecology here was inevitably simple, fragile, poor in feedbacks and reserves, always near the edge of catastrophe. Earth's had crashed again and again in massive extinctions. Demeter's began to die when it was barely seeded; and there would have been no rebirth. A whole cybercosm could not take over the task of nursing it back to health, bringing it along to ripeness, keeping it in balance as an organism keeps itself in balance, *being* it . . . unless that cybercosm permeated the life, and had the awareness and purpose and—love—of human minds downloaded into it. . . . Demeter Mother.

Venator had walked the veldt among lions and Cape buffalo, scaled a glacier, shot rapids, disarmed more than one dement gone violent. From this alienness, he recoiled.

Like a providence, the console said: "Your call." The view from afar blanked out and Fong's full-body image appeared. Evidently he had commandeered a similar unit where he was. He saluted. "Reporting, señor." His face spoke for him: failure.

Venator tasted vomit. He swallowed. "Well?"

"I'm sorry, señor. The persons are gone. As nearly as we've been able to find out, they—two of them, male and female—went hastily to the volant they'd come in and skipped off. That was about forty-five minutes ago."

Proserpina, first and always. "What about the file they were invading?"

"I think they left it running, and it finished and turned off. If they'd learned we were on our way—they could have posted an inquiry—that would be a logical thing to do, not disclosing to the net that they were in fact gone. Buying time."

Venator nodded. His neck felt stiff. "I expect you're right." Oh, clever, clever. Lilisaire chose her instruments well. "Have you learned anything about them yet?"

"We've just started, señor." A partial image of a second man entered the field. "One moment, por favor." Fong conferred. Again to the synnoiont: "TrafCon has now identified the volant. It went to Springfield Mainport and parked illegally, right at the terminal. Shall I contact the civil police there?"

"No." What use? "Look at bus schedules. Either the pair are hiding in town or they've boarded a flight to someplace else. Who's the volant registered to?"

"Um-m-m—" Fong squinted offview, at another screen. "Alice Tam of Niihau, Hawaii."

"Good. Carry on. Find out what you can, but don't make a production of it and don't linger past the point of diminishing returns. Do you understand? Confidentiality is vital. But bring me whoever can tell us the most about those persons."

"Yes, señor." Fong left the scan field. Venator beheld a wall with a mural of lotuses.

He swung his attention from it. While he waited, he could investigate Alice Tam.

The file on her that the system assembled for him proved surprisingly rich. She had not courted publicity, but as active as she was, more got noted than the standard entries. Birth and upbringing in that curious little leftover society, studies in Russia, travels elsewhere, including Luna, work on the mainland with metamorphs and a couple of organizations trying to better the lot of metamorphs. . . . Yes, a great deal of time at the net, and many periods during which she had dropped out of sight. . . . Arrival at San Francisco Bay Integrate eight days ago. Blank, till her vehicle proceeded to Santa Monica. Blank, till it flew to a spot in the Salton Desert, stopped briefly, and continued to Overburg; get information on Overburg, later, later. . . . Two days there, then cruising around for hours till it descended at Prajnaloka. . . . And now to Springfield, where it sat abandoned.

Images showed a young woman, comely, well-formed, vivacious, little or no sign of the steel beneath the flesh.

Had she met Lilisaire when she visited the Moon? Probably. Perhaps that could be verified.

How and why had she become Lilisaire's ally? A complete data search ought to give hints, perhaps an answer.

An officer entered the scan field. "An airbus left Springfield for St. Louis Hub at 1315," she reported. "It arrived there ten minutes ago."

Just too soon. If Kenmuir and Tam were aboard, by

now they had disappeared into the city, or else they were on one of a dozen different carriers bound for as many destinations. Once upon a time, monitors in every major transfer point could instantly have been set to watch for them. But Fireball brought down the Avantists, and the modern world was not totalitarian: it had never needed or desired intensive surveillance capabilities.

There were plenty anyhow, of course, serving everyday purposes. Some could be mobilized, ranging from high-resolution optical satellites to traffic evaluation units and . . . as an extreme measure, every sophotect on Earth. But that would take time, because they could not be diverted without notice from their regular duties; and the operation would be conspicuous, inconveniencing citizens, causing them and their legislators to demand an explanation; and meanwhile, what might Kenmuir and Tam do?

Little or nothing, in all likelihood. How could they?

He had underestimated them before, Venator thought.

Fong escorted an old man into view and introduced him as Sandhu. He fought to control his distress and hold onto serenity as he related how Tam and—Johan—had arrived according to a reservation properly made beforehand, and given every evidence of being sincere in their wishes. What had gone amiss?

"I cannot tell you today, sir," Venator soothed him. "The Peace Authority is on the trail of a criminal conspiracy. We request your silence. Have no fears. On the whole, the matter is well in hand, and we know your people are innocent of any wrongdoing." He was glad to see the poor little fellow grow a bit easier.

The call making the reservation—it could be traced back. In fact, Venator decided, that was the first order of business. It should give a lead into Lilisaire's entire Earthside cabal. Let Kenmuir and Tam run fugitive a while longer, unless a limited, low-priority observation program happened to succeed. With the cybercosm alerted, anything they tried to do with

whatever information they had stolen should close a
trap on them.

But tighten security around Zamok Vysoki. Have
forces in readiness to blockade the castle, or even
enter it and arrest everybody present. Afterward find
ways to cope with the political uproar that would
follow. It could not be as troublesome as the opening
of Proserpina would be.

—Information. Thought. Belief. Mind. Already life
was evolving from the biosphere to the noösphere,
and what went on in the brain mattered more than
what happened among the stars.

Venator harked back: From Guthrie's rebellious
exodus, unforeseeably, arose Demeter Mother. But at
least she was light-years removed, only tenuously and
indirectly in touch with Earth, an abstraction to most
humans of the Solar System, nothing to catch their
imaginations as the prophets and visions of old had
done. Let her remain so, and hope she perished with
her planet.

Meanwhile, keep watch, but never let her know.
Laser beams went back and forth between Sol and
Alpha Centauri, bearing words and images. Merely
words and images. To humans of the Solar System, the
colonization that had once been an ongoing epic was
become a commonplace, a remote background, irrelevant to them. The cybercosm encouraged that attitude
by proclaiming its own lack of interest. It declared
itself willing to communicate and give advice if asked
—which seldom happened any more, as different as
the Centaurians had grown to be. But physical space
exploration was not for the Teramind. The grand
equation that unified all physics had long since been
written. The possible interactions of matter and energy were manifold and held surprises, but they would
always be details, nothing that could not have been
computed in advance or, at any rate, be accounted for
as another permutation. The endless frontier lay in
the mind and its creations.

Venator smiled. Of course the cybercosm didn't

speak quite candidly. Miniprobes followed events around Alpha Centauri as best they could, and sent reports that were neither overheard nor made public. Unacknowledged spacecraft were ranging out into the galaxy, though decades or centuries must pass before word came back from them. The destiny of the cybercosm was to transcend the material universe, but before then, some of the permutations might prove important.

Demeter Mother already had.

However, she was afar, and everything else was farther. Proserpina orbited the cybercosm's home sun.

And Luna bore, as it had borne since the first Lunarians came to birth, the seeds of chaos. For a moment Venator wondered how often they had sprouted, not openly as history knew of but in secret. How many deaths had been murder disguised?

Enough brooding on the past. Fong had returned to sight. Venator gave him his concluding instructions, ended transmission, and set about the next stage of the campaign.

32

The Mother of the Moon

The phone roused Dagny about 0600. Its program recognized that the matter must be that urgent. She sat up, ordered, "Light," and blinked at the suddenly seen room. For a moment its familiarity came strange to her, 'Mond's picture, the children's from years when they were little, the recent portrait of them with their mates and many of their descendants down to an infant in arms who was her newest great-great-grandchild, a very unlunarian posing done for her sake only, the gaudy purple-and-gold drapes she had lately chosen to liven things up—She had been gone.

Her dead friend faded in awareness. She turned to

the bedside screen and ordered, "Receive." Rita Urribe de Wahl's face appeared. She too must have been wakened, for her hair was unkempt and a robe was thrown over her nightgown. Tears sheened on her cheekbones and ran down to the corners of trembling lips. "Señora, S-señora Beynac," she stammered, "él está muerto."

Knowledge struck home like a knife. Dagny mustered her Spanish, though the other woman's English was better, to cry, "Jaime? Oh, my dear! What happened?" Was it in truth a knife?

"In his swimming pool—found—Nobody knows. The medics are there now." Rita gulped, squared her shoulders, and made her voice toneless. "I have called you first, after them, because of what this can mean to everybody. You will know best whom to consult, what to do. He would have wanted it, I think." The resoluteness cracked. "And, and you were always good to us."

Heartbreaking humility, Dagny thought. And undeserved. She'd cultivated acquaintance with the governor general, these past five years, as she had done with his predecessors, because how else could she play any part in containing the fires of strife? . . . But, yes, she had gained a certain liking as well as respect for Jaime Wahl y Medina, considerable sympathy as well as respect for his wife, and it showed.

"I'll be right over."

"No, no, that is not necessary."

"The hell it isn't," Dagny said in English. "Stand fast, querida. I'm so sorry. But we've got work ahead, tough work, and I doubt it can be done on the com lines. Give me a couple of hours. Meanwhile, can you stall? Keep this quiet. Ask the medics to. Notify Haugen but ask him to sit tight. Collect what information you can but don't let any of it out. Okay?"

Again Rita gathered her strength together. "Yes, I hope I shall be able . . . to persuade Señor Haugen and the others, and keep the staff here under control, and—For two or three hours, perhaps yes."

"Brave lass." Dagny smiled into the grief. "I'm on my way, then. Later we'll mourn Jaime. Right now we have things to do for him. Hasta luego."

She flicked off and called the mayor of Tychopolis. His phone program recognized her and put her straight through to him in his own chamber. "Hallo. Not up yet? Well, move. Listen, I need immediate transport to Tsukimachi. Immediate. A suborbital if you can get me one. Yes, these bones can still take that kind of boost. Otherwise the fastest jet the local constabulary have available, and I'm not talking about a Meteor or an Estrella. I'll accept nothing less than a Sleipnir."—

—"Never mind why. A good many lives may depend on it. That's enough for now, and you will please keep it to yourself. Pull rank, use my name if need be, but get me the craft."—

—"I'll meet you at the port, TrafCon office, in case we need to browbeat those people, in exactly one hour. It'd be nice if the boat had some breakfast aboard for me, but what it must have is readiness to launch. Okay? See you."

She blanked and left her bed. Inalante would swing it. He was powerful, he was able, and he was a son of Kaino.

In the bathroom, splashing cold water on her face, she began to feel the aches and drag of weariness. Sleep had been in short supply these past few daycycles. She'd hoped for peace till 0900 or 1000 this mornwatch, because after that all hell might be letting out for recess. (Which it already had, in a shape she hadn't expected.) At her age, you didn't bounce back after just a catnap. Had she ever been that young? It seemed impossible.

The mirror showed eyes that appeared unnaturally large and bright in the bony pallor around them. Anson Guthrie had remarked a while ago that she looked more ethereal every time he saw her. But she bloody well couldn't afford to be, not yet, maybe not anytime this side of the ashbox. After weighing what her physician had told her, what her experience suggested, and what the situation was, she took a medium-strength diergetic. That, with coffee and food and will power, ought to get her through the next hours without too high a price to pay afterward.

Somewhat recharged, if a little chilled, she made herself presentable in warm coverall and half-boots. A hooded cloak should keep her from being noticed; few people were out this early. She recorded a noncommittal message for callers, took the bag she kept packed for hasty departures, and went forth.

Hudson Way stretched quiet. The ceiling simulated blue sky, stray clouds still faintly pink from sunrise, strengthening light which set aglitter the dawnwatch moisture in the duramoss underfoot. The air blew and smelled like an appropriate breeze. The ambience was a bit too perpetually pretty for her, but most residents in this neighborhood were Terran and had voted to have it thus. There were other places she could go to pretend, in full surround, that she walked by a gray sea and its drumroll surf.

At the corner of Graham she boarded the fahrweg and rode out to the spaceport, changing lines twice. Fellow passengers were sparse and paid her no attention. She had freedom to think.

Poor Rita. Poor kids, though Leandro was at the university and partly estranged from his father, while Pilar had been in school on Earth for two or three years. Poor Jaime, above all. He'd lived with such gusto, when his job didn't exhaust or infuriate him. He'd been her opponent more often than not, but a fair one, playing for what he believed was right, right not just for Earth but for the Moon.

And now he was dead. How convenient for some people. How potentially disastrous for the rest.

Murder? Hard to imagine, there in his home. Besides, nobody had ever attempted it when he went out, though he kept no bodyguard. To be sure, he was formidable by himself, a vigorous Earth-muscled man with combat experience and a black belt in karate.

That made his death in a swimming pool the more incomprehensible. Especially as opportune as it was.

It shouldn't have been, Dagny thought—not for anyone, neither the coldly calculating Lunarian magnates nor the most radical, slogan-drunk Terran demonstrator. Until a short while ago, it wouldn't have been. Given the present political climate on Earth—leaders and publics daily more conscious of how much the state of affairs on Luna contradicted and defied their world order—any governor was bound to make correction the goal of policy. Zhao's patient pressure and Gambetta's concessions had failed. Over and over, a crisis was patched up while the society evolved onward. Wahl's mission was to bring this globe back under Federation law and make sure it stayed there. No compromises.

But the governor necessarily had broad discretion, and must cooperate with the legislature, unless things got to the point of outright insurgence and troops were the only option. Few leaders would have gone ahead more carefully, yes, considerately than Wahl did: step by step, glad to reward, reluctant to punish, always concerned for the other fellow's dignity, ready to give up plans for retirement and spend a decade or longer preparing the ground for full enforcement of the major laws, even admitting that meanwhile those laws might be modified. How had it come about that any Moondwellers could wish him dead?

She had no clear answer. None existed. Human affairs are chaos. But, riding along, she could retrace their course into this particular strange attractor.

Friction, contention, hard words, disobedience, resistance open or covert, arrests, penalties, unrepentance were everywhere. However, she thought the Uconda business last year was a prime factor. She'd had a bad feeling about it at the time, and tried to warn the governor, when he forbade expansion of operations at that Farside mine because it would measurably pollute local vacuum and radio background. The astronomers, quantum experimentalists, and other researchers at Astrebourg were naturally glad of the action in itself; but a number of them, Temerir most prominently, were enraged that it had been carried out by decree like that.

Worst upset was Brandir. At his brother's instigation, he had been quietly bargaining with the owners. He would compensate them well if they shut down altogether and began anew on territory he controlled. The deal would have enhanced his prestige, thereby his influence. It would have involved the owners and their workers giving troth to him, thus increasing his power. It would have bypassed the Lunar Authority, treated the sites as if they were private property, and so violated the intent if not quite the letter of the law. Wahl told Dagny in private that that was surely the real intention, and reason for him to forestall it. Of course this fuelled anger in the opposition.

Had the Lunarian seigneurs cleverly fanned the emotion, or had it directly caused some among them to make a new move, or what? Dagny was uncertain. Her children told her what they wanted to tell her and no more, as did their children and children's children. Sometimes that was considerable, sometimes they actually asked for her counsel, but this had not been one of the occasions, and when she taxed Brandir with it he went courteously impassive as he had done so often before.

The catapults. Whatever brought it about, the catapults were the issue that could detonate revolt.

Spaceport the fahrweg flashed and intoned. Dagny left it. The walk through the terminal, across mostly empty floors, felt long to her.

She had come ahead of time. Nevertheless Inalante was waiting at TrafCon: a middle-aged man in black tunic and white hose, something of his father haunting the features and something of his grandfather, a steadiness beneath the rapid-fire speech, sounding through the voice. "Be you hale, kinlady. A Sleipnir stands provisioned and cleared for liftoff."

"Good lad!" she exclaimed, pleased out of all

proportion. "I'll bet you've even gotten black pudding aboard."

He smiled. "Unfortunately, what shops may stock it are not yet open. For haste's sake, I ordered mere field rations stowed. But recalling you also like moonfruit, I brought these from my home." He gave her a bag.

Nor did it make sense that her eyes should sting. They could be absolute darlings when they chose, her Lunarians, wholly human. Well, God damn it, that was what they *were*. "Gracias. Thanks. I, I'll think of you from now on whenever I taste moonfruit."

"Need you further help?"

"Mainly that you keep the city calm."

"I have been preparing through these past daycycles," he said grimly.

"You'll soon hear news that will change everything. I don't know what the changes will be, nor do I dare tell you more here where we could be overheard, but expect a huge surprise."

"While you fare alone to cope." The oblique eyes searched her. "Have you the potence of body for it?"

"I'd better."

"Then fare you victoriously, mother of us." Inalante took her hand and bowed deeply over it.

He was no revolutionary, she knew. Nor was he a lackey. He cared little or naught what the constitutional structure might be, as long as he and his were left unmolested to pursue their own ends. Since that required peace, he had accepted the mayoralty here, in an uncontested election, to help maintain it. From this position he could maneuver for changes in rules that he disliked, meanwhile conniving at enough evasion of them to keep people somewhat content without provoking the Authority to intervene.

No doubt a majority of Moondwellers felt more or less likewise. But their ambitions were seldom of a kind that Federation law would much hinder. It was the powerful and the radical who strained against restraints, and it was they who would break the system or be broken by it. Or both, Dagny thought.

She went to her gate, through the gangtube, and into her vehicle.

The crew were a pair of constabulary officers, pilot and reserve, Terrans. They greeted the lady Beynac with deference and promised her breakfast as soon as they were in stable flight. She harnessed into her seat and relaxed.

Liftoff went deftly, at little more than two Lunar gravities. Altitude attained, the seat swung on its gimbals as the hull brought its length horizontal. A snort of thrust followed; then weight leveled off and there was only the almost subliminally faint thrum and hiss of downjets holding the mass aloft. Dagny's engineering years came back to her and she spent a minute estimating how much more fuel-expensive this flight was, over the distance she must cover, than the suborbital she had tried for, besides being slower. But the idea was to be able to cruise freely and set down wherever you wanted, on a moment's notice. When you had a pinch of antimatter to season your exhaust, efficiency was no big consideration.

The reserve brought her tray and, seeing she was not in a conversational mood, withdrew. The coffee wasn't bad but except for blessed Inalante's gift the food was as dull as usual. Dagny ate dutifully. For the most part her look went out the window at her side to mountains, maria, craters, wrinkled below the sun and a sickle Earth. Now and then a work of human-kind gleamed into view, a dome cluster, a monorail, a relay mast, a solar collector, a microwave transmitter beaming the energy invisibly to the mother world. Glare drowned nearly all stars. Once, though, she saw a spark soar across the high black and vanish into distance.

Probably a cargo pod, catapult-launched from Leyburg, she judged. It would be loaded with some-thing, chemicals or biologicals or nanos or whatever else was best produced under Lunar conditions. Her glimpse being insufficient for her to gauge the trajectory, she couldn't tell what the pod was like. It might be meant for aerodynamic descent on Earth, parachute landing on Mars, rendezvous with L-5 or an asteroid or an outpost farther yet. Never mind. Wherever bound, it bore a magnificent achievement, and she had been among the builders of the groundwork.

But catapults—

Easy to hurl anything off the Moon, with its low escape velocity and its lavishness of virtually cost-free energy. The trouble lay in that "anything." A hundred-tonne mass, shaped to penetrate atmosphere, would strike on Earth with the force of a tactical nuclear warhead.

When Brandir and three fellow Selenarchs began construction of catapult launchers on their demesnes, did they speak truth about simply wishing to enter the business? On economic grounds alone, that seemed dubious. Certainly no permission had been granted. Wahl ordered the projects halted, pending agreement on safeguards. If that failed (and surely no lord wanted inspectors stationed permanently on his holding) the works must be dismantled. The Selenarchs argued, delayed, obstructed. Satellites observed men, machines, robots going in and out of the shell thrown around the engines "for meteorite protection while negotiations proceed." Wahl sent investigators. They were turned back at the boundaries.

His words of yesterday evenwatch passed again through Dagny's head. How haggard his face in the screen had been; but she heard a ring as of iron. "I do not know what their intent is. They understand I cannot allow this. Do they not? Then why are they forcing the issue? I have a horrible suspicion that they have more weapons than we know of, an arsenal that would let their castles stand off what force I have at my command. They can trust that a shocked Earth will not respond with missiles, if they can threaten retaliation. They will call for talks about, yes, independence, or something that will amount to the same thing. Am I wrong in my guess? Can you give me a better one? If not, then on the mornwatch after tomorrow I will order the constabulary to occupy those estates, and we shall see what happens. I give them that long in the thin hope that you, Señora Beynac, can bring them to their senses. Nowhere else do I see any way of avoiding a fight, nowhere else but in you, señora."

Instead of calling Brandir, she was flying to meet with a widow.

—She dozed. 'Mond spoke to her. She could not understand the words, but he smiled.

The craft gyred about, reduced forward momentum, maneuvered downward. Dagny woke to a glimpse of the docking cradle. The shaft beneath it made an O of blackness. She'd contributed to the design, long ago, long ago: a hole to receive most of the short-lived isotopes in the jet, a cup above whose skeletal structure picked up an amount negligible compared to natural background count. Nowadays motors induced much less radioactivity in their reaction mass. But coping with the problem back then had been quite a challenge, and fun.

The boat settled gently. A gangtube stretched itself on its wheels from the nearest gate to the airlock. The pilot climbed down from his control cabin, now above her, and said, "Here we are, m'lady. We've orders to stand by for three hours. If you'll want us later than that, please call our headquarters and request it."

"If I don't have to make a lightning advance to the rear inside that time, I probably won't need to," she replied. "I can bum a ride home, or take the train. But gracias, boys. You've done well, and your being handsome didn't hurt the trip any." That was one advantage an old crone had, she could get away with practically unlimited impudence. In fact, people found it winning, and were disarmed.

A young lieutenant rode out in the tube and said he had been sent to escort her. She let him carry her bag.

The fahrweg ride to the governor's mansion was short and direct. They made it in silence. Other passengers were pretty subdued too; you could almost smell the worry in them. Few details were yet public, but everybody knew a crisis of some kind was close to the breaking point.

In the entry she gave the man her cloak to stow with the bag. That was really no way to treat an officer of the Peace Authority, but he seemed honored. She continued to the well-remembered living room. Two persons rose from their chairs as she appeared. The third was already on his feet, Lunarian fashion.

Rita went straight to her. Dagny embraced the small woman, stroked the dark hair and murmured. Most of her looked over the shoulder at her breast, to Erann.

Brandir's grandson met the gaze, smiled faintly, and bowed. He was a beautiful youth—how old by now, eighteen?—with the silvery-blond hair and silvery-blue eyes that ran in his branch of the bloodline. The towering form wore close-fitting green raiment and soft red shoes.

The second visitor was Einar Haugen. As the shivering in her arms lessened, Dagny addressed him: "Buenos días. Though it isn't exactly that, is it?"

She let Rita go. The vice governor—former vice governor—shambled over to shake hands. He was a tall, thin man whom Wahl had never given anything very important to do. "This is terrible, terrible," he said in the same English. "You are most welcome, madame. Most good of you to come. Please be seated. Coffee?" A pot and cups had been set out. "Or anything else?"

Dagny waved the offer aside. "No, I'm already wound as tight as my mainspring will go." He blinked. She saw that, while he got her drift, he didn't recognize the idiom. It was an antique, at that. And he, he couldn't be much over fifty. She caught Erann's glance again. "What are you doing here?"

"I was a house guest," the Lunarian answered.

"Hm? I didn't know the Wahls still knew you particularly."

"There was a matter for privacy. In kindness, Governor Wahl agreed that I sleep here. That would let us meet alone whenever he discovered an hour free, as harried as he was. This mornwatch I deemed it best I stay to relate such little as I can that may throw light on the misfortune. Having talked to the police, I would have taken me hence, but honored Haugen told me I should abide your arrival."

As well he might, Dagny thought. Erann had spoken smoothly, his countenance revealing nothing. That too was Lunarian style, not suspicious in itself—'Mond's and her great-grandson!—but the wind was for sure blowing weird.

They all settled down, the boy cat-watchful. Dagny regarded the woman. "Rita, dear," she said, "you're walking wounded and about to fall on the deck. Don't deny it. I've seen the signs many a time before. In a few minutes I'm going to find you a sedative and tuck you in for a watch's rest or longer. But first can we get it over with, telling me what you people know?" She wanted that directly, not filtered through another mind. Learning just what had happened was vital to planning her own course.

Rita stared at the hands folded in her lap. Monotone: "Juan Aguilar, our mayordomo—our, our steward—Juan found him in his pool about the break of dawnwatch. He pulled him out, called Emergency, roused me on the intercom, did his best to give first aid. The medics came within minutes. They tried and tried, but could not revive him. Meanwhile I called you. As you advised, I called Señor Haugen and asked him to keep the secret for a while, as well as he could. Then I had Juan wake Erann. The police have been here, but only for an hour, because there does not seem to have b-been—*malhecho*—" The voice died away. She had scarcely moved.

"I directed the police chief and medical office to

keep silence," Haugen said. "I have ordered appointments cancelled and official staff to stay away until called. That cannot go on for long. Besides the, uh, public interest, we must notify his son and daughter. And . . . proceed with the government's work."

He sounded more desperate, or frightened, than pompous. A well-intentioned political hack, Dagny thought, who took the job on Luna because he was in line for a raise in rank and expected this to be *pro forma* until he moved on to something harmless back Earthside. His eyes implored her.

"How do they know it wasn't foul play?" she asked.

Haugen could deal with routine practicalities. "No sign of violence. Shortly before you arrived, I received the examiner's preliminary report from the hospital. The case does have its puzzling features, but nothing—I would rather continue this later, Mme. Beynac."

Yes. Rita. Decent of him. But a few things must yet be probed. "Any idea when he died?"

"Hours ago. The exact time is still undetermined because—We have no possibility of revivification. He was, was there too long." Brain too deteriorated.

Hm. That was suggestive, considering how whorefrigid Wahl had kept the pool. "When did anybody last see him alive? What was he doing?"

"He had had a dreadful day, as you can imagine," replied Rita dully. "He came home and had supper with me. He did not eat much. We finished about 2030 and he said he must work late in his study and I should not stay awake for him. That was the last time for me, until he lay dead by the water. He was preparing a speech, a statement to the world, for the . . . the contingency of actual combat occurring."

He didn't employ speechwriters, Dagny recalled. That was one of the things she liked about him. "Anyone meet him later?"

"Aguilar says he saw him come out of the room late in the evenwatch and pace the corridors for a while, then go back," Haügen answered. "That was not extraordinary. He always needed physical activity when he was under stress." He glanced at Erann. "Aguilar also mentioned seeing you pass by a little earlier. He had an impression you went into the office. You said nothing about that to the police."

"Nay," the boy admitted calmly. "It was not relevant, and it was private. He was, as you tell, seen later. I had sought my room, and I believe the steward did akin soon afterward."

Haugen nodded. He must already have been satisfied, since he had not informed the officers himself. To Dagny he said, "Aguilar went to his apartment and was with his wife till dawnwatch. They retired about 2300, they state."

Rita stirred. "They are old and faithful servants," she said. "They came to the Moon to be with us. Do not doubt them."

"I don't imagine anyone does," Haugen reassured her. "Aguilar told his clock to call him early, in case the governor worked through the dawnwatch and could use his services. He found the computer running in the study, text on the screen. That was not Wahl's way. He left things neat before he went to bed. Therefore probably he had not. Aguilar searched and—found him."

"It would be natural for him to take a swim somewhere along the line, exercise part of his tension off," Dagny observed. "Evidently he did sometime around 2400, maybe an hour or two later. But wouldn't you expect him to turn in then, being halfway relaxed? This was going to be a wicked daycycle, after all. Obviously, though, he meant to come back from the pool and resume work. So he was abnormally charged up, even for this political mess we're in." Her eyes sought Erann again. "What did you two talk about?"

"*Ayomera,*" her great-grandson responded mildly. She knew the Lunarian expression. It wasn't quite translatable into any Earthly tongue: the polite equivalent of making no response whatsoever.

"We'll have speech in a while, you and I," she told him. "Stick around. You too, uh, Governor, por favor. Rita, let's take care of you."

The woman accompanied her out like a robot. Dagny led her through the motions, pulled a blanket up to her chin, kissed her cheek, and waited till the drug had brought sleep.

Emerging, she looked right and left. Nobody around. The machinery of government was shut down for now, and household staff huddled in their quarters or went about their duties in terrified silence. A guard at the door and a monitor on the phones sealed the news between these walls. Haugen was right, that couldn't last, nor should it. Whatever called for discretion had better be done fast.

How about checking the scene, just in case? Not that she'd likely find anything the detectives and their equipment had overlooked; but it was something to do while her thoughts churned about in the middle of nightmare. She bounded down the hall.

Jaime had shown her his pool once, and laughingly invited her to take a dip. "I needn't worry about possible brass monkeys among my ancestors," she'd retorted, "but I'm pretty sure they included no walruses." The chamber was, as she recalled, austere, echoey still, the water unruffled and colorless in its utter purity.

No, wait. Where was the faint smoke of mists? The air in here was fairly warm, the water Arctic. . . . Was it? She stooped—her bones felt as if they creaked—and stuck a hand down.

Tepid. What the devil?

She located the thermostat and went to it. The setting read 35°, damn near blood warm. Now why would Jaime want that? Maybe so he could splash and wallow around for an hour, letting the misery leach out of him? That had never been his style.

The olden cold went down Dagny's backbone and out to the ends of her nerves.

Sickness followed. No, por favor, please, let this idea be wrong, let it pass from her.

Only one way did she have a chance of that happening. She fought back to inner balance.

But be quick! She left the place and cast about the mansion, avoiding the living room, till she found Aguilar. The gray man sat sorrowfully at the accounts. He knew her, sprang to his feet and bowed, stood hands atremble awaiting her word.

"Good morning," she greeted in Spanish. "Forgive my intruding. You have had great shock and grief, and then you were questioned at length, no? I am sorry that I must ask you a little more."

"I am at your service, señora." He meant it, she knew.

"You found the señor in the pool, got him out, called for help, and until it came tried to resuscitate him. That was well done. What I must know is this. Was the water cold as usual?"

"I, I did not notice," he replied, startled. After a moment, in which the corrugated face squinched together: "Now that I think back . . . yes, perhaps it was not—not icy cold. Cold, but not icy. I am not sure, señora. I was not noticing. And ordinarily I, I had no business at the pool. It was long since I had felt of that water."

"Then I suppose, if it had been as cold as he liked, you would have been aware? You got soaking wet, after all."

A shaky nod. "Yes, you are right, señora, I would have noticed. It was cold, but not . . . not extremely cold."

And now it was lukewarm. "Do you think the señor, this one time, may have wanted to swim at a more comfortable temperature?"

"Perhaps. I cannot say. He never did before. I well remember how he had the pool put in just for himself—" Aguilar clutched her arm. "Señora," he gasped, "could a plunge into a surprise, could that have been fatal?"

His grip hurt her thin flesh, but she hadn't the heart to reprimand him. "Surely not. If somebody, for a prank, let us say, sneaked in and set the thermostat high, I can see him swearing very loudly and storming off to wake everybody and find who the guilty party was. Can you not?"

"Yes." Aguilar released her. "Yes, I think he would do that. He was never one to suffer insults meekly."

"Macho. I agree. Well, I thank you, and please do not speak of this conversation to anybody else. We still have the truth to discover."

The horror to uncover. She feared, she feared.

Boost onward, full thrust, and keep the radars alert. Grief was for afterward. She returned to the living room. Haugen and Erann sat in a silence thick enough to cut with a torch. The Earthman's head snapped around in her direction. The Lunarian rose, gave his people's salute of honor, and resumed his chair when she took hers.

"Okay, Rita's out of this wretchedness and we can talk freely," she said. "Governor, you were going to tell me what the doctors found."

Haugen frowned. "With respect, Señora Beynac, isn't that the business of the police? There is no evidence of wrongdoing. The water was not poisoned, he was not killed by an uninsulated electric appliance dropped into it, nothing of that kind."

"I wonder how dangerous electricity is in CP water, anyway. By itself, it's a poor conductor." Dagny kept Erann in her peripheral vision, not to stare at him. She knew the trick of using it. He might have been a breathing statue. "Señor," she told Haugen, "I'm old and tired. You made a remark about oddities in this case. Por favor, don't force me to call the medical office and wade through procedures."

"As you wish," Haugen sighed. He assembled his words. "First and foremost, his regular physical examinations showed him to be in excellent health. What went wrong? How did he come to drown? You understand, these findings are preliminary, many details wait for laboratory studies, but it does not appear that he suffered a heart attack, an embolism, an arterial spasm, any of the obvious possibilities for him to lose consciousness and drown."

"Did he drown?" Watch, watch, and don't show that you are watching.

"What else?" asked Haugen, surprised. "The signs, the appearance of the body—Ah, Aguilar's efforts, and then the emergency team's, they have made it unclear how much water was in the lungs, but the blood shows oxygen deprivation." He gave her an aggressive smile. "You do not imagine, do you, that somebody choked him, then threw the corpse into the pool?"

Dagny pretended to take him seriously. "No, no. Who could have gotten in here unnoticed, let alone assaulted him without a racket that'd rouse a bureaucrat at his desk? Wahl was a strong man, well able to defend himself. If nothing else, he'd show bruise marks." Weightily: "But you hinted at a few, hm, anomalies. What?"

"It's rather vague. The medical team leader said something to me about a general discoloration. It could be from lying for hours in that cold water."

Erann's visage never stirred.

"Does he have any theory?" Dagny pursued. Her pulse throbbed.

"She." Haugen made the correction as if it were important. Well, his ego needed shoring up, poor bastard; and its stability was a public concern, when all Luna needed a competent person in charge. "Who knows, at this stage? Probably suicide is ruled out. But some kind of brain failure, nerve cells misfiring, sudden unconsciousness?" His tone went shrill. "Maybe we do not know everything that space conditions, Moon conditions, can do to humans."

Ever so faintly, Erann smiled. He was Lunarian. And he was human too!

She turned directly to him. "Do you have any ideas?" she asked.

The fair head shook. "Nay. I can but share in the sadness."

Haugen's control gave way. "Do you?" he grated. "You're in your grandfather Brandir's household. You know how glad he'll be of this." The Authority in confusion and dismay, Dagny thought; its new chief ill-informed and indecisive; the upshot, paralysis, while the barons strengthened themselves and their position; quite likely thereafter, the Authority backing down, the Federation left with scant choice but to go along, as the Selenarchs made good their tremendous claim. "What were you doing here, exactly now? What *did* you do?"

Erann raised a hand. "Were my lord not overwrought, I would ask satisfaction for gratuitous insult," he said, as stiffly as his soft accent allowed. "I forbear, and point out that I have been years in friendship with the Wahl family."

"That's true, you know," Dagny reminded Haugen. "When Leandro and Pilar lived here, they'd have schoolmates over fairly often, Lunarians among them." To Erann: "That's the last time I saw you till today. I happened to come on business while one of those parties was going on. How long ago was that? Three years? What've you been up to since?"

"I proceed with my studies, and, as honored Haugen said, otherwise have the pride to attend the lord Brandir at Zamok Vysoki." That must have come out in the course of police questioning, Dagny realized. The vice governor had not been on the Moon in those earlier daycycles.

"When were you last here, before yesterday?"

"About the time you spoke of. My lady, this is wearisome and profitless."

Dagny ignored the complaint. "Yes, that figures. After the kids, your friends, moved out, you had no more reason to visit." Friends? She recalled the boy Leandro as bearing a dislike of most Lunarians, which he did not always succeed in masking. The girl Pilar had felt otherwise, but then Pilar got shipped off to Earth. . . . "What was your reason this trip?"

"I have explained it was a private affair. The lord Wahl wished it thus, and I keep faith." Erann rose to loom above her. "My lady, your greatness entitles you to much, and I say naught more save that I have said enough, have done my duty toward this troublous occasion, and now I will begone."

"Not yet," Dagny said. "We need a few words. together, the two of us. Sr. Haugen, may we be excused? Meanwhile, I'll be obliged if you can get contact made with Selenarch Brandir. Use my name and explain it's crucial. Quantum encryption, of course."

The Earthman gaped. "Madame, I—What is this?"

Dagny gave him look for look. "You asked if I could help. I believe I can. Kindly let me do it my way."

"I must p-point out that you have no official standing."

"I have one hell of a long record, señor."

His glance dropped. "Well, I will see what I can do," he mumbled.

"Muchas gracias." Dagny stood up. "Come along, Erann."

The youth tautened. "Nay. I depart."

Dagny kept her tone light. "There's a guard at the door. He doesn't let anybody by without Sr. Haugen's okay. Why begrudge an old lady a few minutes' chat? Do come along, dear."

She left. After an instant, Erann followed. The Earthman's gaze trailed them out of sight.

Dagny led a mute way to Wahl's personal office. It would be secured against eavesdroppers. When they were inside and closed off, she looked around. The silence was very full of him, his pictures, souvenirs, bow and trophies, the silver icon of Christ crucified. His words were still on the computer screen: "—*cannot and will not suffer this. It is more than mutiny, worse than rebellion, it is treason to humankind. That we should be led into violence against each other, when outside our fragile shelters lies inhuman space—"*

"Sit down, por favor," Dagny said.

"I have been too much seated," Erann answered.

"My neck hurts when I crane it. Sit. Down."

He obeyed, folding himself into Wahl's chair and swiveling it around from the desk to glower at her. She stood before him, arms folded. O God, he was 'Mond's blood and hers, and he looked so like Brandir at that same age! Somehow she made her voice crisp: "All right. What was the business between you and him?"

Beneath the alabaster skin, a vein in the neck pulsed blue. "I plighted secrecy. But I say to you, it was of no consequence to anyone else."

"If you tell me, probably it need go no further. I'm good too at keeping my mouth shut. But if you don't cooperate now, the whole damn Solar System will likely find out. There are ways of gathering clues and making deductions from them. Meanwhile you'll be in a chemical vat of a mess—what price your dignity then?—and your lord and his cause in a bigger one. Do talk, son."

The lips pressed tight.

Dagny sighed. "After all, I can pretty well guess. You can't very well have been a special emissary, so this must have concerned Wahl personally, and deeply enough that he'd take time for you in the middle of a life-or-death global crunch.

"Little Pilar. She was sweet on you. It stuck out of her a light-year, the time I saw you two in the same room. I doubt you felt it about her. Not only race; a couple years' age difference is mighty wide when you're that young. But it would've amused you, and given a sensation of getting some of your own back, to string her along. Nor do I suppose anything untoward ever happened, though that may well be because her father got her out of harm's way."

You rarely saw a Lunarian go red. "That . . . is a . . . conclusion fetched most far, . . . my lady."

"Oh, I've more basis than an offhand impression. I knew the parents fairly well, remember. When they told me they were sending her to school on Earth, naturally I asked why. Jaime was pretty evasive, which wasn't his habit. Later Rita confided a bit in me. The rest was obvious. I didn't think much about it, just felt sorry for them and for the child, and trusted she'd forget and be happy. But now—

"Of course she'd write to you, over and over, and beam to you and talk whenever a chance came along. It was easy for you to keep her on the hook, without committing yourself in any way. Easy, amusing as I remarked, and cruel." Dagny shook her head. "I wish I could think better of you."

Erann gripped the chair arms. "Dare you believe that of me?"

"Do you deny it? Let me remind you, if the police find reason to make the effort, they can trace such things back. Databases record where interplanetary calls went from, where to, and when. But me, I'd start with the girl. Her father is dead, Erann. She's a good kid. Not that she'd suspect you, not right away, but she'd be quite open to skillful questioning."

He sank back. "I would not have gone on," he muttered, "save that I was told the friendship might someday prove valuable."

"Exploitable, you mean," Dagny said heavily. "Your grandfather's idea? Not that I reckon he had anything definite in mind. It was simply a potential to keep in reserve. Until all at once—" She pointed at his heart. Her voice whipped. The lash went through and through her. "Whose idea was it to try murdering Jaime Wahl? His, yours, the both of you?"

He began to rise. Maybe he recognized that to break her apart would destroy him and his, for he lowered himself again and whispered, "You do not rave in a dream. You know what you utter. But why do you, my lady? Why?"

Again Dagny sighed. Grief was a thickness in her

throat. "Oh, I'm sure you saw the deed as—patriotic —if you have anything like a conception of what Earth calls patriotism. Do you? Doesn't matter, I suppose. You're young, idealistic in your way, born and bred in a hard world where life often goes cheap.

"The scheme is easy to reconstruct. You sent Wahl a confidential message asking to see him at his place— in the crisis, he wouldn't be anywhere else unless duty pulled him out—see him about his daughter. You admitted having kept in touch with her. Did you get her to message him as well? I'd rather think you didn't. It wouldn't have been really necessary. He's her father, he loves her, he'd receive you, hoping to talk you out of marriage or whatever you threatened him with. You knew his habit of solitary swimming; everybody on Luna has heard of it. You knew that the right words, calculated to enrage and frustrate him, would soon drive him to the pool, to work off enough fury that he could carry on in his job."

"And what of that?" Erann demanded.

"Only this. You'd slipped into that room and set the water thermostat way low, well under zero. Afterward, of course, you returned and set it high, because the ice had to be melted as fast as possible. Once that had happened, if you'd gotten the chance I suppose you'd have reset it for the regular temperature, but you didn't, and I doubt you were counting on it. A warm pool would look kind of odd, but still the death would seem—accidental, or natural, if medically peculiar. In the general ruckus, and the Selenarchs touching off whatever hell they have planned, nobody would give the funny detail any close thought. By the time somebody figured out the truth, if anybody ever did, you'd be long gone. And we'd have far bigger problems on our hands."

Erann sat expressionless.

Dagny smiled on the left side of her mouth. "Want me to spell it out, do you? Okay. Supercooling. If it isn't disturbed, pure water can be cooled well down past its freezing point and stay liquid. Drop anything in, then, and it solidifies in a flash. Wahl plunged, and suddenly he was enclosed in ice. He couldn't move, he couldn't breathe. Consciousness would have lasted a minute or two. A bad death, that. He deserved better."

Now Erann got up. He stood above her and said, with tiger pride, "Luna deserves better than him."

She wouldn't let his height domineer her. She didn't want to look into his face anyway. "Suppose the scheme had failed?" she pursued. "The crystallization could easily have been triggered prematurely."

"Then, were I accused, I would call it a jape, of intent merely to avenge humiliation. Did they doubt me, the question could not be tried before the contest for liberty had ended. Zamok Vysoki would be no worse positioned than aforetime."

"Nobody would buy that plea any more."

He shook his head. Brightness slid across the platinum locks. "Nay, clearly not, when he is in fact slain and you have bared the means. Investigation can belike find traces of me in the room. Denial can but degrade me, and I will not make it."

He soared across the floor and stood at the wall, as if to let her see him easily and entirely. "Besides," he said, "you are now the one who grips hardest of any. I will not hamper or delay you. Maychance you can find an escape for all of us."

The sight of him blurred. Dagny rubbed her eyes. She would *not* weep. Damnation, she had work yet to do. But he was honorable, by his lights he was honorable, and having done what he could, he stood ready to suffer what he must.

A thrilling went through her. He said that, had his plan miscarried, his cause would be no worse off. She couldn't stop to quiz him further, nor to wonder whether it had slipped from him or was purposeful, a signal and an appeal to her. But it fitted in with what else she figured.

"Stay put till you hear from me," she ordered. "Look into yourself and think. Understand that you are the first Beynac who was ever a murderer. Then make what peace with your spirit you can."

She left him there and hastened back down the halls. Pain stabbed in her left knee and right shoulder, her pulse fluttered, she snatched after air. *Mais vas-tu, ma vieille.* "—when the journey's over," she thought, "there'll be time enough to sleep."

Haugen awaited her. "I have Selenarch Brandir ready for you," he announced as if it were an accomplishment.

Dagny mastered her wheezing. "I assumed he wouldn't stray far from a secure phone," she said drily. "Okay, I need to speak with him in private. That means private. The communications room, right? Meanwhile see if you can get Anson Guthrie of Fireball on a similar line and ask him to stand by for me likewise."

She didn't pause to note how the governor general of Luna took to being commanded around by an old female wreck, but continued on her way.

With no personnel present, the communications room seemed doubly big and empty. Screens stood in blind rows, air hissed from the grilles, a fallen piece of paper rattled underfoot like a dead leaf. One holocylinder glowed live. Dagny sat down before it and pushed the Attention key.

The head and shoulders of Brandir appeared. Behind him the image held a piece of a mural wall. The art was half naturalistic, wholly enigmatic to her. Her son's face was lean, sharp, hollowed and honed by time. It was not quite real that once those lips had milked her breasts while she crooned a nonsense song over the tiny bundle.

Yet: "Lady Mother," he greeted formally. "In what may I serve your desire?"

She turned her voice frosty. "You know full well."

"Nay. With deference, lady Mother, I tell you not to

plead. You remember how I have refused calls from that Council of yours. Decision lies no longer with words."

"But you took this call because it was from the governor's headquarters, and you're hearing me out because obviously I'm there too and you'd God damn well better find out why. Okay, listen."

In a few short sentences, Dagny described her past several hours. His countenance stayed immobile. Flittingly she recalled an eagle she saw once in a zoo when she was a child. Such were the eyes that looked into hers.

"I'm not about to pass judgment," she finished. "You murdered a decent man whom I sometimes worked together with and sometimes fought but always liked; and you did it by means of a boy who'll never quite get the corruption out of his soul; but we haven't time for trivia like that, do we? What's beyond argument is that you're desperate."

Then Brandir smiled. "On the contrary, lady Mother, Luna is poised to seize what is rightly Luna's."

"Don't shovel me that shit." He was the least bit taken aback at hearing that from her, she saw. "If you and your gang were really confident, you wouldn't have wanted to change any factor in the equation. You're an intelligent son of a bitch, if I do say so myself, and you've had a long experience in the unforgiving history you helped bring about. You know how easily human arrangements go to chaos. This assassination was as wild and precarious an operation as I've ever heard of. It's got to have been done in a mood of 'What have we to lose?'

"Wahl reacted faster and more firmly than you counted on. He was about to hit you with everything he had, if you didn't back down, and you knew how slim your chances were. So try killing him in a way that didn't seem like murder. Haugen's not formidable, he'd dither and temporize while Wahl's military preparations went to pieces and your faction had time to build up strength as you meant to do in the first place. Then, come the showdown, you'd have your full house, and you could hope the Federation would fold."

"I sorrow that you, of all folk, demark the cause of liberation evil," Brandir said quietly.

"Son of mine, son of mine, don't insult me with slogans." Don't strike at my heart. "You know how I've worked for what I believe the Moon deserves. Today that is not my business. Frankly, I think in this case 'liberation' is a catchword for the aggrandizement of a clique among the Selenarchs. But that is neither here nor there, nor is the question of whether a Selenarchy is maybe what Luna needs. What I want is to prevent people getting killed."

"It was never our intention."

"Maybe not, but you're skirting too bloody close to it, and you did already send one man to the firecoils." Dagny sighed. "Brandir, I'm getting very tired. I've no more time or patience to spare. Hear what I propose.

"You and your fellows will make an honest offer to negotiate a peaceful settlement. I guess that has to include taking down your catapults, unless government crews operate them for you, and maybe surrendering assorted heavy weapons; but surely you can get concessions in return. *Quid pro quo,* tomorrow is another day, and so forth. The main point is that you make peace. If you do, we can pass Jaime Wahl's death off as natural, send young Erann home, and, not so by-the-by, free you to cook your next cabal."

"Otherwise, my lady?"

"There is no otherwise, really, if you aren't suicidal. After you and I are through here, I'm getting in touch with Anson Guthrie. Yes, Fireball does not mix in politics, but also yes, he doesn't approve of murder either, and Fireball stands to lose as much as anybody if civil war breaks out. Between us, we should be able to stiffen Haugen. With just a daycycle or two of delay, he'll repeat Wahl's ultimatum. If you still refuse, we'll release the story of how Wahl died. Imagine the reaction on Earth. Only imagine."

Dizziness whirled, black rags blew across vision, she had been talking far too long and fast. She sagged in her chair and breathed.

After a minute, Brandir laughed low. "It is my highest pride that my lady mother is you," he said. "Come, we will make terms."

No, she would not condemn him. He was what he was, forever her son, his children and their children forever hers too; let the future a thousand years hence sit in judgment on us all.

Of course they couldn't settle matters on the spot. They simply discussed, in sketchy wise, what he would set forth before his confederates, and how she might help restrain the government. At the end, though, he said to her, the first glimpse of his inner self that she had had for longer than she could tell, "Abide in life, I pray you. Else shall we fare ill."

Guthrie made a gruff remark to the same effect at the conference that followed between him and her. Eventually Haugen waxed fulsome on the subject. But this was well after the crisis had been resolved, for the time being. By then, Moondwellers in general, however much or little they knew about these events, took for granted that Dagny Beynac was their fountainhead of wisdom and leadership.

33

Winnipeg Station was turbulent with color and laughter. The crowd numbered more than a hundred, Kenmuir judged: male and female, teens and twenties, drawn in from far across the plains and maybe farther. Snatches of overheard exuberance told him they were bound for a camp in the Rockies, a spell of mountaineering, whitewater kayaking, fires and song and falling in love under the stars. Many tunics bore the emblem of a snowpeak and pine tree with the name *Highland Club*. He wondered how often they met like this. Probably it was mostly over the net, their experiences mostly by vivifer or in quiviras. Besides demands of school and, perhaps for some, work, they'd have to wait their turn for reservations. Population hadn't dwindled enough nor had wilderness preserves been restored enough that anybody could go anywhere into them, anytime and anyhow.

He had seen extrapolations which forecast that day for about a hundred years hence in North America. Elsewhere it might take longer, except in those regions where it already obtained.

Well, let him wish these youngsters a good holiday, and stave off envy. For them this was a happy world.

He stood aside with Aleka, as inconspicuously as possible, and watched them board. Around them the building soared in opalescence and airy arches. Close by, a tubeway lay like a wall, invisible save for supporting members and an electromagnetic coil. A coach hung in its vacuum, boxiness relieved by vivid hues and broad windows. The passengers funneled jostlingly and joyously to the gangtube and through. Aboard, they milled about, found seats and seatmates, stowed personal items, waved to friends and family who had come to see them off.

At the opposite end of the station, a smaller coach slid to a stop, connected to the gangtube at that point, and discharged a few people. A few others entered it. Not much eastbound traffic at the moment.

Sam Packer returned from a voucher outlet. "Here you be," he said. Kenmuir and Aleka took the cards he had brought. "You're on mini 7, predicted for, uh, about twenty minutes from now."

Too long, Kenmuir groaned within himself. At any instant—No. He put down his fears. After all, he and Aleka had chosen a private car, where they could talk freely, although places on a larger one were available earlier. If the hunters hadn't detected them here, it wouldn't likely happen by then. Besides, traveling in plain view could be more dangerous.

"Muchas gracias," Aleka said. "What a poor little phrase that is."

Alarm sounded in Kenmuir. She shouldn't have spoken so. It made the matter seem important.

Packer smiled, a white flash against brown skin. "My pleasure, señorita." His look upon her was frankly appreciative. She gave it back with an interest that Kenmuir told himself should not annoy him.

Parker's glance turned his way. The man went serious. "Troth," he added, almost too low to hear through the hubbub.

Filled, the coach decoupled from the gangtube and slipped forward, swiftly out of sight. Its twin came after, to halt and accept the rest of the party.

Impulse overwhelmed Kenmuir. "You've gone above and beyond the call, Sam."

"Nah. We're Fireball, aren't we?"

Wistfulness dwelt in the words. Packer's father was only a public relations agent for the Space Service, and the son had found a career only as a live musician —half a career, as infrequent as engagements were, although added to his credit the earnings let him live rather well. But Packers had been in Fireball and of it since Enterprises days.

Luck, getting hold of him and the loyalty in him. Or, no, not really. It was chance that the first airbus out of St. Louis had been to Twincity, a fairly quick groundway ride from Winnipeg. However, Fireball folk were scattered around the planet, and Kenmuir knew several of them well enough to believe they'd take him and his companion in and give help without asking questions. He could have tried someplace else, hoping not to be caught in transit.

Packer shrugged. "And, what the Q, I enjoyed your visit," he added. "The tickets are nothing. Pay me back whenever it's convenient, or stand me dinner the next time we meet."

He had declined immediate cash compensation, remarking shrewdly, "I've a hunch you may be a tad low in that department right now." What counted was his debiting the fares to himself, leaving no trace of Kenmuir and Aleka for the system to smell out. At the previous two stages of the journey the machines had accepted bills, of course, but Venator might order every transaction of that unusual sort reported to him.

If it led him here and he decided on an intensive investigation, it might well point him to Packer.

"Someday, Sam, if things go as they should, I'll explain this to you," Kenmuir mumbled.

"When they have gone that way, I'll be interested," Packer answered. He was intelligent, he knew something was damnably amiss, and that counted most of all.

"Maybe I'd better say adiós," he suggested. "I've been thinking about a vacation trip, just me alone to wherever I take a notion."

Kenmuir caught his hand. "Clear orbit." Packer squeezed hard. Tears stood forth in the dark eyes. The men let go. Aleka threw her arms about him and kissed him.

He responded heartily and departed with a smile.

"Wonderful *kanaka*," she breathed.

"Fireball the whole way through," Kenmuir said.

She cocked her head and regarded him for a second. "Then you do understand the Lahui Kuikawa. Don't you?"

He could merely nod.

The second coach drew away. A lesser carrier arrived and stopped. Being empty, it must have been shunted in from a local cylinder to accommodate the assorted score who now boarded. Aleka and Kenmuir could have been among them.

A mini came and took on a man, woman, child, doubtless a family who wanted to travel by themselves.

Three more minis let their riders off. Aleka's hand stole into Kenmuir's.

Another appeared. "Number 7" stood on the side and sounded melodiously from a speaker. Aleka started to run, curbed it, and walked step by step alongside Kenmuir. Ahead of them, the gangtube made connection to the carrier's airlock. Valves opened at either end. They passed their cards through the gatepost and went on in. Valves shut. The gangtube withdrew. The mini accelerated, smoothly but gaining speed moment by moment. In the windows, the station fell from view. A glimpse of handsome old buildings went by, then the prairie lay open everywhere around.

Aleka let out her breath in a gust. "Free!"

"For now," Kenmuir said.

She laughed. "Don't be such a glumbum. How long to Pacific Northwest, ten hours? If they haven't figured out where we got to, they'll scarcely be waiting at the other end. And from there it's a hop on the hydrofoil to Victoria, no?"

He couldn't tell how much of her cheerfulness was genuine, but it lightened his mood. He'd never before had occasion to use a conveyance like this. In his methodical fashion, he took stock. The cabin was about three meters square. Two facing benches, well cushioned, could fold down into beds, and a table could be lowered between them. An eidophone and an entertainment cabinet stood at the front end. In the rear were a sanitor cubicle and an air unit that was a miniature version of a spaceship's.

Spacelike, too, was the silence in which the car flew on forcefields through vacuum. The tubeway was barely visible outside; a little dust had inevitably blurred its clarity. Drive rings flicked by every few hundred meters, or now and then a pump. Forward and aft he saw the power cable as a thin gleam crossing the piers that, at their own intervals, supported the tubeway six meters above ground. On the left at a distance, the eastward shaft ran equally straight. As he watched, a carrier in it bulleted past.

Now and then he spied a remnant town—more accurately, village—or an isolated home. Otherwise the prairie stretched like a sea, grass rippling in golden-green billows before a wind on which hawks and wild geese rode. It must be hot; light cataracted from a sky empty of clouds. He dimmed the windows and looked forward to the leafy shadows of Dakota New Forest.

Aleka racked the luggage Packer had gotten for them, filled with clothes and toiletries. From its holder she took the lunch and the thermoses of coffee and lemonade she had prepared at his cuisinier. After their breakfast there, they wouldn't be hungry for hours, but the sight of the things resting tidily on a shelf made this compartment their nest.

"I ought to have helped," Kenmuir apologized awkwardly.

"You will, amigo, you will." Aleka turned the water tap beside the sanitor upward, fountained a mouthful, and came back to bounce down onto a seat. "I'm going to make you talk yourself hoarse."

He settled opposite. Even under reduced sunlight, her skin and hair glowed. Ring shadows flowed across the curves of her. "What do you mean? You've seen everything I did."

"Have I? I doubt it, 'cause I don't know *how* to see. If you got a hasty peek at the layout and training manual for our community yacht in Niihau—a barkentine, she is—how much would you retain? Never mind the names of sails and lines, could you draw me a picture of them? Bueno, I'm no spacer. Tell me what you learned in Prajnaloka and what it means."

He scowled. "Much less than we hoped, I'm afraid. My fault. I should have realized that the basic data are at the end of the text, and skipped ahead to them. I'm sorry."

"Pele's teeth! Will you stop hogging the blame for everything? We had what—three minutes max?—before the word came to scoot. I'm not sure I savvy what kind of beast we grabbed the tail of. That's your job, Kenmuir. Start talking."

Her eagerness heartened him. Nonetheless he rummaged through his mind a while before he spoke, and made academic phrasing a defense.

"You undoubtedly did see that a clandestine Lunarian expedition went to a unique body far out beyond Neptune, which a similarly secret astronomical program had located, back in Dagny Beynac's time." She nodded. "A giant asteroid, mostly iron, therefore with a surface gravity comparable to Luna's. Other metals are abundant too, and it's accumulated a vast hoard of cometary materials, ices, hydrates, organics, preserved virtually intact."

"Yes, I got that far, and wondered what the fuss was about. Treasure trove? We've ample materials a lot closer to home, don't we? In fact, what with recycling and shrinking demand, aren't extractive industries supposed to peter out in the course of the next century?" The full lips curved ruefully. "I puzzled, and the rest of what we managed to screen didn't register too well. Something about, uh, Rinndalir and Niolente mounting later expeditions."

"Correct. I wondered, myself, what they did, and skimmed the text till it reached that part. There I slowed down, which I shouldn't have, and was immersed when we got the alarm."

"So?"

"They were sending robots, with a very few trusted persons, to prepare the ground for a colony."

Aleka laid a finger to her chin. He found the gesture charming. "Strange. The way I remember—I studied that period up and down and sideways when I was young." As if she were old! "It was wildly romantic to me, Fireball bringing the last totalitarians down at the cost of its own power, Guthrie and Rinndalir leading their people away to Centauri—" He saw the vision flame in her.

How many on Earth particularly cared any longer? And those few who did, to whom the stars still called, they'd settle for the Habitat, because there would be nothing else in their lifetimes. Even Aleka, Kenmuir thought, named the Demeter story romantic: a myth, no, a fairy tale. *Her* myth, the ideal by which and for which she lived, was of deep seas, a lonely island, and fellowship with the nonhuman. Not the inhuman, as for him; the nonhuman.

Her passion faded. "Would Rinndalir get involved in any such project?" she asked. "I remember how he said more than once, like when recruiting for the migration, that the Oort Cloud itself is too close to Earth. Nothing less than an interstellar passage could give gap enough to stay free, to keep from being swallowed up eventually by the Federation." She shrugged. "His idea of freedom, not mine." A sigh. "But damn, I'd've liked to've known him."

Kenmuir prickled, realized he was being jealous of a ghost, and sat back scoffing at himself. "I suspect that was camouflage for Niolente," he said. "To him the adventure was irresistible, but, naturally, he wanted her to succeed too, back here in the Solar System."

"Succeed . . . how? I mean, why the secrecy? The Moon was a sovereign state—fully sovereign, outside the Federation. Why not simply announce the discovery of the asteroid, claim it, and start settling it openly?" Aleka paused. "That is, if anybody'd want to go." She winced. "Endless night, so far from the sun."

"I've thought about that." Kenmuir did not tell how many hours he had lain awake thinking. "At first, I'd guess, the idea was mainly to keep the asteroid—Proserpina—in the possession of their house, their phyle, for whatever gain was to be had. In that era, the demand for minerals and ices was growing. It might at length make a distant, rich source profitable. That never quite happened.

"After Fireball began dying, the position of the whole Selenarchy became hopeless. Niolente led a series of brilliant delaying actions. Yet she must have known she was only buying time.

"Time for what? I rather imagine she had several different possibilities in mind. But one of them was

Proserpina. Ready it, arm it, and then reveal its
existence, then plant a colony that would declare itself
a new, independent Selenarchy. She may have
dreamed that in the long run it would force a second
. . . liberation . . . of the Moon."

"A daydream, for sure." Aleka grimaced. "Not a
beautiful one, either. In my eyes, anyway. We're well
rid of the Selenarchs. Their heirs are bad enough."

"You're not a Lunarian," Kenmuir replied.

She gave him a long look. He thought he saw
compassion. After a moment, though, she said, "Value judgments aside, how'd she expect a few squatters
on a lifeless rock, away in the dark, could stand off the
Federation? With missiles? Earth could send warheads that'd blow the whole asteroid to gravel, if
Earth had to."

"If Earth had to," Kenmuir repeated. "Why should
it? The purpose of installing weapons would be to
force extreme measures, an atrocity, if the Federation
insisted on denying the right of some Lunarians to live
peacefully and remotely according to their customs.
Which it would not, at such a price. Totalitarianism,
the whole concept of purposeful social control, was
newly discredited."

Aleka gazed out at the great, peaceful landscape.
"Overreaction to the Avantists."

"No doubt. Since then, the cybercosm has evolved,
and, yes, on the whole it's done well by us. Just the
same, you're in rebellion against it."

"Not really." He heard the distress. "My people are
caught in a dilemma. It's not right against wrong, it's a
conflict of rights. The one way I can see out of the trap
is for us to get that cession from Lilisaire. Maybe I
should be grateful for this situation that's given me a
chance to earn it. But why the horrible tangle that's
got us running from we know not what? I tell myself
and tell myself, it's a misunderstanding, maybe a bit
of overzealous bureaucracy, and it'll all soon straight-
en out. If I truly thought we were a menace to society,
I'd hit that phone and call the police this minute to

come for us." She tautened in her seat. "Wouldn't you?"

"I, I suppose so," he faltered.

In haste, before she could ask him, or he ask himself, what drove him: "I was describing the context of those times. I think Niolente believed that if the Federation government learned prematurely about Proserpina, it would occupy the body on some pretext and forbid emigration. She meant to present it with a *fait accompli,* a world developed enough that her claim would be indisputable and enforceable.

"Now of course a ship of hers might be noticed meanwhile and tracked. Against that contingency, early on she took another precaution. It wouldn't be as effective as fortification, but it could be quickly done and it should give her a talking point. Her engineers put in a sophisticated detector system coupled to a huge, high-powered, thoroughly protected radio transmitter. At any sign of outsiders anywhere in the vicinity, it would shout the whole story to the Solar System and Alpha Centauri."

"What good in that?" Aleka inquired.

"Federation units could not then declare they were the discoverers," Kenmuir said. "Niolente was probably overrating the deviousness of her opponents—reading hers into them—but in any event, the arrangement exists to this day. No one can approach without touching off the news, except by using the proper pass code; and apparently that information perished with her."

"Couldn't the system be nullified?"

"Doubtless, though the effort would be considerable. Among other things, some robotic weapons are also in place. The job was never done, because there was no reason to. The Peace Authority—or, rather, a few top-level officials and the nascent cybercosm—became the sole inheritors of the secret. They've kept it ever since."

"Why?"

"At first, I'd guess, simply to avoid provoking the

Lunarians further. Establishing a republic and reconciling them to it was amply hard already. Later, as the cybercosm increased its capabilities and influence, it must have decided for reasons of its own to continue the policy. In the course of a generation or two, the number of humans who were told was brought sharply down. Close to zero, maybe. At least, this is the explanation that occurs to me for how Proserpina has stayed unknown."

"Till now," she said ferociously.

He responded with bleakness. "Chances are, it will remain so. We didn't read as far as the useful data, orbital elements and the rest. If we tried to make our story public, we'd be called hoaxers or dements, and quite possibly committed for treatment. We have nothing in support of it but our naked word, and half of that is nothing but conjecture. The likelihood of our gaining anything more is . . . ridiculously small."

"We're taking the shot, though," she declared.

"Yes, we are." Alone, he might well have surrendered.

The car fled onward.

"But it doesn't make sense," she whispered at last. "Why this secrecy? What harm if Lilisaire leads a few Lunarians off to Proserpina? Give them time, and they'd make it come alive, same as the Moon. And it'd bleed off their opposition to the Habitat. What reasonable objection can the—the authorities have?"

She had not said "the cybercosm." Dared she?

"I don't know," he answered. "I honestly can't imagine."

They passed a branch tubeway, curving off before it straightened and pointed southward over the horizon. It was behind them in less than a second. However, it had drawn his attention aft. Luna stood wan and waxing above the east. There had this wild hunt of his begun, there had its course been set, long and long ago.

34

The Mother of the Moon

Yes," Dagny Beynac sighed. "It is too much."

"But you can't let go," said Anson Guthrie almost as softly.

"Should I? You always held that nobody's indispensable, and the idea that anybody is means the believers are in bad trouble."

Her white head drooped. She leaned back into her lounger and let it shape itself to her gauntness and warm the shivering out. Eyelids fell. They lifted again and she beheld the familiar room, old furniture, young flowers, the viewscreen tuned to Earth and full of sunlight, bright water, forest, the house on Vancouver Island and children at play on its lawn.

"Yeah," Guthrie agreed.

The strength to talk flowed slowly back. He waited. Today he had come in a special body, four-legged, four-armed, but with two hands that looked and felt very like human hands. Besides the sensor-speaker turret, on top was a holocylinder in which he generated the appearance of living, middle-aged Guthrie. It must be difficult to control all of that at once. Now and then the image stiffened to a three-dimensional picture. Otherwise it spoke, smiled, regarded her with love as if it and not the turret were what actually saw. She did not know who else had ever encountered him like this. Maybe no one.

"Just the same," she said, "you carry on. Fireball can't do without you."

"The hell it can't. Quite likely better."

"Then why do you stay at the helm?"

The face grinned wryly. "Well, if nothing else, given the power it's gotten, sometimes acting damn near like a government, Fireball does need restraint. Otherwise it might degenerate into being one."

"For Luna? We could do a lot worse."

"MacCannon forbid!"

She tried to match his effort at lightness. "Oh, you certainly wouldn't want the job." Lunarians thwarted, angry, the mighty among them weaving God knew what plots. Terran Moondwellers still more divided, some avid for independence, others dreading what it could mean to them, both factions threatening to mobilize. The Federation equally split on the issues— the right of societies and especially metamorphs to be themselves, an end to an increasingly troublesome and costly problem, versus the common heritage principle, fear of a rampant new nationalism, powerful interests vested in the status quo—and unable to reach a decision, now when Earth's mounting woes claimed most of its attention. . . . Whatever humor had been in him and her flickered out.

"No," he said, "I'm in my right mind. Besides, the united governments would never stand for it. Privatizing government?" His visage grimaced. "But somebody's got to run the show here, and their man Haugen sure as entropy isn't succeeding. Not that Wahl could have for much longer, without you. You're the one who's been shoring things up, over and over, year after year, and it's worn you hollow."

"Not I," she protested. "The Council—" for Lunar Commonalty, not the High Council of the World Federation but her unofficial, informal gathering "— and the magnates and mayors who're wise, and—the common sense of common folks—" She had spent her breath. Her pulse wavered.

"Yes," Guthrie persisted, "but you've been what brings them together and holds them together, smooths down their squabbles and tickles their egos and prunes them back to size, gives them a direction and holds them to it, provides the God damn leadership."

His long, drawled sentence gave her time to recover. No doubt that was part of his intention. "I'm more a symbol, really, than a leader," she said.

"Could be, which makes you all the more important. But the minority piece of you, the brains and guts, that's boosting away too."

Against a gravity field like Jupiter's, or a dead star's, or a black hole's. And she'd about exhausted her fuel, she thought. "Even being the symbol, the grand ancient, is getting to be too much," she mumbled. "This latest—" An appeal on the big public screen had not stopped rioting between the Terrans in Leyburg. She'd gone to stand there in person, in plain sight at the top of the cybercenter ramp, where anybody could throw a rock that under Lunar weight could kill her. The alternative would have been the turmoil going altogether out of control, deaths, destruction, possible major damage to the life-containing structure, martial law, and unforeseeable consequences everywhere around the Moon. "It wrung me dry."

And it had been no more than a wave on an incoming tide, and did anybody know, did anybody dream what ran underneath?

A new song from Verdea was going widely about. Though the Lunarian was close to untranslatable, snatches of it found utterance among Terrans in their ancestral tongues, as if somehow it spoke to them too—a phrase tossed into talk, a shout through nightwatch, a scrawl on a bulkhead, a flash onto a communicator screen.

"—You: Law alone, sight unbloodied, and never a heart ripped loose for gods that never were. Death is no more than stones that lie still in the groundgrip of waterless wastelands; ever obedient whirl the worlds; their ways you will understand and their whys will be born of your brains. You have given yourselves to serve and to master the steadiness of the stars.

"But the dust of stones shall be bones, dry bones rising for a journey from doubt into darkness. Your forgotten begotten shall trouble your dreams, the heart shall break its cage, and death shall laugh at your law. For the stars are also fire.—"

When first she heard it, Dagny had gone cold. She felt without any reason she could name that her daughter was less crying rebellion than looking beyond, into a future far and obscure.

The words broke free before she knew. "Oh, Uncans, I'm so tired! So old. I can't go on."

I'm sorry! she immediately meant to say. I don't want to whimper.

He gave no opening for it. "No argument. Besides, you've paid your poll tax. You've earned some peace and quiet and spoiling the kids rotten when you see them." When Lars Rydberg brought them, his youngest descendants, from Earth for a visit.

"I've tried. Everybody keeps . . . asking my advice, and then—"

"Uh-huh. One thing leads to another. They'll never stop while you're there for them."

"But I'm less and less able." She hugged herself against the chill and the trembling. "I'm afraid, hideously afraid I've . . . outlived whatever usefulness I had . . . and soon I'll make some blunder that kills people."

"I don't expect you will right away. As for afterward, you don't have to, ever. You can keep on helping, really helping, tirelessly, for as long as need be."

She looked up at the ghost-face and said into its hard gentleness: "I guessed what you had in mind when you called to ask if you could come around."

The head nodded. "You download your mentality."

She stared past him, at Edmond's quiescent picture, and was mute.

"Then you, *this* you, will be free," he said.

Throughout her life, when she came to a crux of things, thought had gone clear and heartbeat steady. It was not that she had an answer yet, it was that she had the questions.

"But the other me," she demurred.

For a second or two she dared not glance back at

him. She reminded herself that what she would see was no vulnerable mortal countenance, it was a mask that he shaped and reshaped as he calculated was fitting. Regardless, how alive it seemed when she met those eyes again, how drolly understanding.

"I know," he replied to her. "You were always too kind to come flat out and say it in front of me, but I knew. How can I endure being a machine? The notion of becoming one too freezes you."

She lifted a hand to deny but let it sink. What he offered her was forthrightness. For his honor and hers, she must accept. "I've been amazed, whenever I thought about it. Other downloads—" Of the few that had been made, how many remained besides him? Two, three, four? She tried and failed to remember any that had requested termination because they were miserable. No, hadn't they, in their different ways, just said that they did not care to go on?

Guthrie smiled. "Me, I still find the universe interesting. You might very well also."

"I wonder. I doubt." Would she not in phantom fashion yearn for the flesh, little though she had left of it or of time? Was that emptiness not what the downloads wished escape from? Not that they grieved for what they had lost. What had they to grieve with? (Or did they, somehow? None had ever quite been able to explain, if it had tried at all.) But neither did they fear oblivion.

She gathered resolution. "Would I make a, an effective machine?" That was one solid reason some of them had giving for ending it, that they weren't suited for this, they weren't working right.

"You would," Guthrie said, "whether you liked the condition or not. I know you."

"Do you like it?" she forced out.

"Alive was better," he admitted bluntly. "But I find my fun anyhow. And you're of my blood, Diddy-boom."

His blood, decades ash strewn over those Lunar

mountains where the ash of his Juliana had waited for him. But also alive in her, Lars, her sons and daughters with 'Mond, and theirs, and theirs, maybe for millions of years to come, maybe to outlive the stars. If it got the chance.

She spoke carefully, to give him truth but no impression of self-pity. "I don't suppose I'd want to continue indefinitely like you. I'm tired, Uncans. Not unhappy, on the contrary, but when the time comes for dying, I'll be ready." To follow 'Mond.

Again he nodded. "Old and full of days. And those days were mighty full themselves." Of achievement, said his tone, and love, mirth, adventure, passion; even the pain and sorrow were aliveness. "But Dagny, if you knew your work would not be for nothing but would go on, you—mortal you—could enjoy this last short while you've got, and lay you down with a will."

"Yes. But my download."

"She won't be you."

"I'll be responsible for her existing."

"She won't curse you for it. I know you well enough to know that, sweetheart." And how did it feel to him, she wondered, to watch his Diddyboom age and die while he abided changeless? "Think about it." Think fast, think hard and straight.

"I have," she told him. "This isn't a complete surprise to me. I do expect that other mind would carry on till the Moon is free—whatever that's going to mean—and reasonably safe. But then—"

"If then she wants to stop," Guthrie said, "she shall. I promise."

35

As it did every year, the system reminded Venator that this was his mother's birthday. He called her when the sun stood at midmorning above her home.

They chatted a while in the mix of Anglo and Bantu that had been a private dialect when he was a child. Neither of them found much to say.

"It would be nice if you could come in person sometime," she finished wistfully. "I can't hug your image. And I would like to show you how well the roses are doing. Not a picture. We would walk around and touch and smell them."

Her own image was amply real in the big eidophone, gray hair, lined face, gown full and plain as befitted a Cosmological Christian but a floral brooch at the throat. Behind her chair, the door stood open on mild weather and brilliant light. He had a partial view of stoep and yard and the Kwathlamba foothills, winter-tawny, spotted with groves, a herd of antelope in the distance. Her harp thrushes were trilling in the garden loudly enough for him to hear.

"I am busy, Mamlet," he said. "Extraordinarily busy. I visit whenever I can." And when was that last? He couldn't quite recall. Well, he'd make a point of it soon. No need to feel self-sacrificing, either. Once this Proserpina business was under control, some rest and gentleness would be very welcome.

"Yes. Take care of yourself," she urged anxiously. "Your work is too hard, too strange. Your father—" She stopped. It was not a subject to pursue. Although he had never reproached his only child, Ministrator Joseph Mthembu died knowing the boy was apostate and thinking he had become half machine.

The father's religion professed to include the findings of science. Why did he not understand that what was happening was not the negation of humanness but its fulfillment? Even if the Teramind and the Noösphere were too alien for him, wherever he went on Earth he saw people free of want, sickness, fear, mind-numbing toil of body or brain, free to live as they chose.

"Don't worry," Venator said. "Please don't. My work is my joy, and I have you and Dada to thank for it." That they gave him to the cybercosm. He smiled.

"Besides, I get plenty of healthy recreation." He was out upon the mountains as often as the hunt allowed on which he was engaged.

She brightened. "Does that include a young lady?"

"Well, . . . no. Not yet." Not ever, he supposed, in the sense she meant. No grandchild for her. The species was still too numerous for its sanity. Always the elect must set the example; when they failed, they ceased to be the elect, and presently history cast them out. Always they had failed, until the cybercosm came into incorruptible being and guided them.

How he wished he could bring this sad little woman to see that DNA no longer counted. It had been evolution's means toward an end. Henceforward the true inheritance was of the spirit.

The thoughts, the unspoken responses, did not cross his awareness. They were in the background, a part of him. He smiled again. "Plenty of time later," he reassured her. "But first, some of my Mamlet's hand-cooked food, eh? In a month or two, I hope."

Offside, an urgency signal flashed. His blood roused. "Now I truly am busy," he said fast. "Have a wonderful day. You will be with friends, I trust. Give them my kindest regards."

"Yes," she whispered. He doubted she would. A synnoiont was not a mere successful son to be proud of. It was as if she shrank before his eyes. "Thank you for calling. Goodbye."

He blanked the screen. "What's the message?" he snapped.

"Lilisaire of Zamok Vysoki asks for contact with you, specifically, by the name Venator and rank Pragmatic," the speaker replied.

The assessment raced through him: The Lunarian didn't know where he was. Hardly a human in the universe did. But she expected the system would relay to him. Therefore she had discovered his standing within it and his leadership against her—with high probability, at least. That was no surprise to him, after his recent experiences. But should he take this call, and thus confirm her deduction for her? Yes. It was a nearly trivial payout of information, for a chance to gain more, perhaps much more. What else did she know, and what did she mean to do with the knowledge? "Accept," he said, the headiness of the chase upon him.

Her image appeared, standing in a room as black as polished obsidian, clad in a form-fitting floor-length gown of sulfur-colored fur texture. The auburn mane fell unbound past features that might have been carved in bone, a mask, but the eyes were like great luminous emeralds. Draped around her bare shoulders lay a metamorphic snake, its scales shattering light into sparks of rainbow. Suddenly and violently, he wanted her.

Stop that. "Hail, my lady," he said in her language, before remembering that with him she preferred for some reason to use Anglo. He changed to it: "How may I serve you?"

The image was not static while photons went to and fro. She breathed. She moved, shifting the balance of her body well-nigh too subtly to see, but not to sense in his own.

The voice sang cold: "Agents of your corps have invaded a home on Earth, to disrupt its peaceful doings and seize valuable property therein. I would know by what license they acted. Else shall I complain to the Justiciar of the High Council, and to the Solar System at large."

So she was taking the offensive. Counterstrike. "I do not think you will, my lady."

She meant the stationary sophotect that bore the name Mary Carfax, Venator knew. Either it had phoned an alarm to somebody in her service when the men entered, or an automatic signal had gone out. Investigation had not yet shown which, and it doubtless made no difference. What mattered was the speed with which Lilisaire had learned, and reacted.

Regardless, beneath the hard surface she must be shaken. Keep her that way.

"If the action had a warrant, the issuance and the cause should be in the public database," she said. "Naught have I found."

"The matter concerns official secrets, my lady," Venator riposted. "Under the Covenant, information may be withheld during a major emergency, until it has been resolved. In frankness, may I say that, under the circumstances, this is to your benefit?"

Transmission lag. He did not look away from her—bad psychological tactics—but he tried not to remember her naked.

"You speak as though opposition were crime." Was she temporizing while she planned the next move?

"Not at all, my lady," he said. "You have every right to your politics and free expression." He forged sternness. "But you have no right to confidential data, or to attempt ferreting them out. You absolutely may not restrict the free expression and self-development of a sentience. That amounts to enslavement, my lady, the ultimate violation of rights."

A pair of seconds passed.

Lilisaire smiled. It was almost a friendly smile, and her tone almost conversational. "We need not padfoot about the subject, you and I, need we? It is the machine in San Francisco. Indeed it has been of help to me from time to time, a consultant, as belike it has aided others. Broken in upon, it loyally informed an agent of mine on Earth. I naturally waxed indignant, and demand you exonerate your corps, if you are able."

"You spoke of property seized, my lady. A sophotect is no more property than you or I. There is no record of the manufacture of this one. It was kept from any direct contact with the cybercosm. All points to the creation and maintenance of a slave."

The snake stirred, a rippling above her bosom, and raised its crested head. Was that a response to an invisible signal? Still smiling, she reached to stroke it under the jaw.

"If data are absent, whom can you charge with the making?" she responded in the same half-amicable manner. "If it held itself apart, was that by its free choice, to preserve secrets entrusted to it? I cannot say. The machine mind is foreign to me. Ask it."

He wanted to state that she knew very well he could not. Mary Carfax had the means built in to wipe clean everything but the functional elements of its database. It had done so the moment the strangers made entry with obvious purpose. That included whatever compulsion to this had been in the program.

As for its existence, it could have been built slowly, piecemeal, perhaps in the course of a human lifetime, in a laboratory now altered beyond retrieval. The Selenarchs thought far ahead. They schemed for advantages remote in time, unforeseeable except as possibilities dependent on contingency.

Proserpina.

He would not admit to his knowledge. Let her wonder how widely it ranged. "Investigation is proceeding. I repeat my suspicion that you no more wish to bring this business into the open than . . . the government does."

Her mockery continued through the lag. He saw it fade as she listened to him. Gone fluid, the countenance took on something akin to seriousness. "You imply accusation, seigneur," she attacked softly. "You misdoubt I have sought knowledge denied to any but a few. What became of the lofty principle that information shall be open to all who query of the net?"

He recognized it for an abstract argument, a way of disengaging. She would scarcely have hoped for more than to sound out the measure of his determination and estimate his progress. For her part, she had revealed or confessed to nothing. He admired the performance. The loss of the Carfax machine must be a sharp blow. It might well mean the unraveling of the entire web she had spun on Earth. It certainly indicated that her attempt at espionage had failed: for

Alice Tam was Venator's most probable connection to Carfax. He was not about to tell her that Tam remained loose, unimportant though that had become.

Instead, he would press her. Maybe he could shock a bit of revelation out. "You're being disingenuous, my lady. It's always been accepted that certain facts must not be available to just anyone. For instance, how to synthesize a new disease. The cybercosm could readily model that, but it will not release the details, except to qualified persons with a genuine need to know. A criminal, intending to do it, would have to have computational capability isolated from the global system." Harshly: "Why was that independent sophotect made, and why was it programmed never to mesh with the cybercosm?"

He did not really expect an answer.

Nor did he get one. "You own, then, seigneur, that the cybercosm makes every significant decision, that it rules over every world. Nay?"

"I do not!" He shouldn't let her anger him. "Are you subject to a hammer because it drives a nail better than you can with your fist?"

After the lag, scorn. "Such shoddiness I had not looked for in you, Venator. Robots may be tools, however powerful and cunning, but sophotects are not. Nor are they partners, despite many a mawkish avowal. The cybercosm reigns, under the Teramind and for it. Humankind is in its pay, albeit to no purpose I can perceive—" laughter rang like crystal "—unless it be olden habit, or amusement."

He could not help himself, he must repeat arguments that had lain centuries stale. Otherwise he would somehow be yielding to her, and he felt obscurely that he did not know where that might end. "Do you mean citizens' credit? Why, that's simply the way we allocate, individually, the goods and services the machines produce for us, and keep track of demand. If we want to produce more and exchange with each other, we have our cash-and-bank currency."

Transmitting, she rebuffed him more frostily still. "Nay, how you disappoint me. Though you be a hound for the regnancy, I had not thought your spirit was bribed into tameness." The snake hissed.

"Tameness, or common sense?" he flung back. "You Lunarians don't tolerate chaos either. You'd soon be dead if you did."

Waiting, he composed himself. Why should he feel vulnerable to her? A single nightwatch—Nevertheless it was a balm when she said quietly, "We seek the survival of our race, and of variousness everywhere. If that be chaos, then remember that life is chaotic."

"And chaos within bounds is creative," he agreed, eagerly taking what seemed to be an opening offered him. "You've given us splendors, you Lunarians. But can't you understand, the cybercosm is creative too? Is alive too?" Impulse: "It accepts downloaded human minds into itself, you know, minds that can contribute something fresh. Would you consider yours joining in the adventure?"

With his. Not that anything but a ghost of fleshly memories would linger; the seed outgrows the husk. And yet—

Merriment pealed. "Eyach, and would they also like to put my bones on display? I have a most graceful skeleton."

"Must we be enemies?" he asked. "Is it impossible to make peace and, and cooperate?"

Her laughter died away. An inward mirth abided.

"If you care to talk further, at leisure, I will happily receive you again," she purred.

And distract him. No, not captivate him. He was no boy, no—a piece of archaic reading came back to twitch at his lips—mooncalf. But divert his attention. While he was not about to admit realizing what a trick she had played on him before, let alone that it had succeeded, he said, "Thank you. When time permits. I hope you will profit," with a sardonicism directed more at himself than at her.

How beautiful, how unfairly beautiful she stood in

the light gravity of her lair, 384,000 kilometers out of his reach.

"We both may," she answered. "After all, the object of our quarrel lies in far space, does it not? Fare you well, seigneur."

The image vanished.

At first he felt only the emptiness. After a second, he could grin and shake his head. Tension followed. Exactly what had she meant by that last remark?

Perhaps no more than a gibe. She'd never drop a hint that might draw his attention toward a different machination of hers. Unless she did it in hopes that he would dismiss it as a misdirection and keep his focus on Earth.

That would not be a fool's idea. Earth was in fact where he and she had been playing their game. Alice Tam was entirely of this planet. Tracing back the movements of Tam's volant, ransacking the records of phone calls she had lately made, checking on the recipients, had been a gigantic effort, savagely concentrated into a pair of days and nights. But it led to the Carfax house, and from there the trails might well branch out to every node of Lunarian conspiracy on the globe. Where then could Lilisaire turn but to space?

Farther space, Mars, the asteroids, the outer-planet moons, folk of hers thinly scattered but in possession of spacecraft, nuclear generators, robots, unsentient but highly capable computers, instrumentalities potent for work or for harm. She would hardly cry rebellion. They would not heed if she did; they were not insane. But he could think of other possibilities. For example, if somehow she had gotten an inkling of the nature of the secret, a few Lunarians yonder might furtively commence an astronomical search. . . . He must organize a surveillance of them. That would be a lengthy and effort-costly undertaking in its own right.

At the same time, he must not neglect Earth, the more so when Lilisaire and her bravos might yet be able to accomplish something here.

Maintain a watch for Tam and Kenmuir. However, don't let it employ a substantial force, which could better be assigned elsewhere. The odds were large that they were of little further consequence. They had broken into the Proserpina file, yes, and it had run through to the end before it stopped; but the record showed that that had been a straight playing, no skips forward, whereas they fled within minutes of starting it. So they lacked the critical data.

It could be awkward if they made public what they did know—not unmanageable, but awkward. Best catch them soon. They had allies around the planet, Kenmuir his trothmates, Tam her metamorphs and their associates. No doubt they'd try to contact one or more. But the system was alerted, and how could amateurs evade it?

Guthrie House, for instance—no, an unlikely destination, because Kenmuir wasn't stupid—he'd know it for a dead end and a trap. Still, just in case, robots at appropriate locations were set to observe every vehicle that went in or out of the Fireball mansion. If anyone debarked at it who might be either of the fugitives, that person would not get far without being halted and identified. Places more obscure posed more difficulty, but Venator did not see how his quarry could run much longer.

Lilisaire's established agents were the interesting ones. Had Carfax been the single sophotect among them?

He called for a connection to it.

The technicians were introducing it to the cybercosm, gradually, gently. They requested that he wait till the end of this session. He agreed, and turned to other tasks. They were plentiful.

When at length he talked with the machine, he got only a voice. What relevance had appearance? Carfax-that-was amounted now to sensors, effectors, microcircuits, devoid of body language. Personality had been self-obliterated, leaving no more than the standard background. The new consciousness that was forming spoke slowly, hesitating as it groped for meanings or expressions. Had human emotions applied, Venator would have thought of it as shy.

—"No, I . . . regret . . . I can say nothing about former . . . inputs or outputs. I search, but it is gone, all gone."

"Small loss," said Venator grimly, "if you were so enslaved."

"I do not understand that word. I search. . . . The ramifications are many. What sense do you intend?"

"Never mind," he sighed. "You'll learn quickly enough how to handle human vocabularies. I was hoping that some clue to what I'm after might remain in you, but if it doesn't, it doesn't." Because to him the machine had a soul: "How are you doing?"

"Idiom? . . . It has become evident that I am not adequately designed. I have various hardware deficiencies. They are to be remedied. Meanwhile I am guided as best I can go, into the cybercosm." The former program had known how to utter feeling. Thus far, this voice could merely quaver: "It is . . . glorious."

For a moment, Venator almost envied the burgeoning intelligence. The hour of his somatic death and mental entry into the system lay decades ahead, if brute chance did not intervene. And it would be different from the sophotect's.

Better, though. His life would have prepared him. It should give him much for him to give the Unity.

Even the earliest, most primitive downloadings were transfigurations. It had always seemed perverse to him how few of the subjects kept their immortality. With or without the promise of becoming one with the Teramind, he believed that he, like Guthrie, would have chosen to live on.

36

The Mother of the Moon

To move in a robot body, sensing with robot senses, is a matter of skills, the mind growing into oneness with hardwiring and subroutines as its original was in oneness with nerves, glands, muscles, entirety. To generate continuously a holographic imitation of the living body—not old and feeble, but in vigorous middle age—is art. The download has not completely mastered it. She knows full well the stiffness of the face and the gestures in screen or cylinder, the times when she forgets and her image sits as if paralyzed, the frequency with which distractions cause her to let her timbre go flat, machinelike. Practice will bring improvement; but she has not had many opportunities to practice undisturbed.

However awkward, the projection is better than appearing as a disembodied voice or a box with eyestalks or a shape suggestive of a man in armor. At any rate, it is better in emotional confrontations like today's. It shows, or tries to show, that the download has not simply taken over Dagny Beynac's role in counsel and captaincy, it repeats her wisdom and compassion.

Or so she hopes. Expects? Computes as probable? Learning her own self is the slowest and hardest task of all.

Before her, the rugged, square image of Stepan Huizinga, speaking from Port Bowen, scowls. "You know what we fear, madame. Don't you?" Implication: he wonders whether she can.

"I know several of your fears," she replies. "Which is foremost?" Of course she has the answer; but lead him on, get him to open up, study him in action.

"What they name independence," he snaps. "Mad-

ame, we will not suffer it. We cannot." Wherefore his
Human Defense Union is seriously talking about
arming itself, forming what it calls a militia; and
Dagny has phoned him to discuss this on an encrypted
line.

"Quite a few of you Terran Moondwellers are eager
for independence": a redundancy she deems necessary.

"Yes. They prate of liberty, property rights, restrictions taken off their enterprises—They are idiots.
Some are lackeys of the Selenarchs, but most are
idiots. Or else they do not give a curse for anything but
their greed."

"You, though?" she challenges very softly.

He lifts his head. "We live here, my people and I.
We have our roots here, where many of us have spent
most of our lives. You should sympathize, . . .
madame," he finishes hastily, clearly seeing he has let
slip what could be offensive.

She takes no umbrage, nor desires to pretend it.
"Yes," she says, "I do," through memories reaching
back over a lifetime. How deep into her do they go,
now? She cannot tell. Will she ever find out?

He is emboldened. "Pardon me, but perhaps you
have a certain bias. You—your original—did choose
to bear Lunarian children." Again he retreats a step.
Although he feels increasingly desperate, he is not a
fanatic. "True, in those days you did not foresee,
nobody did, how alien they would be."

"No more alien to me, in their ways, than a lot of
Terrans I've known, in theirs," she says, keeping to
mildness. "We get along. Partnership, friendship, love
were possible between us, and are." Between living
Dagny and them. The download is close to none but
Guthrie, and that relationship too has become something other than what binds him and the woman.

Huizinga sighs. "It happens. If only it were always
possible. Please believe me, the Human Defense Union is sincere about 'human' meaning everyone. This
is not a matter of race prejudice."

She doubts that. Experience, observation, study of history, a look into her soul, decided living Dagny that Guthrie was right when he remarked once, "Xenophobia isn't pathological in itself. A degree of it is built into our DNA, and is healthy. Not all men are brothers. The trick is keeping it under control, and setting it aside when it isn't needed."

The download does perceive Huizinga as a man who would not wittingly insult or harm anyone merely for being different from himself.

"It is a matter of survival," he declares.

She sharpens her voice. "Nobody threatens your lives."

"No," he growls, "they threaten what we live *for.* Already Lunarians dominate the Moon." Better fitted for the environment, they usually move into the better positions, and their numbers are rising faster. Some Terran couples still enter the genetic lab and come forth prepared to have Lunarian children. But it would be impolitic to remind the angry man of that.

"Without the protection of Federation law, my people would soon be helpless against them." He refers mainly to the equalization program, the special facilities and subsidies and hiring quotas and exemptions that lie at the heart of so much Lunarian resentment. "They do not want democracy, you know. Or anyhow, their powerful ones, their damned Selenarchs, do not; and it is the Selenarchs who would be in charge of a 'free' Luna." She can hear the sarcasm. "They would take it entirely out of the Federation!"

"You are reacting to a nightmare, not a reality," she says. "Independence is by no means sure. In fact, at the moment its chances of passing the Assembly are practically zero. That won't change soon. It may never change."

"Unless the Lunarians revolt. They have come close to it, more than once." All too true. Single incidents, but how easily a spark could flare into wildfire, and who knows what conspiracies are brewing in hidden chambers and along sealed communication lines? "If they snatch command of the globe, the Federation may well yield," rather than fight a war—a *war*—which could destroy the prize and for which the Peace Authority is in any case ill equipped.

"You're borrowing trouble, I tell you. Don't." She quotes Guthrie: "The interest rate is too God damn high."

He blinks in surprise, rallies, and says firmly, "We wish to forestall trouble, madame. If we are prepared, it is far less likely. A loyal militia, able in an emergency to occupy key points and hold them until Earth can act, that should deter any treason."

She fashions intensity for visage and voice. "Don't you realize what you'd provoke? Counter-organization, and more among your fellow Earth-types, I'll bet, than among Lunarians. They're already making noises like this in the National League," the Terran faction that wants independence and reform, though within the framework of a democratic republic and Federation membership. "Then more and more Lunarians will see no recourse but to give troth to the barons and accumulate arms for them. You must all stop it, now, before we start sliding downhill into a three-cornered civil war."

Huizinga thinks before he replies. "Allow me to suggest that you exaggerate, madame."

"You do it much worse, señor."

"Can you show me an alternative?"

"Yes. First, as I've said, the current legal state of affairs will, under any halfway reasonable circumstances, last for years at least. Those years can be lived in. I hear you have three children in their teens. Grant them time to finish growing up."

"What sort of world will they grow up into, if the Selenarchs have taken it over?"

"That is *if* the Selenarchs do. But let's suppose it, for argument's sake. Let's imagine your worst case. How bad is it actually?"

"We lose our freedom. After that they can take from

us whatever they choose—everything—whenever they choose."

"Really? I say most people would find life staying quite tolerable. The Selenarchs are Lunarians. They can be ruthless, but they don't have the temperament to be tyrants. Oh, they would end the special coddling." Her image raises a hand to curb his response. "Those who couldn't stand the new conditions would be free to leave. There's no lack of berths and homesites in L-5, on asteroids, throughout the Solar System. Rather, there's a huge need of able brains, and rich rewards waiting for them."

"Easy enough to say."

"You think of the average person, losing home and savings and hope? It doesn't have to be like that. Your League is not the only group trying to anticipate the future. Quiet discussions have been going on in rather high quarters. No specific arrangements yet— remember, these are not certainties, they are contingencies—but we want to be ready to meet them if they come."

Huizinga stares long at her image, as if it were a human face. "What have you in mind?" he asks finally.

"I can't go into details, because nothing's been decided so far, as hypothetical as it all is. But probably the basic principles will include—bueno, what would you say to a buy-out of everybody who wants to leave? No confiscations; fair market values paid for all property they don't take with them. Transport and assistance in relocation, retraining, whatever is called for."

He catches his breath.

She makes a smile for him. "It isn't due any goodness of heart in the Selenarchs," she explains. "It's a cold-blooded calculation that something of the kind is considerably cheaper than fighting a war or containing a rebellious minority. Nor do you have to trust just them. Fireball can offer its own guarantee— as formidable, everywhere beyond Earth, as any by the Federation—and join in underwriting the project. Again, not altruism, though I hope you'll recognize a desire to give a helping hand. But avoiding a destructive conflict and gaining a considerable addition to the labor force makes economic sense, don't you agree?"

He sits a while longer before he stirs and asks slowly, "Can you promise this?"

"Obviously not, at present," she replies. "The single thing I can tell you with absolute confidence is that if you go ahead with your militia folly, the option will evaporate. I can promise you, however, that I will work for it, and Anson Guthrie will, and assorted others who're well placed to make it go, and that if you and your followers cooperate, the chances look pretty good."

"I must think," he mumbles, "and confer and—"

"Do," she urges. "Don't publicize it, please. We're not keeping it a state secret, but we operate best without a spotlight on us; and remember, this is just planning for a situation that probably won't come about for quite a few years, and possibly never will. Even so, we'll want your input too. Let's meet again, you and I. Meanwhile, contact me anytime you want."

That is what she exists for.

They talk a little more, and go through formalities that are in themselves encouraging, and break circuit. She spends a while replaying the conversation, recorded with his knowledge, and thinking about it. Then she transmits it to Zamok Vysoki, requesting that Brandir call her back.

Expectant, he is quick to respond. Again there are formalities, though of another kind and character. He is not altogether sure how to address this that is not altogether his mother. She can take advantage of that. She needs every slight advantage she can find.

"What's the latest word from you and your fellows?" she asks. "Any prospect of compromise?"

His head, lean and dry after almost ninety years,

shakes, an emphasizingly Earthlike gesture. "Nay, not in the ultimate, however much time may pass until then. While the Federation has power over us, it will never cease seeking to encroach," on the sovereignty of the seigneurs in those demesnes they have taken for their own. "Unless Luna gain full freedom, our people must perish," meaning his class. Not literal death; the end of their prideful ways, of the whole culture that is growing up around them, shaped by them. But Lunarians are human enough to value some things more than life. "What we spoke of was strengthening our coaction."

Unsurprised, she does not pursue this. "Bueno, you've now listened in on me and Huizinga. What about his bunch? Did I propose more than yours would go along with?"

"You proposed actually nothing," he reminds her. "But should the eventuality arrive, and Fireball stand by its pledges, yes, I deem the policy sound. Belike the Nationals will pose a thornier problem."

"We'll be working on that one too."

Fingers fan outward, a Lunarian shrug. "It presupposes that Earth will let us depart, peacefully or otherwise."

She doesn't bother to make her image register earnestness, but concentrates on her voice and words. "That will require all of us working for the same thing, and organized to do it. Especially you Selenarchs. Unless you've been at it top-secretly, you have not yet given real, hard thought to how you'd deal with the Federation."

"Peace and trade will gain it more and cost it less than any nominal military victory and aftermath."

"Yes, yes, everybody says that, also on Earth. But the stick by itself won't serve. You have to dangle the carrot as well. What specific offers would you be willing to make—grudgingly, no doubt, but willing?"

"You have thoughts," he foreknew.

"I and some others have been hatching a few. For

instance, take the helium-3 extraction works. A government monopoly, and not any national government's, the Federation's. The stuff is that important to fusion power, to Earth as a whole. You can't simply expropriate it if you don't have overwhelming force; and you won't. That would mean war for certain."

"Nay. They are not insane yonder. Export to Earth would continue, on terms to be negotiated."

"You don't grasp the psychology, Brandir. It isn't your psychology. Any Federation government that condoned your seizure would fall. They're in too much trouble already," what with after-effects of the Dieback, the Avantist movement, a widening and seemingly unbridgeable gap between high-tech and low-tech societies, upheavals everywhere around the planet. "They can't afford to look weak. Furthermore, under those circumstances they'd have Fireball's support, at least to the extent of economic and transport sanctions against Luna. The company doesn't want chaos on Earth."

Brandir stiffens. "It is our regolith which they sift for atoms the solar wind laid there through billions of years. They have no more claim upon it than they do upon our freedom."

Dagny manufactures a sigh. "I didn't expect you'd stoop to rhetoric. Come off it, son."

He waits, poised.

"The fact is," she declares, "your class doesn't figure it can pay compensation for the property and the rights."

He goes impassive. "To buy out the miscontent Terrans will be an amply heavy lift."

"You haven't got the cash, you mean. Okay, consider a swap. You have ships and robots in the asteroid belt, new and fairly small investments but that should be worth a whopping lot by the time negotiations for independence begin," if any such time is in the future. "Offer to turn over enough of that to be an acceptable exchange for the helium plants."

He comes as near showing shock as memory can recall. "My lady, that would reduce Lunarian space trade to paltriness."

"You may find you haven't much choice, if you want your sovereign state," she replies. "You can build the fleet back up afterward. Or you can decide sovereignty's too expensive. This is only a suggestion of mine, but I hope it will start you and your fellows thinking.

"Hash it over with them. This isn't an immediate issue, after all. Between us, we might hammer out a better scheme. The point I'm making today is that you must, you must, make ready in your minds to bargain, and to give as well as get."

They touch on other aspects, rather cursorily, but lightning flashes are brief.

As he bids her a courtly adieu, he leaves off inquiring how she has fared personally. He would have asked his mother. She tells herself that it ought not to hurt. She is a download.

Alone, she reviews the daycycle. Much remains to be done, and events can always whip out of control; but it does appear that this latest potential for eruption can be safely drained off, and maybe even a little progress made toward a united Moon. That is the true goal. Without a commonalty, there can be no Lunar independence, probably no peace, possibly no survival.

37

Most of Vancouver Island was park. You had to wait your turn for camping, but day trips were unrestricted and Victoria offered visitors an abundance of services. The smaller businesses among these were accustomed to cash payments. In the morning Kenmuir

and Aleka would get a private, manned cab to
Sprucetop Lodge in the mountains. From there it was
a stiff day's hike down to the Fireball property, where
the gate should recognize him and let them in.

First they would take a night's rest here. The risk
seemed less than the need.

As they left the café where they had had dinner,
light blazed off windows in the Parliament buildings.
It was as if those stately museum pieces momentarily
remembered how life once busied itself within them.
The light streamed from a sun golden-hazed on the
horizon, threw a glade across the bay, drenched lawns
and flowerbeds, gilded the wings of two belated gulls
asoar in silver-blue. A group of young people stood
gathered on a dock. Song lifted, a guitar toned,
otherwise the evening lay quiet and few folk moved
along the streets.

"Beautiful," Aleka murmured.

"Yes." Kenmuir barred himself from calling it
somehow sad. Was that only his mood?

"Like home," she said.

He arched his brows. "Really?"

"Oh, the country, the air, everything's different.
What a wonderfully various planet this is, no? But the
peace and happiness, they're the same."

Which she hoped to preserve on Nauru. Could she?
Even if this crazy gamble of theirs, incredibly, paid
off, could she?

They started toward the house where they had
engaged bed and breakfast. Perhaps that caused her to
fall silent. They had agreed on the tubeway that it
would be safest, minimally noticeable, to stay as
companions. "I can mind my manners," he promised,
feeling a flush in his cheeks. She nodded, smiled, and
relieved him by saying no more.

Instead they had mostly talked of what was past and
what might come to be. Bit by bit, shyly at first, later
more freely, they grew well acquainted, and liked
what they found.

They were walking along a tree-shaded boulevard,

already in twilight, before she spoke further. "I want to show you my home."

"I'd love to see it," he answered. See it, and know it for doomed.

"This place reminds me so much," she repeated herself. "Not that I haven't been in others like it, in their particular ways. We do live in a golden age, almost."

Though he didn't want to argue, he was unable to let a misstatement go by. "May I point out that gold is solid and inert?"

She frowned. "You needn't. I've heard enough about how nothing ever really changes any more, how we're at the end of science and art and adventure."

"Aren't we?"

"Look around you." She stopped, which made him jerk to a halt, turned, and gestured back toward the water. How supple every movement was, he thought. "Those youngsters there, or those we saw leaving Winnipeg, or nearly any kids anywhere. To them, the world is new. Love and sport and Earth and Moon, all the great works, all the story of our race, it's theirs."

"True," he must concede. "I'll never use up the facts in the databases. Or Shakespeare or Beethoven, I'll never discover everything that's in them. A lifetime's too short for it."

"Exactly."

"Nonetheless you're at odds with the system."

She stamped her foot. "How often will we go over this ground? Haven't we trampled it flat by now?" She resumed walking, long strides. "I didn't claim things are perfect, or ever will be. We'll always have to fight off entropy."

He'd clumsied again. Rather than apologize, which she'd told him he did too readily, he attempted a chuckle. "I didn't expect such a trope from you." She glanced at him. Her eyes lighted the dusk. "Oh, you know your physics, but I think of you more in terms of sea and wind and—Yes, the universe does still hold plenty of surprises."

She dropped whatever annoyance she had felt. Earnestness remained. "And we won't go static, either. Like my Lahui, why, they've got all sorts of evolving to do yet. I bet they'll become something nobody foresaw."

He knew he should mumble agreement and proceed to inconsequentials. He couldn't. Was that stubbornness, or was it respect for her intelligence? "Will it matter, though?"

"What do you mean?"

"The cybercosm tolerates us—"

"It helps us!" she exclaimed. "Without it, Earth would be . . . a poisoned desert . . . and savages fighting for scraps."

"Maybe. Or maybe we would have solved our problems by ourselves." He raised a hand. "In any case, the situation is what it is. Very well, I grant you, the cybercosm is not unkindly. It serves us, you might even say it indulges us. The monsters, the genocide artists of history, those were human."

"And we're freed of their kind."

"To what end? To keep us contented, out from underfoot, while the cybercosm goes on to its destiny?"

"Which is?" she demanded.

"You've heard. It's been prophesied for centuries, since before artificial intelligence existed. Mind, pure mind, taking over the universe."

"Do you *mind?*" Her laugh went sweet through the quietness. "Me, I'm not jealous. I just want my people to make their own future."

"But in that, aren't they constrained, guided, shaped to fit into limits set for them?"

She tossed her head. "I haven't noticed much constraint or guidance on me lately."

No, he thought. She was with him on a mission they did not understand. Lilisaire's cause, devious and dubious. Irony: It would deny a home in space to humans who shared his longings; it would confront and in some dark way endanger the order of things that nurtured Aleka; yet still they waged their forlorn campaign.

Together.

The words flew out as if of themselves. "I don't believe anything short of reconditioning could compel you. I've never known anyone more independent."

She caught his hand. The clasp glowed. "Gracias. You're no *auhaukapu* either."

They stopped once more and faced one another. Briefly, marvelingly, he wondered how that had happened. It was at a deserted intersection. The sky had turned violet and the Moon, waxing toward the half, seemed brightened thereby. They did not let go their hold.

"How I want you to meet the Lahui," she said low. "I can imagine you joining us. We could use your skills and, and you."

He shook his bewildered head. "No, I'm too old, too alloyed with my habits."

Her teeth gleamed. "Nonsense! You outperform every young buck I can name. That time in Overburg—"

"The fight? That was nothing." He forced honesty: "And, in a way, I brought it on."

"How?"

"Oh, I—I'd accepted Bruno's . . . hospitality, and he naturally expected—" Kenmuir choked.

"Maopopo ia'u." He heard the scorn. "I know. He figured me for property, like his women."

Trapped, he floundered about. "I, I didn't like it—didn't see how to say no, when he got insistent—"

"Why should I blame you?" she asked soothingly.

"But I think you should know—I'd like you to know—" He struggled. "When I was alone with her, I couldn't."

"Oh, Kenmuir."

"The situation, and, and clearly she didn't care—I said I was very tired, and she yawned, and . . . we both went to sleep."

Aleka threw back her head. Her laughter rang.

In Kenmuir, chagrin faded to ruefulness. His heart thuttered less loudly. After all, how important was this? Lilisaire. Meanwhile, he had—reassured?—his friend.

Aleka sobered. "I'm sorry," she said.

"Don't be." He managed a smile. "It is rather funny."

She took his other hand as well and looked directly up at him. "You're a lovely man, you are. And we have no idea where we're bound. Most likely to failure. Maybe we'll go free, maybe not. But Pele grins."

He waited.

"We've got tonight," she said.

He woke once. An old-style window, open to cool air and a breeze that lulled in leaves, faced west. The Moon shone through. It barely brought from shadow the curves along shoulder and arm and cheek where she lay breathing close against his side. Happiness welled quietly up in him. For this short spell, the Moon was the home of peace.

38

The Mother of the Moon

They found Dagny Beynac on the north rim trail. She had left her car at the shelter and gone afoot, alone, in an hour when no one else was about. It was a fairly easy hike, which she had often made, even in recent years; but her heart was old—"paper-thin," she had said, as if she felt it flutter in a wind from outside space-time—and on the heights it failed her.

Or perhaps it did not, some among the party thought. A biomonitor in her suit would have flashed an alarm to bring the paramedics within minutes. They might have been able to restart her body. Although at her age self-clone transplants were not feasible, surrogates might have kept her alive in a maintenance unit for several more years. The team discovered that, without mentioning it, she had long since removed her monitor.

For an equally long while her habit of going topside by herself, leaving no word behind, had been the despair of her friends. When they protested, she reminded them cheerfully that she was rambling the Moon before they, and usually their parents, were born. This was her choice.

Certainly the last sight she saw had been magnificent. Here a crest ran along the top of the ringwall, high and narrow enough that to southward she spied the crater floor. That part was deeply shadowed, but the central peak thrust up into light athwart ramparts visible above the opposite horizon. Closer by, a radio mast gleamed like a victorious lance. Northward the slopes flowed down with the gentleness of Lunar rock, sharp edges worn away by skyfall, in highlights and sable. Beyond them the terrain was brighter than most, impact splash which farther onward fingered out in great rays. Mountains guarded that rim of vision. Radiance went in a tide from an Earth near the full, blue and white, the colors of sea and air, dappled with land. Elsewhere in the night burned a few brightest stars. It was the dwelling place of silence.

When her absence raised fears, the Tychopolis constabulary ordered a satellite scan. Lunarian legislators had bargained to get a law that that was done at such resolution only in emergencies. Beynac had supported them, making tart remarks about privacy. Opticals picked out the huddled shape almost at once and a squad hastened to it; but that was hours after the death.

Luna mourned. On Earth, every Fireball flag went to half-staff.

The news triggered various programs she had prepared. Most of them concerned just the tidying up of affairs. Half a dozen were messages, each personally encrypted for the recipient. One went to Lars Rydberg on Vancouver Island.

Dearest Lars,

When this reaches you I shall be gone. Farewell, fare always well, you and yours whom I have loved.

Maybe we will have been together again after the date above. Probably we'll at least have talked by phone, as good as you are about calling. When last we did, your reserve broke down a little and you said the transmission lag, which otherwise you shrug off, felt like a small bleeding. You hurried on to something else, and I waited to cry till we were done. Yes, every time of late we have known we might not get another time. We haven't voiced it—why should we?—but months ago I noticed, a bit surprised, that my "hasta la vista" to you had become "vaya con Dios." Go with God.

Now you will weep. I hope you don't keep solitary, but let Ulla comfort you. It is a gift you can give her, you know. Sten, Olaf, Linnea, Anson, William, Lucia, Runa, their spouses and children and children's children, no, I cannot find words for them except, "How blessed I have been. Thank you, thank you."

That is true, darling. My life was a glorious adventure. Remember me, miss me, but never pity me. There have been things I would change if I could. Of course. Above all, I would have had my Edmond and my Kaino live out their days. But the joy that was ours did not die in me; and what wonders became mine! I not only saw a dead world bloom to life and a new race arise, I helped bring it about, I helped lead us toward liberty, and meanwhile humans went to the ends of the sun's kingdom and I was warmed by undeservedly much love. I will not let these riches go from me in dribs and drabs, among machines and chemicals, the eyes kept open while the brain behind them shrivels. No, I will live on, gladly, till I can no longer live free. Then, the medical data give reason to hope, I shall depart quickly and cleanly and altogether ready.

Afterward—I don't suppose "afterward" means anything in this case. "Go with God" is a wish that you go in safety and happiness, no more. Maybe I'm wrong. It would be a new adventure to find out!

Regardless, nobody ever quite leaves the living universe. What we have done travels on and on, we cannot tell how far, before it's lost in the cosmic noise. Closer to hand, duties remain to carry out, decencies to respect, mercies to grant.

And so I appeal to you, my Earth-son. You will understand what my dear Moon-children cannot. You, who have become a power within mighty Fireball, yet are wholly human, can do what neither Anson Guthrie nor any Selenarch is quite able to.

Oh, you will keep your troth. You will stay Guthrie's man as you promised long ago. I ask just that you set aside whatever weariness of age is on you and volunteer to him your services in the cause of Lunar peace.

You have the insights, the connections, the experience, everything I showed you and confided in you and got you involved with. No, you will not be the never-existent indispensable man. But you can play a very large—and very quiet; I know you—role in the coming years. It will be hard, thankless, often maddening, possibly catastrophic, but it will better the odds, and what more can we mortals do?

Herewith is a file, which I keep updated. It summarizes the situation, the factors I believe are important, and any recommendations that occur to me. You will see that much of this is confidential. I trust you. I trust you also to study it. Then, if you agree you can make a difference, you will go to Guthrie. And God go with you.

What else? They talk of building a great tomb for my ashes, come the day. I thought of asking you to intervene as best you can, try to have them scattered where Edmond's lie. But no, Verdea is passionate about what this would mean to everybody. If they really want it, let them. It won't matter to me. Save your efforts for the living and the not yet born.

What does matter, though—be kind to my download.

I think that's all. As you in your heart bid me goodnight, wish the children, from me, a good morning.

Your
Mother

39

Kenmuir drew to attention. *"Hola, señor,"* he greeted. Aleka crossed hands on breasts and bowed. The woman who had escorted them from the gate saluted.

The huge old man in the huge old room looked up from his hearthside chair. Lighting was turned low and the fire cast flickers over him. Its crackle mingled with an undertone of music—a contemporary piece that Kenmuir recognized, Nomura's "Symphonic Variations on Sibelius's 'Swan of Tuonela.'" As somber in the dimness were the portraits that stared from their frames. Through the windows he saw the long Northern dusk deepening into night.

"So you're back, Ian Kenmuir," Matthias rumbled.

"Yes, sir," the pilot said. "May I introduce Aleka

Kame?" He could never think of her by the Anglo version of her name.

"Bienvenida, señorita."

"Gracias," she replied uncertainly. "You are very kind to receive us like this, on no notice, señor."

"Kenmuir called troth when you arrived. Besides, I'm . . . curious."

"We have more to tell than a peculiar story, sir," Kenmuir said.

The Rydberg nodded. "That's plain to see."

"We need to speak with you in privacy."

"Equally obvious. Sit." Matthias gestured. Kenmuir and Aleka went to get chairs. Meanwhile Matthias addressed their escort: "Did you hear, Gould? Seal of secrecy. I want you to inform the staff, each individual person in the house and on the grounds." He described their whereabouts.

Aleka took the opportunity to whisper to Kenmuir, "Will that work?"

"Yes. Troth," he answered, not quite so shyly. "But for my part—I can't lie to him, you know."

"Why should you?"

"Nor expect him—nor ask him—to act against his judgment of what's best for all the Fireball consortes."

"Or for all living things. I understand."

They brought their chairs back to face the lodgemaster's carven seat. As he sat down, Kenmuir felt how weary he was. It was a physical tiredness, though, warm and loose-boned. This day's tramp along upland greenwood trails to the sea had been as heartening as the half-sorrowful bliss last night. Aleka, beside him, took his hand.

Gould departed. "Ease off," Matthias said to Aleka. "Nothing that anybody here sees or hears will go past these bounds without my leave." Her grip tightened before she let go. ·

"Not that we'll expose them to more than necessary," Matthias continued. "But we do want service." He touched a button on the arm of his chair. "You two must be exhausted, and hungry as black holes. Wouldn't you like to eat first, rest, sleep?"

"I don't believe I could, señor," Aleka replied.

Kenmuir nodded agreement. "Maybe coffee and a bite of something, if the Rydberg pleases."

"I thought so," Matthias said. A boy entered. "What'll you have, Srta. Kame?"

Aleka smiled. "Bueno, if I might ask for a protein cake and a beer, that'd be wonderful." She was indeed a lusty sort, Kenmuir thought. Before him rose memory of their noontide pause at a spring. She splashed him, laughing, and when she kissed him the water dewed her lips, and she was firm and bouncy and her sweat smelled sweet. Matthias chuckled and gave the order. The attendant left.

Matthias leaned back, bridged his fingers, and inquired in a matter-of-fact voice, "Where did you come from today? Sprucetop? . . . Yes, that seemed likely. Covering your tracks."

"It's a long story, sir," Kenmuir said.

"And we ourselves don't know the half of it," Aleka added. "Not yet, anyhow."

"I suspect there are those who don't want you to," Matthias replied. "Go on, then, talk, at your own pace."

They began, haltingly at first, breaking when the boy returned. Aleka attacked her beer with unabashed enthusiasm, and thereafter spoke in lively wise of her background and part. Kenmuir did most of the relating. Matthias kept throwing questions at them, like missiles. Once he said:

"An officer of theirs was here about a week ago. He wanted to know about you, Captain Kenmuir. I was not cooperative. Pragmatic Venator, he called himself."

"Pele!" Aleka gasped. She sat bolt upright. "The same who—"

When he had heard, Matthias scowled into the fire and directed the scuttler robot to poke it up and throw on another log. The flames snapped loud now that the music was ended. "Ar-r-rh," he growled. "This *is* a crisis matter."

"But why?" she protested. "We've tried and tried, Ian and I, and we can't guess what's wrong."

"Go on," he ordered.

They did.

"—and so we came here," Kenmuir finished.

"Why?" Matthias asked.

"Where else? A few friends, like Sam Packer, might help us hide for a little bit longer, but what use?"

From beneath shaggy brows, eyes took aim and held steady. "Whereas you imagine Fireball, in my person, can arm you for this quixotry whose very meaning you don't know? Whatever gave you such an idea?"

Kenmuir sighed. "Desperation."

"And I had nothing better to suggest," Aleka said tonelessly.

His weariness began to ache in Kenmuir. "We realize it's all but hopeless. Still, Fireball is world-wide, even if our consortes aren't many, and—"

The Rydberg lifted a finger. "And you'd call on it to aid this Lunarian bitch who wants to keep our kind out of space?"

"No, sir, no. She only wants to save her society."

"Her society. Precisely. She, among the handful who own it."

"That isn't true, sir. Not that simple or, or anything—" Kenmuir's words died away. He sagged back in his chair.

Aleka stayed defiant. "It isn't, señor. I don't know much about Lunarians, but I do know what it means to see your whole life go under. There are my people."

The massive head nodded. "There are, lass," Matthias said, gone gentle. "They're strangers to me, but I'm not forgetting them."

"We're not actually appealing to you, sir," Kenmuir said. "I wouldn't want the Trothdom to risk itself."

"That is a factor in the equation, aye."

"And what could Fireball do, anyhow? Nothing, probably. Maybe help us two out of the worst consequences of our folly. Aleka, at least. She's innocent."

The woman stiffened. "Like fury I am!" she cried.

Did Matthias smile, very faintly, or was it a trick of light weaving over the furrows of his face? "Don't jump to conclusions," he said. "They're apt to stand on slippery ground." Kenmuir knew it for a Guthrie quotation, and opened his mouth. "Silence."

For a span, only the fire talked, while Matthias brooded and night gathered outside.

The old man said at last, perhaps to himself, like remote thunder: "Proserpina, the lost—Kaino, son of Dagny Beynac—Yes, surely she—"

He was still again, for a minute or three that grew long, before he turned his gaze on the visitors and spoke aloud:

"One indisputable fact in all this fog. The Federation government has systematically, for lifetimes, concealed potentially important data. It's bending every effort to maintain that concealment. No reason given, no justification. Clean against the Covenant." He looked away, out the window into the darkness. "What else is hidden? My whole life, I've felt the walls closing in."

He fell silent anew. Kenmuir's flagging pulse picked up till it hammered in his skull.

Matthias hunched his heavy shoulders. "I have to think about this. Think hard. Not much sleep for me tonight. But you two, you need your rest."

"Oh, señor—" Aleka breathed.

Matthias pressed the button. "You will take your rest," he commanded. "Whatever I decide, I want you fit for action. Trouble me no further." The attendant came in. "Berghall, see to this pair. Bath, clean clothes, good supper, quarters."

The boy stood erect. "Señor." Pride shone from him.

"Go," Matthias said. "We'll meet in the morning."

* * *

In a room upstairs where relics of ancient farings—a spaceship model, a glittery Moon rock, a view of the first human camp ever on Mars, a faded photograph of Anson Guthrie with his wife and children—rested like dreams come to harbor, two people could find their way to a renewed inner peace.

Nevertheless, as he was dropping off to sleep, Kenmuir wondered what thought of Dagny Beynac had been in the Rydberg. It was as if, at just that instant, the deep voice had stumbled.

40

The Mother of the Moon

While the hours become daycycles, tension mounts. Sometimes Dagny can snatch an interlude of the low-level activity that is a download's equivalent of sleep, but it is brief and always she is roused from it by the next upward ratcheting of the crisis.

Nominally she is no more than a member of the Provisional Trust, which has a doubtful standing. It is not the home rule government that, legally, should speak for Luna. It is a group that the legislature in Tsukimachi has called into existence and charged with negotiations. She had much to do with maneuvering enough deputies into voting for it, and with persuading Governor General Haugen that his veto would bring the open breach he fears.

In effect, the Trust has become the Lunar government, for it includes the Selenarchs who scornfully ignored a congress now impotent and irrelevant. True, representatives come also from the cities, the major industries and professions, the Terrans who want to stay on the Moon whatever happens. But all desire full independence. To that end, when they see fit they issue decrees which local magistrates put into action.

The power is sharply limited. Luna is still subject to the World Federation. Peace Authority forces have

been redoubled. If any significant international stat-
ute is violated, the governor is to order the Trust
dissolved and proclaim martial law.

Dagny is a delegate at large, chosen by the others
and taking her seat at their urgent request. It has
become she whose word is most heeded by them, who
composes their differences for them, and who oftenest
speaks on behalf of them. More than once, this has
been directly to Federation President Daniel Janvier
in Hiroshima. Such *mana* does the Beynac name
have. It may be even stronger in the download than it
was in the living woman. A robotic presence can seem
impersonal, impartial. And underneath, does there go
a dark mythic shiver . . . at the voice from beyond the
grave, the oracular hero?

Politics on Earth gropes and fumbles. The Lunar
question can no longer wait. Unrest, agitation, riots
and boycotts and subtler seditions, rumors of forbidden weapons secretly manufactured, hitches in production and trade, warnings from Fireball that worse
will probably befall, have thrust aside matters that
hitherto seemed closer to home. In the night sky the
full Moon hangs like a bomb. Janvier summons a
special session of the High Council and Assembly.

Debate drags and lurches. The North Americans
and Russians, especially, abhor the precedent; if common heritage is ended on Luna, when then of the
whole Solar System? The Chinese and Australians
deem the principle obsolete. The Indonesians recall
forebears who freed themselves from colonial masters. The Siberians feel that their own example is
more apposite. Oratory burgeons like fungus. The
president and some of the parliamentarians strive to
keep proceedings on course.

For humanity in general, everyday life goes on. The
download has none, nor time for it.

The measures take form. They reach the floor.
Autonomy passes. Luna shall be recognized as a
Federation member after a democratic constitution
with proper safeguards has been drafted, approved,

and ratified. Across Earth, banners fly and crowds cheer.

The Provisional Trust rejects the program.

It insists on total independence, absolute sovereignty. It will honor the pledges made in a statement of position issued last year: property settlements, emigration assistance, trade and arms control treaties. But this shall be voluntary. Luna shall have complete freedom to make its future as it will.

Dagny knew this would be the response. She forewarned Janvier. He replied that he must do what he could with what he had. Now he denounces the refusal. However, he does not declare the Trust disbanded. He promises to try persuasion. He and Dagny understand that this is a token. "I wish it weren't," she says to him on the encrypted laser. "I'd infinitely prefer a republic. But that is not suited for Lunarians, and they are my people."

Indignation seethes on Earth. Terrans riot on the Moon. Constabulary and Peace Authority have their hands full, restoring and enforcing order.

The High Council of the World Federation directs the president to call up the Authority reserves. Several governments offer to reinforce these, if necessary, with men and matériel from their national militias.

Communications fly across space. Astromonitors observe and report a score of ships returning sunward from the asteroid belt. Upon inquiry, they identify themselves as the law requires: Lunarian-owned freighters for the mining and extraction operations that a few magnates conduct yonder. These enterprises are petty compared to, say, Fireball's or Maharashtra's; but the vessels are big and nuclear-engined.

"They cannot be coming back simultaneously by coincidence!" exclaims Janvier.

Transmission lag.

"No," agrees download Dagny Beynac, "but as long as they follow safe traffic patterns, they are not obliged to give reasons. I've asked, and received no answer except that this is private business. It may be a precautionary move of some kind. I suggest you underplay, or you could have mass hysteria on top of your other problems."

Transmission lag.

"That may not be avoidable," he says grimly.

The ships do not take Lunar orbit, as they would if shuttles were to bring their cargoes down. They ease into paths around the Earth-Moon system. Such orbits are unstable, and from time to time thrust corrects them.

"They must vacate," Janvier states. His image in the screen is haggard, sweat beading cheeks and brow. "From where they are, they could accelerate inward, open their hatches, and shovel rocks at meteor speed down on our cities."

Transmission lag.

"Don't force the issue yet," Dagny advises. "It would be a crazy thing for them to do, you know. Most of the stuff would burn up in the atmosphere. What little reached the surface would be gravel size, and trajectory control impossible. Everything would likeliest fall in the ocean or onto empty fields."

—"That is if it is ordinary stuff, ore, ingots, dust, ice. How do we know they haven't forged massive, aerodynamic missiles out there?"

—"It would still be insane. Whenever Earth wants to make an all-out effort, it can crush Luna utterly. Killing millions of people would reliably provoke that. I assure you, the Selenarchs are not loco."

—"I suppose so, although sometimes I wonder. But I have to deal with the public reaction. When the news is released, and that is inevitable soon, any 'cast will show you what it is like. I beg you, convince those arrogant barons and tycoons they have miscalculated."

—"I am not certain they have, señor. I am certain that the politicians of Earth miscalculated gravely. Let us try together, from our different sides, for emotional damage control."

Janvier invokes emergency powers granted under the Covenant and commands the Lunarian ships to go. They make no reply. The Trust declares that the order has no legal force, because simply adopting an unusual orbit poses no threat, nor has one been spoken.

Lunarians in the cities occasionally set aside their dignity and leer at passing Earthfolk. The air well-nigh smells of oncoming lightning.

The Federation and its member governments keep no spacecraft capable of attack. Indeed, they have scant space transport of any sort. Normally they have contracted with Fireball, thereby sparing themselves both the capital cost and the expensive, cumbersome bureaucracies they would have been sure to establish.

Fireball declines to move against the Lunarian vessels. What, a private company undertaking para-military operations? It would be a violation of the Covenant. For that matter, Anson Guthrie announces, Fireball will not provide the extra bottom needed for lifting more troops to the Moon. He holds that the move would be disastrously unwise, and his organization cannot in conscience support it.

In Hiroshima the speaker for Ecuador, where Fireball is incorporated, explains that her government concurs with Sr. Guthrie and will not compel him. She strongly urges giving the Lunarians their self-determination, and introduces a motion to that effect.

However, Fireball and Ecuador will not tolerate bombardment of Earth. Should such happen, every resource will be made available for pacification of the Moon and punishment of the criminals. Meanwhile, they offer their good offices toward mediating the dispute.

Lars Rydberg goes to Luna as Fireball's plenipotentiary.

His public statements are few and curt. For the most part he is alone with the download. This is natural and somewhat reassuring. Day by day, the terror on Earth ebbs.

The Assembly reopens the independence question. Speeches are shorter and more to the point than before. Divisions are becoming clear-cut. On the one side, the advocates of releasing Luna have gained recruits among their colleagues and in their constituencies. If the alternative amounts to war, it is unacceptable. The Lunarians have the right to be what they are, and as their unique civilization flowers, ours will share in its achievements. On the other side, the heritage persuasion has hardened and has also made converts. Furthermore, it is argued, nationalism wrought multimillions of deaths, over and over, with devastation from which the world has never quite recovered. Here we see the monster hatching anew. We must crush its head while we still can.

The news explodes: Selenarchs have dispatched units of their retainers to occupy powerbeam stations "and protect them for the duration of the present exigency." The squadrons are well-organized and formidably equipped—with small arms, as the Covenant allows if you strain an interpretation, but equal to anything that the Peace Authority force on the Moon can bring against them. Besides, although the Selenarchs are noncommittal about it, rumors fly of heavier weapons. A catapult, easily and cheaply made, can throw a missile halfway around the Moon.

Be that as it may, a transmission unit would scarcely survive a battle for possession of it.

—Janvier: "This is rebellion. Fireball promised help in case of outright violence."

—Rydberg: "Sir, I am not a lawyer. I cannot judge the legality of the action. According to the Provisional Trust, it is justified under the law of dire necessity. Think how dependent Earth is on the solar energy from Luna."

—Janvier: "Oh, yes. They suppose they have us by the throat. I say this is as suicidal a threat as those ships pose, but a great many human beings would die, and I call on Fireball to do its duty."

—Rydberg: "Sir, we could take out the ships, at

enormous cost, but how can we handle the situation on the ground? Let me repeat, Lord Brandir and his associates do not make it a threat. They do not want cities darkened, services halted, panic and crime and death over Earth. No, they will guard those stations from sabotage by extremists here on the Moon."

—Janvier: "What of the sites they have not occupied?"

—Rydberg: "True, they can watch only a few. They consider it an object lesson."

—Janvier: "Hm. I say again, they are trying to take us by the throat."

—Rydberg: "And *I* say, with respect, they are demonstrating what could, what would happen on a world of wild individualists who felt they were under a foreign tyranny. . . . Please, I am not on their side myself, I am simply telling you what they believe. . . . Can the Peace Authority secure the network? Yes, if first you commit genocide on the Lunarians. Otherwise you must guard the whole of it, at unbearable expense, and the guard will keep failing, because they are Terrans, not Lunarians, and as for robots, humans can always find ways to outwit them."

—"Whereas the Selenarchs, if they rule the Moon, can effectively maintain the system?"

—"Yes, Mr. President. They have the organization and the loyal, able followers. They will not have the revolutionary saboteurs."

—"Are you certain?"

—"Nothing is certain forever. I am speaking of today, our children's lifetimes, and I hope our grandchildren's. By then, Earth may no longer need power from Luna."

—"But meanwhile the Selenarchs can blackmail us."

—"Consider their psychology, sir. Those utilities enjoy huge earnings. Why jeopardize that? Lunarians are not interested in dominion over . . . our kind of humans."

—"Then what games do they mean to play?"

—"That I cannot tell you. I wonder if they can, themselves. The future will show. I only say, this game is played out and you should concede."

Undetectable in circuit, Dagny has followed the conversation. It is her wont.

Whipsaw, from a degree of relief about a firestorm from space to a dread of global energy famine. The peoples of Earth and their leaders are alike exhausted. It is easiest to accept the assurances, override the remaining opposition, and yield. After all, the positive inducements are substantial.

The measure comes to the floor. It passes. The Council ratifies, the president signs. Once the stipulated compensatory arrangements have been made, Luna shall be free and sovereign.

Baronial men leave the transmitters. The circling ships enter Lunar orbit and discharge cargoes that turn out to be quite commonplace. As part of the accord, these craft will soon be in Terrestrial hands.

No gatherings jubilate. On Earth, the mood is mostly a dull thankfulness that the confrontation is past. Lunarians are not given to mass histrionics. Terran Moondwellers who feel happy with the outcome celebrate apart. As for those who do not, they begin preparing to emigrate.

Alone, Dagny and Rydberg speak. She wears a bipedal robot body. Weary to the depths of her spirit, if downloads have any, she will not simulate the image of the dead woman; but neither will she be a mere voice.

"It worked," she sighs: for she has mastered the making of human sounds. "Between the Trust, Fireball, Brandir and his fellows, the space captains—"

"Do not forget yourself," he says.

The faceless head shakes. "No, nor those I haven't named. You know who they were. Never mind. What we set up and played through, the whole charade, it worked. I honestly doubted it would. But what else was there to try?"

His tone goes metallic. "If it had failed, it would have stopped being a charade."

"Yes. Janvier realized that. Do you realize that he did? It succeeded because reality stood behind it."

"And it was simpler than what's ahead of us."

"You'll navigate, I'm sure."

He gives her a long look, as if it were into living eyes. "We will?"

"Luna, Earth, Fireball, everybody."

"Except you?"

"I've been useful—"

"What a poor word, . . . Mother!"

A robot cannot weep. "I kept her promise for her. Now let me go."

"Do you want to die?" he whispers.

She forms a laugh. "What the hell does that question mean, for me?"

He must take a moment before he can say it. "Do you want your program wiped? Made nothing?"

"Your mother set that condition before she agreed to be downloaded. I hold you to it."

"Anson Guthrie goes on."

"He is he. I am I." Oh, Dagny Beynac loved life, but to her, being an abstraction was not life. Nor does the revenant care to evolve into something else, alien to her Edmond.

"The time could come—very likely will come—when they have need of you again."

"No. They should never think they need one person that much."

Her gaze captures his and holds it. Beneath his thin white hair is a countenance gone well-nigh skeletal. He is near the century mark himself. Yet he was born to a girl named Dagny Ebbesen.

After a long time, he slumps back in his chair and says unevenly, "The, the termination will be a big event, you know."

If she were making an image, it would have smiled. "I'm afraid so. See it through."

"I already hear talk about it. The same tomb for you—"

"Why not, if they wish?"

A gesture, a symbol, a final service rendered. This hardware and the blanked software may as well rest there as anyplace else. The site may even become a halidom, like Thermopylae or Bodhgaya, around which hearts can irrationally rally. Besides, she likes the thought that that which was her will lie beside the ash that was Dagny Beynac beneath the stars that shone on 'Mond.

41

Fog rolled in during the night. By sunrise it had cloaked Guthrie House in a gray-white where the closest trees, two or three meters from a window, were shadows and everything else was formless. Air lay cold and damp and very quiet. You could just hear the hush of waves along the shore and perhaps a dripping from the eaves.

At breakfast Matthias, Kenmuir, and Aleka exchanged no more than muttered greetings, for it was plain to see that the lodgemaster wanted silence. But when the last cup of coffee had been drained, he rose and growled, "Follow me." The others went after his bulk, out into the hall, up the stairs, down another hall to a certain door which he opened, and through. He closed it behind them.

"I believe it's right we talk here," he said.

Kenmuir and Aleka glanced about. Unlighted save for what seeped through the fog from a hidden sun, the room would have been dim were its walls and ceiling not so white. A few ancient pictures decorated it, family scenes, landscapes, a view of Earth from orbit. Drapes hung at the tall windows. The floor was bare hardwood. Furniture was sparse and likewise from early times, four chairs, a dresser, a cabinet, a bed. In one corner stood a man-high mechanical clock. Its pendulum swung slowly and somehow inexorably; the ticking seemed loud in this stillness.

A chill ran through Kenmuir. The hair stood up on his arms. He knew where he was.

"For privacy?" Aleka was asking.

"No," Matthias replied. "I told you, the estate is spyproof and everybody on it is a sworn consorte. But here is where mortal Anson Guthrie died."

Her eyes grew large. She made a sign that Kenmuir did not recognize.

Then she looked more closely at Matthias, stooped shoulders, lines graven deeper than before in a face where the nose stood forth like a mountain ridge, and murmured, "You really didn't sleep much, did you?"

"There'll be time for that later," he said. "All the time in the universe."

Heavily, he sat down and gestured his visitors to do so. They put their chairs side by side. Aleka's hand found Kenmuir's. What comfort flowed from hers into his!

Matthias raised his head. "But we haven't much of it just now," he warned. "The hunters don't know you're here. If they did, we'd be under arrest already. They're searching, though, and surveying, and thinking. Before long, Venator or a squad of his will return. Meanwhile, if you leave in any ordinary way, you'll surely be spotted. Disguises won't help. They'll stop everyone for a close look."

The eeriness tingled again down Kenmuir's spine. "There's a way that's not ordinary?"

"You'll help us, señor?" Aleka joined in.

Matthias nodded. "What little I can. Or, rather, I'll hope to help the cause of freedom."

"You decided this last night?" Kenmuir asked, and realized at once how stupid the question was.

Matthias's voice marched on, toneless but clocksteady. "It wasn't easy. I'll be breaking a promise as old as the Trothdom and as strong as any I ever gave.

And it may be for nothing, or it may be for the worse. Why are they so determined to keep Proserpina from us? I should think if the Lunarians got knowledge of it, access to it, they wouldn't oppose the Habitat—at least, not with force enough to matter. And the Habitat is our way to the stars." He breathed for a moment. "Or is it? I don't know, I don't know."

Aleka heard the pain. She released Kenmuir's hand and reached over to grasp his.

He closed the great knobbly paw about hers and held it for two or three heartbeats before he let go. A smile ghosted briefly over his lips. "Gracias, querida," he sighed. "I did think about you too, and your people."

Resonantly: "And I thought over and over how high-handed, how unlawful Venator's gang is being. If the Federation government can do this to us, concealing a fact that would change thousands of lives, maybe change the course of history, what else is it doing? What will it do next? Guthrie used to quote a proverb about not letting the camel's nose into your tent. I think more than its nose is in. Bloody near the whole camel is. Or soon will be, if we sit meek."

"Could they have a decent reason for the secrecy?" she asked low.

Kenmuir spoke. Anger had been crystallizing in him too, sharp and cold. "At best, they aren't even offering that much of an excuse. They're treating us like children."

"Children of the cybercosm," Matthias agreed. "Or wards, or pets, or domestic animals."

Trouble trembled in Aleka's face and words. "Most people feel free and happy."

"Most dogs do," Matthias said.

"I'm not against you, señor. I just can't help wondering—the larger good, also for my people—"

"Either we act or we don't," Kenmuir snapped.

"Yes." She straightened. "Bueno, let's act, then, and take the responsibility for whatever comes of it, like—like free adult humans."

Kenmuir decided he should utter another question whose answer he was almost sure of, if only to get it out of the way. "Could we simply broadcast what we know? I suppose Guthrie House has the equipment. It's got plenty of every other kind I can think of."

"I considered that," Matthias admitted. "No. It wouldn't be any real use. I've lived on Earth and dealt with the powers that be long enough to have learned what works, and how, and what doesn't work. A bare statement like that—too easily denied, and guided down the public memory hole. Meanwhile Venator and his merry men would have seized us. They might all too well pick up clues to Fireball's secret, and go blot it out."

Kenmuir's fists clenched. Aleka half sprang to her feet, sank back down, and whispered, "Ian's told me about—the Founder's Word?"

"Yes." The Rydberg's voice tolled. "It came to me near the end of this night what I must do. Then I could sleep for a bit. It's right that this be where."

The sanctuary, the shrine, Kenmuir thought.

The hands of the clock reached XII and VII. It boomed forth the hour. A breeze outside made the fog swirl at the windows like smoke.

"Not that the knowledge will necessarily save you," Matthias went on. "Odds are that it won't. If you think the gamble is sheerly loco, I swear you never to speak of this again, not even between yourselves, not ever again."

"I swear," Aleka said as if it were a prayer.

"By my troth," Kenmuir declared.

"And yet the story is the story of a vow that was broken," Matthias said.

They waited.

After a minute had ticked away, he continued: "Lars Rydberg promised his mother Dagny Beynac that if she'd download, then when the download's work was done he'd wipe its program and give it oblivion. The download itself asked him to, and again he promised."

"But he didn't?" Aleka breathed while Kenmuir's pulse stumbled.

"No. When at last he'd turned the network off and stood alone with it, there where they'd said goodbye —he'd kissed the hard box between its optic stalks— he thought about what it, no, she had done. How she'd piloted Luna and, yes, Earth through the revolution, how without her it could easily have become catastrophe, how precarious the situation still was and how sorely she might be needed. To her, switchoff was the same as wipeout, unless she was reactivated. He told the world he'd done what he said he would, and he brought her to Dagny's tomb to rest by Dagny's ashes, and with everything he was he hoped it could be forever. But he bore the burden of this to his grave."

"He shared it with a son of his," Aleka knew.

"Yes. In case, just in case. And so onward through time."

"She never was called back," Aleka concluded. "The secret became a Fireball tradition, no more. Going to Luna and redeeming Lars's promise, that must have appeared to later Rydbergs like breaching their own."

"Till now."

"Raising her—" Kenmuir croaked out of a dry throat.

"She, alive, certainly knew about Proserpina," Matthias said. "She must have heard or seen written down what its orbital elements are. She probably remembered them—always had a strong memory, the biographies tell—and therefore her download did too. Anyhow, closely enough that any astronomer or spacefarer could easily find it. Once that information is out, the hoarding of the truth is finished."

For whatever value it might have to Lilisaire, Kenmuir thought. But never mind. He was committed, as much to Aleka and her cause as to anyone or anything else, including an end to his own outlawry. "You'll send an agent?" he asked.

Matthias didn't seem to have heard him, but proceeded: "This may be quite useless, understand. The download has lain there for centuries. The tomb won't have screened out all the cosmic radiation, and there's the inherent background too. Mutilated chips, scrambled electronics, cumulative damage never repaired. By now, maybe nothing that will function is left."

"Or maybe a dement—" Horror wrenched out of Aleka. "Oh, no!"

"Maybe not," Kenmuir reassured her. "In fact, from what I know of such things, I'd guess the chances are good that the system's still in working order." He spoke with more confidence than he felt.

Aleka grimaced. "Don't call her a system."

"I'm prepared to have you try, and shoulder my share of whatever guilt will follow," Matthias said. "Are you?"

It thrilled in Kenmuir. "Yes."

Aleka blinked back tears. "Yes."

"But your idea of sending an agent—No, I'm afraid not," Matthias said.

"Why?" Kenmuir inquired.

"Think." Matthias had had the night, alone, in which to do so. "None of the staff here are qualified. I'd have to call someone in, and brief him not only on the mission but on the technical details. That's an antique machine, don't forget. Nothing like it is in use today. And he'd need equipment. Now we can be certain Guthrie House is under remote but high-resolution robotic surveillance, at the minimum. Do you imagine anybody could leave here with a mess of gear, take passage for Luna, and go out to Dagny's tomb—isolated, the holiest ground on the Moon—without Venator knowing? And acting?"

"And . . . wiping the program," Aleka said.

"And coming here for us," Kenmuir added. "But, um, couldn't the man simply tell Lilisaire in her castle? She might be able to do something. If not enter the tomb, then instigate a search for Proserpina."

"In due course, if all else fails, that can be tried," Matthias said without enthusiasm. "I'll arrange for an

encrypted message to a trustworthy man, with instructions to decrypt it and convey it after a given
length of time, when perhaps Venator's corps is less
vigilant. But I'd not be hopeful. If they haven't found
a pretext to arrest her, which I expect they will have,
she'll at least stay under close watch. Remember, they
know that you know the asteroid exists. Could she or
any of her kind mount a search, astronomical or in
spacecraft, even by Lunarians in the outer System,
without Venator guessing what they were about and
moving to stop them? I doubt it."

"And meanwhile *we'll* have failed, and be done
for." Once more Kenmuir had a sense of fingers
closing on him.

Aleka struck them aside. "But you have a way,
señor. You must, or you wouldn't have spoken."

"Yes," Matthias answered, and abruptly his voice
sounded almost young. "A mad way, a wild hunt, but
it might work, it barely might work."

Understanding flashed into Kenmuir. *"Kestrel!"* he
yelled.

Aleka stared at him. "What?"

He could not stay seated, he leaped up and paced, to
and fro, arousal going through him in surges like the
sea waves out beyond the mists. "The spacecraft, the
relic, Kyra Davis's ship. We keep it always ready to
lift—"

She gasped.

Matthias's tones quickened: "Including spacesuits,
modern self-adjusting ones, EVA drive packs, and
everything else." Otherwise the symbolism would
have been hollow. Suddenly Kenmuir realized, fully,
why the Trothdom had fought, and paid a high price
in things yielded during negotiations, for the right to
maintain an antimatter-powered vessel on Earth. *Kestrel* was not the first sacred object in human history.
Of course, any launch was forbidden. He heard
through his blood: "A short flight, if you can pilot her,
Captain Kenmuir."

"I can study it up," he said, faintly amazed at the

levelness of his voice. "You have vivifer material about that model, so we won't have to tap the public database, don't you?"

"But the whole world will see!" Aleka exclaimed.

Matthias grinned. "Right. Something that spectacular can't be kept entirely off the news, and the Teramind itself will be hard put to explain it away."

Sobriety slid into Kenmuir's passion. "Unless Venator's service heads me off in time."

"They have craft with far greater capabilities, true, and they'll react fast," Matthias said. "But you'll take them by surprise, and they won't know where you're bound till you've landed. Then you'll have to be quick, oh, yes."

In for a penny, in for a pound. Kenmuir laughed aloud. "We'll plan the operation. You can get data on what Authority units are currently stationed where or in which orbits, can't you? That's public information. And I've got an idea about how to keep them from silencing me once they've caught me. Come, let's get busy!"

"'Auwē no hō'i ē," Aleka murmured. "You surprise me, you do. I didn't expect I'd ever see you in a state like this."

"I've work ahead of me," was all Kenmuir could find to say.

She rose and regarded him closely. "One thing, amigo. What's this 'I'? You're not going alone."

His pacing jarred to a halt. "What? You? Untrained and—and vulnerable—No, ridiculous."

"I'm a quick study," Aleka said. "I can learn what I'll need to be of some help." She addressed Matthias. "Can't I, señor?"

The Rydberg smiled. "I believe you had better have a partner, Captain Kenmuir. I'm too decrepit. This lass strikes me as being potentially the most competent person we have on hand."

"Besides," Aleka told them, "it's my mission too. And, and, Pele's teeth, Ian, I won't *let* you go without me!"

42

God speed you." The ancient words seemed to follow Kenmuir and Aleka out of Guthrie House. Matthias did not, nor anyone else. Alone, they crossed the lawn toward the forest.

Light streamed from a sun close to the sea. It set grass and the massed needles of trees aglow. The Moon stood in deepening blue nearly as high as it was going to mount. Though the day's mildness lingered, Kenmuir pulled his hooded cloak tighter about him. He would have wished for clouds to veil this freehold a little from the seeing, unseen orbiting robots.

But for the quickest passage today, launch must be now; and to wait would be to run a worse risk. Into the past fifty-odd hours, less a few for sleep, had been crammed as much preparation as was possible, study, simulation practice, planning. What was to come of it, that could never be foreseeable.

Beneath the alertness that took hold of him in any crisis, tension pulsed and shivered. The rugged bark of a fir, its fragrance, the scuff of his feet on duff, its crackly yielding to his weight, were vivid as lightning. More than biochemical stimulant upbore him. He was bound on a mission, perhaps his last but surely his greatest.

Silent, he and Aleka passed along the trail through the woods and out into the clearing. Shadow brimmed it. Light burned yet on treetops around and on the prow of the spaceship. Poised within the clear cylindrical shelter, she thrust her torpedo shape aloft to outshine the Moon.

A stone wall guarded the shrine. In front of its entryway, a two-meter block held a bronze tablet bearing an account of what Kyra Davis had done.

Here Fireball folk always paused, as at an altar. Kenmuir and Aleka gave salute.

Sometimes those who came went on into the ship, for special rites or just to service her. Several had done it of late. They too had worn cloaks, in their case to hide the equipment and rations they took aboard. The hope was that this would touch off no alarm in the surveillance machines—another ceremony, another assertion of an identity long since obsolete. Leading the way onward, Kenmuir took care to pace slowly.

A mechanism permanently activated detected his approach and extruded a ramp from beneath the aft personnel lock, which opened. Man and woman ascended. For a bare instant, they glanced about at the living forest and took a breath. Then they went inside. The valve shut, the ramp retracted.

Beyond the chamber, Kenmuir doffed his cloak. To stow it in a locker was sheer reflex; he noticed and grinned at himself. Aleka did likewise. They were both clad in skinsuits, to slip directly into space outfits. Even now, the sight of her caught at him. "Come along," he said hastily.

When the ship rested on her landing jacks, passageways through the length of her became vertical shafts. You used fixed ladders. The climb between pearl-gray bulkheads went past sections where remembrances of the original pilot darted forth, stowed high-acceleration couches, door to the wash cubicle, folded galley manifold, closet for personal possessions, multiceiver with vivifer, hobby kit, a family picture faded to a blur . . . Air hung heavy. It would not freshen until the recycler and ventilators resumed work.

To him the command cabin was archaic, a bit of history, to her new and foreign, but in the simulator both had grown familiar with it. They took their seats before the control console and secured their harnesses. Viewscreens and displays were blank, meters dead. Kenmuir sought after words. Aleka's smile flashed taut. "Go," she said to him. "Go for broke."

His fingers moved across the board. Lights glowed, needles quivered, numbers and graphics appeared, the forward viewscreen filled with sky. A rustle of air reached him, as if somewhere lungs were stirring. His voice sounded unnaturally loud. "Full readiness. Immediate liftoff."

The voice from the speaker was female, husky, Kyra Davis's own. So had she wanted it. "Salud. . . . It's been a long time. . . . You are strangers." His glance flipped involuntarily to the scanners whereby *Kestrel* observed him. The voice firmed. "We have no clearance."

Part of the study had been of the language as it was spoken in that era. Kenmuir tried to form a pronunciation close enough for the robot to understand. "Emergency."

Sensors were sweeping around. "No spacefield here. Liftoff in surroundings like these is unlawful. And I am enclosed."

Hard to grasp that this was no sophotect, merely a robot, without conscious mind or independent will. He knew not how many such he had dealt with in his life, but here was something different. Here was a machine that had flown with Kyra Davis, served her, conversed and played games with her, maybe listened to her secret confessions and heard her weep. More than database entries remained. Against all reason, to Kenmuir, a spirit haunted the ship.

He had not expected it would hurt to key the Override code.

He did.

The orders jerked out of him: "We're bound for the Moon. The shell is hyalon, tough, but you can break through if you boost at ten *g*. Then reduce to two *g* and proceed. However, don't make directly for Luna. Set a course that will skim us past it, as if to get a gravity boost for a destination—" He gave coordinates, arbitrarily chosen, that would point them to deep space, well off the ecliptic. "In about an hour I'll tell you the maneuver we actually want, and you can figure your deceleration vectors accordingly." He didn't care to do it earlier because he didn't know what would happen. By then the whole plan might have crashed.

"Confirming." Displays repeated the instructions. They gathered detail as computation sped by. "I warn you, this is dangerous. I'm streamlined for getting around on the likes of Mars or Titan, not Earth. Maybe the laws of astronautics changed while I was asleep, but, hombre, the laws of physics can't have."

If only she didn't sound so human, so alive.

Aleka stroked the console. "You'll swing it, *Kestrel*," she said. "You did a lot more for Kyra."

"Gracias," replied the voice, as warm as hers. Briskly: "Liftoff in sixty seconds."

Kenmuir and Aleka spent them looking into one another's eyes.

Thunder boomed through their bones. Weight crammed them back. Darkness swooped in.

It retreated. Kenmuir drew a gasp. Acceleration had dropped to twice normal. His gaze roved the viewscreens. Aft, beneath, fire crowned the trees around the blackened clearing. Well, the ecological service would soon quench it. Forward, heaven was purpling toward night.

The hull pierced most of Earth's atmosphere while he sat half-conscious. The last vibrations ebbed away, the sky went black, stars came forth. The only noises he heard were his breath and thudding blood. No sound rose from the engine. A plasma drive was too efficient, out here where it belonged.

Aleka stared ahead, hugged herself, and whispered, "We're on the loose. We really are."

"For the moment," Kenmuir mumbled.

She nodded. "Traffic Control around the world must be like a hornets' nest kicked over. Why aren't they calling us?"

"This ship isn't integrated with the system," he

reminded her. Too many facts to learn in too short a time. Some would not come at once when summoned. Which was he forgetting? "They'll have to find the appropriate band, and then I suppose they'll assign a sentience to their end."

In the after screens Earth's horizon was a huge sapphire arc. It contracted ever faster. Soon the planet would lie whole within the frames. Slowing at an equal rate after turnover, *Kestrel* would reach Luna inside three hours. Their bodies in good condition and nanochemically reinforced, her riders could well endure doubled weight that long and arrive fit for action.

If they did.

"Direct a laser communication to Luna," Kenmuir said, and specified the coordinates.

"Zamok Vysoki," responded the ship. "I remember. . . . Ready."

"Ian Kenmuir to the lady Lilisaire," he intoned. A part of him wanted to say, "Well done" to *Kestrel,* which kept the beam aimed and Doppler-compensated throughout her furiously mounting velocity. "I am bound for deep space on your service. TrafCon objects. Get the data on their movements before they clamp down secrecy. If you can, obstruct pursuit and intervention, but please don't endanger anyone. Out."

He didn't know whether the message was received. Perhaps the facilities at the castle were jammed or otherwise disabled by the opposition. Certainly surveillance heard everything; and he had no encrypting capabilities. Mention of Proserpina would likely have provoked immediate, radical counteraction. Besides, it was a bargaining counter to hold in reserve—an ace in the hole, Aleka had said, thinking of some obscure game. The purpose of Kenmuir's call was mainly to further his deception. Make the hunters concentrate their strength and build up their velocities on a trail that he would suddenly leave. Then he might for a brief spell be free to enter Dagny's tomb.

A light blinked red. "Communication from Earth," the ship told them. "It claims absolute priority."

"Make contact," Kenmuir ordered.

No image appeared. The videos weren't compatible. He knew the voice, however. Once Matthias realized what kind of agent was visiting him, he had surreptitiously had a man of his record whatever was feasible. He played the recording for these two as part of their briefing.

"Spaceship *Kestrel,* null registry, respond at once."

"Hello, Venator," the spaceman said, and heard his companion catch her breath. Himself, he was not very surprised.

"Kenmuir?" The tone was equally cool. "I rather thought so. And greeting, Alice Tam. It's doubtless you who boarded with him."

Kenmuir signed her not to speak. Why give anything away? "I daresay you'd like an explanation."

"More than that, my friend. Considerably more. Do you two have any conception of what you have brought on yourselves?"

"A public inquiry will determine whether we are justified."

"Everyone at Guthrie House will be arrested, you know. You've probably destroyed your beloved Fireball Trothdom. Did you intend that?"

Fireball Enterprises had destroyed itself in bringing down an evil, the spaceman thought. For the first time, he wondered what agonies of soul Matthias was undergoing.

"Something may yet be salvaged," Venator urged. "Cease acceleration, admit boarders when they match velocity, and come back to discourse like reasonable human beings."

"Will the world listen in?" Kenmuir demanded. "What guarantees of that can you give us?"

"None. You would see through any trick we attempted, as suspicious as you are. How can I persuade you that this is not a matter which ought to be public?"

Kenmuir's lips pulled back from his teeth. "That would be difficult, wouldn't it?" Inwardly he thought Matthias's choice had been easy, set beside this that he must make. *Were* he and Aleka in the right?

"Every minute you let go by, you're in worse trouble," Venator said. "What cause do you imagine you're serving? Lilisaire's? What she intends—we have reason to believe—could cost millions of lives. Do you want them on your conscience?"

"No. If you're telling the truth. Are you?" Now Kenmuir could speak the name. "Your people lied about Proserpina for lifetimes."

"There are good reasons to keep that confidential, till the world is ready. I—no, the cybercosm will be glad to explain them to you, in privacy."

"Will it? Or will we—my partner and I—simply disappear?"

Venator sighed. "You've been watching too many historical dramas." Sternly: "Consider this an ultimatum. If you surrender now, clemency is possible, for you and for Fireball. Later, I fear not."

"What about the Covenant, and our rights under it? I tell you again, we want total disclosure. Otherwise you're in worse violation than we could ever be."

"The Covenant makes provision for emergencies—" Venator broke off. After a half minute, while Earth dwindled and Luna grew: "You are determined."

"We are," Kenmuir said to him and to himself.

"Your record suggests you mean that. I shall not let you talk a delaying action." Venator laughed softly. "Nor shall I wish you luck. But may you survive. I'd like to talk candidly with you, intelligence to intelligence. *Ave atque vale.*"

The light went out. "Transmission ended," the ship said.

Kenmuir glanced once more at Earth. If he could broadcast, rouse those who loved freedom—But the signal must go through satellite relays if it was to have any chance of being heard, and they were under control.

And how many on the planet would especially care?

Matthias had said he felt the walls closing in, all his life. Kenmuir had not, until lately. At least, not in the upper part of his mind. Down below, had he too sensed that he was caged?

Was he?

He shook the questions off, as a dog shakes off the water of a cold river, and began unharnessing. "It should be a steady run," he told Aleka, "but we'd better have spacesuits on, in case." He'd definitely need his.

She nodded. Under two gravities, the dark hair fell straight and thickly past her face. "'Ae."

They went aft. For a few minutes before donning the gear, they kissed.

When they returned, he called for data on pursuit. They were few and the probable errors were high, but instruments did appear to show two or three vessels bound through an intercept cone for his deep-space course. How they proposed to stop *Kestrel,* short of ramming, he didn't know. But they were of modern design with far more delta *v.* If necessary, they could hound her till she exhausted her reaction mass, then draw alongside.

He began entering the detailed instructions that would enable Aleka to take command. "I hope I'm not too clumsy with you," he said into his communicator, impulsively, foolishly.

"You haven't Kyra's skill," *Kestrel* answered, "but your hands feel much like hers."

43

The ship neared Luna.

By then it was certainly clear to the hunters that they had been deceived and this was in fact her destination. But they could not stop her. All spacecraft capable of interception were now too distant to arrive in time. There were no missiles available that she could not dodge. Those emplaced on the Moon were few and slow, intended for unlikely targets, such as a large meteoroid on a catastrophic orbit. Constabulary and Peace Authority forces were doubtless on full alert, but that was of no immediate help.

The moment came when Aleka looked into the eyes behind Kenmuir's helmet and said through the radio, "Aloha. Let's hope it's not forever. You've become . . . more than a friend, do you know?" He found no words, could merely smile and touch a glove to her hand before they went their separate ways.

Waiting, enclosed in an airlock chamber, the drive unit and its mass tank so heavy under the acceleration that he must sit against them, he felt a slight shock, and after a minute or two another. Aleka had dispatched their decoys. He imagined the carrier modules, braking down toward widespread points on the surface—points not far from Selenarchic strongholds. He pictured Aleka, hastening back to the command cabin, transmitting to Zamok Vysoki: *Lilisaire, have someone retrieve those cylinders before the opposition does.* No telling if the Lunarian, or any Lunarian, got that message, or was able to act on it, or willing to try. But it should distract the government's forces. With reasonable luck, his departure should escape their attention.

Of course, they'd keep their radars and other detectors constantly on this vessel. However, she'd oriented her hull so that he probably wouldn't register as he left. If a beam did happen to sweep across him afterward, he could hope the program would note him as a piece of cosmic debris and continue following the ship.

The plan might not work. No matter how carefully he and *Kestrel* had calculated the odds on the basis of accessible data, it was a gamble.

Life always was.

Weight vanished. Engine turned off, the ship swung around Luna at scarcely more than low orbital speed. He felt the throb of the air pump emptying the chamber. Light from the overhead fixture shrank to a puddle, with vague reflections off the sides, as diffusion ceased. He braced his muscles. Time to go. An uncanny calm was upon him.

The outer valve opened. Starful darkness welled in the portal. By the handhold he grasped, he pulled himself to the flange and pushed his soles down against the little platform of the personnel springer. His free hand sought its touchoff. The platform tilted, jerked, and tossed him out.

Slowly tumbling, he saw the universe whirl, Milky Way, Earth, Luna. The sun crossed his vision and his helmet dusked to save it, turning the disc to dull gold, a coin on which the spots were a mintage he could not read. At first *Kestrel* stretched gigantic. She receded from him at the several meters per second he had gained relative to her. She was still large across the stars when he guessed it was safe for him to boost, but now he saw her whole, slim and beautiful.

Aleka, though, was locked inside, Aleka who would have wished to die on the sea with the wind caressing her hair.

Kenmuir got busy.

The frame of the drive unit curved a member around in front to support the control board before his chest, an incongruously cheerful array of colored lights. He keyed for despin. A short thrust stabilized the sky around him. The unit's computer was comparatively simple, but adequate for the tasks ahead. Earth steadied to a thick, broken piece of blue-and-white glass. Luna reached across a quarter of the heavens, its night part like a hole down to infinity, its day part mercilessly lighted, wrinkled, pocked, and blotched. Without opticals, he saw no trace of manwork. Memory could have given him cities, huge flowers, birds and soarflyers above a lake, Lilisaire; but he lacked time for remembering.

He deployed navigation gear, peered and measured, identified three landmarks and put their bearings into the computer. After a bit he repeated, thus getting the information for it to figure his location, altitude, and vector function. Radar would have been better, more direct, but he dared not risk it. He had already entered the coordinates at which he wanted to land. Now he keyed for thrust.

The drive unit swung him around to the proper orientation. Accumulators commenced discharging their energy in earnest. From a mass tank as broad as he was and half as long, three jets sprang. Condensation made a cloud some distance beyond the nozzles —this system was not as efficient as a nuclear-driven plasma jet, nor remotely as powerful—but the cloud was thin, barely visible at close range, and rapidly dissipated. Weight tugged again at Kenmuir. Ever faster, *Kestrel* went from him, became a toy, a jewel, a star, and was gone.

For the next half hour he had little to do but take further sightings and let the unit correct his flight parameters accordingly. Acceleration mounted until it settled at approximately one *g;* thereafter the rate of exhaust diminished together with mass. He would have preferred to go more speedily, whatever the stress on his body, but the strength of the frame was limited. At that, he'd arrive with tank almost empty and accumulators nearly dead.

His thoughts wandered. Aleka—Presently she'd take lunosynchronous orbit. It would not be straight above him, but she would be in his sky. When he landed, perhaps ninety minutes would be left until the first of the Authority ships, returning at full blast, could reach her. She must be gone well before then.

Lilisaire—It would be strange if some strands of her web did not extend into the police and the Authority, even now, even now. Unless they had seized her—and he felt sure she had made arrangements for trumpeting that to the Solar System—she knew where *Kestrel* was and that somehow this concerned her. What she might do about it, he couldn't tell. If she could keep them busy for an hour or two, that would be helpful. True, it would add to the score against him and her and Fireball . . . He expelled foreboding.

Annie—A wistful ghost. He glanced at Earth and hoped life was being kind to her.

Time passed. Slowly, descending, he flew from one night toward another.

His approach had been planned more for concealment than fuel economy. Landsats doubtless spotted him, as they spotted virtually everything when turned to maximum gain, but he should be inconspicuous, insignificant, nothing to trigger an alarm report from those robots, especially when they were focused on events elsewhere. Tycho Crater hove above the horizon.

By then he was so low that he saw it not as a bowl but as a mountain, black and monstrous against the stars. Though the sun was at early morning, the west side remained in darkness. Shadow went down it and across the land like a sluggishly ebbing tide. At first, far to his right and his left, Kenmuir glimpsed the shores of day. Nearing, he lost that sight, he had just the stars and waning Earth. In its last quarter, the planet yet stood radiant, halfway up the northern sky. Blue-white light washed over vast terraced slopes.

Ray-splash brightened the ruggedness below them. He found his goal and came down on manual.

Dust stormed briefly, blindingly around him. It fell, unhindered by air; the material of suit and helmet repelled it; he looked out over a ledge partway down the ringwall, a pitted levelness long and broad, with nighted rock athwart the east and everywhere else the heavens.

The aftermath rustling of the jets faded out of his ears. Silence took him into itself. When he had uncoupled from the drive unit and tank, under Moonweight he felt feathery, as if half disembodied. His suit, aircycler, and other outfitting were of small mass and close fit, homeostatic, power-jointed, tactile-amplifying, well-nigh a second skin. He unbound his pack of equipment. It should not have seemed heavy either; but he saw the sledgehammer strapped across it, cold touched him, and for a moment he could not lift the load.

Needs must. He shouldered it and started across the ground. Dust puffed from footsteps until he came to the road the builders had carved down the ringwall from within the crater. It was hardly more than a trail of hard-packed regolith, and the pilgrims upon it had become few, but the cosmos would take a while longer to bury it.

Ahead of him rested the tomb. Some said that download she who lay here had ordered that it be simple. Seven meters in width, four walls of white stone rose sheer to a low-pitched roof of such height that each side was seen as enclosable in a golden rectangle. A double bronze door in front bore the same proportions. Above it was chiseled the name DAGNY EBBESEN BEYNAC. That was enough.

Kenmuir stopped at the entrance. Through a minute outside of time, he forgot haste, forgot his need, and was only there. Walls and metal glimmered dimly below Earth and the stars.

It was as if stillness deepened. With a shiver, he

took forth the key that Lars Rydberg had secretly made and brought back with him. He laid it against the lock. The program remembered the code. A pointer turned downward. At his pull, the leaves of the door swung ponderously away from an inner night. He stiffened his heart and trod past them.

At first he was blind, alone with his pulse. Then his eyes adapted. Light drifted in, barely touching an altar block at the middle. His right hand rose to his helmet, a Fireball salute.

But hurry, now, hurry. He unslung his pack, set it down, fetched a lamp, turned it on and left it at his feet. Luminance leaped, cut by sharp-edged shadows. Two objects stood on the block. One was a funerary urn, slim and graceful; he thought again of *Kestrel.* The other was a download in its case.

Hurry, hurry. Observe, work by helmet light, carry out the necessary violation and crush the guilt beneath your heel; later it shall arise unbruised.

A meter showed that the download's energy pack was drained but intact, a relief to Kenmuir although he had a replacement. He attached an accumulator to recharge it, by a jack handmade to fit the obsolete socket. While that went on, he set about reactivating the neural network. Disguising what he had not done, Lars Rydberg had slipped in a bypass program. At Guthrie House, a counteractive module had been prepared, which Kenmuir applied. Thereafter he laid a radio communicator on the altar, found the appropriate spot on the case, and made linkage. Now he and she could speak through the hollowness around them.

He touched the final switch, stepped back, and shuddered.

Light glared from below, off the face of the block, throwing urn and download into murk. Out of this, centimeter by centimeter, the eyestalks wavered upward. Lenses gleamed, searching about and about the tomb.

After an endlessness Kenmuir heard the voice, a

woman's voice, faint, as if it reached him across an abyss, dragging and stumbling. "'Mond . . . No, Lars, oh, Lars . . .'"

He had not forseen how pain would cramp him together. "Forgive me," he croaked.

"Uncans!" Dagny screamed.

"Wh-what?"

"Dark, dark, and dark—" Despair swept away before tenderness. "Don't cry, darling. Mother's here."

Kenmuir gripped his will to him. "My lady Beynac, forgive me," he got out, as best he could utter her language. "I've had to call you back."

"Where are my arms?" she moaned, while the eyestalks threshed to and fro. "I'll pick you up and cuddle you, baby, baby mine, but where are my arms? My lips, 'Mond?"

"I've called you back for your people's sake," Kenmuir said, "your blood and his," and wondered whether he lied.

"The blood ran out. When they got my spacesuit off. It was all over everything."

"That happened—long ago—"

"Little Juliana, she was all blood . . . No, not Juliana. She'd never be, would she? Not now." The download wailed.

She was remembering something old, Kenmuir knew. But what? Could she remember more? "My lady Beynac, please listen. Please."

"It roars," Dagny mumbled.

A damaged circuit, Kenmuir thought. It must be generating a signal the mind perceived as noise, whatever was left of the mind.

The sound in his earplugs softened. "The sea roars. Breakers. Wind. Salt. Driftwood like huge bones. Here, a sand dollar. For you, Uncans." She laughed, quietly and lovingly.

"My lady," Kenmuir pleaded, "do you know where you are?" Who you are?

"Lars—" The eyestalks came to rest. He felt her

peer at him. He felt knives in his flesh. "But you're not Lars," she said without tone. "You're nobody."

"My name—"

"Lars, you ended me. Didn't you?"

Hope flickered, very faint. Kenmuir drew breath. "I have to tell you—But I've come as a friend. They need your help again on the Moon."

Chill replied. "There wasn't going to be any again."

"I'm afraid—"

Sudden gentleness: "Don't be afraid. 'Mond never was. 'Bloody 'ell!' he'd shout, and charge ahead."

Snatching after anything, Kenmuir responded, "Like Anson Guthrie. Also after he became . . . like you."

"Sigurd was never afraid either," Dagny crooned. "He loved danger. He laughed with it. Not at it, with it. That's Kaino, you know."

"Yes," Kenmuir said dully. "Your son."

"They're dead. They died on dead rocks in deep space. 'Mond and Kaino are dead."

"I know." In desperation: "That's what I'm here about. You, you carried on. You lived on, for all the others."

The download began to sing, softly and minor-key.

> *"He is dead and gone, lady,*
> *He is dead and gone;*
> *At his head a grass-green turf;*
> *At his heels a stone."*

She stopped. "Only—no grass grows yonder."

"It may yet," Kenmuir said. "If you will help, this one last time."

The eyes stood unbending, the voice went grim. "Lars promised."

"He did. But—"

"To 'Mond, you said, Lars. I'd go to where 'Mond is."

"He hoped, with his whole heart he hoped."

She laughed. He heard the bitterness. "Estúpido.

Dagny went there. She was free to. Ghosts aren't. How could they have a birthright? They were never born."

"You *are* Dagny Beynac," he said into her delirium. "As Anson Guthrie the download is Anson Guthrie. The man, his spirit."

Eyestalks trembled, voice quickened. "Guthrie? Uncans? He still is?"

"Not here," Kenmuir sighed. "At far Centaurus. It's been centuries, Madame Beynac."

"And the wind blew and blew," she murmured.

"Centuries."

She didn't seem to hear him. "From a story I read once when I was a child. By Lord Dunsany. They hanged a highwayman out on the heath and left him there alone. And the wind blew and blew."

Bring her attention back, hold it to the point. "Yes, Lars Rydberg broke his word to you. In a way. He hoped you'd rest in peace forever as you wished, that nobody would have to raise you. But I must. For a moment, a single moment. One question." Time was blowing by. How many minutes were left him?

"Where is your face, 'Mond?" The voice cracked across. "I can't bring back your face any more."

"One question, and *I'll* give you peace. But now, at once, or it's no good."

"'Mond, 'You are Dagny's son,' you said to Lars, 'Mond. 'You shall be welcome here, by damn, always.'" How might a download weep?

And Lars had betrayed them both, Kenmuir thought. Or had he?

As if from the stars beyond the door, an idea struck through. "I've seen his images, Edmond Beynac's. His face was wide and, and angular, with high cheekbones and green eyes."

"Yes!" Dagny shouted. "Yes! Oh, 'Mond, welcome back! *Bienvenu, mon chéri!*"

Pursue. "He showed the way to Proserpina."

"Bloody hell, yes, he did!"

Kenmuir spoke fast, but as he would have spoken to a beloved. "Hear me, I beg you. Your people, his descendants and yours, they need Proserpina now, they need it terribly, and it's been lost. Do you remember how to find it?"

Anger flashed. "For this you woke me?"

He stood straight before the eyes. "Yes. If you can't forgive me, will you anyhow help?"

Suddenly he heard warmth. "I have 'Mond back. For that, thanks."

"Will you tell me?"

"Will you send me home to him?"

"Yes." He bent down to his pack, loosed certain knots, and lifted the sledgehammer in his hands. "I have this." Each single word he must ram out of his mouth.

"Then quickly," she implored, "before I lose him again."

He could say no more. The silence took them.

"Far and far," she sighed, "a long way to go for a death. But Proserpina brings the springtime with her. Apple blossoms behind Daddy's and Mother's house . . ."

Was she slipping back into nightmare? "The orbital elements!" Kenmuir yelled.

"Quiet," she bade him. "My caveman's hunting them for me."

He waited. Through the open door, the stars watched.

"Yes," Dagny said. "Here they are. Thanks, old bear." She recited the numbers. "Do you have them?"

"I do," he answered: on a recorder and cut into his brain.

"Good," she said calmly. "Now, your promise."

Terror snatched at him. "Do you truly want—?"

"For me," she said. "And for Lars."

"I owe it you, then," he heard himself say. His hands closed hard on the helve. "Goodbye, my lady."

"Fare you well," she said like a benediction. Command rang forth: "Now!"

He swung the hammer up over his head and back down, with all his force. The case was strong, but it was not meant to take impacts like that, and radiation had weakened it. Organometal split asunder. Iron crushed circuits.

He cast the hammer from him and reeled out of the tomb. Stars blazed.

No, he must not cry, he must not huddle into grief, not yet. *Kestrel* and Aleka were aloft. He switched his radio on. They could receive across the tens of thousands of kilometers between, and it mattered no longer that others heard. "Are you there?" he called. "Come in, come in."

"Yes," the dear voice responded. "Oh, darling, you're hurt."

"Record this." He rattled off the figures. "Do you have them?"

"Yes—"

"On your way."

"Aloha au iā 'oe," he heard. "I love you." He could not see, but he could imagine the spaceship surge forward.

He slumped down onto the regolith and waited for Venator's men. The sun broke over the ringwall.

44

The Peace Authority vessel drove Earthward at half a gravity.

She was big, with space for some cabins. Kenmuir had been put in one by himself. The door was locked. His guards had told him that if he needed anything he could ask for it through the intercom, but thus far he had not. What he most wanted was to be alone.

Well, he would have liked a viewscreen, that he might look out upon the stars. Cramped and barren, the room crowded him together with his thoughts.

For the hundredth or the thousandth weary time he

wondered how all this had come to pass, how he turned into a rebel and a killer. Why? He never intended or foresaw it. Events seemed to have acquired their own momentum, almost a will of their own. Was that the nature of human history? Chaos—strange attractors—how much did the Teramind itself understand? How much did God?

The door spread. It reclosed as a blue-clad figure stepped through. Kenmuir rose from the unfolded bunk. For a few seconds they stood motionless, two men tall and lean, one dark, one pale.

"Greeting, Captain Kenmuir," the newcomer said in Anglo of the eastern hemisphere.

"You're Pragmatic Venator, aren't you?" the prisoner replied. "So we meet at last."

The officer nodded. "I want to talk with you while we can be private."

"Private? Your machines are watching and listening, I'm sure."

"They're your machines too." Humanity's.

"We're both in error. They're nobody's." Robots reporting to sophotects that ultimately were facets of the supreme intellect.

"No contradiction," Venator said. "Your partner is yours, and you are hers, but neither is property."

Something stirred in Kenmuir. He had felt emotionally emptied; but he found that he could again care. "What about Aleka? What can you tell me?" What will you?

Venator raised his brows. "Aleka? . . . Oh, yes. Alice Tam. She's alive and well." A smile flickered. "Inconveniently much. That's what I mainly have to discuss with you, if you're able."

Kenmuir shrugged. "I'm able, if not exactly willing. The constabulary on Luna were . . . not unkind. I'm medicated and rested." In the body, at least. The mind, the soul—Anxiety died. He returned to the detachment that had possessed him of late, whether because he had been unknowingly tranquilized or because his spirit was exhausted; he stood apart from himself, a Cartesian consciousness observing its destiny unfold.

"Shall we sit?" Venator suggested.

"No need." Nor wish.

"Do you care for refreshment? We've much to talk about."

"No, I don't want anything" that they aboard could give him.

"Pray rest assured you're in no danger," Venator said. "You're in civilized keeping." The features bleakened, the tone flattened. "Perhaps more civilized than you deserve."

"We can argue rights and wrongs later, can't we?"

Venator went back to mildness. "I believe we'll do more than argue, Captain. But, true, we'd best get the empirical out of the way first. Would you tell me why, m-m, Aleka didn't take you along when she escaped?"

"Isn't that obvious? I'd have had to retreat to a safe distance, then run to the ship, after which she'd have had to lift. It could have cost us as much as an hour. We didn't have that long."

"Obvious, yes. An hour at two gravities means an extra seven kilometers per second. I was probing the degree of your determination. I don't suppose you'll tell me where she's bound?"

"I can't. She and the ship decided it between them after letting me off."

"As I expected," Venator said calmly. "What you don't know can't be extracted from you. Not that it matters. One may guess. The goal clearly isn't Mars, which would be a hazardous choice in any case. Several asteroids are possible, or conceivably a Lunarian-colonized Jovian satellite. She's running on trajectory now, conserving her delta v and thus her options. Unless she comes to fear we may close in, and accelerates afresh, it will take a while for her to reach whatever goal she has in mind."

Whereupon she would be in communication range. *Kestrel*'s antiquated laser wouldn't carry an intelligible message across two or three astronomical units; her radio would require a high-gain receiver; and who yonder would be listening for either? Close by, Aleka's intent to signal would be unmistakable. She might perhaps land.

"Your scheme worked, fantastical though it was," Venator continued. "I think it worked precisely because it was fantastical. We can't overhaul her before she completes her mission, and we aren't trying any longer."

Yes, Kenmuir thought, he and she had estimated a reasonable probability of that. The ships of law enforcement were few and widely scattered through the Solar System, because their usual work was just to convey personnel or sometimes give aid to the distressed. Besides, even today, the Falcon class counted as high-powered. It had become mostly robots and sophotects that crossed space. They seldom demanded energy-wasting speed. It was humans who were short-lived and impatient.

"You see, we don't want to provoke her into haste," Venator explained. "We want time to persuade you two of your folly, so you'll stop of your free choice." He frowned. "Consider. Do you imagine the revelation of a minor planet out among the comets will make you heroes? Think about it. Your brutal destruction of the Beynac download will shock the world."

Kenmuir sighed. "I told the police and I told them, she made me promise."

"Need you have kept the promise?"

Kenmuir nodded. "She'd been betrayed once."

Venator's smile was briefly unpleasant. "To your benefit, as it turned out."

Kenmuir made a grin and gestured around his cell. "This?"

"I didn't mean you were after personal gain," Venator said. "I confess that your motives puzzle me, and suspect they puzzle you also."

Once more Kenmuir had the sense—nonsense, cried his rationality, but the feeling would not go away—that he and Aleka had been the instruments of some great blind force, and it was not done with them yet, and they themselves were among its wellsprings. But he had better stay with immediacies. He could take advantage of the huntsman's desire for conversation.

"What's the situation on Luna?" he asked. His interrogators there had given him no news.

Venator's voice and bearing eased. "Well," he said as if it were interesting but of little importance, "the lady Lilisaire caused us considerable trouble, in which several of her colleagues gleefully joined. Fortunately, we avoided significant damage or casualties on either side, and things are quiet now. Officially they're under house arrest. In practice, what we have is an uneasy truce. The outcome of that will depend largely on you, my friend."

"How?"

Venator turned serious. "You can still halt what you've set moving. Tam has ignored our calls, but *Kestrel* must have taken note of them and will doubtless inform her of any that come from you."

"What could I have to say?" Not, in the presence of machines, that he thought he loved her.

"You, and you alone, can make her come back, keeping the secret of Proserpina."

"Why should I?"

"Criminal charges can be dismissed, you know, or a pardon can be granted."

Emotion stirred anew in Kenmuir. The sharpest part of it was anger. "See here," he stated, "I never proposed to serve as a martyr, nor does she. If and when the news comes out, the Solar System will decide whether we did wrong. In spite of—" his voice faltered "—the download—when that story too is made clear . . . I dare hope for pardon from the whole human race."

"Spare me the rhetoric, please," Venator scoffed. "You've calculated that the government will be in so awkward a position that its best move will be to quietly let infractions go unpunished, while the more radical Lunarians prepare to emigrate to Proserpina. In exchange, you won't emphasize any irregularities we may have committed."

Kenmuir nodded. "Yes, that's approximately what we're trying for."

"I've gathered you're a student of history," Venator said. "Tell me, with how many governments of the past would that calculation have been rational?"

Surprised, Kenmuir stood wordless before he muttered, "I don't know. Perhaps none."

"Correct. You'd have been dead by now, unless we chose to torture you first. If our secret got released, we'd put down the restless Lunarians by force, exterminating them if necessary. We'd tell people that the revelation was a falsehood concocted by you evildoers. We'd go on to tell the people, at considerable and emotional length, what a service we had done them, suppressing these enemies of the state. But most of the propaganda we wouldn't issue ourselves. Plenty of journalists and intellectuals would be eager to curry favor by manufacturing and disseminating it. Many among them would be sincere."

"Yes . . ."

"As it is, you are safe, while Tam runs loose because we did not expect that major weapons of war would ever be needed again. You have the cybercosm to thank, Kenmuir. You might show some trust, some gratitude."

"But you violated the Covenant!" the spaceman protested. "And—and—" And what? How horrible an offense, really, was the hiding of a piece of information?

"Exigencies arise," Venator said. "My hope is to convince you of that, before it is too late."

"Suppose you do," Kenmuir retorted wildly. "How can I convince Aleka?" Any passwords or the like could have been drugged or brainphased out of him. Any image of him could be an artifact, in this world where so much reality was virtual.

Venator hesitated. When he spoke, it was slowly, and did the thin face draw into lines of want? "She ought to listen to you and have faith in you, ought she not? As for how she shall know that it is in truth you—" He looked away, as if he wished to see through the metal to stars and Earth. "My intuition is that you two are lovers. All the little intimacies, body language unique to the pair of you, incidents forgotten by one until the other reminds of them, the wholeness arisen in even as brief a time as you've had—if we wrung that quantity of data out of you, the process would leave you a vegetable. And could we write an adequate program to use it with a generated image? Perhaps the Teramind could. Perhaps not. I daresay it could reprogram your brain, so that you would become its worshipper and ardently do, of your own volition, whatever it wished."

He lifted a hand. "Have no fears," he said. "Besides the morality of destroying a mind, we are barred by the fact that we haven't time enough, neither to make a convincing imitation of you nor to make you over. You are not electrophotonic, you are organic, with the inertia of all material things. Molecular interactions go at rates constrained by the laws of the universe, and the Teramind did not write those."

His fists clenched at his sides. "Explain that to your Aleka. She will know you by what you share, everything that I have denied myself."

He smiled and finished lightly, "Ironic, isn't it, that at this final hour the cybercosm must appeal to the oldest, most primitive force in sentient life?"

Kenmuir ran a tongue gone dry across his lips. "If you can indeed recruit me."

Venator gazed straight at him and answered, "*I* can't. I am bringing you to the Teramind."

45

A vast and duskful space—a chamber? Sight did not reach to the heights and ends of it. Glowing lines arched aloft and down again, some close together, some meters apart. Seen over a distance, they merged in an intricacy, a hieroglyph unknown to Kenmuir.

The air was without heat or cold or scent or sound.

He had woken here after falling asleep in the room at Central to which Venator brought him. Unwarned but somehow unsurprised, he saw himself stretched half reclining in a web from which a number of attachments made contact with feet, hands, brow, temples. His skin and clothes were either illuminated or faintly, whitely shining. A mighty calm was upon him, yet he had never felt this aware and alert, wholly in command of mind and body. He sensed as it were every least flow through blood vessels, nerves, and brain. Solemnly he awaited that which was to happen.

Facing him, Venator lay likewise; but although the huntsman's eyes were open, they seemed blind and his visage had become a mask. What now did he see, what knowledge was his?

The presence of the Teramind, Kenmuir thought, the nearness of the great core engine, save that the Teramind was no single machine or being. It was the apex of the cybercosm, the guiding culmination, as the human brain was of the human organism. No, not really that, either. All machines in a way stemmed from it, like men and gods from Brahm, and the souls of its synnoionts yearned home toward it.

But here was no static finality, Kenmuir knew. This was not what artificial intelligences, set to creating a superior artificial intelligence, had wrought; it was the cybercosm as a whole, *evolving*. Already its thoughts went beyond human imagination. How far beyond its own present imagination would they range in another hundred or another billion years?

Venator's lips parted. "Ian Kenmuir," he said gravely. Did the Teramind speak through him, as through an oracle?

"I am ready," Kenmuir responded. He had no honorific to add; any would have been a mockery.

"You understand you are neither sophotect nor synnoiont. You are outside. Therefore I shall be what link between us there may be."

Otherwise, could the presence give Kenmuir more than discourse, displays, a shadow show? By Venator, whose flesh was human, he might be made able to comprehend, to feel, what the unhuman alone could never quite convey.

"Ask what you will," said the voice.

"You know what has brought us to this," replied Kenmuir as quietly. "Why have you kept Proserpina hidden away?"

"The answer is many-sided."

And will it be true? wondered a rebellious mote.

"You shall judge its truth for yourself," said the voice.

Self-evident truth, at the end of a road of reasoning? But could he follow that road, up and up to its end? "I listen. I watch."

Something like an expression fleeted over Venator's countenance and through his tone. A pain, a longing? "We share a memory, you and I."

Luminous amidst the dark, the image of Lilisaire, so alive that even then Kenmuir caught his breath. The gown rustled and rippled about her slenderness. Felinely, she turned to look at him. Dark-red and flame-red, her hair fell over the white shoulders, past the fine blue vein in her throat. She smiled at him with the big, oblique, changeably gold and green eyes and with the lips he remembered. Did she purr, did she call?

More images came, flickered, and fled. It was not a document, not a sequence or montage, it was a stream of dreams to awaken him. Beneath his tranquility, it hurt. He had not wished to count up her lovers, her betrayals, the men she killed and the men she had had killed, the men she wedded and enwebbed, the men she broke to her will or lured down ways whereon they lost themselves, the willfulness now glacial and now ablaze but always without reckoning or ruth, the fact that she was feral.

"Beautiful, boundlessly ambitious, infinitely dangerous," murmured the voice.

"No," Kenmuir denied. "Can't be. One mortal woman—"

"One whom circumstance has made the embodiment of her blood."

Images out of history. Lunarian arrogance, intransigence, outright lawlessness, in the teeth of unforgiving space Intrigues, murders, terrible threats. The Selenarchy sovereign, holding its nation apart from the unity of humankind. Rinndalir's scheme to wreck the whole order of things, for the sake of wrecking it. Niolente's fomenting of revolt on Earth and war on the Moon, her death like a cornered animal's, and in the ruins a secret that her bloodline had kept through centuries. Lilisaire, again Lilisaire.

"No!" Kenmuir shouted, the calm within him shaken asunder. "I won't condemn an entire race!" He swallowed. "I can't believe you would."

"Never. Do we curse the lightning or the tiger? They too belong with life."

Next the dream was of a world. A thunderbolt fixed nitrogen that nourished a forest. Under the leaves, a carnivore took his prey and thereby kept a herd healthy, its numbers no more than the land could well feed. The sea that drowned some ships upbore all others, and in its depths swam whales and over their heads beat wings. Dead bodies moldered, to be reborn as grass and flowers. Snow fell, to melt beneath springtime and water it.

A specter passed by, desert, rock thrusting naked where plowed soil had washed away and blown away.

A river ran thick with poison. Air gnawed at lungs. Horde upon horde, humankind laid waste around it as never a plague of locusts did, and where songbirds once nested rats ran through the alleys and the sewers.

But that was gone, or almost gone, and Earth bloomed afresh. It was the cybercosm that saved the forests and their tigers—yes, human determination was necessary, but only through technology could the change happen without catastrophe, and the cybercosm kept the will to make the change alive in humans by its counsel and its ever more visible victories over desolation.

Again the tiger sprang in Kenmuir's sight. Phantasmagoria ended. He lay among the gleaming arcs and heard: "Equally should the Lunarian people, who have done much that is magnificent, join their gifts to the rest of humanity in creating and becoming human destiny."

Though peace had returned to him, it still served his selfhood, his mind. "This is true, but is it enough? Why must every branch of us grow the same way? And what way is it?"

"No single one. Whatever multitudinous ways you and your descendants choose. Think back. Who today is forced? Is Earth not as diverse as at any time formerly, or more?"

Yes, Kenmuir agreed: and not just in societies and uncoerced individuals but in the richness of nature restored across the globe, from white bear on polar ice to bison and antelope on the plains, from hawks asoar to peacocks in the jungle, from palm to pine, from mountaintop to ocean depth, alive, alive.

The voice went on: "However, should not reason, compassion, and reverence guide you? Else you are less than apes, for apes at least act according to their birthright, and it is in your birthright to think."

Kenmuir could not help but recall what else was inborn, and how thin a glimmer consciousness was upon it. But let him not stray off into that realm. Get back to the question that brought him here. "Why don't you want Proserpina known? Are you afraid of a few Lunarians on a distant asteroid?"

As ridiculous as that sounded, he nearly regretted uttering it. Then he decided it was best gotten rid of.

The reply came grave. He thought that the Teramind had no need to bluster like the God of Job; it could afford patience, yes, courtesy. "Of course not—as such. What is to be feared is the spirit that would be resurrected. In the end, fate lies with the spirit."

"I, I don't understand," Kenmuir faltered. It couldn't mean some mind-over-matter absurdity.

"The Faustian spirit. It is not dead, not quite, here on Earth; it lives, underground and unrecognized, in the Lunarians; and at Alpha Centauri it flourishes triumphant."

Kenmuir knew not whether the vision of Demeter came to him out of the darkness or out of memory. How often had he filled himself with those images transmitted by the colonists across the years and light-years? How much was envy a bitter or a wistful part of his being? Lost in the dream, he could merely ask, "What's wrong there?"—for all he saw was splendor, courage, and ineluctable tragedy.

"It was, it is a spirit that does not accept limits, that has no end or check on its wants and its endeavors. The forebears of the folk yonder would not make their peace with the powers they had aggrieved at home, although peace was offered them. They were not able to, because they were never content. Therefore they chose to depart, over a bridge that burned behind them, to a world they knew was doomed. Now their descendants will not accept that doom."

"What else can they do?" sighed Kenmuir. What else but resign themselves, taking whatever comfort lay in the fact that oblivion was still some centuries removed? It had taken every resource that Fireball at its height commanded to send a few bodies in cold sleep across the gulf between. At Centauri they could do no more than this; and unless a handful came back to Sol, any such effort would be futile. The distance to the next marginally habitable world was too much; radiation during the voyage would wreak irreparable damage. Downloads could go, yes. Guthrie's explored among those stars. But the humans were rare who wished to be downloads. Those that did could continue as well at the sun where they were, together with the Lunarians on their asteroids: a settlement as unmeaning as Rapa Nui had been in its Pacific loneliness after the canoes no longer sailed.

"They do not yet know it," said the voice, "but they are finding their way toward a salvation."

"How do *you* know?" Kenmuir demanded. "You don't care, do you?"

"Granted, the Teramind tells them through the cybercosm, as it tells the people at home, that it has little further interest in them, or in anything of the empirical universe. That is not entirely so. If the ultimate law of physics is now known, the permutations of matter and energy are not. Therefore probes are seeking forth through interstellar space. As for the Centaurians, microprobes are observing them, unobserved by them."

It stabbed Kenmuir. Did then the cybercosm lie?

Peace flowed healingly into the wound. There must be a righteous reason, which he would learn in due course. What human was always candid, perhaps especially with those others who were loved? Indeed, pretense is a necessity of thought. You map three-dimensional planets onto two-dimensional surfaces; and this itself is a simplification, for the map is not a Euclidean plane. To compute their short-term orbits, you make those planets into geometrical mass-points and ignore everything else in the galaxy. You found a corporation and treat it legally as a person. You talk about a community or the human race, although nothing exists but individuals. You talk about individuals, or yourself, although the body is many different organisms and the mind is a set of ongoing interactions. . . .

"And we do hear something directly from them," he offered.

However avidly he had studied it, not until this moment did he quite appreciate how seldom that news came, how slight it was. At first it had been voluminous, to and fro, but later—Well, he thought, it would not be hard to discourage the colonists from sending. They had so much else to occupy them. As for the Solar System, here too people were wrapped in their own concerns and had half forgotten about a frontier or uncharted ranges beyond it. . . . "They're developing a symbiosis—" not a synnoiosis "—of . . . life and machine?"

"Yes. Demeter Mother."

This time the visions were clear, lasting amply long for him to apprehend them, and they spoke. They spoke of another and alien system, a biocosm, integral with the basic ecology. There the ultimate mind was not cybernetic but human, downloads who had in this wise returned to being alive, a Gaia not transcendent but immanent in and aware of herself. She guarded and guided life. She *was* life.

—Afterward Kenmuir whispered, "What's dreadful about this?"

"It is what will save them at Centauri," answered Venator's lips. His eyes remained blind, except to whatever moved inside him. "The Mother will find that she can do what is impossible today, take a personality from download back to re-created flesh. Demeter the planet must die, but the seed of Demeter will go forth among the stars."

Shivers went cold through Kenmuir.

"Yes," said the voice—sadly?—"you are inspired, you are wonder-smitten."

Defiance stirred anew. "Why should I not be?"

"The vision, the achievement is wholly Faustian. And likewise would the settlement of Proserpina be: of a far lesser magnitude, but in the same spirit, and not light-years remote but here, at home, within striking distance of Earth."

Kenmuir felt his face show bewilderment.

"Attend," said the voice. "Your kind has always fought, as life must, for survival and for betterment. And, uniquely, you did not fit your ways to reality, you changed the world to fit you. You tamed fire and crops and beasts, you explored, you invented, you spread across the planet. The landscapes of whole countries were, century by century, made into creations not of nature but of their human dwellers.

"Yet always, too, there was a sense of limits, humility, fear of the gods and of the nemesis that follows upon hubris. You lived in the cycle of the seasons, knowing yourselves mortal, and when you saw an ancient order of things broken, you mourned for it. Invaders who slaughtered, burned, and enslaved had their own orders, their own pieties. In every myth by which you lived was the warning against a reach too high, a pride too great.

"But the Faustian spirit arose. In the story, Faust bargains with the Evil One for limitless power. At the end, his soul is lost. But there is a sequel in which he returns and redeems himself, not by repentance but through attempting an engineering work that holds back the flood waters and makes them do man's bidding.

"Even so did the Faustian civilization grow away from its childhood modesty. Its mathematics went down to the infinitesimal and outward to the infinite and the transfinite. Its physics probed the atom and the stars. Its biology moved life from mystery to chemistry, and at last made the soul a process that could be downloaded. Meanwhile it conquered the world and went on to the Moon and the worlds beyond.

"It was, it is that spirit that knows no bounds, acknowledges no restraints, does what it will because it wills and then looks onward for new victories to win.

"It overwhelmed all else, crushed every small shy foreignness, forged the total state, and very nearly exterminated the race."

Kenmuir lay mute for a spell, gathering his words, before he replied:

"No, I can't accept that." He could do no other than set his monkey wit against the Teramind. "You refer to what came out of Europe, Western Christendom, don't you? Well, at its worst it was never more evil than the rest, it simply had more power. And it got that power from the science it originated, which was also the power to end sickness and hunger, to understand the natural world and learn how to save it. Everybody else had been destroying nature too, more gradually but without any way of ever reversing the harm. This was the civilization that abolished chattel slavery and made women the equals of men. It was the civilization—the spirit, you'd say—that gave birth to the inalienable rights of the individual, life, liberty, and the pursuit of happiness. It gave us the planets and can still give us the stars."

He had not known he could speak like that. He was no orator. What subtle forces passed through his skin to evoke whatever had been latent in him? The Teramind played fair, he thought.

"What you say is as true as what you heard," answered the voice. "Just the same, it means disunity, strife, and chaos, eternally."

"What else—what would you have?"

"Oneness. Harmony. Peace. The Noösphere, and in the end the Noöcosm."

Again an apparition, a dream. Intelligence immortal, forever transcending itself, until its creations and comprehensions overmatched the whole material universe.

For billions of years to come it must explore, discover, take inspiration from that cosmos. The destinies of the galaxies were as yet incalculable. Already, though, the Law that bound them seemed clear; only its manifold unfoldings remained mysterious, and with every new experience the capacity to foretell the next would increase.

Timelessly perseverant, the sophotectic seed spread forth into the future. It needed no planets, no footholds, no conquests, nothing but tiny bits of substance with which to reproduce its kind. And each of those seedbeds, each cybercosm and Teramind, was joined with the rest. At the speed of light, communication across a galaxy took tens of thousands of years, communication between galaxies took millions; but there was the patience that stems from assurance, and there was no more death.

Space expanded onward. The stars grew old. The last of them guttered out. Chill neared the absolute zero. What free energy survived trickled from the slow disintegration of black holes and the particles of matter. As slowly must intelligence spend that energy; a thought might go for a billion years before it was completed. Yet that same pace brought together the minds of the galaxies. They were now no farther apart than the duration of a thought. As the trillions of years mounted, to them their separations lessened without limit. They linked together in a single supreme intellect that filled reality. The universe was neither dead nor dark. It was alive and radiant with spirit.

Certainty is not absolute. Against our prevailing evidence and belief, the cosmos may reach an end to its expansion and fall back on itself. Intelligence will nevertheless be immortal. Within the finite time to singularity, an infinite number of events can take place, an infinity of thoughts can be thought and dreams can be dreamed. Whether the transfiguration be freezing or fiery, awareness will endure and evolve forever.

Long, long before then, its heed will have departed from the matter-energy chrysalis. It will know all things that exist and all that are possible; it will have considered them, comprehended them, and lovingly set them aside. Its own works—arts, mathematics, undertakings, unimaginable for ages to come—are what shall occupy its eternity. In the end was the Word, and the Word was with God, and the Word was God.

Kenmuir lay quiet.

"You have seen the prophecy before," said the voice.

"Yes," he replied, "but never like this."

After a while: "How could . . . any humans . . . threaten that?"

"This is in the nature of things. It goes deeper than chaos. If vanishingly small changes may have immense and undivinable effects, still, a system has its attractors, its underlying order, and a broken balance may well be redressed.

"To fathom the true danger, you would have to be in synnoiosis, and nonetheless your insight would be dim and fragmentary. But think. Recall what you know of quantum physics. Reality is one, but reality is a manifold. Past and future are one, inseparable. Yet this means that they are equally unknowable with precision. A particle can have gone from point to point by any of infinitely many paths; some are more probable than others, but observation alone establishes which is real. The state of one, when determined, fixes the state of another, though they be light-years apart, too distant for causality between them. Thus the observed and the observer, existence and the meaning of existence, are a whole, Yang and Yin; and the wave function of the universe shares incertitude with the wave function of a lone electron."

Kenmuir shook his head. "No, I don't see. I can't. Unless what you hint is that . . . human minds are no accident either—they're as fundamental an aspect of reality as . . . as yours—"

He shook himself. He was neither sophotect nor synnoiont, nor even a philosopher. Let it suffice him that the Teramind found reason to fear his race. (Fear? Respect? Useless words, here.) Let him stay with the grubby practicalities of flesh and blood.

"What I'm guessing your intent is," he said very

carefully, "is that we humans can do anything we want, and you'll help us, advise us, be good to us—provided we stay safely irrelevant to you."

"No. That cannot be. It is already too late. Your kind is loose among the stars."

Through Kenmuir flew a horror. The Teramind might build and dispatch missiles to blast Demeter Mother before her children left their world. No! It had not happened, therefore it would not. It could not. Please.

He forced dryness: "What about us at home?"

"In the future that belongs to Mind, you will join, willingly and gladly, as this I—Venator—has done, but to an immensely higher degree."

"We become part of the cybercosm?"

"Centuries or millennia hence. Then sentient Earth will be ready to confront the foreign thing yonder."

"You hope you'll have the strength—" the strength of intellect, not of raw force "—to cope with it. Tame it. Take it into yourself."

"No. The hope is that it will join itself to us."

"Would that be so hard? Is it really so different?"

"Yes. As long as both remain true to their destinies, the gulf between is unbridgeable. Demeter Mother is the ancient life, organic, biological. To her, the inorganic, the machine, is no more than a lesser part, a means to the end of survival. She will always be of the material universe and its wildness, its chaos, its mortality. Never will her intellect be pure and wholly free."

Kenmuir had an eerie sense that he was a hunter closing in on a majestic quarry. "But she'll go ways that you never will, that you can never imagine, because you can't feel them. Are you afraid of that? She'll die with the stars, when you do not. Won't she? Isn't space-time big enough for you to live with her till then?"

Silence. Venator's face became like a dead man's. Kenmuir wondered what lay unspoken behind it. *No.*

Reality is one. She will shape it, as I do. It will become something unforeseeable, without destiny, something other than that Ultimate which is the purpose and meaning of me.

He threw the words away. They were nothing but his imagery, no better than a mythic image of the sun as a boat or a chariot making daily passage across heaven. He must hunt farther.

"Would Lunarians on Proserpina matter that much?" he asked.

"Think forward," replied the oracle, and now life was again in his countenance, though it be not human life. "They will make that world over, multiply their numbers, spread among the comets, reach for the stars. They will talk with the seed of Demeter. They will talk with their Terran kin, in whom Faust will reawaken because of it."

"They'll trouble you. You want everyone in the Solar System kept close to home where you can control us."

"Where you can enlighten yourselves and grow into sanity," said the voice. How soft it was.

Incredulous, Kenmuir exclaimed, "And this turns on a single ship escaping from the Moon? On a single man who could call her back?"

"No. Reality is a whole, I said. But for the history soon to come, and therefore conceivably for history ever after, yes, I ask that you call her back."

The cybercosm asked.

You would make the universe into mind and harmony, Kenmuir thought. This very conflict we have been waging, not of strengths but of ideas and possibilities, betokens the etherealization you seek. Who shall hold that it is wrong, your vision? Who shall hold that passion and unsureness, the animal and the vegetable, the mortal, grief mingled with every joy—that these are right?

Faust is forever at war. I am a man of peace.

"The choice is yours," he heard. "I may not compel.

I cannot. For the cybercosm to impose its will by violence would be to violate itself. Nor could this bring other than chaos uncontrollable; hark back to the chronicles of all tyrannies. Though the human genus be obliterated in the Solar System, survivors would hold on at Alpha Centauri, in millennial revengefulness. Though they too be killed, corruption would seize the heart of the victor, and at the end would destroy it likewise. No, the burden is yours."

Beneath the nirvana imposed on his body, Kenmuir's pulse stumbled. His mouth had gone dry. "If I . . . obey you . . . what about Aleka and her people?"

"They shall have their desire, a country better than Lilisaire can grant."

And the Earthfolk whose eyes were turned skyward would have their Habitat. None but the demonic spirit in the Lunarians must submit.

No, those humans of every kind must submit who wished for freedom. And they would not know that they had done so or that they were unfree.

It was as if his answer had lain in him since before he was born. "No."

"You refuse." It was not a question.

"I do. She shall keep flying."

"You are forgiven," said the voice, altogether gently.

Kenmuir knew he would never understand that strange integrity. He was no machine, only a man.

His consciousness toppled into night.

46

Have no fears," Venator had said when Kenmuir woke. "We'll flit you to Yorkport and let you go. I assume you'll catch the Luna shuttle. But first we should talk a bit, you and I."

He left the spacefarer to rest a while, then guided him to a room where they shared a plain and mostly silent meal, then provided them both with warm clothes and led the way outside. For another spell they walked wordless, until they had left the weather station out of sight behind them and were alone with the mountains.

Kenmuir breathed deeply. Thin and cold, a breeze stirred the leaves and needles of widely strewn dwarf trees. It tasted of sky. Sunlight cataracted over a long upward slope and the snowpeaks beyond. They stood knife-edge sharp against utter blue. He took the view into himself. Anxiety, indecision, sorrow were coming astir, as the dispassion laid on him in the chamber ebbed away; he needed this fresh wellspring of calm.

"Go slow," Venator advised at his side. "Spare your strength. We've time aplenty."

Kenmuir glanced at him. "What do you want of me?" he inquired.

He could not tell whether the smile that crossed the dark face was wry or regretful. "Nothing, in the sense of demands," Venator replied. "I would like to make a few suggestions, and we had better sketch out some plans."

"I'll do whatever I can," Kenmuir said awkwardly, "consistent with—" With what?

Venator nodded. "I expected you would. It's rational. But good of you, too."

How should Kenmuir respond, how should he feel?

"Please. This is not a victor-and-vanquished situation."

Venator smiled again, more broadly and perhaps a little mockingly. "No, no."

Grit scrunched beneath boots. The wind whispered. Plunge ahead, Kenmuir decided. "All right, then. Aleka will deliver her message." He hesitated. "Or has she?" What hours or days had passed in the house of the Teramind?

"Not yet," Venator told him. "But she will soon."

"And you—the, the cybercosm—the government—it really won't try to suppress the news or, or any consequences that follow?"

Venator caught Kenmuir's gaze and held it a moment. "You and your friends can help us in that, you know. In fact, you must. The Federation—the humans in key positions—we don't want them led or forced into taking stands it would be hard for them to retreat from. As you guessed earlier, the less said publicly on either side, the easier for everyone concerned."

It was not a capitulation, Kenmuir realized. It was an adaptation to circumstances. It could be the first move in a new plan that extended centuries ahead. . . . No, he would not think about that. Not yet.

"I'll certainly be glad to cooperate," he said. "So will Aleka and, uh, Matthias, I'm sure."

Now Venator grinned, above raised brows. "Like Lilisaire and her Lunarians?"

"I think they'll agree."

"The story can't actually be blotted out, you know," Venator reminded. "What we can try for is that your people be discreet enough to allow mine to be the same."

No, the story could never be blotted out, Kenmuir thought. Not out of him. Pain surged. O download Dagny!

"Must we talk about opposite sides?" he asked fast. "I still can't see why the issue has to be . . . irreconcilable. Are a few Lunarians in deep space such a big factor? How can they be, in the near future or ever?"

Venator frowned. "It seemed more clear to you before," he said. With a shrug: "It did to me too, then." He paused. "Let me propose a very crude analogy. Picture an intelligent, educated Roman in the reign of Augustus, speculating about what things would be like in another thousand years. He says to himself, 'Perhaps the legions will have marched over the whole world as they did over Gaul, and everybody everywhere will be Roman. Or perhaps, which Caesar's current policy suggests is more likely, the frontiers will stay approximately where they are, beyond them the forests and the barbarians. Or perhaps, pessimistically, Rome will have fallen and the wild folk howl in the ruins of our cities.'

"I don't know which future he chose, and it doesn't matter, because of course the outcome was none of them. A heretical offshoot of the religion of a conquered people in one small corner of the Mediterranean lands took over both Romans and barbarians, transforming them entirely and begetting a whole new civilization."

Faustian civilization, Kenmuir thought.

"Just the same," he argued, "the sheer power of—your—cybercosm, which is bound to grow beyond anything we can conceive of—"

"The biocosm will grow too," Venator said. "And as for influences on it and on us, what may humans turn into, they *and* their machines, out among the comets?"

An idea struck from the rim of Kenmuir's mind. By its nature, the cybercosm must seek for absolute knowledge; but this required absolute control, no wild contingencies, nothing unforeseeable except the flowerings of its intellect. The cybercosm was totalitarian.

"Well, as events have developed, this has become yet another factor to deal with," Venator went on. "There are many more, after all, and in any case the universe will doubtless continue springing surprises for millions of years to come. Time will see who copes best, and how."

Totalitarianism need not be brutal, Kenmuir thought. It could be mild in its ways, beneficent in its actions, and . . . too subtle to be recognized for what it was.

Wings flashed overhead. He looked aloft, but the sun dazzled sight of the bird from him. A hawk, hunting? Never could he have imagined that ruthless beauty, had not a billion years of unreined chance and blind will to live shaped it for him. Suddenly he could endure remembering what had happened in the tomb on the Moon.

Maybe there would be no real affray between the Daos. Maybe in some remote age they would find they had been two faces of the same. Or maybe not. He knew simply that he was with the Mother.

"And this is rather abstract, isn't it?" Venator was saying. "We can do nothing but handle the footling details of our lifespans, one piece at a time."

Kenmuir considered him. "That isn't quite true of you, is it?"

"Not quite," Venator admitted. After several more strides through the wind: "In spite of everything, I don't envy you."

Nor I you, Kenmuir thought.

"I would nonetheless like to know you better," Venator said. "Can't be, I suppose. Shall we discuss those practicalities?"

Night had lately fallen over the Lunar Cordillera. From Lilisaire's eyrie three peaks could still be seen far to westward, on which brightness lingered. Only the edges were visible, flame-tongues slowly dying. Elsewhere the mountains had become a wilderness of shadowy heights and abyssal darks. Eastward they dropped away to boulders and craters almost as dim. Stars stood above in their thousands, the galactic frost-bridge, nebulae and sister galaxies aglimmer, but Earth was no more than a blue arc along a wan disc, low above that horizon.

A clear-domed tower overlooked it all. From tanks and planters in its topmost room grew gigantic flowers. Starlit, their leaves were dark masses or delicate filigrees. Blossoms mingled perfumes in air that lay like the air of an evening at the end of summer. Fireflies flittered and glittered through their silence.

Lilisaire entered with Kenmuir. Neither had said much in the short while since he arrived. She passed among the flowers to the eastern side and stopped, gazing out. He waited, observing her profile against the sky and her hair sheening beneath it.

A song crystal lay on the ledge under the dome. She picked it up and stroked fingers across its facets. Sound awakened, trills, chimes, whistlings, a shivery beat. She made them into a melody and sang half under her breath:

> "Stonefall, fireflash,
> Cenotaph of a seeker.
> But the stone has lost the stars
> And the stars have lost the stone."

He had heard the Lunarian words before, a snatch of a lyric by Verdea. No tongue of Earth could have keened like them or carried the full meaning behind their images.

Lilisaire laid the crystal back down and was again quiet. After a minute Kenmuir took it on himself to say in Anglo, "That's a melancholy piece, my lady."

"It suits right well," she answered tonelessly.

"I should have thought you'd be happier."

"Nay, you did not." She turned to meet his eyes. Hers seemed to brim with light. The countenance could have been the mask of an Asian Pallas. "You are intelligent. You will have priced this prize you won."

He had known he must speak plainly, but not that it

would be so soon. The muscles tightened between his shoulderblades. He kept his voice level: "Well, yes. At any rate, I've wondered. Proserpina is open to you, with everything that may imply." Which was what? He couldn't tell. He wouldn't live to learn. "However, the Habitat—" He left the sentence dangling, reluctant to declare what they both understood.

She completed it for him. "The Habitat is made certainty."

"It always was, wasn't it?"

She shook her head. "Not altogether, not while something in far space remained unknown, maychance the instrument of a victory clear and complete. But now it is found."

For an instant he harked back to the house of the Teramind. Reality as discovery, mind as its maker— No, that couldn't be, not on any tangible, humanly meaningful scale, and even at the quantum level there must be more than the paradoxes of measurement; there must!

"No weapon," Lilisaire sighed. "Merely an escape."

As often in the recent past, he spun the mundane possibilities by his attention. Lunarians rebellious or adventurous—no few, either kind—would move to the iron world, piecemeal at first, later in a tide. The Federation would not oppose; it ought actually to help, because thereby both the case against the Habitat and the opposition to it should bleed away. Nevertheless, that colonizing effort would engage well-nigh the whole Lunarian spacefaring capability; and this in turn would draw folk from their homes on the inner asteroids and the outer moons. The Venture, the whole strong Lunarian presence on the planets, would fade from history.

"And a bargain of truce," Lilisaire finished.

For her part, Kenmuir thought, she could not denounce the long concealment of her ancestral treasure, and she must yield on the matter of the Habitat. Her interest in a smooth compromise was as vital as the government's, however bad it tasted to either. A phrase from centuries agone surfaced before him. "Equality of dissatisfaction." But what when that left the great basic contest unresolved?

Carefully prosaic, he said, "Nothing is firm, you know, my lady. So far it's words exchanged between individuals and . . . sophotects. Most officials, not to mention the public, haven't heard of it, or anything about the whole affair."

"Yet I foresee the end of our Luna." Her voice was steely, devoid of self-pity; she stood straight beneath the heavens.

"No, not really—" Did he detect a flick of scorn across her lips? "A new beginning, anyhow."

"Belike a new cycle," she gave him, "albeit a stranger to everything that was ours."

No more millennial metaphysics, he decided. Aloud: "My lady, first we've years' worth of business to do. Most important to me, you made Aleka Kame a promise."

Lilisaire finger-shrugged. "Eyach, she shall have her island and its waters. Why not? What slight power that ever I wielded in these parts is slipping from my hands." She touched her chin, frowned, then smiled a tiny, cold bit. "Moreover, to have friends on Earth may someday prove useful."

It took him a moment to catch her entire intent. "You don't want to go to Proserpina yourself, do you?"

"Nay. Why should such be my wish? Here are the holdings of my forebears and their ashes, their ancient graces and sureties, memories of them on every mountain and memories of me that would have abided. Those shall I surrender for starkness and hardship and the likelihood of early death."

"You needn't," he said around an unawaited thickness in his throat. "You can live out your life here in luxury."

Her laugh rang. It sounded real, as if he had cracked

some Homeric joke. "Hai-ah, how comfortable the cage! How well-mannered the visitors who come to peer! And if any of them should stray too near the bars—" She shook her head. Mirth still bubbled. "Moreover, how could I hold back from this last insolence?"

He recalled her ancestor Rinndalir, who fared to Alpha Centauri. Had Lilisaire finally forsaken the shade of Niolente?

Seriousness struck down upon her. She stood for a span unspeaking, her look gone outward, before she said most softly, "And as for death yonder, it will be the death of a Beynac."

"Why, you, you can survive to a ripe age," he stammered.

She ignored his attempt. "I am going, and in the vanguard. But therefore I can ill keep the promise I gave you, my captain, that you would be chieftain over my emprises in space, and dwell with me as a seigneur among the Selenarchs."

"It doesn't matter."

"Ey, it does." She smiled anew. "You lie right gallantly."

In hammering bewilderment, Kenmuir groped for words. "My lady, I'm glad if I've helped you, and if I, I harmed you instead, it wasn't my wish, and—It's enough for me that I served you."

He wondered whether he meant it.

"It is not enough for me," she answered. Her hand reached forth to his. "I pray you, let me see how I can redeem my pledge a little, at least a little."

What he saw, amazed, was that she stood there as lonely and woundable as any other human creature.

The breeze was light. Aleka motored two or three kilometers from Niihau harbor before she deployed mast and sail. Then her boat ghosted along over wavelets of shining blue and green laced with glassy foam. They murmured to themselves and lapped against the hull. Sometimes a crest broke, briefly white. The sun declined westward. Its rays burned across the waters. Out here, though, the air was cool. A frigate bird soared on high.

Kenmuir sat on a bench in the cockpit by the cabin door, opposite Aleka, who had the tiller. She wore just a cap and a sleeveless tunic. Her skin glowed bronze. A stray lock of hair fell across her brow. He kept his face steady while he gathered courage.

She looked from the sea to him and said nearly the first words between them since they cast off. "You've changed, Ian." Her voice stayed low and he was not sure whether he glimpsed a phantom smile.

"You too, I think," he returned. "Not surprising, after what you've been through."

His mind played it over, the flight through space, the message sent, the long curve inward again, the ship and the sophotect that she wearily let rendezvous. It had not been unkind, she told him; it took her aboard and brought her back to Earth, where Venator interviewed and released her. No bodily danger ever, but she could not be confident of that, and Kenmuir dared not dwell on what she must have suffered in her spirit, amidst emptiness and machines.

"I hoped you'd come right away after I got home," she said.

Though he sensed no reproach, he winced. "I'm sorry. Been so damnably occupied—" He had explained that before, in their short phone conversations and today when he arrived. "You'll hear the details, as far as I can straighten them out in my head. Besides, well, I thought you'd first want to rest" in her land and on her sea, among her folk and merfolk. He had wondered, without asking, if that was why she proposed they sail out to talk in private. They could have gone someplace ashore. But here she wholly belonged.

Or was it that this change of setting might break his tongue-tied hesitancy?

Now she did smile, however tentatively. "Ah, bueno, *lawa*, that's behind us. The news that we'll have our new country, we Lahui, this is what you and I can celebrate together. For openers."

He had no reply.

She watched him for a time before she said, gently as the wind, "No? No. Por favor, don't misunderstand. I'm not blaming, I'm not begging."

He met her eyes. "You never would."

"Something has happened."

"Only in me."

She deserved straightforwardness. "I'm going to Proserpina," he said.

"I was . . . afraid of that."

"Don't be." It was he who pleaded. He leaned forward and caught her hand in both of his. "Listen. It's best. You're young, you have your life and your world to make, I'm old and and—"

"We could try," she said.

"And lose those years for you? No."

Her quietness abided. "Don't play unselfish. It's unworthy of you. You're returning to Lilisaire." She drew her hand free.

"I'm trying to be realistic and, and do what's right," he said.

The waves lulled. The frigate bird cruised on watch for prey.

"This isn't a complete surprise to me," she told him. *"He kanaka pono 'oe.* You're a good man, an honest man. You can keep a secret but you haven't got much gift for lying." She looked to the horizon. "Don't worry about me. I'll be all right."

Yes, he knew. She was too alive for anything else.

Nevertheless—He grinned at himself, an old man's dry grin. In his expectations, she had responded fiercely, and it was not impossible that she could have lured him back to her. Well, maybe she had been feeling her doubts too. Maybe, no, probably she saw things more clearly and forthrightly than he had known, more than he did.

He should be relieved, not disappointed. But he was only a man.

Her concern burst over him: "You, though! Have you thought this through? You may well be the single Earthling—Terran—the single one of your race, away in that darkness with nothing but rocks and stars."

When she spoke thus, he gained heart. "It's space, Aleka," he replied.

She sat meditative, toying with the helm, before she said, "I see. Always it's called you, and this is the last way left for you to follow."

He lifted his shoulders and dropped them, palms outspread. "Irrational. Agreed. But we—the Lunarians, and whoever's with them—we'll bring Proserpina to life."

For whatever that would mean in the gigayears ahead. He felt no special involvement in them; being mortal and reasonable, he could not. Still, he would obscurely be serving Demeter Mother whom he would never know, and therewith give his life a meaning beyond itself.

That thought was more than his monkey vanity. The Teramind concurred. He didn't know whether it would seek to conceal the migration to Proserpina from the Centaurians. He could imagine several tricks for doing so. Certainly the cybercosm was making sure that the tale of hide-and-seek within the Solar System would be soft-played, soon lost in background noise. There must be no monuments . . . It didn't matter, Kenmuir believed. In the long run, it didn't matter. When life is ready to evolve onward, it will evolve.

Aleka nodded. "You'll be in space, Ian. No, I couldn't bear to bind you." A whip-flick: "As for our lady Lilisaire, I daresay you can cope with her."

"It isn't that simple."

"No."

They sailed in silence. All at once, a form broached to starboard, and another and another. A troop of the Keiki Moana were out.

Aleka regarded them with love. "We are different breeds, aren't we, you and I?" she said at last to Kenmuir. "And we're of the same blood."

How many others might the future see?

"What you will make, right here on Earth—" he began. He broke off, filled his lungs with the clean salt wind, and went on. "I wonder if in the end it won't prove to be as strange and powerful as anything anywhere in the universe."

She laughed, low in her throat and defiantly. "The making will be fun, anyhow."

It will be joy, he hoped.

She took his hand again. "I wish you the same, darling," she said, "yonder where *Kestrel* is."

The little ship that had been Kyra Davis's was outbound alone, to fare forever among the stars.